BOOKS BY

Junichirō Tanizaki

SEVEN JAPANESE TALES (1963)

THE KEY (1961)

THE MAKIOKA SISTERS (1957)

Unesco Collection of Representative Works:
Japanese Series

SOME PREFER NETTLES (1955)

These are BORZOI BOOKS *published in New York by*

ALFRED A. KNOPF

THE MAKIOKA SISTERS

THE NANDORA SISTERS

Junichirō Tanizaki

THE

Makioka Sisters

Translated from the Japanese by Edward G. Seidensticker

ALFRED A. KNOPF   NEW YORK

19   68

L.C. catalog card number: 57–10311

© *Alfred A. Knopf, Inc., 1957.*

THIS IS A BORZOI BOOK,
PUBLISHED BY ALFRED A. KNOPF, INC.

Published October 14, 1957
Reprinted, September 1968

Originally published in Japan as SASAME YUKI. *This volume is one of the works recommended for translation by* UNESCO *and the Japanese National Commission for Unesco, as representative of Japanese culture.*

The Principal Characters

🔳 *The four Makioka sisters:*

TSURUKO, *the mistress of the senior or "main" house in Osaka, which by Japanese tradition wields authority over the collateral branches.*

SACHIKO, *the mistress of the junior or branch house in Ashiya, a small city just outside of Osaka. For reasons of sentiment and convenience, the younger unmarried sisters prefer to live with her, somewhat against tradition.*

YUKIKO, *thirty and still unmarried, shy and retiring, now not much sought after; so many proposals for her hand have been refused in earlier years that the family has acquired a reputation for haughtiness even though its fortunes are declining.*

TAEKO *(familiarly called "Koi-san"), willful and sophisticated beyond her twenty-five years, waiting impatiently for Yukiko's marriage so that her own secret liaison can be acknowledged before the world.*

🔳

TATSUO, *Tsuruko's husband, a cautious bank employee who has taken the Makioka name and who, upon the retirement of the father, became the active head of the family according to Japanese custom.*

TEINOSUKE, *Sachiko's husband, an accountant with remarkable literary inclinations and far broader human instincts than Tatsuo; he too has taken the Makioka name.*

ETSUKO, *Sachiko's daughter, a precocious child just entering school.*

O-HARU, *Sachiko's maid.*

80284

Mrs. Itani, *owner of a beauty parlor, an inveterate gossip whose profession lends itself to the exciting game of arranging marriages.*

Okubata *(familiarly called "Kei-boy"), the man with whom Taeko tried to elope at 19, and whom she still sees secretly.*

Itakura, *a man of no background to whom Taeko is attracted after her betrothal to Okubata is too long delayed.*

THE MAKIOKA SISTERS

BOOK I

"WOULD YOU do this please, Koi-san?"

Seeing in the mirror that Taeko had come up behind her, Sachiko stopped powdering her back and held out the puff to her sister. Her eyes were still on the mirror, appraising the face as if it belonged to someone else. The long under-kimono, pulled high at the throat, stood out stiffly behind to reveal her back and shoulders.

"And where is Yukiko?"

"She is watching Etsuko practice," said Taeko. Both sisters spoke in the quiet, unhurried Osaka dialect. Taeko was the youngest in the family, and in Osaka the youngest girl is always "Koi-san," "small daughter."

They could hear the piano downstairs. Yukiko had finished dressing early, and young Etsuko always wanted someone beside her when she practiced. She never objected when her mother went out, provided that Yukiko was left to keep her company. Today, with her mother and Yukiko and Taeko all dressing to go out, she was rebellious. She very grudgingly gave her permission when they promised that Yukiko at least would start back as soon as the concert was over—it began at two—and would be with Etsuko for dinner.

"Koi-san, we have another prospect for Yukiko."

"Oh?"

The bright puff moved from Sachiko's neck down over her

back and shoulders. Sachiko was by no means round-shouldered, and yet the rich, swelling flesh of the neck and back somehow gave a suggestion of a stoop. The warm glow of the skin in the clear autumn sunlight made it hard to believe that she was in her thirties.

"It came through Itani."

"Oh?"

"The man works in an office, M.B. Chemical Industries, Itani says."

"And is he well off?"

"He makes a hundred seventy or eighty yen a month, possibly two hundred fifty with bonuses."

"M.B. Chemical Industries—a French company?"

"How clever of you. How did you know?"

"Oh, I know that much."

Taeko, the youngest, was in fact far better informed on such matters than her sisters. There was a suggestion occasionally that she took advantage of their ignorance to speak with a condescension more appropriate in someone older.

"I had never heard of M.B. Chemical Industries. The head office is in Paris, Itani says. It seems to be very large."

"They have a big building on the Bund in Kobe. Have you never noticed it?"

"That is the place. That is where he works."

"Does he know French?"

"It seems so. He graduated from the French department of the Osaka Language Academy, and he spent some time in Paris—not a great deal, though. He makes a hundred yen a month teaching French at night."

"Does he have property."

"Very little. He still has the family house in the country—his mother is living there—and a house and lot in Kobe. And nothing more. The Kobe house is very small, and he bought it on installments. And so you see there is not much to boast of."

"He has no rent to pay, though. He can live as though he had more than four hundred a month."

"How do you think he would be for Yukiko? He has only his mother to worry about, and she never comes to Kobe. He is past forty, but he has never been married."

"Why not, if he is past forty?"

"He has never found anyone refined enough for him, Itani says."

"Very odd. You should have him investigated."

"And she says he is most enthusiastic about Yukiko."

"You sent her picture?"

"I left a picture with Itani, and she sent it without telling me. She says he is very pleased."

"Do you have a picture of him?"

The practicing went on below. It did not seem likely that Yukiko would interrupt them.

"Look in the top drawer on the right." Puckering her lips as though she were about to kiss the mirror, Sachiko took up her lipstick. "Did you find it?"

"Here it is. You have shown it to Yukiko?"

"Yes."

"And?"

"As usual, she said almost nothing. What do you think, Koi-san?"

"Very plain. Or maybe just a little better than plain. A middling office worker, you can tell at a glance."

"But he is just that after all. Why should it surprise you?"

"There may be one advantage. He can teach Yukiko French."

Satisfied in a general way with her face, Sachiko began to unwrap a kimono.

"I almost forgot." She looked up. "I feel a little short on 'B.' Would you tell Yukiko, please?"

Beri-beri was in the air of this Kobe-Osaka district, and every year from summer into autumn the whole family—Sachiko and her husband and sisters and Etsuko, who had just started school— came down with it. The vitamin injection had become a family institution. They no longer went to a doctor, but instead kept a supply of concentrated vitamins on hand and ministered to each other with complete unconcern. A suggestion of sluggishness was immediately attributed to a shortage of Vitamin B, and, although they had forgotten who coined the expression, "short on 'B' " never had to be explained.

The piano practice was finished. Taeko called from the head of the stairs, and one of the maids came out. "Could you have an injection ready for Mrs. Makioka, please?"

2

MRS. ITANI ("Itani" everyone called her) had a beauty shop near the Oriental Hotel in Kobe, and Sachiko and her sisters were among the steady customers. Knowing that Itani was fond of arranging marriages, Sachiko had once spoken to her of Yukiko's problem, and had left a photograph to be shown to likely prospects. Recently, when Sachiko went for a wave-set, Itani took advantage of a few spare minutes to invite her out for a cup of tea. In the lobby of the Oriental Hotel, Sachiko first heard Itani's story.

It had been wrong not to speak to Sachiko first, Itani knew, but she had been afraid that if they frittered away their time they would miss a good opportunity. She had heard of this possible husband for Miss Yukiko, and had sent him the photograph—only that, nothing more—possibly a month and a half before. She heard nothing from the man, and had almost forgotten about him when she learned that he was apparently busy investigating Yukiko's background. He had found out all about the Makioka family, even the main branch in Osaka.

(Sachiko was the second daughter. Her older sister, Tsuruko, kept the "main" house in Osaka.)

. . . . And he went on to investigate Miss Yukiko herself. He went to her school, and to her calligraphy teacher, and to the woman who instructed her in the tea ceremony. He found out everything. He even heard about that newspaper affair, and he went around to the newspaper office to see whether it had been misreported. It seemed clear to Itani that he was well enough satisfied with the results of the investigation, but, to make quite sure, she had told him he ought to meet Miss Yukiko face to face and see for himself whether she was the sort of girl that the newspaper article had made her seem. Itani was sure she had convinced him. He was very modest and retiring, she said, and protested that he did not belong in a class with the Makioka family, and had very little hope of finding such a splendid bride, and if, by some chance, a marriage could be arranged, he would hate to see Miss

Yukiko try to live on his miserable salary. But since there might just be a chance, he hoped Itani would at least mention his name. Itani had heard that his ancestors down to his grandfather had been leading retainers to a minor *daimyo* (lord) on the Japan Sea, and that even now a part of the family estate remained. As far as the family was concerned, then, it would not seem to be separated by any great distance from the Makiokas. Did Sachiko not agree? The Makiokas were an old family, of course, and probably everyone in Osaka had heard of them at one time or another. But still—Sachiko would have to forgive her for saying so—they could not live on their old glory forever. They would only find that Miss Yukiko had finally missed her chance. Why not compromise, while there was time, on someone not too outrageously inappropriate? Itani admitted that the salary was not large, but then the man was only forty, and it was not at all impossible that he would come to make more. And it was not as if he were working for a Japanese company. He had time to himself, and with more teaching at night he was sure he would have no trouble making four hundred and more. He would be able to afford at least a maid, there was no doubt about that. And as for the man himself, Itani's brother had known him since they were very young, and had given him the highest recommendation. Although it would be perfectly ideal if the Makiokas were to conduct their own investigation, there seemed no doubt that his only reason for not marrying earlier was that he had not found anyone to his taste. Since he had been to Paris and was past forty, it would be hard to guarantee that he had quite left women alone, but when Itani met him she said to herself: "Here's an honest, hard-working man, not a bit the sort to play around with women." It was reasonable enough for such a well-behaved man to insist on an elegant, refined girl, but for some reason—maybe as a reaction from his visit to Paris—he insisted further that he would have only a pure Japanese beauty—gentle, quiet, graceful, able to wear Japanese clothes. It did not matter how she looked in foreign clothes. He wanted a pretty face too, of course, but more than anything he wanted pretty hands and feet. To Itani, Miss Yukiko seemed the perfect answer.

Such was her story.

Itani supported her husband, bedridden with palsy, and, after

putting her brother through medical school, had this spring sent
her daughter to Tokyo to enter Japan Women's University. Sound
and practical, she was quicker by far than most women, but her
way of saying exactly what was on her mind without frills and
circumlocutions was so completely unladylike that one sometimes
wondered how she kept her customers. And yet there was nothing
artificial about this directness—one felt only that the truth had to
be told—and Itani stirred up little resentment. The torrent of
words poured on as through a broken dam. Sachiko could not
help thinking that the woman was really too forward, but, given
the spirited Itani's resemblance to a man used to being obeyed, it
was clear that this was her way of being friendly and helpful. A
still more powerful consideration, however, was the argument itself, which had no cracks. Sachiko felt as if she had been pinned
to the floor. She would speak to her sister in Osaka, then, she said,
and perhaps they could do a little investigating themselves. There
the matter ended.

Some, it would appear, looked for deep and subtle reasons to
explain the fact that Yukiko, the third of the four sisters, had
passed the marriageable age and reached thirty without a husband.
There was in fact no "deep" reason worth the name. Or, if a reason had to be found, perhaps it was that Tsuruko in the main
house and Sachiko and Yukiko herself all remembered the luxury
of their father's last years and the dignity of the Makioka name—
in a word, they were thralls to the family name, to the fact that
they were members of an old and once-important family. In their
hopes of finding Yukiko a worthy husband, they had refused the
proposals that in earlier years had showered upon them. Not one
seemed quite what they wanted. Presently the world grew tired
of their rebuffs, and people no longer mentioned likely candidates. Meanwhile the family fortunes were declining. There was
no doubt, then, that Itani was being kind when she urged Sachiko
to "forget the past." The best days for the Makiokas had lasted
perhaps into the mid-twenties. Their prosperity lived now only
in the mind of the Osakan who knew the old days well. Indeed
even in the mid-twenties, extravagance and bad management were
having their effect on the family business. The first of a series of
crises had overtaken them then. Soon afterwards Sachiko's father
died, the business was cut back, and the shop in Semba, the heart

of old Osaka—a shop that boasted a history from the middle of
the last century and the days of the Shogunate—had to be sold.
Sachiko and Yukiko found it hard to forget how it had been while
their father lived. Before the shop was torn down to make way
for a more modern building, they could not pass the solid earthen
front and look in through the shop windows at the dusky interior
without a twinge of sorrow.

There were four daughters and no sons in the family. When the
father went into retirement, Tsuruko's husband, who had taken
the Makioka name, became active head of the family. Sachiko, too,
married, and her husband also took the Makioka name. When
Yukiko came of age, however, she unhappily no longer had a father to make a good match for her, and she did not get along
well with her brother-in-law, Tatsuo, the new head of the family.
Tatsuo, the son of a banker, had worked in a bank before he became the Makioka heir—indeed even afterwards he left the management of the shop largely to his foster father and the chief clerk.
Upon the father's death, Tatsuo pushed aside the protests of his
sisters-in-law and the rest of the family, who thought that something could still be salvaged, and let the old shop pass into the
hands of a man who had once been a family retainer. Tatsuo himself went back to his old bank. Quite the opposite of Sachiko's
father, who had been a rather ostentatious spender, Tatsuo was
austere and retired almost to the point of timidity. Such being his
nature, he concluded that rather than try to manage an unfamiliar
business heavily in debt, he ought to take the safer course and let
the shop go, and that he had thus fulfilled his duty to the Makioka
family—had in fact chosen that course precisely because he worried so about his duties as family heir. To Yukiko, however, drawn
as she was to the past, there was something very unsatisfactory
about this brother-in-law, and she was sure that from his grave her
father too was reproaching Tatsuo. It was in this crisis, shortly
after the father's death, that Tatsuo became most enthusiastic
about finding a husband for Yukiko. The candidate in question
was the heir of a wealthy family and executive of a bank in Toyohashi, not far from Nagoya. Since that bank and Tatsuo's were
correspondents, Tatsuo knew all he needed to know about the
man's character and finances. The social position of the Saigusa
family of Toyohashi was unassailable, indeed a little too high for

what the Makioka family had become. The man himself was admirable in every respect, and presently a meeting with Yukiko was arranged. Thereupon Yukiko objected, and was not to be moved. There was nothing she really found fault with in the man's appearance and manner, she said, but he was so countrified. Although he was no doubt as admirable as Tatsuo said, one could see that he was quite unintelligent. He had fallen ill on graduating from middle school, it was said, and had been unable to go farther, but Yukiko could not help suspecting that dullness somehow figured in the matter. Herself graduated from a ladies' seminary with honors in English, Yukiko knew that she would be quite unable to respect the man. And besides, no matter how sizable a fortune he was heir to, and no matter how secure a future he could offer, the thought of living in a provincial city like Toyohashi was unbearably dreary. Yukiko had Sachiko's support—surely, said Sachiko, they could not think of sending the poor girl off to such a place. Although Tatsuo for his part admitted that Yukiko was not unintellectual, he had concluded that, for a thoroughly Japanese girl whose reserve was extreme, a quiet, secure life in a provincial city, free from needless excitement, would be ideal, and it had not occurred to him that the lady herself might object. But the shy, introverted Yukiko, unable though she was to open her mouth before strangers, had a hard core that was difficult to reconcile with her apparent docility. Tatsuo discovered that his sister-in-law was sometimes not as submissive as she might be.

As for Yukiko, it would have been well if she had made her position clear at once. Instead she persisted in giving vague answers that could be taken to mean almost anything, and when the crucial moment came it was not to Tatsuo or her older sister that she revealed her feelings, but rather to Sachiko. That was perhaps in part because she found it hard to speak to the almost too enthusiastic Tatsuo, but it was one of Yukiko's shortcomings that she seldom said enough to make herself understood. Tatsuo had concluded that Yukiko was not hostile to the proposal, and the prospective bridegroom became even more enthusiastic after the meeting; he made it known that he must have Yukiko and no one else. The negotiations had advanced to a point, then, from which it was virtually impossible to withdraw gracefully; but once Yukiko said "No," her older sister and Tatsuo could take turns at talking themselves hoarse and still have no hope of moving her. She said "No" to the end. Tatsuo had been especially pleased with the proposed match because he was sure it was one of which his dead father-in-law would have approved, and his disappointment was therefore great. What upset him most of all was the fact that one of the executives in his bank had acted as go-between. Poor Tatsuo wondered what he could possibly say to the man. If Yukiko had reasonable objections, of course, it would be another matter, but this searching out of minor faults—the fellow did not have an intelligent face, she said—and giving them as reasons for airily dismissing a proposal of a sort not likely to come again: it could only be explained by Yukiko's willfulness. Or, if one chose to harbor such suspicions, it was not impossible to conclude that she had acted deliberately to embarrass her brother-in-law.

Tatsuo had apparently learned his lesson. When someone came with a proposal, he listened carefully. He no longer went out himself in search of a husband for Yukiko, however, and he tried whenever possible to avoid putting himself forward in marriage negotiations.

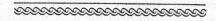

3

THERE WAS yet another reason for Yukiko's difficulties: "the affair that got into the newspapers," Itani called it.

Some five or six years earlier, when she had been nineteen, Taeko, the youngest of the sisters, had eloped with a son of the Okubatas, an old Semba family who kept a jewelry store. Her motives were reasonable enough, it would seem: custom would not allow her to marry before a husband was found for Yukiko, and she had decided to take extraordinary measures. The two families, however, were not sympathetic. The lovers were promptly discovered and brought home, and so the incident passed—but for the unhappy fact that a small Osaka newspaper took it up. In the newspaper story, Yukiko, not Taeko, was made the principal, and even the age given was Yukiko's. Tatsuo debated what to do:

should he, for Yukiko's sake, demand a retraction? But that might not be wise, since it would in effect mean confirming the story of Taeko's misbehavior. Should he then ignore the article? He finally concluded that, whatever the effect might be on the guilty party, it would not do to have the innocent Yukiko spattered. He demanded a retraction. The newspaper published a revised version, and, as they had feared, this time the public read of Taeko. While Tatsuo knew that he should have consulted Yukiko first, he knew too that he could not expect a real answer from her. And there was a possibility that unpleasantness might arise between Yukiko and Taeko, whose interests lay on opposite sides in the matter. He took full responsibility, then, after consulting only his wife. Possibly somewhere deep in his mind lay a hope that, if he saved Yukiko's reputation even at the cost of sacrificing Taeko's, Yukiko might come to think well of him. The truth was that for Tatsuo, in a difficult position as adopted head of the family, this Yukiko, so gentle and docile on the surface and yet so hard underneath, was the most troublesome of his relatives, the most puzzling and the most difficult to manage. But whatever his motives, he succeeded in displeasing both Yukiko and Taeko.

It was my bad luck (thought Yukiko) that the affair got into the papers. And there is no help for it. A retraction would have done no good, down in a corner where no one would have noticed it. And retraction or no retraction, I loathe seeing our names in the papers again. It would have been much wiser to pretend that nothing had happened. Tatsuo was being kind, I suppose, but what of poor Koi-san? She should not have done what she did, but after all the two of them were hardly old enough to know what they should and should not do. It seems to me that the blame must really be laid on the two families for not watching them more carefully. Tatsuo has to take part of it, and so do I. People can say what they will, but I am sure no one who knows me can have taken that story seriously. I cannot think that I was hurt by it. But what of Koi-san? What if she becomes a real delinquent now? Tatsuo thinks only of general principles, and never of the people concerned. Is he not going a little too far? And without even consulting the two of us.

And Taeko, for her part: It is only right of him to want to protect Yukiko, but he could have done it without getting my name

into the papers. It is such a little paper that he could have bought
it off if he had tried, but he is always afraid to spend a little
money.

Taeko was mature for her age.

Tatsuo, who felt that he could no longer face the world, sub-
mitted his resignation to the bank. It was, of course, not accepted,
and for him the incident was closed. The harm to Yukiko, however, was irreparable. A few people no doubt saw the revised newspaper story and knew that she had been maligned, but no matter
how pure and proper she might be herself, it was now known what
sort of sister she had, and, for all her self-confidence, Yukiko presently found marriage withdrawing into the distance. Whatever
she may have felt in private, she continued to insist that the incident had done her little harm, and there was happily no bad
feeling between the sisters. Indeed Yukiko rather tended to protect Taeko from their brother-in-law. The two of them had for
some time been in the habit of paying long visits to Sachiko's
house in Ashiya, between Osaka and Kobe. By turns one of them
would be at the main house in Osaka and the other in Ashiya.
After the newspaper incident, the visits to Ashiya became more
frequent, and now the two of them could be found there together
for weeks at a time—Sachiko's husband Teinosuke was so much
less frightening than Tatsuo in the main house. Teinosuke, an accountant who worked in Osaka and whose earnings were supple-
mented by the money he had received from Sachiko's father, was
quite unlike the stern, stiff Tatsuo. For a commercial-school graduate, he had remarkable literary inclinations, and he had even
tried his hand at poetry. Now and then, when the visits of the
two sisters-in-law seemed too protracted, he would worry about
what the main house might think. "Suppose they were to go back
for a little while," he would say. "But there is nothing at all to
worry about," Sachiko would answer. "I imagine Tsuruko is glad
to have them away now and then. Her house is not half big
enough any more, with all those children. Let Yukiko and Koi-
san do as they like. No one will complain." And so it became the
usual thing for the younger sisters to be in Ashiya.

The years passed. While very little happened to Yukiko, Taeko's
career took a new turn, a turn that was not without import for
Yukiko too. Taeko had been good at making dolls since her school

days. In her spare time, she would make frivolous little dolls from scraps of cloth, and her skill had improved until presently her dolls were on sale in department stores. She made French-style dolls and pure Japanese dolls with a flash of true originality and in such variety that one could see how wide her tastes were in the movies, the theater, art, and literature. She built up a following in the course of time, and, with Sachiko's help, she had rented a gallery for an exhibit in the middle of the Osaka entertainment district. She had early taken to making her dolls in Ashiya, since the main Osaka house was so full of children that it was quite impossible to work there. Soon she began to feel that she needed a better-appointed studio, and she rented a room a half hour or so from Sachiko's house in Ashiya. Tatsuo and Tsuruko in Osaka were opposed to anything that made Taeko seem like a working girl. In particular they had doubts about her renting a room of her own, but Sachiko was able to overcome their objections. Because of that one small mistake, she argued, Taeko was even farther from finding a husband than was Yukiko, and it would be well if she had something to keep her busy. And what if she *was* renting a room? It was a studio, and not a place to live. Fortunately a widowed friend of Sachiko's had opened a rooming house. How would it be, suggested Sachiko, if they were to ask the woman to watch over Taeko? And since it was so near, Sachiko herself could look in on her sister from time to time. Thus Sachiko finally won Tatsuo and Tsuruko over, though it was perhaps an accomplished fact they were giving their permission to.

Quite unlike Yukiko, the lively Taeko was much given to pranks and jokes. It was true that she had had her spells of depression after that newspaper incident; but now, with a new world opening for her, she was again the gay Taeko of old. To that extent Sachiko's theories seemed correct. But since Taeko had an allowance from the main house and was able to ask good prices for her dolls, she found herself with money to spend, and now and then she would appear with an astonishing handbag under her arm, or in shoes that showed every sign of having been imported. Sachiko and her older sister, both somewhat uneasy about this extravagance, urged her to save her money, but Taeko already knew the value of money in the bank. Sachiko was not to tell Tsuruko, she said, but look at this—and she displayed her postal-savings book. "If you ever need a little spending money," she added, "just let me know."

Then one day Sachiko was startled at a bit of news she heard from an acquaintance: "I saw your Koi-san and the Okubata boy walking by the river." Shortly before, a cigarette lighter had fallen from Taeko's pocket as she took out a handkerchief, and Sachiko had learned for the first time that her sister smoked. There was nothing to be done if a girl of twenty-four or twenty-five decided she would smoke, Sachiko said to herself, but now this development. She summoned Taeko and asked whether the report was true. It was, said Taeko. Sachiko's questions brought out the details: Taeko had neither seen nor heard from the Okubata boy after that newspaper incident until the exhibit, where he had bought the largest of her dolls. After that she began seeing him again. But of course it was the purest of relationships, and she saw him very seldom indeed. She was after all a grown woman, no longer a flighty girl, and she hoped her sister would trust her. Sachiko, however, reproved herself for having been too lenient. After all, she had certain obligations to the main house. Taeko worked as the mood took her, and, very much the temperamental artist, made no attempt to follow a fixed schedule. Sometimes she would do nothing for days on end, and again she would work all night and come home red-eyed in the morning—this in spite of the fact that she was not supposed to stay overnight in her studio. Liaison among the main house in Osaka, Sachiko's house in Ashiya, and Taeko's studio, moreover, had not been such that they knew when Taeko left one place and was due to arrive at another. Sachiko began to feel truly guilty. She had been too lax. Choosing a time when Taeko was not likely to be in, she visited the widowed friend and learned of Taeko's habits. Taeko had become so illustrious, it seemed, that she was taking pupils. But only housewives and young girls; except for craftsmen who made boxes for the dolls, men never visited the studio. Taeko was an intense worker once she got herself under way, and it was not uncommon for her to work until three or four in the morning. Since there was no bedding in the room, she would have a smoke while she waited for daylight and the first streetcar. The hours thus matched well enough with what Sachiko had observed. Taeko had at first had a six-mat[1] Japanese room, but recently she had moved into larger quarters: a Western-style room, Sachiko saw, with a little Japanese dressing room on a level slightly above it. There were all sorts of reference works and magazines around the room, and a sewing machine, bits of cloth, and unfinished dolls, and pictures pinned to the walls. It was very much the artist's studio, and yet something in it also suggested the liveliness of a very young girl. Everything was clean and in order. There was not even a stray cigarette butt in the ash tray. Sachiko found nothing in the drawers or the letter rack to arouse her suspicions.

She had been afraid she might find incriminating evidence, and had for that reason dreaded the visit. Now, however, she was immensely relieved, and thankful that she had come. She trusted Taeko more than ever.

Two or three months later, when Taeko was away at her studio, Okubata suddenly appeared at the door and announced that he wanted to see Mrs. Makioka. The two families had lived near each other in the old Semba days, and since he was therefore not a complete stranger, Sachiko thought she might as well see him. He knew it was rude of him to come without warning—so he began. Rash though they had been those several years before, he and Koi-san had been moved by more than the fancy of a moment. They had promised to wait, it did not matter how many years, until they finally had the permission of their families to marry. Although it was true that his family had once considered Taeko a juvenile delinquent, they saw now that she had great artistic talents, and that the love of the two for each other was clean and healthy. He had heard from Koi-san that a husband had not yet been found for Yukiko, but that once a match was made, Koi-san would be permitted to marry him. He had come today only after talking the matter over with her. They were in no hurry; they would wait until the proper time. But they wanted at least Sachiko to know of the promise they had made to each other, and they wanted her to trust them, and presently, at the right time, to take their case to the sister and brother-in-law in the main house. They would be eternally grateful if she would somehow see that their hopes were not disappointed. Sachiko, he had heard, was the most under-

[1] A mat is about two yards by one.

standing member of the family, and an ally of Koi-san's. But he knew of course that it was not his place to come to her with such a request.

Such was his story. Sachiko said she would look into the matter, and sent him on his way. Since she had already suspected that what he described might indeed be the case, his remarks did not particularly surprise her. Since the two of them had gotten into the newspapers together, she rather felt that the best solution would be for them to marry, and she was sure that the main house too would presently come to that conclusion. The marriage might have an unfortunate psychological effect on Yukiko, however, and for that reason Sachiko wanted to put off a decision as long as possible.

As was her habit when time was heavy on her hands, she went into the living room, shuffled through a stack of music, and sat down at the piano. She was still playing when Taeko came in. Taeko had no doubt timed her return carefully, although her expression revealed nothing.

"Koi-san." Sachiko looked up from the piano. "Okubata has just been here."

"Oh."

"I understand how you feel, but I hope you will leave everything to me."

"I see."

"It would be cruel to Yukiko if we moved too fast."

"I see."

"You understand, then, Koi-san?"

Taeko seemed uncomfortable but her face was carefully composed. She said no more.

4

SACHIKO told no one, not even Yukiko, of her discovery. One day, however, Taeko and Okubata ran into Yukiko, who was getting off a bus, just as they started to cross the National Highway.

Yukiko said nothing, but perhaps half a month later Sachiko heard of the incident from Taeko. Wondering what Yukiko might have made of it, Sachiko decided to tell her everything that had happened: there was no hurry, she said—indeed they could wait until something had been arranged for Yukiko herself—but the two must eventually be allowed to marry, and when the time came Yukiko too should do what she could to get the permission of the main house. Sachiko watched carefully for a change in Yukiko's expression, but Yukiko showed not a sign of emotion. If the only reason for not permitting the marriage immediately was that the sisters should be married in order of age, she said when Sachiko had finished, then there was really no reason at all. It would not upset her to be left behind, she added, with no trace of bitterness or defiance. She knew her day would come.

It was nonetheless out of the question to have the younger sister marry first, and since a match for Taeko was as good as arranged, it became more urgent than ever to find a husband for Yukiko. In addition to the complications we have already described, however, yet another fact operated to Yukiko's disadvantage: she had been born in a bad year. In Tokyo the Year of the Horse is sometimes unlucky for women. In Osaka, on the other hand, it is the Year of the Ram that keeps a girl from finding a husband. Especially in the old Osaka merchant class, men fear taking a bride born in the Year of the Ram. "Do not let the woman of the Year of the Ram stand in your door," says the Osaka proverb. The superstition is a deep-rooted one in Osaka, so strongly colored by the merchant and his beliefs, and Tsuruko liked to say that the Year of the Ram was really responsible for poor Yukiko's failure to find a husband. Everything considered, then, the people in the main house, too, had finally concluded that it would be senseless to cling to their high standards. At first they said that, since it was Yukiko's first marriage, it must also be the man's first marriage; presently they conceded that a man who had been married once would be acceptable if he had no children, and then that there should be no more than two children, and even that he might be a year or two older than Teinosuke, Sachiko's husband, provided he looked younger. Yukiko herself said that she would marry anyone her brothers-in-law and sisters agreed upon. She therefore had no particular objection to these revised standards, although she did say that if the man had children she hoped they would be pretty little girls. She thought she could really become fond of little stepdaughters. She added that if the man were in his forties, the climax of his career would be in sight and there would be a little chance that his income would grow. It was quite possible that she would be left a widow, moreover, and, though she did not demand a large estate, she hoped that there would at least be enough to give her security in her old age. The main Osaka house and the Ashiya house agreed that this was most reasonable, and the standards were revised again.

This, then, was the background. For the most part, the Itani candidate did not seem too unlike what they were after. He had no property, it was true, but then he was only forty, a year or two younger than Teinosuke, and one could not say that he had no future. They had conceded that the man might be older than Teinosuke, but it would of course be far better if he were younger. What left them virtually straining to accept the proposal, however, was the fact that this would be his first marriage. They had all but given up hope of finding an unmarried man, and it seemed most unlikely that another such prospect would appear. If they had some misgivings about the man, then, those misgivings were more than wiped out by the fact that he had never been married. And, said Sachiko, even if he was only a clerk, he was versed in French ways and acquainted with French art and literature, and that would please Yukiko. People who did not know her well took Yukiko for a thoroughly Japanese lady, but only because the surface (the dress and appearance, speech and deportment) was so Japanese. The real Yukiko was quite different. She was even then studying French, and she understood Western music far better than Japanese. Sachiko had a friend inquire whether Segoshi— that was his name—was well thought of at M.B. Chemical Industries, and could find no one who spoke ill of him. She had very nearly concluded that this was the opportunity they were waiting for. She should consult the main house. Then suddenly Itani appeared at the gate in a taxi. What of the matter they had discussed the other day? She was, as always, aggressive, and this time she had the man's photograph. Sachiko could hardly admit that she had only begun to consider asking her sister in Osaka—that would make her seem much too unconcerned. They thought it a splendid prospect indeed, she finally answered, but, since the main house was in process of investigating the gentleman, she hoped Itani would wait another week. That was very well, said Itani, but this was the sort of proposal that required speed. If they were in a mood to give a favorable answer, would they not do well to hurry? Every day she had a telephone call from Mr. Segoshi. Had they not made up their minds yet? Wouldn't she show them his photograph, and wouldn't she see what was happening? That was why she had come, and she would expect an answer in a week. Itani finished her business and was off again in five minutes.

Sachiko, a typical Osakan, liked to take her time, and she thought it outrageous to dispose of what was after all a woman's whole life in so perfunctory a fashion. But Itani had touched a sensitive spot, and, with surprising swiftness, Sachiko set off the next day to see her sister in Osaka. She told the whole story, not forgetting to mention Itani's insistence on haste. If Sachiko was slow, however, Tsuruko was slower, especially when it came to marriage proposals. A fairly good prospect, one would judge off-hand, she said, but she would first talk it over with her husband, and, if it seemed appropriate, they might have the man investigated, and perhaps send someone off to the provinces to look into his family. In brief, Tsuruko proposed taking her time. A month seemed a far more likely guess than a week, and it would be up to Sachiko to put Itani off.

Then, precisely a week after Itani's first visit, a taxi pulled up at the gate again. Sachiko held her breath. It was indeed Itani. Just yesterday she had tried to get an answer from the Osaka house, said Sachiko in some confusion, but they still seemed to be investigating. She gathered that there was no particular objection. Might they have four or five days more? Itani did not wait for her to finish. If there was no particular objection, surely they could put off the detailed investigation. How would it be if the two were to meet? She had in mind nothing as elaborate as a *miai*, a formal meeting between a prospective bride and groom. Rather she meant simply to invite them all to dinner. Not even the people in the main house need be present—it would be quite enough if

Sachiko and her husband went with Yukiko. Mr. Segoshi was very eager. And Itani herself was not to be put off. She felt that she really had to awaken these sisters to the facts of life. (Sachiko sensed most of this.) They were a little too fond of themselves; they continued to lounge about while people were out working for them. Hence Miss Yukiko's difficulties.

When exactly did she have in mind, then, asked Sachiko. It was short notice, answered Itani, but both she and Mr. Segoshi would be free the next day, Sunday. Unfortunately Sachiko had an engagement. What of the day after, then? Sachiko agreed vaguely, and said she would telephone a definite answer at noon the next day. That day had come.

"Koi-san." Sachiko started to put on a kimono. Deciding she did not approve of it, she threw it off and took up another. The piano practice had begun again. "I have rather a problem."

"What is your problem?"

"I have to telephone Itani before we leave."

"Why?"

"To give her an answer. She came yesterday and said she wanted Yukiko to meet the man today."

"How like her!"

"It would be nothing formal, she said, only dinner together. I told her I was busy today, and she asked about tomorrow. It was more than I could do to refuse."

"What do they think in Osaka?"

"Tsuruko said over the telephone that if we were going, we should go by ourselves. She said that if they went along, they would have trouble refusing later. And Itani said she would be satisfied without them."

"And Yukiko?"

"Yukiko is the problem."

"She refused?"

"Not exactly. But how do you suppose she feels about being asked to meet the man on only one day's notice? She must think we are not doing very well by her. I hardly know, though. She said nothing definite, except that it might be a good idea to find out a little more about him. She would not give me a clear answer."

"What will you tell Itani?"

"What shall I tell her? It will have to be a good reason, and we cannot afford to annoy her. She might help us again someday. Koi-san, could you call and ask if we might wait a few days?"

"I could, I suppose. But Yukiko is not likely to change her mind in a few days."

"I wonder. She is upset only at the short notice, I suspect. I doubt if she really minds so."

The door opened and Yukiko came in. Sachiko said no more. There was a possibility that Yukiko had heard too much already.

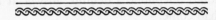

5

"You are going to wear that obi?" asked Yukiko. Taeko was helping Sachiko tie the obi. "You wore that one—when was it?—we went to a piano recital."

"I did wear this one."

"And every time you took a breath it squeaked."

"Did it really?"

"Not very loud, but definitely a squeak. Every time you breathed. I swore I would never let you wear that obi to another concert."

"Which shall I wear, then?" Sachiko pulled obi after obi from the drawer.

"This one." Taeko picked up an obi with a spiral pattern.

"Will it go with my kimono?"

"Exactly the right one. Put it on, put it on." Yukiko and Taeko had finished dressing some time before. Taeko spoke as though to a reluctant child, and stood behind her sister to help tie the second obi. Sachiko knelt at the mirror and gave a little shriek.

"What is the matter?"

"Listen. Carefully. Do you hear? It squeaks." Sachiko breathed deeply to demonstrate the squeak.

"You are right. It squeaks."

"How would the one with the leaf pattern be?"

"Would you see if you can find it, Koi-san?" Taeko, the only one of the three in Western clothes, picked her way lightly through the collection of obis on the floor. Again she helped with the tying. Sachiko stood up and took two or three deep breaths.

"This one seems to be all right." But when the last cord was in place, the obi began squeaking.

The three of them were quite helpless with laughter. Each new squeak set them off again.

"It is because of the double obi," said Yukiko, pulling herself together. "Try a single one."

"No, the trouble is with the cloth."

"But the double ones are all of the same cloth. Folding it double only doubles the squeak."

"You are both wrong." Taeko picked up another obi. "This one will never squeak."

"But that one is double too."

"Do as I tell you. I have discovered the cause."

"But look at the time. You and your obis will have us missing everything. There never is much music at these concerts, you know."

"Who was it that first objected to my obi, Yukiko?"

"I want to hear music, not your squeaking."

"You have me exhausted. Tying and untying, tying and un-tying."

"You are exhausted! Think of me." Taeko braced herself to pull the obi tight.

"Shall I leave it here?" O-haru, the maid, brought the medical equipment in on a tray: a sterilized hypodermic needle, a vitamin concentrate, alcohol, absorbent cotton, adhesive tape.

"My injection, my injection! Yukiko, give me my injection. Oh, yes." O-haru had turned to leave. "Call a cab. Have it come in ten minutes."

Yukiko was thoroughly familiar with the procedure. She opened the ampule with a file, filled the needle, and pushed Sachiko's left sleeve to the shoulder. After touching a bit of alcohol-soaked cotton to the arm, she jabbed with the needle.

"Ouch!"

"I have no time to be careful."

A strong smell of Vitamin B filled the room. Yukiko patted the adhesive tape in place.

"I too am finished," said Taeko.

"Which cord will go with this obi?"

"Take that one. The one you have. And hurry."

"But you know perfectly well how helpless I am when I try to hurry. I do everything wrong."

"Now then. Take a deep breath for us."

"You were right." Sachiko breathed earnestly. "You were quite right. Not a squeak. What was the secret?"

"The new ones squeak. You have nothing to worry about with an old one like this. It is too tired to squeak."

"You must be right."

"One only has to use one's head."

"A telephone call for you, Mrs. Makioka." O-haru came running down the hall. "From Mrs. Itani."

"How awful! I forgot all about her."

"And the cab is coming."

"What shall I do? What shall I tell her?" Sachiko fluttered about the room. Yukiko on the other hand was quite calm, as if to say that the matter was no concern of hers. "What shall I say, Yukiko?"

"Whatever you like."

"Not just any answer will do."

"I leave it to you."

"Shall I refuse for tomorrow, then?"

Yukiko nodded.

"You want me to, Yukiko?"

Yukiko nodded again.

Sachiko could not see the expression on her sister's face. Yukiko's eyes were turned to the floor.

6

"I WILL be back soon, Etsuko." Yukiko looked into the parlor, where Etsuko was playing house with one of the maids. "You promise to watch everything for us?"

"And you are bringing me a present, remember."

"I remember. The little gadget we saw the other day, the gadget to boil rice in."

"And you will be back before dinner?"

"I will be back before dinner."

"Promise?"

"I promise. Koi-san and your mother are having dinner with your father in Kobe, but I promise to be back. We can have dinner together. You have homework to do, remember."

"I have to write a composition."

"You are not to play too long, then. Write your composition, and I can read it when I come back."

"Good-bye, Yukiko. Good-bye, Koi-san." Etsuko called only the oldest of her mother's sisters "aunt." She spoke to Yukiko and Taeko as though they were her own sisters.

Etsuko skipped out over the flagstones without bothering to put on her shoes. "You are to be back for dinner, now. You promised."

"How many times do you think you need to ask?"

"I will be furious with you. Understand?"

"What a child. I understand."

Yukiko was in fact delighted at these signs of affection. For some reason, Etsuko never clung quite so stubbornly to her mother, but Yukiko was not allowed to go out unless she accepted Etsuko's conditions. On the surface, and indeed to Yukiko herself, her reasons for spending so much time in Ashiya were that she did not get along well with her brother-in-law, and that Sachiko was the more sympathetic of her older sisters. Lately, however, Yukiko had begun to wonder whether a still more important reason might not be her affection for Etsuko. She had not been able to find an answer when Tsuruko once complained that though Yukiko doted on Etsuko, she paid almost no attention to the children at the main house. The truth of the matter was that Yukiko was especially fond of little girls Etsuko's age and Etsuko's sort. The main house was of course full of children, but, except for the baby, they were all boys who could not hope to compete with Etsuko for Yukiko's affections. Yukiko, who had lost her father some ten years before and her mother when she was very young, and who had no real home of her own, could with no particular regrets have gone off the next day to be married, but for the thought that she would

no longer see Sachiko, of whom in all the world she was fondest
and on whom she most depended. No, she could still see Sachiko.
It was the child Etsuko she would not see, for Etsuko would be
changing and growing away from her, forgetting the old affection.
Yukiko felt a little jealous of Sachiko, who would always have the
girl's love. If she married a man who had been married before, she
hoped it would be a man with a pretty little daughter. Even should
the child prove to be prettier than Etsuko, however, she feared she
could never quite match the love she had for the latter. The fact
that she had been so long in finding a husband caused Yukiko
herself less anguish than others might have supposed. She rather
hoped that if she could not make a match worth being really enthusiastic about, she would be left here in Ashiya helping Sachiko
rear the child. That would somehow make up for the loneliness.

It was not impossible that Sachiko had deliberately brought the
two together. When Taeko began making dolls in the room assigned to her and Yukiko, Sachiko arranged to move Yukiko into
Etsuko's room, a six-mat Japanese-style room on the second floor.
Etsuko slept in a low wooden baby bed, and a maid had always
slept on the straw-matted floor beside her. When Yukiko took the
maid's place, she spread two kapok mattresses on a folding straw
couch, so that her bed was almost as high as Etsuko's. She gradually began relieving Sachiko of her duties: nursing Etsuko when
she was ill, hearing her lessons and her piano practice, making her
lunch or her afternoon tea. Yukiko was in many ways better qualified to care for the child than was Sachiko. Etsuko was plump
and rosy-cheeked, but like her mother she had little resistance to
ailments. She was always running a high fever or going to bed
with a swollen lymph gland or an attack of tonsillitis. At such
times someone had to sit up two and three nights running to
change the poultices and refill the ice bag, and it was Yukiko who
best stood the strain. Yukiko appeared to be the most delicate of
the sisters. Her arms were very little fuller than Etsuko's, and the
fact that she looked as though she might come down with tuber-
culosis at almost any time had helped frighten off prospective husbands. The truth was, however, that she was the strongest of them
all. Sometimes when influenza went through the house, she alone
escaped. She had never been seriously ill. Sachiko, on the other

hand, would have been taken for the healthiest of the sisters, but her appearance was deceiving. She was in fact quite undependable. If she tired herself, however slightly, taking care of Etsuko, she too was presently ill, and the burden on the rest of the family was doubled. The center of her father's attention when the Makioka family had been at its most prosperous, she even now had something of the spoiled child about her. Her defenses were weak, both mentally and physically. Sometimes, as if they were older than she, her sisters would find it necessary to reprove her for some excess. She was therefore highly unqualified both for nursing Etsuko and for seeing to her everyday needs. Sachiko and Etsuko sometimes had real quarrels. There were those who said that Sachiko did not want to lose a good governess, and that when a prospective bridegroom appeared for Yukiko she stepped in to wreck the negotiations. Although Tsuruko at the main house was not inclined to believe the rumors, she did complain that Sachiko found Yukiko too useful to send home. Sachiko's husband Teinosuke too was a little uneasy. For Yukiko to live with them was very well, he said, but it was unfortunate that she had worked her way between them and the child. Could Sachiko not try to keep her at more of a distance? To have Etsuko come to love her aunt more than her mother would not do. But Sachiko answered that he was inventing problems. Etsuko was clever enough for her age, and, however much she might seem to favor Yukiko, she really loved Sachiko herself best. It was not necessary that Etsuko cling to her mother as she clung to Yukiko. Etsuko knew that Yukiko would one day leave to be married, that was all. To have Yukiko in the house was a great help, of course, but that would last only until they found her a husband. Sachiko knew how fond Yukiko was of children, and had let her have Etsuko to make her forget the loneliness of the wait. Koi-san had her dolls and the income they brought (and as a matter of fact she seemed to be keeping company with a man), whereas poor Yukiko had nothing. Sachiko felt sorriest for Yukiko. Yukiko had no place to go, and Sachiko had given her Etsuko to keep her happy.

To say whether or not Yukiko had guessed all this was impossible. In any case, her devotion when Etsuko was ill was something Sachiko or even a professional nurse could never have imitated. Whenever someone had to watch the house, Yukiko tried to send

Teinosuke and Sachiko and Taeko off while she stayed behind
with Etsuko. She would have been expected, then, to stay behind
again today, but the concert was a small private one to hear Leo
Sirota, and she could not bring herself to forgo a piano recital.
Teinosuke having gone hiking near Arima Springs, Taeko and
Sachiko were to meet him in Kobe for dinner. Yukiko decided to
refuse at least the dinner invitation. She would be back for dinner
with Etsuko.

7

"WHAT COULD be keeping her?"

Taeko and Yukiko were at the gate. There was no sign of Sachiko.

"It is almost two." Taeko stepped toward the cab. The driver
held the door open.

"They have been talking for hours."

"She might just try hanging up."

"Do you think Itani would let her? I can see her trying to back
away from the telephone." Yukiko's amusement suggested again
that the affair was no concern of hers. "Etsuko, go tell your mother
to hang up."

"Shall we get in?" Taeko motioned to the cab.

"I think we should wait." Yukiko, always very proper, would
not get into the cab ahead of an older sister. There was nothing
for Taeko to do but wait with her.

"I heard Itani's story." Taeko took care that the driver did not
overhear her. Etsuko had run back into the house.

"Oh?"

"And I saw the picture."

"Oh?"

"What do you think, Yukiko?"

"I hardly know, from just a picture."

"You should meet him."

Yukiko did not answer.

"Itani has been very kind, and Sachiko will be upset if you refuse to meet him."

"But do we really need to hurry so?"

"She said she thought it was the hurrying that bothered you."

Someone ran up behind them. "I forgot my handkerchief. My handkerchief, my handkerchief. Bring me a handkerchief, someone." Still fussing with the sleeves of her kimono, Sachiko flew through the gate.

"It was quite a conversation."

"I suppose you think it was easy to think up excuses. I only just managed to throw her off."

"We can talk about it later."

"Get in, get in." Taeko pushed her way into the cab after Yukiko.

It was perhaps a half mile to the station. When they had to hurry they took a cab, but sometimes, half for the exercise, they walked. People would turn to stare at the three of them, dressed to go out, as they walked toward the station. Shopkeepers were fond of talking about them, but probably few had guessed their ages. Although Sachiko had a six-year-old daughter and could hardly have hidden her age, she looked no more than twenty-six or twenty-seven. The unmarried Yukiko would have been taken for perhaps twenty-two or three, and Taeko was sometimes mistaken for a sixteen- or seventeen-year-old. Yukiko had reached an age when it was no longer appropriate to address her as a girl, and yet no one found it strange that she should be "young Miss Yukiko." All three, moreover, looked best in clothes a little too young for them. It was not that the brightness of the clothes hid their ages; on the contrary, clothes in keeping with their ages were simply too old for them. When, the year before, Teinosuke had taken his wife and sisters-in-law and Etsuko to see the cherry blossoms by the Brocade Bridge, he had written this verse to go with the souvenir snapshot:

> *Three young sisters,*
> *Side by side,*
> *Here on the Brocade Bridge.*

The three were not monotonously alike, however. Each had her special beauties, and they set one another off most effectively. Still they had an unmistakable something in common—what fine sisters! one immediately thought. Sachiko was the tallest, with Yukiko and Taeko shorter by equal steps, and that fact alone was enough to give a certain charm and balance to the composition as they walked down the street together. Yukiko was the most Japanese in appearance and dress, Taeko the most Western, and Sachiko stood midway between. Taeko had a round face and a firm, plump body to go with it. Yukiko, by contrast, had a long, thin face and a very slender figure. Sachiko again stood between, as if to combine their best features. Taeko usually wore Western clothes, and Yukiko wore only Japanese clothes. Sachiko wore Western clothes in the summer and Japanese clothes the rest of the year. There was something bright and lively about Sachiko and Taeko, both of whom resembled their father. Yukiko was different. Her face impressed one as somehow sad, lonely, and yet she looked best in gay clothes. The sombre kimonos so stylish in Tokyo were quite wrong for her.

One of course always dressed for a concert. Since this was a private concert, they had given more attention than usual to their clothes. There was literally no one who did not turn for another look at them as they climbed from the cab and ran through the bright autumn sunlight toward the station. Since it was a Sunday afternoon, the train was nearly empty. Yukiko noticed that the middle-school boy directly opposite her blushed and looked at the floor as they sat down.

8

ETSUKO was tired of playing house. Sending O-hana upstairs for a notebook, she sat down in the parlor to work on her compostion.

The house was for the most part Japanese, the only Western-style rooms being this parlor and the dining room that opened from it. The family received guests in the parlor and spent the better part of the day there. The piano, the radio, and the phonograph were all in the parlor, and during the winter, since only the parlor was heated, it was more than ever the center of the house. This liveliest of rooms attracted Etsuko. Unless she was ill or turned out by guests, she virtually lived there. Her room upstairs, though matted in the Japanese fashion, had Western furnishings and was meant to be her study; but she preferred to study and play in the parlor, which was always a clutter of toys and books and pencils. Everyone dashed about picking things up when there was an unexpected caller.

Etsuko ran to the front door when she heard the bell, and skipped back into the parlor after Yukiko. The promised gift was under Yukiko's arm.

"You are not to look at my composition." Etsuko turned the notebook face down on the table. "You brought what I asked for? Let me see." She pulled the package from Yukiko's arm and lined up the contents on the couch. "Thank you very much."

"This was what you wanted?"

"Yes. Thank you very much."

"And did you finish your composition?"

"Stop. You are not to look at it." Etsuko snatched up the notebook and ran toward the door. "There is a reason."

"And what is that?"

Etsuko laughed. "Because I wrote about you."

"You think you ought not to write about me? Let me see it."

"Later. You can see it later. Not now."

She had written about the rabbit's ear, said Etsuko, and Yukiko figured slightly in the narrative. She would be embarrassed to have Yukiko look at it now. Yukiko should go over it carefully that night after Etsuko herself was in bed. She would get up early to make a clean copy before she started for school. Sure that Sachiko and the others would go to a movie after dinner and be late coming home, Yukiko had a bath with Etsuko and at about eight thirty took her upstairs. Etsuko, a very bad sleeper, always talked excitedly for twenty minutes or a half hour after she was in bed. Putting her to sleep was something of a chore, and Yukiko always had to lie down and listen to the chatter. Sometimes she would go off to sleep herself and not wake up until morning, and sometimes, getting up quietly and throwing a robe over her shoulders, she would go downstairs to have a cup of tea with Sachiko, or the cheese and white wine Teinosuke occasionally

brought out. Tonight a stiffness in the shoulders—she often suffered from it—kept her awake. Sachiko and the rest would not be
home for some time, and it seemed a good chance to look at the
composition. Making very sure that Etsuko was asleep, Yukiko
opened the notebook under the night lamp.

THE RABBIT'S EAR

*I have a rabbit. Someone brought him and said, "This is
for Miss Etsuko."*

*We have a dog and cat in our house, and we keep the rab-
bit by itself in the hall. I always pet it in the morning before I go
to school.*

*Last Thursday I went out into the hall before I went to
school. One ear stood up straight but the other was floped over.
"What a funny rabbit. Why not make the other ear stand up?" I
said, but the rabbit did not listen. "Let me stand it up for you,"
I said. I stood the ear up with my hand, but as soon as I let go
it floped over again. I said to Yukiko, "Yukiko, look at the rabbit's
ear." Yukiko pushed the ear up with her foot, but when she let go
it floped over again. Yukiko laughed and said, "What a funny ear."*

Yukiko hastily drew a line under the words "with her foot."

Etsuko was good at composition, and this too seemed well
enough written. Looking in the dictionary to see whether "floped"
might just possibly be an acceptable spelling, Yukiko corrected
only that. There did not seem to be any mistakes in grammar.
The problem was what to do about that foot, however. She finally
decided only to strike out the three unfortunate words. It would
have been simplest to say "with her hand," but Yukiko had in fact
used her foot, and she did not think it right to have the child telling a lie. If the sentence became a little vague, there was nothing
to be done about it. But what if the composition had been taken
off to school without Yukiko's having seen it? Etsuko had caught
her in an unseemly pose.

Here is the story of that "with her foot":

The house next door to, or rather behind, the Ashiya house had
for the last six months been occupied by a German family named
Stolz. Since only a coarse wire-net fence stood between the two
back yards, Etsuko immediately came to know the Stolz children.

At first they would glare through the fence and Etsuko would glare back, like animals warily testing each other, but before long they were moving freely back and forth. The oldest was named Peter, and after him came Rosemarie and Fritz. Peter appeared to be nine or ten, and Rosemarie, exactly Etsuko's height, was probably a year or two younger than Etsuko. Foreign children tend to be large. Etsuko and the Stolzes were soon great friends. Rosemarie in particular came over after school each evening, and Etsuko used the affectionate "Rumi" by which the German girl was known in her own family.

The Stolzes had, besides a German pointer and a coal-black cat, an Angora rabbit which they kept penned in the back yard. Etsuko, who had a cat and dog of her own, was not interested in the cat and dog next door, but the rabbit fascinated her. She was fond of helping Rosemarie feed it and of picking it up by the ears, and presently she was coaxing her mother to buy a rabbit for her. Although Sachiko had no particular objection to keeping animals, it would be sad, she thought, to have an animal die for want of good care. And of course they already had Johnny, the dog and Bell, the cat, and it would be a nuisance to have to feed a rabbit too. And there was nowhere in the house to keep it, since it would have to be penned apart from Johnny and Bell. Sachiko was still deliberating the problem when the man who cleaned the chimney came around with a rabbit. The rabbit was not an Angora, indeed, but it was very white and very pretty. Etsuko, upon consultation with her mother, decided that it would best be kept in the hall, out of reach of Johnny and Bell. The creature was a puzzle to Sachiko and the rest. Unlike a cat or a dog, it was completely unresponsive. It only sat with wide, staring, pink eyes, a strange, twitching creature in a world quite apart.

This was the rabbit of which Etsuko had written. Yukiko was in the habit of waking the girl, helping with her breakfast, seeing that she had everything she needed for school, and then going back to bed herself. It had been a chilly autumn morning. Yukiko, a kimono thrown over her nightgown, had gone to the door to see Etsuko off and found the girl earnestly trying to make the rabbit's ear stand up. "See what you can do with it," Etsuko had ordered. Yukiko, hoping to solve the problem and see Etsuko off in

time for school, and yet unwilling to touch the puffy animal, had
tried lifting the ear between her toes. As soon as she took her
foot away, the ear "floped over" again.

"What was wrong with what I had?" Etsuko looked at the cor-
rection the next morning.

"Did you really have to say I used my foot?"

"But you did."

"Because I did not want to touch the thing."

"Oh?" Etsuko did not seem satisfied. "Maybe I should say so,
then."

"And what will your teacher think of my manners?"

"Oh?" Etsuko still did not seem entirely satisfied.

9

"IF TOMORROW is bad, how would the sixteenth be? The sixteenth
is a very lucky day."

So Itani had said when Sachiko was caught by that telephone
call. Sachiko was forced to agree. Two days passed, however, before Yukiko too agreed. Yukiko set as a condition that Itani keep
her promise and only introduce the two, avoiding any suggestion
of a formal *miai*. Dinner, then, was to be at six at the Oriental
Hotel in Kobe. With Itani would be her brother, Murakami
Fusajirō, who worked for an Osaka iron dealer (it was because he
was an old friend of the man Segoshi that Itani had first come
with her proposal, and he was of course a man without whom the
party would not be complete), and his wife. Segoshi would be a
sad figure all by himself, and yet it was hardly an occasion to justify calling his family in from the country; but fortunately there
was a middle-aged gentleman named Igarashi who was a director
of the same iron company and who came from Segoshi's home
town, and Murakami invited him to come along as a sort of substitute for the relatives expected at a *miai*. Including Sachiko,
Teinosuke and Yukiko there would be a total of eight at the dinner.

The day before, Sachiko and Yukiko went to Itani's beauty parlor. Sachiko, who meant only to have her hair set and had sent Yukiko in first, was awaiting her turn when Itani took advantage of a free moment to confer with her.

"May I ask a favor?" Itani sat down and, bringing her mouth to Sachiko's ear, lowered her voice almost to whisper. She always spoke in the brisk Tokyo manner. "I'm sure I don't need to tell you, but could you try to make yourself as old as possible tomorrow?"

"Of course . . ."

But Itani had begun again. "I don't mean that you should dress just a *little* more modestly than usual. You have to dress *very* modestly—make up your mind to it. Miss Yukiko is very attractive, of course, but she's so slender. There is something a little sad about her face, and she loses a good twenty per cent of her charm when she sits beside you. You have such a bright, modern face—and you would attract attention anyway. So could you try at least tomorrow to set Miss Yukiko off? Make yourself look say ten or fifteen years older? If not, you might be just enough to ruin everything."

Sachiko had received similar instructions before. She had been with Yukiko at a number of *miai*, and had been the subject of some discussion: "The older sister seems so lively and modern, and the younger one a little moody," or, "The older sister completely blotted out the younger." There had even been occasions when she had been asked not to come at all, and only Tsuruko at the main house had attended Yukiko. Sachiko's answer was always that people simply did not see Yukiko's beauty. It was true that she herself had a somewhat livelier face, a face that might be called "modern." But there was nothing remarkable about a modern face. Modern faces were to be found everywhere. She knew it was odd of her to be praising her own sister so extravagantly, but the beauty, fragile and elegant, of the sheltered maiden of old, the maiden who had never known the winds of the world —might one not say that Yukiko had it? Sachiko would not want Yukiko to marry a man who could not appreciate her beauty, indeed a man who did not demand someone exactly like her. But ardently though she defended Yukiko, Sachiko could not suppress a certain feeling of superiority. Before Teinosuke, at least, she was

boastful: "They say I overshadow poor Yukiko when I go along."
Teinosuke himself would sometimes suggest that Sachiko stay
home or, ordering her to retouch her face or put on a more
modest kimono, would say: "No, you are still not old enough.
You will only lower Yukiko's stock again." It was clear to Sachiko
that he was pleased at having so impressive a wife. Sachiko had
stayed away from one or two of Yukiko's *miai*, but for the most
part she went in Tsuruko's place. Yukiko occasionally said that
she would not go herself if Sachiko was not with her. The difficulty was, however, that no matter how sombre Sachiko tried to
make herself, her wardrobe was simply too bright, and after a
miai she would be told that she still had not looked old enough.

"That is what everyone says. I understand completely. I would
have tried to look old even if you had not mentioned it."

Sachiko was the only customer in the waiting room. The curtain that marked off the next room was drawn back, and Yukiko's
figure, under the dryer, was reflected in the mirror directly before
them. Itani no doubt relied on the noise of the dryer to drown
out her words, but it seemed to Sachiko that Yukiko's eyes were
fixed on them as if to ask what they were talking about. She was
in a panic lest their lips give them away.

On the appointed day, Yukiko, attended by her sisters, started
dressing at about three. Teinosuke, who had left work early, was
there to lend his support. A connoisseur of women's dress, he
was fond of watching such preparations; but more than that, he
knew that the sisters were completely oblivious of time. He was
present chiefly to see that they were ready by six.

Etsuko, back from school, threw her books down in the parlor
and ran upstairs.

"So Yukiko is going to meet her husband."

Sachiko started. She saw in the mirror that the expression on
Yukiko's face had changed.

"And where did you hear that?" she asked with what unconcern she could muster.

"O-haru told me this morning. Is it true, Yukiko?"

"It is not," said Sachiko. "Yukiko and I have been invited to
dinner at the Oriental Hotel by Mrs. Itani."

"But Father is going along."

"And why should she not invite your father too?"

"Etsuko, would you go downstairs, please?" Yukiko was looking straight ahead into the mirror. "And tell O-haru to come up. You will not need to come back yourself."

Etsuko was generally not quick to obey, but she sensed something out of the ordinary in Yukiko's tone.

"All right."

A moment later O-haru was kneeling timidly at the door. "You called?" It was clear that Etsuko had said something. Teinosuke and Taeko, sensing danger, had disappeared.

"O-haru, what did you tell the child today?" Sachiko could not remember having spoken to the maids about today's meeting, but it must have been through her carelessness that they guessed the secret. She owed it to Yukiko to discover how. "What did you say?"

O-haru did not answer. Her eyes were on the floor, and her whole manner was a confession of misconduct.

"When did you tell her?"

"This morning."

"And just what did you have in mind?"

O-haru, who was seventeen, had come to the house at fourteen. Now that she had become almost a member of the family, they found it natural to address her more affectionately than the other maids. Someone always had to see Etsuko across the national highway on her way to and from school, and the task was usually O-haru's. Under Sachiko's questioning, she let it be known that she had told the whole story to Etsuko on the way to school that morning. O-haru was a wonderfully good-natured girl, and when she was scolded she wilted so dismally that it was almost amusing.

"I was wrong to let you overhear that telephone conversation, but you did overhear it, and you should have known well enough that it was secret. You should know that there are some things you talk about and some things you do not. Do you tell a child about something that is completely undecided? When did you come to work here, O-haru? Not just yesterday, you know."

"And not only this time." Yukiko took over. "You have always talked too much. You are always saying things you should have left unsaid."

Scolded by the two in turns, O-haru stared motionless at the

floor. "Very well, you may leave." But O-haru still knelt before
them as if she were dead. Only when she had been told three or
four times to leave did she apologize in a barely audible voice
and turn to go.

"She *will* go on talking, no matter what you say to her."
Sachiko studied the face in the mirror. Yukiko was obviously upset. "But it was careless of me. I should have tried to talk over
the telephone so that they could not understand. I never dreamed
they would tell Etsuko."

"It is not only the telephone. For ever so long I have noticed
how you talk with O-haru there listening."

"And when have we done that?"

"Any number of times. You stop talking when she comes into
the room, but when she goes out you begin again in the loudest
voices, and there she is just outside the door. She must have
heard any number of times."

Sachiko, Yukiko, Teinosuke, and sometimes Taeko had these
last few nights had a number of conferences after Etsuko was in
bed. Occasionally O-haru would come in from the dining room
with something to drink, and, since the dining room was separated from the parlor by three sliding doors with openings large
enough to admit a finger between them, a conversation in the
parlor could be heard quite distinctly in the dining room. Late
at night, when the house was quiet, it was necessary to talk in
particularly low voices to avoid being overheard, and there was
no doubt that they had not been as careful as they might have
been. Yukiko was perhaps right. But if she had been so upset,
and if the point seemed worth mentioning now, why had she
not warned them at the time? She had such a low voice that,
unless she especially called their attention to it, they were not
likely to notice that she was being more subdued than usual. It
was of course a nuisance to have a gossip like O-haru about, but
it could be just as trying to have someone who never said enough,
Sachiko could not help thinking. It appeared from Yukiko's use
of the plural "voices," however, that Teinosuke was the principal
object of her criticism, and one could perhaps forgive her for
having kept quiet out of deference to him. Teinosuke, it was true,
had a very penetrating voice.

"You really should have told us at the time."

"We are not to talk about it in front of them. It is not that I dislike these meetings—you know that—but there they are, watching and telling each other I have failed again." Yukiko's voice was choked, and a tear drew a line over the face in the mirror.

"You know perfectly well, Yukiko, that we have always been the ones who do the refusing. You know that. The other side has always been ready and waiting, and we have not been quite satisfied ourselves."

"Do you suppose the maids think so? They will only think I have failed again, and even if they know the truth, they will say. . . ."

"I think we should talk about something else. We were wrong, and it will never happen again. See what you are doing to your face." Sachiko wanted to retouch the face, but she was afraid she would only invite more tears.

I 0

Teinosuke had fled to the garden cottage that served as his study. He was beginning to worry about the time. It was after four, and there was no sign that the sisters were ready. Something struck the dry foliage in the garden outside. Leaning across his desk, he slid open the paper-panelled window. An autumn shower had suddenly clouded a blue sky. Here and there a raindrop traced its line over the greenery and fell rustling on a leaf.

"It is raining!" He ran into the main house and called up the stairs.

"It *is* raining." Sachiko looked out the window. "Only a shower, though. It will be over in no time. You can still see the blue sky."

But the tiled roofs were already wet and glistening, and the pounding suggested more than a shower.

"You ought to reserve a cab. Have it here at five-fifteen. And I will not wear a kimono in the rain. How would blue serge be?"

There was hardly a cab to be had in Ashiya when it rained. They telephoned immediately, as Teinosuke suggested; but five-fifteen came, and five-twenty, and no cab. The rain only became more violent. Every garage in the city gave the same answer: it being a lucky day, there were scores of weddings, all of which needed cabs; and the cabs left over had unfortunately been taken when the rain began. As soon as a cab came in, however, it would be sent around. Leaving at five-thirty and going straight to Kobe, they could be at the Oriental Hotel by six. The half-hour too passed. Teinosuke telephoned the hotel and was told that the party was present in force and waiting for them. At five minutes to six a cab finally arrived. Safely inside after the driver had come with an umbrella to escort them one by one through the downpour, Sachiko felt a cold drop run down her neck. She remembered that it had rained at Yukiko's last *miai* too, and at the one before that.

"Here we are a half hour late." Teinosuke apologized to Itani almost before he said hello. She came out as they were checking their coats. "There are weddings everywhere, and then it began to rain. We just couldn't find a taxi."

"I saw bride after bride on my way here," said Itani. While Sachiko and Yukiko were checking their coats, she signalled that she wanted to talk to Teinosuke alone.

"I'll introduce you to Mr. Segoshi in a minute. First I wanted to ask whether you had finished investigating him."

"As a matter of fact, the people in Osaka have investigated Mr. Segoshi and are very happy with what they've found out. At the moment they're looking into the matter of his family. There is just one more report due. Might we have another week?"

"I see . . ."

"We should try to be quicker, I know, with you going to all this trouble. But they're so old-fashioned, and they will take their time. We're grateful for all you've done, though, and I must say that I approve completely myself. I told them as strongly as I could that it would do no good to go following all the old forms —that it would only mean putting Yukiko's marriage off still longer. I said that if there was no objection to the man himself they shouldn't worry too much about the family. As a matter of fact, I think everything will go off very well if they like each other this evening."

Teinosuke and Sachiko had agreed upon the excuses they would make, but Teinosuke was quite sincere on at least this last point.

They exchanged only the simplest greetings in the lobby and hurried to the elevator for the second floor, where Itani had reserved a private dining room. Itani and Igarashi were at the head and foot of the table, and Segoshi and the Murakamis on one side. Yukiko, Sachiko, and Teinosuke sat in that order on the other side, with Yukiko opposite Segoshi. Itani had suggested the day before that Segoshi and Yukiko sit in the middle, the one between the Murakamis and the other between her sister and brother-in-law. Sachiko had objected, however, that that would be too reminiscent of a formal *miai*.

"I can't help thinking I don't belong here." The soup had come, and Igarashi chose a suitable moment to open the conversation. "I come from the same town as Segoshi, it's true, but you can see how much older I am. He really ought to have a schoolmate here to help him. All we have in common, you might say, is that our families happen to live near each other. Not that I'm not glad to be here—don't misunderstand me—as a matter of fact it's too fine a party for me. But I argued all the way, and this man Murakami told me I had to come. Mrs. Itani is a good talker, I'm told, but I don't imagine her brother here has ever lost an argument even with her. Do you mean to refuse this important invitation? he said. Think what that would mean, he said—the whole affair would be ruined. We need one old man there, he said, and we can't let that bald head get away. So here I am."

Murakami laughed. "But the director doesn't seem to mind being here, now that we've made it."

"The director—no more of that. I'm here to enjoy myself, and I don't want to hear a word that reminds me of business."

Sachiko remembered that there had been just such a bald, clowning chief-clerk in the Makioka shop. Today, with the larger of the old shops for the most part reorganized as joint-stock companies, "chief clerk" had become "director." The old cloak and apron had been changed for the business suit, and the Semba dialect for standard Japanese, but the "director" himself was even now less an executive than an old apprentice, a man who had come as a boy to learn the business. Every Osaka shop had one or two of them, the bowing, bald-headed, talkative clerks who

knew how to keep the master happy and how to make people
laugh. It seemed likely that Itani had decided to invite Igarashi
lest the conversation lag.

Segoshi sat smiling through this exchange. He was very much
as Sachiko and the rest had imagined him, though younger than
in the picture—they would have taken him for no more than
thirty-six or thirty-seven. The features were regular, but quite lacking in charm and distinction. It was, as Taeko had said, a most
ordinary face. Indeed there was something very ordinary about
the man in general—the height, the frame, the clothes, down to
the choice of necktie. One searched in vain for the Parisian influence. Still he looked like a good, honest office worker, likable
enough in his way.

He could be worse, thought Teinosuke. "And how long were
you in Paris, Mr. Segoshi?"

"Two years exactly. It was a long time ago, though."

"When was it?"

"Fifteen or sixteen years ago. Just after I finished school."

"You were sent to the main office when you graduated, then?"

"No, the trip had nothing to do with the company. I didn't
go to work until I was back in Japan. My father had just
died. The estate didn't come to very much, but I did have a little
money to spend, and off I went. If I had any aim in mind, I
suppose it was to improve my French. And then I had a vague
idea that I might find work. It turned out to be nothing more
than a pleasure trip, though. I accomplished nothing—my French
was no better afterwards, and of course I didn't find work."

"Segoshi is a very unusual person," Murakami put in. "Most
people hate the idea of coming home once they're in Paris, but
Segoshi was so homesick he had to come back."

"Really? And why was that?"

"I hardly know. I suppose I expected too much."

"You went to Paris to find how good Japan was—there's nothing wrong with that. And is that why you want a Japanese-style
wife?" Igarashi's manner was joking, but he shot a glance at
Yukiko, who was looking at her plate.

"I suppose your French has improved a great deal since you've
been back," said Teinosuke.

"I'm afraid not. It's a French company, but the staff is almost entirely Japanese. Only two or three executives at the top are French."

"And you have no chance to speak French?"

"When an M.M. ship comes in I have a little conversation practice, and that is the sum of it. Except of course for writing letters."

"Miss Yukiko is studying French too," put in Itani.

"Only to keep my sister company."

"And who is your teacher?" asked Itani. "Japanese? French?"

"A French lady . . ."

". . . who is married to a Japanese," Sachiko took up. Yukiko was never very talkative when she was out of the house, and she was especially helpless when the occasion demanded not the Osaka dialect, but standard Japanese. Her sentences had a way of never quite ending unless Sachiko rescued her. Sachiko herself had a little trouble bringing out exactly the right words, but she was able to disguise the more obvious features of her Osaka accent and talk with a certain fluency on almost any subject.

"And can the lady speak Japanese?"

"She couldn't at first, but lately she has been learning, and now . . ."

". . . and now," said Sachiko, "she is really too good. We're forbidden to use Japanese when we're having French lessons, but somehow we slip into it."

"I've listened to them from the next room and heard hardly a word of French," said Teinosuke.

"That is not true." Sachiko slipped into the Osaka dialect in spite of herself. "We speak a great deal of French, and you cannot hear it."

"That's so. Now and then you would say something in the tiniest whisper, and I suppose it was French. I doubt if you'll improve at that rate. But I suppose that is always the way when ladies take up languages."

"It is very kind of you to say so. . . . But I do not spend all my time on French, you will remember. I learn any number of things from her when she uses Japanese—cooking and knitting and how to make French pastries and so on. You liked the cuttle-fish the other day so well that you ordered me to go back to learn more. Have you forgotten?"

Everyone was amused at this little tiff. Mrs. Murakami took
the cuttlefish seriously, however, and Sachiko had to describe it
in detail: a French way of cooking cuttlefish, she explained, with
tomatoes and a touch of garlic.

I I

SACHIKO noticed that Segoshi drank down whatever was poured
for him. He was clearly a good drinker. Murakami seemed to be
a teetotaler, and Igarashi, a flaming red from what little he had
already drunk, waved the boy away each time he came around
with a bottle. Teinosuke and Segoshi, on the other hand, were
able to keep each other company. Neither showed the slightest
sign of drunkenness. Itani had already told Sachiko that, while
Segoshi of course did not drink every night, he liked his liquor,
and, when the opportunity came, was always ready to drink his
share. Sachiko was far from disapproving. She had lost her mother
when she was very young, and she and her sisters had kept their
father company when he had a drink with his dinner. All of them,
beginning with Tsuruko, knew how to drink. Tatsuo and Teinosuke, the husbands of the two older sisters, were moreover in the
habit of having a drink now and then, and it seemed to them all
that a teetotaler would be a most unsatisfying husband. No one
of course wanted to marry a drunkard, but a man who enjoyed
an occasional drink seemed best. Although Yukiko had, it was
true, never insisted that a prospective husband be a drinker,
Sachiko suspected that her sister felt much as she did. Yukiko was
not the sort to make her views known, and unless she had a
husband who would drink with her she might well take to brooding. The husband for his part would be likely to find the silence
depressing. In any case, the picture of Yukiko married to a teetotaler seemed unbearably dreary.

"Suppose you have something to drink," she whispered, hoping
to bring Yukiko into the conversation. She motioned with her
eyes to the glass of white wine, and now and then, by way of

encouragement, had a sip of her own. "Would you pour her a little more, please?" she said to the boy.

Yukiko too had noted what a good drinker Segoshi was. Thinking she should be a little more lively herself, she now and then took an unobtrusive sip of wine. Her feet were wet and cold from the rain, however, and the wine only made her dizzy.

"You like white wine?" Segoshi asked.

Yukiko laughed and looked at her plate.

"One small glass or two," said Sachiko. "But I've been very impressed, watching you. Do you know how much you could drink if you had to?"

"A quart or two, I suppose, with no trouble."

"And do you do tricks when you're drunk?" asked Igarashi.

"I'm afraid I have no talents. I just talk more than usual."

"Miss Yukiko plays the piano," said Itani. "They tell me the whole family likes foreign music."

"But not only foreign music," Sachiko was quick to explain. "We had koto lessons when we were children, and lately I've been thinking I would like to learn again. Sometimes I take the koto out to see what I still remember. My youngest sister has started taking dancing lessons, you know, and I have any number of chances to hear the koto."

"Miss Taeko is taking dancing lessons, is she?"

"Yes. Yamamura school. She seems so fond of foreign things, but lately she's begun to go back to what she knew when she was a girl. She really handles herself very well—but then it's only a matter of relearning, I suppose."

"I don't know much about it," said Igarashi, "but I think this Yamamura school is a fine thing. What we need to do is keep our Osaka arts, not imitate everything that comes in from Tokyo."

"The director—I'm sorry, Mr. Igarashi—Mr. Igarashi is very good at Utazawa singing. He's been practicing for years."

"But the trouble with Utazawa," interposed Teinosuke, "—of course it's different when you are as good as Mr. Igarashi—is that when you first begin, you want an audience, and before long you're spending your time at geisha houses where they'll always listen to you."

"You're quite right. That's the trouble with Japanese music in general," said Igarashi. "It isn't for home consumption. But with me it's different. On that point I'm as stiff and proper as the best of them. Isn't that so, Murakami?"

"As stiff as iron. The business is in your blood."

Igarashi laughed. "But there's something I have to ask the ladies. That thing you all carry—a compact is it called. What is inside it? Just powder?"

"Just powder," said Itani. "Why?"

"On a train about a week ago, the lady up wind from me—she was straight out of a fashion magazine—took out a compact and began patting away at her nose, and just then I had a fit of sneezing. Does powder do that sort of thing to you?"

"There must have been something wrong with your nose. I'm not at all sure it was the powder."

"I would agree with you if it were only the one time, but I've had the same experience twice now."

"You must be right, now that I think of it," put in Sachiko. "I've been sneezed at myself two or three times. The more elegant the powder the more it seems to make people sneeze."

"I've never had that experience," said Mrs. Murakami. "I'll have to try using more expensive powder."

"But it's no laughing matter. We mustn't let this go too far. Possibly we should have a law against powdering the nose when someone is sitting down wind. Mrs. Makioka has been kind enough to apologize, but the woman the other day ignored my sneezing."

"Speaking of trains," said Sachiko. "My youngest sister says she always wants to go around yanking loose threads out of strange men's coat lapels when she is on a crowded train."

Itani had felt much the same urge. "And I can remember how I used to want to pull the stuffing out of quilts when I was a girl."

"There's something of that in all of us," said Igarashi. "When I have a little to drink, I always want to ring someone's doorbell. Or I'm waiting for a train, and I want to press the button that says 'Do not touch,' and have to fight to keep myself away."

Itani sighed happily. "I *have* had fun this evening." It seemed that even when the fruit was brought she had not yet talked enough. "Mrs. Makioka—not to change the subject, but have you noticed how young wives—of course you're young yourself, but

I mean *younger* wives, women in their early twenties who have only been married two or three years—have you noticed how clever and scientific young wives are these days—in managing their houses, and bringing up their children, and whatever they do? It makes me think how fast times are changing."

"That's very true. The schools seem to teach them entirely different things from what I learned. I feel ages older when I talk to one of them."

"My niece, for instance, came in from the country, and I was told to watch over her while she was in school in Kobe. She got married not long ago, to a man who works in Osaka. He makes ninety yen a month, and with bonus and with thirty yen a month his family sends for the rent, I suppose he has, in all, a hundred fifty or sixty a month. I went to see how they were managing, and I found that as soon as they had the ninety yen they took out all sorts of envelopes marked 'gas' and 'light' and 'clothes' and 'miscellaneous' and so on, and set everything in order for the following month by dividing the money up in the envelopes. You can imagine how little they have to spare, but she was very clever about putting together a meal the night I was there. And the house is nicely furnished too, not nearly as shabby as you would expect. Of course there's a certain amount of cheating involved. When I started home I gave her money to buy my ticket, but instead she bought a strip of tickets and kept the rest herself. I couldn't help thinking what nonsense it was to say that I should be watching over her."

"Parents need more watching than children these days," said Sachiko. "There's a young wife near me. The other day when I stopped by to ask her something she made me come in. She had no maid, but everything was beautifully in order. I wonder if young wives all prefer Western clothes and have foreign furniture —anyway, this lady always wears foreign clothes. There was a perambulator in the middle of the room, and the baby tight inside. The mother asked me to take care of it for just a minute, and stepped out of the room. Not a minute later she was back with tea for me and warm bread and milk for the baby. And how would you like a cup of tea, she said, and no sooner had she sat down than she looked at her watch. It was time for Chopin. Did I like Chopin? She switched on the radio, and began feeding the baby. Entertaining the guest, listening to Chopin, getting the baby fed—she managed everything at once. It really seemed very clever of her."

"And the way they bring up children these days. That's changed too," said Itani.

"The lady complained about exactly that. She said it was very nice of her mother to come to see the baby, but that just when she herself had finished teaching it not to want to be picked up, along would come the old lady to pick it up and hug it unmercifully, and the training would have to begin all over again."

"It does seem to be true, now that you mention it, that children cry less than they used to. I understand that once a child is old enough to get up by itself, the mother pays no attention when it falls. She walks on as though nothing had happened, and soon the child comes after her without a whimper."

In the lobby after dinner, Itani told Sachiko and Teinosuke that, if Yukiko did not mind, Segoshi would like to see her alone for perhaps fifteen or twenty minutes. Yukiko agreed, and the others talked of nothing in particular while the two sat a little apart.

"What did Mr. Segoshi have to say?" Sachiko asked as they were on their way home in a cab.

"All sorts of things," said Yukiko almost inaudibly. "And not really anything."

"I suppose he was testing you. He asked questions?"

Yukiko did not answer. The rain had settled into a slow drizzle, as though the long spring rains were coming out of season. The wine seemed finally to be having its effect. She looked at the blurred confusion of headlights reflecting from the national highway.

I 2

"ITANI stopped by my office today," Teinosuke said to Sachiko the following evening.

"And why did she do that?"

"She said she knew she should have gone to see you instead, but she had business in Osaka, and then she thought I might not be as slow as you."

"What did she have to say?"

"It was good news for the most part. But we ought to go out where no one will hear us." He led the way to his study.

The others, it appeared, had stayed to talk for twenty or thirty minutes after the Makiokas left. Segoshi was extremely enthusiastic. He thought Yukiko's appearance and manner quite as elegant as one could desire, but he also thought she looked rather delicate and he wondered if she might be ill. And when Itani's brother had investigated Yukiko's school record he had noticed that she was absent more often than normal. He too wondered whether Yukiko might not have been sickly in her school days. Teinosuke answered that he knew nothing about Yukiko's bad school attendance, and that he would have to ask his wife and Yukiko herself, but he could assure Itani that in the years he had known her Yukiko had not been ill even once. It was true that she seemed delicate, that she was almost too slender, and that she could hardly be called robust. When it came to catching colds, however, he could say most positively that Yukiko had more resistance than any of her sisters. She was better able to stand a physical strain than anyone except the sister in Osaka. They were quite right, nevertheless, to suspect that her delicate appearance might be a sign of weak lungs, and indeed more than one person had had the same misgivings before. Teinosuke would therefore talk to his wife, to Yukiko, and to the main house in Osaka, and urge them to put these doubts at rest by having a physical examination, and perhaps even an X-ray. Itani replied that his assurances were quite enough, that they need not go to such trouble. But Teinosuke insisted: it was better to have matters entirely in the open. They had not had a doctor's report recently, and this would be a good occasion for one. They would feel better themselves, and so would the people in the main house, and Segoshi's delight would no doubt be boundless when he had before him a photograph to show that there was not the faintest cloud on Yukiko's lungs. Even if nothing were to come of the present negotiations, said Teinosuke to his wife, the X-ray would not be a waste of money. It would be evidence to present if similar doubts should arise in the future. He was sure the Osaka house would have no objection, and he suggested that Sachiko take Yukiko to the Osaka University Hospital the very next day.

"But why was she absent from school so often?"

"Schools in those days were not as fussy as they are now, and Father was always taking us to the theater when we should have been in school. I used to go too, and if you were to investigate I think you would find that I was absent even oftener than Yukiko."

"Will Yukiko mind being X-rayed?"

"But why go all the way to Osaka? Dr. Kushida can do it."

"There was the question of that spot too." Teinosuke pointed at his left eye. "She spoke of that. She said that she had not noticed herself, but that men seemed to be good at catching small details. Someone said after we left last night that he thought he saw just a trace of a dark spot over Yukiko's left eye, and someone else agreed with him, and someone said that they were wrong, that it was just the way the light struck. Itani wants to know whether there really is a spot."

"I noticed last night that it was showing. What wretched luck —it has finally attracted attention."

"But she was not especially worried."

The spot over Yukiko's left eye—just above the eyelid—a faint shadow that had recently begun to come and go in cycles. Teinosuke had first noticed it perhaps three to six months before. How long had Yukiko had that spot on her face, he asked Sachiko. Sachiko herself had but recently noticed it, and indeed it was not always there to be noticed. Sometimes it would fade away so that it was barely visible even when one was looking for it, and sometimes it would quite disappear. Then, for a period of perhaps a week, it would suddenly be darker again. Sachiko, who had begun to notice that the spot was most in evidence at about the time of Yukiko's periods, was much concerned about what Yukiko herself might be thinking. Yukiko would have noticed earlier than anyone. And might it not be having an unfortunate psychological effect on her? Yukiko's personality, it was clear, had not so far been twisted by her difficulties in finding a husband, and that was perhaps because she had quiet confidence in her beauty. But

what effect would this new blemish have? Unable to approach
Yukiko directly, Sachiko could only watch for some change in
her sister's manner. Whether Yukiko had not yet noticed, or
whether she was not particularly worried, however, she showed
nothing. One day Taeko came in with a women's magazine some
two or three months old. "Have you read this?" she asked Sachiko.
In the advice column was a letter from a twenty-eight-year-old
woman, unmarried, who had exactly Yukiko's trouble. She had
recently discovered a mark on her face and noted how it faded,
disappeared, and came back again in a monthly cycle. The disturbance was fairly common among women who married late,
the answer said, and was nothing to worry about. The mark generally disappeared when the woman married, and in any case it
could usually be cured by moderate hormone injections. Sachiko
was greatly relieved. As a matter of fact, she herself had had a
similar experience. Some years before, shortly after her marriage,
she had had a dark spot over her eye, rather like a candy smear
over a child's mouth. Her addiction to aspirin was responsible,
said the doctor, and the spot would disappear of its own accord.
In about a year it did indeed disappear. Perhaps, then, the sisters
were particularly susceptible to such spots. Remembering how that
spot of hers—it had been a far darker spot than Yukiko's—had
left her so painlessly, Sachiko was not as upset as another might
have been in her place. The magazine piece put her fears completely at rest. Taeko apparently hoped that Sachiko would find
some way to show it to Yukiko. Despite her apparent unconcern,
Yukiko did no doubt feel a certain uneasiness. Show her this,
said Taeko. Tell her there is nothing to worry about. It will clear
up in no time once she is married, but it would be better to do
something now. Suppose she were to have injections. Of course
it is Yukiko, and she is not likely to welcome the idea, but possibly if we were to choose the right time . . .

Sachiko had mentioned the spot to no one, and this was the
first time she and Taeko had talked of it. So Taeko too was worried. Sachiko saw that something more than sisterly affection was
behind Taeko's uneasiness: the longer Yukiko's marriage was put
off, the longer she herself would have to wait. Who then should
show the magazine to Yukiko? They concluded that Taeko
would be the better choice. If Sachiko were to do it, the whole

incident would be somehow inflated, and Yukiko would have grounds for suspecting that even Teinosuke had been brought into the discussions. Taeko would do better, and she should take the matter up lightly, as though it were really of little consequence. One day when Yukiko was seated at her dresser, Taeko, contriving to make it seem that she had come in quite by accident, said in a low voice:

"That spot over your eye is nothing to worry about, Yukiko."

The spot was darker again.

"Oh?" said Yukiko.

To avoid her sister's eyes, Taeko looked at the floor. "There was an article about it in a magazine. Did you see it? I can show it to you."

"I may have seen it."

"Oh? The spot will go away when you are married, it said, or if you have injections."

Yukiko nodded.

"You know about it then?"

Yukiko nodded again.

The nod was so ambiguous that Taeko could have taken it as a sign that Yukiko simply did not want to talk about the matter. Still it seemed to have in it a note of affirmation. Possibly Yukiko was embarrassed to have her sister know that she had read the article.

Taeko, very timid before, was much relieved. "Suppose you have a few injections," she suggested. But Yukiko did not seem happy at the idea, and put her off with vague answers. For one thing, Yukiko was not the sort to go off to a strange skin doctor unless someone led her by the hand. For another, she seemed less worried about the spot than were those around her.

Some days later Etsuko noticed the spot. She stared curiously at Yukiko. "What is that thing over your eye?" she demanded. Sachiko and the maids, who were unfortunately in the room, fell silent. But Yukiko herself was strangely unconcerned. She muttered an unintelligible answer, and the expression on her face did not change by so much as a shade.

What worried Sachiko most was going out with Yukiko when the spot showed. Yukiko was their marketable article, and it was not only at *miai* that they had to consider who might be looking at her. They wished she would stay at home for the week or so when the spot was expected to be darkest; or, if she must go out, that she would try to hide it.

Yukiko herself was quite indifferent. Sachiko and Taeko agreed that Yukiko's face lent itself well to heavy make-up. A heavy coating of powder, however, had the perverse effect, when the mark was clearest, of making it stand out under a slanting light like a leaden cloud. But although Yukiko might better have used rouge at such times, she disliked rouge (her preference for powder was indeed one reason why she was suspected of having weak lungs; Taeko for her part wore rouge even when she went without powder). She would wear the usual heavy white powder, nothing else.

She occasionally had the misfortune to meet an acquaintance. Once Taeko offered her a compact—they were on a train together, and the spot was darker than usual.

"Suppose you put a little rouge on."

But Yukiko, as always, seemed quite unworried.

13

"AND WHAT did you say to her?" Sachiko asked her husband.

"I told her the truth. I said that the spot was not always so clear, and that there was nothing to worry about—so I had read in magazines, I said. And I thought since we would be having an X-ray taken, we might as well have her go to the University to be examined by a skin specialist. Now that the question has come up, we will have to do at least that much. I said I would see if I could persuade you to agree."

Yukiko being in the habit of spending her time in Ashiya, the people at the main house knew nothing of the spot over her eye, and Teinosuke was afraid he might have been irresponsible in leaving it so long untended. The difficulty had developed but recently, however, and had not complicated earlier *miai*; and then Teinosuke, remembering the surprising speed with which Sachiko's mark had disappeared, was not as disturbed as he might otherwise have been. Since the comings and goings of the spot were moreover predictable, Sachiko could tell in general when it would be unwise to have a *miai*. But Itani had been so insistent, and Sachiko herself had been a little sanguine, not to say careless. Even if the mark has not entirely disappeared by the day named, she had thought, it will hardly be noticeable.

That morning, after Teinosuke left for work, Sachiko had asked Yukiko's impressions of the dinner party. It appeared that Yukiko would leave everything to her sisters and brothers-in-law. Afraid that if she approached the subject tactlessly she might upset the negotiations, Sachiko waited until that night, when Etsuko was in bed and Teinosuke had withdrawn, to mention the possibility of a skin examination. Yukiko was surprisingly quick to agree. With the mark growing fainter by the day, Sachiko thought they might best wait until it appeared again the following month. But Itani had been wise to go to Teinosuke: he insisted on an examination the very earliest day possible. Sachiko called the next day at the Osaka house to report on the negotiations and to urge haste, and in the process to tell her sister that Yukiko would be going to the Osaka University Hospital. The day after that Sachiko and Yukiko started for Osaka, telling the maids in an offhand way that they were going shopping.

Both the internal examination and the skin examination came out quite as expected. The X-ray, which was developed while they waited, revealed not a mark on the lungs. The report on the blood test came some days later: precipitation thirteen milimeters, reactions negative. Sachiko was called aside after the skin examination. The point was to get the young lady married as soon as possible—the doctor did not bother with preliminaries. But she had heard that the ailment could be cured by injections, replied Sachiko. It could, of course; but the mark was so slight that one hardly noticed it, and far the best thing would be for the young lady to marry. It appeared that the magazine article had been correct.

"Will you report to Itani, then?" asked Teinosuke.

Although Sachiko had no particular objection to doing so, she suggested that inasmuch as Itani thought Teinosuke the more responsible of the two, he might well do the reporting himself. Sachiko was not annoyed at being left out, but she did dislike being rushed. Very well, said Teinosuke; he would conduct the negotiations in as businesslike a manner as Itani. The next day he telephoned from his office, told Itani of the examination, and sent off the report and X-ray by registered special-delivery mail. A day later, at four o'clock, he had a return telephone call. Itani announced that she would visit him in an hour, and at precisely five o'clock she appeared. She thanked him for the speed with which he had acted. She had immediately passed the information on to Segoshi, who was most grateful for so detailed a report, and especially for their pains with the X-ray. He was now quite without misgivings, and he hoped they would forgive him for having raised the issue at all. These preliminaries out of the way, Itani proceeded to her main business: hesitant though he was to ask such a favor, Segoshi would like to see Yukiko alone for a little longer than last time—for say an hour. Might they hope that Yukiko would agree? Although Segoshi was no longer young, said Itani, there was something a little shy and naïve about him, possibly because he had never been married. That earlier evening he had been so flustered that he could not for the life of him remember what he had said. And then the young lady herself was so quiet—not that there was anything wrong with her being quiet, of course. What with its being their first meeting, however, she had been extremely reserved, and Segoshi wondered if they might meet again, and this time really learn to know each other. They would be likely to attract notice in a hotel or restaurant, and Itani thought they might better come to her house, dirty little place though it was. Segoshi would be free the following Sunday.

"Do you think Yukiko will agree?" Teinosuke asked his wife.

"I think the question is whether the family in Osaka will agree. Nothing has really been decided yet, and they will say we are going too far too soon."

"I suspect Segoshi wants to see how bad the spot is."

"You are probably right."

"Might it not be best to have him see her now? It hardly shows."

"I quite agree. And if we refuse, he will think we are trying to keep her hidden."

The next day, thinking there might be trouble if she used the telephone at home, Sachiko went out to call Osaka from a public telephone. As she had expected, Tsuruko wanted to know why it was necessary to have them meet so often. Sachiko explained in the most elaborate detail her reasons and Teinosuke's for wanting to permit a second meeting. Possibly they were right, replied Tsuruko, but she could not make the decision alone. She would talk the matter over with Tatsuo and give their answer in a day or so. Sachiko went out to the public telephone again the next day, to catch Tsuruko before the latter called her at home. Tatsuo had agreed, said Tsuruko, but with careful specifications on the time, the place, and the degree of supervision.

A bouquet for Itani in her hand, Sachiko went with Yukiko on the day appointed. For a time the four of them talked together over tea, and presently Yukiko withdrew with Segoshi to the second floor. They came down some thirty or forty minutes later than the arrangements had called for. Leaving before Segoshi, the two sisters went to the Oriental Hotel—Sachiko remembered that it was Sunday and Etsuko would be waiting at home. While they were having tea in the lobby, Yukiko gave her report.

"He certainly talked today," she said.

And Yukiko too had talked, on any number of subjects. Segoshi had asked first about the four sisters: why Yukiko and Taeko spent more time in Ashiya than at the main house in Osaka, what might have been the truth about the newspaper incident, what had happened since. He had gone rather far, but Yukiko had answered freely where it seemed proper, though she had carefully refrained from saying anything that might show Tatsuo in a not very favorable light. It was unfair of him to be asking all the questions, said Segoshi. How would it be if Yukiko were to ask some? But Yukiko was not so disposed, and he went ahead to talk about himself. He preferred what might be called "classical" graces to "modern," and that was why he had never married. If he were to take Yukiko for his bride, however, he would have a better bride than he deserved—the expression "difference in station" came up repeatedly in the course of the conversation. Although he had had no very intimate relations with women, he said, there was one confession he had to make: he had been friendly with a Paris shop girl. Apparently she had deceived him (on this point the details were not clear), and thereby made him homesick and turned him back to pure Japanese tastes. Only his friend Murakami knew of the affair, added Segoshi. This was the first mention he had made of it to anyone else. He hoped Yukiko would believe him when he said that his relations with the girl had been of the purest.

Such in general were the matters Yukiko reported to her sister. It was not hard to guess the feelings of a man who chose to reveal himself so completely.

Itani followed up her advantage. She telephoned Teinosuke the next day to say that Segoshi's misgivings were now quite at rest. He knew that the spot over Yukiko's eye was, as they had said, nothing to worry about. All he could do was wait to see whether he himself had passed the test. Itani wondered when the people at the main house might finish their investigations. Teinosuke had to admit that it was not unreasonable of her to feel a little impatient. She had first approached Sachiko more than a month before, and twice, once at the Ashiya house and again at the Oriental Hotel on the night of the *miai*, she had been put off with the same answer: "May we have another week?" Sachiko had first gone to discuss the matter at the main house only ten days or two weeks before, and there would have been little reason to expect an answer yet even had she been speedier. The main house was extremely slow and deliberate. It had been cowardly of her, pressed by Itani, to ask for only a week and to have Teinosuke do the same. The family record which the main house had requested had as a matter of fact arrived only two or three days before, and, if the home town too was to be investigated, the detective agency would require time. And just to make absolutely sure, the main house meant to send someone for a last check when it seemed likely that the proposal would be accepted. There was nothing to do but ask for four or five days more, and then four or five days more, and in the meantime Itani made a trip to Ashiya and a trip to Teinosuke's office to urge haste. They could not act too quickly, she would say; the negotiations could so easily be upset. And she would point out that the wedding ought to take place before the end of the year. Finally she telephoned Tsuruko, whom she had never met. The startled Tsuruko immediately called Sachiko, who could imagine the consternation on the face of this phlegmatic sister. Tsuruko, so much slower than Sachiko even, would sometimes take as much as five minutes to answer a question. Itani's volleys left her quite helpless. Among other things, Itani again warned that marriage negotiations were delicate in proportion as they were promising.

14

THUS THE MONTH passed. One day in December Sachiko was called to the telephone—the call was from "the lady at the house in Osaka." They had been slow, said Tsuruko, but now they knew fairly well what they needed to know. She would come that day to tell everything. "And what I have to say is not pleasant," she added as she hung up.

The warning was quite unnecessary. "We have failed again," Sachiko had said to herself the moment she heard her sister's voice. Back in the parlor, she heaved a sigh and sank into the armchair. She did not know how often Yukiko's marriage negotiations had progressed almost to the point of a formal engagement and then come to nothing—so often that the process had become routine. Try though she might to tell herself that the match this time was not a particularly desirable one, she knew that she was deeply disappointed, far more disappointed than at earlier failures. For one thing, she had always until now agreed with the main house that the proposal in question should be refused; but this time she had somehow believed that all would go well. No doubt because they had had this Itani woman pushing them, the part she and Teinosuke had played was unusual. Teinosuke generally stood outside the negotiations, allowing himself to be pulled in only when his services were quite necessary, but this time he had, so to speak, flexed his muscles and gone to work. And Yukiko's attitude too had been different. She had agreed to the hasty *miai*, and had twice been alone with the man. She had not objected even to the X-ray and the skin examination—never before had she been so docile. Was she changing,

then? Deep in her heart was she beginning to worry about
having gone so long unmarried? And, though she showed nothing,
was she disturbed at the shadow over her eye? Everything considered, Sachiko had wanted the negotiations to succeed this
time, and had really believed that they would.

She did not entirely give up hope until she had heard what
Tsuruko had to say. The details were enough to convince her
that nothing could be done. Tsuruko had taken advantage of an
hour or two in the afternoon when her older children were
still at school, and when Yukiko, who from two o'clock had a
lesson in the tea ceremony, was out of the Ashiya house. After
about an hour and a half they heard Etsuko come in the front
door. Tsuruko stood up to go. She would let Sachiko consult
with Teinosuke on how best to convey their refusal, she said.

This was Tsuruko's story: Segoshi's mother, a widow for more
than ten years, lived in seclusion in the old family house. She
was said to be ill. Her son rarely called, and her sister, also a
widow, cared for her. Ostensibly the illness was palsy, but tradesmen who knew the house said that there was evidence of mental
disorder. The woman seemed unable to recognize her own son.
There had been a hint of this in the report from the detective
agency, and the main house in Osaka, vaguely uneasy, had sent
someone off to approach certain reliable informants. It grieved
her to have it thought, Tsuruko added, that they at the main
house deliberately ruined every prospect of which people were
kind enough to tell them. That was not their intention at all. They
no longer worried a great deal about family or money, and it
was indeed because they thought this match so desirable that
they had sent their own agent out into the country. They had
hoped somehow to overcome this last difficulty. But, after all, the
fact that there was a strain of insanity in the family was rather
a special difficulty. What could they do? It was strange that
whenever talk came up of a husband for Yukiko, some really
insurmountable difficulty always presented itself. Yukiko seemed
to be unmarriageable, and Tsuruko found it hard to shrug off
as only a superstition the belief that women born in the Year
of the Ram had trouble finding husbands.

Tsuruko had barely left when Yukiko came in. A corner of
the little damask tea-ceremony napkin showed at the neck of her

kimono. Etsuko had gone off to play with the Stolz children.

"Tsuruko has just been here." She waited for a response, but Yukiko was as silent as ever. "Tsuruko says we must refuse."

"Oh."

"We have heard that his mother has palsy, but the trouble really seems to be mental."

"Oh."

"There is nothing to be done, Yukiko."

"I see."

"Rumi, come on over." They heard Etsuko's voice in the distance, and soon the little girls were running toward them across the lawn.

Sachiko lowered her voice. "I can tell you the details later. I wanted you to know at least that much."

"Yukiko is back." Etsuko pressed her face to the glass door, and four little legs were lined up side by side in cream-colored woolen socks.

"Play inside today, Etsuko. The wind is cold." Yukiko opened the door. "You come in too, Rumi." Her voice was quite as usual.

So the matter ended for Yukiko, but for Teinosuke it was not so simple. When he heard the news that evening, he did not try to hide his annoyance. So they had broken up another perfectly good match. Once singled out by Itani to lead the negotiations, he had become enthusiastic, and he had told himself that if the main house again appeared with out-of-date arguments about form and prestige, he would plead as strongly as he could the reasons for accepting the proposal: Segoshi was marrying for the first time, and since he looked younger than he really was, he and Yukiko would not seem at all badly matched. Because of these two points alone it would be a great shame to decline the proposal in the vague hope that someone who filled certain other qualifications might appear. Even when Sachiko had finished her story, he found it hard to give up hope. But clearly the main house had made its decision. And supposing Teinosuke were to be asked whether he could take responsibility, whether he could guarantee that if Yukiko married a man in whose veins flowed such blood there would, in the future, be nothing wrong with the man himself or with children who might be born? He had to admit that the thought made him

uneasy. The spring of the year before—had it been?—they had
had a similar proposal. That man was also in his forties, it was also
a first marriage, and the family had money. Everyone was most
excited. The day had been set for exchanging betrothal gifts
when suddenly the Makiokas learned that the man was deeply
involved with a woman and was taking a wife to screen the
affair. They had of course immediately ended the negotiations.
Yukiko's *miai*, when one explored them thoroughly, almost always had their dark sides; and so it was that the people in the
main house were cautious. The desire for a match out of all
proportion to what they could reasonably expect had the perverse
effect of dazzling them and throwing them off guard. Wealthy
bachelors past forty generally had something wrong with them.

Possibly Segoshi's insane mother had in fact been responsible
for his not having married earlier, but it did not seem likely
that he had meant to deceive them. No doubt he thought that,
since the investigation was taking so long, Teinosuke and the
rest had learned of the mother, and that even so they were
interested in the proposal. His modesty—his insistence on his
low status and his general unworthiness—perhaps carried a strong
mixture of gratitude. He had not denied the rumor spreading
among his fellows at M.B. Chemical Industries that he was
about to take a fine bride, and Teinosuke, hearing reports
that the reliable and industrious Segoshi had become too restless
to work, could not help feeling that they were needlessly hurting
a most admirable gentleman. Had the investigation and the
refusal been prompt, no one would have been hurt; but Sachiko
had delayed, and the main Osaka house had hardly acted with
dispatch. And worst of all, they had tried to cover the delay
by suggesting that the investigation was almost over, and by
giving the most hopeful of reports—by indicating that the approval of the main house was virtually assured. That had not
been simply mischievous of them. They had really felt that this
time they would be successful. Still the end result was a wrong
that could have been avoided, and Teinosuke felt that he had
himself to reprove before he reproved Sachiko or the people
at the main house.

Teinosuke, who had been adopted into the Makioka family,
had made it a principle not to become too deeply involved in

Yukiko's marital problems; and now, at the thought that discussions in which he had played so central a part were a failure (an unavoidable failure, of course), and at the further thought that his own rashness had caused pain and had possibly made Yukiko's future yet unhappier, he felt first of all that he must apologize, if but silently, to Yukiko. One worried little, moreover, when a marriage proposal was refused by a man, but when the refusal came from a woman, it was most embarrassing and degrading for the man, no matter how deviously it was phrased. There could be no doubt, then, that the Makioka family had invited the hostility of a great many families. Sachiko and her sister at the main house, quite ignorant of the world, had a way of blithely luring a prospective husband to the point of a formal betrothal before rejecting him. What Teinosuke feared most of all was that the accumulated resentment might lead to tragedy for poor Yukiko.

But the problem of the moment was how to refuse Segoshi. Sachiko meant to run away, that much was clear, and Teinosuke concluded that, to pay in part for his mistakes, he must take up the bad hand he had been dealt and try to make Itani understand. How should he proceed? There was little more to be done about Segoshi, but it would be unwise to make Itani unhappy; she might be of service later. She had put a great deal of time and effort into the negotiations—the trips to the house in Ashiya and the office in Osaka were in themselves no small matter. Itani's beauty shop was prosperous enough to keep her and her several assistants busy, and yet she had taken time to run about on those errands. Even if, as rumor would have it, she was fond of arranging marriages, what she had done was not to be dismissed as ordinary courtesy. She had spent a good deal of money on cab fares, to mention but one detail, and there had been that night at the Oriental Hotel. Teinosuke had assumed that, although Itani was formally the hostess, the expenses would be shared by him and Segoshi, but when he tried to pay her on the way out she refused his money. She had invited them, she said, and the party was hers. Teinosuke let the matter pass, thinking that she would be called on to do much more before the marriage was finally arranged, and that they could see later

about paying for all her services. But now something had to be
done.

"She will refuse money," said Sachiko. "Let me take her a
present. I am not sure I can think of anything just at the
moment. . . . Suppose you talk to her, and I will see what Tsuruko has to say about a present."

"You always manage to take the pleasant jobs." Teinosuke
looked annoyed, but there was little he could do.

15

ITANI's visits stopped around the first of December. Perhaps
she had sensed that the negotiations were not going well. If she
had, Teinosuke's task would be easier. He did not want to be
overheard, he said when he telephoned for an appointment,
and he would prefer to visit her at home. Leaving the office a
little later than usual, he stopped to see her on his way back to
Ashiya.

She sat before him in an armchair, half hidden in the shadow
cast by the deep green lamp shade. Teinosuke had about him
a boyishness surprising for a man in his profession—one might
have taken him for a young man of letters—and the fact that he
could not see Itani's face very clearly made it easier for him to
break the unpleasant news.

"I would rather not have to tell you this—but we have finally
investigated the gentleman's family. Everything seems to be all
right, except that his mother is ill."

"What?" Itani cocked her head in surprise.

"She is generally thought to have palsy, we've been told, but
we have a report that the trouble is mental."

"Not really!" Itani's usual poise quite left her. "Not really!"
she said again, and then again, emphasizing the words each time
with a shake of the head.

Teinosuke wondered whether she had known of the woman's

illness. Her earlier haste, and now this confusion, made him suspect that she had indeed.

"I hope you won't misunderstand, Mrs. Itani. I don't mean to blame you in any way. It would be the proper thing to put together a pleasant excuse, I suppose, and we thought of doing just that. But you have gone to so much trouble that we could never be satisfied with an excuse you wouldn't accept."

"I quite understand, and I'm not in the least angry. On the contrary, I must apologize to you. I've really been too careless."

"You mustn't say that. The truth is that we are very unhappy with ourselves. People begin to think that the Makiokas are so worried about form that they go on refusing perfectly good proposals, and I want you, at least, to know that this time we have a good reason. And I hope most sincerely that we haven't made you angry. May we ask you to speak to Mr. Segoshi?"

"You are being very kind. I don't know what you may be thinking, but this is the first I have heard of the illness. We are very lucky that you investigated so carefully. And you are quite right to refuse. It is sad for Mr. Segoshi, but I'll try not to upset him too much."

Greatly relieved, Teinosuke took his leave shortly after he had finished his business. Itani repeated time after time that she was not in the least angry. Indeed she felt most apologetic, and she would somehow redeem herself by bringing Miss Yukiko a really good proposal. He need have no misgivings—she would take care of Miss Yukiko, and she hoped he would pass this assurance on to his wife. Since Itani was not given to sugary words, Teinosuke concluded that she was indeed less put out than he had feared.

Some days later Sachiko bought a kimono and accessories in Osaka and left them at Itani's house with a message. Itani herself was out. The next day Sachiko received a most friendly letter of thanks. Itani had been of no use to them, and her rashness had caused needless pain. There was no reason whatsoever to reward her. But she would redeem herself somehow, she again insisted.

One evening ten days or so later, as the year was drawing to an end, a cab pulled up at the gate. She had very little time, said Itani. She had only come to say hello, and she could

stay no more than a moment. Sachiko was in bed with a cold,
but Teinosuke, back from work, persuaded Itani to come into
the parlor. What had happened to Mr. Segoshi, he asked after
they had talked for a time. It was sad. He had seemed such an
admirable gentleman. It was truly sad, Itani agreed. Mr. Segoshi
probably thought they already knew about his mother, Teinosuke
continued. Again Itani agreed. He had seemed strangely cool
and reticent at first, perhaps because of his mother, and it was
only gradually that he had warmed to the prospect. That being
the case, said Teinosuke, they had been grievously wrong to
take so much time with the investigation. But he hoped that
Itani would not be frightened off, and that they would count
on her help again. Itani suddenly lowered her voice. "If you
don't mind his having a good many children," she said, as if
probing very tentatively, "I do as a matter of fact have another
prospect." Teinosuke thought he saw the real reason for the visit.

The details were these: the man was manager of a branch
bank south of Nara. He had five children, but the oldest, a boy,
was a student in Osaka, and the second, a girl, could be expected
to marry soon. There would only be three at home. The Makiokas
need have no concern about Miss Yukiko's livelihood, since the
family was one of the wealthiest in the region. As soon as Teinosuke heard that the man had five children and lived in a country
town, however, he knew that there was no hope. Apparently
noting a certain lack of enthusiasm, Itani retreated. She knew,
she said, that they would not find the proposal an attractive
one.

But why, then, had she come? Perhaps deep in her heart
she was unhappy with them, and wanted to hint that this was
the sort of match they must expect.

Teinosuke went upstairs when he had seen her to the door.
Sachiko lay sniffing at an inhaler, a towel over her face. "I
hear Itani has another proposal," she said presently, wiping her
face.

"Who told you?"

"Etsuko arrived long ago with the news."

"True to form." Etsuko had come quietly into the parlor
and was listening most intently to his conversation with Itani
until he chased her from the room. It was, he said, no conversation

for a child. She had taken everything in from the dining room.
"Even when they are young they enjoy talk about husbands."

"The man has five children."

"You even heard that?"

"Of course. The oldest boy is in school in Osaka, and the
oldest girl is to marry soon."

Teinosuke was more and more astonished.

"And he lives in Shimoichi, and he is the manager of some
bank."

"Remarkable. You can never be too careful with children."

"We really must watch ourselves. And think what would have
happened if Yukiko had been here."

Both Yukiko and Taeko went each year to spend the first
days of the New Year at the Osaka house. Yukiko, a little ahead of
Taeko this year, had left the day before. The thought of the
difficulty they might have had on their hands had she still been
in Ashiya was frightening.

Sachiko was susceptible to attacks of bronchitis. Since she
had been warned by the doctor that bronchitis could easily
turn into penumonia, she was extremely careful with even the
slightest cold, and would spend as much as a month in bed
each winter. This time, happily, the cold seemed to have gone
no farther than the throat. Her temperature was returning to
normal.

The end of the year approached. Sachiko, who meant to
stay in her room a day or two more, was reading a New Year
magazine on the twenty-fifth when Taeko came to announce
her departure for Osaka.

"But we have a whole week still. Last year you waited until
New Year's Eve."

"I did, I suppose."

Taeko was to give her third doll exhibition in January, and
had been hard at work in her studio for the better part of the
last month. Afraid she might forget her dancing, moreover,
she had been going once a week for a lesson in Osaka. It seemed
to Sachiko a very long while since she had really talked to this
youngest sister. Knowing how the people at the main house
wanted Yukiko and Taeko to be with them, she had no thought
of keeping either sister in Ashiya. Still it was odd that Taeko,

who hated being in the main house even more than Yukiko did, should be leaving so early. Sachiko did not go so far as to suspect connivance with young Okubata. It made her a little sad, however, to see how Taeko, always precocious, was each year growing farther away from her.

"I have no more to do on the dolls. In Osaka I can go for a lesson every day." It was not exactly an apology, although Taeko did seem to be admitting that her sudden departure called for an explanation.

"And what are you practicing now?"

"A New Year dance called 'Manzai,'" answered Taeko. "Can you still play the accompaniment?"

"I remember most of it, I think. 'May this year too be happy . . .'"

Taeko went through the hand motions as Sachiko hummed the accompaniment. "Wait just a minute. These clothes will never do." She ran off to her room, and almost immediately was back dressed in kimono, a dancing fan in her hand.

> *"Says the lovely maid, the lovely maid, the lovely maid*
> *of Miyako,*
> *'Mussels and clams, won't you buy my clams,*
> *Large fish, and small fish,[1] and mussels, and clams,'*
> *And on the shelf beside her, scarlet and gold,*
> *Brocades and damasks, and* chirimen *silks.*
> Tonton chirimen, ton chirimen."

They had, as little girls, been especially delighted with the way in which the samisen refrain echoed in solfeggio the word *chirimen*, "crepe." "The Lovely Maid of Miyako, *Ton Chirimen*" had become almost a nursery song, and Sachiko remembered it alone of the *jiuta*, the old Osaka songs. The picture of the Semba house twenty years before floated up in her memory, and the faces of her father and mother. Taeko used to dance this same "Manzai" on New Year's Day, accompanied on the samisen by her mother or sister. The figure of the little dancer, a hand lifted artlessly, was as clear in Sachiko's mind as if she had seen it yesterday. And this was the same sister? (The other

[1] The song refers to congratulatory fish associated with the New Year.

sister too, and both of them still unmarried—what would her mother and father be thinking in their graves?) Sachiko did not try to hide her tears.

"When will you be back, Koi-san?"

"On the fourth."

"We will have you dance for us, then. Practice every day, and I will try to learn the samisen part well."

They had fewer guests here in Ashiya than when they had lived in Osaka, and, with the younger sisters away, the first days of the New Year were always a little too quiet. It was good for Sachiko and her husband to be alone now and then, but Etsuko, intensely lonely, could hardly wait for Yukiko and Koi-san to come back. On the afternoon of New Year's day, Sachiko took out her samisen and began practicing "Manzai." For three days she practiced, and by the third day Etusko too had learned to take up the *tonton chirimen, ton chirimen.*

16

TAEKO's exhibition ran for three days, this time in a Kobe gallery. Through the efforts of Sachiko, who knew everyone, most of the dolls were sold on the opening day. Sachiko brought Yukiko and Etsuko on the third day to help clean up.

"Etsuko, suppose we have Koi-san take us to dinner tonight," suggested Sachiko when they had finished. "She has lots of money."

"A splendid idea," Yukiko joined in. "Where will it be, Etsuko? A Western restaurant? A Chinese restaurant?"

"Go ahead and make your plans. You might remember, though, that I have not yet collected." Taeko did not feign poverty well, however. She was smiling in spite of herself.

"Quite all right, quite all right. I can pay for it, and you can pay me later." Knowing that Taeko could count on considerable profits even after she had paid the bills, Sachiko was determined to coax forth a dinner invitation. As Itani would have noted,

Taeko, unlike Sachiko, was blessed with sound business sense.
She was not quick to open her purse.

"We will go to the Tōgarō," said Taeko. "The Tōgarō is the
cheapest place I know."

"Really, Koi-san. You could at least take us to the Oriental
Grill."

The Tōgarō was half butcher shop and half Cantonese restaurant.

"Good evening." A young foreign woman was paying her
bill as they went in.

"How nice to see you, Katharina," said Taeko. "This is the
Russian lady I spoke to you of. My sisters."

"How do you do. I am Katharina Kyrilenko. I went to the
exhibition today. You sold all. Congratulations." Her Japanese
was far from perfect.

"Who was that foreigner, Koi-san?" asked Etsuko afterwards.

"A pupil of Koi-san's," said Sachiko. "I often see her on the
train."

"A very pretty girl, I have always thought."

"Does that foreigner like Chinese cooking?" asked Etsuko.

"She grew up in Shanghai, and knows everything about Chinese
cooking. She says the dirtiest restaurants—restaurants most foreigners refuse to go to—are the best, and this is the best in all
Kobe."

"Is she Russian?" asked Yukiko. "Somehow she looks less
Russian than—I hardly know what."

"She went to an English school in Shanghai, and was a nurse
in an English hospital, and was once married to an Englishman.
You would hardly think she was old enough, but she even
has a child."

"Really? And how old is she, then?"

"I wonder. About my age? Or a little younger?"

According to Taeko, the White Russian Kyrilenko family had
a small two-storey house, four rooms in all, not far from her
studio. There Katharina lived with her old mother and a
brother. Taeko had for some time had a nodding acquaintance
with Katharina, and then one day, a month or two before,
the latter had appeared at the studio and announced that she

wanted to learn to make dolls, especially Japanese dolls. Taeko immediately found herself being called "the professor." In some confusion she suggested that "Taeko" might be more appropriate, and the two quickly became close friends. Taeko occasionally stopped by the Kyrilenko house on her way to and from the studio.

"She said not long ago she often saw you on the train. She said she thought you very attractive, and wanted to meet you."

"What do they live on?"

"The brother has a business, importing wool, I believe. But to judge from the house they are far from well off. Katharina was given a settlement when she divorced her husband, and says she has enough to live on. She manages to keep herself fairly trim, you can see."

They talked of the Kyrilenko family over the metal bowls of Chinese food, the prawns and the pigeon-egg soup that Etsuko liked, and the glazed duck skin that Sachiko liked, and so on. Katharina's child, a little girl three or four years old to judge from her picture, had been taken to England by her father. Taeko had no idea whether dolls were only a hobby for Katharina, or whether she meant one day to turn her new skill to profit. For a foreigner she was clever with her hands and quick to learn, and in very little time she had mastered all the problems of pattern and color combination.

The family had been broken up at the time of the Revolution. Katharina grew up in Shanghai, where she was taken by her grandmother. The brother went to Japan with his mother, and was said to have studied in a Japanese middle school and to have some knowledge of Japanese writing. In contrast to Katharina, an Anglophile, the brother and mother were extraordinarily pro-Japanese. In one of the two downstairs rooms of their house hung pictures of the Emperor and Empress, and in the other pictures of the last Czar and his consort. The brother was of course very good in Japanese, and Katharina had learned a surprising amount in the short time she had been in the country. The most entertaining Japanese was that of the old mother. Taeko had been rather puzzled at first.

"The Japanese the old one talks! She speaks at a fearful rate and misses the important words. She looked a little surprised the other day when I told her my home was in Osaka, and it only came to me later that she was telling me to make myself at home."

Taeko was an excellent mimic. She liked to entertain them by burlesquing the little mannerisms she was so quick to notice. Her imitations of "the old one" were almost too good. There before them would be the old Russian woman they had never met.

"She seems to have been very remarkable. She was a doctor of law in Russia. 'I no good Japanese,' she says. 'French, German, I speak.'"

"She must once have had money. How old is she?"

"Past sixty, I would say. But you would never guess it. She is as lively as a young girl."

Three or four days later Taeko came home with another story about "the old one." Taeko had been shopping in Kobe, and she was having a cup of tea at Juccheim's when the old woman came in with Katharina. They were going skating, they said. If she was free, would she like to join them? Though she had never skated, Taeko had confidence in her athletic abilities. She decided to have a try when they assured her that they could teach her in no time. After an hour or so she was skating well, and the old woman was lavish in her praise.

"You, very good. I think this no first time."

But the astonishing one was "the old one" herself. The moment they were on the rink she sailed off with complete aplomb, straight and confident, treating them now and then to a truly breathtaking display of virtuosity. All the other skaters stopped to watch.

"I had dinner at Katharina's," said Taeko, coming home late one evening.

The Russians, she had found, were a race of remarkably heavy eaters. First came cold appetizers, and then all sorts of bread, and hot dish after hot dish, meats and vegetables heaped to the brim. Taeko had had enough with the appetizers alone. No more thank you; I really could not possibly—but the Kyrilenkos ate on. What was the matter with her? Wouldn't she have more of this, or perhaps this? And as they ate they gulped down beer and Japanese saké and vodka. Taeko was not surprised at the brother, but Katharina kept him company, and "the old one" ate and drank with both of them. It was nine o'clock, and Taeko got up to leave. No, she couldn't go yet—they brought out cards and played for an hour or so. At past ten they started on another dinner. Taeko could barely bring herself to look at the food, but the others ate and drank—it might be more accurate to say that they tossed liquor down—as happily as before. A most astonishing set of stomachs, thought Taeko. The Russians explained that Japanese saké, and even a strong liquor like vodka, had to be drunk fast if it was to be enjoyed. The food was not especially remarkable, Taeko thought, although she was interested in the soup, a sort of ravioli soup to judge from her description.

"She says I am to bring my sisters and brother-in-law next time. Would you like to go for a look?"

Katharina was busy on a Japanese doll with long, flowing sleeves, an old-style coiffure, and, in one hand, a New Year battledore. Since Taeko was the model, Katharina sometimes came to the Ashiya house to work, and in the course of time she became acquainted with the rest of the family. Teinosuke had remarked, it was true, that she should have a try at Hollywood, but there was in fact not a suggestion of Yankee coarseness about her. Indeed something gentle and ladylike in her manner made it easy for her to be friendly with Japanese women.

On February 11, the anniversary of the founding of the Empire, Katharina appeared at the door with her brother, who had on plus fours. They were hiking to Kōza Falls, she said, and had only stopped by to say hello. Walking through the garden to the terrace, they had a cocktail or two and talked to Teinosuke for perhaps a half hour.

"Now we must meet the old one," said Teinosuke.

Sachiko agreed. "But after listening to Koi-san, I feel as if I already knew her."

17

TAEKO had aroused their curiosity, and they found it hard to go on refusing. Finally in the spring—actually on a chilly March evening—they went to the Kyrilenko house. The whole family had been invited, but, knowing they would be late getting home, they left Etsuko behind, and Yukiko to keep her company. Sachiko and Teinosuke set out with Taeko. Perhaps a quarter of a mile from the station the bourgeois mansions gave way to rice paddies, and beyond the paddies was a pine-covered hill. The Kyrilenko house stood in a cluster of little houses, the smallest of all, and yet very clean and pretty, like something out of a fairy tale. Katharina led them to the farther of the downstairs rooms. There was a cast-iron stove in the center, and when the four of them were seated—on the sofa, in the one easy chair, and on a hard wooden chair—they were in great danger of brushing the stove or the chimney, or knocking something off the table. The bedrooms were apparently upstairs. They gathered that, besides these two rooms downstairs, there was only a kitchen somewhere in back. The next room, through an open door, seemed no larger than this one. Teinosuke wondered how six of them could possibly sit down for dinner. What was even stranger, however, was the fact that only Katharina was with them. The brother and "the old one" of the stories were nowhere to be seen. Though the Makiokas knew that foreigners generally dined later than Japanese, they had neglected to ask the exact time. Perhaps they had come early. But even when it was dark outside, the house was quite still, and nothing was being done about dinner.

"Here. My first doll." Katharina took up a dancing doll from the bottom shelf of a triangular cupboard.

"You really made this?"

"Yes. But it had many bad things. Taeko repaired them."

"Look at the obi," said Taeko. The dark cloth of the obi, which was tied so that the ends trailed down, was decorated with Japanese chess pieces. No doubt Katharina had drawn on her brother's knowledge of things Japanese. "This is not something I taught her. Katharina designed it by herself, and even painted the pieces."

"Look at this." Katharina took out an album of photographs from her Shanghai years. "Here. My husband. Here, my daughter."

"How pretty. She looks exactly like her mother."

"You think so?"

"I do indeed. Do you never feel lonesome for her?"

"She is in England. I cannot see her. That is all."

"Do you know where in England she is? Could you see her if you were to go there?"

"I do not know. But I want to see her. Maybe I will go to see her." There was nothing sentimental in Katharina's tone. She seemed quite philosophical.

Sachiko and Teinosuke had for some time been feeling hungry. They glanced uncertainly at their watches and at each other.

"And your brother? Is he out this evening?" Teinosuke took advantage of a lull in the conversation.

"My brother, he is always late, every night."

"And your mother?"

"My mother went shopping in Kobe."

"I see."

It was possible, of course, that the old woman had gone off to buy provisions for dinner, but when the clock on the wall struck seven they began to feel as though the signals had gone wrong. Taeko, responsible for having brought them, was soon looking quite openly at the dining room. Whether Katharina noticed or not, she said nothing. Now and then she got up to put more coal in the stove, which was so small that it needed re-fueling almost immediately. They really had to think of something to talk about, since silence only made them hungrier, but when they ran out of subjects, they could only listen to the fire. A mongrel dog, largely pointer they would have said, pushed open the door and, picking a warm spot among the feet, lay down happily with its jowls on its forepaws.

"Boris," said Katharina. The dog rolled its eyes at her.

"Boris," said Teinosuke, for want of anyone else to talk to. He stroked the dog's arched back, and presently another half hour went by.

"Katharina," he said suddenly. "Have we made a mistake?"

"I beg your pardon?"

"Koi-san, have we come on the wrong day?" He spoke in the Osaka dialect, which Katharina could not understand. "If so, she must be terribly embarrassed. Maybe we should say good-bye."

"But how could I have been wrong? Katharina."

"Yes?"

"You ask her, Sachiko. I have no idea how to."

"Maybe your French would be useful at a time like this," said Teinosuke.

"Does Katharina speak French, Koi-san?"

"I think not. She knows English, though."

"Katharina, I . . . I am . . ." Teinosuke began in faltering English. "I am afraid . . . you were not expecting us tonight."

"Why not?" Katharina looked at him in astonishment. "We invited you for tonight, and we were waiting for you." Her English was fluent, though she spoke with a certain tenseness.

As the clock struck eight, Katharina left the room. They heard a clattering in the kitchen, and a moment later she had the table in the next room lined with dishes and platters, and was inviting them to take their places. Their first reaction when they saw the appetizers (when might she have prepared them?)— smoked salmon and salted anchovies and sardines in oil, and ham and cheese and crackers, and meat pie and all sorts of bread—was one of relief. All three were hungry, and they ate as rapidly as good form allowed. Presently, however, as Katharina urged them to take more, they were passing bits of food under the table to Boris. Katharina meanwhile busied herself making tea and refilling cups.

The front door slammed, and Boris bounded into the hall.

"The old one seems to be back," whispered Taeko.

"The old one" disappeared from the hall into the kitchen with five or six little bundles under her arm. Katharina's brother came into the room, followed by a gentleman perhaps in his fifties.

"We began our feast without you," said Teinosuke.

"Please, please." Kyrilenko rubbed his hands together. He was rather small and delicate for a foreigner, and the cheeks of his long, thin face, which reminded one of a Kabuki actor, were red from the chill of the early-spring wind. He spoke a few words to Katharina in Russian. Teinosuke and the rest caught only "Mamochka, Mamochka," which they took to be an affectionate diminutive for "Mother."

"I met my mother in Kobe and we came home together. And this is my friend Vronsky." He patted the other gentleman on the shoulder. "Taeko already knows him, I believe."

"We have met. My brother-in-law, my sister."

"Vronsky," mused Teinosuke. "There is someone by that name in *Anna Karenina*."

"You are very well informed. You read Tolstoy, do you?"

"All Japanese read Tolstoy and Dostoyevsky," said Kyrilenko.

"How do you happen to know Mr. Vronsky?" asked Sachiko.

"He lives in a rooming house not far from my studio. He is terribly fond of children." Taeko spoke in the Osaka dialect. "Everyone in the neighborhood knows about 'the Russian who likes children.' They call him 'the Russian who likes children' more often than they call him Mr. Vronsky."

"Is he married?"

"No . . . as a matter of fact, there seems to have been an unhappy affair."

There was something gentle, a little weak, about Vronsky. They could see that he might be partial to children. The corners of his rather sad eyes were wrinkled in a smile as he listened to this discussion of himself. He was larger than Kyrilenko, but he seemed somehow more like a Japanese, with his close-knit frame, his swarthy skin as of one who has long been exposed to the sun, his thick hair now flecked with gray, his black eyes. They wondered if he might not once have been a sailor.

"You didn't bring Etsuko?" asked Kyrilenko.

"She has her homework to do."

"What a shame. I told Vronsky here I would show him a very pretty little girl this evening."

"I wish we had known."

"The old one" came in to greet them.

"How nice you come. Taeko's other sister, little girl, why they not come?"

The accent was exactly as Taeko had reproduced it. Taeko was looking away with studied composure, and that only made it harder for the others to keep from laughing. "The old one," they called her; but she had none of the portliness foreign women fall into as they grow old. The figure, trim and straight, especially as seen from the rear, the slender, well-shaped legs above high-heeled shoes, the firm step as the hells clicked across the floor, swift and deer-like, untamed one might have said—seeing these, they had no trouble imagining the old woman as she swept blithely off across that skating rink. When she smiled, they noted that several teeth were missing. The flesh sagged at the jaws and throat, and the face was covered with small wrinkles, like a piece of crepe silk; but the skin itself was a pure, clear white, and from a distance, with the wrinkles obscured one might well take her for twenty years younger.

"The old one" cleared the table, and covered it afresh with the food she had brought: oysters, caviar, sour pickles, pork and chicken and liver sausages, and again all sorts of bread. The drinking began: vodka and beer were brought out, and heated saké, in drinking glasses rather than the tiny cups more commonly used. Of the Russians, "the old one" and Katharina seemed fond of saké. There was, as Teinosuke had feared, not room for all of them to sit down. Katharina leaned against the mantle, and "the old one" helped herself from behind the rest when she was not busy bringing out new dishes. Since there were not enough knives and forks, Katharina sometimes picked something up in her hand. She turned scarlet when one of the guests caught her. They had to pretend not to notice.

"Stay away from the oysters," Sachiko whispered to Teinosuke. The oysters showed every sign of being not deep-sea oysters, but quite ordinary oysters picked up at a near-by fish market. The Russians, who ate them with great gusto, were on that point, at least, not as discriminating as their Japanese guests.

Careful not to attract attention, the Japanese were passing on to Boris what was left of the too-generous helpings.

Teinosuke had been mixing his drinks, and his voice was growing louder. "And what is that?" He pointed to a framed picture beside that of the Czar.

"That is the palace at Tsarskoe Selo, near Petrograd," said Kyrilenko. They refused to call the city "Leningrad."

"That is the famous Tsarskoe Selo palace, is it."

"Our house, very near palace at Tsarskoe Selo. Czar, horse, ride out of palace. You see? I watch him every day. I think I hear voice, talking."

"Mamochka," said Kyrilenko. After an explanation in Russian, he interpreted for her. "What she wants to say is that she could not actually hear his voice, but the carriage passed so near that she thought she could. Our house was almost next door to the palace. Of course I can barely remember it myself."

"And Katharina?"

"I hadn't started to school. I remember nothing."

"And why the pictures of the Japanese Emperor and Empress in the other room?"

The old lady's expression was suddenly very serious. "Of course. We, White Russians, live here. Because of them."

"All White Russians feel that way. Japan will fight longest against the Communists." After a pause, Kyrilenko added: "What do you think will happen in China? Do you think the Communists will win?"

"I really know very little about politics. It would be nice, though, if Japan and China could be friends."

"What do you think of Chiang Kai-shek?" Vronsky had been sitting in silence, an empty glass in his hand. "And of what happened last December in Hsian? Chiang Kai-shek was kidnapped by Chang Hsüeh-liang. And then rescued. Why?"

"There must be more to it than we read in the newspapers."

Teinosuke had considerable interest in international affairs, and was well enough informed on at least what appeared in the papers. He had never been more than a passive onlooker, however, and, the times being what they were, it seemed better not to let reckless talk invite trouble. In particular before foreigners, whose motives and ways of thinking were so mysterious, he had resolved to offer no opinions. But for these people, driven from their homeland and forced to wander, the international question was one they could not forget for a single moment. It was their very life. For a time they debated among themselves. Vronsky seemed to be the best informed, and the other Russians would listen while he developed some point at length. They used Japanese as much as possible, but Vronsky, when the discussion became complicated, tended to lapse into Russian. Occasionally

Kyrilenko would interpret for Teinosuke and the rest. "The old one" was an accomplished debater, and not one to listen quietly while the men argued. She had no trouble holding her own, except for the fact that when she became excited her Japanese collapsed, and neither the Russians nor the Japanese had any idea what she was talking about. "Say it in Russian, Mamochka," Kyrilenko would now and then put in.

Presently, for some reason that the Japanese did not understand, the discussion became a quarrel between Katharina and "the old one." The latter quite indiscriminately assailed the English— English character, English policies—and Katharina fought back. She had been born in Russia, she said, but when she was driven to Shanghai she lived on the generosity of the English. She was educated by the English and she paid not a cent in return, and it was the English who had helped her make her way as a nurse. What could be wrong with such a country? But "the old one" answered that Katharina was still too young to understand. Soon the two were glaring at each other, and Kyrilenko and Vronsky interceded to prevent a real fight.

"Mamochka and Katharina are a great problem. They are always fighting about England," said Kyrilenko.

When they had spent some time at cards in the other room, they were summoned again to the dining room. The Japanese were not up to another feast, whatever it might be, and the result as far as they were concerned was only stuffing Boris fuller. Still Teinosuke managed to drink with Vronsky and Kyrilenko to the end.

"Be careful," said Sachiko when, after eleven, they started back through the rice paddies. "You are staggering."

"The wind feels good."

"Really, I wondered what could have happened. Katharina all by herself, and not a thing to eat or drink, and there I was getting hungrier and hungrier."

"Then when she finally brought it out I began to eat with both hands. But how do you suppose Russians manage to eat so much? I can drink with them well enough, but I am no match when it comes to eating."

"The old one seemed delighted to have all of us. They enjoy guests even in that tiny house."

"They must be lonely. They must want to make friends with Japanese."

"That Mr. Vronsky," called Taeko from the darkness one or two steps behind them. "It is really very sad. It seems that he was in love when he was young, but he and the girl were separated at the time of the Revolution. He learned some years later that she was in Australia, and went to Australia himself. He did find her, but almost immediately afterwards she died. And with that he decided he would never marry."

"There was something very sad about him."

"He had a dreadful time in Australia. He was even a miner for a while. Afterwards he went into business and made some money, and now they say he has five hundred thousand yen. Katharina's brother has borrowed from him, I suspect."

"What a nice smell," said Sachiko. They were walking down a hedge-lined street. "The cloves are in bloom somewhere."

"Only one more month to the cherry blossoms. I can hardly wait."

"Me, hardly wait too," said Teinosuke, after the manner of "the old one."

18

NOMURA MINOKICHI, *born September, 1893.*
PERMANENT RESIDENCE: *20 Tatemachi, Himeji, Hyōgo Prefecture*
PRESENT RESIDENCE: *559 4-chōme, Aodani, Nada Ward, Kobe*
EDUCATION: *Graduated from the School of Agriculture, Tokyo Imperial University, 1916*
OCCUPATION: *Fisheries technician, Agriculture and Forestry Office, Hyōgo Prefecture*
FAMILY: *Married in 1922 to Tanako Noriko. One son and one daughter. Daughter died at the age of two. Wife died of influenza in 1935. Son died in 1936 at the age of thirteen. Both parents died early. Only sister, whose married name is Ota, lives in Tokyo.*

The small photograph, on the back of which Mr. Nomura himself had written this information (he used a pen rather than the formal writing brush such occasions really called for), had come late in March from Mrs. Jimba, a classmate of Sachiko's. Sachiko had almost forgotten how, late in November the year before, as the Makiokas were marking time in the Segoshi negotiations, she had met Mrs. Jimba in Osaka. They talked for twenty or thirty minutes, and in the course of the conversation Yukiko's name was mentioned. She is not married yet, then, said Mrs. Jimba, and Sachiko asked her friend to let them know of any likely prospects. At the time, the negotiations with Segoshi seemed promising, and Sachiko meant only to be pleasant; but Mrs. Jimba evidently took the matter to heart.

This was the substance of her letter:

She wondered how matters were with Yukiko. She had carelessly not thought to mention the fact earlier, but a cousin of Mr. Hamada Jōkichi, to whom Mr. Jimba was much obliged, had not long before lost his wife, and an urgent request, complete with photograph, had come from Mr. Hamada that they help find a suitable second wife. Mrs. Jimba had thought of Yukiko. Her husband did not know the man personally, but, since he had Mr. Hamada for a guarantor, there could be no question about his worth. She would send the photograph under separate cover, and they might perhaps conduct an investigation based on the material they would find on the back. If they then decided that the man seemed a promising candidate, Mrs. Jimba would be glad to arrange an introduction at any time. Such a matter should really be discussed face to face, of course, but, since she did not want to seem to be pressing them, she thought she might first try writing.

The photograph arrived the next day.

Sachiko immediately sent off a note of thanks. With the Itani affair of the year before still fresh in her memory, she was careful not to make easy promises. She was most deeply grateful for Mrs. Jimba's thoughtfulness, she wrote, but she hoped Mrs. Jimba would not mind waiting a month or two for an answer. Yukiko had just been through the ordeal of unsuccessful marriage negotiations, and it might be best to wait a while before beginning again. Sachiko wanted this time to be very deliberate, and if,

after a thorough investigation, it seemed that they would want
to ask Mrs. Jimba's good offices, they hoped they might be able
to do so. As Mrs. Jimba knew, Yukiko was well past the age
when most girls marry, and it would be too sad—Sachiko herself
could hardly bear it—if failures were to pile one on another
too rapidly. So she wrote, making no attempt to hide the facts.

She and Teinosuke had decided that this time they would
conduct their own investigation at their own pace. If it seemed
advisable, they would consult the main house, and in the course
of time broach the matter to Yukiko herself. The truth was
that Sachiko was far from enthusiastic. They could of course know
little until they had investigated, and they had no information
about the man's resources. Even so, Sachiko knew immediately
that the conditions were far worse than with Segoshi. In the
first place, the man was two years older than Teinosuke. In the
second place, it was not his first marriage, though of course the
children were dead and would be no trouble. But what made
Sachiko quite sure that Yukiko would never accept was the
face in the photograph, the face of an old man. Photographs
could be misleading, but it seemed likely that, although the
man might look older than the photograph, he would not look
younger. They did not ask that he be especially handsome, or
that he be younger than Teinosuke. It would be sad to see
Yukiko exchanging marriage cups with an old man, however,
and the older sisters, even now that they had found her a husband,
would not be able to lift their heads before the assembled relatives. If it was unreasonable to ask for a young bridegroom, Sachiko hoped that they might at least find someone healthy, vigorous, buoyant. Everything considered, she could work up little excitement over the photograph. She did nothing for a week or so.

Then it occurred to her that Yukiko might have seen an
envelope marked "Photograph" in the mail. If so, might she not
think something was being hidden from her? Yukiko as always
showed nothing, and yet she had quite possibly been hurt by
the Segoshi affair. Sachiko had thought it better to refrain from
bringing up another proposal so soon, but it would only look
like a conspiracy if indeed Yukiko was wondering why Sachiko
did not have the honesty to tell her of the new photograph.

Indeed, in view of Sachiko's own lack of enthusiasm, an easy solution might be to consult Yukiko at the outset, and hear the views of the person most concerned.

One day, when Sachiko was dressing to go shopping in Kobe, Yukiko came into the room.

"I have another photograph, Yukiko." Without waiting for an answer, Sachiko took the photograph from a drawer. "Read what is on the back."

Yukiko glanced at the photograph in silence, and turned it over.

"Who sent it to you?"

"You remember Mrs. Jimba? Her name was Imai when we were in school."

"Yes."

"We happened to speak of you one day in Osaka, and I asked her to let me know if she heard of any good prospects. She seems to have taken it seriously."

Yukiko did not answer.

"There is no need to decide immediately. As a matter of fact, I thought of investigating the man before I spoke to you, but I decided it would not do to have you think I was hiding something." Yukiko had laid the photograph on a shelf, and was looking absently down at the garden from the veranda. "If you would rather not think about it yet, you can wait. And if the man does not interest you, you can pretend you never heard of him. I think, though, that I ought at least to go ahead with the investigation. After all, Mrs. Jimba *was* kind enough to send the picture."

"Sachiko." Forcing herself to smile, Yukiko turned to her sister. "I want you to tell me when something like this comes up. I feel much better when I know something is being done. It is hearing nothing at all that upsets me."

"I see."

"But the *miai*. I would like you always to put it off until you have finished investigating. There is nothing else you need worry about."

"I see. That makes things easier."

Sachiko finished dressing and went out, with a promise to be back for dinner. Yukiko hung the discarded kimono on the

clothes rack and folded the obi and accessories into a neat pile.
For a time she leaned on the railing and looked down at the
garden.

This section of Ashiya had been farms and fields until the
mid-twenties, when the suburbs of Osaka began to encroach
on it. For all its being rather small, the garden had in it two
or three old native pines, and beyond the hedge it gave way
to the hills of the Rokkō chain, off to the north and west.
Yukiko always felt that she had come to life again when she
was back in Ashiya after four or five days in the Osaka house.
She looked to the south. Just below her were the lawn and
flower beds, and beyond them was an artificial hillock, from
between the boulders of which a shrub trailed branches of tiny
white flowers down into a dry lake. On the right shore of the
lake, a lilac and a cherry were in bloom. The cherry had
been planted two or three years before—Sachiko, extremely fond
of cherry blossoms, wanted to go cherry viewing at home. Each
spring, when the proper season came, she dutifully spread a carpet
under the tree, but for some reason there were never more than
a few sickly blossoms. The lilac, on the other hand, was always
a rich mass of blossoms. To the west of the lilac were a plane
tree and a sandalwood not yet in bud, and to the south of the
sandalwood was a syringa. Mme Tsukamoto, the French lady
from whom Sachiko took lessons, felt most nostalgic when she
saw the garden. This was the first syringa she had come upon
in Japan, she said, although it was very common in France.
The syringa, which bloomed with the yellow *yamabuki*[1] by
Teinosuke's study after the lilac had fallen, had only begun to
send out buds. Farther on was the net-wire fence that separated
the garden from the Stolz yard, and under the plane trees by the
fence, on grass warm in the afternoon sun, Etsuko and Rosemarie
were playing house. From the second-floor railing Yukiko could
see all the properties: the dolls' beds, cabinets, chairs, and table,
and the Western dolls themselves. The two little girls, quite lost
in play, did not know they were being overheard.

"This is the father," said Rosemarie, taking up a doll in her
left hand. "And this is the mother." She pressed the faces together,

[1] A shrub related to the rose.

and there was a resounding smack. Rosemarie seemed to be
providing the sound effects. "The baby came." She took a baby
doll from the skirts of the "mother." "Baby came, baby came,"
she repeated happily.

Foreign children believed that babies were brought by storks
and fastened to trees, Yukiko had always heard, but at least
Rosemarie knew the truth. Yukiko smiled on and on as she
watched the play.

19

TEINOSUKE had laughed when, on their honeymoon in the Hakone
mountains south of Tokyo, he asked Sachiko what her favorite
fish was and learned that it was the sea bream. The sea bream
was far too ordinary a fish to have for a favorite. Sachiko
said, however, that the sea bream, both in appearance and in
taste, was the most Japanese of all fish, and that a Japanese who
did not like sea bream was simply not a Japanese. Teinosuke
suspected that his wife was secretly boasting of her native Osaka.
The Osaka region produced the best sea bream, and, it would
seem to follow, was most truly Japanese. And when Sachiko
was asked what flower she liked best, there was no hesitation
in her answer: the cherry blossom.

All these hundreds of years, from the days of the oldest
poetry collections, there have been poems about cherry blossoms.
The ancients waited for cherry blossoms, grieved when they
were gone, and lamented their passing in countless poems. How
very ordinary the poems had seemed to Sachiko when she read
them as a girl, but now she knew, as well as one could know,
that grieving over fallen cherry blossoms was more than a fad
or a convention. The family—Sachiko, her husband and daughter,
her two younger sisters—had for some years now been going
to Kyoto in the spring to see the cherry blossoms. The excursion
had become a fixed annual observance. Sometimes Teinosuke
or Etsuko would be missing because of work or school, but at

least the three sisters were always together. For Sachiko there was, besides pleasant sorrow for the cherry blossoms, sorrow for her sisters and the passing of their youth. She wondered whether each excursion might not be her last with Yukiko, at least. And her sisters seemed to feel much the same emotions. Not as fond of cherry blossoms as Sachiko, they still took great pleasure in the outing. Long before—at the time of the Spring Festival in Nara, early in March—they began waiting for it, and planning what they would wear.

As the season approached, there would be reports on when the cherries were likely to be in full bloom. They had to pick a week-end, for the convenience of Etsuko and Teinosuke, and they all had the anxiety of the ancients over the weather, anxiety which had once seemed to Sachiko merely conventional. With each breeze and each shower their concern for the cherries would grow. There were cherries enough around the Ashiya house, and cherries to be seen from the window of the train into Osaka, and there was no need to go all the way to Kyoto; but Sachiko had firm views on what was best. When it came to sea bream, only Akashi bream seemed worth eating, and she felt that she had not seen the cherry blossoms at all unless she went to Kyoto. Teinosuke had rebelled the year before and taken them instead to the Brocade Bridge; but Sachiko had been restless afterwards, as though she had forgotten something. She complained that spring did not feel like spring, and finally took Teinosuke off to Kyoto in time for the late cherries at Omuro. The annual procedure was fixed: they arrived in Kyoto on Saturday afternoon, had an early dinner at the Gourd Restaurant, and, after the spring dances, which they never missed, saw the Gion cherries by lantern light. On Sunday morning they went to the western suburbs. After lunch by the river at Storm Hill, they returned to the city in time to see the weeping cherries in the Heian Shrine; and with that, whether or not Teinosuke and Sachiko stayed on another night by themselves, the outing proper was finished.

The cherries in the Heian Shrine were left to the last because they, of all the cherries in Kyoto, were the most beautiful. Now that the great weeping cherry in Gion was dying and its blossoms were growing paler each year, what was left to stand for the Kyoto spring if not the cherries in the Heian Shrine? And so, coming back from the western suburbs on the afternoon of the second day, and picking that moment of regret when the spring sun was about to set, they would pause, a little tired, under the trailing branches, and look fondly at each tree—on around the lake, by the approach to a bridge, by a bend in the path, under the eaves of the gallery. And, until the cherries came the following year, they could close their eyes and see again the color and line of a trailing branch.

Choosing a week-end in mid-April, they set out. Etsuko, who put on a kimono scarcely ten times a year, and would have been uncomfortable in any case, was wearing a kimono a little too small for her. An intent expression on her holiday face (it was touched up very slightly with cosmetics), she concentrated on keeping her sandals from slipping off and her kimono from coming open. At dinner, a bare knee finally slipped through. She was clearly more at home in Western clothes. She still had her own childish way of holding chopsticks, moreover, and the kimono sleeve seemed to get in her way. When a particularly slippery vegetable shot from the chopsticks, slithered across the veranda, and came to rest in the moss outside, she was as pleased as the rest. The year's expedition was off to a good start.

The next morning they strolled first of all along the banks of Hirosawa Pond. Teinosuke took a picture with his Leica of the four of them—Sachiko, Etsuko, Yukiko, and Taeko—lined up in that order under a cherry tree whose branches trailed off into the water. They had a happy memory of the spot: one spring, as they had been walking along the pond, a gentleman had asked them most politely if he might take their picture. Writing down their address, he promised to send prints if the snapshots turned out well; and among the prints that arrived some ten days later was a truly remarkable one. Sachiko and Etsuko, turned away from the camera, were looking out over the rippled surface of the lake from under this same cherry tree, and the two rapt figures, mother and daughter, with cherry petals falling on the gay kimono of the little girl, seemed the very incarnation of regret for the passing of spring. Ever since, they had made it a point to stand under the same tree and look out over the pond, and have their picture taken. Sachiko knew too that in the hedge that lined the path there would be a camellia loaded with crimson blossoms. She never forgot to look for it.

They climbed the embankment of Osawa Pond for a brief look at the cherries there, and went on past the temple gates—the Temple of the Great Awakening, the Temple of Clean Coolness, the Temple of the Heavenly Dragon—to arrive at the Bridge of the Passing Moon, beyond which, rising from the river, was Storm Hill with its cherry blossoms. At Storm Hill there were always throngs of Korean women in the plain yet richly dyed clothes of their peninsula, bringing a touch of the exotic and cosmopolitan to spring in the old capital. This year too, under the cherry trees along the river, they were gathered in twos and threes and fives, some of them stirred by the cherry-blossom saké to a rather unladylike ebullience.

The year before, the Makiokas had had lunch at the Pavilion of the All-Merciful, and the year before that at one of the tea houses by the bridge. This year they chose the precincts of the Temple of the All-Conquering Law—that temple to which, in April each year, the twelve-year-olds of Kyoto are brought to pray for a happy adolescence.

"Remember the tongue-cut sparrow,[1] Etsuko? This is where he lived." They had crossed the bridge back toward the city, and were starting through the bamboo groves near the Temple of the Heavenly Dragon.

A chilly wind had come up by the time they passed the Nonomiya, the Shrine in the Fields, where in ancient times court maidens retired for purification before leaving to become Shrine Virgins at Ise. At the Enrian Hermitage a shower of cherry petals was falling, to decorate their kimono sleeves. Again they walked through the Temple of Clean Coolness, and, taking a train, arrived back at the Bridge of the Passing Moon yet a third time. After a rest they hailed a cab and drove to the Heian Shrine.

Those weeping cherries just beyond the gallery to the left as one steps inside the gate and faces the main hall—those cherries said to be famous even abroad—how would they be this year? Was it perhaps already too late? Always they stepped through the gallery with a strange rising of the heart, but the five of them cried

---

[1] Of a well-known Japanese fairy tale.

out as one when they saw that cloud of pink spread across the late-afternoon sky.

It was the climax of the pilgrimage, the moment treasured through a whole year. All was well, they had come again to the cherries in full bloom. There was a feeling of relief, and a hope that next year they might be as fortunate, and for Sachiko, at least, the thought that even if she herself stood here next year, Yukiko might be married and far away. The flowers would come again, but Yukiko would not. It was a saddening thought, and yet it contained almost a prayer that, for Yukiko's sake, she might indeed no longer be with them. Sachiko had stood under these same trees with these same emotions the year before and the year before that, and each time she had found it hard to understand why they should still be together. She could not bear to look at Yukiko.

The willows and oaks beyond the cherry grove were sending out new buds. The oleanders had been clipped into round balls. Sending the four ahead, Teinosuke photographed them at all the usual spots: White Tiger Pond, with its iris-lined shore; the stepping stones called the Bridge of the Reclining Tiger, reflected from the water with the four figures. He had them line up under the truly glorious branches that trail down over the path from the pine-topped hillock to the west of the Pond of the Nesting Phoenix. All sorts of strangers took pictures of the Makioka procession. The polite would carefully ask permission, the rude would simply snap. There the family had had tea, here they had fed the red carp—they remembered the smallest details of earlier pilgrimages.

"Look, Mother. A bride."

A wedding party was just leaving the Purification Hall. The curious had gathered to see the bride into her automobile, and the Makiokas caught only a glimpse of the white headdress and the brilliant bridal cloak. This was not the first time they had seen a bride at the Heian Shrine. Sachiko always felt a stabbing at the heart and walked on, but Yukiko and Taeko seemed strangely undisturbed. Sometimes they would join the crowd and wait for the bride to appear, and afterwards they would tell Sachiko how she had looked and how she had been dressed.

Sachiko and Teinosuke stayed another night in Kyoto. On Monday they visited a nunnery which Sachiko's father, then at the height of his prosperity, had built on Mt. Takao, to the west of the city, and spent a quiet half day exchanging reminiscences with the old abbess. The maples carried but a touch of new green, and over the bamboo drain a single bud of Indian quince was opening. In the stillness, one seemed to know the very heart of the nunnery. Delighted with the mountain water, Sachiko and her husband drank glass after glass. They walked the mile or so back down the mountain while it was still daylight. Although she knew that the cherries at Omuro would not yet be in bloom, Sachiko wanted to rest there a moment and taste the herb-scented spring cakes for which the temple is famous. But if they dallied too long they would want to stay another night—this had happened before— and shortly after five they left Kyoto Station, with regrets for the mountains and valleys to the north and east and west that they had had to leave unvisited.

One morning some days later, when Teinosuke had left for work and Sachiko was cleaning his study, she noticed a sheet of paper on the desk. In the margin, beside several lines written in the cursive style, was this poem:

> Near Kyoto, on a day in April:
> "The beauties gather in festive dress.
> For the cherries are in bloom,
> At Saga in old Miyako."

Sachiko had been fond of poetry when she was in school, and recently, under the influence of her husband, she had taken to jotting down poems as they came to her. Teinosuke's poem aroused her interest. A verse that she had not been able to finish at the Heian Shrine presently finished itself in her mind:

> Under the falling flowers, at the Heian Shrine:
> "The cherry blossoms that fall
> And leave us to mourn the spring—
> I shall hide them here in my sleeve."

She wrote it beside Teinosuke's verse, and left the paper as she had found it. Teinosuke said nothing when he came home that evening, and Sachiko herself quite forgot her poem. The next morning as she started to clean the study, she found a new verse penned in after hers. Possibly it was a suggested revision.

"Let me hide at least a petal
In the sleeve of my flower-viewing robe,
That I may remember the spring."

20

"I THINK you ought to stop," said Sachiko. "You will only wear yourself out, trying to do it all at once."

"But I can never stop once I begin."

It was Sunday. Although they had been there for the cherry blossoms but a month before, Teinosuke thought he would like to go to Kyoto again, this time for the new spring greenery. Sachiko had been feeling sluggish all day, however, and Teinosuke decided he might better stay home and cut the grass.

Although the previous owner of the house had assured them that grass would not grow in the garden, Teinosuke was determined to have a try. He did indeed succeed in producing a lawn, but it was a very sickly lawn, always late to turn green in the spring. He worked twice as hard over it as most men would have. Discovering that the feebleness of the grass was owing at least in part to the fact that sparrows ate the early shoots, he worked almost full time each spring stoning sparrows. The rest of the family must help him, he insisted, and as the season approached they would say: "The time for the throwing of stones has come." In a sun hat, kimono, and loose trousers, Teinosuke would go out on sunny days to dig weeds and cut the grass.

"A bee, a bee! An enormous bee!"

"Where?"

"Over there. See?"

On the terrace, under a reed awning, Sachiko was sitting in a chair of untrimmed birch logs. The bee skimmed her shoulder, circled a potted peony three or four times, and droned on to a bed of red and white Hirado lilies. Quite absorbed in trimming the grass, Teinosuke was advancing on the dark tangle of shrub-

bery and bamboo by the fence. Sachiko could see only the wide
brim of his hat beyond a cluster of lilies.

"The mosquitoes are more of a problem than any bee. They
manage to bite their way through the gloves."

"I did tell you to stop, did I not?"

"But a more important question is why you are not in bed."

"I only feel worse in bed. I thought I might be more comfortable here."

"How exactly do you 'feel worse'?"

"My head is heavy, my feet are draggy, I feel like vomiting. I
wonder if it might not be the start of something really serious."

"Come, now. You have a case of nerves. And that," he announced in a loud voice, "is all I mean to do." The bamboo leaves
rustled as he stood up. He threw down the knife he had been using
to dig out plantain roots, took off his gloves, wiped the sweat
from his forehead with a mosquito-bitten hand, and, rubbing at
the small of his back, went over to rinse his hands under the faucet
beside the flower bed.

"Have we any Mosquiton?" He was scratching a wrist as he
came up to the terrace.

"O-haru, bring the Mosquiton, please."

Teinosuke went down into the garden again and began picking
lilies. At their best four or five days before, the lilies were beginning to look faded and dirty. In particular, he objected to the
white ones, yellowed like bits of old scrap paper. He earnestly
pulled off the petals, and then the stamens that had been left behind like whiskers.

"Here is the Mosquiton."

"Thank you." He went on working for a time. "Have them clean
all this up. Wait a minute—what have we here?" He looked into
Sachiko's eyes as he took the Mosquiton from her. "Come out in
the light."

The terrace, under the reed awning, was already dusky. Teinosuke led his wife out into the direct light of the evening sun.

"Your eyes are yellow."

"Yellow?"

"The whites."

"What does that mean? Jaundice?"

"I suppose so. Did you eat anything greasy?"

"You know perfectly well that I had steak yesterday."

"That explains it."

"That *does* explain it. That explains why I have felt so strange all day." Sachiko had taken alarm at the tone of Teinosuke's voice. But if it was only jaundice, there was nothing to worry about. She looked strangely happy.

"Let me see, let me see." Teinosuke pressed his forehead to hers. "Not much fever. But it will not do for you to get excited. Go to bed, and we can have Dr. Kushida come look at you."

Dr. Kushida, an excellent diagnostician, was always much in demand. He was out on calls until eleven every night, not even going home for dinner. Since it was not easy to catch him, Teinosuke himself always went to the telephone and talked to the elderly nurse when they thought they really needed a doctor, but unless the illness seemed serious, they could not be sure that he would come promptly, or indeed that he would come at all. Teinosuke generally had to make the symptoms more impressive than they actually were. Now it was past ten, and still they were waiting.

"It looks as though Dr. Kushida has deserted us."

But just before eleven an automobile stopped at the gate.

"Jaundice. There's no doubt about it."

"I had a very large steak yesterday."

"That's the reason. Over-eating." Dr. Kushida had a hearty way with his patients. "Have clam broth every day, and you'll be well in no time." He always swept in like a gale, conducted a brisk examination, and swept out again.

Sachiko stayed in bed the following day. She did not feel really ill, and yet she did not feel well. For one thing, the weather was of the heavy, muggy sort, neither stormy nor clear, that comes before the beginning of the June rains; and for another, she had been unable to take a bath for several days. Feeling damp and sticky, she changed nightgowns repeatedly, and had O-haru sponge her back with alcohol.

Etsuko came into the room.

"What is that flower, Mother?" She pointed at the flower in the alcove.

"A poppy."

"I think you should take it away."

"Why?"

"Look at it—it sucks you up inside it."

"I see what you mean." The child had a point. Sachiko herself had been feeling strangely oppressed by something in this sick room, and, without being able to say what it was, she could not help thinking that the cause was right before her eyes. Etsuko had put her finger on it. In the fields, the poppy was a pretty enough flower, but the single poppy in the alcove was somehow repulsive. You felt as though you were being "sucked up inside it."

"I see exactly what she means. It takes a child to see what is wrong," said Yukiko admiringly. She took away the poppy and put flags and lilies in its place. But Sachiko still felt oppressed. It would be better to have no flowers at all, she concluded, and she asked Teinosuke to hang a poem in the alcove, a fresh, clean sort of poem. Although it referred to the quick evening showers that come in late summer and early autumn and was therefore a little unseasonal, Teinosuke decided upon this poem by Kagawa Kageki: [1]

> A far-off evening shower, on the Peak of Atago.
> Soon it will be roiling our Clear Cascade.

Perhaps the change made a difference. Sachiko began to feel better the next morning. At about three in the afternoon the doorbell rang.

"Mrs. Niu is at the door. A lady named Mrs. Shimozuma and a lady named Mrs. Sagara are with her."

Sachiko wondered what to do. Had Mrs. Niu been alone, Sachiko would have invited her upstairs. She had not seen Mrs. Niu for some time, and the lady had twice called while she was out. But she did not know Mrs. Shimozuma well, and she could not remember having met Mrs. Sagara at all. It would help if Yukiko would go down to receive them, but that was too much to expect. Yukiko was quite unable to talk to strangers. Sachiko could not turn Mrs. Niu away after all those fruitless calls—and besides, she was bored. Sending down word that she was unwell, in and out of bed, and that her appearance would therefore be nothing to do them honor, she had O-haru see the guests into the parlor. She

[1] Poet and scholar, 1768–1843.

rushed to the mirror, but it was a half hour before she had finished powdering her neglected face and making herself fairly presentable in a fresh kimono.

"This is Mrs. Sagara." Mrs. Niu nodded toward a lady dressed in the American manner. One knew at a glance that she had just come back from abroad. "We were friends in school. Her husband's with N.Y.K. They were in Los Angeles."

"How do you do," said Sachiko. She regretted immediately that she had come down. Haggard as she was, she had had doubts about meeting any stranger, and she had not dreamed that the stranger would be so fearfully stylish.

"You've been ill? What's the trouble?"

"I have had jaundice. If you look you can see the yellow in my eyes."

"You're right. They're very yellow."

"You're still not feeling well?" asked Mrs. Shimozuma.

"Today I am much better."

"We shouldn't have bothered you. It's your fault, Mrs. Niu. We should've left our names at the door."

"That's not fair. The truth of the matter, Sachiko, is that Mrs. Sagara here came very suddenly. I'm to show her around. I asked her what she wanted to see, and she said she'd like to see a typical Osaka lady."

"And what do you mean by typical?" asked Sachiko.

"I don't really know—typical in all sorts of ways. I thought and I thought, and finally I chose you."

"Very foolish of you."

"But now that you've been chosen, you really must talk to us even if you don't feel well. Oh, yes." Mrs. Niu undid a bundle she had laid on the piano stool. Inside were two boxes of wonderfully large tomatoes. "From Mrs. Sagara."

"How beautiful. Where did you find such large ones?"

"They're from Mrs. Sagara's. Tomatoes like these aren't for sale."

"I should think not. And where do you live, Mrs. Sagara?"

"North Kamakura. But I came back from abroad only last year, and I've been there only a month or two."

There are many strange ways of pronouncing "been," but Mrs.

Sagara had an affectation all her own. Sachiko could not possibly
have imitated it. She wanted to laugh when she thought what
Taeko might have done.

"You have been traveling since you came back?"

"I was in the hospital for some time."

"Oh?"

"A nervous breakdown."

"Mrs. Sagara's trouble is luxury," said Mrs. Shimozuma. "But
it must almost be fun to be in St. Luke's."

"It's near the harbor, and very cool—it'll be pleasant from now
on into the summer. But the fish market is so near, and you sometimes get a very smelly breeze. And then there are those noisy
temple bells."

"They still ring bells in the Honganji, do they, even now that
they have put up that odd building?"

"Oh, they do indeed." Mrs. Sagara managed to give even that
phrase her own elegant accent.

"It would be more appropriate if they were to blow a siren."

"And you can hear the church bells too."

Mrs. Shimozuma heaved a sigh. "Maybe I should become a
nurse. Do you think that'd be a good idea?"

"It might be just what you're looking for," said Mrs. Niu lightly.
Sachiko had heard rumors that Mrs. Shimozuma's marriage was
not happy, and she sensed a deep meaning in the words.

"I've just remembered," Mrs. Niu continued. "It's supposed to
be good for jaundice to keep a rice ball under each arm."

"Really!" Mrs. Sagara, flicking open a cigarette lighter, looked
at Mrs. Niu in astonishment. "You do have interesting bits of information."

"They say if you keep the rice balls under your arms they turn
yellow."

"What a filthy idea," said Mrs. Shimozuma. "You've been keeping rice balls under your arms, Mrs. Makioka?"

"This is the first time that treatment has been suggested. I have
been told to take clam broth."

"Whichever treatment," said Mrs. Sagara, "it's a very inexpen-
sive ailment."

Sachiko knew, from the presents they had brought, that they
hoped to be invited for dinner, but the two hours to dinner prom-

ised to be very long indeed. She always felt uncomfortable with bright, stylish Tokyo matrons like Mrs. Sagara. One of the more expert of Osaka ladies at standard Tokyo speech, Sachiko still found that Mrs. Sagara put her on her guard—or rather, made Tokyo speech seem repulsive. Sachiko avoided it purposely. And then Mrs. Niu, who always used the Osaka dialect with Sachiko, was today keeping Mrs. Sagara company. Tokyo speech had made her an entirely different person, Sachiko thought, a person with whom she could not possibly feel at home. Although there was nothing strange in the fact that Mrs. Niu, who, though born in Osaka, had gone to school in Tokyo and had long associated with Tokyo people, should have a good Tokyo accent, Sachiko had never before realized how far into the Tokyo recesses her friend had penetrated. There was nothing here of the usual sedate Mrs. Niu. The way she rolled her eyes, the way she curled her lips, the way she held her forefinger as she lifted a cigarette to her lips— perhaps Tokyo speech was not authentic unless it brought its own gestures and facial expressions. The woman was suddenly cheapened in Sachiko's eyes.

Normally Sachiko would have stood a little discomfort rather than turn guests away. Today, however, she only became more irritable as she listened to the three of them. Presently her unhappiness showed on her face.

"Mrs. Niu—I really think we should go." Mrs. Shimozuma at length saw the point and stood up. Sachiko made no effort to detain them.

21

IT WAS NOT a particularly serious attack of jaundice, and yet Sachiko was a very long time recovering. The June rains had begun before she was quite well again.

One day Tsuruko telephoned to ask how she was, and incidentally to pass on a bit of news: Tatsuo was to manage a branch bank in Tokyo, and very shortly the family would leave Osaka.

"And when will that be?"

"Tatsuo says next month. He means to go on ahead, though, and the rest of us will follow when he has a house. But then we have school to think about, and we will have to leave before the end of August."

Sachiko could tell even over the telephone that her sister was almost in tears.

"How long have you known about it?"

"It was very sudden. Not even Tatsuo knew."

"But next month—that is really too soon. What will you do about the house?"

"We have hardly given it a thought. No one dreamed we would ever have to move."

Tsuruko was fond of long telephone conversations. On the point of hanging up, she would begin all over again. For a half hour she told Sachiko how distressing it was to reach the age of thirty-six and suddenly be asked to leave a city from which one had not ventured in one's whole life.

Relatives and acquaintances came around with congratulations, said Tsuruko, and no one took the trouble to imagine how she felt. When, occasionally, she let fall a hint, they only laughed and told her not to be so old-fashioned. It was indeed as they said, Tsuruko tried to tell herself: she was not going off to a foreign country, or even out to some inaccessible spot in the provinces. She was going to the capital, she would be at the very feet of His Imperial Majesty. What was there then to be sad about? But Osaka was her home, and she wept sometimes at even the thought of having to leave. The children were all laughing at her.

Sachiko herself could not help being a little amused. Still she thought she knew how her sister felt. Tsuruko had lost her mother early, and had had to take care of her father and sisters, and when the father was dead and the sisters were grown, there were her own husband and children and she had to work to revive the family fortunes. She had known more hardship than any of them; and yet she had also had a more conservative education, and there remained in her something of the sheltered maiden of old. It was very strange for a lady of the Osaka middle classes to reach the age of thirty-six without once having seen Tokyo. Osaka women, it was true, did not travel as much as Tokyo women, and Sachiko and the younger sisters had rarely been east of Kyoto. Still they had each had occasion—a school outing, perhaps—to visit Tokyo once or twice. Tsuruko, early burdened with housework, had never had time for travel, but beyond that she was convinced that no city compared with Osaka. As for the Kabuki, she was quite satisfied with the Osaka actor Ganjirō; and as for restaurants she wanted nothing better than the Harihan or the Tsuruya. Since she had no desire to go off looking at strange places, then, she always sent her sisters instead, and happily stayed behind to watch the Osaka house.

The house was built in the old Osaka fashion. Inside the high garden walls, one came upon the latticed front of the house. An earthen passage led from the entrance through to the rear. In the rooms, lighted even at noon by but a dim light from the courtyard, hemlock pillars, rubbed to a fine polish, gave off a soft glow. Sachiko did not know how old the house was—possibly a generation or two. At first it must have been used as a villa to which elderly Makiokas might retire, or in which junior branches of the family might live. Not long before his death, Sachiko's father had moved his family there from Semba; it had become the fashion for merchant families to have residences away from their shops. The younger sisters had therefore not lived in the house long. They had often visited relatives there even when they were young, however, and it was there that their father had died. They were deeply attached to the old place. Sachiko sensed that much of her sister's love for Osaka was in fact love for the house, and, for all her amusement at these old-fashioned ways, she felt a twinge of pain herself—she would no longer be able to go back to the old family house. She had often enough joined Yukiko and Taeko in complaining about it—surely there was no darker and more unhygienic house in the world, and they could not understand what made their sister live there, and they felt thoroughly depressed after no more than three days there, and so on—and yet a deep, indefinable sorrow came over Sachiko at the news. To lose the Osaka house would be to lose her very roots.

It had been inevitable that Tsuruko would leave Osaka. Tatsuo, having given up the family business and gone back to his bank, could be transferred at any time. But Tsuruko, and Sachiko herself, had chosen to overlook the inevitable. Some eight or nine

years before, it was true, Tatsuo had almost been sent off to
Fukuoka. He had pleaded family reasons for staying in Osaka,
even at his old salary, and, although there had been no clear understanding on the point, it had seemed afterwards that the bank
would respect his status as the head of an old family. Tsuruko had
somehow taken it for granted that they would be allowed to live
forever in Osaka, but the bank had had a change in management
and policy, and then Tatsuo himself wanted to get ahead in the
world, even if it meant leaving Osaka. He was most dissatisfied to
see his colleagues move ahead while only he stayed behind. He
had many children, and while his expenses were growing, economic developments were making it more difficult for him to rely
on the property he had inherited from his foster father.

Tsuruko might well feel that she was being evicted. Deeply attached herself to the old house, Sachiko thought of going immediately both to console her sister and to see the house again. There
were delays and delays, however, and two or three days later she
had another telephone call. Tsuruko did not know when they
would be able to return to Osaka, but they had decided in any
case to let "Otoyan" and his family have the house for the time
being at a low rent—in fact he would be half renter and half care-
taker. Since August was so very near, Tsuruko had to begin getting
ready; but, spend her days though she would in the storehouse,
she could only stare absent-mindedly at the disordered heaps. The
utensils and furnishings and art objects had been left untouched
since her father's death. She was sure that among the things she
herself did not need there would be something Sachiko might
want. Would Sachiko come for a look?

"Otoyan" was their affectionate name for Kanei Otokichi, an
old man who had long before worked in their father's Hamadera
villa, and who now had a grown son. With the son working in a
large department store, Otoyan no longer had any particular responsibilities. He frequently visited the Osaka house.

Sachiko went to Osaka the next afternoon. The doors of the
storehouse, beyond the court, were open, and Tsuruko was on the
second floor. Even out of doors the air was heavy and sticky, as
it so often is in the rainy season. In the storehouse the smell of
mildew was strong. Tsuruko, a scarf tied around her head, was
quite lost in the task of sorting out household goods. Before her

was an open chest full of small boxes, and beside it were five or
six ancient-looking boxes with such labels as "Twenty Trays,
Shunkei Lacquer." Tsuruko was busily untying cords and opening
boxes. After making sure that the contents were indeed "One
Shino Candy Dish" or "One Kutani Decanter," she would decide
whether the boxes were to be taken along or left behind or otherwise disposed of.

"Do you need this?" asked Sachiko. Her sister gave a vaguely
negative snort, and went on with her work. Sachiko had come
upon a Chinese inkstone. She remembered the day her father had
bought it. He really was a very bad judge of art, and, since he
tended to think that the expensive must be good, he had occasionally made a foolish buy. Sachiko was with him when, quite without protest, he paid the several hundred yen a favored antique
dealer asked for this stone. Astonished that inkstones could come
so high, the child Sachiko wondered what her father, who was neither a calligrapher nor an artist, meant to do with the thing, but
even more puzzling were the two pieces of red-flecked alabaster
which, Sachiko remembered, had come with the inkstone. Later,
choosing suitable congratulatory mottoes, her father took them to
be carved into seals for a physician friend who composed Chinese
verses and who had reached his sixtieth birthday. The engraver returned them with apologies: they contained impurities, and he
could do nothing with them. Sachiko had come upon them a
number of times afterwards, pushed out of sight somewhere.

"Do you remember those two pieces of—alabaster, I think it
was?"

"Yes."

"What ever happened to them?"

Tsuruko did not answer.

"What ever happened to them?"

Tsuruko was meditating upon a "Book Box, Decorated Kōdaiji
Lacquer." She was having trouble with the cleated lid.

So it always was with Tsuruko. People who did not know her
well would be overcome with admiration—what a thorough, industrious housewife—when they saw her so hard at work that she
did not hear what was said to her; but she was as a matter of fact
by no means as self-contained as she appeared. When a crisis
came, she would stand looking vacantly into space for a time.

Then she would go to work as though possessed. Utterly selfless, one would have thought, and intent only on serving others. The truth was that she was too excited to know what she was doing.

"She was very funny," Sachiko said to her sisters that evening. "She sobbed into the telephone yesterday, and she wanted me to come talk to her because no one else would. And then when I went today she hardly spoke to me."

"But wait and see," said Yukiko. "Before long we will have her weeping for us again."

Two days later, Tsuruko telephoned to ask if Yukiko would not help her. We will see which mood she is in now, said Yukiko. About a week later she was back.

"The packing is nearly finished, but she is still bewitched."

She had been asked to go to Osaka, Yukiko reported, to watch the house while Tsuruko went with Tatsuo to take formal leave of his family in Nagoya. The two of them left on Saturday afternoon, the day after Yukiko arrived, and returned late Sunday night. And what, then, had Tsuruko been doing in the five or six days since? She had been at her desk practicing calligraphy. And why was she practicing calligraphy? She now had to write notes of thanks to all the relatives on whom they had called, and this for Tsuruko was a heavy task. She was determined in particular not to be out-done by her sister-in-law, the wife of Tatsuo's elder brother—a lady who was an expert calligrapher. Always when she wrote to this sister-in-law she sat down with a dictionary on her left and a copybook on her right. Looking up each character to make sure that she had it in the proper cursive style, and deliberating over the choice of each word, she would write draft after draft, until in the end the letter had taken the better part of a day. And this time she had not one but five or six letters to write. Even to pre-pare the drafts was no easy matter. All day she sat at her desk, and she showed the drafts to Yukiko. Was this all right? Had she left anything out? Only one letter had been finished by the time Yukiko returned to Ashiya.

"How like her. When she has to go calling on a bank executive, she starts three days ahead of time memorizing what she will say, and she goes around mumbling it to herself."

"It was too sudden, she said, and all she could do was sit around in tears, but now she has made up her mind, and everyone will be

surprised at how fast she is off for Tokyo. She says she will surprise
us all."

"She lives for that sort of thing. We must all act surprised—
that will delight her."

So the three of them dissected Tsuruko.

22

TATSUO, who was to begin work in Tokyo on July 1, left Osaka
late in June. He planned to stay with relatives while he looked and
had other people look for a house to be rented cheaply. Presently
a letter came saying that he had chosen the house. It was decided
that he would return to Osaka on the twenty-eighth, a Saturday,
that they would all leave for Tokyo on the twenty-ninth, and that
relatives and friends would gather at the station for one last farewell.

From the beginning of August, Tsuruko went about making a
call or two a day on relatives and bank officials. When she had finished the last of the calls, she came to spend two or three days with
Sachiko. This was no formal leave-taking like the other calls.
Tsuruko had been left reeling by all the preparations, she had
worked as though "bewitched"; and now, partly to rest, partly to
be with her three sisters for the first time in a very great while, she
meant to forget everything, she said. Leaving Otoyan's wife to
look after the house, she brought along only her youngest child,
who was two, and a maid to take care of her. When had the four
of them last gathered under one roof, able to talk quite at their
leisure? Tsuruko could count the number of times she had visited
Ashiya, and the visits had been no more than an hour or two
stolen from household chores, and when Sachiko visited Osaka
the children were always so noisy that it was quite impossible to
talk. For two of the sisters, then, it was the first time since before
they were married that they could really have a good, long conversation. There were any number of things they wanted to say,
and any number of things they wanted to hear. Subjects had piled

up through more than ten years. But when at length the time
came, the exhaustion of her recent labors, or perhaps the exhaustion of more than ten years' work, caught up with Tsuruko. What
she wanted was simply to call in a masseuse and lounge about the
house. Since Tsuruko knew little of Kobe, Sachiko thought of taking her to the Oriental Hotel and to a Chinese restaurant on Nanking Street, but Tsuruko said that she wanted only to lie down
with no one to bother her, that all she needed was the simplest
of food, that they need not worry about entertaining her. And so
the three days passed without their really having talked about anything.

Some days before Tsuruko was to leave Osaka, Aunt Tominaga
suddenly came to call on Sachiko. Aunt Tominaga, an elderly sister of Sachiko's father, had never before visited the Ashiya house.
Only important business could have brought her out from Osaka
on a hot summer day. Sachiko thought she knew what it was. She
was right: it concerned Yukiko and Taeko. Aunt Tominaga was
of the view that, although the younger sisters might well stay with
Sachiko while the main house was in Osaka, it would be better
for them now to go to Tokyo. After all, they belonged in the main
house. Yukiko, with nothing to detain her, should go to Osaka the
next day and on to Tokyo with Tsuruko. Taeko on the other hand
had work to finish. They would have to let her stay behind for a
time; but she too, Aunt Tominaga hoped, would leave for Tokyo
in no more than a month or two. No one, of course, had in mind
making her give up her work. She could continue it perfectly well
in Tokyo, and indeed Tokyo might have advantages over Osaka.
Tatsuo had said that, with Taeko beginning to win recognition,
she might have a studio in Tokyo, provided of course that she
showed herself to be truly sincere. Tsuruko, Aunt Tominaga explained, knew that she should have discussed the matter herself
when she was in Ashiya, but she had wanted only to rest. Lazy
and irresponsible though it was of her, she hoped the aunt would
forgive her and go speak to Sachiko in her place. Aunt Tominaga
was therefore in a sense Tsuruko's messenger.

The two sisters in question, though they had said nothing to
each other, had both been gloomy in the knowledge that they
would one day have to hear the argument the old aunt now
brought. With their sister frantically busy getting ready to move,

they should have gone to Osaka to help her without being asked, and the fact that they had stayed away so studiously—and the further fact that, even when Yukiko was called to Osaka, Taeko had found it convenient to be busy, had shut herself up in her studio, spending only her nights in the Ashiya house, while Tsuruko was there, and had been careful not to go to Osaka at all—these facts suggested a scheme to forestall the attack and to make it known that they would prefer to stay where they were.

It was a matter of which she would speak to no one else, Aunt Tominaga continued, but why did Yukiko and Taeko so dislike being in the main house? She had heard that they did not get on well with their brother-in-law. Tatsuo, however, was not at all the sort of man they seemed to think him. He was quite without malice. The only difficulty was that he was the son of an old Nagoya family, and he tended to be overly proper. If the two sisters were to leave the main house and stay in Osaka, it might lead to talk and reflect on Tatsuo's name as head of the family. And Tsuruko would be in a difficult position, caught between her husband and her sisters. The aunt had come to Sachiko because she thought the latter might be clever at making the two see the light. Not, of course, that anyone would hold it against Sachiko if they refused to go even after she tried to reason with them. They were both grown women, old enough indeed to have married long ago; and if they said they would not go, one could not lead them off like children. Aunt Tominaga had discussed the problem with Tsuruko, however, and had concluded that Sachiko's arguments would be the most effective. She hoped Sachiko would do what was to be done.

"Yukiko and Koi-san are both away?" The aunt used pure Semba speech.

"Koi-san is so busy that she rarely comes home." Sachiko too was led into the old dialect. "Yukiko is here, though. Shall I call her?"

Sachiko suspected that Yukiko had fled upstairs when she heard the aunt's voice, and that she would be timidly awaiting the verdict. From the head of the stairs, Sachiko could see through the reed blind a huddled, forlorn figure on Etsuko's bed.

"Aunt Tominaga has finally come."

Yukiko did not answer.

"What will you do, Yukiko?"

Although it was autumn by the calendar, these last two or three days had been as hot as the worst of the summer. And the room was badly ventilated. Surprisingly for her, Yukiko had on a one-piece georgette dress. She knew that she was too thin to wear Western clothes, and even in summer she preferred the strictest Japanese dress, down to the wide, binding obi. Perhaps ten days each summer were quite unbearable in kimono, but even then Yukiko wore Western dress only in the daytime and showed herself only to the family—and not to Teinosuke if she could avoid it. When he did catch a glimpse of that slight figure in Western dress, he knew that the day had been an unusually warm one. At the sight of the almost startlingly white skin on the fragile arms and shoulders, and of the shoulder bones pathetically clear through the dark-blue dress, he felt as though a cooling draft had swept over him.

"She says she wants you to go back to Osaka tomorrow, and on to Tokyo with Tsuruko."

Yukiko said nothing. Her head was bowed, and her arms were limp as the arms of a cloth doll. Her bare foot rested on a large rubber ball, which she now and then rolled a little in search of a cooler spot.

"And Koi-san?"

"She says that Koi-san can stay behind to finish her work, but that she will have to go later. That is what Tatsuo wants."

Again Yukiko was silent.

"I imagine she thinks I am holding you back. She has really come to argue with me. I hope you see how difficult this makes things for me, Yukiko."

Sorry though she was for Yukiko, Sachiko resented the implication that she was keeping her sister as a sort of governess. Perhaps people were saying that by contrast with the sister in the main house, able to take care of all those children, the sister in Ashiya had to have help with even the one daughter. Perhaps Yukiko too felt that Sachiko was under obligation to her. If so, Sachiko's pride was damaged—after all, she was a mother. It was of course true that Yukiko helped; but Sachiko would not be *entirely* lost without her. Yukiko would in any case some day leave to be married. Since Etsuko was a child one could reason with, she would no doubt come through the first loneliness, and she would not wail as forlornly as Yukiko possibly hoped. Sachiko had meant only to console this unmarried sister. She did not mean to resist Tatsuo. It seemed reasonable, then, to send Yukiko back now that the main house had summoned her; and it would be good to show Yukiko and the world in general that she was something less than indispensable.

"Suppose you go back for a while. Make Aunt Tominaga look successful."

Yukiko said nothing. She knew that with Sachiko's position so clear, she had no choice.

"But of course we can have you come again. Remember the picture Mrs. Jimba sent? I have done nothing about it, but you might have to come back for a *miai*—we can always find some excuse."

"Yes."

"I can say you promise to go back to Osaka tomorrow?"

"Yes."

"Suppose you brighten up, then, and come downstairs."

Sachiko talked to Aunt Tominaga while Yukiko was changing into a cotton summer kimono.

"Yukiko will be down in just a minute. She says she understands, and she promises to go back. It might be a good idea not to say anything more."

"Good, good. I have been a success, then." The old lady was in high spirits.

She must stay for dinner, said Sachiko. Teinosuke would be home very shortly. But Aunt Tominaga thought it more important to tell Tsuruko the good news. While it was a great pity that she had not seen Koi-san, she hoped Sachiko would pass on her message. She started back to Osaka after the worst of the afternoon heat had passed.

Yukiko left the next day, with the most routine of farewells, as if she would be back in no more than a week. The three sisters being in the habit of using one another's kimonos, Yukiko had brought only a thin summer kimono and a few changes of underwear to Ashiya with her. She had a novel in her hand, and there was but one small bundle for O-haru to carry to the station. Etsuko, who had been playing in the Stolz yard at the time of

Aunt Tominaga's visit, was told that Yukiko was going to Osaka to help Tsuruko and would be back very soon. She did not cling to the departing Yukiko quite as stubbornly as usual.

There were eleven in the party that left from Osaka station: Tatsuo, Tsuruko, their six children (the oldest was thirteen), Yukido, a maid, and a nurse. Sachiko of course should have been them off, but she knew that Tsuruko would disgrace them by bursting into tears. Teinosuke went by himself. A guide was posted in the waiting room from early in the evening, and among the hundred well-wishers were old geishas and musicians who had been patronized by Sachiko's father. Though perhaps not as impressive a gathering as it might once have been, still it was enough to honor an old family leaving the family seat. Taeko, who had kept her distance to the end, ran up to the platform just before the train pulled out, and, taking advantage of the crowd and the excitement, escaped after only a word or two of farewell. Someone called to her as she walked toward the gate.

"Excuse me, but I believe you are one of the Makioka girls."

Taeko turned around. It was O-ei, an old geisha famous for her dancing.

"Yes, I am Taeko."

"Taeko—which was Taeko, I wonder."

"The youngest."

"Oh, Koi-san. How you have grown. You must be out of school by now."

Taeko laughed. People were always mistaking her for a girl graduate of perhaps twenty, and she had learned not to correct them. But it amused her that O-ei should have made the mistake. Back in their Semba days O-ei, already well along in years, had visited them so often that the Makioka daughters all called her by her first name. Since Taeko had been perhaps ten at the time, some sixteen or seventeen years before, O-ei should have known that she was no school girl. Still it was true that the dress and hat she had chosen that evening made her look especially young.

"And how old are you, Koi-san?"

"Far from as young as you think."

"Do you remember me?"

"I do indeed, O-ei. You look exactly the same."

"You flatter me. I am an old, old woman. And why are you staying in Osaka?"

"I persuaded them to leave me with my sister in Ashiya for a while."

"It will be lonely with the main house gone."

Taeko said good-bye to O-ei and started for the gate. She had not gone three steps when someone called to her again.

"Taeko?" This time it was a gentleman. "Remember me? Sekihara. It has been a long time. We're all very pleased that Makioka got himself promoted."

Sekihara, a college friend of Tatsuo's, worked for a Mitsubishi-owned company. Unmarried at the time Tatsuo was adopted into the Makioka family, he had often called on them. Later he married and served for some years in London, and he had returned to the main Osaka office several months before. Taeko knew that he was back, but it was eight or nine years since she had last seen him.

"I noticed you a few minutes ago, Koi-san." Sekihara immediately slipped from "Taeko" back to the familiar "Koi-san." "It's been a long time."

"How many years has it been, I wonder. It is good to have you back, in any case."

"Thank you. I was sure it was you on the platform, but you looked too young."

Again Taeko laughed her practiced laugh.

"Was that Yukiko on the train with Makioka?"

"Yes."

"I wish I'd had a chance to speak to her. You're so young, both of you. Pardon me for saying so—but when I was abroad I'd think of the old Semba days, and I was sure both of you—Yukiko, and you too—would be married by the time I got back. I was very much surprised when I heard from Makioka that you were still single. It was the strangest feeling—as though the last five or six years hadn't happened. I know it's rude of me, but I did have the strangest feeling. And then this evening I had another surprise. There you were, both as young as the last time I saw you. I could hardly believe my eyes."

Taeko laughed.

"I mean it. You're still girls, and we shouldn't be surprised to find you single." Sekihara's eye wandered admiringly from the hat down to the shoes. "And where was Sachiko tonight?"

"She stayed away on purpose. She thought it would embarrass everyone to have them weeping over each other."

"I did notice that Tsuruko had tears in her eyes. It was very charming."

"Everyone laughed and asked why anyone should weep at going to Tokyo."

"Not I. It was good to see after all these years how a real Japanese lady behaves. You're staying here?"

"I have a little work to finish."

"I hear you've become an artist. I always knew you had talent."

"The English have made you over, I see."

Taeko remembered that Sekihara liked his liquor, and she suspected that he had had a little already this evening. She made her excuses when he suggested a cup of tea.

23

September 18

DEAR SACHIKO,

Forgive me for not writing. I have been much too busy these last few days.

Tsuruko managed to keep back the tears while we were in the station, but once we started the dam broke, and she hid herself in her berth. Then Hideo began to run a fever. He said his stomach ached, and he went off to the toilet every few minutes. Tsuruko and I hardly slept the whole night. To make things worse, the lease to the house was canceled at the last minute by the landlord. We heard of it the day before we left, but we could not change our plans, and have had to move in with the Tanedas. You can imagine how it is for them, having eleven of us pour in on them at once. We called a doctor for Hideo and found that he

had intestinal catarrh. Yesterday he began to feel a little better.
Everyone has been looking for a house, and we have finally found
one in Shibuya, three rooms upstairs, four rooms down, no gar-
den, fifty-five yen a month. It was built to rent, and I can imagine
the sort of place it is. I do not see how we can all live in such a
tiny house, but we are a nuisance to the Tanedas and have de-
cided to take it, even if we have to move again soon. We move
on Sunday. The address is Ōwada, Shibuya Ward. We are to have
a telephone next month. It is a healthy location, I hear, and it is
convenient for Tatsuo, and for Teruo, who has been put in a mid-
dle school.

I wanted you to know at least how we are. My best to
Teinosuke, Etsuko, and Koi-san.

As ever,
YUKIKO

P.S. *It feels like autumn this morning. How is the weather there?*

In Ashiya too the coolness of autumn had come overnight. Sachiko and Teinosuke were facing each other across the breakfast
table, Etsuko having left for school, and it came to Sachiko, who
was reading of Japanese carrier-based raids on Swatow and Chao-
chow, that the coffee in the kitchen smelled better than usual.

"It is autumn," she remarked, glancing up from the paper.
"Does it seem to you that the coffee smells stronger this morning?"

Teinosuke muttered something. He was lost in the newspaper.
O-haru brought in Yukiko's letter on a tray when she came with
the coffee.

Sachiko had just been thinking of Yukiko, in Tokyo some ten
days now. She quickly tore open the envelope. Even the handwriting—the letter had obviously been scribbled off in a spare moment
—suggested how busy her two sisters were. The Tanedas were the
family of an older brother of Tatsuo's, a man who Sachiko knew
worked in the Ministry of Commerce and Industry. Sachiko had
met him only once, at her sister's wedding more than ten years before, and could hardly remember his face. She was sure that Tsuruko knew him little better. Tatsuo, who had been living with the
Tanedas for a month, was with his own family, but how difficult

it must be for Tsuruko and Yukiko, forced in a strange city to impose themselves on a senior branch of the Taneda family. And as if that were not enough, one of the children was ill.

"From Yukiko?" Teinosuke looked up from the paper and reached for his coffee.

"I can see now why she has not written. They have been having a dreadful time."

"What is the matter?"

"Read it." Sachiko handed the three sheets of paper to him.

Five or six days later they received a formal printed note announcing the change of address and thanking them for coming to the station. After that there was silence. Otoyan's son Shōkichi, who went to Tokyo to help with the moving, visited Sachiko immediately after his return to Osaka on Monday. He reported that the moving had proceeded smoothly; that houses for rent in Tokyo were far less elegant than in Osaka, the sliding doors in particular being shabby and cheap; that downstairs in the Shibuya house there were a two-mat room,[1] two four-and-a-half-mat rooms, and a six-mat room, and upstairs only a four-and-a-half-mat room and an eight-mat room; that, since the mats were the smaller Tokyo measure, the eight-mat room was no better than a six-mat room in Osaka or Kyoto; that it was thus a cramped little house indeed; that it was fresh, bright, and new, however, and, with a good southern exposure, far healthier than the dark old Osaka house; that, though there was no garden, the neighborhood was full of parks and mansions, and in general seemed quiet and dignified; that in a busy shopping district but a few minutes away there were several movie theaters, which fascinated the children and made them actually glad they had left Osaka; and that Hideo had recovered and was starting to a near-by primary school this week.

"And how is Yukiko?"

"Very well. Mrs. Makioka says that when the boy was ill Miss Yukiko was better than a nurse would have been."

"She has always been good. I was sure she would be a great help."

"The sad thing, though, is that with such a small house Miss Yukiko has no room of her own. They use a room upstairs both

---

[1] The Tokyo mat (about two yards by one) is slightly smaller than the Osaka-Kyoto mat.

for the boys' study and for Miss Yukiko's bedroom. Mr. Makioka says they will move into a larger house as soon as they can. He says this is unfair to Miss Yukiko." Shōkichi liked to talk. He lowered his voice and continued: "Mr. Makioka is very happy that Miss Yukiko is back, and wants to see that she stays. He is doing his best to please her, that much is easy to see."

Sachiko thus knew what was happening in Tokyo. From Yukiko there was no word, however. Although Yukiko did not make letter-writing quite the chore Tsuruko did, still it was not easy for her. She was letting herself be as bad a correspondent as ever. With no room of her own, she probably found it difficult to collect herself for the effort of writing.

"How would it be if you were to write to Yukiko?" Sachiko suggested to Etsuko one day.

Etsuko chose a picture postcard, a photograph of one of Taeko's dolls. Still there was no answer.

"Suppose we each write something," said Teinosuke. It was some twenty days later, on the night of the autumn full moon. Everyone thought this an excellent idea, and after dinner Teinosuke, Sachiko, Taeko, and Etsuko gathered near the veranda of a Japanese-style room downstairs. The traditional moon-viewing flowers and fruit had been set out. When O-haru had ground the ink, Teinosuke, Sachiko, and Etsuko each composed a poem. Taeko, who was not good at poetry, did a quick ink wash of the moon coming through pine branches.

> *The clouds are passing.*
> *The pines reach out for the moon.*
> —TEINOSUKE

> *The night of the full moon.*
> *Here, one shadow is missing.*
> —SACHIKO

> *The moon tonight—*
> *Yukiko sees it in Tokyo.*
> —ETSUKO

After these three came Taeko's ink wash. Teinosuke suggested changes in Sachiko's poem, which in the first draft had read "there

is one shadow too few," and in Etsuko's, which had read "a moon-
light night" instead of "the moon tonight."

"Now we will have O-haru write something."

O-haru took the brush and wrote with surprising readiness,
though in a tiny, awkward hand.

> *The autumn moon shows itself*
> *There among the clouds.*
>   —HARU

Sachiko took a plume of autumn grass from a vase and folded
it into the letter.

24

SHORTLY AFTERWARDS a rather sentimental answer came from Yukiko. Quite overcome with delight, Yukiko had read the poems
over and over again. She herself had sat alone looking at the full
moon from an upstairs window, and the letter brought memories,
as though it had happened the evening before, of her last moon-
viewing in Ashiya.

There followed the usual silence.

O-haru slept with Etsuko after Yukiko left. Not half a month
later, however, Etsuko took a dislike to her and drove her out in
favor of O-hana, and in another half month O-hana was driven
out in favor of O-aki, the scullery maid. Etsuko was a bad sleeper
for a child. As always, she talked excitedly for a half hour or so
after she went to bed. Unlike Yukiko, the maids would not listen
to her, and it annoyed her to have them go to sleep first. The more
annoyed she became, the harder it was to sleep. Presently, in the
middle of the night, she would storm down the hall and slam open
the door to her parents' room.

"I have not slept a wink," she complained loudly, bursting into
tears. "That O-haru. There she is, snoring away. I hate her. I de-
test her. I am going back in there and kill her."

"You are not to get excited, Etsuko. When you are excited you have trouble sleeping. Try telling yourself it makes no difference whether you can sleep or not."

"But I might sleep late in the morning and be late for school again."

"Must you shout so?" Sachiko's voice too would rise. Climbing in bed with the child, Sachiko tried to soothe her. Nothing seemed to help, however. She could not sleep, she could not sleep. Soon Sachiko would lose her temper and start scolding, and Etsuko would be screaming louder. The maid meanwhile slept happily on, quite oblivious of the commotion. So it was every night.

Though they knew of course that the "B-shortage" season had come, they had neglected their vitamin injections in the excitement of seeing the main house off for Tokyo. The whole family was to some extent suffering from beri-beri. Perhaps, thought Sachiko, that was the trouble with Etsuko. Putting her hand over the child's heart, she noted a slight palpitation. The next day, under protest, Etsuko was given a vitamin injection. After four or five more injections, which Sachiko administered on alternate days, the palpitation stopped, Etsuko's complexion seemed to improve, and she no longer complained of fatigue. But the insomnia was worse. Since the ailment did not seem serious enough to require a visit from Dr. Kushida, Sachiko talked to him over the telephone, and was told to give the child an adalin tablet each night. Unfortunately one tablet was not enough, and two tablets made her oversleep. Sometimes they let her sleep in the morning, and when she awoke she looked at the clock by her pillow and began wailing. She would be late for school again. It embarrassed her to be late, she would not go to school at all.

If, on the other hand, they awoke her in time for school, she pulled the quilt over her head and protested that she had not slept a wink. When she awoke again, she would be in tears because she was late. Her likes and dislikes among the maids fluctuated violently, and she frequently used strong words: "I'll kill you," or "I'll murder you." Her appetite, never good for a growing girl, was worse than ever. She would eat no more than a bowl of rice, and with it only the sort of food old people like—salted seaweed, bean curds—and she would wash the rice down with tea. Very fond of Bell, the cat, she liked to pass food under the table. If the food was even a little greasy, Bell got the better part of it.

She was extremely fastidious, on the other hand. She would complain that Bell had touched her while she was eating, or that a fly had lighted somewhere, or that the maid's sleeve was dirty. Her chopsticks had to be washed two and three times in boiling water. Presently, to save time, the maids were bringing her a pot of tea with which to wash the chopsticks at the beginning of every meal. Flies were a particular problem. She had a great horror of flies—when they lighted on her food, of course, and even when they flew near. That fly definitely touched something, she would say, and quite refuse to eat; or she would nag the others for assurances that it had not. When something slipped from her chopsticks, even upon a clean tablecloth, she refused to eat it.

One day, walking with Sachiko, she saw a dead rat, crawling with maggots. A hundred yards or so beyond, she called to her mother: "Did I step on it? Do you think I stepped on it?" She clung to Sachiko and spoke in a frightened little voice. "Are there any maggots on me?"

Startled, Sachiko looked into the child's face. They had made a detour of at least eight or ten yards to avoid the rat.

Could a child only in the second grade have a nervous breakdown? Sachiko had thought little of Etsuko's difficulties and had been quick to scold, but the rat incident aroused her. She had Dr. Kushida come the next day. Nervous prostration was not uncommon in children, said Dr. Kushida, and very probably that was Etsuko's trouble. Though he was sure it was not the serious ailment they seemed to think it, still, to make very sure, he would introduce them to a specialist. Dr. Kushida himself could take care of the beri-beri, and he would call a specialist—Dr. Tsuji in Nishinomiya would do—that very day. Dr. Tsuji appeared in the evening. After questioning Etsuko, he concluded that she was indeed suffering from nervous prostration. He gave detailed instructions on how she was to be treated: it would be necessary first of all to cure the beri-beri; they might have to give her medicine to stimulate her appetite and modify her strange eating habits; although she should be allowed to go to school late and to leave early as the spirit moved her, it would not do to have her quit school or try a change of air—with something to occupy her, she would have less time for brooding; they should take care not to excite her and they should not scold her when she was unreasonable, but should try patiently to make her understand.

It did not follow, of course, and Sachiko preferred not to think, that Etsuko had become ill because Yukiko had left her; yet Sachiko, at the end of her wits, could not help feeling that Yukiko would manage to be more patient with the child. In the circumstances, there was no doubt that Tatsuo would let Yukiko return to Ashiya—and that Yukiko, if Sachiko wrote to her of Etsuko's condition, would return even without his permission. But Sachiko, reluctant though she was to make an issue of the matter, did not want it said that she had surrendered after a scant two months. She passed her days, then, telling herself that she must wait just a little longer, that she must struggle on alone while she could.

As for Teinosuke, he was opposed to calling Yukiko back. This fussiness, this way of washing chopsticks in hot water or tea, and of refusing to eat something that had fallen on the tablecloth—it was quite in the style of Sachiko and Yukiko, he argued, from long before Etsuko's illness. It was unwise and should be stopped immediately; it was the cause of the child's nervous troubles. They should be a little more adventurous, they should steel themselves to eating even the food a fly had crawled over, and demonstrate that one virtually never became ill as a result. They were wrong to be so noisy about antiseptics and sanitation and to pay no attention to order and discipline. They must begin immediately to order the child's life.

So Teinosuke argued, but his recommendations had little effect. To Sachiko it seemed that one as strong and healthy as Teinosuke would never understand the feelings of one like herself, so quick to catch each passing ailment. To Teinosuke, it seemed that the chances of catching a disease from chopsticks were one in ten thousand, and that this constant disinfecting only lowered one's resistance. When Sachiko said that grace and elegance were more important for a girl than his "order," Teinosuke answered that she was being old-fashioned, that the child's eating habits and play hours should follow a strict pattern. Teinosuke was a barbarian who knew nothing about modern sanitation, said Sachiko; Sachiko's methods of disinfecting were ineffective in any case, answered Teinosuke. What good did it do to pour hot water or tea over chopsticks? That would kill no germs, and besides Sachiko could not know what had happened to the food before it was brought to her. Sachiko and Yukiko misunderstood Occidental ideas of sanitation and cleanliness. Remember the Russians? How they had eaten raw oysters without a second thought?

Teinosuke preferred not to be too deeply involved in domestic problems, and particularly with regard to Etsuko's upbringing he was of the view that matters might best be left to his wife. Lately, however, with the outbreak of the China Incident, he had become conscious of the need to train strong, reliant women, women able to support the man behind the gun. One day he saw Etsuko at play with O-hana. Taking a worn-out hypodermic needle, Etsuko gave her straw-stuffed Occidental doll a shot in the arm. What a morbid little game, Teinosuke thought. That too was the result of a dangerous preoccupation with hygiene. Something must be done.

But Etsuko trusted Yukiko more than anyone else in the house, and, with Sachiko backing Yukiko, a clumsy effort to intervene could only lead to quarreling. He therefore awaited his chance, and Yukiko's departure seemed to provide it. The truth was that he pitied Yukiko deeply, and, important though the rearing of his daughter was, he feared the emotional effect it might have on Yukiko were he to drive a wedge between her and the child. He might make her feel that she was unwanted, a nuisance. Now the problem had resolved itself, and he was sure that Sachiko without Yukiko would be more easily managed. Although he was extremely sorry for Yukiko, then, and although he would not have refused to let her come back had she asked, he could not agree to calling her back for Etsuko's sake. Yukiko knew how to control Etsuko, and she would be a great help, but it seemed to him that at least one reason, even if a remote one, for Etsuko's nervousness was the way Yukiko and Sachiko had trained her, and that he and Sachiko should bear the trials of the moment and take this opportunity to lessen Yukiko's influence. Would it not be well to change their training methods, gradually, of course, so as not to stir up rebellion? For the present they should not ask Yukiko back.

In November Teinosuke had two or three days' business in Tokyo. He visited the Shibuya house for the first time. The children were thoroughly used to Tokyo life, he found, and had learned to use standard Tokyo speech at school and the Osaka dialect at home. Tatsuo and his wife and Yukiko were to all appearances well and happy. Cramped place though it was, they said, they hoped he would stay with them. But it was a cramped place indeed, and he took a room at an inn after doing his duty and staying with them one night. The next day, when Tatsuo and the older children had gone out and Yukiko was upstairs cleaning house, Teinosuke had a chance to talk to Tsuruko.

"Yukiko seems to have settled down nicely."

"Well, you may not have noticed, but . . ."

So the story began. When they first arrived, Yukiko had cheerfully helped with the house and with the children, but—not that she refused to help even now, of course—but sometimes she would shut herself up in the little room upstairs. When Tsuruko began to wonder what might have happened and went up to investigate, she would find Yukiko at Teruo's desk, lost in thought, sometimes even weeping. This was happening more and more often—at first it had been only once every ten days or so. Sometimes even after Yukiko came downstairs she would pass a half day without saying a word, and occasionally she would be unable to hide her tears from the others. Tsuruko and Tatsuo had been very careful. They could think of no reason why she should be so unhappy. Possibly, then, it was that she longed for Osaka—in a word, they could only conclude that she was homesick. They thought to distract her by having her take lessons in tea ceremony and calligraphy, but she showed not the slightest interest. They had been truly delighted, Tsuruko continued, at Aunt Tominaga's success and Yukiko's quiet return, and they had not dreamed that to be with them would be so unpleasant. If indeed they drove her to tears, perhaps they should try to change. But why should they be so disliked? Tsuruko herself began to weep. Still, she continued, hurt though they were, they could not but be moved at the depth of this forlornness, and they sometimes felt that, if her longing for Osaka was so great, they might better let her do as she wanted. Tatsuo would never consent to having her live permanently in Ashiya, but they might say they were leaving her there until they moved into a larger house, and they might see whether a week or ten days in Ashiya would revive her spirits. They would have to find an appropriate excuse, of course, but it was sad to see Yukiko grieving, sadder indeed for those who had to watch than for Yukiko herself.

It was a very short conversation, and Teinosuke offered only vague condolences. They must be very upset indeed, he said, and part of the responsibility unquestionably lay with Sachiko. He did not mention Etsuko's illness.

Back in Ashiya, he told Sachiko everything he had heard.

"I never thought she would dislike Tokyo so," he concluded.

"Do you suppose she dislikes being with Tatsuo?"

"Possibly."

"Or she wants to see Etsuko?"

"There must be all sorts of reasons. Yukiko is just not the kind to live in Tokyo."

Sachiko thought how even as a child Yukiko had endured in silence, only sobbing quietly to herself. She could see, as though before her eyes, that figure bent weeping over the desk.

25

ETSUKO was given sedatives and put on a diet. They discovered that she would eat Chinese food even if it was a little greasy; and the beri-beri left with the cold weather, and her teacher agreed not to worry too much about homework. In due time, and with less discomfort than they had expected, the child began to recover. The need for rescue had disappeared, but when she heard Teinosuke's story Sachiko thought she could not rest until she had seen Yukiko again.

She wondered if she had been cruel to Yukiko the day of Aunt Tominaga's visit. She should not have done what she did—she had almost ordered Yukiko from the house. She should have interceded to ask for more time. Taeko after all had been allowed two or three months. The determination to show that she could get along by herself must have been especially strong that day. And Yukiko had been so docile and unresisting—Sachiko could hardly bear to think of her. Yukiko had gone off in fairly high spirits, taking almost nothing with her; and that, when one thought about the matter, was obviously because she had faith in Sachiko's assurances that they would find a pretext to call her back. Yukiko was quite justified in thinking that she had been deceived and made a fool of. After sending her off in the secure knowledge that she need stay only long enough to soothe the feelings of the main family, they had shown no sign of plotting for her return. And no one said a word about Taeko, who was still in Ashiya.

Sachiko wondered what her husband would think. In view of Tsuruko's tone, they need expect little resistance from the main house. Would he say even so that it would be best to wait? Or would he agree that there could be no objection to asking Yukiko down for ten days or two weeks, now that four months had gone by and Etsuko was quieter?

On January 10, as Sachiko was coming to the conclusion that she might best wait until spring before raising the question, a letter came from Mrs. Jimba, who had been silent since sending the photograph. Had they thought about the proposal, she asked. Sachiko had told her not to expect an immediate answer, but was Yukiko favorably disposed? If it seemed that a marriage could not be arranged, Mrs. Jimba wondered whether she might trouble Sachiko to return the photograph. If, on the other hand, Yukiko was inclined, however slightly, to accept, it was still not too late. Mrs. Jimba did not know whether or not they had investigated the gentleman, but there was only one thing she thought they should know in addition to what he himself had written on the back of the photograph: that he was quite without property, and depended entirely on his salary. Perhaps Yukiko would be displeased at this news. The gentleman had investigated the Makiokas thoroughly, however, and, having somewhere had a chance to see for himself how attractive Yukiko was, had sent through Mr. Hamada the warmest assurances that Yukiko was the bride he wanted, no matter how long he had to wait. Mrs. Jimba added that she herself would gain favor with Mr. Hamada if they would agree to meet the prospective bridegroom.

For Sachiko, Mrs. Jimba's letter was a godsend. She wrote to Tokyo immediately, enclosing the letter and the photograph. They had this proposal, she said, and Mrs. Jimba seemed in a hurry to arrange a *miai*—although, in view of the unfortunate experience

they had had with Segoshi, Yukiko would no doubt be unwilling
to have a *miai* before they had finished investigating the man.
If there was no objection, therefore, she would hurry with the
investigation; but she wanted to know first what Tatsuo and
Tsuruko thought. Five or six days later came an answer, a surprisingly long one for Tsuruko.

January 18

DEAR SACHIKO,
*Late though it is, I want to wish you a Happy New Year.
I am delighted to hear that you had a pleasant holiday season.
We ourselves, being in a new city, hardly felt that the New Year
had come at all, and our celebrations were most confused. I have
always heard that the cold in Tokyo is particularly hard to bear,
and in fact I have never seen anything like it. Not a day passes
without that cold, dry north wind. This morning the towels were
frozen like boards and crackled when you picked them up. I do
not remember that this ever happened in Osaka. They say it is
warmer in toward the city, but here we are high up and far out.
Nearly all of us, even the maids, have been in bed with colds, and
only Yukiko and I have managed to escape with no more than
colds in the head. It does seem to be true, though, that the air
is cleaner than in Osaka. A kimono I have been wearing for ten
days is still fairly clean. Tatsuo's shirts were always dirty after
three days in Osaka, but here he can wear them four days.
     On the matter of Yukiko, we are most grateful for all the
trouble you have gone to. I showed the picture and letter to
Tatsuo, who seems to have had a change of heart. He no longer
raises the objections he once did, and he says he is willing to leave
everything to you. He only points out that a fisheries technician
in his forties cannot expect to go much farther, and that since
the man has no property it will not be easy to live on his income;
but if Yukiko has no objections he will raise none. He says too
that if Yukiko is willing you can arrange a miai whenever it is
convenient. We should of course wait until we have finished
investigating the man, but if he is as eager as you say, possibly
we should put off the detailed investigation and have the miai
first. Teinosuke has no doubt told you of the trouble we have
had with Yukiko, and I have, as a matter of fact, been trying*

*to think of a way to send her back to you for a while. I mentioned
the matter to her yesterday, and found her disgustingly eager.
She agreed immediately to the miai, seeing that it meant a chance
to go back to Osaka. She has been all smiles this morning. I
really am quite put out with her.*

*If you will arrange a schedule, we can send her off to
you whenever you suggest. We will say for the record that she is
to come back four or five days after the miai, but it will not
matter if she stays a little longer. I can manage Tatsuo.*

*I have not written since I came here, and now that I have
begun I see that I have trouble stopping. I feel as though someone
had poured cold water down my back, though, and my fingers are
nearly frozen. I am sure it is warm in Ashiya, but take care all
the same that you do not catch cold.*

My best regards to Teinosuke.

As ever,
TSURUKO

Sachiko, who knew little of Tokyo and to whom names like
Shibuya meant nothing, could only imagine something like the
distant views she had had of the Tokyo suburbs from the Loop
Line, of well-wooded hills and valleys and intermittent clusters of
houses, and overhead a sky whose very color made one shiver—of
a wholly different world, in short, from Osaka. As she read of
Tsuruko's "frozen" fingers, she remembered how the main house
in Osaka, true to the old fashion, had been almost without heating.
There was of course the electric stove in the guest parlor, but that
was rarely used except for special guests on the coldest days.
The main family for the most part was satisfied with a charcoal
brazier, and Sachiko herself felt as though someone "had poured
cold water" on her when she made her New-Year call and sat
talking with her sister. Too often she came home with a cold.
According to Tsuruko, stoves had at length become common in
Osaka in the twenties. Even her father, with his taste for the
latest luxuries, had put in gas heaters only a year or so before he
died. He then found that the gas made him dizzy, and the daughters had thus grown up knowing only the old-fashioned brazier.
Sachiko herself had done without heating for some years after she
was married, indeed until she moved into this Ashiya house; but

now that she was used to stoves and fireplaces, it was hard to imagine going through a winter without them. She could not believe that she had really passed her childhood with only the primitive brazier. In Osaka, Tsuruko had persisted in the old fashion. Yukiko, with that strong core of hers, could stand the cold, but Sachiko was sure that she herself would very soon have come down with pneumonia.

With Mr. Hamada acting as go-between, it took a very long time to choose a date, but presently they learned that Mr. Nomura had consulted the horoscope and preferred to have the *miai* before the day in early February that signifies the beginning of spring. On January 29 Sachiko sent for Yukiko. Remembering their telephone trouble of the year before, she had had Teinosuke install a desk telephone in his study, out in the garden cottage. On January 30 she received a postcard that had evidently crossed her letter. The Tokyo house was in a turmoil. The two youngest children had influenza, and the youngest, three-year-old Umeko, was in danger of developing pneumonia. They thought of calling a nurse, but, since the house was so small and there would be nowhere for her to sleep, and since they knew from their experience with Hideo that Yukiko was better than a nurse, they had finally decided against it. Selfish though they knew it was of them, they wondered if Mrs. Jimba could be asked to wait a little longer. Sachiko, seeing that Yukiko was not likely to be free for some time, passed the request for postponement on to Mrs. Jimba. The latter replied that Nomura was willing to wait as long as necessary. Even so, Sachiko could not help feeling sad for Yukiko, always the nursemaid, always the loser.

While they were waiting, the investigation progressed. The detective agency reported that Mr. Nomura was a senior civil servant third grade, with a yearly salary of 3600 yen, and that, with bonuses, he had a monthly income of about 350 yen. Although he was the son of a Himeji innkeeper, he no longer had property in that city. His sister was married to one Ōta, a pharmacist in Tokyo, and two uncles, one an antique dealer who gave lessons in tea ceremony, the other a clerk in the records office, still lived in Himeji. The only relative of whom he could be proud, a man whose ward he had been, so to speak, was a cousin, Mr. Hamada Jōkichi, president of the Kansai Electric Company. (It was this

Mr. Hamada to whom Mrs. Jimba's husband was indebted, Mr. Jimba having worked his way through school as gatekeeper for the Hamadas.) The report from the agency said little more, except that Mr. Nomura's wife had died in 1935 of influenza, and that the deaths of the two children had not been from hereditary ailments.

Teinosuke meanwhile asked acquaintances what they knew of Mr. Nomura's character and behavior. He found that, although the man apparently had no real vices, he did seem to have one strange quirk: occasionally and quite without warning, one of his fellow workers said, he would begin talking to himself. He talked to himself only when he thought he was alone, but sometimes he was overheard. By now there was no one in the office who did not know of the odd habit. His dead wife and son had known of it too, and had often laughed, Teinosuke was told, "at the funny things Father says."

To give an example: one of his fellow workers was in the toilet one day when someone came into the compartment next door. "Excuse me, but are you Mr. Nomura?" a voice asked twice. On the verge of answering, the fellow worker suddenly realized that the voice was that of Mr. Nomura himself. Since Mr. Nomura obviously thought he was alone, the man held his breath and did his best not to be noticed. Finally he grew tired of waiting and slipped out. There could be no doubt that Mr. Nomura knew he had been overheard. Unable to guess who the man next door might have been, however, he presently came out and took up his work quite as if nothing had happened. The things he said were harmless—and indeed made the listener want to burst out laughing. Although the urge to talk to himself seemed to come upon him in unguarded moments, it was clear from the way in which he waited until he thought no one was around that he was able to control himself. Sometimes when he was sure there was no danger of being overheard, he would break forth in such a loud voice that the startled listener thought he had lost his mind.

It was not a really serious defect, but they need hardly be so eager to find a husband for Yukiko that they had to accept such a man. A greater defect, Sachiko thought, was the fact that he looked so old in his pictures, a good fifty or more, well beyond the forty-five reported. She was sure that Yukiko would not like him and that he was doomed to fail in the first *miai*—this was hardly a proposal to be enthusiastic about. Still, since it would give them a pretext for calling Yukiko back, Sachiko and Teinosuke felt that they must at least go ahead with the *miai*. The proposal being one that was not likely to be accepted in any case, they concluded that there was no need to tell Yukiko the unpleasant details, and they decided to keep the secret of the man's strange habit to themselves.

26

"LEAVE TODAY on Seagull Express—Yukiko."

Etsuko was back from school. The long-awaited telegram was brought in as her mother and O-haru were helping arrange her festival dolls.

It was the practice in Osaka to celebrate the Doll Festival in April, a month later than in Tokyo, but this year they were bringing the dolls out a month ahead of time. They had heard some four or five days earlier that Yukiko would be coming. A dancing doll Taeko had made for Etsuko—it was of the actor Kikugorō—had suddenly reminded Sachiko of the festival.

"Etsuko, how would it be if we were to put out your festival dolls? They will want to say hello to Yukiko too."

"But do we bring them out in March, Mother?"

"We have no peach blossoms yet," said Taeko. The doll stands are traditionally decorated with peach blossoms. "And they say that a girl who brings her dolls out at the wrong time of the year has trouble finding a husband."

"Mother did say that, I remember. She was always in such a hurry to put away the dolls after the festival. But it makes no difference if you bring them out early. Only if you leave them out too long."

"Really? I had not heard that part."

"Be sure to remember it. Is it like our Koi-san not to know these things?"

The dolls, ordered in Kyoto for Etsuko's first Doll Festival, had been put out each year in the parlor. Although the parlor was in the foreign style and therefore not entirely appropriate for an old festival, the dolls seemed to fit best in the room where the family gathered.

Sachiko suggested, some days later, that they begin the festival immediately, in early March, and leave the dolls out through the April festival customary in Osaka. It would please Yukiko, back after six months in Tokyo, she said, and Yukiko might even be able to stay with them through the whole month. Everyone thought that a fine idea. Today, March 3, they were busy arranging the dolls.

"See, Etsuko. Just as I said," boasted Sachiko.

"You were right. She is coming for the festival."

"She is coming with the dolls."

"It must mean good luck," said O-haru.

"Will she get married this time?"

"Etsuko, you are not to speak of that in front of Yukiko."

"Oh, I know that much."

"And you too, O-haru. Remember the trouble we had last year."

"Yes."

"But you do know about it, and I suppose you may talk when Yukiko is not around."

"I understand."

"Shall we telephone Koi-san?" asked Etsuko excitedly.

"Shall I telephone her?"

"You do it, Etsuko."

Etsuko ran off to telephone Taeko's studio.

"Yes, today. She comes today. Get home early. The Seagull, not the Swallow—O-haru is going to Osaka to meet her."

Arranging the diadem on the head of the Empress doll, Sachiko listened to the shrill voice.

"Etsuko, tell Koi-san to meet the train herself if she has time."

"Listen, Koi-san. Mother says if you have time you should meet Yukiko yourself. Yes. Yes. It gets to Osaka at about nine. You are going, then? And O-haru can stay home?"

No doubt Taeko knew what Sachiko meant. Although Aunt Tominaga had taken Yukiko back to the main house the year before on the understanding that Taeko was to follow in two or three months, the main house was in such confusion that there had been no thought of summoning her, and, freer than ever, Taeko might well think she had cleverly let Yukiko draw the booby prize. It was her duty at least to meet the train.

"And shall I call Father too?"

"Why call Father? Father will be home any minute now."

Teinosuke, back at seven, thought how good it would be to see Yukiko. Reproving himself for having felt, if only for a time, that he did not want her in Ashiya again, he fussed over details—she would want a bath as soon as she arrived, he said, and, though she had perhaps had dinner on the train, she might want something more before she went to bed. Sending for two or three bottles of the white wine Yukiko was so fond of, he made sure as he wiped away the dust that he had good vintages. Etsuko was told that she would have time the next day to talk to Yukiko, but she quite refused to be sent off to bed. At about nine-thirty, O-haru led her away by the hand. Soon afterwards they heard the bell at the gate. The dog Johnny ran out.

"Yukiko!" Etsuko bounded downstairs.

"Welcome back, welcome back."

Yukiko stood in the doorway pushing off Johnny. Possibly from the strain of the trip, she was astonishingly pale beside Taeko, who followed with her suitcase. Taeko was looking healthier than ever.

"And where are my presents? What have you brought me?" Etsuko promptly opened the suitcase. She had no trouble finding a package of colored cutting paper and several handkerchiefs.

"I am told you collect handkerchiefs."

"I do. Thank you very much."

"Look farther down, now."

"Here it is, here it is." Etsuko came on a package that carried the mark of a well-known Ginza shop. Inside was a pair of red-enameled sandals.

"How beautiful," said Sachiko. "Tokyo is so much better for this sort of thing. Take very good care of them, Etsuko, and you can wear them next month when we go to see the cherry blossoms."

"Yes. Thank you very much."

"You were waiting just for the presents, then?"

"We have had enough of you, Etsuko. Suppose you take all this upstairs."

"Yukiko is to sleep with me tonight."

"Yes, yes. But Yukiko has to have a bath first. You go ahead with O-haru."

"You are to hurry, Yukiko."

It was in fact nearly twelve when Yukiko came from the bath. Afterwards the three sisters and Teinosuke had their cheese and white wine. A wood fire was crackling in the stove.

"How warm it is in this part of the country. I noticed the difference as soon as I got off the train."

"The Spring Festival has already begun in Nara."

"Is the climate really so different from Tokyo?"

"As different as you can imagine. The air in Tokyo never feels soft against your skin. And those dry winds. The other day I was in the city shopping and a gust of wind blew the packages right out of my hands. They rolled and rolled, and there I was chasing them and at the same time trying to hold down my skirts. People are right about those dry winds."

"It is amazing how quickly children take to the language of a place. I noticed even when I was in Tokyo last November. They had been there no more than two or three months, and they all had the most beautiful Tokyo accents. The younger they were the better the accents."

"I suppose Tsuruko is too old to learn," said Sachiko.

"Much too old. And besides, she has no intention of learning. All the passengers on the bus turn and stare when she breaks out with her Osaka accent, but she never seems to mind. She lets them stare. And sometimes someone says, 'That Osaka accent isn't bad at all.'" For this last remark, Yukiko herself took on a Tokyo accent.

"Women that age are all the same," said Teinosuke. "They care less than nothing what people think. I know an old geisha—she must be in her forties—who always uses an Osaka accent on a Tokyo conductor when she wants to get off a streetcar. She says she can make them stop wherever she wants."

"Teruo is ashamed to go out with his mother because of that accent."

"I imagine most children would be."

"Does Tsuruko feel that she has really moved?" asked Taeko. "Or is she still just off on a trip?"

"She finds it easier than Osaka, she says. She likes being able to do what she wants with no one watching her. And she says that Tokyo women pay less attention to fashions. They make a great thing of being individuals, and they wear exactly what they think suits them."

Perhaps the wine was responsible—Yukiko was in high spirits, quite delirious at being back in Ashiya after half a year, at being able to talk late into the night with Sachiko and Taeko.

"I suppose we ought to go to bed," said Teinosuke.

But the talk went on, and he had to get up again—how many times did this make?—to put wood on the fire.

"I will be joining you in Tokyo before long," said Taeko. "But I understand the house is very small. When do they mean to move?"

"I wonder. There is no sign that they are looking for a new place."

"They might not move at all, then?"

"I suspect not. Last year they said it would be impossible to live in such a tiny house, and they talked and talked of moving, but this year I have heard little about it. They seem both of them to have changed their minds."

Yukiko then told them something surprising. These were her own inferences, she said. She had heard nothing directly from Tsuruko or Tatsuo. It was a desire to advance in the world that had made them resolve to move, however, much though they disliked the prospect; and since one might say, with but a little exaggeration, that this desire to advance had been brought on by certain difficulties in the supporting of a family of eight on the property left by the sisters' father, might it not be that, though they complained at first of the tiny house, they had learned that it was not at all impossible for them to endure even such cramped quarters? The low rent, only fifty-five yen, they found most alluring. They spoke a little apologetically of how low it was even for so unpretentious a house, and they had in a sense been made captives of the low rent. It was not at all odd that they should be moved by such considerations. Whereas in Osaka they did have to maintain certain forms for the sake of the family name, in Tokyo no one had ever heard of the Makiokas, and they could dispense with ostentation and accumulate a little property. Tatsuo's salary was higher now that he had become a branch manager, Yukiko pointed out, and yet he was far thriftier than he had been in Osaka. Both Tatsuo and Tsuruko had become remarkably clever at economizing. With six children to feed, it made a difference if one planned in advance the buying of even a single vegetable, but what astonished Yukiko most was how the menu had changed from the Osaka days. Tsuruko planned meals with stew or meat chowder or rice curry, so that the whole family could have their fill on but one simple dish. They almost never had meat except a bit floating here and there in a stew. Sometimes the two sisters had dinner with Tatsuo after the children had finished, and as a special treat they would have tuna, say— tuna was edible even in Tokyo, though sea bream was out of the question. It seemed that these special dinners were less to please Tatsuo than to please Yukiko. Tatsuo and Tsuruko worried about her: they thought she might find it trying to be surrounded by children.

"Or so it would seem from watching them. But wait and see. They will decide not to move."

"Can they really have changed so just from moving to Tokyo?"

"I suspect Yukiko is right," said Teinosuke. "And why should anyone object? Tatsuo has his opportunity to stop worrying about appearances and to concentrate instead on building up a little capital. The house may be cramped, but they can stand it if they decide to."

"They should come out in the open, then. Why do they go on apologizing because I have no room of my own?"

"That is how people are. You should not expect them to change overnight. They still have to keep up a *few* forms."

"And will I have to move into that little house too?" Taeko finally asked the question that was most important to her.

"I have no idea where you would sleep."

"You think I am safe for the time being, then?"

"They seem to have forgotten all about you."

"We have to get some sleep." Teinosuke looked up in astonishment as the clock on the mantle struck half past two. "I imagine
Yukiko will be tired."

"We ought to talk about the *miai*, but that I suppose can wait
until tomorrow."

Yukiko did not answer. She went upstairs ahead of the others.
Etsuko was asleep with all the presents, even the box the sandals
had come in, carefully lined up by her pillow. Looking down at
the quiet face in the soft light of the night lamp, Yukiko felt
again the pleasure of being back in Ashiya. O-haru lay sprawled on
the floor between Etsuko's bed and Yukiko's.

Yukiko shook the maid two or three times and sent her downstairs.

27

THE OCCASION for calling Yukiko back from Tokyo had been a
letter from Mrs. Jimba informing them that, although the hour and
place could be determined later, she would like to have the *miai*
on the eighth, a lucky day; but they had to postpone it again
because of a quite unexpected development on the night of the
fifth. Sachiko had that morning crossed the Rōkko mountains by
bus—she could as well have taken a train—with two or three
friends to visit a woman convalescing at Arima Springs. They took
a train back, but that night after she went to bed she was taken
with pain and hemorrhage, and Dr. Kushida gave them the
startling news that it seemed to be the beginning of a miscarriage.
They immediately called a specialist, who confirmed Dr. Kushida's
diagnosis. The next morning Sachiko had her miscarriage.

Teinosuke sat up all night, and in the morning, though he
left for a time to see to the disposition of the foetus, he was with
Sachiko as the pain receded. He decided not to go to work. All
day he sat looking into the charcoal brazier, his hands resting on
the poker, and sometimes, as he felt Sachiko's tear-filled eyes turn
toward him, he would look up.

"It makes no difference. And there is nothing to be done now."

"You forgive me?"

"For what?"

"For being careless."

"Oh, that. No, as a matter of fact this makes me more hopeful."

A tear spilled down over Sachiko's cheek. "But it is such a shame."

"Say no more about it. We will have another chance."

Time after time during the day the conversation was repeated. Teinosuke, looking into his wife's blanched face, found it hard to hide his own disappointment.

It had occurred to Sachiko that she might just possibly be pregnant. But nearly ten years had passed since Etsuko's birth, and doctors had even told her that surgery might be necessary before she could have another child. And so she had been careless. She knew that her husband wanted a son. She herself, even though she did not hope to be as prolific as her sister, found it too lonely with but one daughter. To be very sure, and indeed as a sort of petition to the gods, she had meant to see a doctor if this menstrual irregularity continued a third month. The thought had crossed her mind the day before that she would do well to take care of herself. But what foolishness—this second thought was strong enough to cancel out the caution. She could not bring herself to object to an outing that seemed to give her friend such pleasure. She had had her reasons, then, and she need not apologize. But as Dr. Kushida chided her for the blunder, she could not keep back tears of regret. Why had she made that promise in the first place? And why, having made it, had she been so careless as to take a bus? Teinosuke tried to console her. He had become resigned to the fact that she would have no more children, he said, and, far from being saddened, he found that this unexpected pregnancy filled him with new hope. Sachiko could see nonetheless that he was deeply disappointed. His gentleness only made her reprove herself the more for what had been a serious blunder, not just a trifling misstep.

By the second day Teinosuke's spirits had recovered. He set out for work at the usual hour. Sachiko, alone in her bedroom, could only turn the tragedy over and over in her mind. Since, with the *miai*, it should have been a time for rejoicing, she wanted to hide her sorrow from Yukiko and the rest. But when she was alone the tears would come, however much she tried to hold them back. Had she not been so careless, the child would have been born in November. By this time next year it would have been old enough to laugh when you tickled it. And she was sure it would have been a boy, a great delight to Teinosuke, and to Etsuko too. Sachiko could perhaps have consoled herself had she really suspected nothing, but in her heart she had known that she was pregnant. And why, then, had she not refused to take that bus ride? It was true that she had not been able on the spur of the moment to think of a polite way to refuse. But if she had tried, she could have hit upon an acceptable excuse for following by train.

She could never have regrets enough. Possibly, as Teinosuke hoped, she would have another child; but if she did not, the regret would be with her the rest of her life. No matter how many years passed, she would be telling herself that the child would now be this age, and now this age. She felt tears coming to her eyes again.

In view of the repeated delays, someone should have gone in person to apologize to Mrs. Jimba; but Teinosuke had never met her, and Mr. Jimba had not yet put in an appearance. Teinosuke finally wrote a note for Sachiko on the evening of the sixth. It was difficult to ask yet another postponement, he said, but Sachiko had taken cold, and was running a fever. Selfish though it was of them, might they have the *miai* put off beyond the eighth? He wanted to make it quite clear that Sachiko's illness was absolutely their only reason for asking more time. The cold was not particularly serious, and he was sure she would be over it in a week. He sent the letter special delivery.

Whatever meaning she might have read into it, Mrs. Jimba appeared on the afternoon of the seventh, and asked if she might see Sachiko, only for a moment, to inquire how she was. Thinking it might be well to demonstrate that she really was ill, Sachiko had Mrs. Jimba shown upstairs. At the sight of the face she knew so well, she felt a wave of affection. She must tell everything. A *miai* being so happy an occasion, she said, she had not wanted to write of her illness, but she knew that she could hide the truth no longer. Telling briefly what had happened on the night of the fifth and adding a remark or two about her sorrow, she emphasized that, although what she said was meant only for Mrs. Jimba, and that the latter should make whatever excuses seemed appropriate, she was telling the whole truth. She was sure Mrs. Jimba would not be annoyed, and she hoped Mrs. Jimba would again choose an auspicious date—she herself would be up and around in another week, the doctor had assured her.

What a pity, said Mrs. Jimba. Teinosuke must be terribly disappointed. Seeing the tears in Sachiko's eyes, she hastily changed the subject. If Sachiko would be well in a week, how would the fifteenth do? When she received the special-delivery letter that morning, she had immediately discussed the matter with Mr. Hamada and had been told that, the week of the vernal equinox being of course taboo, the only appropriate day was the fifteenth, unless they meant to wait until the following month. The fifteenth was exactly a week off. Might Mrs. Jimba set the *miai* for that day? She had as a matter of fact been asked by Mr. Hamada to see if the fifteenth would be satisfactory. Sachiko felt that she could plead ill health no longer. The doctor having given her assurances, it was not impossible, if she made the effort, that she could go out in a week. Without consulting Teinosuke, she agreed in a general way to Mrs. Jimba's proposal.

But though her progress seemed satisfactory, she was still in and out of bed on the fourteenth, and still troubled by light hemorrhages.

"Do you think you should have made that promise?"

Teinosuke had had misgivings from the start. It was a very important occasion, and, since Mrs. Jimba knew the true story, they might arrange to have Teinosuke alone go with Yukiko, rather than risk having Sachiko ruin the party. The only difficulty was that without Sachiko there would be no one to introduce them. Yukiko said that she did not want Sachiko to strain herself. They should ask for another postponement, she said, and if that meant the end of the negotiations, it meant the end of the negotiations. Probably they would not be successful anyway—the fact that such difficulty should have arisen at such a time augured ill. Sachiko felt the old sympathy for Yukiko, forgotten in her own sorrows, come surging back. It would be foolish perhaps to say that past experience had led them to expect the worse when Yukiko was having a *miai*. Still, just as they were praying that all would go well, there had come first the illness of the niece in the main house, and then a miscarriage, surely a bad omen; and Sachiko could not help feeling a little frightened at the way in which they all seemed pulled into a conspiracy to ruin Yukiko's future. Yukiko, on the other hand, was strangely undisturbed. Even to look at her touched Sachiko deeply.

When he left for work on the fourteenth, Teinosuke tended to feel that Sachiko should stay at home. Sachiko for her part was determined to appear at the *miai*. With matters thus undecided, a telephone call came at about three from Mrs. Jimba. She wanted to know how Sachiko was. Very well for the most part, said Sachiko, quite involuntarily. Mrs. Jimba followed her advantage. The fifteenth would be acceptable, then. Mr. Nomura had decided that they should meet at five in the lobby of the Oriental Hotel, and she hoped the Makiokas had no objection. The Oriental Hotel was only a convenient place to meet. After a cup of tea, they would go on to a restaurant somewhere—what restaurant had not yet been decided. Though the meeting was of course a *miai*, it was to be no more than an informal little dinner party, and they could discuss the matter of the restaurant when they met in the hotel. There would be six in the party: Mr. and Mrs. Jimba, representing Mr. Hamada, would be with Mr. Nomura, and she supposed there would be three Makiokas. Sachiko had fairly well made up her mind to go, but as Mrs. Jimba pressed her to agree to all the arrangements, she made one special request: since she was still having light hemorrhages and since this would be her first day out, she would be most grateful, much though it pained her to have to ask the favor, if Mrs. Jimba would arrange the *miai* with as little moving about as possible. She hoped they might take cabs, even to go a very short distance. That being understood, she said, she saw no reason why she should not go out.

Yukiko was at Itani's having her hair dressed when Mrs. Jimba called, and on her return she objected to only one detail: that they were to meet in the Oriental Hotel. She did not consider it a bad omen, she said, that they had met Segoshi for the last *miai* at the same place, but she hated to have the maids and the waiters recognize her, and look knowingly at each other as if to say that the old maid was already back for another try. Sachiko had not been entirely unprepared for this objection. Sure that once Yukiko had spoken she would not be easy to move, Sachiko went out to the study and telephoned Mrs. Jimba to ask if they might consider meeting elsewhere. Two hours later Mrs. Jimba called back. She had discussed the matter with Mr. Nomura, and they could not at the moment think of a better place than the Oriental Hotel. They could of course go directly to the restaurant, but she had been afraid that if she and Mr. Nomura arbitrarily decided on a restaurant that too might upset the Makiokas. She wondered if Sachiko had anything to suggest. The truth was that, though they hated to seem selfish, they hoped Sachiko might try to change Yukiko's mind. The Oriental Hotel would be so convenient for all of them, and it was after all only a place to meet— and there was no cause at all for these misgivings of Yukiko's. Sachiko talked the matter over with Teinosuke, who was just back from work. They concluded that it would be best to respect Yukiko's wishes. Much though she hated to force the issue, said Sachiko, might she not hope that Mrs. Jimba would concede that one point? Mrs. Jimba said that she would ponder the problem and call back the next morning. On the morning of the fifteenth she called back to ask whether the Tor Hotel would be more suitable. So the question was settled.

~~~~~~~~~~~~~~~~~~~~~~~~~~~~~~~~~~~~

28

THE SPRING FESTIVAL in Nara was over, and yet the day appointed for the *miai* was chilly. The air was still, but the sky was a dull gray, as though they might have snow. The first thing Teinosuke asked when he got up was whether the hemorrhages had stopped. Home from work early in the afternoon, he asked again. If Sachiko was not feeling well, they could still refuse for her. Sachiko answered that she was losing less and less blood. As a result of those trips to the telephone the afternoon before, however, the bleeding had in fact increased. She sponged her face and neck (she had not been able to take a bath for some days) and sat down before the mirror. The loss of blood had clearly had its effect. But then she had once been ordered by Itani to make herself as old and unobtrusive as possible, and she thought perhaps she had wasted away to just the proper point.

Mrs. Jimba, who was waiting at the hotel entrance, hurried up to them.

"Introduce me to your husband, Sachiko." She beckoned to a gentleman who waited deferentially a step or two behind her. "This is mine."

"I am very glad to meet you. My wife seems to have caused you a great deal of trouble."

"On the contrary, we've been very selfish about the arrangements for this evening."

"Sachiko." Mrs. Jimba turned to Sachiko and lowered her voice once the formalities were over. "I shall introduce you to Mr. Nomura—that is he over there—but as a matter of fact we have only met two or three times at Mr. Hamada's, and are not especially friendly. I really know very little about him, and possibly you should ask directly if you want to know anything."

Mr. Jimba waited in silence through this hushed conference. Then, with a bow, he motioned them toward Mr. Nomura.

Sachiko and Teinosuke had noticed, sitting in the lobby, a gentleman they recognized. He nervously put out his half-smoked cigarette and stood up to meet them. Though he was better built than they had expected, he did indeed look older than the photograph. His face was covered with small wrinkles, and his hair—they had not been able to tell from the photograph—was gray and thin, and yet somehow bushy, shaggy, and generally untidy. One would have said at first sight that he was in his mid-fifties. Two years older than Teinosuke, he looked at least ten years older. Since Yukiko, on the other hand, looked seven or eight years younger than she really was, they could have been taken for father and daughter. Sachiko felt apologetic for even having brought her sister.

After the introductions they gathered around a tea table. The conversation did not go well. There was something unapproachable about the man Nomura, and Mr. and Mrs. Jimba, who should have been helping fill in the pauses, were stiff and hesitant before him. Even granting that Jimba ought to behave with respect toward the cousin of an old benefactor, to Teinosuke this deference seemed to approach obseqiousness. He and Sachiko would ordinarily have had the tact to keep a conversation going, but tonight Sachiko quite lacked spirit, and only succeeded in passing something of her apathy on to her husband.

"And what sort of work do you do, Mr. Nomura?"

There followed a brief exchange in which they learned that Nomura was in charge of restocking trout streams, that his principal work was supervising and inspecting, and that the trout at Tatsuno and Takino were especially good.

Meanwhile Mrs. Jimba bustled about. She called Sachiko aside and talked to her for a time. She then talked to Nomura, went out to a telephone booth, and called Sachiko for another conference. Finally she was back at her seat, and it was Sachiko's turn: Sachiko called Teinosuke aside for a conference.

"The question is where we are to have dinner. Do you know a Chinese restaurant called the Peking, up in the hills?"

"I have never heard of it."

"Mr. Nomura goes there often, and says he would like to have dinner there. I told Mrs. Jimba I had no objection to Chinese food, but I simply could not sit in a foreign chair this evening. Most of the customers are Chinese, she says, but there are one or two Japanese rooms. She called to reserve one. Is it all right?"

"If it is all right with you. But try not to move around quite so much."

"She keeps calling me."

Sachiko went off to the women's room and was gone for twenty minutes. When at length she came back, paler than ever, Mrs. Jimba called her again.

"Let me take it," said Teinosuke. "My wife is not feeling at all well, and perhaps you could talk to me instead."

"I see. As a matter of fact, it's about the taxi. I've called two, and I wondered if we might not put Yukiko and Mr. Nomura and myself in one, and my husband in the other with you two."

"Is that what Mr. Nomura would like?"

"He hasn't said. I only thought it might be a good arrangement."

"Oh."

Teinosuke had trouble hiding his annoyance. Mr. and Mrs. Jimba had been told yesterday that Sachiko was braving considerable physical discomfort and even endangering her health, and the Makiokas had given hints enough this evening that she was not well; and yet neither Jimba nor his wife had bothered to ask after her or give her a word of comfort. Perhaps they thought it bad luck to refer to her illness at such a time. Still they could have tried unobtrusively to see that she was made comfortable. Or perhaps he was being unfair. Was it not possible that Mr. and Mrs. Jimba, for their part, felt that after they had undertaken all the arrangements and been put off time after time, Sachiko could be expected to make *some* sacrifice? Did they not think that, inasmuch as the meeting was to help no one if not Yukiko, Sachiko could bear a little physical discomfort, and that she was quite mistaken if she expected them to feel obligated? Perhaps he was being too sensitive, but it occurred to him that they might agree with Itani: Yukiko, having passed the marriageable age, was in serious trouble, and they were only trying to help—and Sachiko and her family should feel in debt to them. On the whole, however, it seemed most reasonable to conclude that they were too intent on pleasing Nomura to think of the others. Jimba worked for the Kansai Electric Company, of which Nomura's cousin Hamada Jōkichi was president.

Whether Mrs. Jimba was determined to do her duty by Mr. Hamada, or whether she was only echoing Nomura's wishes, it simply was not good sense to suggest that Yukiko ride with Nomura. Teinosuke wondered if she might not be trying to make a fool of him.

"Will it be all right, then? If Yukiko has no objection . . ."

"Yukiko is Yukiko, and she'll have no objection, I'm sure. But if everything goes well, there should be plenty of opportunities later."

"I see." Mrs. Jimba studied the expression on his face for a time, her nose wrinkled in a sardonic little smile.

"And then I think it would only make Yukiko stiffer than ever. It would not have at all the effect we want."

"I see. It was only a thought."

But Teinosuke found more to annoy him. When he heard that the Peking was in the hills, he was careful to ask whether the cab could go to the gate. He was assured that there would be no difficulty. Although the cab did indeed stop at the gate, however, there was a long, steep flight of stairs to climb before they arrived at the restaurant itself, and once inside they were shown to the second floor. Sachiko, leaning on Teinosuke's arm, fell behind the others. In fine spirits and quite indifferent to her distress, Nomura was praising the view when they reached the second flood.

"How do you like it, Mr. Makioka? One of my favorites."

"What a fine spot you've found." Jimba nodded his agreement vigorously.

"And when you look down on the harbor from here, there is something exotic about it. A little like Nagasaki."

"Very true. It does feel like Nagasaki."

"I often go to Chinese restaurants on Nanking Street, but I had no idea there was a place like this in Kobe."

"It's near the office, you know, and we often come here. And the food is rather good."

"Speaking of exotic things, look at this building. Very unusual, like something you might see in a harbor in China. Restaurants run by Chinese are generally ugly, but this one has a quality all it own—the railings and the carvings and the decorations and everything."

"See the warship." There was nothing for Sachiko to do but muster her strength and try to be polite. "What flag is it flying?"

Mrs. Jimba came upstairs looking perplexed.

"Really, I cannot tell you how sorry I am, Sachiko, but the Japanese rooms are all full. They want to put us in a Chinese room. Over the telephone they assured me they would have a Japanese room for us. But the boys here are Chinese of course. No matter how often you tell them, they *will* not understand."

It had struck Teinosuke as odd that a Chinese room seemed to be ready for them. If the boy had misunderstood Mrs. Jimba, Teinosuke could hardly hold her responsible; but even so, he had to conclude that, since there surely should have been a way to make the point clear even to an unreliable Chinese boy, Mrs. Jimba was showing a certain lack of consideration. And Nomura and Jimba, far from apologizing, were still busy praising the view.

"You will try to bear it, then?" Mrs. Jimba took Sachiko's hand in both of her own, and left no room for refusal.

"Oh, but this is a wonderful room. And such an interesting

place." Sachiko was more worried about her husband's irritability
than about her own discomfort. "We should bring Etsuko and
Koi-san some time."

"The child might enjoy looking down at the ships, I suppose."
Teinosuke still looked far from happy.

The hors d'oeuvres were served with Japanese saké and Chinese
shao-hsin wine. Sachiko sat across the table from Nomura. Jimba
spoke of the Anschluss, about which the newspapers had been
excited that morning, and for a time the conversation turned to
the resignation of Schuschnigg and Hitler's entry into Vienna.
It tended to be a dialogue between Jimba and Nomura, with
the Makiokas only putting in a word now and then. Although
she struggled to make it seem that nothing was amiss, Sachiko
had inspected herself once at the Tor Hotel and once before
they sat down in the restaurant, and found that the bleeding
was worse. The hard, straight chair helped little, and soon she
was left quite inarticulate by physical discomfort coupled with a
fear lest she spoil the party. Teinosuke, who only grew angrier,
knew that his wife was hard at work and that her task would
only be heavier if he did not try to be pleasant. He undertook
with the support of the saké to see that there were no gaping
holes in the conversation.

"Here, Sachiko. You should like this." Mrs. Jimba, who had
been pouring for the men, turned to Sachiko with a decanter.

"None for me this evening, thank you. But you ought to
have a little, Yukiko."

"Yes, please do."

"I think I might try this." Yukiko took a sip of the shao-hsin,
in which sugar crystals were floating. She was acutely embarrassed
at the glumness of her sister and brother-in-law and at the way
Nomura persisted in staring at her. Finally she was huddled so
low over the table that her slender shoulders seemed quite to
disappear. Nomura, excited at having a prospective bride before
him, became livelier as he drank. Clearly proud of having Hamada
Jōkichi for a cousin, he was careful to keep that gentleman's
name in the conversation, and Jimba too talked incessantly of
"the President," no doubt to suggest how great an interest Hamada
took in looking after this cousin. What surprised Teinosuke
most was the thoroughness with which Nomura had investigated

the Makioka family—Yukiko herself, of course, and her sisters, and their dead father, and the people at the main house, and the misstep that had put Taeko in the newspapers. They invited him to ask questions about any doubtful points, and the detailed interrogation that followed made it clear that his investigation had taken him everywhere. Perhaps Hamada himself had mobilized the investigating forces—in any case, someone had been sent to interview Itani, Dr. Kushida, Mme Tsukamoto, and a piano teacher from whom Yukiko had once taken lessons. Nomura even knew—they could only assume that he had heard from Itani—the reasons for the rupture in the negotiations with Segoshi and for the visit to the Osaka University Hospital. (Itani had told Sachiko that someone had come inquiring after Miss Yukiko, and that, to the extent that there seemed no reason not to answer, she had answered all the questions. Sachiko started at the thought of that spot over Yukiko's eye. She had not been worried this evening about the spot, which had disappeared since Yukiko's return from Tokyo. Surely Itani had not mentioned it!)

Teinosuke, on whom fell the duty of answering Nomura's questions, soon noted that Nomura was an extremely nervous man. It seemed not at all surprising that the fellow should talk to himself. Nomura's manner suggested that he went into all the fine points because he was confident his proposal would be accepted. In increasingly good spirits, he had become a different man from the rather dour person they met at the Tor Hotel.

Teinosuke wanted to cut the conversation off and go home as soon as possible, but as they left another difficulty arose. Mr. and Mrs. Jimba, who were returning to Osaka, were to see the Makiokas to Ashiya in a cab and ride on to Ashiya Station. Teinosuke was startled, therefore, to see that but one cab had been called. Nomura lived in the same general direction—a little out of the way perhaps—and could just as well come with them, someone suggested. Teinosuke knew how far out of the way a trip to Nomura's would take them. Worse, the roads were rough and the slopes steep in that part of the city. He wanted to look back in alarm each time they hit a new bump or rounded another curve, but he was wedged too tightly into the front seat to turn around.

Nomura suddenly announced that he would like to have them all in for a cup of coffee. It was a miserable little house, he said, but the view down over the harbor was even better than that from the Peking, and besides, they would want to see how he lived. Their refusals had no effect, and when Mrs. Jimba joined in to support him—they really must, since he had been so kind as to invite them, and there was, she had heard, no one in the house before whom they need feel the slightest constraint; there were only a girl and an old lady who worked for him, and it would surely be helpful to know how he lived—Teinosuke began to give way. Without consulting Yukiko, he could hardly refuse now that the cup of coffee had been tied to the marriage negotiations themselves. It seemed necessary moreover to defer to Mr. and Mrs. Jimba, who might be of help in the future. And after all, Nomura was only being kind. Presently Sachiko suggested that they should at least step inside.

To reach Nomura's house, they had to climb some forty or fifty yards up a narrow, steep, slippery path. Nomura was lively as a child. He hurried to have someone open the shutters and he proceeded to show off the view of which he was so proud, and invited them to see his study, and afterwards every room in the house, including the kitchen. It was, they found, a cheaply built two-storey six-room house. Nomura even dragged them to the Buddhist altar, over which hung pictures of his dead wife and children. In the living room, Jimba was praising the view, which he found quite as Nomura had described it, far better than that from the Peking, but Teinosuke and the rest felt that they could never feel safe in such a place: the veranda gave way to a cliff, and it was as though they were being sucked over.

They hurried off into the waiting cab as soon as they had finished their coffee.

"Mr. Nomura was in a fine mood tonight," said Jimba.

His wife agreed. "He was indeed. I have never seen him talk so much. It was because he had a young and beautiful audience. Sachiko, you can see how Mr. Nomura feels, and everything is up to you now. He has no property, of course, but he has Mr. Hamada behind him. He will never have to worry about a living, that much is sure. And possibly we can get guarantees from Mr. Hamada."

"Thank you very much." Teinosuke did not want to continue the discussion. "We will ask the people in the main house."

But as he got from the cab, he began to wonder if he had not been too abrupt. By way of apology he thanked the Jimbas for the evening not once, but three times.

29

MRS. JIMBA appeared in Ashiya two days later, on the morning of the seventeenth. She was most apologetic when she heard that the *miai* had sent Sachiko back to bed, and she left after but a half hour at Sachiko's bedside. Mr. Nomura had insisted, she said, that she come to plead his case. Having seen his house, they knew well enough how he lived. He was in such quarters only because he was a bachelor, and he had assured her that he would move into a house worthy of the name once he found a wife. He meant to do everything for his new wife, most especially if he should succeed in winning Yukiko. He was not wealthy, he admitted, but he knew at least that Yukiko would not be left wanting. Mrs. Jimba had also called on Mr. Hamada, and, seeing that Nomura was so enthusiastic, Mr. Hamada had urged her to do whatever was to be done to advance the negotiations. The fact that Nomura had no property would of course make the new bride's position a little uncertain, but Hamada would think of something—they should leave money matters to him. Hamada would be rather at a loss if they asked him what concrete guarantees he was prepared to make, but he could say that while he lived, Nomura would not be left destitute. And since a man of such stature was prepared to say so much, added Mrs. Jimba, ought they not to have confidence? Mr. Nomura, it was true, had a somewhat frightening face, but he also had a human warmth all his own. He was so good to his first wife, people said, that his ministrations in her last illness had brought tears to their eyes. And had he not had her picture out the night they visited him? The Makiokas could go on and on once they set out looking for defects, but inasmuch as the most important thing for a woman was that her husband love her and be good to her, Mrs. Jimba hoped most sincerely that they would look upon the proposal generously and give her their answer as soon as possible.

Sachiko, preparing the way for a later refusal, tried to answer so that the responsibility would seem to rest with the main house: there would be no trouble learning whether or not Yukiko herself approved—but as for the main house, which after all was most directly concerned—Sachiko and her husband were only acting as agents, so to speak, and the investigation was being conducted by the main house.

Sachiko's recovery was slow and Dr. Kushida had ordered absolute quiet. She did not have a chance to speak to Yukiko, then, until perhaps the fifth morning after the *miai*, when the two of them chanced to be alone in the sick room.

"What did you think of Mr. Nomura, Yukiko?"

Yukiko only nodded. Sachiko went on to report the substance of the conversation with Mrs. Jimba.

"And that is what she said. But you are so young, Yukiko, and he looks so old beside you. It seems wrong, somehow." She watched carefully for a change in Yukiko's expression.

"I do think he would do exactly as I wanted. I could live as I pleased." Yukiko had nothing more revealing to say.

Sachiko thought she knew what her sister meant: that she would be allowed to visit Sachiko whenever she liked. In most houses it would not be easy, but she would have this small consolation if she were to marry "the old gentleman." The average man would find it intolerable that his bride had accepted him only because she thought she could control him, but probably the old gentleman would want to marry Yukiko even knowing her reasons. Once she was married, of course, she might not find it as easy to go out as she had thought. Yukiko being the woman she was, the old gentleman's affections might bind her more tightly than she would care to say. Perhaps she would soon forget Sachiko's house—certainly she would forget it once she had children.

One could, if one chose, be grateful that the man wanted so earnestly to marry this too-long-unmarried sister. It was a little hasty, Sachiko concluded, the great antipathy she had taken. "If that is how you feel, Yukiko, perhaps you are right."

But Yukiko would come forth with nothing definite, however Sachiko pressed her. "I am not sure I would want to be made *too* much of," she said, smiling.

The next morning Sachiko, still in bed, sent off a note to Tokyo reporting that the *miai* had taken place. There was no answer. She was in and out of bed through the week of the equinox. One day, lured by the spring sky, she went out to sun herself on the veranda of her bedroom. Yukiko had gone down into the garden from the terrace below. On the point of calling out, Sachiko saw that her sister was enjoying the quiet moment after Etsuko had left for school. Yukiko circled the flower bed, inspected the budding branches of the lilac by the pond, picked up the cat Bell, and knelt for a moment under a round-clipped gardenia bush. Sachiko, who could only see her head bob as Yukiko rubbed her cheek against Bell, knew well enough without seeing her face what Yukiko was thinking: that she would soon be called back to Tokyo, and that she hated to leave spring in this garden behind. And she was perhaps praying that she might still be here to see the lilac in bloom. Although no word had come from Tsuruko in Tokyo, it was clear to the rest of the family that Yukiko was waiting in dread and asking to be left here even one day longer.

The reserved, quiet Yukiko was fonder of going out than one would have guessed. Sachiko, had she been well, would have made it a point to go each day to see a movie or do some shopping. Unable to wait for Sachiko's recovery, Yukiko was restless each sunny day if she could not call Taeko to wander about Kobe with her. She would set out happily after the two of them had arranged to meet, and it seemed that the marriage negotiations had completely left her mind.

Taeko, thus summoned time after time to keep Yukiko company, occasionally complained to Sachiko. Just now she was busiest, and it was too much to be called out during the busiest part of each afternoon.

"Yesterday something funny happened," she said one day.

The evening before, when they were buying candy in a Kobe shop, Yukiko had suddenly turned to Taeko in consternation.

"What shall I do, Koi-san? There he is, there he is." Who was, Taeko asked. Yukiko only fluttered about. "There he is, there he is." An old gentleman Taeko did not know hurried out from the back of the shop, where he had been drinking coffee. "If you have nothing else to do, why not have a cup of coffee with me? I won't take more than fifteen minutes of your time." Yukiko, more and more confused, flushed scarlet and murmured something unintelligible. "You really must have a cup of coffee," the gentleman said two or three times. Finally, seeing that Yukiko would only go on muttering to herself, he gave up, apologized politely for having bothered them, and went back to his table. "Hurry, Koi-san, hurry." Yukiko pressed the shop girl to wrap the candy faster, and flew out the door. Who was it, Taeko asked. "That man. The man I met the other day." Taeko at length guessed that it was Nomura.

"There is no one quite like Yukiko. She could just as well have refused, but there she stood muttering and gurgling."

"She is really quite hopeless. No better than a sixteen-year-old."

Sachiko asked whether Yukiko had said anything about the man. Taeko had, in fact, been entrusted with a message for Sachiko. Although Yukiko was leaving the question of her husband to Sachiko and Tsuruko and would marry the man they told her to, Nomura was out of the question. Willful though it was of her, she hoped Taeko would ask Sachiko to break off the negotiations. Taeko, astonished at how much older the man looked than he was said to be, thought it but natural that Yukiko should dislike him, and was sure that his appearance was at least one point against him, but Yukiko had had nothing in particular to say of that. Rather she complained that she had been distressed at having to see the pictures of his dead wife and children after the *miai*. True, it was a second marriage, said Yukiko; but had she not a right to feel uncomfortable at having the pictures set right out in front of her? She quite understood that the man, still alone, would want to pray for the repose of his wife's soul; but he hardly needed to take guests into the room where the pictures were on display. He might have hurried to put them away—what could he have had in mind, leading them straight to the altar and the row of pictures over it? That more than anything else had destroyed Yukiko's hopes of ever learning to like him. He understood nothing of a woman's finer feelings.

Sachiko had finally recovered. One afternoon two or three days later she started dressing to go out.

"I am going to Mrs. Jimba's to refuse for you, Yukiko."

"Oh."

"Koi-san told me."

"Oh."

Sachiko, as she had planned earlier, left Mrs. Jimba to infer that the refusal had come from the main house. Upon her return she told Yukiko only that things had been settled amicably, and Yukiko asked for no details. Some days later, as the Doll Festival approached, a note came from Jimba enclosing the bill from the Peking and asking that they pay half of it. They sent a money order by return mail, and thus the negotiations with Nomura came to an end.

There was still no word from the main house. Now that Yukiko had been with them a month, Sachiko began urging her to go back to Tokyo—she could come again, said Sachiko, and, rather than cause trouble, it might be better to go back for a time. Because it was the custom for Etsuko to give a tea party for her school friends each year on April 3, the Doll Festival, and because it was also the custom for Yukiko to make cakes and sandwiches for the occasion, Yukiko said that she would leave when the festival was over; but in no more than three or four days, she added, the Kyoto cherries would be in full bloom.

"You can go back after you see the cherries," said Etsuko. "You are not to go back any earlier. You understand?"

The most eager of all to keep Yukiko a little longer was Teinosuke. She had stayed this long, he said, and she would only regret missing the Kyoto cherry blossoms; and besides it would not do to have an important member missing from an annual observance. His real motive was this: since her miscarriage, Sachiko had become extremely emotional, and sometimes, when the two of them were alone, she would choke up with tears; he thought it might distract her to go cherry-viewing with her sisters.

The outing was set for the week-end of the ninth and tenth. Yukiko left it undecided whether she would stay long enough to be with them; but on Saturday morning she went upstairs and started to dress. When she had finished her face, she opened her suitcase, and, taking out the package at the very bottom, undid the cord. It was a kimono especially chosen for viewing cherry blossoms.

"Did you see what she brought with her?" laughed Taeko, who was helping Sachiko with her obi. Yukiko had left the room for a moment.

"She keeps quiet and has everything her way," said Sachiko. "Wait and see how she manages her husband."

Even among the cherry-viewing crowds, Sachiko wept a little each time she passed someone with a baby. Rather upset, Teinosuke took her home with the others on Sunday night. Three or four days later, in mid-April, Yukiko returned to Tokyo.

BOOK II

Sachiko had been careful, since the attack of jaundice, to watch the color of her eyes. A year had passed. Again the Hirado lilies were beginning to look dirty and ragged. The reed awning was up for the summer, and the birch chairs had been set out on the terrace. It came to Sachiko, looking out over the garden one afternoon, that exactly a year before, Teinosuke had noticed the tinge of yellow in her eyes. As he had done then, she went down into the garden and began picking off the faded blossoms. She knew how he hated them, and she meant to have the garden clean and neat for him—he would be home in an hour or so. When she had been at work for perhaps a half hour, she heard someone come up behind her.

"This gentleman says he would like to see you." O-haru, a strangely solemn expression on her face, handed Sachiko a calling card.

It was Okubata's. When he called that once—was it two years before?—he had not been encouraged to call again, and they had avoided mentioning his name before the maids, and yet Sachiko was sure, from her studied composure, that O-haru knew of the newspaper incident, and had been adroit enough to associate Okubata with Taeko.

"Show him into the parlor. I will be just a minute."

Sachiko washed her hands, sticky from the flowers, and, after a trip upstairs to see that she was presentable, went to receive her caller.

"I have kept you waiting."

Okubata had on a light-colored jacket one recognized immediately as English tweed, and gray flannel trousers. He leaped up with an almost affected briskness and brought himself to attention like a soldier. Three or four years older than Taeko, he would now be thirty or thirty-one. When Sachiko had last seen him, there had been something boyish about him, but in two years he had filled out—he was on his way to becoming a solid gentleman, one might have said. Still, as he looked at her with an ingratiating smile, and, his head thrust slightly forward, began talking in his high, nasal voice, she could see that very much of the wheedling, pampered Semba boy remained.

"I have often thought of calling, but I have never been sure you would want to see me. As a matter of fact, I have been at the gate two or three times without being able to come in."

"How sad. And what was the trouble?"

"I lost my nerve." He laughed lightly, quite at his ease.

Whatever Okubata may have thought, Sachiko's attitude toward him had changed since their last meeting. She had been told a number of times by Teinosuke, whose business frequently took him to the geisha quarters and who heard all the rumors, that Okubata was no longer the clean youth they had once known. He was seen about the Sōemon geisha district. Worse, it seemed that he was keeping company with a certain lady there. Did Koi-san know the sort of person he had become, Teinosuke wondered. If not, and if, only waiting for Yukiko to be married, she still considered herself engaged to him, might it not be better to tell her? There was, Teinosuke could not deny, something to be said in the fellow's favor. Possibly he had fallen into a fit of despondency over the difficulties in marrying Taeko, but there was a suggestion of cynicism in his avowals of "pure love." Since this was moreover hardly the way to behave in a time of national crisis, even Teinosuke and his wife, who had secretly been on Okubata's side, would find it difficult, unless he reformed, to work in his behalf when the time came for marriage negotiations—so said Teinosuke.

Guessing that he was more disturbed than his manner indicated, Sachiko decided to ask Taeko about her relation with Okubata. She tried not to let it seem that she was forcing the issue. Taeko replied that a fondness for geishas had run in the Okubata family from at least the time of young Okubata's father, and that even now his uncles and brothers frequented the tea-houses. It was wrong, then, to blame only "Kei-boy," as she called him. And Teinosuke was quite right—Kei-boy behaved as he did because he could not marry her. He was young, after all, and a little dissipation was only to be expected. True, she had not heard before of his keeping company with a geisha, but that was probably a malicious rumor. Barring real evidence, she would refuse to believe it. Because there was no denying, however, that his behavior might invite criticism with the China Incident in progress, she would tell Kei-boy to stay away from the teahouses. He did whatever she said, and a word from her would make him reform. Her composure seemed to proclaim that she was not one to find fault with Kei-boy, that she already knew everything, and that there was nothing to be surprised at. Sachiko almost felt that she herself had lost face from the encounter.

But Teinosuke continued to worry and to make inquiries in the pleasure quarters, even though he saw, and told Sachiko, that Taeko's confidence left no room for them to interfere. Then, just as he was happily noting that the rumors had died down (perhaps Taeko's warning had had its effect), a small incident made it seem likely that Kei-boy's dissipation had only gone underground. At about ten one night, some two weeks before, when Teinosuke was seeing a client home, the headlights of the cab for an instant picked up Kei-boy staggering down the sidewalk with the help of a lady one would take for a barmaid. Telling the story to Sachiko that night, Teinosuke asked that nothing be said to Taeko. There the matter had ended; but now, with the young man before her, Sachiko felt something sly and insincere in him. She wanted to agree with Teinosuke: "I find it very hard to be friendly toward him any more."

"Yukiko? Oh, yes, people have been very kind, and we keep having proposals."

Guessing that these inquiries about Yukiko were an indirect way of saying that he wanted his own marriage to Taeko somehow speeded up, Sachiko thought she saw the reason for the visit. It would presently be stated openly, and what would she answer? On his earlier visit, she had only said that she would see, and she was confident that she had made no commitments. This time, Teinosuke's feelings having changed so, she would have to be even more careful. They had no intention of blocking the marriage, of course, and yet, inasmuch as it would not do to have Kei-boy take them for active allies, she would have to give carefully vague answers.

Kei-boy suddenly pulled himself up and flicked an ash into the ashtray. "As a matter of fact, I came to ask a favor about Koi-san." Something about his tone and choice of words suggested that he already considered Sachiko his sister-in-law.

"Oh? And what might that be?"

"You know, of course, that Koi-san has been going to Mrs. Tamaki's sewing school these last few weeks. I have no objection to that in itself, but she seems to have lost interest in her dolls. She is doing no work on them worth mentioning. When I asked her what she had in mind, she said she was finished with dolls. She said she wanted to learn all there was to learn about sewing, and some day to specialize in it. She has orders coming in, and she has her pupils, and she has to go on with the dolls for a while at least. But when the right time comes she wants to leave everything to the pupils and give her time to sewing. And she says that with your permission she wants to go to France for six months or a year. She wants to be able to tell people she has studied designing in France."

"No! Did she really say that?" Sachiko knew that Taeko had taken up sewing in the spare time her dolls left, but this was another matter.

"She did. I have no right to interfere in her affairs, I know, but she has come this far by herself, and she has built up a name because she has her own original style. Why should she want to give it all up? No—I might understand that, but why should she want to take up sewing? She says that for one thing, no matter how good you are at doll-making, you are never more than a fad, and people soon tire of you and stop buying. She says that sewing is something necessary and practical, and the demand for it never falls off. But why should a girl from a good

family want to earn money by taking in sewing? She is going
to be married soon, and a girl who is going to be married ought
to stop worrying about how to support herself. I may not be very
dependable, but I have no intention of letting her starve. I
would rather she stopped pretending to be a working woman.
She is clever with her hands, and I can understand that she
has to have something to do; but think how much better it
would look if she were to take something up as a hobby, not to
make money. Something we might call artistic. No one needs to
be ashamed when a woman from a good family takes up doll-
making in her spare time. But I wish she would stop that dressmaking. I told her I was sure the people in the main house
would agree with me, and I told her to ask them and find out
for herself."

Okubata usually had an unpleasantly lazy drawl, as if to show
how unhurried one could be when one had money; but today
he was aroused. His words seemed to run into one another.

"You have been very good to tell me all this. Of course I
will have to hear what Koi-san herself has to say."

"Do, by all means. I may be going too far, but if she really
has made up her mind, might I ask you to put in a word to
stop her? And as for the trip abroad, I certainly do not say it
would be wrong. I think it would be a fine thing for her to go
to France, if only she had something better to study. You must
forgive me for saying so, but I would even like to pay the expenses
myself. And I might go with her. But I cannot approve of this
going abroad to learn sewing. I feel very sure you would never
give your permission, and I hope you will ask her to give up the
idea. If she has to go abroad, it will not be too late after we
are married. And that will be much more convenient for me."

There were many points on which Sachiko would have trouble
coming to a conclusion without talking to Taeko, but she noted
with a mixture of hostility and amusement that Okubata talked
as though he were already publicly recognized as Taeko's future
husband. It appeared that he had expected her to greet him
with the warmest sympathy and to welcome him into a frank
and open discussion, and that he had purposely chosen an hour
when, if all went well, he might even be allowed to see Teinosuke. After he had presented his "petition," he continued to

probe for Sachiko's views. Sachiko did her best to keep the conversation away from the main point. Thanking him for all the kind advice about Taeko, she treated him with the most impersonal politeness. She hastily left the room when she heard footsteps outside.

"Kei-boy is here."

"What does he want?"

Teinosuke waited in the doorway while Sachiko gave him a whispered summary of Okubata's business.

"In that case, there seems to be no need for me to see him."

"I think it would be better if you did not."

"Try to send him off, then."

But Okubata lingered on for another half hour. Finally, when it became clear that he was not to see Teinosuke, he said a cheerful goodbye and left. Sachiko offered only routine apologies for not having entertained him better. She avoided mentioning Teinosuke.

2

IF OKUBATA was telling the truth, then there were a number of points Taeko must explain, but Taeko, who said she was very busy, left each morning at about the same time as Teinosuke and Etsuko, came back latest of all, and perhaps one evening in three had dinner out. There was no opportunity to speak to her that night. The next morning Sachiko stopped her as she was about to follow Etsuko and Teinosuke out.

"There is something I must ask you, Koi-san." Sachiko led the way into the parlor.

Taeko denied none of what Okubata had said—that she meant to turn from doll-making to sewing, and that she wanted to study in France, no matter for how short a time. Sachiko, as she questioned her sister, began to see that Taeko had very good reasons for the change in her plans, and that she had come to it only after considerable thought.

Taeko had wearied of dolls, she said, because she did not want to go on forever wasting her time on girlish frivolities. She hoped rather to work at something more useful. Western-style sewing most fitted her talents, tastes, and skills, and since she would not be starting from scratch, her progress should be rapid. (Long interested in Western clothes, she knew how to use a sewing machine. She made her own clothes, and clothes for Sachiko and Etsuko too, from models in such foreign magazines as *Jardin des Modes* and *Vogue*.) She was quite confident that she would soon be able to stand alone. Scoffing at Okubata's view that doll-making was artistic and dressmaking vulgar, she said that she had no desire for an empty title like "artist." If dressmaking was vulgar, let it be vulgar. Okubata was not as alive as he should be to the national emergency: this was hardly a time for dolls and children's make-believe. Was it not disgraceful for even a woman's work to be so far from every-day life?

Sachiko could find no reason to object and was soon completely convinced. But she saw in Taeko's new plans evidence that her sister's affection for young Okubata had finally died. Because her elopement had been noised in the newspapers, pride made it difficult for Taeko to admit her mistake and discard Okubata at once, but had she not in effect already discarded him, and was she not merely waiting for a good opportunity to make a formal break? This determination to learn sewing—had it not come because she felt that, once she had left Okubata, she would have no choice but to make her way alone? Sachiko suspected that the young man only revealed his inability to understand Taeko's deeper motives when he asked what could made "a girl from a good family" want to earn money. If Sachiko was right, then it was not hard to see why Taeko was determined to go to France: no doubt she did mean to study dressmaking, but was not her main purpose rather to part company with Okubata? Taeko could be expected to think up a pretext for going alone.

As the conversation progressed, Sachiko saw that she had been half right and half wrong. Thinking that it would be best for Taeko to renounce Okubata with no pressure from outside, and that Taeko had the sagacity to do at least that, Sachiko proceeded with her questioning most circumspectly, but it became apparent, from bits of information Taeko dropped with outward unconcern, that, whether from the old pride or from deeper motives, she had no intention at the moment of giving Okubata up. She meant to marry him shortly, it would seem. She knew better than anyone, Taeko said, that Kei-boy was a classic example of the pampered Semba child. He had literally no redeeming features. Neither Sachiko nor Teinosuke could tell her anything she did not already know. Eight or nine years before, when she had first fallen in love with him, she had been a carefree girl, and she had not seen how hopeless a specimen he was; but love was not something that came and went depending on whether the man in question showed promise. She could not find it in her to reject her first love for reasons of expediency. She had no regrets, and she was resigned to the fact that she was meant to love the unpromising youth. It did worry her, however, to think how they would live after they were married. Okubata was an executive in the family corporation and could expect his brother to give him a share of the family property when he married. He therefore took the sanguine view that there was nothing to worry about. Taeko for her part could not help feeling that he would only eat up his capital. Even now he was by no means staying within his income, and she had heard that every month, with bills from teahouses and tailors and haberdashers to pay, he would go crying to his mother for money from her personal savings. That could last only while she lived, of course. Taeko was sure that if anything were to happen to the mother, Kei-boy's brothers would very shortly put a stop to the extravagance. However wealthy the Okubata family might be, Kei-boy was the third son, and, with his oldest brother already head of the family, he could not expect a large settlement, especially if the brother disapproved of his marrying Taeko. And since, even if the settlement should be a fairly large one, Okubata would very probably indulge in speculation and become an easy target for swindlers, the day might well come when he would be turned out penniless by his family. Taeko could not shake off these forebodings. Because she did not want people to point at her with superior wisdom when the unhappy day came, she meant from the start to have her own independent livelihood— better, to have a means of supporting her husband. That, said Taeko, was one reason for her decision to learn dressmaking.

Sachiko could see too that Taeko was determined not to join the main family in Tokyo. Yukiko had said that they were much too crowded to be summoning new additions, but it seemed clear that even if the summons were to come, Taeko would now ignore it. Taeko said that with her brother-in-law so bent on economy, she would not mind if he reduced her allowance. She had her savings and the income from her dolls. The expenses at the main house being heavy—there were six growing children to look after, and there was Yukiko—Taeko wanted somehow to lessen the burden, she said. She hoped that one day she might get along with no allowance at all. But there were favors she wanted in return. She wanted her brother-in-law's permission to go to France, perhaps the following year, and she wanted him to let her have part, or all, of the money her father had left for her wedding expenses. She did not know how large a sum Tatsuo was holding, but she thought it would probably be at least enough to pay for six months or a year in Paris and for passage both ways. If she used up the whole of it and there was nothing left to pay for her wedding, she could not complain.

Taeko then asked Sachiko to choose a good time—it did not have to be immediately—for approaching the main house. Taeko would not mind going herself to state her case. The idea of having Okubata pay for the trip was out of the question. He was fond of making such offers, but what in fact could he do? Taeko knew the answer better than Okubata himself. Possibly he meant to go crying to his mother again, but Taeko disliked the thought of taking money from him before they were married. Even after they were married, she had no intention of touching his property, and indeed she meant to keep him from touching it himself. She wanted to make her way alone, she would see to it that he did not come bothering Sachiko again, and she hoped that Sachiko would worry herself no more.

Teinosuke, upon hearing all this from his wife, said he thought it best not to interfere. They should see how serious Taeko was, and if it appeared that her decision was final, they could take up the task of winning over the main house. So the matter ended.

Taeko was as busy as ever. She denied that she was no longer interested in dolls. It was true that she would as soon stop work, but for many reasons she had to work harder than ever: orders were coming in, and she wanted to save a little more money, and it was costing her a great deal to live, and so on. And, she added, the knowledge that sooner or later she would give up doll-making only made her the more eager. She wanted to leave behind as many masterpieces as she possibly could. She also went for an hour or two every day to Mrs. Tamaki's sewing school, and she still kept up her dancing.

It appeared that the dancing was more than a hobby. She hoped to become a teacher. She went once a week to practice under Yamamura Saku, the second dance mistress to carry that name. Saku, a granddaughter of the Kabuki actor Ichikawa Sagijūrō, was popularly known as Sagi-saku. Of the two or three schools that called themselves Yamamura, Sagi-saku's was said to be truest to the old tradition. Her studio was in second floor rooms up a narrow alley in one of the pleasure quarters, and most of her pupils were professional ladies. Only a few were amateurs, and among them still fewer could really be called chaste young women. Taeko always brought her dancing kimono and fan with her and changed in a corner of the studio. As she waited among the professionals for her turn, she would watch the dancing and now and then nod to a geisha acquaintance. Her behavior was not at all improper when one considered her age, but she was uncomfortably aware that the others, even Saku, took her to be no more than twenty, and thought her a pert and knowing young lady indeed. Saku's pupils, amateurs and professionals alike, were much grieved to see the Osaka dance lose to the Tokyo dance. In their devotion to the Yamamura school and their desire to show the Osaka dance to the world, some of the more enthusiastic among them had formed a club called the Daughters of Osaka, which presented a dance recital once a month at the home of Mrs. Kamisugi, widow of an Osaka lawyer. Taeko occasionally danced in the recitals—such was her devotion to the art.

Teinosuke and Sachiko always took Etsuko and Yukiko to the recitals in which Taeko was to appear. Presently they came to know the other Daughters of Osaka. Toward the end of April, Taeko brought a request from one of the officers that they be allowed to use the Ashiya house for the June recital. The Daughters had been inactive since July of the preceding year because of the China Incident. But since theirs was such an unpretentious organization, no one could object to its having an occasional recital even in time of crisis, said one of the members, provided it took care to purge itself of frivolity, and they might well change the meeting place occasionally, lest the burden on Mrs. Kamisugi be too heavy. Sachiko, very fond of the dance, replied that the group would be most welcome, though she could not offer the facilities Mrs. Kamisugi could. Because it would be a nuisance to bring Mrs. Kamisugi's portable stage from Osaka, they decided to move the furniture from the two Western-style rooms on the first floor of the Ashiya house, to have the dances before a gold screen in the dining room, and to seat the guests on the parlor carpet as on the matted floor of an old-style theater. The dressing room was to be upstairs, the recital was to be from one to four on the afternoon of the first Sunday in June, and Taeko was to dance "Snow."

From the beginning of May, Taeko went to Osaka two or three times a week to practice, and for a week from about the twentieth Saku herself came out to Ashiya every day. Saku, who was fifty-seven and naturally delicate, and who to make matters worse had in recent years been suffering from a kidney ailment, almost never went out. For her to go all the way from the south end of Osaka to Ashiya in the summer heat was quite unprecedented. No doubt she wanted to show her gratitude to Taeko, so devoted to the Osaka dance that she did not hesitate to mingle with professional ladies, but in addition she may have seen that she could not continue to live in retirement if she meant to revive the fortunes of the Yamamura school. Etsuko, who had been resigned to the fact that Saku's studio was not the place for her, announced that she too would like to take up dancing. Saku replied that she would not at all mind visiting Ashiya ten days or so a month.

Saku generally told them when they might expect her the following day, but she never arrived on time. She would be an hour or two late, and when the weather was bad she would not come at all. Taeko, busy with her dolls, soon found the answer: she had someone telephone when Saku arrived, and while she was hurrying home, Etsuko had a lesson.

After Saku had talked twenty minutes or a half hour with
Sachiko, they would slowly begin to clear away the furniture.
Humming the accompaniment and demonstrating the steps and
gestures, Saku would soon be gasping for breath. Sometimes
she would arrive with blanched face and report that she had
had a kidney attack the evening before. Fond of telling people
that she had to stay healthy for her dancing, however, she appeared
not to let the illness worry her. She was also fond of saying that
she was no talker, but as a matter of fact she was an excellent
conversationalist and mimic, and she had no trouble leaving
Sachiko helpless with laughter. Perhaps it was a talent she had
inherited from her actor grandfather. Her face, when one thought
about it, was rather long and bold for her frail body, and suggested
theater breeding. One could not help thinking how it would
have become her, had she been born long ago, to shave her
eyebrows and blacken her teeth, and wear long, trailing skirts
in the old manner. A thousand expressions moved over her face
as she went through one of her imitations. She could take on
another's mannerisms as she would put on a mask.

Back from school, Etsuko would change to the unfamiliar
kimono—she almost never wore Japanese clothes except to go
viewing cherry blossoms—and Japanese socks that happened to
be a little too large for her, take up the Yamamura fan with
its flower-and-wave pattern, and dance the opening lines of "Ebisu
Fair":

> *The April cherries bloom at Omuro.*
> *To the sound of samisen and drum,*
> *One face turns to the other.*

In the long summer afternoon, the last of the Hirado lilies
glowed as if aflame. It was still daylight when Etsuko finished
and Taeko began her "Snow." The two younger Stolz children,
who played in the parlor with Etsuko almost every evening after
school, stared curiously in from the terrace, resigned to having
lost their playmate and playground. Sometimes the older boy,
Peter, would join them. One day Fritz came inside.

"Miss Saku." He imitated Sachiko.

"Ye-e-es?"

"Miss Saku." Rosemarie joined in.

"Ye-e-es?"

"Miss Saku."

"Ye-e-es?" With the utmost seriousness, Saku kept up her part of the game with the little blue-eyed foreigners.

3

"Koi-san, the photographer wants to know is it all right for him to come in."

Opening the recital with a special attraction, Saku had had Etsuko dance first. Etsuko was still in her dance kimono when she came upstairs.

"Please."

Taeko, dressed for her dance, was leaning against a pillar while O-haru helped her into her socks. Only her eyes turned toward Etsuko—the heavy Japanese coiffure did not move. Etsuko of course knew that this young aunt, to be ready for the recital, had for some ten days been wearing kimono rather than foreign dress and tying her hair up in the Japanese manner, and yet the change seemed to come as a fresh surprise. Taeko's kimono was the undermost of Tsuruko's three wedding kimonos. Because the gathering was to be such a small one, and because the times did not permit extravagance, Taeko had decided not to have a new kimono made. Discussing the problem with Sachiko, she remembered that the wedding kimonos were still at the main Osaka house. Sachiko's father, in his most prosperous period, had commissioned three famous artists to paint the designs, representations of the "three scenic spots of Japan": the shrine at Itsukushima on a black ground, the pine-covered islands of Matsushima Bay on a red ground, and the strand at Amanohashidate on a white ground. The kimono was almost new, having been worn only at the wedding some sixteen or seventeen years before.

In the white kimono and a black damask obi, Taeko seemed larger and more mature than usual and somehow more like Sachiko. Her full, rather round face had taken on a weight and dignity lacking when she wore foreign clothes.

"Photographer." Etsuko called to a young man, twenty-six or twenty-seven, who stood looking in at Taeko. Only his head showed over the stairs. "She says for you to come in."

"Please, Etsuko. It is rude to call the gentleman 'Photographer.' Say 'Mr. Itakura.' "

Itakura was already in the room. "Stand exactly as you are, Koi-san." He knelt down in the door and aimed his Leica at her. He took five or six pictures in quick succession, from the front, the back, the left, and the right.

Etsuko's dance had been followed by "Dark Hair," "The Maiden at the Well," and "Great Buddha." After the fifth dance, "Gift from Edo," by one of Saku's leading disciples, there was an intermission for refreshments. The audience in the parlor, limited to the families of the dancers, came to no more than twenty or thirty people. In the very front row, Fritz and Rosemarie Stolz had been watching solemnly from the very beginning, a little uncomfortable on Japanese-style cushions. Their mother sat outside on the terrace. She had said when she heard of the recital that she must see it, and she came in through the garden at a signal from Fritz that Etsuko was about to begin. No, the terrace would do nicely—she watched from a rattan chair someone brought her.

"You are being very good today, Fritz." Saku came from behind the gold screen, where she had been helping the dancers. She wore a formal black kimono embroidered with her family crest.

"They are behaving beautifully," said Mrs. Kamisugi. "What nationality are they?"

"They are friends of the little girl here, German children. We have become great friends ourselves. They call me 'Miss Saku.' "

"Really? They seem most interested."

"And see how properly they sit."

"Little German girl—I am sure someone told me your name." Saku had trouble remembering Rosemarie's name. "Are you and Fritz comfortable on the floor? Stretch your legs if you like."

Fritz and Rosemarie sat in stern silence. They hardly seemed the Stolz children with whom Etsuko played every day. "Can you eat this food, Mrs. Stolz?" Teinosuke noticed that Mrs. Stolz was using the chopsticks most inexpertly as she attacked the dish on her knee—and that it was a Japanese delicacy of a sort foreigners were thought not to eat. "You must find it impossible. Bring Mrs. Stolz something she can eat, someone." He saw O-hana pouring tea. "Bring a piece of cake for Mrs. Stolz. Take that other away."

"No, really. I am doing very well."

"You mean you can eat it?"

"I like it . . . very much," said Mrs. Stolz in hesitant Japanese.

"Really? You really like it? Bring the lady a spoon."

It appeared that she was telling the truth, and she left not a grain of rice on the plate when O-hana had brought her a spoon.

Taeko's dance was to come after the intermission. Teinosuke, very much on edge, had been up and down the stairs any number of times. Just when they thought he had finally settled down among the guests, he would be off up the stairs again.

"It is almost time."

"I am quite ready, as you can see."

Sachiko, Etsuko, and the photographer Itakura sat at Taeko's feet. Refreshments had been brought to them too. Taeko, a napkin spread over her lap, took the food in tiny bites, so as not to disturb her make-up. Her full lips, opened into a round "O," seemed fuller than ever, and after each bite she took a sip from the teacup O-haru held for her.

"You are not eating?" Sachiko asked her husband.

"I ate downstairs. Is it all right for Koi-san to eat so much? I know they say an army never fights on an empty stomach, but do you dance when you are stuffed?"

"She had almost no lunch. She says she is so weak from hunger that she might collapse right in the middle of her dance."

"But the singers in the puppet theater go without food until they have finished a performance. I know dancing and singing are different, but ought you to be eating so much?"

"I am really eating very little. It looks like more because I have to take such tiny bites."

"I have been admiring her," said Itakura.

"Why?"

"She struggles away at it like a goldfish eating bread, and yet she does manage to put it down."

"I thought you were staring harder than you needed to."

"You do look like a goldfish, Koi-san." Etsuko laughed happily.

"I have had lessons in how to eat."

"From whom?"

"From geishas who come to Miss Saku's. Once they have on their make-up, they have to keep their lips dry. The trick is to put food deep in the mouth without touching the lips. They practice when they are very young, on the drippiest things they can find."

"You have a most remarkable store of knowledge."

"And did you come to see the dancing, Mr. Itakura?" asked Teinosuke.

"Yes. But more to take pictures."

"You mean to use the pictures on postcards?"

"Not this time. It is not often you see Koi-san with her hair up. These pictures are to remember the occasion by."

"He is taking them for nothing," said Taeko.

Itakura had opened a small studio where he specialized in "art photography." Once an apprentice in the Okubata shop, he had gone to America before being graduated from middle school, and had studied photography in Hollywood for five or six years— it was said that he had hoped to become a movie photographer, but had not found his chance. When, upon his return, he opened a studio, his employer, the brother of Taeko's "Kei-boy," lent him money and introduced him to prospective customers, and Kei-boy recommended him to Taeko, just then looking for someone to take advertising pictures. He now did all the photographs for her pamphlets and postcards, and was himself able to advertise through her. Knowing of her affair with young Okubata, he was most respectful toward her, sometimes behaving almost as if he were a servant. A certain American-style forwardness helped him work his way into any opening offered, and—they hardly knew how—he had somehow become very close to the Makioka family, on the best of terms with the maids. He liked to tell O-haru that he would have Sachiko talk her into marrying him.

"It is free?" said Teinosuke. "Maybe we should all have our pictures taken."

"Let me take a picture of the whole family. Suppose you line up with Koi-san in the middle."

"What order do you suggest?"

"Mr. and Mrs. Makioka behind the chair. And now Miss Etsuko on Koi-san's right."

"We must put O-haru in too."

"O-haru will fit in to the left."

"If only Yukiko were here," said Etsuko.

"That would be nice," Sachiko agreed. "She will be very sorry when she hears what she missed."

"You should have invited her down, Mother. You had a whole month."

"I did think about it. But after all, she only went back in April."

Itakura looked up startled. He was sure that as he turned his range-finder toward them he had seen tears in Sachiko's eyes. Teinosuke noticed at almost the same time. What could be the reason? He was often caught off guard by her tears when something would remind her of the child she had lost, but today there must be another reason. Seeing Taeko in that white kimono, had Sachiko thought of the day long before when her other sister had worn the same kimono? Did she wonder when Taeko would put on a wedding kimono in earnest? And had it made her sad to think that they must first find a solution to the problem of Yukiko? He felt an answering wave of emotion as it occurred to him that someone besides Yukiko would be sorry to have missed the recital. But possibly Okubata had arranged for Itakura to be here in his place—very probably he had.

"Satoyū." The pictures finished, Taeko called to a girl perhaps twenty-two or three, evidently a geisha, who was kneeling before a mirror in a corner of the room. Her dance was to follow Taeko's. "May I ask you a favor?"

"And what might it be?"

"Would you step across the hall with me for a minute?"

There were a number of professionals among the dancers today, two geishas and several teachers. This Satoyū, a geisha from the Sōemon quarter, was a favorite pupil of Saku's.

"I have never danced in long skirts before. I am not at all sure I can manage. Would you give me a little coaching on how not to trip?"

"But I am not sure myself that I can keep from tripping."

"Oh, come now." Taeko led the young geisha across the hall. They could hear samisen and *kokyū* [1] being tuned below.

"Koi-san, Mr. Makioka says to hurry." Itakura went to call her when she had been shut up with Satoyū twenty or thirty minutes.

The door opened and Taeko came out, satisfied with what she had learned.

"Would you mind holding up the train please?" She had Itakura help her downstairs.

Teinosuke, Sachiko, and Etsuko followed. Teinosuke quietly took his place in the audience.

"You know who that is, Fritz?" He tapped the German boy on the shoulder.

Fritz nodded curtly and turned to watch the dancing.

4

It was the morning of July 5, just a month after the dance recital.

Even for the rainy season, there had been more rain than usual. It rained all through June and on into July, when the rainy season should have been over. From the third through the fourth it rained, and on the morning of the fifth the slow rain turned into a downpour. Even so, no one foresaw that but two hours would bring the most disastrous flood in the history of the Kobe-Osaka district. At about seven, Etsuko, bundled against the rain, but not especially worried, started out as usual with O-haru. Her school was some three or four hundred yards south of the National Highway, not far from the west bank of the

[1] A sort of bowed samisen.

Ashiya River. O-haru, who usually came back after seeing the child across the highway, felt that in such a storm she must go as far as the school. She was not back at the house until eight-thirty. Her interest aroused by the flood warnings the youths of the Home Defense Corps were spreading, she made a detour along the embankment, and she reported that the water was frightening around Narihira Bridge, almost as high as the bridge already. Still no one suspected the danger. "Do you think you should go out in this rain?" said Sachiko when some ten or twenty minutes after O-haru's return Taeko put on a green oiled-silk raincoat and overshoes and started to go out, but Taeko, off this morning not to her studio but to the sewing school, only laughed and said that a small flood might be interesting. Sachiko did not try to stop her. Only Teinosuke decided to wait until the rain had let up a little. He was killing time over some papers in his study when he heard the siren.

The rain was at its very worst. He looked out and saw that, although the lowest part of the garden, under the plums by the study—water was likely to collect there after even a trifling shower—had become a pond two yards square, there was nothing to suggest a crisis. Since the house was a half mile or so from the west bank of the Ashiya River, he felt no particular alarm. But then he thought of Etsuko's school, much nearer the river. If the embankment had given way, might it not have been by the school? Would the school be safe? Not wanting to frighten Sachiko, he tried to calm himself. After some minutes he ran into the main house. (He was soaking wet even after the five or six steps that separated his study from the house.) The siren was probably nothing serious, he said to Sachiko. As he put on a raincoat over his kimono and started out for a look around the neighborhood, O-haru came from the kitchen, her face pale and her clothes sodden from the hips down. A terrible thing, she said; she had been worried about the school after seeing the flood waters in the river, and she had run out in alarm when she heard that siren. The water, she said, had come as far as the next street east, and was running in a torrent from the mountains to the sea, north to south. She had made a try at crossing, but after two or three steps the water was up to her knees. Just when she was beginning to fear that she would be swept away, someone

shouted at her from a roof nearby. She was sternly reprimanded—
what the devil did a woman mean trying to cross a torrent like
that? The fellow was in what seemed to be a Home-Defense
uniform—but she saw that it was the young green grocer. "Yao-
tsune, what are you doing here?" At that, he recognized her too.
"Where do you think you are going, O-haru? Have you lost
your mind?" Not even a man could go farther, he said, and
near the river the destruction was fearful—houses were falling
people were dying. There had apparently been landslides in the
upper reaches of both the Ashiya River and the Kōza River,
O-haru learned; houses and mud and boulders and trees had
dammed up against the north side of the railroad bridge, and
the embankments had given way on both sides. The streets
below the breaks were seething maelstroms, in some places as
much as ten feet deep. People were calling for help from second-
storey windows. How was the school? she asked. He did not
really know, but since the destruction was worst to the north of
the National Highway, possibly the lower areas had escaped. He
had heard too that the danger was far greater on the east bank
than on the west. She could not rest until she had seen for
herself, said O-haru. Might there not be a roundabout way she
could take? But the man replied that you could go nowhere
without running into water, and that it only got deeper the
farther east you went. The deep water was bad enough, but
the current was so strong that you were in danger of being
swept away to sea; and it was the end if a boulder or a tree
came down on you. The men of the Home Defense Corps were
crossing on ropes at the risk of their lives, but that was nothing
for a woman to try. O-haru gave up and came home.

Teinosuke tried to telephone the school, but the line was already out. "Very well, I shall go see for myself," he said. He did
not remember what Sachiko answered. He remembered only that
she gazed at him with tear-filled eyes and clung to him for a
moment. He changed his kimono for his oldest foreign-style clothes
and put on a macintosh, a rain hat, and rubber boots. Before he
had gone fifty yards he saw that O-haru was following him. Instead of the loose summer dress she had worn on her earlier
venture, she had on a cotton kimono with the sleeves tied up and

the skirt hitched up into the obi to show the red under-kimono. There was no need for her to come along, he shouted; she was to go home immediately. But she answered that she would go with him only a little of the way. It might be better to go south, she said, and led him south, parallel to the river, until they came to the national highway. Following a circuitous route as much to the south as possible, he came to within a hundred yards of the Kobe-Osaka electric line without getting especially wet, but to reach the school he had to cross a torrent. The water was fortunately only about as high as the tops of his boots. As he approached the old National Highway, he was surprised to note that it was even shallower. From there he could see the school, and the faces of the children in the second-storey windows. "Fine, fine, the school is safe," he heard a happy voice behind him, speaking to no one in particular. O-haru was still with him. He had been following her, and he could not remember when he had passed her. The current was fairly swift. With his boots full of water, he had to brace himself at each step to keep from being swept away. O-haru, much shorter than he, was already wet to the waist. Having given up protecting herself from the rain, she was using her umbrella as a staff and clutching at fences and telephone poles as she followed some distance behind him. O-haru was famous for talking to herself. "How nice," or, "Whatever will he do now?" she would say in the movies, the delight or the suspense too much for her. The other maids all complained that it embarrassed them beyond measure to go to the movies with her, and Teinosuke could not help feeling a little amused as he saw how the old quirk had come out in this crisis too.

Sachiko moved restlessly about the house after Teinosuke left. When the rain seemed to let up a little, she went outside. Stopping a cab from the garage in front of the Ashiya River Station, she asked about the school. He had not been in that section of town himself, the driver said, but it appeared to be as safe as any. Though cut off by flood waters, the school itself, on high ground, had no doubt escaped. Sachiko was much relieved. If the Ashiya River was bad, added the driver, the Sumiyoshi River was far worse. The Government line, the electric line, and the National Highway all being cut, he had no exact information; but people

walking from the west reported that, although there was little
water as far as Motoyama and by following the tracks one could
reach that station without getting wet, everything farther west was
under a sea of muddy water; that waves were thundering from the
mountains, piling one on another and breaking over in a violent
backwash; that all manner of debris was coming down with them;
that nothing could be done to help the people clinging to bits
of matting and wood in the torrent.

Sachiko had to worry about Taeko, then, instead of Etsuko.
Taeko's sewing school was no more than two or three hundred
yards from the Sumiyoshi River, and, from the driver's story,
must certainly be in the middle of the flood. Taeko generally
walked to the National Highway and took a bus from there. The
driver remembered having passed her on the way down—she had
had on a green raincoat, he said; and if she was starting out then,
she must have reached the school very shortly before the flood
came down. Sachiko should be much more worried about the sewing school than about Etsuko's school. For no reason at all,
Sachiko ran back into the house and called out in the loudest
voice she could muster:

"O-haru!"

O-haru had gone out with Mr. Makioka and had not yet come
back, she was told. With that she screwed up her face and wailed
like a little child.

O-aki and O-hana stared at her in mute surprise. Embarrassed,
Sachiko fled from the parlor to the terrace, and, still sniffling,
down to the lawn. She saw Mrs. Stolz's pale face over the net-
wire fence between the two gardens.

"Mrs. Makioka. Your husband? Etsuko's school?"

"My husband has gone after Etsuko. But the school seems to be
all right. And your husband?"

"To Kobe. Peter and Rumi. I am very worried."

Of the three Stolz children, Fritz was still too young for school,
but Rosemarie and Peter went to the school run by the German
Club, high in the Kobe hills. It had once been the usual thing for
the father and the two children to start out together in the morning, Mr. Stolz's office being in Kobe; but with the China incident, business had fallen off, and, as his trips to Kobe had become

less frequent, the two children would often start out by themselves. This morning too the father had stayed home. Later, worried about the children, he had determined to go to Kobe. At the time, of course, they had not known how serious a flood it was, and it had not occurred to them that the railway lines would be out, and Mrs. Stolz only hoped he had gotten through safely. It was not easy to talk to Mrs. Stolz, who was less adept at Japanese than her children, but somehow, mixing in her own almost nonexistent English, Sachiko managed to convey her meaning.

"I am very sure he will be back safe. And the flood is only in Ashiya and Sumiyoshi, and the children in Kobe will be quite all right. I really think so—you have nothing to worry about."

After repeating her assurances several times, Sachiko went back into the house. Very shortly Teinosuke and O-haru brought Etsuko in through the front gate, which Sachiko had left open.

Etsuko's school had not been damaged. Because much of the surrounding land was flooded, however, and there was a possibility that the water would rise higher, classes had been dismissed and the children had been gathered on the second floor, where they waited for fathers and brothers to call for them. Etsuko had therefore not felt in danger herself, and had only been wondering about the house. Teinosuke was among the earliest parents to arrive. After thanking the principal and Etsuko's teacher, he started back with Etsuko and O-haru over more or less the same route. It was then that Teinosuke was glad O-haru was with him. She had astonished everyone when, mud and all, she fell upon Etsuko in her delight at seeing that the child was safe; and on the way back she walked upcurrent to shield Teinosuke. The water was two or three inches higher and the current much swifter than when they had crossed but a short time before. Teinosuke had to carry Etsuko on his back. He found that it was extremely difficult to walk, and if O-haru had not been there to divide the current for him he would have been in danger venturing even one step into it. The task was not an easy one for O-haru, who was sometimes in water to her waist. They followed a street to the west, cross current, and at the intersections they were sometimes in real danger. At one intersection there was a rope for them to cling to, at another they were pulled out by a Home Defense patrol; but at a third there was no such help, and they barely managed to get across by clinging to each other and leaning on O-haru's umbrella.

Sachiko had no time to be happy or to thank them. She could hardly wait for the end of the story.

"Yes, but what about Koi-san?" She was in tears again.

5

IT USUALLY took no more than a half hour for Teinosuke to go to and from the school. Today it had taken upwards of an hour. By the time he returned, information about the Sumiyoshi flood was fairly detailed, if somewhat confusing: the district west of Tanaka had become one great, swirling river; the sewing school was in the worst of the flood; south of the National Highway, the Kōnan Market and the golf course had literally become an arm of the sea; people and animals were dead and injured by the score, houses were collapsing. The news Sachiko had gathered, in short, was all bad.

But Teinosuke, who had been through the Tokyo-Yokohama earthquake, knew how reports could be exaggerated. Citing the earthquake, he sought to comfort the already despairing Sachiko. Since it was said that one could go as far as Motoyama, he would go see for himself. If the flood was really as bad as reports had it, he said, he could not hope to go farther, but he doubted very much that it was. He had seen at the time of the earthquake that even in the worse calamities surprisingly few people died. Long after the outsider had concluded that there was absolutely no hope, people somehow managed to get through. In any case, it was much too soon to begin weeping. Sachiko was to compose herself and wait for him. She was not to worry if he was a little late. He would do nothing rash. He would turn back as soon as it appeared that he could go no farther. Taking along a light lunch and shoving a little brandy and some first-aid medicines into his pocket, he started out in low shoes and plus-fours—he had had enough of the rubber boots.

The sewing school was a little more than two miles away by the Government Line. Teinosuke, who was fond of walking, knew the area well and had passed the school itself a number of times. He pinned his hopes chiefly on the fact that the Kōnan Girls' Academy lay across the street south of the tracks, perhaps a mile beyond Motoyama Station, and the sewing school a little to the west of it, a hundred yards or so directly south from the tracks; and that if he could follow the tracks as far as the academy, he might be able to go on to the sewing school, or at least to see whether or not it was damaged. O-haru was after him again, but this time he was firm: she was not to come, he said harshly. She was to stay with Sachiko and Etsuko, whom he did not want to leave alone. About fifty yards north of the house he came to the tracks. For the first few hundred yards there was no water at all, except two or three feet in the open rice paddies. As he left the wooded section, the water to the south disappeared, but near Motoyama the south side of the tracks was again under water. The tracks themselves still being dry, he did not feel endangered. Each time he met a group of students from one of the Kōnan academies, however, and asked what lay beyond, he received the same answer: this was nothing to what he would find the other side of Motoyama—he had only to go a little farther and everything would be one solid sea. He wanted to go on to the west of the Kōnan Girls' Academy, he said, and they all answered that that was the worst flooded section of all. The water had still been rising when they had left school, and by now probably even the tracks were under water.

At Motoyama the water was indeed frightening. Teinosuke went into the station to rest a moment. The street in front of the station was already under water, and students and station attendants were taking turns sweeping out the water that seeped through the barrier of sandbags and matting at the entrance. Teinosuke feared that if he loitered too long he too might have to man a broom. Finishing his cigarette, he started along the tracks in a yet fiercer downpour.

The water was as yellow and muddy as the Yang-tze, and here

and there spotted with something viscous and chocolate-colored. Soon Teinosuke himself was in water. He noticed with surprise that he was crossing the bridge over the little Tanaka brook, now a roaring torrent. Beyond the bridge the water was shallower again; but though the tracks were dry, the water was fairly high on both sides. He stopped and looked ahead, and saw what the students had meant when they said he would find "one solid sea." It would have been out of place, perhaps, to use words like "grand" or "majestic," but as a matter of fact Teinosuke looked first at the flood less with horror than with a sort of reverent awe. This was a region of fields, pine groves, and brooks, dotted by old farm houses and the red roofs of foreign-style houses on land sloping gently from Mt. Rokkō to Osaka Bay—Teinosuke was fond of saying that even for this bright, dry Osaka-Kobe region, it was bright and dry and good for walking. Now it had become a torrent that made one think of the Yang-tze or the Yellow River in flood. Even for a flood it was extraordinary: great waves rolled from Mt. Rokkō one after another, breaking and roaring and sending up sheets of foam, as if in an enormous caldron. It seemed less a river than a black, boiling sea, with the mid-summer surf at its most violent. The railroad stretched ahead like a pier out into the sea, in some places almost under water, in others a twisted ladder of rails and ties, the land beneath having been torn away. He noticed a pair of little crabs scuttling along at his feet. No doubt they were from one of the brooks, and had fled to the tracks before the rising water.

If he had been alone, he would probably have turned back, but he was with another group of students from the Kōnan Boys' Academy. The excitement had begun an hour or two after they reached school. With classes dismissed, they had walked through the swirling water as far as Okamoto Station only to find that the electric line was not running. They then walked on to Motoyama and found that the Government Line too was cut. After resting for a time in the station (it had been they who were sweeping back the water), they became uneasy at the rising water, and de- cided to divide into two groups, one headed for Osaka, the other for Kobe, to see how far they could go along the tracks. All healthy, vigorous boys, they had no sense of danger, and they would shout with delight when one of their number fell into the water.

Following close after them, Teinosuke stepped uncertainly from one tie to another where the ground had been cut away and the torrent roared below. He had not noticed in the roar that someone was calling them. Fifty yards or so ahead a train was stalled, and students from the same school were leaning out the windows and urging them on. And where do you think you are going? the students on the train wanted to know. It was dangerous to go on, the Sumiyoshi River was terrible, there was no crossing, why not get on the train and wait? Teinosuke gave up any thought of going farther and climbed in with them.

It was a third-class car on an express for Kobe. There were numerous people aboard besides the students. Several families of Koreans were huddled together off by themselves, no doubt driven from their homes by the flood. An old woman who seemed to be ill had her maid with her, and before long she was praying aloud. A clothes peddler shivered in a linen half-kimono and drawers, his wares in a large, muddy cloth bundle beside him, his kimono and woolen stomach-band spread to dry. Their number having increased, the students were livelier than ever. One of them took a box of caramels from his pocket and passed it around to his friends. Another pulled off his rubber boots, dumped out the gravel, and sat staring at his white, puffy feet. A third, taking off his student's uniform, proceeded to dry himself. Others, reluctant to sit down in their wet clothes, stood in the aisles. They took turns at the windows. Look, a roof. A mat. Some wood. A bicycle —look, look, a bicycle!

"A dog. Shall we help it in?"

"It must be dead."

"It is not, it is not. Look, on the tracks."

A muddy, medium-sized cur, part terrier, one would have guessed, huddled shivering in the shelter of the car. Two or three of the students climbed down with much shouting to help it into the train. Once inside, the dog shook itself and lay quietly before the boys who had helped it, looking up at them with frightened, bewildered eyes. It only sniffed at the caramel one of them offered.

Teinosuke, too, was wet and cold. He took off his raincoat and jacket and spread them on the seat, and, after a swallow or two of brandy, lighted a cigarette. Though his wrist watch said one, he was still not hungry. Looking to the north, he saw that the train was directly opposite the Second Motoyama Primary School, from the windows of which water was pouring as through a giant sluice. It would be no more than fifty yards or so to the Kōnan Girls' Academy, then. On an ordinary day he could have been there in two minutes. The students were quieter. As if by agreement, they had all taken on solemn expressions. Even to the young, there was no denying that the time for laughter had passed. The tracks along which Teinosuke had walked from Motoyama Station were under water, and the short stretch the train stood on was now an island in the flood. Soon it too might be under water, or the water would be gnawing away the embankment.

The level of the flood was meanwhile creeping up the embankment, here six or seven feet high. A muddy wave from the hills broke with a roar as of the surf upon a beach, throwing a sheet of spray into the cars. The passengers hastily closed the windows to the north. Outside, muddy current struck muddy current, boiling and whirling and foaming. A man in a postman's uniform came running from the car ahead, and after him fifteen or sixteen other passengers, and the conductor.

"Would you all move back one more car, please. The water ahead is over the tracks."

The passengers picked up their baggage and their wet clothes and boots and hurried into the car behind.

"Can we use the berths?" It was a third-class sleeper.

"Go ahead. This is no time to worry about fares," said the conductor.

Several of the students tried lying down, but most of them were soon up and looking out the windows again. The roar of the water was more and more ominous. The old woman was praying earnestly, and the Korean children were crying.

"It is over the tracks." Everyone got up to look out the windows to the north. The water was washing near the edge of this embankment, and had already begun to pour over the north embankment.

"Will we be all right here?" asked a woman thirty or so, probably a suburban housewife.

"Well—you might try if you think you can make it to a safer place."

Teinosuke stared absently at a cart tumbling over and over in the stream. He had promised his wife that he would do nothing rash, that he would turn back as soon as the way began to look dangerous. Now he faced a crisis, hardly knowing how it had happened. Even so he did not think of death. He was not a woman or a child, he could still tell himself, and when the time came he would escape somehow. He was worried about Taeko: he remembered that her school was a one-storey building. He had dismissed his wife's fears as exaggerated and unreasonable, but had not the knowledge that someone near her was in very great danger come to her intuitively? The figure of Taeko dressed to dance "Snow" but a month before came into his mind, the more poignant for its freshness. And he thought too of how they had lined up for a family photograph with Taeko in the middle, and how for no reason tears had come to Sachiko's eyes. Perhaps even now Taeko was on a rooftop crying for help—was nothing to be done, now that his goal was before his eyes? Must he sit here inactive? He felt he could not go back to Sachiko unless he braved a little danger. He saw her grateful face in alternation with the desperate, tear-stained face he had left at the door.

The water to the south of the tracks had receded a little. Here and there sand was showing. To the north, waves were breaking still higher over the track for Osaka.

"The water is lower on this side," said one of the students.

"It is. We can get through."

"We can go as far as the Girls' Academy."

The students jumped down and were on their way, and most of the other passengers, Teinosuke among them, followed with brief-cases under their arms and bundles strapped to their backs. As Teinosuke stepped down from the embankment, a huge wave broke over him like a waterfall, and a log shot out from one side. He managed somehow to escape the muddy rush, but when he came to what he took for dry ground, he sank to his knee in the sand. He lost a shoe pulling himself free, and immediately the other leg was in the sand. Five or six paces with first one leg and then the other in sand to the knee, and he came to a swift current some six feet wide. The people ahead of him managed to cross after stumbling several times. The current was strong beyond comparison with the one he had carried Etsuko across. Two or three times he thought he was lost, and when at length he reached the other side, he sank to his hips in the sand. Falling against a telephone pole, he again pulled himself free. The back gate of the Kōnan Girls' Academy was before him, no more than ten or fifteen yards away; but in the ten or fifteen yards was another current some ten feet wide, and it was not easy to see how he could cover even that short distance. Finally the gate opened and someone pushed a rake toward him. He was pulled safely inside.

6

AT ABOUT one o'clock the rain began to let up. The water showed no sign of receding until about three, when the rain had quite stopped and spots of blue were visible here and there through the clouds.

As the sun came out, Sachiko went down from the terrace into the garden. Two white butterflies were dancing over the lawn, which was greener and fresher for the rain. Among the weeds between the sandalwood and the lilac a pigeon was fishing for something in the puddles. The tranquil scene carried not a hint that there had been a flood. The utilities were cut off, but there was no shortage of water, since the Makioka house had a well. Expecting Teinosuke and the rest to come home covered with mud, Sachiko ordered that the bath be heated. Etsuko had gone out with O-haru to look at the river, and the house was quiet. Maids and house-boys from neighboring houses came one after another for water, which they had to lift by hand. The well motor was not running. Sachiko could hear splashing back by the kitchen, and the voices of O-hana and O-aki as they exchanged reports with the callers.

At about four came the first inquirer after their safety: Shōkichi, the son of the man who was living in the main Osaka house. Since there had been nothing out of the ordinary in Osaka, no one had guessed the damage between Osaka and Kobe until, at about noon, an extra came out. Quitting work, Shōkichi had picked up a few essential supplies and started out immediately.

He had been on the way ever since. He had tried the Government Line and the electric and he had taken buses. Sometimes he had had to stop a cab or a truck and demand a ride, and sometimes he had walked. His knapsack was full of food, he carried his shoes in one hand, and his muddy trousers were rolled up to the knees. When he saw the destruction around Narihira Bridge, he had wondered what might have happened to the Ashiya house, but he had felt a little foolish when he came to this street and found that the flood seemed a fabrication. "Well, young lady, it is good you are safe," he said to Etsuko when she came back. He was a great talker. Presently he caught himself and asked whether there was anything he could do. What of Teinosuke and Koi-san? With that Sachiko told him of her anguish since morning.

Each new report had only increased her concern. She heard, for instance, that in the upper reaches of the Sumiyoshi River a valley some hundreds of feet deep had so filled with sand and boulders that there was no longer a trace of it; that boulders weighing tons and trees stripped of their bark and turned into bare logs had piled up on the railway bridge across the Sumiyoshi and made it quite impassible; that a mound of corpses was heaped against the Kōnan Apartments, in low ground south of the tracks and some two or three hundred yards this side of the Sumiyoshi River; that with the corpses encrusted in sand identification was quite impossible; that Kobe too had suffered considerable damage; and large numbers of passengers had died in the flooded underground of the Kobe-Osaka Electric. There was no doubt a good deal of exaggeration in all the reports, but Sachiko was deeply disturbed by one of them: the story of the corpses at the Kōnan Apartments. Taeko's sewing school was across the road and no more than fifty yards to the north; and if indeed there were mountains of corpses it could only mean great destruction in the area north of the apartments. This alarming conclusion was confirmed by information O-haru brought back. O-haru, as worried as Sachiko, had asked everyone she met for news of the sewing school, and her informants had agreed that in all the land east of the Sumiyoshi River the neighborhood of the sewing school was the most severely hit. Even though the flood had begun to recede everywhere else, she was told, it was as bad as ever there, in some places as much as ten feet deep.

Teinosuke was not a reckless sort, and he had promised when he left that he would do nothing rash. Still, as the hours went by, Sachiko began to add worries about him to worries about Taeko. If the land around the sewing school had been so badly hit, he could not possibly have made his way through. He must surely have turned back—and why was he not yet home? Might he have gone just a little farther and a little farther until, without his knowing it, he was in the flood? But for all his cautiousness, he was not one to give up easily when he had set out to do something, and, having found one road blocked, perhaps he was trying another and yet another, and waiting for the water to recede along one of them. It would take time for him to make his way back through the water, assuming he had found and rescued Taeko, and there would be nothing surprising about his not reaching home until six or seven. Thus Sachiko turned over all the possibilities from the best to the worse, until the very worst had come to seem the most likely. There was not the slightest chance that she was right, said Shōkichi, but, since she was so disturbed, he would go out and look for himself. Sachiko knew that there was very little likelihood of his meeting Teinosuke along the way. Even so, she thought she would feel better if he went. Would he mind very much?—Shōkichi got ready immediately, and at about five Sachiko saw him off from the back door.

The front door and the back door opened on different streets. For the exercise, Sachiko walked around to the front. She went on into the garden from the gate, left open that day because the bell was not working.

"Mrs. Makioka." Mrs. Stolz was standing at the fence again. "Etsuko's school. All right. You feel better?"

"Yes, Etsuko came home safely, thank you. But I am terribly worried about my sister. My husband has gone out to look for her." In language Mrs. Stolz could understand, Sachiko repeated the story she had told Shōkichi.

"Really?" Mrs. Stolz clucked sympathetically. "I understand you are worried. I am sorry."

"Thank you. And what about your husband?"

"He is not home. I am very worried."

"Do you suppose he really went all the way to Kobe, then?"

"I think so. Kobe, flood. And Nada, and Rokkō, and Oishikawa, water, water, water. My husband, Rosemarie, Peter. What has happened to them? Where are they? I am very worried."

Mr. Stolz was a strongly built man whom one felt at a glance one could rely on, and he was a most intelligent German type. It did not seem possible to Sachiko that he could be harmed. As for Peter and Rosemarie, their school was on high ground even for Kobe, and no doubt they had only found the way blocked and were late getting home. But Mrs. Stolz was imagining the worst. Sachiko's attempts to comfort her had little effect. "I heard about it, the water in Kobe is terrible, many people are dead," she said. Looking into that tearful face, Sachiko could not think of the German woman as a foreigner. At a loss for comforting words, she found herself only repeating the usual stilted phrases—everything was all right, she certainly hoped everything was all right.

While she was having her troubles with Mrs. Stolz, she heard someone at the gate. The dog Johnny ran out to investigate. Would it be Teinosuke and the others? Sachiko's heart pounded. But through the shrubbery she saw a dark blue suit and a Panama hat.

"Who is it?" O-haru had come down from the terrace.

"Mr. Okubata."

"I see." Sachiko looked just a little confused. Although it had not occurred to her that Okubata would come calling, it was quite the most natural thing in the world that he should. But what could she do with him? She had decided, and she had been told by Teinosuke, that if Okubata came again she should be as cool and distant as possible, and turn him away at the door. But today was different. He had come all this way to inquire after Taeko, and if he asked permission to wait for her, it would be inhuman to send him off. And as a matter of fact today, only today, Sachiko felt that she would like to have him wait for Taeko and share their happiness when she came back safely.

"He asked after Koi-san, and when I said she was not yet back, he asked to see you."

Okubata knew well enough that his relations with Taeko were being kept secret. A lack of self-possession that could bring him to make such an inquiry of the maid who came to the door seemed to Sachiko something she could forgive only in a crisis— but today she found this evidence of confusion rather appealing.

"Ask him in, please." It was a good opportunity to break free of
Mrs. Stolz, who still waited by the fence. "I am terribly sorry, but
I have a caller."

She went upstairs to retouch her face. Her eyes were swollen
from weeping.

The electric refrigerator was not working. Sachiko had one of the
maids take Okubata a glass of barley-tea cooled at the well. When
she came down herself, he shot up at attention, exactly as on his
earlier visit. The blue-serge trousers were neatly creased and almost
spotless, a striking contrast to Shōkichi's. He had heard that the
train was finally running from Osaka to Aoki, he said. He had come
as far as Ashiya station and walked only the mile or so from there.
In places there had been water, but nothing serious—he had only
to take off his shoes, roll up his trousers, and stroll across.

"I should have come earlier, but I heard about the flood only a
little while ago. I knew this was one of the days Koi-san would
be at the sewing school. Was she still at home when it began?"

Sachiko's main reason for deciding to see Okubata had been
that she thought he would best understand her feelings. If she told
him how extremely worried she was about her husband and sister,
at least a part of the terrible uncertainty might leave her. But as
she sat across the table from him, she wondered whether it would
not be better to say very little. No doubt he was worried about
Taeko, but there was something just a little artificial about the
concern written on his face. Sachiko began to suspect that he
thought this a good opportunity to work his way into the Ashiya
house. In answer to his questions, she told him in as businesslike
a fashion as possible what she knew: that the water must have
risen very shortly after Taeko arrived at her sewing school; that
the land around the sewing school was the worst flooded of all;
that, noting her concern for Taeko, Teinosuke had decided to
go as far as he could in the direction of the school, and had left
the house at eleven that morning; that an hour or so before,
Shōkichi from the Osaka house had arrived and left again; and
that she was most uneasy because no one had come back.
Okubata fidgeted; then, as she had expected, he asked whether he
might wait there for a time. "Please do, as long as you like,"
Sachiko said pleasantly, and went back upstairs.

The guest would wait, she told one of the maids, and should be given a magazine or two and a cup of tea. She did not go downstairs again herself. She noted that Etsuko had made several trips to peek in at Okubata from the hall.

"Etsuko, come here, please," Sachiko called from the head of the stairs. "That is a bad habit of yours. Must you go looking into the parlor when there is a guest?"

"I was not."

"You are not to lie to me. I saw you. It is very rude."

Etsuko flushed and hung her head, and rolled timid eyes up at her mother; but almost immediately she started downstairs again.

"You are not to go downstairs. You are to stay up here."

"Why?"

"You can do your homework. You will probably have school tomorrow."

Sachiko sat Etsuko down with her books, and, after lighting incense under the desk to drive off mosquitoes, went back to her own room and knelt looking out from the veranda at the street up which she hoped soon to see Teinosuke and Taeko coming. She heard a deep voice next door—"Hilda, Hilda!"—and turned to see Mr. Stolz walking around to the back of his house. After him came Peter and Rosemarie. Mrs. Stolz, who had been doing something in back, threw herself upon him with a happy shriek. The garden was still light, and through the leaves of the plane tree and the sandalwood at the fence, Sachiko looked down upon the sort of embrace one is treated to in foreign movies. When Mrs. Stolz had finished kissing her husband, Peter and Rosemarie had their turns. Sachiko, who had been leaning against the veranda railing, quietly pulled back out of sight.

"Mrs. Makioka!" Mrs. Stolz was apparently unaware that she had been seen. She danced about the garden, and her voice was quite mad with happiness. "My husband is back. Peter and Rosemarie are back."

"I am so happy for you." Sachiko stepped out to the veranda again, and at the same moment Etsuko was at the window of the next room.

"Peter! Rumi!"

"Banzai!"

"Banzai!"

The three children raised their hands in the cheer, and Mr. and Mrs. Stolz waved with them.

"Did your husband go to Kobe?" Sachiko asked.

"He found Peter and Rumi. On his way to Kobe. They came home together."

"How nice, Peter, that you were able to meet your father." A little impatient with Mrs. Stolz's Japanese, Sachiko spoke instead to the boy. "And where did you find your father?"

"Not far from Tokui, on the National Highway."

"Did you really walk all the way to Tokui from Kobe?"

"We took a train from Sannomiya to Nada."

"The trains are going through as far as Nada?"

"Yes. And then I walked on to Tokui with Rumi, and we met Father."

"You were lucky to find him. And how did you come from Tokui?"

"We walked along the National Highway. And along the tracks too, and higher up in the hills. And in some places where there was no road at all."

"How dreadful. Was there still a good deal of water?"

"Not a great deal. Just a little, here and there."

There were many obscure points in Peter's story when she pressed him for information. It was not clear how they had come, and which sections were still flooded, and what they had seen along the way, but if a little girl like Rosemarie had come through, and without even getting muddy, they could not have met any serious obstacles. Sachiko was more and more uneasy. If children could come all the way from Kobe in so short a time, then Teinosuke and Taeko should have been home long ago. Had they then made some tragic mistake? The mistake would have been Taeko's. And had Teinosuke, with perhaps Shōkichi, found himself in trouble as he tried to bring her out?

"Your husband and your sister. Are they back?"

"Not yet. And here your husband is. What can have happened to them? I am terribly worried." Sachiko could not control the tremor in her voice. Mrs. Stolz, her face partly hidden by the trees, clucked sympathetically.

"Mrs. Makioka." O-haru knelt in the doorway. "Mr. Okubata

asked me to tell you he is going to have a look at the sewing
school."

7

OKUBATA was standing at the door, in his hand an ash cane with
a gleaming gold head.

"I heard what they said. Those foreign children came through.
What can have happened to Koi-san?"

"I wonder too."

"There is no reason for her to be so late. I am going out to see
what I can find. I may stop by later."

"Thank you. But it is almost dark. Possibly you should wait a
little longer."

"I am too nervous. And I can be there and back in the time I
would be waiting."

"Oh?" Sachiko felt she must be grateful to anyone kind enough
to show concern for her sister. In the end she was not able to
keep Okubata from seeing her tears.

"I will see you later, then. There is really no need to be so
upset."

"Thank you. Do be careful." She saw him to the door. "You
have a flashlight?"

"Yes."

Okubata picked up two objects that lay under his Panama hat,
and hastily shoved one into his pocket. He did not try to hide the
flashlight, but the object tucked out of sight was clearly a Leica
or a Contax—probably it embarrassed him to be caught with his
camera all ready.

For a time after he left, Sachiko stood leaning against the gate
and staring off into the darkness. She finally went back into the
parlor. In an effort to calm her nerves, she lighted a candle and
sat down. When O-haru came in and announced timidly that dinner was waiting, she saw that it was indeed well past dinner time,
but she had no appetite. Have Etsuko eat first, she said. O-haru

came downstairs a minute or so later to report that Etsuko too
would rather wait. It was strange for Etsuko, who hated being
alone upstairs, to be so quiet now that her homework must be
finished. Perhaps she knew that if she hung on her mother as was
her habit she would find herself in trouble. No calmer after twenty
or thirty minutes, Sachiko went upstairs and, without speaking to
Etsuko, on into Taeko's room, where she lighted a candle. She
stood as if bound to the four photographs over the south lintel.

They were photographs of Taeko's "Snow." All through the
dance, Itakura had clicked his shutter industriously, and in the
evening, before Taeko changed clothes, he had had her pose before the gold screen for several more pictures. Taeko picked these
as the four she liked best, and had them enlarged. All four belonged to the specially posed group. Itakura had been extremely
particular about the lighting and the effects, and Sachiko was
much impressed to see how carefully he had watched the dance.
He would ask for certain passages—"There was something about
'a freezing bed,' I believe, Koi-san," he would say, or, "How about
the passage where you listen to a hailstorm at night?"—and he
even remembered particular poses well enough to demonstrate
them himself. The photographs were among his masterpieces.
Looking up at them, Sachiko remembered with astonishing clear-
ness, down to a glance or a gesture, the inconsequential things
Taeko had said and done that day. She had danced surprisingly
well, considering that she was dancing "Snow" in public for the
first time. Sachiko was not alone in thinking so; Saku, the dance
mistress, had also praised Taeko. And even if it was her own
sister, thought Sachiko, and even if much of the credit should
go to the devoted teacher who came all the way to Ashiya each
day, still Taeko's progress must be owing in very large part to her
peculiar qualifications, to the fact that she was naturally graceful
and that she had danced since she was a child. Quick to weep
when anything moved her, Sachiko had not been able to keep
back her tears that day—Koisan had come so far, then, she said
to herself—and now, looking up at the photographs, she felt
the tears come again. Of the four photographs, she especially
liked that of the passage where the dancer, her heart far away, listened for a midnight temple bell: an open umbrella behind her,
Taeko knelt with her flowing sleeves brought close together, and,

bending the upper part of her body to the left and throwing her head a little to one side, listened intently to that bell fading away in the snowy night air. Watching Taeko practice to a hummed accompaniment, Sachiko had thought it the pose she liked best, and perhaps the clothes and the high Japanese coiffure on the day of the recital made it even more effective. Sachiko was not sure herself why she was so taken with it, unless she found there more than anywhere else a certain delicate winsomeness and grace quite lacking in the usual Taeko, so showy and up-to-date. Taeko alone of the four sisters was the brisk, enterprising modern girl who went ahead quite without hesitation—sometimes even to the point of making herself a little unpleasant—when she had decided where she was going; and yet one could see from this photograph that there was in her too something of the old Japanese maiden, something quietly engaging that pulled at Sachiko as the usual Taeko did not. And then the Japanese coiffure and the old-fashioned make-up had erased Taeko's girlishness, and given her a beauty more in keeping with her years, and this too Sachiko found pleasing. It was perhaps not by accident—it was perhaps an unhappy omen—that her sister had exactly a month earlier been photographed in this particularly beautiful pose and dress, thought Sachiko. The photograph of herself and Etsuko and Teinosuke with Taeko in the middle—might it not become a horrid memorial? Sachiko remembered how moved she had been at the sight of Taeko in her other sister's wedding clothes, how ashamed she had been of her tears; and it had been her prayer that she would soon see this younger sister dressed with similar care for her own wedding. Was the prayer then to come to nothing, and had that in fact been the last time Taeko would put on festive dress? Trying to fight back the thought, Sachiko found the photograph a little frightening. She looked down at the shelf beside her. On it was one of Taeko's most recent dolls, a girl playing at battledore and shuttlecocks. Two or three years before, Taeko had gone time after time to the Kabuki Theater in Osaka to watch the sixth Kikugorō, and she seemed to have studied his dancing well. The face was not Kikugorō's, but somewhere in the lines of the figure Taeko had captured his particular traits so successfully that the great actor himself stood there before one. Koi-san was really very clever. The youngest sister, she had had the least happy childhood, and she was wisest in the ways of the world. Sachiko herself and Yukiko sometimes found Taeko treating them as if they were younger than she. It had been wrong of Sachiko, in an excess of affection and concern for Yukiko, to neglect Koi-san. From now on she would give the two of them impartial care. Koi-san could not die. If she would but come home safely, Sachiko would talk Teinosuke into agreeing to the trip abroad, and they would let her marry Okubata if she liked.

It was quite dark, still darker for the fact that the electricity was out. In the still distance, she could hear the croaking of a frog. Beyond the foliage in the garden she suddenly saw a light. It was a candle in the Stolz dining room. Mr. Stolz was talking in a loud voice, and after him Peter, and then Rosemarie. No doubt they were gathered around the dinner table, recounting their adventures to Mrs. Stolz. The flickering candle told of the happiness next door and emphasized Sachiko's own misery. Just then she heard Johnny run out across the lawn.

"Hello, hello." It was Shōkichi's hearty voice.

"Mother!" Etsuko called excitedly.

"They are back, they are back!" An instant later the two were running downstairs.

The hall was so dark that Sachiko could not make out the faces. The first voice was Shōkichi's, and he was followed by Teinosuke.

"Koi-san?"

"Koi-san is here," said Teinosuke. But why did Taeko herself not answer?

"What is the matter, Koi-san? What is the matter?"

As Sachiko peered into the darkness, O-haru came up behind her with a candle. The uncertain light fell here and there in the hallway. Sachiko saw Taeko staring at her with wide eyes. The kimono was not one Sachiko remembered, and there was no trace of the foreign clothes in which Taeko had left the house that morning.

"Sachiko." Taeko's defenses collapsed. With a great, wailing sob she sank to the floor.

"What has happened, Koi-san? Are you hurt?"

"No," said Teinosuke. "But she had a time of it. She was finally brought out by Itakura."

"Itakura?" Sachiko looked into the darkness behind the three, and saw no sign of Itakura.

"Bring a bucket of water," Teinosuke ordered. He was covered with mud, and—what had happened to his shoes?—he was wearing wooden pattens. The pattens, his feet, his legs were one solid layer of mud.

8

SACHIKO heard the story of Taeko's escape in turns from Teinosuke and Taeko herself.

At eight forty-five that morning, shortly after O-haru came back from seeing Etsuko to school, Taeko left the house. Although the rain was heavy, the bus on the National Highway was running as usual. At about nine she stepped through the gate of the sewing school, only a few yards from the highway. It was extremely informal and easy-going for a school. With rumors abroad that the river might rise, only a few students were present, and with those few becoming more and more restless, Mrs. Tamaki decided to call a holiday. She asked Taeko to stay for a cup of coffee, and the two of them chatted for a while in Mrs. Tamaki's house, next door to the school. Mrs. Tamaki, seven or eight years older than Taeko, had a husband who was an engineer and a son who was in primary school. Besides managing her school she acted as adviser on women's clothes to a Kobe department store. Just beyond the school gate was the gate to the neat little one-floor Spanish-style house —actually, though the gates were separate, the school and the house shared the same grounds. Taeko was a special favorite of Mrs. Tamaki's, often invited in for a talk. Today Mrs. Tamaki was giving her advice on the trip to France. Having herself spent a number of years in Paris, Mrs. Tamaki strongly approved of Taeko's plans. Although she did not know how much use they would be, she would like to write a few letters of introduction, she said as she put the coffee on the alcohol burner.

The rain was meanwhile worse. What shall I do? Can I possibly go home in this? Wait here until it lets up a little—I will be going out myself. While they were talking, Mrs. Tamaki's son, nine-year-old Hiroshi, came in panting. Why was he not in school, Mrs. Tamaki asked. They had been told after an hour or so that they could go home, because they would have trouble getting through after the water rose. "You mean it looks as if the water might rise?" "What are you talking about—it was coming up behind me, and I had to run as fast as I could to keep from getting caught." They heard water while the boy was talking, and looked out the window to see that a muddy stream running through the garden promised very soon to be up over the floor. Mrs. Tamaki and Taeko hastily closed the door. Then, under the veranda on the other side, they heard a roar as of the tide, and water poured in through the door young Hiroshi had left open.

The three of them had to lean against the door to keep it from breaking open again when they had closed it, and the water pounded angrily outside. They ran to put up a barricade of tables and chairs. Very shortly Hiroshi, who sat at his ease in an armchair tight against the door, let out a delighted laugh: the door had come open, and the chair, with Hiroshi in it, was floating free. "Terrible, terrible!" said Mrs. Tamaki. "See that the records don't get wet." They ran to move the records from the cabinet to the piano, already half under water. The water was waist-deep. Three small tables, the glass coffee-maker, the sugar bowl, and a vase of carnations were floating about the room. Taeko, will the doll be all right? Mrs. Tamaki was worried about the French doll, one of Taeko's, that stood on the mantel. The water would surely not rise that high, said Taeko. The three were still rather enjoying themselves, shouting at each other in the best of spirits. They all had a good laugh when Hiroshi, reaching to grab the brief case in which he had brought home his school books, bumped his head on the bobbing radio. But after perhaps a half hour, there came a moment when the three fell silent. Almost immediately, Taeko remembered afterwards, the water was above her waist. As she clutched at a curtain, a picture fell from over her head; the curtain had probably brushed against it. It was a picture Mrs. Tamaki was especially fond of, Kishida Ryūsei's portrait of the girl Reiko. Mrs. Tamaki and Taeko could only look after it regretfully as it floated off and settled in a corner of the room. "Are you all right, Hiroshi?" The tone of Mrs. Tamaki's voice had changed. Grunting a reply, Hiroshi climbed to the piano. Taeko thought of a foreign movie she had seen when she was very small, in which a detective was trapped in an underground room with water rising around him inch by inch. The three were some distance apart, Taeko still clinging to her curtain at a window to the west, Hiroshi on the piano across the room from her, and Mrs. Tamaki on a table that had been propped against the door, but had by now floated to the middle of the room. Probing with her foot for something to stand on as she clung to the curtain, Taeko came on one of the tables. She kicked it over and stood on the edge. (They found afterwards that the water, heavy with sand, had fastened things down. When it receded, the tables and chairs were quite immobile. Many houses were left after the flood only because of the sand that held them in place.)

Taeko thought of the possibility of taking refuge outside, and she might have broken a window (because of the rain, the windows had been closed except for two or three inches at the top), but, while the water inside was settling into a stagnant, muddy pool, beyond that one thin layer of glass, it was surging by in a torrent. Aside from a wisteria arbor some five or six feet from the window, the garden offered no trees or buildings to which they might flee. It was only too clear, moreover, that they would be swept away if they tried to reach the arbor. Hiroshi, standing on the piano, rubbed his hand over the ceiling. He was quite right— if they could break their way out through the ceiling their problem would be solved, but what could a small boy and two women do?

"Where is Kane, Mother?"—Hiroshi thought of the maid. "I think she was in her room a little while ago," said Mrs. Tamaki. "What do you suppose could have happened to her? Can you hear her voice, Mother?" But this time Mrs. Tamaki was silent. The three of them stared into the water that lay between them; soon it was within three or four feet of the ceiling. Taeko stood the table upright (she found that it was heavy with mud and pulled at her foot), and clutched the curtain rod. Only her head was above water. Mrs. Tamaki was in much the same predicament, but fortunately an aluminum chandelier for indirect lighting hung from three sturdy chains above her head, and she could reach for it when she was in danger of losing her balance. "Will we drown,

Mother? Will we, Mother?" Mrs. Tamaki did not answer. "We
will drown, Mother." "What nonsense!" For the rest, Mrs. Tamaki's lips moved ineffectually, and it was clear that she could not
think of a reassuring answer. Taeko glanced at Mrs. Tamaki, up to
the throat in water, and thought she saw the face of one who was
looking at death. She knew that she wore much the same expression herself. And she knew too that when a person is finally convinced that nothing can save him, he becomes strangely calm and
relaxed.

She was sure she had been standing there a very long time,
three or four hours at least. As a matter of fact it was less than
an hour. Water was beginning to pour in through the opening at
the top of the window. While she was struggling to close it (indeed from a little before), one hand still fast to the curtain rod,
she sensed that someone was walking about on the roof. A man
jumped to the wisteria arbor, worked his way to the edge nearest
Taeko's window, and, lowering himself into the water, sank out
of sight for a moment. Then, careful not to release his hold on
the arbor, he turned to face Taeko. One glance at her and he
went to work. At first Taeko could not guess what he was about,
but in a moment she saw that he was trying to hold fast to the
arbor and at the same time reach across to the window. He wore
a leather jacket and a leather aviator's helmet, under which only
the eyes seemed alive. Taeko saw that it was the photographer
Itakura.

She had not recognized him at first: she had never seen him in
that jacket, which he was said to have worn a great deal in America, and his face was hidden by the helmet; she had not expected
to see anyone here, least of all him; her vision was obscured by the
downpour and the spray; and, most important, she was much too
distraught to recognize him. "Itakura, Itakura," she called out,
less to Itakura himself than to Mrs. Tamaki and Hiroshi. She concentrated on the window, this time to lower it, and, tight though
it was from the pressure of the water, she managed to lower it
until she could lean out. As she stretched to take Itakura's hand
in her own right hand, the torrent hit her with all its fury. She
was afraid the curtain rod would be torn from her grasp. "Let go
with your other hand." Itakura spoke for the first time. "I have
this one. Let go with the other." Taeko gave herself up and did as

she was told. Their two arms snapped taut, and a moment later Itakura had pulled her to him. (Afterwards he said he had not known himself that he had such strength). "Take hold, like this," he said. Taeko clutched at the arbor with both hands; but she was in far more danger than inside the house. "No, no—I am finished." "Hold on for just a minute—hold on tight—for just a minute."—as he spoke, Itakura fought his way to the top of the arbor. Opening a hole in the vines, he pulled her up after him.

Well, I at least am safe—that was Taeko's first thought. It was possible that the water would rise above the arbor too, but then they could flee to the roof—Itakura would think of something. Shut up in that narrow room, she had not suspected the changes that had taken place outside. She saw now what the last hour or two had brought. She saw what Teinosuke had seen from the railroad bridge in Tanaka. There was this difference, however: Teinosuke looked out over "the sea" from the eastern shore, whereas Taeko, in the middle of it, saw those mighty waves all around her. She had but a moment before thought she was saved. Now, looking at nature gone mad, she wondered if she and Itakura could possibly escape. But the immediate problem was what to do about the others. "Mrs. Tamaki and Hiroshi are still inside—can you do something?" As she was urging Itakura on, a dull, heavy blow shook the arbor. A log had come down in the torrent. "Just what we need," he said. Lowering himself into the water, he proceeded to lay a bridge across to the window. He pushed one end of the log inside, and, with Taeko's help, made the other fast with wisteria vines. When he had crossed over, he disappeared inside for rather a long time. Taeko heard afterwards that he had torn up the lace curtains to make a rope. He threw one end to Mrs. Tamaki, who was fairly near, and she threw it on to young Hiroshi. After he had brought the two of them to the window, Itakura helped Hiroshi across the bridge and followed with Mrs. Tamaki.

It seemed as if Itakura's activities had taken a fairly long time, and again as if they had taken almost no time. Even afterwards, no one could really be sure. The self-winding watch Itakura had brought back from America—that, too, he was very proud of— was said to be water-proof, but in the course of the morning it had stopped. The downpour continued, the water rose, and they had to flee from the wisteria arbor to the roof, again using the log for a bridge (two or three very helpful pieces of wood had meanwhile floated down to reinforce it). On the roof Taeko for the first time composed herself to wonder what could have brought Itakura down from the skies in the crisis. He had had a feeling that morning, he said, that there would be a flood. As early as spring, he had heard an old man remark that there was a flood in this part of the country every six or seven years, and that this was a flood year. He had therefore been greatly disturbed at the succession of rainy days, and when, that morning, the Home Defense Corps was out with its flood warnings and there were excited rumors that the Sumiyoshi embankments would give way, he felt that he had to go see for himself what was happening. He walked along the banks for a time and noted that there was considerable danger of a flood. Near the sewing school he ran into the water.

But it was strange, even with these forebodings, that he should have gotten himself up especially in that leather jacket, and come precisely to the sewing school. He knew that this was one of Taeko's days at the school. Had he then meant from the beginning to be where he could run to her rescue if by some chance she should be in danger? That was the question, perhaps too touchy a question to dwell on for very long. In any case, Taeko was told that as he fled from the water he had suddenly remembered where she was, and had plunged in again at the thought that she might be in danger. Afterwards she heard at great length of his fight with the water. Like Teinosuke, Itakura approached along the tracks and through the Kōnan Girls' Academy. Since he was some two or three hours earlier than Teinosuke, he still found it possible to make his way beyond. No doubt he was not lying when he said that three times he was swept away and barely escaped drowning, and that he was quite alone in the torrent. It was after he reached the sewing school that the waves were at their highest. He finally had to climb to the roof, and while he was staring absently at the flood he noticed that someone was waving insistently from the roof of Mrs. Tamaki's house. It was Kane, the maid. When she knew he had seen her, Kane pointed in the direction of the parlor window and, raising three fingers, wrote the name "Taeko" in the air. Itakura plunged into the water again. Half swimming, half sinking, he fought his way to the arbor. It was clear that he had truly risked his life in this last, most perilous bout with the water.

9

THESE RESCUE OPERATIONS were taking place at about the time Teinosuke was stranded in the train. After making his way to the Kōnan Academy, he rested until about three o'clock in the second-floor room that had been set aside for flood refugees. When the rain stopped and the water began to recede, he decided to go on to the sewing school. The way was of course not as easy as it would ordinarily have been. The water had left behind mounds of sand in some places as high as the eaves of houses, so that the scene resembled nothing so much as a north-country town in the snowbound winter months. The worst problem was the quicksand. He had lost one shoe in the earlier quicksand, and he now threw the other away and went on in his stockings. A walk that would usually have taken no more than two or three minutes now took twenty or thirty.

The land about the sewing school had been completely transformed. The school gate was almost buried in sand and mud, only the tips of the gate posts showing, and the building itself was buried except for the slate roof. Teinosuke had imagined crowds of students awaiting rescue on the roof, but for some reason—had they escaped, had they been swept away in the water, had they been buried under the sand?—there was not a student in sight. Almost despairing, he crossed to Mrs. Tamaki's house over what had once been the lawn and the flower beds south of the school. The top of the arbor, along which trailed wisteria vines, was barely above the ground, and beside it rested two or three logs. And on the red roof were Taeko, Itakura, Mrs. Tamaki, Hiroshi, and one other, the maid Kane, who had joined them.

When he had finished telling Teinosuke his story, Itakura explained that although he had been wanting to see Koi-san home, she was much too exhausted, and Mrs. Tamaki and the boy did not know what would happen to them if he left. He was wondering what to do next.

It is hard for one who has not had a similar experience to imagine the terror that still gripped Taeko and Mrs. Tamaki and Hiroshi, so intense a terror that afterwards it seemed almost funny. Even when the sky had cleared and the water receded, they could not believe they were safe, and they sat trembling violently. Itakura tried to rouse Taeko. Mr. and Mrs. Makioka would be worried, he said, and he would see her home, but Taeko, though admitting he was right, felt somehow that further perils awaited her. She could not bring herself to leave the roof for the mud and sand, now within easy stepping distance from the eaves. And Mrs. Tamaki worried about what she would do when Itakura and Taeko were gone. Her husband would no doubt be along soon, but in the meantime the sun might go down, leaving them to spend the night on the roof. Hiroshi and the maid Kane joined their laments with hers. Teinosuke found them pleading with Itakura to stay just a little longer.

Falling exhausted on the roof, Teinosuke himself had little desire to move. At perhaps four-thirty (his watch, too, had stopped), when he had been lying there for upwards of an hour watching the sky clear and the sun come out, several emissaries arrived from Mrs. Tamaki's family. Teinosuke and Itakura saw their chance to leave. In places they had to carry Taeko, still weak and dazed. Even without her they would have had trouble crossing the Sumiyoshi River, which had left its old bed and was pouring over the National Highway between the Kōnan Academies and Tanaka. Halfway across, they met Shōkichi and became a party of four. At Tanaka, Itakura suggested that they rest for a time at his house, which was very near—as a matter of fact he was rather worried about it. Eager though Teinosuke was to get home, it seemed best to let Taeko rest a little. They spent about an hour at Itakura's. The downstairs rooms, living quarters for the unmarried Itakura and his sister, had been considerably damaged, the water having risen about a foot above the floor. Teinosuke and the rest were invited to the studio upstairs, where they drank ginger ale rescued from the water. Taeko took off her voile dress and changed to a kimono Itakura had his sister bring out for her. Teinosuke, who had returned barefoot, borrowed a pair of wooden pattens.

Itakura insisted on seeing them part of the way home, even though Teinosuke pointed out that Shōkichi was there to take his place. In the outskirts of Tanaka, he finally turned back.

Sachiko expected Okubata to come again. He did not appear that evening, however, and the next day Itakura came to make inquiries in his place. Okubata had arrived at Itakura's house the night before, some time after Itakura returned from seeing Teinosuke and the rest off. Okubata reported that he had been waiting at the Makioka house for Taeko to come back, but had gone out, worried that she should be so late, to see what he could see, and that, walking along the National Highway, he had found himself in Itakura's neighborhood. Although he had hoped to go on as far as the sewing school, it was now pitch dark, and the road to the west had turned into a river. Fearing that it would be impossible to push his way across, he thought he might be able to learn something from Itakura. He need not worry, said Itakura, telling him in a general way what had happened since that morning. Okubata left immediately for Osaka—he really should stop by the Makioka house again, he knew, but he wanted Itakura to call the following morning and tell them he had gone home only after hearing that Taeko had come through safely. And, added Itakura, he had also been asked by Okubata to inquire after Taeko—to make sure that even if she was uninjured she had not caught cold.

Taeko had quite recovered. She came down with Sachiko to thank Itakura and to reconstruct the hours of peril. It did seem strange that, after sitting through a two-hour downpour in only a summer dress, she had not caught cold. But at such times, remarked Itakura, extra strength comes from somewhere. Soon he took his leave.

The fight against the water had been a very great strain after all. The next morning Taeko was sore in every joint, and especially worried about a soreness under the arm that might well turn into pleurisy. Fortunately it passed in a few days. Two or three days later there was a light shower, and she started up in terror at the sound of the rain on the roof. She had never before thought much about rain, but a new fear had taken root in her heart. When it began raining one night, she lay waiting for the flood until morning.

RESIDENTS OF Kobe and Osaka were astonished when they opened their newspapers the next morning and read of the flood damage. For several days a steady procession of callers, coming partly to inquire after the safety of the family, partly to view the damage, kept Sachiko busy; but as the utilities returned to normal, the excitement subsided. There was a shortage of labor and equipment to clear away the mud and sand. The streets, a cloud of dust in the hot sun, made Teinosuke think of Tokyo and Yokohama after the great earthquake. At the Ashiya River station a new platform was built over the debris that covered the old platform, and trains crossed the river on a new bridge above the old one. Since the bed of the river was, in places, almost as high as the banks, there was danger of floods from even a light shower, and something had to be done immediately, but the army of workmen, like a swarm of ants in a mountain of sugar, made little headway. The pines along the embankment were buried under a solid layer of dust. Unfortunately the blazing hot weather continued day after day and the cloud of dust only became more suffocating. There was little this year to bespeak the elegant suburb Ashiya.

It was on a summer day, in the cloud of dust, that Yukiko returned after two and a half months in Tokyo.

News of the flood had come out in the Tokyo morning newspapers. Not knowing the details, the people in the main house were most uneasy. It was clear that the worst damage had been along the banks of the Sumiyoshi River and the Ashiya River, and what most concerned Yukiko, as she read of drowned students in the Kōnan Elementary School, was Etsuko's safety. The next day Teinosuke called from his office in Osaka and answered questions as Tsuruko and Yukiko came to the telephone in turns. Yukiko— it was as if she wanted his advice—said she was so worried that she was thinking of leaving for Osaka the next day, but Teinosuke answered that although he would be pleased to see her there was no need for her to make a special trip. The situation was as he had described it, and the Government lines were not yet running west from Osaka. That evening, as he told Sachiko of the conversation, he said he suspected that they would be seeing Yukiko soon; this was the pretext she had been waiting for. A letter arrived for Sachiko some days later. Yukiko yearned to see Taeko and could not rest until she had inspected the damage to the city she was so fond of. She might be calling on them without warning one day very soon.

Purposely neglecting to send a telegram, Yukiko left Tokyo on the Swallow Express. She changed at Osaka for the electric line and, lucky enough to catch a taxi in Ashiya, arrived at Sachiko's just before six in the evening.

O-haru met her at the door, took her suitcase, and saw her into the parlor. The house was quiet.

"Is Mrs. Makioka out?"

"She has gone over to the Stolzes'." O-haru turned on the electric fan.

"And Etsuko?"

"They have all gone over to the Stolzes' for tea—Koi-san too. They should be back any time now. Maybe I should go call them?"

"No, never mind."

"They said they thought you might come today. Miss Etsuko has been excited ever since this morning. Shall I go call them?"

"No, no, please. I can wait."

Yukiko stopped O-haru, who was already on her way to the Stolz house—they could hear children's voices in the garden—and went out to sit in a birch chair under the terrace awning.

From the cab window, the damage around Narihira Bridge had seemed worse than she expected, but here everything was as it had always been. Not a leaf was disturbed. In the evening calm, hardly a breath of air touched the garden. The heat was intense, and the quiet gave the light and dark greens of the foliage a special limpidity. The green of the lawn seemed to rise up and flow through her. When she had left in the spring, the lilac had been in bloom and the yellow *yamabuki* in bud; and now the Hirado lilies and the azaleas had fallen, and only a gardenia or two was left to perfume the air. Thick leaves at the fence half hid the two-storey foreign-style house next door.

Near the fence, the children were playing train. Though Yukiko could not actually see them, she gathered that Peter was the conductor.

"Next stop, Mikage. This train does not stop between Mikage and Ashiya. Passengers for Sumiyoshi, Uozaki, Aoki, and Fukae will please change to a local." He had all the mannerisms of a conductor. One would not have dreamed that it was a little foreigner speaking.

"Rumi, we will go on to Kyoto," said Etsuko.

"Yes, we will go to Tokyo."

"Not Tokyo. Kyoto."

But Rosemarie had apparently never heard of Kyoto, and no matter how often Etsuko said "Kyoto," the answer came back "Tokyo." Etsuko found this exasperating.

"No, no. Kyoto, Rumi. Kyoto."

"Yes, we will go to Tokyo."

"No, there are a hundred stops on the way to Tokyo."

"Yes. We will be there the day from tomorrow."

"What did you say, Rumi?"

Rosemarie had stumbled a little over the words; but Etsuko would have had trouble with "the day from tomorrow" in any case.

"What did you say? That is not Japanese, Rumi."

"What is the name of this tree?"

The leaves rustled as Peter started up one of the trees. It was on this side of the fence, but the branches trailed over into the Stolz yard. The children were always climbing from a foothold on the fence.

"Aogiri," answered Etsuko.

"Aogirigiri?"

"Not aogirigiri. Aogiri."

"Aogirigiri."

"Aogiri!"

"Aogirigiri."

Yukiko was not sure whether Peter was making fun of Etsuko or whether he really could not pronounce the word.

II

SUMMER VACATION had begun. Every day the Stolz children and Etsuko played together. In the morning and evening they played train in the garden or climbed the trees along the fence, but in the hot part of the day they were indoors, playing house when the girls were alone, playing war when Peter and Fritz joined them. The four would move the heavy armchairs and sofas about to make forts and strong points, which they then attacked with air guns. Peter was in command, and the others fired at his orders. The German children, even Fritz, not yet in school, invariably shouted "Frankreich, Frankreich" at the enemy. Sachiko and the rest, who at first did not know what "Frankreich" meant, were more impressed than ever at the thoroughness of German child-training when Teinosuke translated for them. It was something of a trial for the Makioka family, however, to have the furniture in the parlor always ready for war. If an unexpected guest arrived, the maids had him wait in the hall while the whole family worked at dismantling forts and strong points. One day Mrs. Stolz looked in from the terrace. Was this what the boys were in the habit of doing? she asked. She went away with a wry smile, but whether or not she scolded her sons, they showed no sign of mending their violent ways.

In the daytime, Sachiko and her sisters generally turned the parlor over to the children and took their ease in the small Japanese-style room next to the dining room. Across the hall from the bath, and as a result often used for undressing or dumping dirty clothes, the room was dark and cave-like. Deep eaves sheltered it to the south, where it looked out over the garden. The sun was thus kept at a distance, and, with a low western window at floor level, and with a breeze passing through for the better part of the day, the room was generally considered the coolest in the house. The three sisters would fight for the place nearest the window as they rested there during the hot afternoons. Each year in the hot weather they lost their appetites, grew thinner, and began to suffer from "shortage of B." Of the three, Yukiko, always slender,

showed the loss of weight most clearly. She had had a stubborn
case of beri-beri since June. Although one reason for her trip to
Ashiya had been to try a change of air, the beri-beri only got
worse upon her arrival. She was constantly being given injections
by Sachiko or Taeko. The latter two were also suffering in some
measure from beri-beri, and the chain of injections, one to another
and on to the third, became a daily ritual. Sachiko had, early in
the summer, changed to a one-piece Western dress cut low in back.
From around the twenty-fifth or twenty-sixth, Yukiko too surrendered and, frail as a cord doll, appeared in a georgette dress.
Taeko, usually the most active of the three, had evidently not recovered from the shock of the flood. This summer she showed
little of her usual energy. The sewing school was of course closed.
Though her studio had escaped damage and she had no reason
not to work on her dolls, she seldom went near the place.

Itakura often called. Customers being few since the flood, he
spent his time taking pictures for an album of flood-damage photographs. He wandered about with his Leica when the weather was
good, and he would appear at the back door in shorts, his face
sunburned and sweaty, and demand water of O-haru. Draining a
glass of ice water at one gulp, he would carefully wipe his shorts
and shirt, white with dust, and march in through the kitchen to
the little room where the sisters were resting. He had been at
Nunobiki today, he would say, or Mt. Rokkō, or Koshigi Crag, or
Arima Springs, or Minoo, and he would tell them in his own
very individual way what he had seen, often illustrating his talk
with photographs.

Sometimes he would want to go swimming. "Mrs. Makioka, we
are going swimming. Get up," he would order as he came into the
room. "You will ruin your health lying around like this."

When Sachiko gave an evasive answer, he virtually pulled her to
her feet. It was no distance at all to Ashiya Beach, he would say;
there was nothing like a swim to cure beri-beri. "O-haru, get out
the swimming suits and call a cab." When Sachiko wanted to take
Etsuko swimming and simply did not have the energy, she would
send the girl off with Itakura. Day by day he became friendlier,
and his speech became freer and even a little rude. He took to
opening cupboards without being invited to, and otherwise making himself objectionable, but he was redeemed by the fact that

whatever they asked him to do he did without protest. And he was a most entertaining talker.

They were enjoying the breeze as usual one afternoon when an unusually large bee flew in from the garden. It alighted first on Sachiko's head, where it marched around in circles.

"A bee, Sachiko, a bee!" screamed Taeko. The bee moved on to Yukiko's head and then to Taeko's, and back to Sachiko's. The three of them, as good as naked, scrambled about the small room. The bee followed them as if it were teasing, and when they ran screaming into the hall, it was with them.

"It is after us, it is after us!" They ran on into the dining room, and from there to the parlor, where Etsuko and Rosemarie were playing house.

"What is it, Mother?" The two girls were startled.

The bee hit a window, and the clamor began again.

Half for the sport, Rosemarie and Etsuko joined in. They dodged about the room as if they were playing blindman's buff with the bee; and the bee, whether it was excited, or whether such is the way with bees, would start out into the garden and fly back into the room. The five of them fled into the hall again. In the midst of the confusion Itakura's face appeared under the curtain at the kitchen door. He was ready to go swimming. He had on a straw hat, and, over his swimming suit, a cotton kimono, and he had a towel around his neck.

"What is going on, O-haru?"

"A bee is after them."

"Is that all?" The five sped past in a tight group, their arms high and their fists clenched as if they were training for a race.

"Hello. You seem to be having trouble."

"A bee, a bee! Catch it, quick," Sachiko called in a piercing voice as she raced on down the hall.

The five mouths were open and the eyes shone, and the faces were strangely contorted.

Itakura took off his hat and calmly chased the bee out into the garden.

"I was terrified, really terrified. It was a very stubborn bee."

"But the bee was more frightened than you were."

"You are not to laugh. I was really terrified." Yukiko, still panting, forced her white face into a smile. The beating of her heart,

already agitated from beri-beri, was clear under the thin summe
dress.

12

EARLY IN AUGUST Taeko had a letter from one of Yamamur;
Saku's pupils saying that the dancing teacher was worse, and had
entered a hospital near her home.

It was usual for dance practice to be discontinued during the
hot months, July and August, but this year Saku had not beer
well even at the June recital, and she had decided then to take ;
vacation until September. Although Taeko had not been withou
concern for Saku's health, she had neglected to call because a trip
to the teacher's house, in the south of Osaka, meant several train
changes. Always before it had served her purpose to go to the
studio, and she had never visited Saku at home. But now Saku
had developed uremic poisoning, and her condition was serious

"Suppose you go tomorrow, Koi-san. I will go later myself."

Sachiko was afraid those long trips to Ashiya in May and June
might have brought on the new attack. She had thought at the
time, as she noticed the pale, puffed face and the heavy breathing
and as she reflected on how, whatever Saku herself might say abou
keeping strong for her dancing, there was nothing worse for kid
ney trouble than over-exertion, that it might be better to put ;
stop to the trips. But Taeko and Etsuko were so enthusiastic, and
Sachiko was carried away by the teacher's own enthusiasm. She
had let the matter pass. Now she feared that that had been a mis
take. Planning to call in a very few days herself, she thought she
should send Taeko as soon as possible.

Taeko had meant to go in the cooler morning hours. There was
a conference about a present, however, and there were various
other matters to delay her, and she finally set out in the hottest
part of the afternoon. When she came home panting at about
five in the evening—she could not describe how hot that part of
Osaka was, she said—she peeled off her dress, wet and clinging

nd disappeared into the bath, naked but for a pair of underpants. After a time she reappeared in a large towel, a damp cloth around her head, and took out a gossamer-silk kimono.

"You will just have to excuse me." Throwing the kimono over her shoulders, she sat down with her back to her sisters and her naked bosom turned toward the electric fan.

Although Saku always complained of not feeling well, Taeko reported, there had been nothing particularly out of order through July. Then, on the thirtieth, she had held ceremonies at her house to confer a professional name on a certain disciple. Saku was not generous about conferring names and thus accrediting her disciples as Yamamura teachers in their own right, but this time she made an exception. Dressing with the most solemn formality, for all the heat, she hung out the picture of her predecessor, the old head of the school, and with great dignity conducted the ceremony that had been handed down by her grandmother. The next day, when she went to pay a call at the disciple's house, she looked more ill than usual; and the day after that, the first of August, she collapsed.

The south side of Osaka, unlike these suburbs between Osaka and Kobe, was a jam of little houses, almost without trees. Taeko was dripping with perspiration by the time she managed to find the hospital, and there, in a room that faced west into the beating afternoon sun, the teacher lay with but one woman, a disciple, to watch over her. Though the face was not as swollen as Taeko had expected, Saku did not recognize her when she knelt beside the bed. The woman nursing her said that Saku recovered consciousness only now and then, that for the most part she was in a coma. When occasionally she became delirious, it was always the dance she talked of. The lady stepped into the hall as Taeko started to leave, about a half hour later, and reported that there was no hope. Taeko had guessed as much. Making her way home under the blazing sun, she knew what a strain it had been for the ailing teacher to make that trip every day—it was a trial for Taeko herself to go even once.

The next day Sachiko visited the hospital with Taeko, and five or six days later they had notice of the teacher's death. When they went with condolences, they had occasion for the first time to call at her house; and they found it an astonishing house—

little better than a tenement—for a woman who bore the proud
Yamamura name, and who almost alone handed on the dance tra
dition so much a part of old Osaka. There she had wrung out a
miserable existence, a desperate existence, even. And was that not
because she was a woman with little talent for making her way
in the world, a woman whose conscience did not permit her to
do damage to the old forms and make concessions to the fashion
of the day? Her predecessor had been dance mistress to the gei
shas in the South Quarter, and had overseen their annual dance
recital; but Saku herself announced upon succeeding to the name
that she wanted no part of geisha recitals and the like. The gaudy
Tokyo styles being in their heyday, she knew that if she became
dance mistress to one of the geisha quarters, certain functionarie
would interfere to make her adopt the new fashions she so dis
liked. This rigidness kept her from becoming a worldly success
She had few pupils, and she was not blessed with a happy persona
life: reared by a grandmother, she never married, although there
was said to have been a man who had paid her geisha debts. She
had no children. No relatives were with her when she died. Only
a very few people attended the funeral, at Abeno, in the late sum
mer heat. Almost all the funeral guests went to the crematory nex
door, where they exchanged memories as they waited for the ashes
Saku had hated to ride in anything, and had particularly disliked
ships and automobiles. Very religious, she made her visit on the
twenty-sixth of every month to the Kiyoshikōjin Shrine, and she
had made the "round of the hundred twenty-eight shrines." In
February each year, on the day that traditionally marks the be
ginning of spring, she visited the Jizō chapels in the Uemachi sec
tion of Osaka and offered a rice cake for each year of her age. She
was most patient in explaining to her pupils the key spots in
dance, but she could also be demanding. She was very particular
for instance, about this passage from "The Salt Makers":

> Come, a box-tree comb in your hair,
> And help me take brine from the tide.

And at the verse about the moon and the two reflections, she in
sisted that the dancer think of the unreal moon in the brine
buckets. Again, there was a passage from "The Curse":

I suppose you too will be sorry now.
Think well on what you have done.

The dancer, half kneeling, went through the motions of driving a nail, and Saku required that the eyes express intense determination. Conservative and retiring, she yet felt that she could not sit idly by and see the Osaka dance overwhelmed by the Tokyo dance, and she thought the opportunity might come for her to take her dance to Tokyo. Her pupils planned to celebrate her sixtieth birthday by hiring a hall in the South Quarter and giving a really elaborate recital—it had not occurred to them that she might not live until her sixtieth birthday. Taeko, a relatively new pupil who had known Saku for but a few years, sat respectfully by with Sachiko and listened. She had hoped, as a favorite pupil, to receive a professional name in the Yamamura school, and the hope had come to nothing.

13

"MOTHER, the Stolzes are going back to Germany," said Etsuko one evening after she had been playing next door.

Across the fence the next day, Sachiko asked Mrs. Stolz whether Etsuko's story was true. It was, said Mrs. Stolz. Her husband said Japan was at war. The Kobe office, almost no business. No business since the first of the year. They waited, hoping the war would end, they did not know when. Her husband thought about many things, decided to go back to Germany. Mrs. Stolz went on to describe how her husband had been in business in Manila before coming to Kobe two or three years before, and how they hated to go back to Germany now that he had established himself in the Far East. They had been very lucky to have such good neighbors, and all of them, and especially the children, were extremely sad at having to go. Mr. Stolz and the oldest son, Peter, would leave this month and go home by way of America. Mrs.

Stolz and Rosemarie and Fritz would go to Manila next month
and spend some time with a sister's family, and return to Europe
from there. The sister's family too was returning to Germany; and
since the sister was at the moment ill in Germany, Mrs. Stolz
would see to packing and closing the house for them, and would
take the three children back with her. Mrs. Stolz and the younger
children would not leave for perhaps three weeks, but Mr. Stolz
and Peter already had their reservations. They would leave Yokohama on the *Empress of Canada* late in August—so quickly had
they had to make their plans.

Since the end of July, Etsuko had again shown symptoms of
nervousness and beri-beri, though not as severe as the year before,
and had begun to lose her appetite and complain that she could
not sleep. They thought it best to have her see a specialist in
Tokyo while the symptoms were still mild. And then Etsuko, who
had never seen Tokyo, spoke enviously of how this friend and
that friend had bowed to the Imperial Family, and it would be a
great delight for her to be shown Tokyo, and Sachiko herself had
never seen the Shibuya house, and thought that this would be a
good occasion to call on Tsuruko. Everything considered, then,
they had decided that early in August the three of them, Sachiko
and Yukiko and Etsuko, would go to Tokyo. Then came the death
of the dancing teacher to interfere with their plans, and they began to wonder if they would be able to go in August at all. It
would be good, however, to see Peter and his father off from
Yokohama—but unfortunately the sailing came on the Festival of
the Dead, and it was absolutely essential that Sachiko pay a visit
in her sister's place to the family temple in Osaka, where services
were held each year.

They had to be contented with a little farewell party on the
seventeenth, to which they invited Rosemarie, Peter, and Fritz.
Two days later the Stolzes gave a party at which Etsuko was the
only Japanese among the friends of Rosemarie and Peter. On the
twenty-first Peter came over alone to say good-bye. After shaking
hands with them all, he reported that he and his father were leaving Sannomiya Station for Yokohama the next day. They expected
to reach Germany from the United States early in September, and
he hoped the Makiokas would find a way to visit Hamburg, where
the family would be living. As he wanted to send Etsuko some-

thing from America, he wondered what she would like. Etsuko, after talking the matter over with her mother, asked for shoes. Very well, answered Peter, he would borrow one of Etsuko's shoes for size. Back almost immediately with paper, pencil, and tape measure, he said that his mother had suggested measuring Etsuko's foot instead. He put the foot on the paper and carefully took down the dimensions.

On the morning of the twenty-second Etsuko and Yukiko went to Sannomiya Station. That evening at dinner they told of the Stolzes, father and son. It appeared that Peter was extremely sad to be leaving. When could Etsuko be in Tokyo, he asked. Would she come to the ship? It sailed the evening of the twenty-fourth. They could meet that day. He was still repeating the invitation when the train pulled out, and he seemed very sad. How would it be, said Sachiko, if Etsuko at least were to go to Yokohama? Sachiko herself could not leave until after the twenty-fourth, but how would it be if Etsuko and Yukiko were to take the night train on the twenty-third, and, getting off in Yokohama, go directly to the ship? Sachiko would be in Tokyo on about the twenty-sixth. Etsuko could have someone show her the sights and she could wait for her mother at the Shibuya house. A fine idea, thought Etsuko.

"Will you be able to leave tomorrow evening, Yukiko?"

"I have all sorts of shopping to do . . . "

"But with all day tomorrow. . . ."

"If we take too late a train, Etsuko will be sleepy. There would still be time if we left early the following morning."

"Suppose you do that, then," said Sachiko lightly. She was touched to see that Yukiko wanted to stay even one night longer.

"What a hurry to be off." Taeko's tone was a little mocking. "It seems as though you just arrived."

"I would just as soon stay longer, of course. But if it will make Etsuko and Peter happy. . . ."

When she had arrived in July, Yukiko had thought she might be allowed to stay for about two months, and no doubt she was sad to think that she had to leave even a little early. Etsuko would be with her this time, and Sachiko would follow, and it would not be as if she were returning to Tokyo alone. Sachiko and Etsuko would not be in Tokyo long, however—they would have to come back in time for school—and Yukiko would have to stay on. She saw that though she did indeed like to be near Sachiko and the others, one reason for wanting to live in Ashiya was her love for this Kobe-Osaka district, and that though one reason for disliking Tokyo was that she did not get along well with her brother-in-law, still it was the air of Osaka and Kobe that best suited her.

Sachiko, sensing all this, said little the following day except that she left everything to Yukiko and Etsuko. Yukiko spent the morning about the house. Then, seeing how eager Etsuko was to make the trip, she dressed hastily and after a vitamin injection set out in the afternoon with O-haru—she did not say where she was going. At about six she came back with several parcels from Kobe shops.

"I have these," she said, taking from her obi two tickets for the Fuji Express the following morning. The Fuji left Osaka at seven and arrived in Yokohama at three, and they could thus be at the pier a little past three. That would give them two or three hours before sailing time. So the plans were made; and they flew about taking out suitcases and informing Mrs. Stolz and so on.

Etsuko, so excited that she had no thought of sleep, was led upstairs by Yukiko—they would have to be up early the following morning. Yukiko took her time with her own packing, and talked to her sisters until after midnight. Teinosuke was at work in his study.

"We really ought to go to bed, Yukiko," said Taeko, with an impolitely wide yawn. Taeko, much the worst-mannered of the three, stood in sharp contrast to Yukiko, and especially in the hot months her slovenliness was really too noticeable. This evening, for instance, she had come from the bath in a cotton kimono and an undress obi, and as she talked she sometimes pulled the kimono open at the neck and fanned her bare bosom.

"If you are sleepy, you might go on ahead."

"You are not sleepy?"

"I have been too busy. I doubt if I could sleep anyway."

"Do you need another injection?"

"It might be better to wait until just before I leave in the morning."

"It is a shame you have to go, Yukiko." Sachiko saw that the spot over the eye, which had not appeared for some time, was faintly visible again. "I hope we can think of something to bring you down again before the end of the year. Next year is unlucky, you know."

The Stolzes, father and son, had left from Sannomiya, in downtown Kobe. So that they might have even a few more minutes at the house, Etsuko and Yukiko decided to take the express from Osaka instead. Even so, they had to be at Ashiya Station by six. Sachiko had meant to see them only to the door, but when it became clear that Mrs. Stolz and her children were going as far as the station, she went along, as did Taeko and O-haru.

"I sent a telegram last night. I told them what time," said Mrs. Stolz, while they were waiting for a local train.

"Peter will be on deck, then?"

"I think so. Etsuko, you are very kind. Thank you." Mrs. Stolz turned to Rosemarie and Fritz. "Tell Etsuko thank you," she said in German. Sachiko and the others understood only the *danke schön.*

"Come as soon as you can, Mother."

"It will be no later than the twenty-sixth or twenty-seventh."

"Promise."

"I promise."

"Hurry back, Etsuko." Rosemarie ran after the train. "*Auf Wiedersehen.*"

"*Auf Wiedersehen,*" said Etsuko, waving from the window.

14

SACHIKO planned to take the Seagull Express on the twenty-seventh. With all the presents she would have three suitcases, more than she could manage by herself. It occurred to her that she might let O-haru too see the sights of Tokyo. Taeko could keep house for Teinosuke, and there were all sorts of reasons why it would be good to have O-haru along: for one thing, Sachiko might want to send Etsuko back in time for school and stay on in Tokyo her-

self. It had been so very long since her last visit, and she did not
want to hurry. She might see a few plays before she came back.

"O-haru is here too!" Etsuko was at the station with Yukiko
and Teruo, Tsuruko's oldest son.

"That is the Marunouchi Building over there, and that is the
palace," she said when they were in the cab. She was by now very
much the old Tokyo hand. Sachiko noted how her color had improved, and thought that even in so short a time her face had become fuller.

"Etsuko, we had a beautiful view of Mt. Fuji from the train.
Tell Etsuko about it, O-haru."

"A really beautiful view, all the way to the top. And not a bit
of snow."

"It was a little cloudy when we saw it," said Etsuko. "The top
was under clouds."

"O-haru was luckier, then." O-haru always referred to herself
in the third person when she was talking to Etsuko.

"Look, O-haru—the Double Bridge." Teruo had taken off his
cap, and Etsuko noticed that they were passing the bridge from
which respects were paid to the Imperial Family.

"We all got out of the car and bowed the other day," said
Yukiko.

"We really did, Mother."

"When?"

"The other day—the twenty-fourth. Mr. Stolz and Peter and
Yukiko and I—we all got out and lined up there."

"The Stolzes came to Tokyo?"

"Yukiko brought them."

"You had that much time to spare, then?"

"Only just that much. We could hardly take our eyes off our
watches."

Yukiko and Etsuko had rushed to the pier and found Mr. Stolz
and Peter waiting impatiently on deck. They sailed at seven,
Yukiko was told. That left four hours. After she considered the
possibility of going to the New Grand Hotel for tea and concluded that it would still be too early, she suggested that they all
go to Tokyo. They would need a half hour each way on the train,
and they would have some three hours to tour the city. Yukiko
knew that Peter, and even Mr. Stolz, had never seen Tokyo. Mr.

Stolz seemed to hesitate a little. He agreed only after asking repeatedly whether she was quite sure they would have time. Once in Tokyo, they had tea in the Imperial Hotel, and at about four-thirty they set out in a cab, first to pay their respects at the Double Bridge, then to see the sights: the War Ministry, the Diet Building, the Prime Minister's Residence, the Navy Ministry, the Ministry of Justice, Hibiya Park, the Imperial Theater, the Marunouchi Building. Sometimes they only looked out from the cab, sometimes they walked around for a few minutes, and by five-thirty they had made the rounds. Yukiko and Etsuko meant to see the Stolzes back to Yokohama, but Mr. Stolz insisted that that was unnecessary, and at length, afraid the excitement since early that morning might be too much for Etsuko, Yukiko decided to say good-bye at Tokyo Station.

"Was Peter pleased?"

"He was surprised at what a fine city Tokyo is. Remember how surprised he was, Etsuko?"

"All the big buildings—he looked dizzy."

"Mr. Stolz had seen Europe, but Peter only knew Manila and Kobe and Osaka."

"And he thought Tokyo was every bit as good as people said."

"How about you, Etsuko?"

"What do you mean? I am Japanese. I knew already."

"I was the only one who had been in Tokyo. I had a terrible time explaining everything."

"Did you explain in Japanese?" asked Teruo.

"That was the problem. I explained in Japanese to Peter, and he interpreted to his father. But Peter had trouble with words like 'Diet Building' and 'Prime Minister's Residence.' I had to use my English sometimes."

"Lucky you knew the English for Diet Building and Prime Minister's Residence." Teruo alone spoke with a proper Tokyo accent.

"I only mixed in a little broken English. I remembered the Diet Building, but for 'Prime Minister's Residence' I had to say: 'This is where Prince Konoye lives.'"

"And I spoke German," said Etsuko.

"Auf Wiedersehen?"

"Yes. I said Auf Wiedersehen several times."

"Mr. Stolz kept thanking us in English."

Yukiko, usually so retiring, hand in hand with Etsuko, the aunt in summer kimono, the niece in Western clothes, the two of them showing a foreign gentleman and his son through the Imperial Hotel and the government buildings and office buildings—what a remarkable expedition it must have been, thought Sachiko. And how trying for Mr. Stolz, dragged along by his son, unable to understand the explanations, keeping a worried eye on his watch.

"Have you ever been in that museum, Mother?"

"Of course. You are not to go treating me as though I just came in from the country."

Sachiko did not in fact know Tokyo as well as she pretended. When she had been perhaps sixteen, she had stayed, once or twice, with her father at a downtown inn, and she had been shown the city, but that was before the earthquake. Since then she had spent only two or three nights at the Imperial Hotel on her way back from her honeymoon. She had not been in Tokyo even once in the nine years since Etsuko's birth. Though she might tease the girl, then, she had to admit that she had been a little excited herself as for the first time in so many years she saw the grandeur of the capital, the rows of tall buildings at the heart of the city. In Osaka too, Midō Boulevard had been widened. With modern buildings all through the old Semba district south of the river, the view from the Alaska Restaurant on the tenth floor of the Asahi Building was in its way an impressive one, but in the final analysis Osaka was no match for Tokyo. The changes from the Tokyo she had last seen, only beginning to recover from the earthquake, were quite beyond what she had imagined. Those great, towering piles, and the pyramid-shaped roof of the Diet Building down the avenues to the west—she knew how long those nine years had been. She looked back over changes in the city and changes in her own life.

Sachiko did not really like Tokyo, however. Radiant clouds might trail from His Imperial Majesty, but for Sachiko the beauty of Tokyo was the beauty of the Palace and its pine-covered grounds, and no more: the beauty of that island in the most modern part of the city, a medieval castle with mossy walls and banks along its moat, set off against the finest modern buildings. Of the Palace grounds, which had no rival in Osaka or Kyoto,

Sachiko was sure she would never tire. But for the rest there was little in Tokyo that pleased her. Magnificent though the Ginza might be, there was something dry and harsh in the air that made her sure she would always be a stranger there. And she especially disliked the drab streets in the outlying districts. As the cab approached Shibuya, she felt somehow chilly even in the summer night. It was as though she had come to a distant, utterly foreign country. She did not know whether she had ever before been in this part of Tokyo. In any case, the streets seemed to her quite unlike those of Kyoto and Osaka and Kobe—they seemed rather like what one would expect in a frontier city farther to the north, or even in Manchuria. And this was no end-of-the-line alley; it was a busy street in the main part of Tokyo. The shops were imposing and there was considerable evidence of prosperity as they started up the hill beyond Shibuya. Why then was it so lacking in warmth; why were the faces so cold and white? Sachiko thought of her own Ashiya, and of Kyoto. If this were Kyoto, she could feel at home in a street she was seeing for the first time. She would even want to stop for a chat with someone. But in Tokyo, wherever she went and however diligently she searched, she never felt that she had ties. She was an alien. She could hardly believe that a true child of Osaka, and her own sister at that, could be living in this section of this city. It was as if, in a dream, she was walking through a strange city, suddenly to come upon the house where her mother or her sister lived, and to say to herself: "So *this* is where Mother is living." How strange that Tsuruko could endure the place. Until they reached the house, Sachiko could hardly believe she was about to see her sister.

The cab turned left into a quiet residential street, and almost immediately it was surrounded by children. The oldest was about nine.

"Aunt Sachiko!"

"Aunt Sachiko!"

"Mother is waiting."

"There is the house, right over there."

"Be careful, be careful! Keep away from the cab," said Yukiko. The cab was coming to a stop.

"Are those really Tsuruko's children? The big one is Tetsuo, then?"

"Hideo," Teruo corrected her. "Hideo and Yoshio and Masao."
"How they have grown. Except for the Osaka accent, I would
never have guessed who they were."
"They all have good Tokyo accents when they want to," said
Teruo. "They're trying to make you feel at home."

15

SACHIKO had heard about the Shibuya house from Yukiko. The
wild disorder, however, the clutter that left hardly a place to
stand, was far worse than she had imagined. Although it was true
that the house was new and could be called bright, the pillars
were thin, the floors were weak, and the whole house shook when
one of the children ran up or down stairs. The paper paneling on
the doors, already full of holes, looked all the shabbier for the
cheap, whitish frames. Sachiko disliked the old Osaka house, so
dark and inconvenient, but she had to admit that it had a certain
repose quite lacking here. And then the Osaka house did have
a garden, albeit a very small garden, and Sachiko had fond memories of the view from the back tea room through the court to the
earth-walled storehouse. Here in Shibuya, with barely room inside
the fences for a few plotted plants, there was nothing at all that
could be called a garden. The children were too noisy downstairs,
said Tsuruko; she had given Sachiko the room upstairs that passed
for a guest room. Sachiko recognized in the alcove a painting by
Seihō [1]—it was of trout—that had been brought from Osaka. Her
father had collected Seihō paintings, and this was one of the few
they had kept when they sold his collection. Sachiko recognized
much besides the painting: the red-lacquer table in the alcove,
the motto over the door in the handwriting of Rai Shunsui,[2] the
gold-lacquer cupboard by the wall, the clock on it. She could see
the corner of the Osaka house where they had all been kept. No
doubt Tsuruko had brought them out to help her remember the

[1] Takeuchi Seihō (1864–1942), a Kyoto painter.
[2] Confucian scholar, 1746–1816. Father of the more famous Rai Sanyō.

good days and to brighten up what was much too ugly to be called a guest room. But the treasures had a perverse effect: they only set off the shabbiness of the room, and for Sachiko it was strange indeed to find relics of her father in a dreary section of Tokyo. It seemed to show the depths to which Tsuruko had fallen.

"How clever of you to find a place for everything."

"When the baggage came, I had no idea what I would do with it all. Somehow I did manage, though. When you pack a house full, you can put an amazing amount into it."

Tsuruko sat down for a talk after she showed Sachiko to her room. The children came storming up after her, and pulled and tugged at the two sisters. They were to go downstairs—they were smothering her—see, they were getting their aunt all wrinkled.

"Masao, suppose you go downstairs and tell O-hisa to hurry with something cool for your aunt. Do as I tell you, Masao."

Tsuruko held the youngest child, Umeko, on her lap. "Yoshio, go down and bring us a fan. Hideo, you are the oldest. The oldest is to go downstairs first. I have not seen your aunt in a very long time, and we have a great deal to talk about. Do you expect me to talk with you hanging on me?"

"How old are you, Hideo?"

"Eight."

"You are very big for your age. At the gate I thought it was Tetsuo."

"And he still has to hang on his mother, just as if he were the youngest of all. Tetsuo keeps himself busy with his studies. He is not quite so much of a baby."

"O-hisa is the only maid you have?"

"O-miyo was with us until a little while ago, but she wanted to go back to Osaka. I decided that with Umeko able to walk I hardly needed a nurse."

Sachiko, expecting to find Tsuruko faded and worn, looked admiringly at her sister. She still knew how to take care of herself. Her hair was neat, her dress was proper and tasteful. With a husband and six children—fourteen, eleven, eight, six, five, and three —to look after, and only one maid to help her, she had a right to look far more wasted and slovenly. She might well have looked ten years older than she was. But Tsuruko, a proper Makioka, would have been taken for a good five or six years younger than her thirty-seven. Tsuruko and Yukiko resembled their mother, a Kyoto woman, and Sachiko and Taeko their father. One could see something of the Kyoto beauty in the first and third sisters. Unlike Yukiko, however, Tsuruko was amply built. Just as the two younger sisters were shorter by steps than Sachiko, so Sachiko was a step shorter than Tsuruko. Her figure well proportioned to her height, Tsuruko seemed larger than her slight husband when they went out together. She was far from the delicate, fragile Kyoto beauty Yukiko was. Sachiko, who had been twenty at the time of Tsuruko's wedding, could remember how striking her sister had been that day. Clean featured and rather long of face, Tsuruko had worn her hair—when loose it trailed to the floor and reminded one of the long-haired Heian beauty of a thousand years ago—in a high, sweeping Japanese coiffure. One thought, looking at the figure, feminine and at the same time grand and imposing, how the robes of the ancient court lady would have become her. The most extravagant rumors about the bride Tatsuo was taking were no more than the truth, said Sachiko and the other sisters. Fifteen or sixteen years had passed, Tsuruko had six children, life had become less easy, and yet, though something of the bloom had passed, she still looked young. No doubt she was saved by her height and the fullness of her body. Sachiko looked closely at her sister, rocking Umeko in her arms, and saw that the smooth, white skin at the throat was as firm as ever.

Teinosuke had suggested that it would be a great imposition for Sachiko and Etsuko to stay at the Shibuya house. He would telephone or write to make reservations at an inn, he said, and Sachiko could move after only a night or two with her sister. But Sachiko did not like the idea of going to an inn—she might have been less reluctant if Teinosuke had been with her—and besides, not having seen her sister for so long, she had all sorts of things to talk about, and the Shibuya house would be far more convenient than an inn. And with O-haru to help in the kitchen, they would not be such a nuisance. Soon, however, she began to see that she might better have taken Teinosuke's advice. Tsuruko assured her that it was not always this noisy. The children were in the house all day long because of the summer vacation, and in two or three days it would be quieter. But since the three youngest

had not yet started to school, it did not seem likely that Tsuruko
would have much time to herself. Finding a spare moment now
and then, she would come up to Sachiko's room. The three children would immediately be up after her, and sometimes she would
have to spank one of them, and the clamor would only be louder.
Once or twice every day the screams were quite deafening. Sachiko
knew from the Osaka days that her sister tended to be short with
the children—how otherwise could she have managed them? But
even granting that no one was to blame, Sachiko thought it sad to
have so little time for conversation. After the first two or three
days, in the course of which Etsuko was taken by Yukiko to see
the Yasukuni Shrine and the Sengakuji Temple and the other
famous places, they found that it was too warm for sight-seeing.
Very soon Etsuko was bored. Another reason for not staying at an
inn had been Sachiko's hope that Etsuko, who had no brothers
and sisters, might find it fun to play with a little girl younger than
she, and might become friendly with her cousins, but Umeko was
so completely her mother's child that she even turned Yukiko
away, and she proved to be too much for Etsuko. School would
begin soon, Etsuko pointed out, and if she did not hurry back
Rumi would be off for Manila. Since she had been treated more
gently herself, she would steal frightened, intimidated glances at
Tsuruko when the latter began to punish one of the children.
Fearing that Etsuko might come to dislike Tsuruko, in many ways
the kindest of the sisters, and that the spankings might have an
unfortunate effect on her nerves, Sachiko concluded that the best
thing would be to send Etsuko on home with O-haru. However,
Dr. Sugiura of Tokyo University, to whom they had an introduction from Dr. Kushida, was out of town and would not be back
until early in September. The whole trip would be wasted unless
they saw him.

If they were to stay on, might it not be better to go to an inn?
True, Sachiko herself had never stayed at the Hamaya; but it was
managed by a lady who had been a waitress at the Harihan Restaurant in Osaka, whom Sachiko's father had known, and whom
Sachiko herself remembered ("the young lady," Sachiko had been
in those days). It was not as if she would be staying at a completely strange inn. Teinosuke had said moreover that the inn was
a small one, a made-over restaurant, that the guests were for the

most part congenial people from Osaka, that most of the maids
spoke the Osaka dialect, and that it was a place to make one forget
that one was in Tokyo. Because of all this, might it not be better
to move? But seeing the trouble Tsuruko was taking to entertain
her, Sachiko could not bring the subject up. Tatsuo too was most
solicitous. He said that it was quite impossible to have a comfortable meal at home, and took them out to a foreign-style restaurant said to be well known in Tokyo, and gave a little party
at a Chinese restaurant called the Peking, to which the children
were brought lest Etsuko be lonely. For all the tight-fisted ways
he was said to have developed, Tatsuo seemed as fond as ever of
taking people out. Or was it that he still felt the old impulse to
father them all? Sachiko did not know. Perhaps he was unhappy
over reports that he did not get along well with his sisters-in-law.
He pointed out that Sachiko knew only the Harihan and the Tsuruya and other expensive restaurants. Very near the Shibuya house,
he said, were any number of little restaurants that catered to the
pleasure quarters. The food was better than in large, famous restaurants, and, since proper wives and daughters were quite willing to be seen in such places, Sachiko too might find them interesting. If she liked, he would give her a taste of the real Tokyo. Leaving Tsuruko to watch the house, he would set out happily with
Sachiko and Yukiko for one of his little restaurants. Sachiko remembered, a little fondly, how the sisters had had their fits of
perverseness in the days when Tatsuo was new in the family, and
how he had occasionally sent them off in tears; but now, seeing
how good-natured and indeed how weak he was, and how intent
he was on entertaining them—more intent than Tsuruko even—
Sachiko could not bring herself to cross him. She concluded that
there was nothing to do but stay in the Shibuya house. They
would leave as soon as possible after seeing Dr. Sugiura.

16

It was the night of the first of September.

Sachiko and Yukiko had dinner with Tatsuo and Tsuruko, the children having eaten earlier. The talk turned from the Tokyo-Yokohama earthquake—September 1 was the anniversary—to the recent Ashiya flood, and as the matter of Taeko and the young photographer Itakura came up, Sachiko told them in some detail of what had happened. She herself had not been in danger, she said, and she only knew what Taeko had told her. No doubt it was not by way of retribution, but that very night the worst typhoon in over ten years hit Tokyo. For almost the first time in her life Sachiko knew two or three hours of real terror.

Reared in the Osaka region, where storm damage is lighter, Sachiko did not know how terrifying a wind could be. It was true that some four or five years earlier—had it been the autumn of 1934?—the pagoda of the Tennōji Temple had fallen in a typhoon, the Eastern Hills of Kyoto had been stripped quite bare, and Sachiko herself had been frightened for perhaps a half hour, but since the damage was light in Ashiya, they were astonished to learn from the newspapers that the wind had been enough to knock over a pagoda. That typhoon was hardly one to compare to this Tokyo typhoon. Her fears were multiplied at the thought that if the Tennōji Pagoda had fallen before the wind then, the Shibuya house would never stand before the wind now. Because the house was so cheaply built, the typhoon seemed five and ten times more violent than it really was.

The wind came up before the children were in bed, at eight or nine o'clock, and by ten o'clock it was fierce. Sachiko as usual went to bed upstairs with Yukiko and Etsuko. Etsuko clung to her as the house began to shake. Calling Yukiko over too, the child was soon lying with an arm tight around each. There was nothing to worry about—the wind would die down, they said; but they were clinging to her as desperately as she was clinging to them. The three lay huddled in a tight cluster, their faces pressed together. Teruo, who slept with Tetsuo in the small room across the hall, looked in and asked if they ought not to go downstairs. Might it be safer downstairs?—ought they to go downstairs?—he could hear people running about down there. Sachiko could not see his face, but his voice was tense and unnatural. Not wanting to frighten Etsuko, she said nothing. She was beginning to fear that the house might fall, however. Each time the beams moaned she thought the time had come, and she was in no mood to argue with Teruo. "Etsuko, Yukiko, suppose we go downstairs," she said, taking Etsuko by the hand. The house was just then shaken by a gust of wind which they thought must surely blow it over. The stairs, flimsy as shingles, seemed about to crumple under her feet, while the walls on either side ballooned like sails. Dirt and sand came in through the yawning cracks between the plaster and the pillars. Certain that she was about to be crushed to death, Sachiko threw herself down the stairs, almost knocking Teruo over before her. Upstairs they had not noticed because of the wind, and the leaves and branches and tin roofs and sign boards sailing through the air; but now they could hear the frightened voices: "I'm scared, Mother; I'm scared." The four youngest children, headed by Hideo, were clustered about their parents. As Sachiko came in, Yoshio and Masao ran over to her. Etsuko was left to Yukiko. Tsuruko held Umeko in both arms, and Hideo cowered at her sleeve (his behavior was extraordinary: during lulls in the wind, he would twist at his mother's sleeve and listen intently, and when he heard the wind coming up again in the distance, he would cover his ears and, with a low and yet hoarse and penetrating moan, press his face against the floor). Four adults and seven children, like a group statue of Terror. Whatever may have been Tatsuo's feelings, the three sisters at least were resigned to being crushed to death. Had the wind been a little stronger and had it lasted a little longer, they might well have been. Sachiko thought that in her fright she had been imagining things, but here downstairs she could see that at each fresh gust of wind the pillars and the plastered walls were indeed separated by cracks two and three inches wide—she wanted to say six inches or a foot, watching by the one flashlight. The cracks opened before the wind and closed in the lulls, and each time they were wider than before. Sachiko remembered how the Osaka house had shaken in the Hachiyama earthquake, but an earthquake is over in a moment. This opening and closing of the walls was quite new to her.

Even Tatsuo, doing his best to remain calm, began to feel uneasy at the billowing walls. Was this the only house that was rocking so, he wondered aloud—the other houses in the neighborhood were more solidly built. The Koizumis' would be standing up well enough, said Teruo. It was a solid, one-storey house. Suppose they go to the Koizumis'? They did not want the house to fall on them. The house would not fall, answered Tatsuo—but then, it might be better to leave—but they could hardly get the Koizumis out of bed. This was no time to think about being polite, said Tsuruko; and the Koizumis would surely not be sleeping through the storm. Suddenly everyone was in favor of leaving. The Koizumi house was the neighboring one to the rear, its gate but a step from the Makioka kitchen. Mr. Koizumi, a retired civil servant with a wife and one son, had been of some help to Teruo, who went to the same middle school as the son. Tatsuo and Teruo had called on him once or twice.

Meanwhile O-haru and O-hisa were talking in the maid's room; and soon O-haru came in to say that she would go see how things were with the Koizumis. If it seemed appropriate, she would ask them to take in the whole Makioka family. O-haru of course had no idea who the Koizumis might be, but she had complete confidence in herself, and she evidently meant to present her petition once O-hisa had shown her the house.

"Suppose we get started, O-hisa."

"Be careful—the wind might blow you away."

Without waiting for permission, O-haru led O-hisa off through the back door. The Koizumis would not mind a bit, she said, back a few minutes later. Mr. Teruo was right—the Koizumi house was not even trembling, the storm seemed like a far-off dream. As she spoke, O-haru turned to take Etsuko on her back.

"Miss Etsuko could never make it alone. Why I was blown back twice myself, and finally had to crawl over. And there are all sorts of things blowing through the air. Put a quilt over your head, now."

Tatsuo still showed no sign of leaving. He would stay to take care of the house, he said, as Teruo, Tetsuo, Sachiko, Yukiko, and

Etsuko went off with O-haru. Tsuruko could not decide what to
do; but when, after O-haru had gone off with Masao ("Come on,
young man, we are getting out of here!") and was preparing to
take Yoshio in his turn, she could stand it no longer. Giving Yoshio
to O-hisa, she left the house with Umeko in her arms. O-haru had
been most heroic—coming back the second time, she had barely
escaped being crushed by a balcony that sailed down the street.
O-hisa having taken Yoshio, she turned to the terrified Hideo, and,
brushing aside Tsuruko's protests that the boy was quite big
enough to walk by himself, took him on her back.

So all of them, even the maid O-hisa, had left. Half an hour
later Tatsuo appeared somewhat sheepishly at the Koizumis' back
door. The wind was worse than ever; but the walls and pillars of
the Koizumi house were so solid that no one thought of the danger. How strange that a better-built house should make such a
difference. The wind subsided at about four in the morning, and
the Makiokas returned trembling to their frail, uninviting little
house.

17

ALTHOUGH THERE WAS a clear autumn sky the next morning, the
memory of the typhoon was still with Sachiko like a nightmare.
Worried about the effect on Etsuko's nerves, she decided that the
time for deliberation had passed. She put in an emergency call to
Osaka and asked Teinosuke to make reservations at the Hamaya
Inn. She would like if possible to move that day, she said, and toward evening she had a call from the Hamaya. Reservations had
been made from Osaka, and a room was waiting for her. She set
out with Etsuko after a brief farewell to her sister. She would have
dinner at the inn, she said, and if Tsuruko did not mind she would
like to leave O-haru in Shibuya for three or four more days. She
hoped her sister might find time to visit the inn.

Yukiko and O-haru went into the city with them. The four had
dinner at a German restaurant recommended by the inn, and after

they had strolled along the Ginza and looked at the night shops—
it must have been at about nine—Yukiko and O-haru said
good-bye at the subway station. It was the first night Sachiko had
ever spent at an inn alone with Etsuko. The terror of the night
before came back still more vividly. Even though she had taken
sleeping medicine and a sip or two of the brandy she kept for just
such an occasion, she was still awake when the first streetcar passed
the following morning. Etsuko too had had trouble sleeping. She
was going back to Osaka the next day, she said fretfully. She would
not wait for the doctor. She was likely to get worse at this rate.
She would go back ahead of Sachiko; she wanted to see Rumi. The
next morning, however, she was snoring happily. At about seven
o'clock, reconciled to the fact that she herself was not to sleep,
Sachiko got up quietly so as not to disturb Etsuko. Asking for
newspapers, she went out to sit on the veranda overlooking the
Tsukiji canal.

At home, she was intensely interested in the two problems of
the day, the Japanese advance on Hankow and the Sudeten dis-
pute, so interested that she could hardly wait for the morning newspapers; but here, perhaps because of the unfamiliar Tokyo papers,
she found that the news did not seem real. She turned to watch the
people on the banks of the canal. Since the inn she had stayed at
with her father was in an alley behind the Kabuki Theater, the
roof of which she could see, this was not the alien ground she
found Shibuya to be; but new buildings had gone up, and the view
along the canal was very different from the view she remembered.
Then too she had come to Tokyo during spring vacation, and
this was the first time she had seen it in September, and even here
in the middle of the city the air was chilly against the skin. Osaka
would not be chilly so soon. Did autumn come early to Tokyo,
cold city that it was? Or was this only a cold wave after the typhoon, a short break in the hot weather? Or was one more sensitive to the cold when one was away from home?

In any case, she had four or five days to wait before she could
take Etsuko to see Dr. Sugiura. How were they to pass the time?
Sachiko had thought that the great actor Kikugorō would be playing in September, and that Etsuko could go to the Kabuki. Since
Etsuko liked the dance, she would like the dance-drama too; and
it being quite possible that the Kabuki would have collapsed by

the time she was grown, she really must see Kikugorō now—
Sachiko remembered how her father had taken her to the theater
whenever the Osaka actor Ganjirō was playing. But the really good
Kabuki had not yet opened at any of the theaters. Aside from a
stroll each evening along the Ginza, then, there was very little she
wanted to do. Suddenly, she was homesick. She began to agree
with Etsuko that they should put off the examination and leave
for Osaka immediately. And if she could be so homesick in less
than a week, she understood how Yukiko might sit in the Shibuya
house and weep to be back in Ashiya.

At about ten there was a call from O-haru. Tsuruko would like
to visit the inn, and O-haru would show her the way. A letter had
come from Mr. Makioka. Was there anything else Sachiko needed?
Nothing, answered Sachiko. She did want to have Tsuruko for
lunch, however, and she hoped they would hurry. This would be a
good chance to send Etsuko off with O-haru and to have a quiet,
leisurely meal with her sister for the first time in a very great while.
Where, she wondered, might they go? She remembered that
her sister was fond of eels, and that there was an eel restaurant
called the Daikokuya to which her father had often taken her.
Was it still in business, she wondered. The lady at the desk did
not know. There was a famous place called the Komatsu, but the
Daikokuya—she looked in the telephone book and found that
there was indeed a Daikokuya. After making reservations, Sachiko
sat down to wait for her sister. Etsuko could go to the Mitsukoshi
Department Store with O-haru, she said as she and Tsuruko set
out together.

Yukiko had finally succeeded in luring Umeko upstairs, and
Tsuruko had dressed in a great rush and slipped out. No doubt
poor Yukiko had a problem on her hands by now—but Tsuruko
had escaped, and she meant to enjoy herself.

"This reminds me so of Osaka. I had no idea there were
such places in Tokyo." Tsuruko looked out over the canal from the
restaurant.

"It really is very much like Osaka. Father used to bring me here
when we came to Tokyo."

"Do you suppose it was once an island?"

"I wonder. This is the place, certainly, but these rooms on the
canal are new."

In the old days, there had been houses along but one side of the street. Now, with houses on the canal side too, the waitresses apparently brought the food across from the main building. The canal rooms were built on the stone embankment at a bend in the canal, and the view was even more like Osaka than Sachiko had remembered. The cross formed by two branch canals joining the main canal at the bend made one think of the view from the oyster boats at Yotsuhashi, "Four Bridges," in Osaka. Although there were, across one arm or another, not the four bridges of Yotsuhashi, there were at least three bridges here. Unfortunately this old downtown district, which had once had the dignity and repose one expects of such districts, had been rebuilt after the earthquake. The buildings, the bridges, and the paved roads were all new. With so few people passing by, one was reminded of a rude, unfinished frontier community.

"Shall we have ginger ale?"

"We could." Sachiko looked at her sister. "But what would you really like?"

"Ginger ale would be good, I suppose. It is only noon."

"Suppose we have some beer."

"If you will drink half of it."

Sachiko knew that Tsuruko was the best drinker in the family. There were times when she fairly longed for a drink—especially of Japanese saké. Beer, however, would do as well.

"You must not have much time these days for a good drink."

"As a matter of fact, I keep Tatsuo company at dinner. And then we do have guests."

"What sort of guests?"

"Tatsuo's brother from Azabu. We always have something to drink when he comes. He says saké tastes better in a shabby little house full of children."

"It must be hard for you."

"Not really. We never go out of our way to entertain him. He eats with the children, and we give him a little to drink, and that is what it comes to. And then O-hisa can plan a meal with no orders from me."

"She really has learned to take care of things very well."

"In the early days we both disliked Tokyo, and we used to have our cries together. 'Send me back to Osaka, send me back to

Osaka,' she would say. But lately she has stopped. I hope I can keep her until she gets married."

"Is she older than O-haru?"

"How old is O-haru?"

"Nineteen."

"They are the same age, then. You must keep O-haru too. She seems like such a good girl."

"I have had her nearly six years now—she was fourteen when she came. She would never go to work for anyone else, I know, even if I ordered her to. But she is really not as good as she seems."

"So Yukiko says. But the way she worked night before last— O-hisa was fussing and holding back, but not O-haru. Tatsuo was quite amazed."

"At times like that she is very good. She was a great help in the flood too. But . . ."

To go with the beer, Sachiko offered her sister a review of O-haru's faults.

It was not unpleasant to have one's maid praised, and Sachiko, not wanting to unmask O-haru, always listened quietly when she heard something flattering about the girl; there were few maids who enjoyed such a good name. O-haru had a clever way with people. She was most liberal in giving away her own things and the Makiokas', and her generosity made her very popular with tradesmen and craftsmen who were in and out of the house. Sachiko was often surprised, moreover, at the way in which Etsuko's teachers and her own friends came out of their way to tell her what an admirable maid she had.

The woman who best understood the problems Sachiko faced was O-haru's stepmother. When she came occasionally to see that all was going well, she would go over the whole story again: whatever anyone said, she could never forget Sachiko's kindness in keeping such an unmanageable girl; she had been reduced to tears herself any number of times, and she knew well enough the troubles Sachiko would be having; if Sachiko were to let the girl go, they could never find another place for her. They hoped Sachiko would continue to put up with all the embarrassments and inconveniences—she need not pay O-haru anything, and she need not be afraid to scold the girl. Since O-haru only took advantage of kindness, it would be quite the best thing to scold her incessantly.

When the laundryman introduced O-haru, then fourteen, and asked Sachiko to hire her, Sachiko was much taken with the girl's general appearance and manner; but within a month she began to see what she had hired, and to understand that the stepmother was not being polite and self-effacing when she called O-haru "unmanageable." What struck one most was O-haru's uncleanliness. Sachiko soon realized that the dirty hands and fingernails—she had noticed them the first time she saw the girl—were a sign less of poverty and hard work than of pure laziness. O-haru had a great dislike for laundering and bathing. Sachiko was energetic in her efforts to correct the shortcoming, but as soon as she looked away, O-haru was as bad as ever again. Unlike the other maids, who had baths every night, O-haru would loll about the maids' room and presently go to sleep without even undressing. She had no objection to wearing the same dirty underwear for days on end. One simply had to take off her clothes and lead her to the bath, or pull out all the dirty underwear and stand over her while she washed it. All in all, she was more trouble than a baby. The other maids, more directly her victims than Sachiko, were soon complaining. The closet was full of dirty clothes, they said; and when in desperation they took out O-haru's laundry and did it themselves, they were astonished to find in it a pair of underpants that belonged to Sachiko. In her reluctance to do her laundry, O-haru had apparently even taken to borrowing Sachiko's underwear. And, they added, O-haru smelled so bad that they could hardly go near her. It was not only that she was unwashed—she ate incessantly, she had chronic dyspepsia, and her breath was really enough to make one hold one's nose. They suffered most acutely when they had to sleep with her, and they began to report that they were acquiring fleas. Any number of times Sachiko persuaded O-haru to accept the inevitable and go home, but the father and stepmother came in turn each time and begged her with elaborate apologies to take the girl back on whatever terms. O-haru was the only child of the first wife, and the second wife had two children of her own, and since O-haru was not as diligent as she might be and her grades in school were far worse than those of the other two, there was constant tension when she was in the house—the father restraining himself before the second wife, the stepmother uncomfortable before the father of the first wife's child. The parents would plead with Sachiko. They hoped that she would see her way to keeping O-haru until she was old enough to be married. The stepmother stated the case more strongly than the father: O-haru had a ridiculously good name in the neighborhood, and even the younger children would take her part, until the poor woman found herself the very model of the wicked stepmother. O-haru had this fault and that fault, she would point out, and not even her husband would listen to her. She could not imagine what made him protect the girl as he did. Only Sachiko could understand how she felt. Sachiko, seeing how difficult the woman's position must be, would in the end find herself sympathizing rather than being sympathized with.

"You can tell how she is from the way she wears her clothes. The other maids laugh and tell her she is wide open in front, but that does not worry her in the least. I suppose scolding never makes a person over."

"But she is such a pretty girl," said Tsuruko.

"She is very particular about her face, whatever happens to the rest of her. She is always stealing my cold cream and lipstick . . . You say O-hisa can plan a meal without being told. After five years there is not a single thing O-haru can do unless I tell her exactly how it is to be done. I come home hungry at dinner time and ask her what she has ready, and she says she has not really thought about dinner."

"And she seems so clever."

"She is far from stupid. But she is too sociable. She likes talking to people, and she hates chores. She knows perfectly well that the house has to be cleaned, but if I stop watching her, she lets it go. She never gets up in the morning unless someone calls her. And she still goes to bed with her clothes on."

Sachiko thought of incidents and illustrations with which to entertain her sister: how a chestnut or two would always disappear between the kitchen and the dining room; how O-haru's eyes would dart about in consternation when someone called her unexpectedly, and she would turn away to gulp down whatever she happened to be eating; how, as she gave Sachiko a massage in the evening, she would doze off and fall over, and in the end be stretched out full length beside Sachiko; how she had several times

gone to bed with the gas on, or, forgetting to turn off the iron,
scorched the clothes and almost set the house on fire; how on
such occasions Sachiko had decided that she had had enough,
and had bundled the girl off home, and then had been persuaded
by the parents to take her back; and how O-haru, off on an errand,
would find interesting people along the way, and take hours coming back.

"What do you suppose she will do when she gets married?"

"A husband and family may change her. But do keep her,
Sachiko. She is a very likable girl."

"After five years I almost think of her as my daughter. She may
be a little tricky at times, but she has none of the touchiness you
expect of a stepchild. And she does have her good points. Even
when she seems more trouble than she is worth, I can never be
really angry with her."

18

AFTER LUNCH they went back to the inn, where they talked until
evening. Tsuruko suggested that they send O-haru with O-hisa to
see the sights at Nikko—she had been such a help with the children. To keep O-hisa from returning to Osaka, Tsuruko had
promised her a trip to Nikko, but for want of a suitable companion
it had been put off and put off; and was this not the opportunity
she had been waiting for? Although Tsuruko knew little about
Nikko, she had heard that one could see the shrines and Kegon
Falls and Lake Chūzenji and be back in Tokyo the same day.
Tatsuo too was enthusiastic, and of course would pay the expenses.

Sachiko could not help thinking that O-haru had played her
cards cleverly. Still O-hisa would not be allowed to go alone, and,
since O-haru seemed already to know, it would be a crime to spoil
the fun. Tsuruko telephoned two mornings later: she had broken
the news the evening before; they had been too happy to sleep,
and had set out early that morning; she had sent them off prepared

to spend the night if they had to, but she expected them back by seven or eight in the evening; and Yukiko would very shortly visit the inn.

As Sachiko put down the receiver, thinking that when Yukiko arrived the three of them might go to the Art Academy, the maid came in and handed a special-delivery letter to Etsuko, who turned it over with a strange expression on her face and laid it on the table before her mother. The letter, in a foreign-style envelope, was addressed to Sachiko in care of the Hamaya. The handwriting was not Teinosuke's—but only Teinosuke knew where she was staying.

She turned it over. It was from Okubata.

Trying to hide the return address from Etsuko, she hastily tore open the envelope. The three pieces of stiff Western stationery, crammed with writing on both sides and folded lengthwise and crosswise, crackled like a movie sound-effect as she spread them open.

The contents were shocking.

September 13
DEAR SACHIKO:

Forgive me for writing so suddenly. You will be upset to hear from me, I know, but I cannot let the opportunity pass.

I have as a matter of fact been wanting for some time to write, and I have been afraid Koi-san might stop the letter. Today I saw her, at the studio, for the first time in several days, and learned that you and Etsuko are staying at the Hamaya. I happen to know the address, since friends of mine stay there when they are in Tokyo, and I am sure that this time my letter will reach you. I must ask you to forgive me.

I will be as brief as possible. I suppose I should begin with the suspicions that have been bothering me. They are entirely my own, but I wonder if something is not happening between Koi-san and Itakura. Much though I would like to think, for Koi-san's sake, that their relations are clean, I suspect that we have at least the beginnings of a love affair.

I first began to notice it at the time of the flood. It seemed very strange that Itakura should run off to rescue her, and it was more than just kindness that made him leave his own house and sister and risk his life for her. In the first place, how did he know she was at the sewing school, and why was he so friendly with Mrs. Tamaki? He must have been in and out of the school for some time, and he may have been meeting Koi-san there and leaving messages for her. I have investigated and found evidence to make me very suspicious, but I need not go into it now. I would rather you investigated for yourself. I am sure you would find much to surprise you.

I have presented my evidence to both Koi-san and Itakura, and they have denied everything. It is strange, though, that Koi-san should now be avoiding me. She rarely comes to the studio, and when I telephone the Ashiya house O-haru generally tells me, whether it is true or not, that she is out. Itakura says what you would expect him to: that he has seen Koi-san no more than two or three times since the flood, and that nothing else will happen to upset me. But I have my ways of checking on him. Is it not true that he has been visiting your house almost every day since the flood? And is it not a fact that he has gone swimming alone with Koi-san several times? I have my ways of investigating, and there is no use in his trying to hide the facts. Maybe he tells you that I have ordered him to bring messages to Koi-san, but I have given no such orders. The only possible business he could have with her would be to take pictures, and since I have forbidden him to do any more work for her he no longer has even that excuse. And yet he goes to your house oftener than before, and Koi-san has stopped going to her studio. It is all right when you are around to watch her, I suppose; but I hate to think what might be happening now, with Teinosuke out of the house in the daytime and you and Etsuko and even O-haru in Tokyo. (You of course would not know that he seems to be visiting your house every day even now.) Koi-san is trustworthy and not likely to make mistakes, but Itakura is thoroughly untrustworthy. He has wandered around America and tried his hand at many things, and as you know he is remarkably good at meeting the right people and working his way into whatever house he chooses. And when it comes to borrowing money and deceiving women he is only too accomplished. I have known him since he was a boy in our shop, and I can tell you anything you need to know about him.

There are many favors I want to ask for myself, but they

can wait; the problem of separating the two comes first. Even assuming that Koi-san means to break her engagement to me (she says she does not), she will have no future if there are rumors about her and a man like Itakura. I cannot believe that a Makioka could be serious about him; but it was I who introduced them, and it is my duty to tell everything to the person who is supposed to be watching over her.

I do not doubt that you will have ideas of your own. If there is anything you think I can do, I will of course call on you whenever you say.

I must ask you not to tell Koi-san I have written. It could do no good, and might possibly do harm, if she were to know.

I am writing in a very great hurry, to be sure that my letter will reach you at the Hamaya. I suppose you have had trouble reading it, but I hope you will understand the haste. Writing everything as it has come to me, I have said much that is foolish and rude. You must forgive me.

Sincerely,
OKUBATA KEISABURŌ

Leaning on her elbows and shielding the letter between her hands, Sachiko reread several key passages. Then, to avoid Etsuko's prying eyes, she put it back into the envelope, folded it double, slipped it into her obi, and went out to sit in a rattan chair on the veranda.

It had been too sudden. She could think of nothing until the beating of her heart subsided. How much would be true? Now that she had Okubata's accusations before her, she had to admit that she had been too lenient with Koi-san. She had let Itakura become too familiar. She had been careless in letting him come and go as he would, whether or not he had business, and in not thinking it strange that he should come so often. But in the role that so concerned Okubata—as a candidate for Koi-san's hand—they had not even thought about the young man. They knew nothing of his antecedents. All they knew was that he had worked as a boy in the Okubata shop. The truth was that from the outset they had considered him on a level below them. He had suggested playfully, had he not, that they might let him take O-haru for his bride? Who then would have thought that he might have designs on Koi-san herself? Had the playfulness been only a trick?

But Sachiko could not believe that, even if Itakura had such ambitions, Koi-san could think of taking them seriously. She could not believe the accusations as they concerned Koi-san. Whatever mistakes Koi-san had made in the past, had she no pride? However faded and fallen, was she not always a Makioka? Tears came into Sachiko's eyes. Okubata was worthless, but one could imagine, and even approve of, his marrying Koi-san. But could Koi-san even consider a liaison with the other young man? Had not her whole manner toward him, her way of speaking to him, been as to one beneath her? And had he not seemed to accept it, almost to enjoy it?

Was there then no basis for Okubata's suspicions? He spoke of evidence, but the fact that he had not even hinted at what the evidence was might mean that he had only vague misgivings. To keep Koi-san from making a mistake, he had perhaps stated his warnings in the most exaggerated terms. Sachiko did not know what his "ways of investigating" might be, but it certainly was *not* a "fact," for instance, that Koi-san and Itakura had gone swimming alone together. Lenient though Sachiko might be, she would not allow such complete indifference to the proprieties. It was Etsuko who had gone alone with Itakura. Whenever Koi-san went swimming, Etsuko and Yukiko and Sachiko were with her; Koi-san and Itakura had really been left alone very little. The other sisters had not meant especially to chaperon her, but since Itakura was such an entertaining talker, they always came in to listen. Sachiko had not once noted anything strange in his behavior or Koi-san's. Had Okubata then built a fantasy on irresponsible rumors?

Sachiko wanted very much to think so, but something, she could hardly say what, came to her as she read the letter. She had thought Itakura a member of a class with which they had nothing in common; and yet she could not say that she had on no occasion had suspicions of the sort Okubata described. She had vaguely sensed that there was something behind the devotion to Koi-san and those constant visits to the Ashiya house. And she could imagine how deep would be the gratitude of a girl who had been rescued at such peril. Consciousness of class always intervened, however, to make her dismiss the matter as not really worth thinking about. If the truth must be told, she had avoided thinking about it. Her consternation came from the fact that what she had not wanted to see, what she had feared to see, was with no preliminaries and no hesitations hauled out before her by Okubata.

Already homesick, she felt, after reading the letter, that she could not waste even another day in Tokyo. She must hurry home and learn the truth as soon as possible. But how ought she to proceed? How could she keep from angering Koi-san and Itakura? Should she talk to her husband? Or should she take full responsibility upon herself, and discover the truth in the strictest secrecy, telling neither Teinosuke nor Yukiko? Would it not be best, if Okubata's allegations should prove true, to separate the two without wounding them and without letting anyone else know? Sachiko turned the possibilities over one after another in her mind. The really urgent need was to keep Itakura from the Ashiya house. "He seems to be visiting your house every day even now"—that was the sentence that most disturbed her. If indeed the seeds of an affair were sprouting, then this was their chance to grow and flourish. "I hate to think what might be happening now, with Teinosuke out of the house in the daytime and you and Etsuko and even O-haru in Tokyo."

How careless she had been! Who if not Sachiko herself had hit upon the idea of taking Yukiko and Etsuko and O-haru to Tokyo, and leaving only Taeko behind? It was as though she had built a nursery especially for those sprouting seeds—or for seeds that would send out sprouts if there had been none before. Should she blame her sister and Itakura, or should she blame herself? In any case, there was no time to be wasted. Even as she sat there, time was passing. She was seized with an intolerable restlessness. If she had to wait a day or two before she could go back to Osaka with Etsuko, what defense measures should she take in the meantime? The quickest solution of course would be to telephone Teinosuke and have him prevent Taeko's seeing Itakura. But that would not do. She wanted to keep Teinosuke from learning of the affair. Another possibility was to tell Yukiko everything, send her back to Osaka that night, and have her watch unobtrusively over Taeko. Yukiko would be easier to talk to than Teinosuke. But even assuming that Yukiko would agree, Sachiko would have no excuse for bundling her off to Osaka when she had only just returned to the main family. The step least likely to arouse suspicion, then, would be to send O-haru back immediately. She need tell the girl nothing. O-haru's presence in the Ashiya house would impose certain restrictions on Koi-san even if it did not entirely keep her from meeting Itakura.

But Sachiko hesitated again. O-haru was such a talker. There was no telling what rumors she would start if she became suspicious. A clever girl, she might guess why she was being sent back early. And, on the other hand, she might allow herself to be bribed. For all her cleverness, she yielded easily to such temptations. She would be no problem at all for a talker as persuasive as Itakura. Sachiko concluded that she could entrust the mission to no one. She must go back to Osaka. After the examination, today or tomorrow, she must take a night train back, however late it might be.

Seeing Yukiko's parasol on the bridge by the Kabuki Theater, she went quietly back into the room, sat down at the dresser, and powdered her face. Then, as if she had remembered something, she opened her cosmetics case—she tried not to let Etsuko see— and poured the cap of the pocket flask a third full of brandy.

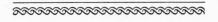

19

SACHIKO was no longer interested in art exhibits—and yet a little art might take her mind off her troubles. In the afternoon the three of them set out for Ueno Park. After two exhibits, Sachiko was exhausted, but not Etsuko, who still had to see the zoo. It was six before they finally dragged themselves back to the inn. As for dinner, Sachiko could not bear the thought of going out to a restaurant. She invited Yukiko to have something with them at the inn. They had finished their baths and were sitting down for dinner when O-haru came in flushed and sweating, her summer dress quite wilted. She and O-hisa had taken the subway from Asakusa, and she had come alone from the Ginza to thank Sachiko. And this is for Miss Etsuko—she took out some candy and several postcards.

"Thank you. But you should take this to Shibuya instead."

"I have much more. I sent it on with O-hisa."

"Really, you should not have bought so much, O-haru."

"Did you see the falls?" Etsuko was looking at the postcards.

"Yes, thank you, I saw everything. The shrines, the falls, the lake."

For a time, the talk was of Nikko. O-haru was challenged when she said that she had seen Mt. Fuji too.

"Not Mt. Fuji!"

"Definitely Mt. Fuji."

"From where?"

"From the train."

"You can see Mt. Fuji from the Tōbu Line?"

"You just saw a mountain that reminded you of Mt. Fuji."

"No, it was definitely Mt. Fuji. Everyone on the train was pointing at it."

"Can you really see Mt. Fuji? I wonder. From where on the Tōbu Line would it be?"

Sachiko, who had been thinking about Dr. Sugiura since that morning, had O-haru call his office from the inn. He had just returned to the city, and he could see them the following morning, the sixth. Reconciled to the possibility that, even though he was due back on the fifth, the doctor might be delayed two or three days, Sachiko was much relieved. She asked the inn to reserve three berths for the following night, if possible berths in a series. "You are going back tomorrow?"—Yukiko was startled. With the examination in the morning, answered Sachiko, she might be a little pressed, but if she did her shopping in the afternoon it would not be impossible to take a night train. Although Sachiko herself had no special reason to rush home, Etsuko was already late for school. They might go shopping together if Yukiko and O-haru would come to the inn at about noon. Sachiko knew she should go once more to the Shibuya house, she said as she saw Yukiko and O-haru off after dinner, but she simply could not find the time. She hoped Yukiko would apologize for her.

She was indeed "pressed" the next day. After the examination at Dr. Sugiura's office and a trip to a pharmacy for the medicine he prescribed, she and Etsuko took a cab from Tokyo University and arrived at the inn to find Yukiko and O-haru waiting. Yukiko wanted first to know the results of the examination. Dr. Sugiura's diagnosis had in general agreed with Dr. Tsuji's. Dr. Sugiura added that the illness was particularly common with children who had outstanding artistic abilities. There was nothing to worry about. Depending on how she was trained, the girl might excel in one field or another. The important thing was to discover where her talents lay. He advised dieting and wrote out a prescription, and only the prescription departed from what Dr. Tsuji had advised. In the afternoon, the four went shopping. The hot weather had returned, and though there was a breeze, it was a stifling day. They had to make frequent stops to refresh themselves, at the German Bakery, at the Colombin, on the seventh floor of the Mitsukoshi Department Store. O-haru, who followed after them with only her head showing over the packages, was sweating as freely as the day before. Each of the others also had two or three packages. It was time for dinner when they returned to the Ginza to pick up odds and ends. Deciding not to go again to the German restaurant (they needed a change, she said), Sachiko suggested the New Grand instead. Dinner would take less time there than at the inn, and it would be good to spend these last moments with Yukiko— who knew when they would see her again?—over a glass of beer and the foreign cooking of which she was so fond. They rushed back to the hotel, packed, and went to the station. After a brief conversation with Tsuruko, who had come to see them off, they boarded a sleeper on the eight-thirty express.

Tsuruko took advantage of a moment when Etsuko had stepped down to the platform with Yukiko. Sachiko was standing in the car door.

"Have you had any more proposals for Yukiko?" Tsuruko spoke in a very low voice.

"Not since the one you know of. But I am hoping for something soon."

"This year? Next year is bad, you know."

"I know. I have been asking everyone."

"Good-bye, Yukiko." Etsuko waved a pink georgette handkerchief from the door. "When are you coming again?"

"I wonder."

"Make it soon."

Yukiko did not answer.

"You will come soon, Yukiko? Be sure to come soon."

They had two lower berths and one upper. Sachiko put O-haru and Etsuko opposite each other and took the upper herself. She lay down in an under-kimono, but she made no real effort to sleep. The image of Tsuruko and Yukiko and their tear-filled eyes lingered on and on. This was the eleventh day since her arrival in Tokyo; and she thought she had never before had so restless and unsettling a trip. First those noisy children, then the typhoon, and she had crawled off to the Hamaya only to be hit by the letter from Okubata. The one day she had really enjoyed was the day she had had lunch with Tsuruko. It was true that their primary mission was accomplished: they had seen Dr. Sugiura. But they had not once gone to the theater. And all yesterday and today Sachiko had raced through the dusty streets of Tokyo in the worst of the heat. What a dizzying two days they had been. Only on a trip could one think of rushing about to so many places in so short a time. The memory alone was enough to exhaust her. She felt less as if she were lying down than as if she had been thrown down from some high place, and yet she could not sleep. Knowing well enough that a sip or two of brandy might make her doze off, she did not have the energy to get up for it. And with her all the while was the unhappy question that would have to be answered as soon as she reached home. It took shape and vanished and took shape again, cloaked in doubts and shadows. Was Okubata right? And if he was, what should she do? Did Etsuko suspect anything? Had she told Yukiko of the letter?

20

ETSUKO started back to school after a day's rest. Sachiko, on the other hand, only felt more exhausted. She would call in a masseuse and lie down for a nap in the middle of the day, or she would go out to sit on the terrace.

Perhaps because it reflected the tastes of one who preferred spring, the garden had little in it to attract the eye: a rather forlorn hibiscus in the shade of the hillock, and a clump of *hagi* [1] trailing its white flowers off toward the Stolz fence. The sandalwood and the plane trees, such a profusion of leaves in summer, were limp and tired. The green of the lawn was much as it had been when she left, and yet the sun seemed a little weaker. The garden carried just a suggestion of coolness, the smell of a sweet olive reminded her that in Ashiya too autumn was near. They would soon have to take in the reed awning. These last two or three days she had felt an intense affection for the familiar garden. It was good to go away now and then. Possibly because she was not used to traveling, she felt that she had been away at least a month. She remembered how Yukiko treasured every minute, how she would walk through the garden, stopping here and there, when she had to go back to Tokyo. Yukiko was not the only child of Osaka, Sachiko knew. This was a most unremarkable little garden, but even here, smelling the pines, looking at the mountains and the clear sky, she thought that there could be no finer place to live than the suburbs of Osaka. How unpleasant Tokyo was, how dusty, gray, pushing. Yukiko was fond of saying that the very feel of the Osaka air was different, and she was right. Sachiko would not have to move. She could not begin to describe how much luckier she thought herself than Tsuruko or Yukiko. Sometimes she would say to O-haru:

"You had a very good time for yourself, going off to Nikko. But for me there is not one good thing in Tokyo. Home is the best place in the world."

Taeko reported that she had been meaning to start work on her dolls again (she had left them untouched through the summer), but that she had not wanted to leave the house while Sachiko was away. The day after Sachiko's return, she set out for her studio. There was no telling when the sewing school would open again, and the dancing teacher was no longer living. With nothing to keep her busy except her dolls, then, she thought she might take up French. Why not have Mme Tsukamoto come in, suggested Sachiko. She herself had stopped when Yukiko went to Tokyo,

[1] *Lespedeza japonica*, sometimes translated "bush clover."

but if Koi-san was interested they might study together. That would never do, laughed Taeko—she was only a beginner and she would not be in a class with Sachiko; and besides, the French woman charged too much.

Itakura called while Taeko was out. He only wanted to say hello. After about twenty minutes or a half hour on the terrace he went around to the kitchen to hear about Nikko.

It was true that Sachiko wanted a good rest before she grappled with her problem, but as a matter of fact the suspicions she had brought back from Tokyo showed a strange tendency to fade as the days passed. The shock when she had opened the letter, the fears that had clutched at her heart all through the following day, the nightmare that had tormented her on the train—the feeling of intolerable urgency—began to leave her the moment she was at home in the clear morning sunlight. She began to feel that there was no need at all for haste and confusion. Had it been a matter that concerned Yukiko, she would have refused from the start to listen. She would have dismissed the rumors as libelous, whatever they were and whoever brought them, but there had been that newspaper incident, and Taeko was basically different from Sachiko and Yukiko. Sachiko could not trust her altogether; that was why Okubata's letter had struck home.

Meanwhile, Taeko was her usual bright self. She could not possibly have such a dark secret, thought Sachiko. The earlier consternation began to seem a little funny—perhaps in Tokyo Sachiko had caught something of Etsuko's nervousness. That wearing, rankling city must surely affect the nerves of one as delicate as herself. Had her fears been morbid, then, and was her view of the situation now the right one?

About a week after her return she found an opportunity to ask Taeko.

Taeko, back early from the studio, was in her room looking at a doll she had brought with her. It was a doll on which she had taken special pains: an old woman in sombre kimono and garden sandals, crouched under a stone lantern. She was listening to autumn insects, one was to imagine.

"You have done a beautiful job, Koi-san."

"It is rather good, I think."

"Beautiful. Much the best thing you have done lately. You were

right to make in an old woman. There is a sort of sadness about
it. . . ." Sachiko paused when she had finished praising the doll.
"Koi-san, I had a strange letter while I was in Tokyo."
"Oh?" Taeko was still gazing at the doll.
"From Okubata."
"Oh?" She turned to face her sister.
"Here it is." Sachiko handed Taeko the letter, still in its foreign
envelope. "Do you know what is in it, Koi-san?"
"I think I can guess. Is it about Itakura?"
"Yes. Read it if you like."
Taeko was able when the occasion demanded to take on a calm,
unhurried air that made it next to impossible to know what she
was thinking. She quietly opened the letter and read through the
three sheets, front and back, without so much as moving an eye-
brow.
"What a fool. He has been threatening to tell you."
"It came as a real shock. I wonder if you can imagine how sur-
prised I was."
"You should have ignored it."
"He asked me not to tell you he had written. But it seemed simplest to speak to you. I suppose there is no truth in it?"
"He thinks because he is not to be trusted himself other people are not to be trusted either."
"But how do you really feel about Itakura?"
"Feel? I have no feelings one way or the other—at least the sort
of feelings he is talking about. But I am grateful. He did save my
life."
"I see. That is what I thought."
Okubata's suspicions had been aroused, according to his letter,
after the flood; though he had said nothing to her, however, Taeko
discovered later that, for some time before the flood, he had been
behaving disagreeably toward Itakura. Itakura at first dismissed
his complaints lightly, suspecting them to be only evidence of a
rather childish anger at the undeniable fact that Itakura could and
Okubata could not visit the Ashiya house. After the flood, Okubata's complaints, opener and more bitter, came to be directed at
Taeko too. Okubata said that he meant to talk only to her, that he
was ignoring Itakura, and that he hoped she would say nothing
to the fellow; and Taeko, not dreaming that the haughty Okubata

had already spoken to Itakura, did in fact say nothing. Itakura, for his part, said nothing of his own difficulties.

The result of Okubata's efforts was a quarrel with Taeko. Afterwards she refused to come to the telephone when he called, and took care that he had no chance to meet her. His distress was so real, however, that she finally took pity on him. Recently, for the first time in a very great while, she had agreed to see him—on the third of the month, as the letter said. (Taeko was apparently in the habit of meeting Okubata on her way to or from the studio. Although his letter had them meeting in the studio, the details on where and in what manner they met were far from clear. Taeko said vaguely that they took a walk through the pine groves about the place.) Okubata then announced that he had evidence, charged her with the offenses he had described to Sachiko, and insisted that she break off relations with Itakura. When she answered that it was not right to snub the man who had saved her life, he made her promise that she would see Itakura as little as possible, that she would keep him from going too often to the Ashiya house, and that she would have no further business relations with him—that she would no longer have him take her advertising photographs. To carry out these promises, she had to give Itakura her reasons, and when she did she learned that a similar promise had been forced from him, and that he too had been sworn to silence.

That in general was Taeko's story. Since then—since the third of the month—she had not seen Itakura and he had not come looking for her. He had called on Sachiko because he was afraid it would arouse her suspicions if his visits were suddenly to stop, said Taeko, and he had purposely chosen a time when she herself could be out.

This explanation might do for Taeko, but what of Itakura? Even if Okubata had no reason to doubt the one, he might well doubt the other. Taeko need not feel in the least indebted to Itakura, he argued. There had been a good reason for the heroism. Would so cunning a man brave such danger if he did not expect a reward? Say though he would that he was just wandering around the neighborhood, he had had everything planned in advance. Why be grateful to an ambitious schemer who did not know his place in the world—a man so lacking in honor that he could think of stealing the fiancée of his old employer?

Itakura protested strongly. Okubata was quite mistaken. It was precisely *because* Taeko was Okubata's fiancée that he himself had been so concerned at the time of the flood. He had rescued her from a sense of obligation, and it pained him to be misunderstood. And he did have common sense: he could not imagine Koi-san's marrying into a family like his.

And how did Koi-san weigh the two arguments? To be quite honest, she could not deny having sensed Itakura's real motives. He was clever enough not to reveal them too openly, but there was more behind his bravery than a feeling of indebtedness to the Okubata family. Whether consciously or not, he had worked that day for Taeko, and not for his old employer. But that made no difference. As long as he kept his distance, she could pretend she noticed nothing. Itakura was very useful. He would run about on errands for her, and she might as well use him, especially since he seemed to think it a privilege to be used. Such in any case was her view of her relations with him. But Okubata, a timid, nagging sort of man, misunderstood completely. She and Itakura had therefore decided that they would see each other as little as possible. Okubata's doubts should now be at rest, and probably he regretted having written to Sachiko.

"But he is so strange. It would be far better for him to ignore Itakura."

"What seems like nothing at all to you, Koi-san, is not so simple for him."

Taeko no longer hid the fact that she smoked. She took a white tortoise-shell cigarette case and a lighter from her obi and lighted a gold-tipped imported cigarette, by that time something of a rarity. Silent for a moment, she rounded her full lips into an "O" and blew several smoke rings.

"While we are on the subject." Her face was turned to one side. "Have you thought about my trip to France?"

"I have been thinking about it."

"Did you talk to Tsuruko?"

"We talked about all sorts of things, and I was on the point of mentioning it. But then I decided not to. It involves money, and we have to be careful. I think we should let Teinosuke do the talking."

"And what does he say?"

"That if you are really serious he will see what is to be done. But he thinks there might be a war."

"Will there be, do you think?"

"Who knows. He thinks it would be a good idea to wait a little longer, though."

"I suppose he is right. But Mrs. Tamaki is going to France, and she says she will take me with her."

Sachiko had been thinking her problem would be solved if she could keep Itakura, and Okubata too, at a distance; and one possibility would be to send Taeko abroad. With the situation in Europe changing more and more rapidly, she hesitated both because it would worry her to send her sister off alone and because she was quite sure the main house would never agree. It might help matters if Mrs. Tamaki were to be with her.

Mrs. Tamaki did not mean to stay long, said Taeko. It had been many years since she was last in Paris, and just as she had been thinking that she should go for a look at the most recent fashions, the flood had made it necessary to rebuild her school. She meant to take advantage of the interruption, and to be away perhaps six months. Taeko would do well to study in France for a year or two, Mrs. Tamaki felt, but if she was lonely at the thought of staying on by herself the two of them could come back together. It would certainly do her no harm to stay for six months only. Mrs. Tamaki would arrange for her to come back with some impressive title. It was not likely that war would begin so soon—Mrs. Tamaki meant to leave in January and return in July or August—but if it did, well, they would have to give themselves up to fate. Each would be a support to the other, and since Mrs. Tamaki had friends in both Germany and England, they could always find asylum somewhere. The opportunity was not likely to come again, said Taeko. She was prepared to brave a little danger.

"And with Itakura to worry about, Kei-boy has decided it will be all right for me to go."

"I think so myself. But I will have to talk to Teinosuke."

"See if you can get him to argue with the people in Tokyo."

"There is no hurry, is there, if she is not leaving until January?"

"But the sooner the better. When will Teinosuke be going to Tokyo again?"

"He will have to go two or three times before the end of the year, I suppose. You must get to work on your French, Koi-san."

21

MRS. STOLZ, Fritz, and Rosemarie were leaving for Manila on the *President Coolidge,* which sailed the fifteenth. Rosemarie, impatient that Etsuko's visit to Tokyo should be taking so long, was after Taeko and the maids every day. She was not back yet? Why was she not back yet? Then she was back, and Rosemarie waited each day for school to be out. Etsuko would throw down her books and run for the fence.

"*Rumi, komm'!*" Rosemarie would clamber over the fence, and they would jump rope barefoot on the lawn. Sometimes Fritz and even Sachiko and Taeko joined them.

"*Ein, zwei, drei, vier.*" Etsuko could count to twenty or thirty in German, and she had her favorite phrases: "*Schnell! Schnell! Bitte, Rumi. Noch nicht.*"

One day Rosemarie's voice came through the thick leaves at the fence: "Take care of yourself, Etsuko."

"*Auf Wiedersehen,* Rumi. Write to me when you get to Hamburg."

"You write too."

"I will. I promise. Say hello to Peter."

"Etsuko!"

"Rumi! Fritz!"

Fritz and Rosemarie burst into *Deutschland über Alles.* Sachiko went out to see what was happening. The two German children, high in a plane tree by the fence, were waving their handkerchiefs at Etsuko, who waved back. The ship had apparently just sailed.

"Rumi! Fritz!" Sachiko too ran over and began waving her handkerchief.

"*Auf Wiedersehen,* Etsuko's mother."

"*Auf Wiedersehen.* Take care of yourselves. And come back to Japan some day."

"And you come to Hamburg, Etsuko and Etsuko's mother."

"We will, we will. We promise. As soon as Etsuko is big enough. Take care of yourself, Rumi." Sachiko's eyes clouded over at the silly little game.

The Stolzes being very strict with their children, there was always that call "Rumi!" from across the fence when the girl had been playing too long; but Mrs. Stolz saw how much these last few days meant to the children. Free from the usual summons, Rumi would play with Etsuko on into the evening, lining up dolls in the parlor, changing their clothes, and in the end catching the cat Bell and dressing her too. As they took turns at the piano, Rosemarie would say: "Have another, Etsuko."

That meant: "Play another, Etsuko."

Mr. Stolz's departure had been so sudden that Mrs. Stolz was left to pack and to close the house. Every day Sachiko would see her at work. From the second-floor veranda one looked down at the back of the Stolz house whether one wanted to or not, and without meaning to spy, Sachiko saw almost as if it were being played on a stage for her how furiously Mrs. Stolz and the maids worked. She had often admired the kitchen utensils, always arranged by size around the stove and the cook's table, and always as polished and shining as weapons in an armory. The cleaning, the laundering, the cooking were so regular that the Makiokas had only to glance next door to know what time it was.

There had once been an incident involving the two young Japanese maids—the two who had preceded the maids now in the Stolz house. To Sachiko they had seemed models of willingness and industry, but Mrs. Stolz had disagreed. She was really too stern, they sometimes complained to Sachiko's maids. Determined to show by her own example that not a moment of the day need be wasted, she would push them on to another job as soon as they had finished one. It was true, they admitted, that they were better paid than if they worked in a Japanese house, and that they learned many useful things, but they scarcely had time to breathe the whole day long. Admirable housewife though Mrs. Stolz was, she was not easy to work for.

One morning O-aki, out sweeping the sidewalk, went on to sweep the Stolz sidewalk too. It was little enough to repay them for sweeping the Makioka sidewalk so often, she thought. Unfortunately Mrs. Stolz saw her, and scolded the maids fiercely: what was this, letting someone else do the work they should be doing? The maids fought back. They were not avoiding work, and they had not asked O-aki to sweep the sidewalk. She had done it out of kindness and only the one morning. They would see that she did not do it again. Possibly because Mrs. Stolz did not understand what they were trying to say, she was not prepared to forgive them. In the end the maids said they thought it best if they went looking for new jobs. Go, then, retorted Mrs. Stolz. Sachiko, hearing the story from O-aki, sought to intercede, but the maids were firm: much though they appreciated her kindness, they would rather she said nothing. Their resentment went beyond the morning's incident. They worked as hard as they could, and yet Mrs. Stolz, not even a little grateful, told them in every other breath how stupid they were. It was true, they supposed, that they were not as bright as she, but when she had other maids she would begin to appreciate how diligent they had been. If she were to see the light and apologize, they might reconsider. Otherwise this would be a good chance to leave. Mrs. Stolz made no effort to keep them, and the two maids departed together. After the present maids came, it began to seem that the earlier maids had had reason to be angry. Mrs. Stolz once admitted to Sachiko that it had been a mistake to let them go.

The incident suggested much about Mrs. Stolz's nature; but the fact that she was not all sternness, that she had her gentle and affectionate side, became clear to Sachiko at the time of the flood: Mrs. Stolz, hearing that two or three half-drowned flood refugees had taken shelter at a near-by police box, gathered shirts and underwear for them, and urged the maids to give away any summer kimonos they did not need; pale and tearful, she worried about her husband and children, and even Etsuko; and when her family came home safely in the evening, she ran out with that delirious squeal to meet them. Sachiko could still see her clinging fiercely to her husband, there under the sandalwood tree. Was such warmth not admirable? No doubt all German ladies were outstanding, but Mrs. Stolz must be outstanding even among Germans. There could be few so fine and noble. The Makiokas had been lucky to have such neighbors; the two families had seen too little of each other. Sachiko had heard that foreigners kept aloof from Japanese, but the Stolzes had been quite unreserved from the start—they had sent over a beautiful cake when they moved in, and Sachiko regretted now that she had not followed Etsuko's example. Mrs. Stolz could have given her some good recipes.

There were other neighbors who were sorry to see the family go, and tradesmen who were delighted at being able to buy a sewing machine or an electric refrigerator at a remarkably low price. Mrs. Stolz tried to sell unneeded household goods to friends and acquaintances. Pieces no one wanted she sold for a lump sum to a furniture store.

"Nothing left in the house. We eat from this till we leave," she laughed, pointing to a picnic basket.

Knowing that she meant to add a Japanese room to her house in Germany, the neighbors gave her antiques and wall hangings and the like. Sachiko offered a brocade that had belonged to her grandmother. Rosemarie gave Etsuko a doll and carriage she was especially fond of, and Etsuko gave in return a colored photograph of herself at the dance recital, and the kimono she had worn that day (pink silk, it was, decorated with flowery parasols).

Rosemarie was allowed to spend her last night in Ashiya with Etsuko, and "noisy" would not begin to describe that night. Etsuko gave her bed to Rosemarie and borrowed Yukiko's couch. The two were in no hurry to sleep.

"How long will this go on?" Teinosuke pulled the covers over his head as the two girls came storming down the hall. Finally he switched on the lamp at his pillow. "Two o'clock in the morning!"

"Not really!"

"Do you think you should let them get so worked up? Mrs. Stolz will be annoyed with us."

"But it is the last night. How can she possibly mind?"

"Ghost!" There were steps outside the bedroom door. "Father, what is 'ghost' in German?"

"Tell her the German for 'ghost.' "

"*Gespenst.*" Teinosuke was surprised that he remembered.
" 'Ghost' is *Gespenst* in German."

"*Gespenst.*" Etsuko tested the word. "Rumi, this is a *Gespenst.*"

"Let me be a *Gespenst* too." The party was livelier than ever.
"Ghost!"

"*Gespenst!*"

The two ran shouting up and down the hall. Soon, with
Rosemarie in the lead, they invaded Sachiko's bedroom. They
had sheets over their heads, and they pranced about the room
and out into the hall again. "*Gespenst!* Ghost!" In bed at about
three, they were still too excited to sleep. And Rosemarie was
homesick. She was going back to her mother's. Teinosuke and Sachiko had to get up in turns to comfort her. It was daybreak before
the house was finally quiet.

Bouquet in hand, Etsuko went to the pier with Sachiko and
Taeko. The ship sailed at seven. There were few children to
see Rosemarie and Fritz off, among Rosemarie's friends only
a German girl named Inge (Etsuko, who had met her occasionally at the Stolz house, liked to call her *ingen-mame,* "kidney
bean") and Etsuko herself. The Stolzes boarded ship early in
the day, and the Makiokas set out after dinner. As the taxi
passed the customs gate, the *President Coolidge* was suddenly
over them, a nightless city bathed in floodlights. The walls and
ceiling of the Stolz cabin were a creamy green, and the bed
was a mound of flowers. Mrs. Stolz sent Rosemarie off to show
Etsuko the ship. With only a nervous fifteen minutes to spare,
however, Etsuko remembered little afterwards except that everything was wonderfully luxurious and that she climbed up and
down a great many stairs. She returned to find her mother and
Mrs. Stolz in tears. Very soon the warning gong sounded.

"Beautiful—like a department store moving off." Taeko who
had on a thin summer blouse, shivered in the autumn breeze
from the harbor. For some time they could pick out Mrs. Stolz
and the children on deck; and when it was no longer possible
to distinguish one from another, they could still hear Rosemarie's
voice, shrill and determined: "Etsuko, Etsuko!"

22

Manila
September 30, 1938

Dear Mrs. Makioka:

This is the month for typhoons in Japan, and I am much worried about you. You have had too many misfortunes these last few months. I hope you have no more. I suppose that all the boulders and the sand and mud on the national highway and in Ashiya have been cleared away. And I suppose that everything is back to normal, and that people are enjoying life once more. Perhaps you have good neighbors in the house we lived in. I often think of our pretty garden, and of the quiet streets where the children rode their bicycles. They had many pleasant times. How good you were at keeping them entertained! I must thank you again for all your kindness. They often speak of you, and sometimes they feel very homesick for you and Etsuko. Peter wrote from the ship to tell us what a pleasant time they had in Tokyo with your sister and Etsuko. It was very good of your sister. We are most grateful. The other day I had a cable from Hamburg. Peter and his father arrived safely and are staying with my sister, who has three children of her own. I suppose Peter has become the fourth.

We are an enormous family here too. There are eight children, and I am the only hen in the coop. Sometimes the children quarrel, but for the most part they get along well. Rosemarie is the oldest of all, and knows it. Every afternoon we go out on our bicycles through the beautiful streets and stop for ice cream.

Take care of yourselves. And please give my very best regards to your husband, your sisters, and dear Etsuko. You are to come to Europe when everything is quiet again. All we can hear now is the rattle of swords, but I do not think we will have war. No one wants it. I am sure Hitler will take care of the Czech problem.

Sincerely,
HILDA STOLZ

P.S. I am sending a little piece of embroidery. I hope you like it.

Mrs. Stolz's letter, written in English, reached Sachiko on about the tenth of October, and a delicate hand-embroidered tablecloth arrived two or three days later. Sachiko put off writing her thanks—it seemed such a chore, and besides, who would translate for her? Teinosuke asked to be excused. One evening, strolling along the Ashiya River, she met the Japanese wife of a German named Hening, a lady to whom Mrs. Stolz had introduced her. Mrs. Hening said the translation would be no problem. Although she did not write German well herself, she could ask her daughter, who wrote both German and English. But even then Sachiko had trouble collecting herself for a letter to a foreign country. It was some time later that she finally sat down at her desk and had Etsuko sit down at hers, and sent the letters off to Mrs. Hening.

Soon afterwards Etsuko received a package from New York— the shoes Peter had promised to buy in the United States. In spite of the care with which he had taken the measurements, they were too small. Elegant patent-leather party shoes, they were a great sorrow to Etsuko, who tried in spite of the pinch to force her feet into them.

"What a shame. If only they had been too large instead of too small."

"But how could he have made such a mistake? Did he measure too close?"

"Maybe your feet have grown. We should have told him to allow a little room. I am sure his mother would have thought of that if she had been here."

"What a shame, though."

"Oh, give it up, Etsuko. You are not going to wear them, no matter how you try." Sachiko did not know what to say of the well-meant present, and in the end she did not write to thank Peter.

Taeko was almost never around the house in the daytime: she was off at her studio, hoping to fill all the orders for dolls before she went abroad. Mrs. Tamaki had arranged for her to take French lessons at the especially low price of ten yen a month for three lessons a week, from the wife of an artist who had studied in Paris for six years. Back from school each day, Etsuko would look through the net-wire fence at the Stolz house and listen to the autumn insects in the weed-choked yard. With a companion so near at hand, she had seen very little of her school mates and had rather grown away from them. Eager though she might be now to make new friends, it was not easy to find friends who suited her. The Makiokas thought another family with a daughter like Rumi might move into the Stolz house, but the house was designed for foreigners, and most foreigners had left the Far East. Sachiko too was bored. She practiced her calligraphy and gave koto lessons to O-haru. One day she remarked in a letter to Yukiko: "Etsuko is not the only one who is lonely. Everything seems sad this autumn. I wonder if it is a sign of age—I have always liked the spring, and this is the first time I have understood the autumn."

It had been an eventful year: Yukiko's *miai* in the spring, the dance recital in June, the flood and Taeko's narrow escape, the death of the dancing teacher, the departure of the Stolz family, the trip to Tokyo, the typhoon, the dark shadow cast by that letter from Okubata—and now, with everything quiet, it was as if a gap had opened in her life. She could not help thinking how close she was to her younger sisters. Since she got along well with her husband, and since Etsuko was an only child, albeit a rather difficult child, Sachiko's life was if anything too peaceful, too lacking in storms and trials. The unsettling agents had always been her sisters. Not that they were a bother to her: she was delighted at the color they gave the life of the family. Sachiko among the four sisters had in largest measure inherited her father's love of excitement. She disliked too quiet a house. Out of deference to her married sister and her brother-in-law she could not purposely lure her younger sisters away. Still she rejoiced in the fact that they preferred her house to the main house, and it seemed natural that they should be where there was more room and where children were less of a problem. Though he kept a worried eye on the main house, Teinosuke understood his wife's feelings and always welcomed Yukiko and Taeko. Everything considered, then, her feelings for the two had not been what one usually understands by the affection of sister for sister. She was sometimes startled at the thought that she spent more time worrying about her sisters than about her husband and daughter, but they were like daughters—they were on a level with Etsuko in her affections, and at the same time they were her only friends. Left alone, she was surprised to note that she had no friends worthy of the name. Her relations with other housewives had for the most part been cool and formal. Because of her sisters she had not needed friends. She knew that she was as sad to lose Yukiko and Koi-san as Etsuko was to lose Rosemarie.

Teinosuke was quick to sense this gloom. "Kikugorō is coming to Osaka next month," he said, looking up from the entertainment column of his newspaper.

Suppose they go on the fifth. And might Koi-san not want to go too? Kikugorō was dancing one of her favorite roles. Taeko, however, said that since she would be especially busy the first part of the month, she would choose another day. Teinosuke and Sachiko took Etsuko instead.

Sachiko was thus able to make up for the September failure and to show Etsuko the Kikugorō Kabuki; but in the lobby between plays Teinosuke noticed what must have escaped Etsuko, that Sachiko's eyes were filled with tears. Though he knew how quick she was to weep, he found this too strange.

"What is the matter?" He led her quietly into a corner. The tears were streaming over her face.

"Have you forgotten? It was in March, on exactly this day. Today might have been its birthday." Sachiko pressed her fingers to her eyes.

23

MRS. TAMAKI was leaving in January, and it was already mid-November. More and more nervous, Taeko asked when Teinosuke might be going again to Tokyo. Although he usually made a business trip once every two months or so, he had not had occasion to go for some time. Shortly after the Kikugorō performance he left for two or three days in Tokyo.

His trips always being on short notice, Sachiko heard of this one only the afternoon before, when he telephoned from Osaka.

She immediately summoned Taeko home from the studio to consider how Teinosuke might best present her case. The real reason—or one reason—for her desire to go to France and become a true modiste was the possibility that she might have to support Okubata. Permission to go to France on such grounds, however, presupposed permission to marry Okubata, and the troublesome question of her marriage was not likely to be solved in such a short time. And Teinosuke did not relish becoming a marriage go-between. Since Taeko wanted only to go to France and hoped to avoid needless complications, might it not be better for her to set aside the problem of her relations with Okubata, at least for the time being? What pretext should they give, then? Sachiko suggested this: although Taeko did not consider her life ruined by the incident, still her name *had* once been in the newspapers; it did not seem likely that she would make a really good marriage, therefore, and she wanted to be able to support herself. She would not refuse a good proposal if one came along, they might add, and indeed she thought that returning from France with a degree of some sort might improve her prospects—people who had dismissed her as a juvenile delinquent would have cause to reconsider. Suppose she asked permission on these grounds, with the understanding that the main house need not pay for her wedding?

Taeko had no objections. She wanted Sachiko to do as she thought best.

Sachiko suggested another possible argument when she talked to Teinosuke that evening. Wanting to keep Taeko from both Okubata and Itakura, she had her own reasons for favoring a trip abroad; but since she had discussed the Itakura affair with no one, not even her husband, she could ask Teinosuke only to speak of Okubata—to mention the fact that Okubata had appeared at the Ashiya house two or three times recently; that although he had appeared sincere, he could no longer be considered a clean, wholesome youth; and that Teinosuke had learned of his fondness for the teahouses, and thought him a not very promising person. Teinosuke could then point out that it might be well to let Taeko have her way and go abroad, her interests happily having turned to sewing, and that, though undeniably

at the age of discretion, she had made a mistake once and
ought for a time to be kept where Okubata could not reach her.
The money was after all Taeko's, thought Sachiko, and surrender-
ing it could bring no hardship to the people in the main house.
Still, they were old-fashioned. They were not likely to approve
of a woman's going abroad, and it might be well to frighten
them a little, to hint that Taeko was about to elope again.

Teinosuke stayed in Tokyo a day longer than he had planned.
Feeling that Tsuruko would be more approachable than her
husband, he chose two o'clock on the afternoon of the third
day for his visit to Shibuya. Tsuruko said that she could not
give him an answer until she had talked to Tatsuo. She would
have to write to Sachiko, and, seeing that Koi-san was in such
a hurry, she would write as soon as possible. She was sorry they
had to bother Teinosuke so often with family matters.

Sachiko did not expect a quick answer. She knew how slow
her sister was, and she knew too that Tatsuo needed time for his
decisions. Ten days passed, and the end of November drew near.
Suppose Teinosuke raise the question again—but Teinosuke was
not enthusiastic. He had opened the discussions, he said, and
they were no longer an affair of his. Finally Sachiko herself
wrote to ask what had been decided about Koi-san, and to point
out that if she was to go at all it would have to be in January.
The silence continued. Possibly Taeko should go to Tokyo—she
might hurry them a little. Taeko was ready to leave for Tokyo
in two or three days when, on November 30, a letter came.

November 28

DEAR SACHIKO,

*Forgive me for not having written sooner. I hope you
are well. I was much relieved to learn from Teinosuke that
Etsuko's troubles are over. Soon it will be the New Year, my
second New Year in Tokyo; and how I dread the winter! Tatsuo's
sister-in-law says it takes three years to get used to the Tokyo
winter. Through her own first three winters she had nothing but
colds. I envy you, being able to live in Ashiya.*

*Teinosuke must be very busy, and it was good of him
to explain Koi-san's problems to us in such detail. I always feel*

guilty about having to bother him. I should of course have answered sooner, but as always I have been so busy with the children that I have not been able to collect myself for a decent letter; and then the fact that Tatsuo's opinion is the opposite of your own has made it difficult for me to write, and I have been putting the letter off from day to day. I hope you will forgive me.

In a word, Tatsuo sees no reason for Koi-san to be so touchy about the newspaper affair. It happened eight or nine years ago, and no one even remembers. If she really thinks she cannot marry and will have to support herself, then she is simply being too sensitive. It may sound strange from a relative, but Tatsuo says that with her looks, training, and talent he can guarantee her a very good marriage indeed, and that she is absolutely not to worry. We find it odd, then, to be asked to give her money. I am told that there is no money specifically in Koi-san's name. We have thought about her wedding, but there is no money that we have to turn over on demand. Tatsuo is moreover quite opposed to her becoming in any way a working woman. He hopes that she will always have it as her goal to make a good marriage when the time comes, and to become a good wife and mother. If she must have a hobby, doll-making will do. Dressmaking is quite out of the question.

This is not the time for a decision on Okubata. We would like to have the question left open. Koi-san is a grown woman, and we have no intention of being as strict as we once were. If you will quietly keep watch over her, there is no reason why she should not see him from time to time. We are far more upset at the idea that she thinks of making a career as a seamstress.

I hate to ask it after all the trouble Teinosuke has gone to, but could you pass this on to Koi-san? I cannot help thinking that all of her troubles come down to her being so long unmarried. It seems more urgent than ever to find someone for Yukiko, and as soon as we possibly can. Are there to be no more proposals this year?

I have left a great deal unsaid, I am sure, but I shall stop here. My best regards to Teinosuke, Etsuko, and Koi-san.

TSURUKO

"What do you think of it?" Sachiko showed the letter to Teinosuke that evening. She had not yet spoken to Taeko.

"There seems to be a difference of opinion about the money."

"That is the point."

"What have you heard yourself?" Teinosuke asked.

"I am not really sure who is right. But I do remember hearing that Father left money with Tatsuo. It might be better not to say anything to Koi-san."

"There is too much at stake. Tell her as soon as possible, and be sure she understands."

"What about Kei-boy?" Sachiko asked. "What did you say about him? You made it very clear that he is not as nice as he once was?"

"I said in general what I thought. But I had a feeling she would rather not talk about him. I did say that for the time being they ought not to see too much of each other. I meant to say if she asked me that we were opposed to the marriage, but she changed the subject."

" 'We would like to have the question left open.' Do you suppose they want her to marry him?"

"I suspect so. I thought so when I talked to her," Teinosuke answered.

"You might have done better to bring up the question of the marriage first, then."

"I wonder. They would probably have said that there was even less reason to go abroad."

"You are probably right."

"In any case, it is more than I can manage. Let Koi-san talk to them herself. No more for me," Teinosuke said.

Sachiko was reluctant to transmit Tatsuo's views unmodified, since Taeko was even more hostile to the main house than Yukiko; but Teinosuke thought it best to hide nothing. When she showed the letter to Taeko the next day, the results were exactly as she had expected. Taeko said that she was no longer a child, that she did not need the guidance of any Tatsuo, that she understood her affairs better than anyone else. And what was so wrong with a woman who worked? The people in Tokyo still worried about family and position, and it seemed to them a disgrace that the Makioka family should produce a seamstress. But was that not ridiculously old-fashioned? She would go herself and explain everything, she would make them see how wrong they were. And she was furious about the money.

Always before, when she attacked Tatsuo, she had refrained from criticizing Tsuruko, but this time her anger was aimed rather at Tsuruko: Tsuruko was wrong to let Tatsuo say what he did. It was true that the money was not in Taeko's name, but had she not heard from Aunt Tominaga, and any number of times from Tsuruko herself, that Tatsuo had money in trust for her? And now they chose to cloud the issue. They kept having children and needing more money, and no doubt Tatsuo had changed his plans, but how could Tsuruko support him? Very well, Taeko knew what to do. She would have her money. She wept and stormed, and Sachiko was in a real sweat to calm her. Sachiko understood well enough, but should Koi-san lose control of herself? Maybe Tei-nosuke had explained badly. And in any case she should try to understand their own position. Although it would be very fine indeed for her to have everything out in Toyko, could she not proceed more cautiously? Sachiko and her husband would be most embarrassed if Koi-san went picking a fight—it was not to find themselves in a fight that they had sided with her.

In a few days, Taeko was her old placid self again. It became clear that she had only given vent to the rage of the moment, and that she did not have courage to carry out her threats. Even so, Sachiko was uneasy.

Then one afternoon, possibly around the middle of December, Taeko came home from her studio earlier than usual.

"I have stopped my French lessons."

"Oh?" Sachiko tried not to seem interested.

"And I am not going to France."

"Oh? That seems a shame, now that your mind is made up. But I think you are right. Tatsuo and Tsuruko have been so worried."

"It makes no difference about them. Mrs. Tamaki has decided not to go."

"Really? And why has she changed her plans?"

"The school is opening again in January, and she says she has no time."

Mrs. Tamaki had meant to go to Europe while the school

was being repaired. It had been found, however, that rebuilding would have to begin from the very foundations. Setting out in search of a new site—to rebuild would take both time and money with materials and manpower so short—she had been lucky enough to find at a most reasonable price a foreign-style house that could be used almost unaltered as a sewing school. She had decided that she wanted to reopen the school immediately. Her husband, worried about the tensions in Europe, had all along been opposed to the trip. Mr. Tamaki knew a military attaché recently back from Europe, and had heard that Germany, France, and England, although on the surface friendly since the Munich Conference in September, had by no means reached an accord; that the English, unprepared for war, had only compromised to put the Germans off guard; and that the Germans, quite aware of this, meant to go the English one better. War could not possibly be avoided. For all these reasons, Mrs. Tamaki had decided not to go to France. Taeko too had changed her plans. But whatever the main house in Tokyo might say, she added, her plans to learn sewing were not to be changed. She would begin her lessons again when the sewing school opened in January. And since she felt more and more strongly the need to do without an allowance from the main house, she was in an even greater hurry to learn her trade.

"That is very well for you, Koi-san, but think of us. What excuse can we make if you go on with your sewing?"

"You can say you know nothing about it."

"Do you really think we can?"

"I will make it look as though I am working on my dolls, and you can say that I seem to have stopped the sewing."

"Think of the trouble when they find out."

There was something a little threatening about Taeko's eagerness to be independent and her determination to collect the lump sum of money from the main house even if it meant being disagreeable. Sachiko foresaw the day when she and her husband would be caught in a cross fire. Whatever Taeko said, she could only answer: "Think of the trouble."

24

WHAT WERE Taeko's real motives for setting out to become a professional woman? Did one not find certain inconsistencies if, as she said, she still hoped to marry Okubata? Married to so worthless a person, she should be prepared to support him, but he was the pampered son of a good family, a man who wanted for nothing, and the day when he might worry about his next meal seemed a very distant one indeed. The excuse was not enough to justify a course in sewing and a trip to Europe. Taeko ought rather to be planning for a home with the man she loved. Since the precocious girl had always been one to lay her plans carefully, she might well be preparing for distant eventualities, and yet Sachiko was troubled. She would find herself wondering whether Taeko did not in fact dislike Okubata, whether she was not seeking a way to break with him. The trip abroad might be her first step, and the sewing her means of supporting herself once she had made the break.

Sachiko was becoming suspicious again.

She was puzzled about the Itakura affair. She had seen nothing of Itakura since that short visit, and there was no sign that he telephoned or wrote to Taeko, but with Taeko away from home the better part of the day, the two of them could arrange whatever they pleased. It was most unnatural that Itakura should have disappeared. The suspicion arose that he was seeing Taeko in secret. It was the vaguest of suspicions, with no evidence to support it, but for that very reason it grew stronger as the days passed. Soon Sachiko came to feel that she could not be wrong. For one thing, Taeko's appearance, her manner, her facial expressions, her dress, her speech were changing. Of the four sisters, Taeko had always been the most open and direct—to put her case favorably, the most modern—but lately that directness had been strangely transformed into a certain rudeness and vulgarity. It bothered her little to display herself naked, and sometimes, even before the maids, she would bare her bosom to the electric fan, or she would come from the bath looking like a tenement woman. She seldom sat with her feet tucked properly under her. She preferred to throw them out to one side, or, worse still, to sit with her legs crossed, her kimono coming open at the skirt. Quite indifferent to the prerogatives of age, she would start eating or go into or out of a room ahead of her sisters, or take a place higher at the table. Sachiko was left wondering what horror might be coming next when they went out or had guests. In April, at the Gourd Restaurant in Kyoto, Taeko went in ahead of them all, took a place higher than Yukiko, and started eating before anyone. Afterwards Sachiko whispered to Yukiko that she never again wanted to dine out with Koi-san. And in the tearoom of the Kitano Theater in the summer, Taeko sat silently by while Yukiko poured tea. She had long been guilty of such rudeness, but recently it had become worse. One evening Sachiko noticed that the door to the kitchen was half open. Through the trap door between the heater and the bath, also five or six inches open, she caught a glimpse of Taeko in the tub.

"Would you please close the door to the bathroom, O-haru."

"Leave it open, leave it open!" shouted Taeko.

"You left it open on purpose?" asked O-haru in surprise.

"I left it open to hear the radio."

Taeko had left all the doors open between the parlor and the bath so that she could sit in the tub and listen to a symphony concert.

Another time—was it in August?—Sachiko was having her afternoon tea when the young man from the Kozuchiya came to deliver kimonos. She listened to the conversation from the dining room.

"But you are putting on weight, Miss Taeko. That kimono is almost ready to split at the hips."

"It may not split," answered Taeko. "But you can be sure I will have people following me."

The young man roared with laughter.

Sachiko was aghast. She had not dreamed that her sister could descend quite to that level. Since the young man was not one to sport openly with customers, there must be something in Taeko's manner that urged him on. No doubt such exchanges were the usual thing when Sachiko was not around. With her dolls and her dancing and her sewing, Taeko was on familiar terms with a wider range of classes than her sisters, and it was natural that she should be better versed in the crude and vulgar, but Sachiko, who had to then only been amused at Taeko and her tendency to treat her shut-in sisters as children, thought that matters had finally reached a point where she must interfere. Though by no means as old-fashioned as Tsuruko, she was still distressed to think that anyone in the family could carry on such a conversation. Taeko was under the influence of someone, she was sure, and she began to note something that reminded her of Itakura's joking manner, his general outlook, his vulgarity.

There were reasons why Taeko should be different from the rest of them. It was not entirely fair to reprove her. She alone of the four sisters had known almost nothing of their father's prosperous days, and she had but the dimmest memories of her mother, who had died just as the youngest daughter was starting school. Their pleasure-loving father gave the daughters everything they wanted, and yet Taeko had never really known—had never had an immediate sense of—what had been done for her. Yukiko, so little older, had vivid memories of her father, and would often recount how he had done this for her on one occasion, and that on another, but Taeko was too young, and the favors she received had never been entirely real. Although her father might have let her go on with her dancing, that too had been stopped soon after her mother died. She remembered chiefly how her father would describe her as the darkest and plainest of them all, and indeed she must have been a most untidy girl, with her face quite uncared for and her clothes so shapeless that she could have passed for a boy. She liked to say that some day she too would finish school and dress up and go out as her sisters did. She too would buy pretty clothes. But before she had her wish, her father died, and the good days were over for the Makioka family. Very shortly afterwards came the "newspaper incident."

As Yukiko said, Koi-san's behavior was natural enough for an impressionable girl who had never enjoyed the affection of her parents, and who, always at odds with her brother-in-law, was unhappy at home. Though someone was perhaps to blame for the incident, the main fault lay rather in the girl's surroundings. Koi-san's grades in school had been no worse than those of her sisters, Yukiko pointed out. In mathematics she had been the best of the four. Still there could be no doubt that the incident had branded her and to an extent twisted her. And Tatsuo, in the main house, had never been as good to her as to Yukiko. He did not really get along well with either of the sisters, but he had very early labelled Taeko the heretic. While showing some affection for the older sister, he hinted that he thought the younger a nuisance. In the course of time this favoritism became evident in the allowances he gave the two, and even in their clothes and accessories. Yukiko had her trousseau ready. Taeko on the other hand had virtually nothing that could be called expensive except a few things she had bought with her own money or had had Sachiko buy for her. It was true, as the people in the main house said, that since Koi-san had money of her own they must be fair and give Yukiko more. Had Taeko herself not told them that she would rather they gave more to Yukiko? As a matter of fact she was less than half the burden on the main house Yukiko was. Sachiko sometimes noted with a mixture of surprise and admiration how clever Koi-san was at saving money even while she followed the latest foreign styles—she did remarkably well, even granting that she had a sizable income. (Now and then Sachiko wondered whether a necklace or a ring might not have come from the display cases of the Okubata store.) Of the four sisters, Taeko knew best what it meant to have money. Sachiko had grown up in her father's prosperous years, whereas Taeko had been at her most impressionable when the family fortunes were on the decline.

Fearing that this unusual sister would sooner or later be the cause of another scandal, and that she herself and her husband might be implicated, Sachiko thought of sending Taeko off to the main house, but it was clear that Taeko would not agree to go, and it seemed likely moreover that the main house was not willing to take her. Tatsuo would have been expected, after hearing Teinosuke's story, to say that he wanted Koi-san where he could watch her, and he had said nothing of the sort. Once so afraid of what people would think, he had overcome his resentment at having his sisters-in-law in Ashiya. Still he must also have economic reasons for his silence: he had come to look upon Taeko as semi-independent, and he only had to send her a little spending money each month. Troublesome though the youngest sister was, then, Sachiko could not but feel sorry for her.

But they had to have an honest talk.

The New-Year festivities passed, and Sachiko came to suspect that Taeko had taken up sewing again.

"Has Mrs. Tamaki's school opened?" she asked one morning as Taeko started to leave the house.

"Yes."

"There is something I must talk to you about, Koi-san." Sachiko led her sister back into the parlor, and they faced each other across the stove. "There is the sewing, of course, but there is something else I have been wanting to ask you. I hope you will not hide anything from me."

Taeko stared at the burning wood. Her skin glowed in the fire light, and she seemed to be holding her breath.

"I might begin with Kei-boy. Do you still mean to marry him?"

For the first few minutes Taeko was silent. As Sachiko tried various ways to reveal her suspicions, she saw that her sister's eyes were filled with tears. Taeko pressed a handkerchief to her face.

"Kei-boy has been deceiving me," she sniffled. "You remember you said he was seeing a geisha?"

"Yes. Teinosuke heard of it in some teahouse."

"It was true."

Led on by Sachiko's questions, Taeko made her confession: When in May she had heard from Sachiko of the geisha, she had on the surface dismissed the story as no more than a rumor. As a matter of fact, it had become an issue from about then. Okubata had long been fond of the teahouses, but his excuse was that in his gloom at being unable to marry Taeko he only went out now and then in search of consolation. He hoped she would be generous with him. He wanted her to believe that he only had an innocent drink or two with the ladies, and that this in no way marred his chastity. Taeko accepted the explanation. As she had told Sachiko, Okubata's brothers and uncles were great pleasure-lovers, and her own father had frequented the quarters. She had therefore been prepared to accept a certain amount of dissipation as inevitable. She would not make a nuisance of herself, provided that Okubata remained celibate.

Then, from a trivial incident, she came to see that he had been quite brazenly lying to her. In addition to that geisha in the Soēmon Quarter, he had a dancer, and she had had a child. When the secret was discovered, Okubata offered a model apology: the affair with the dancer had taken place long before; the child having only been foisted on him—it was quite impossible to know who the father was—he had been relieved of his paternal responsibilities too. As for the geisha, he had no apology to offer, he could only vow that he would not see her again. But Taeko sensed from his flippant manner that he thought it a matter of little concern to have lied to her. She could never trust him again. Having actually seen the receipt for the separation money he paid the dancer, she knew that he could not be lying about at least that. There was no evidence that he had parted with the geisha, however, and Taeko could not be sure there had not been other affairs besides. Although Okubata protested that he was still determined to marry her, and that his affection for these women was not to be mentioned in the same breath with his love for her, she could not but feel that she too might be thrown away as the plaything of a moment. In sum, she began to dislike him. Even so, she did not find it easy to break the engagement. The foolish girl had trusted him, and now her own sisters would point at her and laugh. But she wanted to be away from him for a time. She wanted to think matters over quietly by herself.

There could be no doubt that the trip abroad was a means toward that end, and, as Sachiko had guessed, Taeko meant to learn sewing so that she could support herself afterwards.

Her distress was at its worst when the flood came. Until then she had thought of Itakura as—well, a sort of servant. With the flood, her feelings toward him underwent a very quick change. She knew that Sachiko and Yukiko would think her frivolous, but they had never known how it was to be saved when you had given yourself up for lost. Kei-boy said that Itakura had his reasons. Very well, suppose he had. He had still risked his life; and in the meantime what was Kei-boy himself doing? Far from risking his life, had he shown even a trace of real concern, of real affection? It was the flood that killed the last of her love for him. As Sachiko knew, he appeared at the Ashiya house after trains were running from Osaka. Setting out to look for her, he went only as far as Tanaka, and decided that he could not get through the little water that was running across the street there. After a time he wandered into Itakura's house, and thereupon went back to Osaka. He arrived at Itakura's in an immaculate blue suit and a Panama hat, a walking stick in his hand and a camera over his shoulder—it was a wonder no one gave him a cuffing for his elegance. Had it not been because he was afraid of spoiling the crease in his trousers that he turned back at Tanaka? Was the contrast not too complete with Teinosuke and Itakura and even Shōkichi, mud from head to foot? She had long known how particular Okubata was about his appearance, and she had not expected him to plunge into the mud with them, but he had not even shown ordinary human sympathy. If he was really so pleased and relieved to know that she was safe, should he not have gone again to the Ashiya house? He had said that he would stop by later, and had not Sachiko too expected him? And did he think that he had acquitted himself of his responsibilities by inquiring after her? It was at such times that one saw the real worth of people. She had been resigned to enduring his spendthrift ways, his fickleness, his general uselessness, but she had quite lost hope when she saw that he was unwilling to sacrifice the crease in his trousers for his future wife.

25

TEARS STREAMED over her cheeks and she sniffled occasionally; but she had told her story thus far clearly and with great composure. Her tone became heavier as they moved on to the question of her relations with Itakura. Her replies to Sachiko's questions being limited to affirmation or denial, Sachiko had to fill in the gaps for herself. This was the story Sachiko pieced together:

Itakura came to seem in many ways a pleasant contrast to Okubata. Laugh though she might at the people in the main

house, Taeko was not wholly unconscious of family and position, and she tried to hold herself back; but her heart worked
against her conservative mind. She was not one to lose her head,
whatever the crisis, and even after she fell in love with Itakura
she was by no means blind to his faults. Particularly because of
her failure with Okubata, she looked far into the future and
weighed the profit and loss, and after examining the balance as
cooly as she could, she concluded that her happiness lay in
marrying Itakura. Sachiko, who had guessed a good deal of the
truth without even considering that her sister might want to
marry the man, was stunned. Taeko, however, had taken the
man's defects into her calculations: that he was an uneducated
person who began as an apprentice, that he came from a family
of tenant farmers in Okayama Prefecture, that he had the peculiar
coarseness of emigrants returned from America. All that was true,
said Taeko, but as a man Itakura ranked several grades higher
than Okubata, the pampered child of wealth. His physique was
splendid, and he would not hesitate to plunge into a fire if it
seemed necessary. And best of all, he could support himself and
his sister—he stood in sharp contrast to a man who lived by
begging from his mother and brother. Going off to America
without a cent, he had made his way with help from no one, and
learned his trade—and art photography required not a little intelligence. Although his formal education left much to be desired,
he had his own sort of intelligence and sensibility. He was more
of a student, she had discovered, than Okubata with his university diploma. Family and inherited property and diplomas had
lost their appeal for her; Okubata had been enough to show
her how worthless they were. She meant now to be quite practical. She asked only that her husband satisfy three conditions:
he must have a strong body, he must have a trade, and he
must be willing to offer up his very life for her. In Itakura all
three conditions were satisfied, and there was another point in
his favor: with three brothers back on the farm, he had no family
responsibilities. (The sister who kept house for him would go
home once he was married.) She would have his affections to
herself. Her position would be far easier than that of the wife
of the oldest and wealthiest family imaginable.

The perceptive Itakura had early guessed her feelings, one would judge from his behavior. Taeko had but recently confessed them. The year before—early in September, when Sachiko was in Tokyo and Okubata's suspicions forced Taeko and Itakura to be more cautious—they had debated what to do, and Taeko had declared herself for the first time. Thus Okubata succeeded in bringing them together. When it became clear that Taeko was actually proposing marriage, Itakura seemed unable to believe his ears— perhaps he was but making a show of propriety, perhaps he was indeed caught by surprise. He said that he had not dreamed of such good fortune, and that he would like two or three days to think matters over. Beneath his surprise and hesitation there seemed to run another vein: it was such a stroke of luck that considerations of personal advantage and disadvantage had no meaning. But ought not Koi-san to make sure that she would not regret her decision? He himself would no longer be able to see the Okubata family, he said, and Koi-san would probably be cast out by the main branch of her family and even by the Ashiya branch. And they would be misunderstood and even ostracized. He could fight his way through, but could Koi-san? People would say that he had cleverly bagged a Makioka daughter. But it made no difference what people in general said—Kei-boy's reproaches would be harder to bear. Then Itakura's tone changed: Kei-boy would not understand in any case, and it was rather to the old master and the old mistress (Kei-boy's mother) and to the young master (Kei-boy's brother) that Itakura himself was indebted. Kei-boy was a younger son to whom he owed nothing directly. Angry though Kei-boy would be, the old mistress and the young master might even be grateful to Itakura. They were quite possibly still opposed to Kei-boy's marrying Koi-san. Itakura suspected that such was indeed the case, although Kei-boy had said nothing. So, while making a show of hesitation, Itakura contrived to accept Taeko's proposal.

They made their plans in great detail: for the time being they would keep their engagement absolutely secret; a problem to be solved before that was how to break Taeko's engagement to Okubata; they should do nothing rash, but should take their time and if possible bring Okubata to renounce her voluntarily. For Taeko the best step possible would be to go abroad; their marriage could well be put off two or three years, and in the meantime they should prepare themselves to meet possible economic sanctions; and Taeko should therefore go ahead with her sewing. Then, suddenly, the opposition of the main house and Mrs. Tamaki's change in plans made it impossible for Taeko to go abroad. Meanwhile, Okubata followed her about, partly to annoy Itakura, she believed. As long as she was in Japan, he would never break the engagement. If, on the other hand, she were to send a letter from Paris insisting that he give her her freedom, and if she were to keep out of sight for a time, he might finally resign himself to what had to be. Now he would be more difficult than ever. Concluding that she had stayed in Japan for Itakura, he would trail her even more closely. In a distant foreign country she could stand being away from Itakura for six months or a year, but with him almost beside her, and with Okubata clinging to her, she found she could not live without him. There was no alternative, then. Since it was becoming impossible to deceive the world and Okubata, they might as well face the difficulties and be married as soon as possible. There were only two reasons for hesitating: they were not entirely ready to support themselves, and Taeko, prepared though she was for ostracism, feared catching Yukiko in the wake of the affair. She wanted to wait until a marriage had been arranged for the latter.

"And you have only made the promise, then? You have gone no farther?"

"We have gone no farther."

"You are telling me the truth?"

"There has been nothing more than the promise."

"Would you think a little longer, then, before you do anything more?"

Taeko did not answer.

"Please, Koi-san. How can we face people, and especially the people in Tokyo?" Sachiko asked in a shrill, excited voice. She saw a pit opening before her eyes. Taeko was strangely calm.

26

For two or three mornings Sachiko called Taeko into the parlor
after Teinosuke and Etsuko had left. She wanted to see how
firmly Taeko's mind was made up, and she found no sign that
her sister could be moved. Sachiko was willing to make concessions if only Taeko would give up the idea of marrying the man:
whatever the main house might think, she and Teinosuke approved of breaking the engagement to Okubata, and, depending
on the circumstances, they might even intercede to see that
Okubata no longer bothered her; although it would be difficult to
recognize the sewing lessons openly, Sachiko could pretend to
know nothing about them; she and her husband would not
really oppose Taeko's becoming a professional woman; and, impossible though it was to do anything at the moment, they would
argue Taeko's case when the time came and see that she received
her money from the main house.

But Taeko only answered that she and Itakura were willing as
their final concession to wait until Yukiko was married. They
hoped Yukiko's marriage would be arranged as soon as possible.

Matters of position and class quite aside, continued Sachiko,
she did not trust Itakura as a person. Since he had worked his way
up from shop apprentice to photographer, he was different from a
pampered youth like Okubata; and yet—Sachiko knew she should
not say so—he had about him the cunning of a man who has seen
too much of the world. Taeko spoke of his intelligence, but
Sachiko herself had observed only that he tended to be very
pleased with himself over things that made no difference. He was
a simple and indeed a rather inferior youth, and his tastes were
far from cultivated. And as for his having become the sort of
photographer he was—he needed only a certain craftsman's in-
stinct. Koi-san, blind to his defects at the moment, would do well
to think long and carefully. It had been Sachiko's observation
that marriages did not last when the husband and wife came from
different stations in life. To be quite honest, she was at a loss to
understand how a woman as discerning as Koi-san could pos-

sibly want to marry such a man. Koi-san would very soon tire of him. Sachiko did find chatterers like Itakura entertaining, but an hour or so was all she could stand.

Taeko admitted that something of the cunning Sachiko noted was inevitable in a man who, as a boy, had been a shop apprentice and who had later seen the world—it had been made inevitable by his surroundings—but there was for all that something surprisingly clean and honest about the man. He was at heart not the sly one Sachiko took him for. It was also true, as Sachiko had pointed out, that Itakura made much of trivialities, and he was disliked as a result; but might that not be evidence of something innocent and childlike? Perhaps he was uneducated, perhaps he was inferior. Taeko was as aware of his defects as anyone, and she would prefer that Sachiko not worry. She did not demand elegant tastes and a subtle mind, she had no objection to a noisy and even a coarse man. Indeed a husband from the lower classes would be easier to handle and less of a worry. Itakura considered it a great honor to be taking her for his bride. His sister too, and his family out in the country—they were overcome with joy at the thought of how high they could hold their heads now. When Taeko went to Itakura's house, he would tell his sister she had no right to be so familiar with Koi-san—in olden times she would have had to kowtow in the next room. They treated her with proper deference, she would have Sachiko know. Taeko was becoming boastful. Sachiko could almost see Itakura, always pleased with himself, announcing that he was going to marry a Makioka daughter. And they had apparently told his family—the thought revolted Sachiko.

She was comforted to see that Taeko did not mean to do anything rash until Yukiko was married. The crisis was therefore not immediate, and Sachiko feared a rebellion if she set out now to bring her sister under control. Since it would be at least six months before Yukiko could be married, Sachiko must argue with Taeko calmly and unhurriedly and prepare the way step by step for a change of heart. For the time being Taeko should be allowed complete freedom. But how sad for Yukiko. No doubt Yukiko would find it distasteful to think that Taeko was waiting for her, and expecting her to feel indebted. There were other reasons why Yukiko had not married, but certainly one reason was the harm done her by that newspaper incident. She owed her sister nothing. Yukiko would probably say that she was in no great rush to be married, and that she felt no resentment toward Taeko for the incident; her fate was not to be determined by anything so trivial. Taeko should go ahead and be married without a thought for her. Taeko for her part might not be trying to saddle Yukiko with a debt, and yet it was a fact that she had been impatient at the latter's slowness. She would hardly have thought of eloping with Okubata, however young she was at the time, if Yukiko had been married or on the point of being married. Although the two sisters never quarreled, one could not deny that their interests conflicted deeply.

Since that day—since she received the letter from Okubata in September of the preceding year—Sachiko had told no one of the Itakura affair. Now it had become too heavy a burden to carry alone. She had always sided with Taeko. She had understood and sympathized, she had encouraged the doll-making, she had rented the studio, she had silently acquiesced in the relations with Okubata, she had interceded with the main house each time there was a disagreement—and this was her reward. But perhaps it was because of her efforts that matters were no worse. There was no telling what scandals they might have had otherwise. The world in general and the people at the main house would probably not agree with her, however, and what distressed her most was the thought of the private detective who was sent out to investigate the family each time there was talk of a husband for Yukiko, and who, each time, dragged Taeko's misbehavior out afresh for the world to see. Sachiko herself did not know the exact details—what exactly had taken place between Taeko and the two men—but Taeko's affairs must seem thoroughly shameful to the disapproving eye. Yukiko's purity should be apparent to everyone. As far as she was concerned, the Makiokas had nothing to hide from investigators, but this scapegrace sister so easily attracted notice that the investigation tended to be concerned more with Taeko and her doubtful points than with the principal herself. And it was even possible that things hidden from the family were known abroad. Might not unwholesome rumors be circulating about Sachiko too, and might they not be responsible for this lack of suitors? There had been no new proposals since the spring of the year before, even though Sachiko had asked all her friends to tell her of likely prospects. For Yukiko's sake, something must be done. When these rumors reached the main house, Sachiko would have a great deal to explain. Teinosuke and Yukiko too would want to know why she had not confided in them. And there might be more chance to make Taeko reconsider if Teinosuke and Yukiko were to have their turns arguing with her.

One evening toward the end of January, Teinosuke was reading a magazine in his study when Sachiko came in and looked solemnly at him, as if there were important matters to be discussed.

"Koi-san seems to have made the promise last September when I was in Tokyo. Etsuko and O-haru were with me, and Itakura came here every day."

"I am responsible too, am I?"

"That is not what I meant. I only wondered if you noticed anything."

"Not a thing. I did think even before the flood, though, that he was a little too friendly."

"But he is that way with everyone, not just Koi-san."

"I suppose so."

"How was he in the flood?"

"Very impressive. He did everything. I suppose Koi-san was very pleased."

"But can't she see how vulgar the man is? I cannot understand her. She flares up and tells me he has this good point and that good point and the other good point. She was sheltered when she was young, and she is too trusting. He has managed to get around her."

"She knows what she is doing. Maybe he is a little vulgar, but she knows a dependable man when she sees one."

"That is exactly what she says."

"That *is* one way to look at it."

"No! You really think she should marry him?"

"Not necessarily. But he would be a better match than Okubata."

"I think just the opposite."

And so she discovered to her surprise that they did not agree.

Under Teinosuke's influence she had begun to dislike Okubata, and even now she did not feel friendly toward him; but when she compared him with Itakura she found him much to be pitied. Even though he was a classic example of the pampered youth, even though he was quite useless, even though one knew at first glance how frivolous and shallow he was—he was an old friend, the child of an old Semba family. He was one of them. Sachiko could foresee great difficulties if her sister were to marry him, but at least for the time being they would not have to worry about what people thought. If on the other hand she married Itakura, she would be held up to public ridicule. Okubata seen by himself was not a happy choice, but he was certainly better than Itakura, and he could be their weapon to turn away the latter.

Teinosuke was more liberal. The question of family aside, he said, there was no point on which Okubata could be given a higher mark than Itakura. Koi-san was right. The conditions for a husband were love, health, and the ability to make a living, and if Itakura satisfied all three, what need was there to worry about family? Teinosuke himself was not particularly fond of Itakura, and only chose him in preference to Okubata, and, knowing that the people in the main house would never approve, he did not feel enthusiastic at the thought of pleading Koi-san's case. But since she was not one to be married in the traditional manner, she should be left free to marry the man she chose. Precisely because she knew herself so well, they should be very cautious about interfering. Yukiko was different, not a person they could turn out to make her way alone. They should do everything for her. They should find her a husband, and be sure that he came from a good family and had money. But Koi-san could take care of herself.

Although Teinosuke would have to give his views if asked, what he said was for Sachiko only. He did not want Sachiko announcing what he thought to the people in the main house, or even to Koi-san. He wanted to remain an outsider.

"And why is that?"

"She is too complicated," he muttered. "There are things I will never understand."

"There are indeed. I took her part in everything, even to the point of letting myself be misunderstood, and now to have her turn on me . . ."

"That is what makes her interesting."

"She could have told me earlier. But to deceive me. This time I am furious with her, really furious."

Sachiko looked like a spoiled child when she wept. The flaming cheeks and the angry tears always made Teinosuke think how it must have been long ago when she quarreled with her sisters.

27

SACHIKO worried about Yukiko, helpless in the main Tokyo house, a different sort from Taeko, who would do what she wanted regardless of the trouble it might cause and the rumors it might start. Sachiko thought she could never apologize enough to Yukiko. She had been asked so earnestly by Tsuruko that September night in Tokyo Station to find a husband for Yukiko; she had hoped she might have a candidate before the end of the year, this year being an unlucky one for Yukiko; and she had then hoped to find someone before the day early in February when the horoscope year would begin. That day was but a week off.

If rumors about Taeko were indeed frightening off prospective husbands, then she must hold herself partly responsible. She had long thought of calling Yukiko back for a conference—Yukiko who would best understand her dissatisfaction with Taeko—and she had hesitated only because of the psychological effect she was afraid it might have on Yukiko to hear of Taeko's misbehavior. Now, however, she was more afraid of what would happen if Yukiko were to hear from someone else. And with Teinosuke, whose advice she had so counted on, taking this extraordinary position, she had no one left but Yukiko. She was trying to think of an excuse for summoning her sister when notice came of a recital in memory of Taeko's old dancing teacher.

RECITAL

YAMAMURA SCHOOL, *in memory of the late Yamamura Saku*
ONE O'CLOCK, *February 21, 1939, Mitsukoshi Hall, Kōrai Bridge,
Osaka.*

THE DANCES (*not necessarily in this order*): *Perfumed Sleeves*
(*Elegy*), *Nanoha,*[1] *Dark Hair, Love Among the Saucepans,
The Battle of Yashima, Gift from Edo, The Curse, Snow, The
Coy One, Bird of Miyako, Eight Scenes, Tea, Moon of
Remembrance, The Maiden at the Well.*

THE DANCERS *and their order of appearance will be announced on
the day of the recital.*

*Although there will be no charge, admission will be by invitation
only. Applications will be accepted from members of this
society and their families until February 19. A letter with
return envelope will be appreciated from anyone who wishes
to attend.*

THE DAUGHTERS OF OSAKA
(*Pupils of Yamamura Saku*)

Early in February, Sachiko sent the printed post card off to
Tokyo. To her older sister she wrote a brief note: for all their
hopes that they would soon have to call Yukiko back to Osaka,
the old year had passed without a single proposal, and here it was
February; although there was no real business at the moment,
Sachiko wanted very much to see Yukiko, and she was sure that
Yukiko would by now be feeling a little homesick; if there were
no particular objection, might Yukiko not be allowed to visit
Ashiya for a time?—there happened to be a Yamamura recital,
the announcement of which she was enclosing, and Taeko, who
was dancing, wanted Yukiko to be present. To Yukiko she wrote
in more detail: with the crisis in China, dance recitals were becoming rare, and this might well be the last for a very long time;
Koi-san, quite out of practice, had at first refused the surprise
invitation to dance, and had at length accepted because such an
opportunity might not come again and because she felt she must
offer something in memory of the teacher; it was just possible
that this would be Yukiko's last chance to see Koi-san in a recital;
unable to learn a new dance on such short notice, Koi-san had

---

[1] Colza or rape, an early-flowering brassicaceous herb.

hastily set about relearning "Snow", which she had danced the
year before; she would at least have to have a different kimono,
however, and the kimono Sachiko had had dyed at the Kozuchiya
(it had a delicate, unobtrusive pattern) seemed to fit the order;
Koi-san was being trained by a leading disciple of the old teacher,
a woman who had a studio in Osaka; Koi-san was thus her usual
busy self, what with practice every day in Osaka, and more practice in the evening to Sachiko's accompaniment, and her doll-
making and all; Sachiko was kept busy at the koto (she had no
confidence that she could do "Snow" on the samisen); although
Sachiko found it hard to be angry with so diligent a worker, still
Koi-san had been a great trial to her, and there were incidents of
which she could not write in a letter, but which she would recount in detail when she saw Yukiko; and Etsuko insisted that
Yukiko, who had missed the last recital, must be present this time.
There was no answer from either Tsuruko or Yukiko. They began
to think that the latter would again arrive unannounced. Late
on the afternoon of February 11—a holiday, the anniversary
of the founding of the Empire—Taeko was having a dress
rehearsal in the parlor.

"Yukiko!" Etsuko was the first to hear the bell.

"Come in, come in," O-haru followed Etsuko to the door.
"They are all in the parlor."

The furniture had been cleared away except for one sofa, and the
rug was rolled up. In the center of the room stood Taeko, parasol
in hand, her Japanese-style coiffure tied up with bright pink
ribbons. Her kimono was the one Sachiko had described, a bronze-
purple with a fine pattern of snow-covered camellias and plum
blossoms. In a corner of the room, Sachiko sat on a cushion, her
koto before her. It was decorated with chrysanthemums in gold
lacquer.

"I thought I would find you all at this." Yukiko nodded to
Teinosuke, who sat on the sofa in a winter kimono, his long underwear showing at the hem. "I could hear the koto from outside."

"We wondered what could have happened to you." Sachiko's
hands rested on the koto. Yukiko liked noise and gaiety for all
her apparent melancholy, and Sachiko saw a wave of emotion
cross the white face (possibly Yukiko was tired).

"You came on the Swallow?"

Yukiko did not answer Etsuko's question. She turned instead to Taeko. "Is that a wig you have on?"

"Yes. They finally had it ready today."

"It looks wonderful on you, Koi-san."

"I thought I might want to wear it sometimes myself," said Sachiko. "Koi-san and I had it made together."

"You can wear it too, Yukiko."

"When you get married."

"Listen to the woman! Do you really think it would fit me?"

Yukiko laughed happily at Sachiko's joke. But she was right: because of the rich hair, one did not notice that she had an extremely small head.

"You came at just the right time," said Teinosuke. "With Koi-san's wig ready, we thought we would have her dance in full costume. A special performance for me. The twenty-first is a Tuesday, and I am not at all sure I can go."

"And I have to be in school," said Etsuko.

"They should have made it a Sunday."

"That would have attracted too much attention. It would not do to attract attention at a time like this."

"Would you go over that passage again please?" Taking the parasol in her right hand, Taeko held it with the handle upright.

"No, begin at the beginning," said Teinosuke.

Etsuko too was in favor of beginning again for Yukiko.

"But Koi-san will be exhausted, going through it twice."

"Think of it as practice, and do it again," said Sachiko. "Of course I am freezing, here on the bare floor. You may not have noticed."

"How about a pocket-warmer," suggested O-haru. "It will make a great difference if you sit on a pocket-warmer."

"Possibly I should."

"I can have a rest while you fuss about your pocket-warmer." Taeko put down the parasol and, sweeping aside the long skirts, walked over to the sofa. "May I have one too?" She lighted the cigarette Teinosuke gave her.

"And I," said Yukiko, leaving for the bathroom, "ought to wash my hands."

"This sort of thing always makes Yukiko so happy. I know: you can take us out to dinner. Yukiko came all the way from Tokyo, and Koi-san has been dancing for us."

"And I am the one who pays?"

"Of course. It is your duty. There is not a thing in the house, and I have meant all along to be taken out to dinner."

"I would be happy with almost any kind of feast," said Taeko.

"Would you like to go to the Yohei or the Oriental Grill?"

"Either one will do. We can ask Yukiko."

"After all that time in Tokyo, she might want some good fish."

"Suppose we have a bottle of white wine, then, and go on to the Yohei," said Teinosuke.

"I will have to dance very hard to pay for my dinner." As O-haru came in with the pocket-warmer, Taeko put out the lipstick-smeared cigarette and began arranging her skirts.

28

ALTHOUGH IT SEEMED that Teinosuke, busy closing books for a certain company, might have to miss the whole concert, he telephoned from the office that morning asking Sachiko to let him know when Taeko would be dancing. At about two-thirty, Sachiko called to say that if he left then he would be just in time. Unfortunately a client appeared, and at a warning from O-haru, after he had wasted another half hour, that if he did not come at full speed he would be late, he swept the client from the room, and, without bothering to put on a hat, ran for the elevator and across the street to the Mitsukoshi Building. He arrived at the hall on the eighth floor to find that Taeko was already dancing. Since the recital was a private one limited to Taeko's group, to the Osaka Society, and to readers of the latter's newspaper, there should not have been a large audience. Such recitals were becoming rare, however, and with all sorts of people using their influence to get tickets, almost every seat was taken, and spectators were even standing at the back of the hall. Looking over their shoulders toward the stage, Teinosuke noticed, perhaps two yards from him, a man with a Leica raised to his face. There could be no doubt that it was Itakura. Pulling back into a corner, Teinosuke stole an occasional glance at the photographer, who had his overcoat collar turned up and who hardly looked away from the camera. No doubt he meant to hide his face, but the overcoat, a relic of his Los Angeles days, was so suggestive of the movies that it only attracted attention.

The dance went smoothly. Taeko had done this "Snow" a year before. But she had practiced only a month, and this was her first performance on a real stage—she had until then danced either on Mrs. Kamisugi's portable stage or in the Ashiya house—and it was inevitable that there should be something a little inadequate about her dancing, as if she were trying to occupy too large a space. Aware of the danger, Taeko had sought to hide her defects behind the samisen accompaniment, and she had particularly asked the daughter of Sachiko's koto teacher, Kikuoka Kengyō, to play for her. And yet there was no sign of stage fright. For all Teinosuke could see, she was as composed as ever. The calm deliberation with which she danced made it difficult to believe that but one month's practice could have prepared her for so grand a stage. Perhaps the rest of the audience did not notice, but to Teinosuke there was a rather irksome feeling of defiance, of brazenness, almost, something that challenged the critic to praise or damn as he saw fit. Still, she was twenty-eight years old, an age at which a geisha would be well past her prime, and it was not strange that she should have this touch of bravado. He had thought when she danced the year before that the metal beneath the gilt was finally showing through—Taeko usually looked ten years younger than she was. Did the dress of long ago make women look older, then? Or only Taeko, because traditional dress offered such a contrast to her usual foreign brightness? Or was it this defiant manner that aged her?

The moment the dance ended, Itakura tucked his camera under his arm and hurried out. An instant later a man ran headlong through the audience and almost flung himself at the door through which the gaudy overcoat had disappeared. For a moment Teinosuke did not realize that the second figure was Okubata. Teinosuke too ran out into the lobby.

"Why did you take Koi-san's picture? Have you forgotten that you promised not to?" Okubata was trying to control his voice. Itakura looked at the floor, like a child being scolded. "Give me the camera."

Okubata began searching his man as a detective would search a suspected criminal, running his hands over the pockets. He took the camera out briskly and put it into his own pocket. Then, reconsidering, he pulled at the lens with a trembling hand and threw the camera to the floor as hard as he could. It was the work of a moment. Okubata was gone by the time the other spectators noticed, and Itakura had picked up his camera and was walking dejectedly away. He had stood as if unable to raise his head before the son of his old master, and even when the Leica he prized as his very life was skidding across the floor he did not seem to think of resorting to the physical strength in which he had such confidence.

Teinosuke returned to his office after paying his respects backstage and complimenting Taeko. It was not until late that night, when Etsuko and his sisters-in-law were in bed, that he told his wife of the incident. Itakura, whether on his own initiative or at Taeko's request, had apparently planned to slip in and to stay only long enough for pictures of "Snow." Okubata, who had been hidden in the audience, intercepted him as he was hurrying off, mission accomplished. Though it was hard to say when Okubata had arrived, no doubt he had suspected that Itakura would be present. Like Teinosuke, he had been watching from afar. He would not let Itakura escape—such in any case was the only explanation Teinosuke thought possible. He could not tell whether they knew he had seen the little drama.

She had been afraid Okubata would be at the recital, said Sachiko, and she had dreaded having to speak to him. Koi-san assured her that he had not been informed; and besides, he had to spend two or three hours in the shop every afternoon except Sunday. Still Sachiko was uneasy. There had been two or three lines in the newspapers, and Okubata, if he saw them, might have guessed that Koi-san would be dancing. Having cast a worried eye over the audience from time to time, Sachiko was sure he had not been present before Taeko's "Snow." Yukiko, who spent more time in the audience than backstage and would have

noticed, had said nothing. Perhaps Okubata had slipped in at
about the same time as Teinosuke. Or perhaps he had been in
disguise. Sachiko did not know about Koi-san, but she herself
had not seen Itakura, and of course had had no intimation of
what happened in the lobby.

"They were able to keep from being seen backstage. It would
have been very awkward for them if we had noticed."

"Itakura held himself back, and nothing came of it. But we
cannot have two men fighting over Koi-san in public. We will
have to do something before the rumors start."

"Why do you refuse to worry with me, then?"

"I am worrying. Only it is not my place to interfere. Does
Yukiko know about Itakura?"

"One reason I asked her down was that I wanted to talk to her.
I have been looking for a chance."

Sachiko had meant to wait until the recital was over, and two
or three mornings later she was left alone with Yukiko after Taeko,
who said that she wanted to have her picture taken in her dancing
costume and would like to borrow Sachiko's kimono again, had
left in a taxi with her suitcase and wig box and parasol.

"I am sure she is going to Itakura's." Sachiko proceeded to
summarize the events between that shocking letter from Okubata
in September and the scene in the Mitsukoshi lobby.

"Was the Leica broken, then?"

"I wonder. Teinosuke says that the lens at least must have
been damaged."

"And they are taking pictures again because the film was
spoiled?"

"Probably." Sachiko saw that Yukiko had listened to the
story calmly. "This time I really, *really* think I have been stabbed
in the back. I am furious, more furious the more I think of it.
There is no point in going into all the details, but I am not the
only one. Has anyone been hurt as you yourself have, Yukiko?"

"Me? I have not been especially bothered. . . ."

"You are not to say that, Yukiko. Think of it all, since that
newspaper affair. Maybe you would rather I changed the subject,
but think of the trouble every time there is a chance of your
getting married. And after the way I have protected her and taken

her part—to go off and make such a promise to such a man and not say a word to me."

"Have you spoken to Teinosuke?"

"Only after I could not keep it to myself any longer."

"And what did he say?"

"He said he did have opinions, but he would rather not be involved."

"Why?"

"He finds Koi-san hard to understand. Frankly, he does not trust her, and he would rather have as little to do with her as possible. Just between the two of us, he really thinks it would be a mistake to interfere. He thinks someone like Koi-san should be left to do what she wants, even to marry Itakura. He says she can take care of herself, and we should let her. I feel just the opposite, and I have not been able to talk to him."

"Maybe I should have a good talk with Koi-san."

"I do wish you would, Yukiko. There is nothing for us to do but take turns trying to talk sense into her. She does say she will wait until after you are married, of course."

"If it were any other man, I would not mind seeing her married first."

"But Itakura *is* impossible."

"Am I wrong in thinking there is something a little vulgar about Koi-san herself?"

"You may be right, I am afraid."

"In any case, Itakura is no brother-in-law for me."

Sachiko had expected Yukiko to understand, but for one so reserved to express herself so clearly suggested even stronger opposition than Sachiko's own. The two sisters agreed that they would be delighted to have Okubata marry into the family if he was the alternative to Itakura. Sachiko saw that her task must be to sell Okubata.

29

With Yukiko back, the Ashiya house was gay and noisy again. Yukiko, so inarticulate that one hardly knew she was about, added little to the noise, but one could see from the difference she made that something bright was hidden behind that apparent melancholy and reserve. And it was like a spring breeze to have all the sisters under one roof. The mood would be broken if one of them were to go.

Someone had finally rented the Stolz house. Every night the kitchen blazed with light. The new renter, a Swiss, worked as adviser to a Nagoya company and was away from home most of the time. The house was managed by his young wife, who groomed herself like an Occidental but who had the face of a Chinese or a Filipino. Since there were no children, the place was far from being as lively as when the Stolzes were there. Still, it made a great difference to have someone in that Western-style house, so desolate and run-down that it had begun to look like a haunted house. Etsuko had hoped for a little girl to take Rosemarie's place. She had many school friends, however, and they had already formed their own little set, inviting one another back and forth to tea parties and birthday parties and the like. Taeko, as busy as ever, spent more time away than at home. She had dinner out one night in three. Teinosuke suspected that she did not want to be where her sisters could argue with her. He feared a permanent breach, and in particular he was afraid that Yukiko and Taeko might turn away from each other. But one evening, looking for Sachiko in the Japanese room across from the bath, he slid the door open to find Yukiko sitting on the veranda with her knees tucked under her chin, while Taeko cut her toenails for her.

"Where is Sachiko?"

"She has gone to see Mrs. Kuwayama," answered Taeko. "She should be back soon."

Yukiko quietly pulled her bare feet out of sight and took a more lady-like posture. As he closed the door, Teinosuke saw Taeko kneel to gather up the shiny parings. It was only a glimpse, and yet there was a beauty in the scene, sister with sister, that left a deep impression on him. Though they might disagree, there would not often be serious conflicts between them.

One night early in March, Teinosuke dozed off to be awakened by his wife's tears against his face. He could hear a faint sobbing in the darkness.

"What is the matter?"

"Tonight—tonight—it is exactly a year." The sobbing was more distinct.

"I wish you would try to forget. It does you no good to remember."

With the taste of tears in his mouth, Teinosuke thought how happy Sachiko had seemed when they went to bed. This flood of tears was too sudden. But it had been in March, he remembered, that Mr. and Mrs. Jimba invited them to meet Nomura, and perhaps, as Sachiko said, exactly a year had passed since the miscarriage. Natural though it was that his wife should continue to grieve after he himself had forgotten, these attacks were most puzzling. When the family had gone cherry-viewing the year before, and when they had gone to the Kabuki in the fall, he had seen just such a flood of tears, and he had seen too that Sachiko was her usual self immediately afterwards. This time it was the same. In the morning she looked as though nothing had happened.

Also in March, Katharina Kyrilenko sailed for Germany on the luxury ship *Scharnhorst*. Teinosuke and the rest, while meaning to repay the Kyrilenkos for the party two years before, had only seen them occasionally on the train. Taeko continued to bring reports of "the old one" and the brother and sister and Vronsky. Though less enthusiastic about dolls, Katharina had not entirely given them up. Just when Taeko was beginning to forget about her, she would appear with a new doll to be criticized. She had made considerable progress these two or three years. In the course of time she had acquired a "friend," a young German named Rudolf, and it was Taeko's theory that the doll-making suffered because Rudolf was more interesting. Rudolf worked in the Kobe office of a German company. Taeko, who had been introduced to him one day in Kobe, frequently saw him out walking with Katharina. One knew immediately that he was a German, she said: he was tall and strongly built, and not so much handsome as rugged. Katharina had apparently decided to go to Germany because, for one thing, she had grown to like Germany since she met Rudolf, and for another, Rudolf had arranged for her to stay with his sister in Berlin. But her real destination was England, where the daughter by her former husband was living. She would have a springboard once she arrived in Germany.

"Is Yudōfu sailing with her, then?"

Taeko called Rudolf "Yudōfu," "Steamed Curds" (a pun on "Rudōfu," the nearest a Japanese could come to pronouncing his name), and Sachiko and the others spoke of this gentleman they had never met as if that were really his name.

"Yudōfu is staying in Japan. Katharina is going alone with an introduction to the sister."

"Will she go to England for the little girl, then, and back to Berlin to wait for Yudōfu?"

"I doubt it."

"This is the end of Yudōfu?"

"I rather imagine so."

"That seems very businesslike of her."

"But I think that is really best," Teinosuke put in. They were talking over the dinner table. "I doubt if they were really in love— they were just playing."

"Unmarried people *have* to behave that way when they come to Japan alone." Taeko apologized for the two.

"When does she sail?" asked Teinsouke.

"At noon, day after tomorrow."

"If you have any time day after tomorrow," said Sachiko to her husband, "you might go see her off. It was wrong of us not to have them over for dinner."

"We never quite got around to it, did we."

"And so you should see her off. Etsuko will be in school, but the rest of us mean to go down to the ship."

"Yukiko too?" asked Etsuko.

Yukiko smiled and shrugged her shoulders. "Just to see the ship."

After about an hour in his office, Teinosuke took an express for Kobe. He had almost no time to talk to Katharina. Only "the old one," Kyrilenko, Vronsky, the Makioka sisters, a gentle-

man Taeko told them was Rudolf, and two or three other foreigners and Japanese saw Katharina off. Teinosuke and his family
left the pier with the Kyrilenkos. By the time they said good-bye
on the Bund, Rudolf and the other foreigners had already disappeared.

"The old one does manage to hide her age," said Teinosuke.
"The old one" looked especially young from the rear. She walked
off, as always, with a quick, deerlike step.

"I wonder if she will ever see Katharina again. She is old, no
matter how young she looks."

"And neither of them shed a tear," said Yukiko.

"She even seemed embarrassed when we cried."

"It takes courage to go off to Europe alone, with a war about
to begin. It takes courage for the old one too. But then I suppose
this seems like nothing after the Revolution."

"Born in Russia, grew up in Shanghai, drifted to Japan—and
now she is off for Germany and England."

"I suppose the old one is in a bad temper. Remember how she
dislikes the English?"

" 'I, Katharina, always fight. Now she go. I, not sad. Happy.' "
For the first time in a great while, they had Taeko's imitation of
"the old one." Having just heard "the old one" herself, they stood
roaring with laughter in the middle of the street.

30

"But Katharina has improved—grown up," said Teinosuke.
"I kept wondering if she was so good looking the last time I saw
her." They had walked up from the Bund, and they continued
the conversation as they sat in a row—Sachiko, Teinosuke, Yukiko,
Taeko—at the Yohei, where they had made reservations that
morning.

"It was just her make-up. And she was dressed very carefully."

"She has changed her make-up since she met Yudōfu," said
Taeko. "The whole tone of her face has changed. She has the

most amazing confidence in herself. Just you watch, Taeko, she said. I'll find myself a rich husband in Europe."

"She is not bothering to take along much money, then?"

"In a pinch she can always be a nurse. She was a nurse in Shanghai, you know. She probably has only enough money to keep her for a little while."

"And she and Yudōfu have said goodbye?"

"I imagine so."

"Yudōfu is no fool," said Teinosuke. "His only responsibility is to write a letter to his sister. And did you notice the way he waved at her once or twice and then marched off ahead of everyone?"

"I did indeed. A Japanese could never have done that."

If a Japanese tried to behave like Rudolf, Teinosuke said, it would be "Sudōfu," "Soured Curds," and not Yudōfu. But Sachiko missed the point.

"What is 'Sudōfu'? A French novel?"

"By Molnar. Remember?"

There was room for ten customers around the L-shaped counter. The Yohei was therefore quite packed with only the Makiokas, a man who looked to be a broker from the neighborhood, two or three of his employees, and beyond them two young women, no doubt geishas, chaperoned by an older geisha, and there was barely room for one person to pass behind the chairs. The door was constantly opening. A newcomer would ask—even beg—for a place; but as is so often the case with proprietors of sushi[1] restaurants, the old man made rudeness a part of his trade. Unless the applicant was a steady customer who had a reservation, he would be turned off with a snort as if to say that he ought to be able to see for himself what his chances were. The passer-by, unless he happened to come at a slack time, had little chance of being admitted. Even the steady customer who had made his reservation, but who appeared fifteen or twenty minutes late, would be told to go walk around the block for an hour or so. The old man had learned his trade at the Yobei, a famous old sushi restaurant in Tokyo, no longer in business. The name of his shop was in fact a modification of "Yobei." He was a native of

[1] Balls of vinegared rice, highly seasoned and usually topped with strips of raw or cooked fish.

Kobe, however, and he made his *sushi* to fit the Kobe taste. Although he did give his customers the vinegared rice and fish any Tokyo *sushi* man would, the Kobe influence was evident in his choice of materials. He always used white Kobe vinegar, never yellow Tokyo vinegar, and always a thick soy sauce not seen in Tokyo. He offered only fish taken before his very eyes, so to speak, here along the shores of the Inland Sea. No fish was unsuitable for *sushi*, he insisted—on that point at least he agreed with the old Yohei. He tried conger eels and blowfish and dace and even oysters and sea urchins, and scraps of halibut or clam, and sometimes red whale meat. Nor did he limit himself to fish: he used mushrooms too, and bamboo sprouts and persimmons. But he was opposed to tuna, that most common of *sushi* ingredients; and scallops and omelettes and the commonplace *sushi* that goes with them were never seen in his restaurant. Though he sometimes cooked his fish, the prawns and abalone were alive and moving when they reached the customer.

Taeko had long known the old man. One might say that she discovered him. Eating out often, she was wonderfully well informed on the little restaurants in downtown Kobe. She had found this one in the days when, in an alley opposite the stock exchange, it was even smaller than now, and she had introduced Teinosuke and the rest. She first gave them a description with gestures: he looked like the dwarf with the enormous, mallet-shaped head one sees in illustrations to horror stories; he turned customers off most haughtily, and he attacked a fish with his carving knife as though it had insulted him. When Teinosuke went to see for himself he found the man ridiculously like Taeko's description. His customers lined up before him, he would ask what they wanted, and then proceed to give them what he himself preferred: he would cut enough sea bream, for instance, to go around, and after that he would give everyone prawns and halibut. And it annoyed him when a customer had not finished the first round in time for the second. "You still have some left," he would say to anyone who carelessly let two or three pieces accumulate. His fish varied from day to day, but he always had prawns and sea bream, of which he was especially proud, and he liked to begin a course with the bream. He did not welcome the un-initiated person who asked for tuna. When a customer displeased him he would pepper the *sushi*, and grin as his victim started choking.

Sachiko, with her particular fondness for sea bream, soon became a regular customer, and Yukiko was as fond of this *sushi* as she. With a little exaggeration, one might say that it was one of the pulls that brought Yukiko back from Tokyo. She thought of the house in Ashiya when she became homesick, but somewhere in a corner of her mind there was also a picture of this restaurant, and the old man, and the glistening bream and prawns under his determined knife. Although Yukiko for the most part preferred Western food, she would find that after two or three months of Tokyo tuna, she could almost taste the bream of Akashi. That white flesh, newly cut, gleaming like mother of pearl, became the image of the bright Osaka-Kobe region, and of her sister and niece and the house in Ashiya. Sensing that Kobe *sushi* was one of the particular pleasures Yukiko came back for, Teinosuke was always careful to take her once or twice to the Yohei. He would sit between Sachiko and Yukiko, and make sure that his wife and sisters-in-law had saké in their cups.

"Delicious. Absolutely delicious." Beyond the shy Yukiko, who sat huddled over her saké, Taeko was expressing her pleasure quite openly. "This is the sort of thing we should have treated the Kyrilenkos to."

"We really should have," said Sachiko. "We could have asked the brother and the old one to come along with us this evening."

"I did think of it. But then we only had reservations for four, and I doubted if they would eat raw fish."

"Nonsense," protested Taeko. "Foreigners love *sushi*." She looked inquiringly at the old man.

"They eat it, all right." The old man reached down with a water-swollen hand to restrain the prawns, which were scampering over the counter. "They come in now and then."

"And have you forgotten how Mrs. Stolz ate it?" asked Sachiko.

"But there was no raw fish in the *sushi* you gave her."

"They eat raw fish too," said the old man. "It depends on the kind, though. They don't seem to like tuna much."

"Why is that?" asked the broker.

"I don't know, but they don't seem to. Tuna and bonito they don't much eat."

"Remember Mr. Roots?" One of the younger geishas, turning to the older one, spoke in a soft voice. She did not seem in the least self-conscious about her Kobe accent. "He would eat raw fish only if it were white."

"I do remember." The old geisha was busy with a toothpick. "The red seems to bother foreigners."

"It must not look very appetizing," said Teinosuke. "A lump of raw, red fish on top of the dead-white rice."

"Koi-san," Sachiko called down the counter. "What would the old one say about a place like this?"

"Not here, not here!" Taeko resisted the impulse to do an imitation of "the old one."

"You've been down to the harbor?" The old man cut open a prawn and spread it over a ball of rice, which he then cut into sections an inch or so wide. One prawn was set before Sachiko and her husband, the other before Yukiko and Taeko. They were such large prawns that a whole one per person would have left room for nothing else.

Teinosuke took up a piece of the still-wriggling prawn. "We saw someone off on the *Scharnhorst,* and while we were about it we did a little sight-seeing."

"German ships are very different from American ships," said Sachiko. "Even a luxury ship like the *Scharnhorst.*"

"Remember how bright and cheerful the *President Coolidge* was?" Taeko agreed with her sister. "The *Scharnhorst* made you think of a battleship."

"Eat it up, young lady, eat it up." The old man was impatient. Yukiko had not touched the *sushi* before her.

"But the thing is still moving." It was always a trial for Yukiko to have to eat as fast as the others. She liked the "dancing *sushi*" of which the old man was so proud, the prawns that were still moving when they were set out to be eaten; she liked it as well as the sea bream. But she wanted at least to wait until it had stopped moving.

"That is what makes it good."

"Go ahead and eat it. Are you afraid it will haunt you?"

"Would I be afraid of a prawn's ghost, I wonder," mused the broker.

"What about a frog's ghost, Yukiko?"

"A frog's ghost?"

"It happened when we were in Tokyo. Tatsuo took us out to
have barbecued chicken one evening. The chicken was very good,
but for the last course they killed a frog, and it let out a horrible
croak. Yukiko and I were as white as two sheets. Yukiko said
she could hear that croak the rest of the night."

"I would rather talk about something else." Quite sure that it
was no longer moving, Yukiko took up a piece of the "dancing
sushi."

31

CHOOSING A weekend in mid-April, Teinosuke, the three sisters,
and Etsuko made their annual pilgrimage to Kyoto. On the
train back, Etsuko suddenly ran high fever. She had complained
of feeling tired for about a week and had not been as lively as
usual in Kyoto, and when they found, upon reaching home, that
she had a temperature of about one hundred and four, they immediately called Dr. Kushida, who suspected scarlet fever and
said he would come again. The next morning he said there could
be no doubt about it—one symptom of scarlet fever was this
bright flush over the whole face, except around the lips—and
was in favor of sending her to an isolation ward. Since Etsuko
violently disliked hospitals, however, and since the disease, though
contagious, was not usually passed on to adults and did not often
appear more than once in the same house, he finally agreed to
treat her at home, provided it was in a room apart. Fortunately
Teinosuke's study was in a cottage off from the main house.
Brushing aside his protests, Sachiko moved Teinosuke into the
main house and turned his study, one room with a small ante-
room, into Etsuko's hospital suite. In addition to electric heating
and gas, the study had been fitted with a sink for light cooking
when, some four or five years before, Sachiko had convalesced
there from a severe attack of influenza. Teinosuke moved his desk
and some of the book shelves and cabinets to the master bedroom

on the second floor. After he had disposed of everything else that was likely to be in the way, Etsuko moved in with her nurse, and communication was broken off between the study and the house. Not completely broken off, of course. Someone had to bring out food, and someone was therefore needed for liaison. Because the other maids prepared food and were to be kept away from the patient, the task was first given to O-haru, who had no fear of contagion and who loved to be of service, but her courage had its disadvantages. After two or three days Yukiko pointed out that O-haru's disdain for antiseptics and the carefree way in which she touched first Etsuko and then everything else in the house could only result in spreading the disease. O-haru was therefore replaced by Yukiko, who had had enough experience to be extremely cautious, and who was as fearless as O-haru. Yukiko entrusted nothing to the maids. She did the cooking and the serving and the washing herself, and she went almost without sleep for the week the fever was at its highest. She and the nurse took turns refilling the ice bag every two hours.

Etsuko made good progress; the fever began to fall. Even so, said Dr. Kushida, it would be forty or fifty days before the scarlet had dried into scabs and peeled away and recovery was complete. Yukiko, who had meant to go back to Tokyo shortly after the excursion to Kyoto, decided to stay on. Sending an explanation and a request for more clothes, she threw herself into her work, happy to be in Ashiya even if it meant working as a nurse. She strictly forbade anyone else to go in and out of the study. Sachiko, ordered to keep away (she was always the first to catch a disease, Yukiko pointed out), had so little to occupy her that Yukiko suggested a day at the theater. There was no need to worry about Etsuko. The suggestion quite hit the mark: Kikugorō was in Osaka again, dancing one of Sachiko's favorite roles, and nothing was to keep her from the theater *this* month, she had thought. Then came the illness. But however much she wanted to see Kikugorō, she could not go jauntily off leaving behind a child with scarlet fever. She had to be satisfied with a phonograph recording of the accompaniment to her favorite role. Koi-san, she remarked, might want to go on alone, and apparently Taeko did slip off to the theater.

Etsuko, meanwhile, was bored. She lay all day listening to the

phonograph, and soon there was a protest from the Swiss gentleman who had moved into the Stolz house. He was a rather difficult person. A month before they had been asked if they would
not do something about the barking dog. The protests came
through Mr. Satō, who owned the Stolz house and who lived two
doors from Sachiko. The Satō maid would be sent over to deliver a two- or three-line note in English that had come from the
Swiss. This was the note about the dog:

MY DEAR MR. SATŌ:

*I am very sorry, but I must trouble you about the dog
next door. I am kept awake every night by the barking. I wonder
if you would mind calling this to the attention of the owner.*

And now about the phonograph:

MY DEAR MR. SATŌ:

*I am very sorry, but this time I must trouble you about a
phonograph. The people next door have been playing phonograph records morning and night, and it is a great nuisance. I
should be most grateful if you would point this out, and ask them
to be more quiet.*

The Satō maid delivered the notes with an apologetic smile:
"We have had this from Mr. Bosch, and we thought we should let
you see it." The dog Johnny had only once or twice barked
through the night, and they had done nothing about that protest.
The phonograph was a different matter. Etsuko's sick room had
its own board fence, separate from the net-wire fence, to cut
off the view from outside, but it was nearer than the main
house to the house next door, and Teinosuke had frequently been
disturbed by the noise Rosemarie and Peter made. It was natural,
then, that the phonograph records should disturb the touchy
Swiss.

These protests seemed to indicate that Mr. Bosch, who worked
for a Nagoya company, spent some of his time in Ashiya, and yet
no one in the Makioka house had the slightest idea what he was
like. Mr. Stolz and his wife and children were always appearing on
the balcony and in the back yard, but although the Makiokas
did have an occasional glimpse of Mrs. Bosch, they had so far not
seen Mr. Bosch at all. There was now a board fence around the

balcony just high enough to conceal a sitting person. Mr. Bosch
evidently did not want to be seen, and evidently too he was most
eccentric. According to the Satō maid, he was a sickly, nervous
person who suffered from insomnia. A detective appeared at the
Makioka house one day and said that there was some doubt
whether the foreigner was really Swiss at all, and there was cause
for suspicion that he might be engaged in sinister operations.
If the Makiokas noted anything strange, they should report immediately to the police. With the husband a man of uncertain
origins who was constantly on the road, and the wife apparently
of mixed Chinese blood, there were indeed grounds for suspicion.
The wife, added the detective, did not seem to be really a wife at
all. Mr. Bosch was only living with her for the time being. Her
nationality too was in doubt. Though a Japanese would have
taken her for Chinese, she insisted she was born somewhere to the
south—precisely where was not clear. The one time Sachiko
visited the woman, she noted that the furniture was of Chinese
sandalwood. It therefore seemed likely that she was Chinese and
wanted for some reason to hide that fact. In any case, she was
obviously an enchantress who combined Oriental allure with
Occidental poise. She reminded one of Anna May Wong, half
French and half Chinese, who was once a Hollywood movie star.
There was an exotic something about her that was likely to appeal
to a certain kind of European. With time heavy on her hands
when her husband was traveling, she would send a maid over to
see if Sachiko could pay a visit, or she would meet Sachiko in
the street and ask her in, but after hearing what the detective
had to say, Sachiko thought it better to keep her distance.

O-haru was incensed. Why should the young lady not play the
phonograph when she was ill? Did that foreigner not know what
it was to be neighborly? Teinosuke answered that if Mr. Bosch
was so eccentric, there was little they could do, and besides it was
not seemly in time of national crisis to be playing a phonograph
from early in the morning. Thereafter Etsuko entertained herself at cards. But Yukiko objected to the card-playing: when the
patient was recovering, she said, and the scabs were beginning to
peel, there was most danger of contagion. Etsuko might well pass
the disease on to those who played with her—in particular, to
O-haru and the nurse "Mito." "Mito," who had been so named

by Etsuko because she resembled the movie star Mito Mitsuko, had had scarlet fever herself and was immune, and O-haru for her part said she would not in the least mind an attack of scarlet fever. Unlike the other maids, she ate Etsuko's left-overs—the sea bream, for instance—as if she would not again have such an opportunity. Although at first Yukiko had forbidden O-haru to come into the sick room, Etsuko was soon lonely, and Mito said the chances of contagion were very small even without such elaborate precautions. As Yukiko's reprimands lost their effect, O-haru came to be in the sick room all day long. Even worse, the two of them, O-haru and Mito, were fond of taking Etsuko by an arm or a leg and peeling off the scabs. See how far you can peel, one of them would say, clutching a loose end and ripping off a strip of skin. O-haru would then make the other maids unhappy by gathering up the skin to display in the main house ("See how the young lady is peeling!"). In time, they became quite hardened to the practice.

Early in May, when Etsuko was well on her way to recovery, Taeko announced that she was going to Tokyo. She could not rest until she had seen her brother-in-law about her money. She had, it was true, given up her plans for a trip abroad, and she was in no hurry to be married, but she now had other plans. If she was to have her money at all, she needed it immediately. She might find her brother-in-law in no mood to let her have it—well, she would make him reconsider. Since she had no intention of doing anything that would embarrass Sachiko or Yukiko, but meant only to talk matters over quietly, she hoped they would not worry. There was no reason why she had to go this month, but she had suddenly wanted to go when it occurred to her that she could most conveniently stay at the Tokyo house while Yukiko was away. She could not see herself staying long in that cramped house with all those screaming children and would be back as soon as her business was finished. It would be good to see the Kabuki, but she had seen Kikugorō so recently that she thought she could do without the plays this month.

Whom did she mean to talk to, and what were the "plans" of which she spoke, Sachiko asked. Taeko, afraid she would find her two sisters united against her, was not quick to answer. At length she hinted that she meant first to talk to Tsuruko, and if nothing came of that conversation she would not hesitate to go directly to Tatsuo. It was not at all clear what the "plans" were, although after much questioning Sachiko did draw from her reluctant sister enough information to guess that Taeko hoped, with Mrs. Tamaki's backing, to open a small dress shop. In that case, thought Sachiko, there was little chance indeed that she would get her money. Tatsuo was no doubt as firm as ever in his resolution to pay for a wedding of which he approved, and for nothing else, and he was strongly opposed to Taeko's becoming a professional woman. And yet there did seem to be one slight chance: Taeko might succeed if she attacked Tatsuo directly. He had a timid streak, and he had been persecuted by his sisters-in-law in his younger days; and since the firm position he took when no one challenged him was likely to collapse when he faced opposition, there was no telling what success Taeko might have if she tried bullying him a little. Probably she saw her opportunity. Though Tatsuo would try to flee, she was ready to stay on in Tokyo until she caught him.

Sachiko was worried. Had Taeko deliberately picked a time when neither of her sisters could go with her? She said she meant to talk matters over quietly, but might she not be resolved to assail Tatsuo even at the risk of being thrown out of the family? If so, she would not want Sachiko or Yukiko along. Possibly Sachiko was imagining dangers, but one could not be sure what the impulse of a moment might bring. Tatsuo might even conclude that Sachiko had deliberately sent Taeko off to bother him. He might feel that Sachiko had stayed behind because she wanted no part in the discussions, but on the other hand it would not be impossible for him to assume that Sachiko meant to watch with lofty amusement while he grappled with the problem. And Sachiko's position would be very difficult if Tsuruko too were to look accusingly at her—to ask why she had not kept Taeko back, why she had sent Taeko off to upset them. If she were to leave Etsuko with Yukiko and go off to Tokyo herself, however, she would find herself in the middle of a fight over money, and, worst of all, she was not sure in her own mind whose side she would take. Yukiko said that without a doubt Itakura was behind Koi-san's "plans." The dress shop might be only an excuse, and the plans might change once Koi-san had her money. For all her

apparent worldliness, Koi-san was too good-natured. The money
would be used as Itakura saw fit. She should therefore not be
given a thing until she broke with him. So said Yukiko, and there
was much to her argument. Still Sachiko had reasons for not
wanting to interfere. She was distressed at the fact that her
sister apparently meant to reject their advice and marry Itakura
whatever they said, and yet, when she thought of the courage with
which the girl was setting out to make her own way, she felt
that she could not help in what might seem like persecution.
However Taeko chose to spend the money, it was the means by
which she sought to stand alone, and she was capable of standing alone. If indeed Tatsuo was holding money in trust, it
should be given to her. Sachiko would find herself in a fight over
money, then, whether she wanted to or not. She might even be
forced to side with the main house. In all honesty, she could not
say that she had the courage and determination to stand with
Taeko against Tsuruko and her husband.

32

YUKIKO was completely opposed to letting Taeko go off alone.
There could be no excuse for Sachiko's remaining behind, she
said. She herself could take care of Etsuko and manage the house.
There would be nothing to worry about. And they could stay
on as long as they liked, and need not think of rushing back.
Taeko seemed a little upset when she heard of Sachiko's plans.
Sachiko explained that she was going along only because she
worried about what the people in Tokyo would think, and that
she had no wish to interfere. Taeko was free to challenge whomever she would. Though Tatsuo and Tsuruko might want Sachiko
to take part in the discussions, she did not want to do so. If
finally she could no longer refuse, she would be wholly neutral.
She would do nothing to Koi-san's disadvantage.
Sachiko wrote to Tsuruko describing Taeko's objectives in a

general way, and adding that she would prefer not to be consulted herself, since Koi-san seemed hostile to mediation.

Sachiko stayed again at the Hamaya Inn. Taeko, to avoid giving the impression that they were plotting together, decided to stay at the Shibuya house at least until her business was finished. They left Osaka on the Swallow Express, and that evening Sachiko took Taeko to the Hamaya and from there called Tsuruko in Shibuya: she wanted to see Koi-san to Shibuya immediately, but as she was very tired and as Koi-san did not know the way, they wondered if Teruo might not be troubled to come for her. She would come herself, said Tsuruko. If Sachiko and Taeko had not yet eaten, they might all three have dinner together. Could they meet her somewhere on the Ginza? Sachiko thought she would like to eat at either Lohmeyer's or the New Grand, and it was she who had to give the old Tokyo resident instructions on how to reach Lohmeyer's.

Sachiko and Taeko had their baths and set out for the Ginza. They arrived at Lohmeyer's to find that Tsuruko already had a table. She made it clear that this time she would pay the bill. Because Sachiko generally had more spending money, it had been the rule that the bill was hers, but this time Tsuruko was determined to be the hostess. She was especially attentive to Taeko. Living in such a small house, she repeated over and over, half apologetically, they had sent for Yukiko and perhaps had made it seem that they wanted only her with them. While they were taking a very long time, however, they did mean to call Koi-san too one day. After a bottle of German beer each, the three sisters wandered about the Ginza in the early-summer evening. Sachiko said good-bye at the entrance to the subway.

She had decided not to go to Shibuya during the two or three days the discussions were in progress and she therefore had to entertain herself. She might call on old school friends now married and living in Tokyo, she concluded. The next morning, while she was reading her newspaper, she had a call from Shibuya: Taeko would like to visit the inn. Did she have something to discuss? No, she was just bored. And what of her business? She had described it to her sister that morning, but Tatsuo was so extremely busy that there was nothing to be done for the time being. She thought she would have more fun at Sachiko's. Sachiko replied that she was going to see a friend in Aoyama and would be out until evening, but that perhaps Taeko could come by at five or six. Sachiko was kept on and on at Aoyama, and had dinner there. When she returned to the inn at seven o'clock, Taeko promptly appeared. Taeko had waited for Teruo to come home from school and the two of them had gone to see the Meiji Shrine. At five they stopped by the inn and found Sachiko out, and they waited and waited, and presently began to feel a little hungry. Though the landlady offered to provide dinner, the memory of that German beer was too strong, and Taeko took Teruo to Lohmeyer's. She had just seen him off on the subway (and she had apparently arranged to stay at the Hamaya). As she went on with her story, it became clear that her reception at Shibuya had been very cordial. Her brother-in-law, leaving for work in the morning, urged her to stay and enjoy herself now that she was in Tokyo. Cramped house though it was, they could easily find room for her with Yukiko away. He himself was busy at the moment, but in five or six days he would have time to take her wherever she wanted to go. But of course he had time off for lunch. If she would come to the Marunouchi Building at noon, they could have lunch together. He would order tickets to the Kabuki, and the three sisters could go to the theater in the next few days. All in all, he had been so considerate that he made her a little uncomfortable. She could not remember having been treated more kindly. After Tatsuo and the children left, Taeko talked to her sister for an hour or so and discussed her business in some detail. Tsuruko listened intently, without a sign of displeasure, and answered that she did not know what Tatsuo would say. He was busy with a bank amalgamation and came home late every night, and the problem would have to wait until the following week. They would have time to consider it then, and in the meantime Taeko should enjoy herself. Since it was her first visit to Tokyo in so long, they could have Teruo show her the city; or, since Sachiko was no doubt bored, how would it be if Taeko went to the inn? She did not know what would happen finally, said Taeko, but she had left everything to Tsuruko.

The day before, Mt. Fuji had been largely hidden in clouds. That did not bode well for the success of her mission, laughed

Taeko. She was still uncertain, and extremely suspicious of these blandishments, but even while she was reaffirming her intention to resist soft words, it was clear that she was not displeased at having been so warmly received.

The night before, by herself on the second floor of the inn, Sachiko had been lonelier than even a lone traveler should be, and quite unable to sleep. It had seemed dreary indeed that she would have to spend five or six more days in Tokyo. Now, unexpectedly, there were two of them in the large ten-mat room, Sachiko and Taeko side by side, for the first time in how many years? In the old Semba days the sisters had slept together—they were still sleeping together the night before Sachiko was married. She did not know how it had been when she was very young, but at least after she started school she slept in the six-mat room on the second floor with her two younger sisters. Only Tsuruko had a separate room. Sometimes, so small was the room, the three of them used but two mattresses. She and Taeko had rarely been alone—between them was Yukiko, careful on the warmest nights that her kimono was neat, never untidy even when she slept. Sachiko could almost see that figure, slender and fragile and always completely proper, lying between her and Taeko.

As they had done when they were girls, they talked carelessly of this and that before they got out of bed in the morning.

"What are your plans for today, Koi-san?"

"I have none."

"Would you like to see anything in particular?"

"Everyone talks about Tokyo, but there is not a thing I really want to see."

"We belong in Osaka, you and I. How was Lohmeyer's yesterday?"

"We had something different—Wienerschnitzel."

"Did Teruo like it?"

"While we were eating, a friend came in with his mother and father and sat down across the room from us."

"Oh?"

"Teruo turned bright red. I asked him what was the matter, and he said the friend would never believe I was his aunt."

"I suppose not."

"The waiter kept speaking to us as though we were young

lovers and giving us suspicious looks, and he stared at me with his mouth open when I asked for beer. He must have thought I was a school girl."

"When you wear foreign clothes, you look as young as Teruo. The waiter thought you were a juvenile delinquent."

Shortly before noon, there was a telephone call from Shibuya: Tsuruko had Kabuki tickets for the next day. With nothing else to do, Sachiko and Taeko had tea on the Ginza, after which they took a taxi for a tour of the government buildings and the Yasukuni Shrine.

"See how popular that arrow pattern is," Taeko remarked as they passed Hibiya Park. "I counted seven between the German Bakery and the Nippon Theater."

"You have been counting all this time?"

"See, another. And another over there." For a moment, Taeko was silent. "And see how those middle-school boys walk along with both hands in their pockets. Very dangerous. Where was it, I wonder—a middle school somewhere near Osaka. Students were forbidden to have pockets in their uniforms. That strikes me as a very good idea."

Taeko had always been precocious. And after all, she was old enough that one need not be startled by such remarks.

Sachiko nodded her agreement.

33

THE CURTAIN was about to go up on the last play of the afternoon, *Stammering Matahei*. They listened with admiration to the names being called over the loud-speaker. It was a wide and varied audience the Kabuki drew: Mr. X from Nishinomiya, Mrs. Y from Shimonoseki, and even someone from the Philippines. Suddenly Taeko held up a finger to silence them.

"Mrs. Makioka of Ashiya." There could be no doubt about it: "Mrs. Makioka of Ashiya, Hyōgo Prefecture."

"Would you see what they want, Koi-san?"

Taeko was back in a few minutes. She picked up the handbag and lace handkerchief in her seat. "May I speak to you a minute?" Sachiko followed her into the lobby.

"What is it?"

"A maid just came from the inn."

When she had been told that someone had asked for her, Taeko had gone to the door to find a maid from the Hamaya waiting there. The maid, who had an Osaka accent, reported that there had been a call from Ashiya. The landlady had not succeeded in getting through to the Kabuki Theater, and had finally sent the maid to deliver the message in person. And what was the message? She herself had not been at the telephone, said the maid, but according to the landlady it was something about a sick person who had taken a turn for the worse. Not the little girl, however. The lady on the telephone had said over and over again that it was not the little girl, who had scarlet fever, but rather the person in the ear-nose-and-throat hospital—Koi-san would know whom she meant. The landlady promised to relay the message to the Kabuki Theater immediately. She asked if there was anything else to be done and was told that at least Koi-san should come back on the night train, and telephone if there was time before she left.

"It is Itakura, then?"

Taeko had mentioned on the train that Itakura, whose ear had been bothering him for five or six days, was in the Isogai Hospital in Kobe. Having been told that the beginnings of a papillary infection made surgery necessary, he had the day before had the ear operated on. The operation was apparently successful. Since her plans were made and Itakura assured her that there was no cause for worry, she had decided not to postpone her trip— and Itakura was so strong that you felt nothing could kill him. But there had been a relapse. The call, she gathered, was from the lady in Ashiya, said the maid. Yukiko, possibly after talking to Itakura's sister, must have concluded that something should be done. Papillary infections were not serious if treated in time, but when the operation was late, the infection often spread through the chest and sometimes even proved fatal. If Itakura's sister found it necessary to call Yukiko, then all was not well.

"And what will you do, Koi-san?"

"Go back to the Hamaya, and leave as soon as I can." Taeko was quite calm.

"And what shall I do?"

"Stay on to the end. It will hardly do to walk out on Tsuruko."

"But what shall I say to her?"

"Whatever seems best."

"Did you tell her about Itakura?"

"No." In the doorway, Taeko threw a cream-colored lace shawl over her shoulders. "But you can if you like." She ran down the stairs.

It was fortunate for Sachiko that the curtain had gone up and Tsuruko's attention was concentrated on the stage. As they were making their way out through the crowd afterwards, Tsuruko asked what had happened to Koi-san.

"A friend came and took her off a little while ago."

Sachiko saw her sister as far as the Ginza. Back at the inn, she found that Taeko had just left. The landlady had reserved a berth for that night and Taeko had taken the ticket and run for the station. She had also telephoned Ashiya, but the landlady had not heard the details of the conversation. Taeko did however ask her to tell Sachiko that although the story was not entirely clear, a virulent infection seemed to have set in shortly after the operation, that the patient was in great pain, and that Koi-san would take the train through to Sannomiya Station and go from there directly to the hospital the following morning. Koi-san had left a small suitcase at Shibuya and wanted Sachiko to pick it up before she left, said the landlady, who had guessed something of the relationship between Taeko and Itakura. Very restless, Sachiko put in another emergency call to Ashiya, and found Yukiko as difficult to understand as ever. It was not that the connection was bad; Yukiko's voice was simply inadequate, though she was doing her best. A frail little voice in any case—a fleeting, ephemeral voice, one might have said—it was extremely unreliable over the telephone. There was in fact nothing so exasperating as a telephone conversation with Yukiko. Knowing how inept she was, Yukiko usually had someone else talk for her, but she could not entrust a matter concerning Itakura to O-haru, nor could she leave everything to Teinosuke. For want of a better solution, she had to take the call herself. Her voice would trail off to something no louder than the hum of a mosquito, and it seemed to Sachiko that she spent more time saying "Hello" than actually talking about the business at hand. But in the fragments she managed to salvage from the lapses and hesitations, she learned that there had been a call from Itakura's sister at four in the afternoon. Although he had seemed to be making good progress, Itakura had taken a sudden turn for the worse the evening before. Had the inflamation spread through the chest, then? No, there was nothing wrong with the chest. It was the leg. What exactly was wrong with the leg was not clear, but the patient leaped with pain if anything brushed his leg, and he could only lie moaning and writhing. He had not yet asked for Koi-san, according to the sister. Seeing that he faced a crisis, and concluding that the case was no longer one for an ear-nose-and-throat specialist, the sister thought she should call in another doctor. Alone and quite at a loss, she had telephoned for Koi-san as a last resort. Was there no more recent report? asked Sachiko. Yukiko replied that she had telephoned to say that Koi-san would leave on a night train, and had been told that the pain was growing worse—Itakura was almost mad with pain—and that the sister had telegraphed her family in the country. Her parents would be in Kobe the following morning. Koi-san had already left, said Sachiko. Having no reason to stay on in Tokyo herself, she would take a train the next morning. Just before she hung up, she asked after Etsuko, and learned that the girl was really too healthy. She kept trying to flee the sick room, and the scabs were gone except for traces on the soles of her feet.

Sachiko wondered how she could explain this sudden departure. Finally resigned to the fact that no excuse would be really convincing, she called Shibuya the following morning: Koi-san had left on urgent business, and since she meant to follow today she wondered if she might visit the Shibuya house. In that case, answered Tsuruko, she herself would come to the Hamaya. Soon she arrived with Taeko's suitcase. She was the most phlegmatic of the four sisters, so phlegmatic that they had come to think of her as a little obtuse, and she did not press to know what the "urgent business" might be. Even so, Sachiko could see that her sister was puzzled at this running off without waiting for an answer to the troublesome question Koi-san herself had raised. After announcing that she must leave immediately, Tsuruko proceeded to stay for lunch.

"Is Koi-san still seeing Kei-boy?" she asked suddenly.

"Now and then, I believe."

"And she is seeing someone else?"

"Have you heard rumors?"

"There was talk of a prospect for Yukiko. Nothing came of it, and we said nothing to her. But there was an investigation."

The person who had been acting as go-between had only meant to be kind, Tsuruko was sure. Although Tsuruko had not learned the details, it appeared that strange rumors were current about Koi-san—that she had recently become intimate with a young man who, unlike Okubata, came from the lower classes. No doubt the rumors were quite groundless, said the go-between, but still he thought Tsuruko should know of them. Tsuruko suspected that Koi-san's behavior rather than any defect in Yukiko was responsible for the failure of the marriage negotiations. Because she had the most complete trust in Sachiko and Koi-san, she would not ask to what extent the rumors were true, or who the young man was, but it was her opinion and Tatsuo's that there could be nothing better for Koi-san than to marry Okubata. They meant to make him a proposal as soon as they had Yukiko safely married. For the reasons outlined in the letter, therefore, they could not give Koi-san the money she wanted. Her manner had suggested that she was ready for a quarrel and they had been discussing how best to send her back to Osaka. Tsuruko was relieved at the turn events had taken.

"It really would be best for her to marry Kei-boy. I think so myself, and so does Yukiko, and we have both been arguing with her."

Sachiko's words may have sounded like an apology. In any case, Tsuruko did not push the matter. By the time lunch was over, she had said everything she had to say.

"Thank you very much." Immediately after dessert she stood up to leave. "I may not be able to see you off this evening, I am afraid."

34

BACK IN Ashiya the next morning, Sachiko heard this from Yukiko:

When, two afternoons before, she had been told that there was a call from Itakura's sister, Yukiko, knowing nothing of Itakura's illness and never having met the sister, was sure the call must be for Taeko. But no, it was for Miss Yukiko, the maid insisted, and Yukiko went to the telephone. The sister said that she knew of Koi-san's trip to Tokyo, apologized profusely for disturbing Yukiko, and told her the details of the illness. The day of the operation—the day before Taeko's departure for Tokyo— Taeko had visited the hospital and found Itakura comfortable and in good spirits, but from that evening his leg began to itch. Although at first it was enough if they rubbed the leg for him, his complaint by the next morning had become "It hurts, it hurts." Now, the third day after the operation, the pain was still more intense. Worse, the head of the hospital paid no attention, and only pointed out that the incision was healing satisfactorily. He fled after changing the bandage once in the morning, and for two days now he had left the patient to suffer by himself. The nurses were remarking apologetically that the doctor had really botched things this time. Itakura's sister, who had closed the Tanaka house to be with her brother, had concluded that she could no longer bear the whole responsibility. She had not been able to think of anything, she said, her voice choked with tears, except to have Taeko come immediately—no doubt her brother would scold her later. (She seemed to be calling from outside the hospital.) One could imagine Yukiko, as uncommunicative as ever, forcing the sister to do all the talking; but the tone and choice of words made it obvious that the sister, whom Taeko had described as a twenty-year-old country girl quite unaccustomed to the city, had summoned all her courage to make the call. Yukiko said she understood and would telephone Taeko immediately.

Taeko had gone directly from Sannomiya Station to the hospital. Back home for an hour or so during the evening, she described how frightening it was to find Itakura, usually so sturdy and so indifferent to pain, reduced to whimpering and moaning. Told that Taeko was back, he had looked up at her with twisted face and gone on moaning. The pain left him no room to think of others. He had moaned all through the night, and neither eaten nor slept. There was no sign of a swelling, however. It was difficult to tell exactly where the pain was—from the left knee to the foot, apparently. The moaning was louder when he turned over or when someone chanced to touch the leg. Why should an ear operation affect a leg, asked Yukiko. Taeko did not know the answer. Not only did the head of the hospital refuse an opinion, but he had been running away ever since Itakura first began to complain. From what the nurse said, and from what Taeko herself would guess as a layman, germs had entered at the time of the operation and settled in the leg.

Dr. Isogai was forced to take action when the parents and a sister-in-law, who had arrived early the same morning, began holding consultations in the hall. That afternoon he called a surgeon. After a conference with Dr. Isogai, the surgeon withdrew, to be followed almost immediately by another surgeon, who also examined the patient, had a conference with Dr. Isogai, and withdrew. Dr. Isogai, said the nurse, had seen that the infection was out of control. Having been told by the best-known surgeon in Kobe that it was too late even for amputation, he had in great haste called in a second surgeon, and again been refused. Taeko added that she herself, after seeing Itakura and hearing the sister's story, had known that there was not a moment to lose. She had been in favor of consulting a reliable doctor, whatever the head of this hospital might think, but country people are slow. Itakura's family only stood in the hall conferring and wondering what to do. Though Taeko was aware that they were wasting precious time, she could not be too forward. She had met them only that morning. When she made a suggestion, they said she was probably right and did nothing.

Such was the story the evening before. At six this morning she had come home again to rest for an hour or two, and said that Dr. Isogai had finally called in a Dr. Suzuki who agreed to operate, though he was doubtful about the results. Even then the parents could not make up their minds. The mother in particular said that if Itakura was going to die, they should at least let him die a whole man. The sister on the other hand insisted that they must do everything possible, hopeless though the case might be. The sister was right, of course. Not that it mattered—Taeko was now sure that nothing would help.

One had trouble knowing how far to believe the nurse, who was hostile to Dr. Isogai and would criticize him on the least provocation, but it was her story that the doctor was an old man and an alcoholic besides. His hand thus being shaky, he had made two or three serious blunders that she herself knew of. Even the finest specialist, Dr. Kushida said afterwards, could not absolutely guarantee that germs would not enter from an ear operation and attack the legs, since after all a doctor was not a god, but if there was the slightest possibility that an infection had slipped in, the doctor should not waste a moment in calling a surgeon when the patient complained of a throbbing anywhere in the body. Even then, it was a battle with time, and the least delay might make the final difference. One could sympathize with Dr. Isogai, then, in having botched the operation, but one could not find terms— cruelty, neglect, incompetence—to describe the failure of a doctor who abandoned a suffering patient for three whole days. It was Dr. Isogai's good luck that he faced a family of naïve, poorly in- formed farmers who would not make trouble for him. It was Ita- kura's bad luck that he had not known what a questionable physician he was choosing.

Sachiko had a number of questions: from which telephone Yukiko had called, whether the maids knew, whether she had told Teinosuke. Yukiko replied that she was in the sick room with O-haru when the first call came, and that O-haru, Etsuko, and the nurse "Mito" heard the conversation; that O-haru and Mito looked a little strange and said nothing, but that Etsuko made a great nuisance of herself (what had happened to Itakura, why was Koi-san coming home, and so on); that Yukiko, knowing how quick O-haru would be to tell the other maids, and not wanting Mito to hear more, used the telephone in the main house for the other calls; and that she told Teinosuke both of the original call and of all she had done since. Teinosuke was much concerned, she added, and after hearing the story in detail from Taeko that morning had urged her to make the parents agree to an operation.

Sachiko wondered what to do. "I ought to go to the hospital myself, for just a little while."

"But you should call Teinosuke first."

"I will have a nap first."

Sachiko had been unable to sleep on the train. She went upstairs to lie down, but was too nervous to sleep even now. After washing her face and ordering an early lunch, she went to call Teinosuke. Although there was no keeping Taeko from the man's bedside, said Sachiko, she knew that if she too went to the hospital it might seem that the Makiokas were publicly acknowledging the betrothal. Still Itakura *had* rescued Taeko at the time of the flood, and Sachiko thought it would rest badly on her conscience if she ignored what might well be his last illness. She did not think he would live. Strong though he was, there was something about him, she had thought, that suggested an early death. Teinosuke agreed. Perhaps she should visit the hospital for a few minutes. But might not Okubata be there? Might it not be better to stay away? They concluded that she should go if there seemed to be no danger of meeting Okubata, but that she should not stay long, and that if possible she should bring Taeko home with her. Calling Taeko to ask about Okubata, she was told that at the moment only Itakura's relatives were at the bedside, that no one else had been told, and that whatever happened Taeko saw no need to call Okubata. Itakura would be excited unnecessarily. She had thought of having Sachiko come to the hospital, however: they were still debating whether to call in the surgeon or not. Taeko and the sister were warmly in favor of an operation; the parents were still undecided. Sachiko might be able to help.

She would leave after lunch, said Sachiko. Over an early lunch she discussed with Yukiko the possibility of letting Mito go: it would not do to have reports about Taeko leak out, and Mito was no more than a playmate for Etsuko. Mito herself was beginning to suggest that her work was finished, said Yukiko. As she left in a taxi at noon, Sachiko asked Yukiko to tell Mito that, short notice though it was, they would not need her services after that day. If she would wait and perhaps have dinner with Sachiko, she would be free to go afterwards.

The hospital—such it was called—was a shabby two-storey

building in a narrow alley. On the second floor there were only
two or three rooms, Japanese style. Itakura had a six-mat room
with a view of a clothesline. Crowded and badly ventilated, it
smelled of perspiration. He lay facing the wall in a steel bed, his
body slightly bent. All the while Sachiko was being introduced
to the relatives—parents, sister, and sister-in-law—he was moaning
in a low voice, rapidly and quite without pause: "It hurts, it hurts,
it hurts." Taeko knelt by the pillow.

"Yone-yan. Sachiko has come."

"It hurts, it hurts, it hurts."

He lay on his side and stared at the wall. Sachiko, behind
Taeko, peered timidly down and saw that he was far from as
gaunt as she had expected, and his color was far from as bad. The
blanket was pulled down to his hips. He wore only a light cotton
kimono, the sleeves of which were pulled up, and his chest and
arms seemed as powerful as ever. The bandage over his ear was
held in place by a cross of tape, one strip from the jaw to the top of
the head, another from the forehead to the neck.

"Yone-yan," said Taeko again. "Sachiko is here."

It was the first time Sachiko had heard her sister call Itakura
"Yone-yan." At the Ashiya house she had always spoken of him as
"Itakura," and Sachiko herself, and Yukiko, and even Etsuko
had been in the habit of somewhat discourteously referring to
him by his last name. His full name was Itakura Yūsaku, and this
"Yone-yan" was a diminutive of "Yonekichi," his trade name as
an apprentice in the Okubata shop.

"How awful to find you like this," said Sachiko. "You always
seemed so healthy." She sniffled into a handkerchief.

"See, the lady from Ashiya is here." This time the sister spoke
to him.

"No, leave him alone," said Sachiko. "I thought it was the left
leg that hurt."

"It is. But because of the ear, he has to lie on his left side."

"How terrible."

"And that makes it hurt all the more."

There were beads of sweat on Itakura's rough-grained face.
Now and then a fly would light on the face, and Taeko would
brush it away as she talked. Itakura stopped moaning.

"I have to go," he said.

"Mother, he has to use the bedpan." The mother was leaning against the wall.

"Excuse me." She bent to pick up the bedpan, in newspapers under the bed. "Quiet, now."

"It hurts!" The moaning, which had been low and steady and trancelike, became the screaming of a lunatic. "It hurts, it hurts, it hurts!"

"You will just have to stand it. There is nothing else to do."

"It hurts, it hurts! You are not to touch me. You are not . . ."

"Try to stand it. What else am I to do?"

Sachiko looked curiously at the sick man, wondering what could have brought this failure of courage. The left leg had to be moved several inches, and Itakura took some minutes turning so that he faced partly up. He was quiet for a time, trying to control his breathing. Then he set about the task of using the bedpan. His mouth was open, and he looked up at them with frightened eyes quite strange to Sachiko.

"Has he been eating?" Sachiko asked the mother.

"No, not a thing."

"He just drinks lemonade."

The left leg protruded from under the blanket. There seemed to be nothing wrong with it, except that the veins were a little swollen and it was a little too white. And possibly Sachiko was imagining even that much. As Itakura rolled over again, the screams were as terrible as before. This time, "it hurts" was puncuated with screams of: "I want to die. Let me die;" and "Kill me. Kill me right now."

The father was a quiet man who seemed too timid and good-natured to have opinions of his own. The mother was considerably more forceful. Whether from lack of sleep or from weeping or from some ailment, her eyes were swollen and watery, and she was always pressing them shut. Although there was, for that reason, something a little dull and absent about her expression, it was evident that she had taken charge of the patient. Itakura, who seemed very dependent on his mother, would do whatever she said. Because the mother resisted, said Taeko, they had not called in a surgeon. Even after Sachiko arrived, they divided into two factions, the sister and Taeko in one, the parents in the other, and held whispered conferences in the corners of the room, or in the hall. The sister-in-law tried to mediate; she talked first with one faction and then with the other. The parents spoke in such low tones that Sachiko could make out nothing they said. The mother seemed to be complaining, and the father listened. Taeko and the sister called the sister-in-law aside and told her over and over that the parents would be guilty of murder if they did not agree to an operation, and that she must somehow try to convince the mother. The sister then talked to the mother; but the mother argued stubbornly that since her son would die anyway she wanted him to die with a whole body. When the sister-in-law tried to overcome that argument, the mother counterattacked: was the sister-in-law prepared to guarantee that the cruel operation would be a success? The sister-in-law next tried to pacify the sister: she simply could not prevail; hers was not the sort of argument old people understood. And the sister talked to the mother. The mother, said the sister in a tearful voice, saw only what was immediately before her eyes, and did not know her duty as a parent. So that they would have nothing to reproach themselves with afterwards, they should try surgery whether it would succeed or not. Time after time the round of arguments was repeated.

"Sachiko." Taeko called her sister to the far end of the hall. "I cannot stand a minute more of this."

"But it is not at all unreasonable for a mother to feel as she does."

"Anyway, we are too late. I am sure of that. But the sister has asked me to see if you might not be willing to talk to the mother. The mother is stubborn with the family. With important people, she nods and does as they tell her."

"And I am an important person?"

Sachiko was most reluctant to enter the discussions. She sensed how deep the old woman's resentment would be if outside interference were to bring unhappy results, and she knew moreover that the chances were eight or nine in ten that the results would be unhappy.

"You only need to wait a little while. She sees that she will have to do as everyone says. She will go on objecting until she has satisfied herself."

More worried about persuading Taeko to come home now that
she had done her duty, Sachiko waited nervously for an opening.

A nurse about to go into Itakura's room stopped when she saw
Taeko.

"Dr. Isogai would like to speak to one of the relatives."

Taeko passed this information on to the people in the room.
The sister and sister-in-law were kneeling beside the pillow; the
mother and father were at the foot of the bed. The two old
people debated for a time which should go, and presently they
went together. Fifteen minutes later they came back, the father
looking most upset, the mother in tears and muttering something
in his ear. Afterwards it appeared that Dr. Isogai had instructed
them in the most positive terms to transfer the patient to a surgical
hospital. To have him die here would be no small inconvenience.
The doctor argued that he had done everything possible to treat
the ear; that, since the most complete care had been taken in
the disinfecting, there could have been no error in the operation
itself; and that the leg ailment must therefore be quite another
matter. The ear was healing, as they could of course see, and the
patient no longer belonged in this hospital. Out of consideration
for other patients, Dr. Isogai had called in Dr. Suzuki the night
before and persuaded him to take the case. Since then valuable
time had been lost through indecision, and maybe the time for
surgery had already passed. In any case the hospital could not
take responsibility for further delays. Thus Dr. Isogai made it
appear that the whole crisis had been brought on by the parents
and their slowness. They only bowed and thanked the good
doctor. When they were back in the room, the mother scolded the
father as if it had been entirely his fault that the doctor had
gotten around them so successfully. Sachiko knew that the complaints resulted from an excess of grief. The mother, resigned at
length to the inevitable, had found the proper moment to end
her resistance.

It was growing dark as they prepared to move Itakura. Dr.
Isogai behaved with extreme coldness. His manner suggested that
the patient was a great nuisance, and he did not once come out to
see the family. The work of moving was left to a doctor and
nurse from the Suzuki Hospital. Whether or not he knew that
in the conferences of these last hours it had been decided to

amputate his leg, Itakura only moaned like some strange animal. The family accepted the fact that the strange animal was what their son and brother had become, and no one asked his opinion about the operation. One thought bothered them, however: what of the screams when they moved him to the ambulance? The halls were only a yard wide, there was no landing on the narrow spiral staircase, and it was obvious from the screams when Itakura had to use the bedpan that the pain would be intense when they carried the stretcher out. The family seemed less concerned for the strange animal than for themselves, who would have to listen. Sachiko asked the nurse if something could not be done. There was no cause for worry, said Dr. Suzuki. They would give him a sedative. And indeed he was quieter when, after an injection, he was taken away by the doctor, the nurse, and his mother.

35

SACHIKO called her sister aside while Itakura's father, sister, and sister-in-law were cleaning the room and paying the bill. She wanted to go home, she said, and Teinosuke had told her to bring Koi-san with her if possible. Taeko replied that she would wait for the results of the operation. Unable to dissuade her, Sachiko finally saw the four of them to Dr. Suzuki's and went on to Ashiya in the same cab. As Taeko started into the hospital, Sachiko called her back again: though she could understand Koi-san's desire to help, still it appeared—perhaps they had only been shy before the Makiokas—that the Itakura family really did not need help. How would it be then if Koi-san were to slip out? Of course much would depend on exactly what happened, but Sachiko hoped Koi-san would not forget for one second their great fear of rumors that she and the sick man were formally engaged. She hoped her sister would think always of the Makioka name, and most especially of the effect on Yukiko. Sachiko felt that she may have gone a little too far. What she hoped to convey, with much delicacy and indirection, was that it could do no good to have Koi-san's affairs known now that Itakura was to die. There was no doubt that Taeko knew what she meant.

To be honest, Sachiko could not keep back a certain feeling of relief now that the possibility of Taeko's marriage to a man of no family had been eliminated by natural and wholly unforeseen circumstances. It made her a little uncomfortable, a little unhappy with herself, to think that somewhere deep in her heart she could hope for a man's death, but there was the truth. And she was sure she would not be alone: Yukiko would be with her, and Teinosuke; and Okubata, if he knew, would be dancing the happiest dance of all.

"Why are you so late?" Teinosuke, already back from work, had been waiting for her in the parlor. "They said you left at noon, and I just had someone call the hospital to find out what was keeping you."

"I had to stay on and on. I wanted to bring Koi-san back with me."

"And did you?"

"No. She decided to wait for the operation. I think she is right."

"They will operate?"

"Yes. They were still arguing whether they should or not when I got there, and when they finally made up their minds I took them all to the Suzuki Hospital."

"Will he live?"

"Probably not."

"It seems very strange. What is the matter with the leg?"

"No one really told me."

"Did you find out the name of the disease?"

"Dr. Isogai ran off whenever we tried to ask, and Dr. Suzuki seemed not to want to talk while Dr. Isogai was there. I imagine it is blood-poisoning."

As Sachiko paid "Mito," all ready to leave, for her forty days' services, and sat down to dinner with Teinosuke and Yukiko, there was a telephone call from the Suzuki Hospital. The conversation was a long one, the general drift of which Teinosuke and Yukiko could follow from the dining room: the operation was over and Itakura was resting more easily; because there would have to be transfusions, everyone except the two old people had

had blood tests; Itakura and his sister were both Type A, whereas Taeko was Type O; although they could thus use the sister's blood for the time being, they would need one or two more donors; Taeko's blood, Type O, would do, but the family was determined not to ask for it; unhappily, the sister had suggested telling Itakura's fellow apprentices in the Okubata shop, and two or three of them had been informed and would very shortly arrive at the hospital; Taeko did not want to see them, or, worse yet, to see Kei-boy, who might have heard; she had therefore decided to go home; the apprentices being old friends of Itakura's, the sister seemed to think that they might be willing to donate blood; since Taeko was exhausted, she hoped someone would send a cab for her; and, finally, she wanted a bath and something to eat as soon as she reached home.

"Does the family know about Koi-san and Kei-boy, then?" asked Teinosuke when Sachiko was back in the dining room. He was careful to lower his voice.

"I doubt it very much. If they did, do you think they would think of letting Itakura marry her?"

"Never," Yukiko agreed. "He cannot have told his parents about Kei-boy."

"But possibly the sister knows."

"Those men from the shop—do they see a great deal of Itakura?"

"I wonder. I have not heard anything about old friends."

"But if there are people like that around his studio, then there is not much doubt that Koi-san's affair is an open secret."

"You remember how Kei-boy told me he had ways of investigating? He probably was thinking of the men in the shop."

Although a cab was ordered immediately, it was more than an hour before Taeko appeared. The cab had had a flat tire on the way, and she had waited a fairly long time at the hospital. The wait was no problem, but she had had to see the men from the Okubata shop, and the man she most wanted to avoid, Kei-boy himself. (It was not likely that he was in the shop at such an hour. Taeko assumed that one of the men had called him.) She stayed as far from Kei-boy as she could, and he was tactful enough to keep his distance. When she started to leave, however, he came up and asked why she did not stay longer—he asked with every appearance of politeness, but a note of sarcasm could easily be read into the words. When the men from the shop, on their own initiative, asked to have their blood tested, Kei-boy stepped forward and said that he too would have a blood test. It was difficult to see what he had in mind, though with that bustling officiousness of his, he was probably but following a sudden impulse. Taeko had had her own blood tested because she had thought she could do no less when the sister and the sister-in-law were tested. The whole family had tried to discourage her, she said.

"Where did they amputate?" asked Sachiko. The three sat for a time at the dinner table with Taeko, who had taken a bath and changed to a cotton summer kimono.

"Here." Taeko stretched out her leg and drew a hand across her thigh. Then, in confusion, she waved as if to brush away the mark.

"And were you watching?"

"Just a little."

"In the operating room?"

"I was in the next room, with a glass door between. I could watch if I wanted to."

"How brave of you—even if you were not especially watching."

"I tried not to see—but I would be frightened and want to take just a look. His heart was beating so, and his chest was rising and falling like this. Does a general anaesthetic always do that to a person, I wonder. You could never have stood seeing that much, Sachiko."

"We will talk about something else."

"That was nothing. I did see something really terrible."

"Stop, stop. Please."

"It will be a long time before I can eat beef again."

"Stop it, Koi-san." This time it was Yukiko who protested.

"I found out the name of the disease, though." Taeko turned to Teinosuke. "Gangrene. Dr. Suzuki would not talk while we were in the other hospital, but he told us later."

"Is gangrene as painful as all that? It was from the ear, then."

"I have no idea."

They learned afterwards that Dr. Suzuki was not in good repute with other members of his profession. Indeed it was strange that he agreed to take a case two leading surgeons had already refused, and a case so hopeless that even he could make no promises. It must have been just such incidents that had given him a bad name. Though unaware of the doctor's shortcomings, Taeko had thought, when she saw the large hospital with apparently no other patients, that it was not a prosperous establishment. Perhaps because the building was a converted Western-style house that made one think of those put up some seventy-five years earlier, in the first days after the opening of the ports, and because footsteps echoed hollow against the high ceilings as in a haunted house, she felt a sudden chill when she stepped inside the door. Coming out of the anaesthetic, Itakura looked up at her and said: "So I am a cripple." But the moaning animal at Isogai Hospital had become a human being again. Clearly he had known all along how serious his condition was, and what those repeated conferences meant. In any case, it was a great relief to Taeko that the moaning at least had stopped. She began to wonder if he might not survive with but the one leg gone. She began to imagine him on crutches. But it was only a two- or three-hour reprieve, in the course of which the men from the Okubata shop and Kei-boy himself arrived. She saw her opportunity to leave. The sister, who alone knew of the triangle, helped her slip out unobtrusively. At the door, Taeko told the sister to call her if there was a change, whatever the hour. She also told the driver that she might have to get him out of bed before the night was over.

Exhausted though she was, Taeko talked with her sisters and Teinosuke for some time. At four in the morning she was called back to the hospital. Sachiko, half asleep, heard the cab, and said to herself as she dozed off: So Koi-san has left again. She did not know how much time passed before O-haru slid the bedroom door open.

"Mrs. Makioka. Koi-san called from the hospital to say that Mr. Itakura is dead."

"What time is it?"

"About half past six, I think."

Sachiko could not go back to sleep. Teinosuke knew of the telephone call, but Yukiko and Etsuko, asleep in Teinosuke's study, did not learn of it until they got up at about eight.

Taeko came home at noon to tell them all that had happened: when Itakura again took a turn for the worse, the sister and the men from the Okubata shop gave repeated blood transfusions, to no avail; the poison attacked the chest and head, and the patient, though for a time liberated from the pain in the leg, died in the most intense agony; Taeko hoped never again to see such a painful death; his mind was clear to the end, however, and he took leave of his family and friends one by one, and thanked Kei-boy and Taeko and wished them happiness; asking to be remembered to the family in Ashiya, he mentioned them all by name, Mr. and Mrs. Makioka, Miss Yukiko, Miss Etsuko, and even O-haru; the men from the Okubata shop, with their work to do, returned to Osaka after spending the night at the hospital, but Taeko herself and Kei-boy went to Tanaka with the body, and it was from there that she had just returned; Kei-boy, who stayed on to help after she left, was addressed as "the young master" by the Itakura family; and the wake would be tonight and the next night, and the funeral in two days, at the Tanaka house. Though Taeko's face was worn, she was calm and shed no tears.

Taeko went to the wake for about an hour the second evening. She wanted to stay longer, but Okubata had been there for two nights and seemed to be looking for a chance to talk to her.

Teinosuke thought that he and his family should go to the funeral. What most concerned him, however, was the welfare of his two sisters-in-law. There was no telling whom they would meet. It would be especially embarrassing, after the newspaper incident, to meet the Okubata family on such an occasion. He decided to stay away and to send Sachiko with condolences, choosing an hour when there were not likely to be many at the wake. Taeko went to the funeral, but not to the cremation. There were so many people at the funeral, she said, that even she wondered how Itakura could have made all those acquaintances. Kei-boy, in among the men from the shop, was his usual officious self.

The ashes were buried in an Okayama temple, and the Makiokas were not informed when the photograph studio was closed. Perhaps the Itakura family had decided that further correspondence would be presumptuous. Sachiko knew that Taeko went quietly to Okayama once a week until the thirty-fifth day after the death.[1] Without calling on the family, she visited Itakura's grave.

Yukiko and Etsuko, lonely without "Mito," had O-haru sleep with them in the study. It was for only two nights; the night before Itakura's funeral they moved back to the main house. Teinosuke reoccupied the study after it was fumigated.

Forgotten in all this excitement, a letter had come late in May via Siberia. It was in English, addressed to Sachiko.

Hamburg
May 2, 1939

DEAR MRS. MAKIOKA:

I must apologize for not having answered your very kind letter sooner. I had no time to myself either in Manila or on the boat. I had to take care of all the baggage. My sister is ill even now here in Germany, and I brought her three children back with me. I had five in all to take care of. I had hardly a moment to myself between Genoa and Bremerhaven, where my husband met us. It is good that we all arrived home safely. My husband seemed very well, as did Peter, who was with friends and relatives at Hamburg Station. I have not yet seen my mother or my other sisters. We must first think of making ourselves a home, and that has been a great deal of trouble. We looked at many places before we finally found the one that seemed right for us, and we are now buying furniture and kitchen supplies. All our work should be finished in another two weeks or so. The large trunks and crates have not yet arrived, but we expect them within ten days. Peter and Fritz are staying with friends. Peter, who is extremely busy with his school work, asks to be remembered to you. We have friends returning to Japan this month, and we will send a little present for Etsuko, which we hope you will accept as a very small mark of our affection. When are you coming to Germany? I shall take great pride in showing you Hamburg. It is a fine city.

Rosemarie has written a letter to Etsuko. Etsuko must write too. She must not worry about mistakes in English. I make

---

[1] There are memorial observances every seventh day for forty-nine days after a death.

plenty myself. Is someone living in the Satō house? I often think of that lovely place. Please give our regards to Mr. Satō. And to your family. Did Etsuko receive the shoes Peter sent from New York? I hope you did not have to pay customs on them.

Sincerely,
HILDA STOLZ

Enclosed was a sheet at the top of which Mrs. Stolz had written: "This is Rosemarie's letter, which I have translated for her."

Tuesday, May 2, 1939

DEAR ETSUKO:

I have not written for a long time. I will write now. I met a Japanese man who lives in Mrs. von Pustan's house. He works for the Yokohama Specie Bank. His wife and three children are with him. Their name is Imai. The trip from Manila to Germany was very interesting. We had a sand storm once coming through the Suez Canal. My cousins got off the ship at Genoa. Their mother took them to Germany on a train. We went by ship to Bremerhaven.

Under my bedroom window here in the boarding house a blackbird has a nest. First she laid the eggs. Now she has to hatch them. One day when I was watching the father bird came with a fly in his mouth. He tried to give the fly to the mother bird but the mother bird flew away. The father bird was very smart. He put the fly down in the nest and flew away. The mother bird came right back. She ate the fly and sat down on the eggs again.

We will have our new apartment soon. Our address will be: First Floor Left, 14 Overbeck Strasse. Please write, and give my regards to everyone.

Sincerely,
ROSEMARIE

P.S. *We saw Peter yesterday. He sends regards too.*

BOOK III

YUKIKO HAD ARRIVED in mid-February and stayed on through March, April, May—almost four months. She never spoke of going back to Tokyo, and she seemed to have settled quietly in Ashiya. Early in June there was, surprisingly, word from Tsuruko of a marriage proposal. Surprising for two reasons: it was the first such proposal in two years and three months, the first since Mrs. Jimba had mentioned Nomura, and whereas, since Tatsuo's trouble with the Saigusa proposal years before, word had come first to Ashiya and been passed on to Tokyo, this time it was Tatsuo who acted first, and relayed the information to Ashiya through his wife. The new proposal, as Sachiko read of it in her sister's letter, did not seem very promising. It was not the sort one would leap at: Tatsuo's oldest sister had married into the Sugano family, large landowners at Ogaki, near Nagoya; the Suganos were friendly with the Sawazakis, a well-known Nogoya family, the previous head of which had occupied one of the seats in the House of Peers reserved for leading taxpayers; and the present head of the family, through the good offices of Tatsuo's sister, would like to meet Yukiko. Mrs. Sugano of all Tatsuo's relatives knew Sachiko and her sisters best. Sachiko, perhaps nineteen at the time, had once gone with Tatsuo, Tsuruko, Yukiko, and Taeko to watch the cormorant fishing on the Nagara River, and they had spent a night at the Sugano house; two or three years later, all of them had been invited to a mushroom picking. Sachiko remembered the place well: you drove for twenty or thirty minutes along a country road to a lonely country village; you turned off what would seem to be a prefectural highway and saw the gate at the end of a deep, hedged lane. Though there were otherwise only a few dreary farmhouses in the neighborhood, the mansion of the Suganos, which dated from the Battle of Sekigahara in 1600, was most imposing, with the memorial hall for the family funeral tablets rising grandly across the courtyard from the main building. Sachiko remembered too that beyond the mossy garden was a vegetable patch, and that in the autumn little girls climbed the heavily laden trees to shake down chestnuts. The food was simple, largely home-grown vegetables, but very good, the new potatoes and the baked lotus roots being especially good. The lady of the house, Tatsuo's sister, was a widow. Possibly because she had little else to think about, she had for some time been considering Yukiko's problems, the Makiokas heard, and she had set about finding a good husband. No doubt she enjoyed being a matchmaker.

Tsuruko's letter had little to say about the present head of the Sawazaki family, or about the circumstances that had led to talk of a *miai* with Yukiko. There had, she said, been this statement from Mrs. Sugano that she would like to have Yukiko in Ogaki to meet Mr. Sawazaki. The Sawazaki fortune ran into tens of millions of yen, ridiculously out of proportion to what the Makioka family now had, but inasmuch as it was a second marriage, and the man had already sent someone off to Osaka to investigate Yukiko and the Makiokas, the prospect did not seem entirely hopeless. But the most important thing to remember was Mrs. Sugano's kindness; to ignore it would be to put Tatsuo in a most difficult position. Since Mrs. Sugano had said only that she wanted Yukiko to come to Ogaki, and that she would explain later, Tsuruko did not really know what the situation was, but in any case she hoped Yukiko would not be difficult. And besides, Yukiko had been in Ashiya a long time now, and they had been thinking of calling her back; she could stop in Ogaki on her way to Tokyo. Mrs. Sugano had not said who was to accompany Yukiko. Though Tsuruko herself could go down from Tokyo (Tatsuo was unfortunately very busy), it would be quite ideal if Sachiko would go instead. Might they ask her to?

There was to be nothing formal about the *miai*. They might set out as if on a pleasure trip.

Tsuruko wrote with great blandness. But would Yukiko agree? That was Sachiko's first question, and when she showed the letter to Teinosuke, he too felt that there was something a little unexpected about it, something not quite in keeping with Tsuruko's usual good sense. It was true that the gentleman was not completely unknown, the Sawazakis of Nagoya being famous in Osaka too. But to send Yukiko off as ordered, without learning a thing about the present head of the family—could it escape being called rash and ill-considered? Since the Sawazakis were so far above the Makiokas, might they not think the latter lacking in dignity and restraint, unaware of their proper place? And the people in the main house ought to have known, after so many proposals had been refused, that Yukiko wanted each new one investigated most carefully. Back from the office the next day, Teinosuke said that there were many things he did not understand. He had talked with two or three people in the course of the day, and learned what he could about the head of the Sawazaki family: that he was about forty-five years old, a graduate of the Waseda University business school; that his wife, who had died two or three years before, had come from a noble court family; that they had three children; that though it was the previous head of the family who had sat in the House of Peers by virtue of the taxes he paid, the family's fortunes had deteriorated little if at all since; and that the Sawazakis were still one of the richest and most important families in Nagoya. But Teinosuke was not able to get a clear answer when he asked about the disposition and deportment of the man himself. He could not understand, said Teinosuke, why a millionaire who had been able to marry into a court family should now be seeking, even for a second wife, a daughter of the declining Makiokas. There must be reasons why he could not make a more suitable marriage—but Mrs. Sugano would hardly be sending Yukiko into the arms of a man she knew to have serious defects. Perhaps Mr. Sawazaki, searching at any cost for a wife in the pure Japanese style, a sheltered lady of the old type, had heard of Yukiko and decided, half from curiosity, that he would like to meet her. Or perhaps he had heard that Yukiko's niece was closer to Yukiko than to her own mother, and had concluded that Yukiko would make a good stepmother for his children. If she got along well with children, then nothing else mattered. Might he not have some such uncomplicated motive for wanting to meet her? One of the two explanations must be the correct one, and of the two was not the first the more likely? In his curiosity to see whether the Makioka daughter was really as elegant as reported, had the man possibly taken the half-cynical view that he had nothing to lose by seeing her? One could easily think so, and the people at the main house, without having followed that possibility through, were pushing Yukiko on simply because Tatsuo could not say no to his oldest sister. The youngest in the Taneda family, Tatsuo found it hard to lift his head before his brothers and sisters even now that he had become a Makioka. A suggestion from this oldest sister of all, really more like an aunt, was an order. Though Yukiko would not be pleased, said Tsuruko, Sachiko must somehow force her to agree. It mattered little at the moment whether a marriage was arranged or not; Tatsuo would be greatly distressed if Yukiko would not at least go to Ogaki. It was true that the proposal did not seem promising, but marriage proposals were so easily labelled and filed away, and it would certainly do Yukiko no harm to be in the good graces of the Sugano family.

Almost immediately a letter came from Mrs. Sugano. She had learned from Tatsuo that Yukiko was in Ashiya. To avoid roundabout negotiations, she had decided to write directly. Sachiko and Yukiko had of course had the details from Tsuruko, but the matter was not to be taken so seriously. Mrs. Sugano preferred to think that all of them—Sachiko, Yukiko, Taeko, and possibly Etsuko, whom she had never seen—were only coming for a visit. These ten years had seen little change in her out-of-the-way home. And now the firefly season was coming. The place was not particularly famous for fireflies. With swarms of fireflies in the night, however, the nameless little streams that ran through the rice paddies would all be very beautiful for another week or so. Unlike maple leaves and mushrooms, fireflies would really interest them. The firefly season moreover was very short: for another week it would be at its height, and then it would be over. There was also the weather to be considered. Fireflies were unimpressive when the weather had been good for too long, and on the

other hand, a rainy day was bad. The day after a rain was ideal.
Could they set aside the coming week-end, and arrive by Saturday
evening? An unobtrusive meeting might then be arranged with
Mr. Sawazaki. Mrs. Sugano did not know exactly what the details
would be, but she thought he would be willing to come from
Nagoya. The meeting could be at her house, and it need last no
longer than a half hour or an hour. And even if this week-end
should prove inconvenient for Mr. Sawazaki, she hoped the
Makiokas would come to see the fireflies.

It seemed that the people in Tokyo had urged her to write.
Although Sachiko herself was inclined to dismiss the proposal as
altogether too unpromising, in their hearts her sister and brother-
in-law were apparently hoping that a dream might come true.
And Sachiko herself had become very timid in marriage negotiations, and did not have the courage to refuse a proposal arbitrarily.
There had, it was true, been a similar proposal some five years
before. The man had belonged to a class above the Makiokas,
and when, much excited, they had set about investigating, they
had found to their very great disappointment that there was
evidence of a domestic scandal. Though grateful to Mrs. Sugano,
Teinosuke could not help wondering whether they were being
made fools of again. He was even a little angry: was it not insulting, he said, to demand that Yukiko come for a *miai* before
any of the usual preliminary steps had been taken? But this was,
after all, the first proposal in two years and three months. Thinking how proposals had showered upon them until two or three
years before and then had suddenly stopped, Sachiko could not
help feeling that she had to take a certain amount of the blame
herself: for one thing, the Makiokas had made too much of
family and prestige and had set their sights too high, turning
away proposal after proposal; for another, Taeko's bad name
seemed to be having its effect. Now came this new proposal, just
when Sachiko was suffering the keenest pangs of self-recrimina-
tion. She even thought sometimes that the world had lost interest and that no one would come with another proposal, and
she feared that to dismiss this proposal, unpromising though it was,
would only be to invite more hostility. Others might follow even
if nothing came of this one. If they turned it away, on the other
hand, they could not expect another for the time being. And

was this not a bad year for Yukiko? Even while she laughed at her sister and brother-in-law and their "dream," Sachiko could hear a voice that refused to let her call it a dream herself. Teinosuke advised caution, but was he not going too far? However wealthy the Sawazakis might be, was Yukiko so ridiculously unqualified to become the second wife of a man with two or three children? The Makiokas had their pedigree too. She said so to Teinosuke, and he had no answer. He felt that he could offer no apology to Yukiko or to her parents in their graves.

After talking for an evening, Teinosuke and Sachiko decided to leave everything to Yukiko. The next day Sachiko told her sister of the two letters, and was surprised to see that Yukiko did not seem especially displeased. As usual, Yukiko did not really say yes or no, but behind her brief replies Sachiko sensed something like a willingness to be convinced. Perhaps even this proud lady was growing impatient and would no longer be difficult on the subject of *miai*. Sachiko had been careful to say nothing that might hurt Yukiko's feelings and Yukiko had no cause to think of the proposal as ridiculous or extravagant, or to suspect that someone might be making fun of her. Usually when she heard that there were children she was particular to ask about them— whether they were well behaved, what their ages were, and so on —but this time she was less meticulous. She would have to be going back to Tokyo in any event, she said, and if they would all go with her to Ogaki, she thought she would not find the fireflies unpleasant. Yukiko wants a rich husband, laughed Teinosuke.

Sachiko sent off her letter to Mrs. Sugano: they were going to take advantage of her kindness, and hoped she would continue to favor them; Yukiko would be most pleased to meet the gentleman; it appeared that there would be four of them—herself, Yukiko, Taeko, and Etsuko; though she hesitated to plead her own convenience, Etsuko had been out of school for a long time and it would therefore be better if they could go to Ogaki on Friday rather than Saturday; and she hoped that nothing would be said; to Etsuko of the *miai*. Her real reason for moving the date up was that she wanted to see Yukiko off as far as Gamagōri. They would spend Friday night with Mrs. Sugano, and go on to spend Saturday night in Gamagōri. On Sunday afternoon, Yukiko would leave Gamagōri for Tokyo, the others for Osaka. Etsuko would be back in school the following week.

2

THOUGH SACHIKO would have preferred foreign clothes for a train ride in the summer heat, she was off for a *miai* and had to tie herself up in a smothering kimono and obi. She looked enviously at Taeko, in simple girlish dress not much different from Etsuko's. Yukiko, for her part, would have preferred to carry her good clothes in a suitcase since it was not proper to dress ostentatiously in time of crisis, but the details had not been settled clearly enough for her to be sure that the man would not be waiting when they arrived, and in the end she dressed with much more care than usual.

"She looks so young." Teinosuke, who was seeing them as far as Osaka, glanced at Yukiko across the aisle. As though it were a fresh discovery, he whispered his admiration to Sachiko. And indeed there were few who would have believed that Yukiko was in that troublesome thirty-third year. Thin and sad though the face was, the make-up set it off wonderfully well, and the kimono was, of all Yukiko owned, the one that best suited her, a delicate summer kimono and under-kimono of semi-diaphanous georgette, the sleeves two feet long. On a quiet purple ground, the bold plaited-bamboo pattern was broken here and there by flowers and white waves. They had telephoned Tokyo to have it sent by express when they decided to make the trip.

"She does look young. There are very few people her age who could wear that kimono."

Yukiko looked at the floor, aware that she was being discussed. If one had been searching for faults, one could have remarked on that dark spot over the eye. The evening before Yukiko and Etsuko had left for Yokohama to see Peter Stolz off—it must have been in August—Sachiko had noticed that the spot was back after having disappeared for some time, and since then, though it was sometimes dark and sometimes faint, it had never entirely left her. There were times when a stranger might not have noticed at all, but a shadow was always to be detected by those near her. And the spot had become quite unpredictable. Whereas it had once come and gone in a monthly cycle, one could never be sure now when it would be dark and when it would fade. Teinosuke, much disturbed, said that if injections would do any good then injections she should have, and Sachiko urged her sister to see a specialist. They had been told by the doctor at Osaka University, however, that a long series of injections would be necessary, and that since the spot would disappear in any case when Yukiko was married, it was hardly worth the trouble. And the spot did not seem to bother people once they were used to it. Much though it might upset the family, it was a very small blemish indeed. More important, Yukiko herself did not seem worried. They had therefore done nothing.

When viewed from a certain angle, the spot stood out under heavy powder like mercury in a thermometer. Teinosuke had noticed it as he watched Yukiko at the mirror that morning, and he was sure it would attract attention. Sachiko guessed what he was thinking. Each of them knew that the other saw this unfortunate development as a new shadow over a proposal unpromising from the start.

Etsuko suspected that the trip was for more than fireflies. "Why are you wearing a kimono, Mother?" she asked as they changed trains in Osaka Station.

"I thought Mrs. Sugano might be offended if I wore foreign clothes."

"Oh." Etsuko was not satisfied. "Why?"

"Why? You know how particular country people are when they get old."

"What are we going to do today?"

"I have told you, I believe, that we are going to look at fireflies."

"But you and Yukiko are so dressed up."

"You know how it is when you go hunting fireflies, Etsuko." Taeko came to Sachiko's rescue. "You must have seen it in pictures—princesses with all sorts of court ladies, and long sleeves trailing off like this." Taeko demonstrated with gestures. "They have fans in their hands and they run around the lake and over the bridge after fireflies. You have to run around in a pretty kimono—otherwise a firefly hunt hardly seems like a firefly hunt."

"What about you, then?"

"I have never owned a good summer kimono. Sachiko will be the princess, and I will have to be a servant in foreign dress."

Though Taeko had recently been in Okayama for the third of her visits to Itakura's grave, she seemed in good spirits. The tragedy had left no visible scars. Now and then she would send her sisters into spasms of laughter, and she managed her boxes of candy and tins of cake like a juggler.

"Look, Yukiko, Mt. Mikami."

Etsuko, who seldom went east of Kyoto, was enjoying her second trip around Lake Biwa, and remembering all the famous places she had had pointed out to her the year before—Mt. Mikami, the long bridge at Seta, the site of Azuchi Castle, and so on. Just beyond Notogawa the train pulled to a stop—on a curved embankment through the rice paddies, they saw as they leaned out the windows. It was impossible to tell what the difficulty was. A pair of crewmen climbed from the locomotive and walked back and forth peering under the cars, but whether they did not know what was wrong or were not saying, they gave only vague answers to the passengers' question. They thought it would be five or ten minutes at most. Presently a second train pulled up. The crewmen came for a look, and one of them ran back toward Notogawa.

"What is it, Mother?"

"I have no idea."

"Did we run over something?"

"Do you see anything?"

"But they ought to know we are in a hurry."

"Silly train, stopping in a place like this."

Sachiko too thought at first that someone had been run over, but they seemed to have been spared at least that ill omen. For all Sachiko knew it might be the usual thing for a train, not on a remote branch line or a small private line, but on the main line of the Government Railways—it might be the usual thing for such a train to waste upwards of a half hour out among the rice paddies. She did not travel much, and she could not really say. Still she thought it odd. And the foolish, absent-minded way the train had slowed down and clanked to a stop, almost as though it were making fun of Yukiko's *miai*. Always when Yukiko had a *miai* something came up to spoil the day. Sachiko had been hoping that this time they would escape—and now, when they had all safely boarded the train and everything seemed in prospect of going well—now, to have this happen. She felt her face cloud over, try though she would to hide her dejection.

"We are in no hurry. Suppose we have lunch while the train is resting," joked Taeko. "We can have a much pleasanter lunch."

"An excellent idea." Sachiko set about reviving her spirits. "The lunch will lose all its flavor in this heat unless we hurry and eat it."

Taeko was already taking down bundles and baskets from the rack above.

"How are the egg rolls, Koi-san? Has anything happened to them?"

"The club sandwiches are in more danger. We will have them first."

"You *are* an eater, Koi-san. Your mouth has been full ever since we left Osaka." Yukiko seemed to have none of the forebodings that troubled her sisters.

Some fifteen minutes later the train moved jerkily off. A new locomotive had come out to meet it.

3

THEY HAD last been invited to Ogaki, for a mushroom picking, the autumn before Sachiko was married. She was already engaged, and the wedding came two or three months later. It would have been 1925, fourteen years before, when Sachiko was twenty-two, Yukiko eighteen, and Taeko fourteen. Mrs. Sugano's husband had greatly amused them with his heavy midland accent. They remembered how Tatsuo frowned when finally they were unable to hold back their laughter. Proud of being related to a family that figured in the chronicles of Sekigahara, Tatsuo had been looking for an excuse to display the Suganos to his wife and sisters-in-law. He also took much pleasure in showing them the battle-field and the ruins of the barrier gate at Fuwa. Their first visit was in the worst of the heat, however, and they were exhausted by the time he had finished dragging them over dusty country roads in a battered automobile. On their second visit they had to see the same famous places again. Sachiko was thoroughly bored. She had a pride an outsider would not understand in being a native of Osaka, and since the great heroes of her child-hood were the losers at Sekigahara,[1] she had little interest in that battle.

The second visit was in a sense to help unveil the garden cottage, just then finished. Called the "Pavilion of Timelessness," it was connected with the main house by a long L-shaped gallery, and it was for the old man's pleasure—naps, chess, special guests. Though it showed more attention to detail than the rest of the house, there was nothing that struck one as discordant or ostenta-tious. Indeed the cottage had about it the pleasant expansiveness of the well-to-do country family. Shown again to the Pavilion of Timelessness, they noted that it had mellowed into an even quieter, more tranquil little house than they remembered.

As they were looking out over the fresh garden foliage, Mrs. Sugano came in to greet them formally, and to introduce her daughter-in-law and grandchildren. The daughter-in-law, whose husband, the present head of the family, worked in an Ogaki bank, held a baby in her arms. A boy five or six years old hid shyly behind her. The daughter-in-law's name was Tsuneko, the boy was Sōsuke, and the baby girl was Katsuko. The introductions finished, Mrs. Sugano set about renewing the acquaintance, and again the youthfulness of the sisters came up for discussion. When she had heard the automobile and had gone out to receive them at the gate, said Mrs. Sugano, she had seen Taeko climb from the automobile, and wondered if it was young Etsuko—but then of course her eyes were not as good as they might be. Then came Yukiko and Sachiko, whom she took for Taeko and Yukiko—

[1] Osaka Castle was the main seat of the anti-Tokugawa faction, defeated at Sekigahara.

and a little girl—and no Sachiko. She was first able to identify
them properly when she came out to the cottage. Tsuneko too
was surprised: she had never met them, she said, but she had
heard enough about them to know fairly well how old they would
be. She had been unable to decide which was which when she
saw them get out of the automobile. She hoped they would
forgive her for asking, but was not Miss Yukiko a year or two
older than she? Tsuneko was thirty, explained Mrs. Sugano. It
was natural that Tsuneko, married for some years and already the
mother of two children, should have aged, and for all the special
care she had obviously taken with her dress, she looked almost
like Yukiko's mother. And Taeko too, Mrs. Sugano went on.
When she first came here, she was a little bigger than the girl
(pointing to Etsuko); and if the next time was 1925 and she
was fourteen or so then—Mrs. Sugano blinked with astonishment—it seemed as if the last ten years and more had not happened. She should not have confused Taeko and Etsuko, but
even here face to face she could not see that Taeko had aged
in the least. A year or two, no more. Taeko looked like a girl of
sixteen or seventeen.

After tea, Sachiko was called to the main house, and five or
ten minutes with Mrs. Sugano proved enough to make her regret
that they had accepted the invitation. What astonished her most
was the lack of information. Mrs. Sugano knew nothing of the
matter that most worried them, Mr. Sawazaki's character. She
had never even met the man. The Suganos and the Sawazakis
had long respected each other as old families, and the former
head of the Sawazaki family had been most friendly with Mrs.
Sugano's husband, but since her husband's death she had had
little or nothing to do with the younger Mr. Sawazaki. As far as
she could remember, he had never visited this house, and she
had never met him. She had not written to him before she set
about arranging the *miai*. Through mutual acquaintances, she
heard that he had lost his wife two or three years before, that
he was looking for a second, that nothing had come of proposals
thus far, and that, though he was past forty and had children by
his first wife, he hoped to take for his second an unmarried lady
in her twenties. Having had Yukiko on her mind for some time,
Mrs. Sugano thought she might arrange a meeting, even though

Yukiko was past the specified age. She knew that she should have found an appropriate go-between, but just any go-between would not do, and she had concluded that rather than waste time on empty forms she would act immediately. A little rashly, she had written to the gentleman: she had such and such a lady among her relatives, and she wondered if he would like to meet her. When she heard nothing from him, she concluded that he was not interested, but then it appeared that he had been quietly investigating on the basis of her letter. After about two months an answer finally came. This was the letter, she said, and handed Sachiko a very brief note: Mr. Sawazaki had much valued the friendship of the old gentleman and regretted that he had neglected Mrs. Sugano herself since her husband's death; he was most grateful for her letter and thanked her from his heart; though he should have answered sooner, he had been occupied with his own vulgar affairs; he would very much like to meet the lady; if he could be given two or three days' notice, his Saturdays were generally open, and he thought they might arrange the details by telephone. Sachiko could only describe the letter as routine. She was astounded: how to explain it, when old families like the Suganos and the Sawazakis were so extremely careful to observe the most elaborate of forms at such times? And was it not a piece of impetuousness, effrontery almost—quite out of keeping with her years—for Mrs. Sugano to send off a letter to a stranger without even consulting the Makiokas? Sachiko had never before encountered this impetuous streak in Mrs. Sugano's nature. Whether or not it had become worse with age, she thought she could see a suggestion of the authoritarian that made her understand why Tatsuo so feared this oldest of his sisters. And it did not entirely make sense for Mr. Sawazaki to have accepted the invitation. Perhaps he was afraid of insulting the Sugano family.

Sachiko tried not to show her dissatisfaction. Mrs. Sugano went on, not quite by way of apology, to explain that she tended to be quick and impatient and greatly disliked tedious formalities, and that she had thought everyone would understand everything once a meeting was arranged. The details could be taken care of later. She had not investigated Mr. Sawazaki, but in view of the fact that she had heard no disagreeable rumors either about him or about his household, she felt sure that he could have no serious

defects. They might save time by questioning him directly on
points they did not understand. She could answer none of
Sachiko's questions. Mr. Sawazaki had two or three children—she
was not quite sure whether it was two or three, and she did not
know whether they were boys or girls. Still she seemed pleased
with herself for having arranged a meeting. She had called Mr.
Sawazaki as soon as she had received Sachiko's letter, she said,
and he would come from Nagoya the next morning at about
eleven. Though she could promise no feast, she would have
Tsuneko get something ready, and she thought just the three of
them, herself, Sachiko, and Yukiko, should see him. They could
all go hunting fireflies tonight. She would arrange tomorrow for
young Mr. Sugano to show Taeko and Etsuko the battlefield. She
would send them off with their lunch (she was delighted with her
plans) and the *miai* should be over by two. One never could tell
about marriage negotiations. Knowing that Yukiko was in that
troublesome thirty-third year, Mrs. Sugano had been astonished
to find that she looked no more than twenty-four or twenty-five—
did she not satisfy Mr. Sawazaki's conditions in full?

Sachiko could not help wishing that she had an excuse to put
the *miai* off and to devote this trip to the fireflies. She had
brought Yukiko on the basis of but one letter from Mrs. Sugano
because she had had complete faith in the latter and had assumed
that the groundwork was carefully laid, and now she saw of how
little importance both the Suganos and the Sawazakis seemed to
think Yukiko. She knew that Yukiko would be hurt if she knew
the truth, and that Teinosuke would be even angrier than she
was herself. It was not hard to imagine the contempt Mr. Sawazaki
must have for a lady who proposed by letter to him and his tens
of millions—nor was it hard to see that he was less than serious
about the negotiations. Had Teinosuke been along, they could have
pleaded what should be common sense—that they would like to
investigate the man, and that they would like at least to go through
the form of having an intermediary. A woman alone, helpless before the widow's enthusiasm, could do nothing so bold. And
Sachiko had to think of her brother-in-law in Tokyo. Sad though
it was for Yukiko, there was nothing to do but follow Mrs.
Sugano's wishes.

"Suppose you change clothes if you are too warm, Yukiko. I am thinking of changing myself."

Back in the cottage, Sachiko signaled to Yukiko that the *miai* was not today, and started to untie her obi. She tried to blame her dejected gesture on the heat. She would say nothing about the unpleasant details to either Yukiko or Koi-san. Since she was only making herself unhappy, for today at least she would forget. Tomorrow was another day, and this evening they could hunt fireflies. It was not Sachiko's nature to brood, and she set to work mending her spirits. Even so she felt a clutching at her heart as she looked at Yukiko, unaware of what had happened. With a show of jauntiness, she took out an informal summer kimono.

Etsuko was suspicious. "Are you wearing that to the firefly hunt, Mother?"

"I am feeling just a little warm." Sachiko reached to hang up the discarded kimono.

∞∞∞∞∞∞∞∞∞∞∞∞∞∞∞∞∞∞

4

THE HOUSE was a strange one, but it was probably less the strange house than sheer exhaustion that kept Sachiko awake. She had gotten up early, she had been rocked and jolted by train and automobile through the heat of the day, and in the evening she had chased over the fields with the children, two or three miles at least. But she knew that the firefly hunt would be good to remember. She had seen firefly hunts only on the puppet stage, Miyuki and Komazawa murmuring of love as they sailed down the River Uji, and, as Taeko had said, one should put on a long-sleeved kimono, a smart summer print, and run across the evening fields with the wind at one's sleeves, lightly taking up a firefly here and there with one's fan. Sachiko was enchanted with the picture.

The firefly hunt was in fact rather different. If you are going to play in the fields, you had better change clothes, said Mrs. Sugano,

laying out four muslin kimonos—prepared especially for them?—
each with a different pattern, as became their several ages. Not
quite the way it looked in the pictures, laughed Taeko. In the
dark, however, it hardly mattered what they had on. They could
still see each other's faces when they left the house, but by the
time they reached the river it was almost pitch dark. "The river"
was actually no more than a ditch through the paddies, a little
wider than most ditches, with plumes of grass bending from either
bank and almost closing off the water. A bridge was still faintly
visible a hundred yards or so ahead.

They turned off the flash lights and approached in silence.
Fireflies dislike noise and light. But even at the edge of the river
there were no fireflies. "Maybe they are not out tonight," someone
whispered. "No, there are plenty of them. Come over here."
Down into the grasses on the bank, and there, in the delicate
moment before the last light goes, were fireflies, gliding out over
the water, in low arcs like the sweep of the grasses. On down the
river, and on and on, were fireflies, lines of them wavering out
from this bank and the other and back again, sketching their uncertain tracks of light down close to the surface of the water,
hidden from outside by the grasses. In the last moment of light,
with the darkness creeping up from the water and the moving
plumes of grass still faintly outlined, there, far as the river stretched
—an infinite number of little lines in two long rows on either side,
quiet, unearthly. Sachiko could see it all even now, here inside
with her eyes closed. Surely that was the impressive moment of the
evening, the moment that made the firefly hunt worth-while.

A firefly hunt has none of the radiance of a cherry-blossom party.
Dark, dreamy, rather—might one say? Perhaps something of the
child's world, the world of the fairy story in it. Something not to
be painted, but set to music, the mood of it taken up on piano or
koto. And while she lay with her eyes closed, the fireflies, out there
along the river, all through the night, were flashing on and off,
silent, numberless. Sachiko felt a surging inside her, as though she
were joining them, soaring and dipping along the surface of the
water, cutting her own uncertain track of light.

It was rather a long little river, as she thought about it, that
they had followed after those fireflies. Now and then they crossed
a bridge over or back, taking care not to fall in, and watching for

snakes with eyes like fireflies. Six-year-old Sōsuke ran ahead in the darkness, thoroughly familiar with the ground. His father, who was guiding them, called uneasily after him, "Sōsuke, Sōsuke." No one worried about frightening the fireflies, there were so many, and unless they called out to one another, they were in danger of being separated, drawn apart in the darkness by fireflies. Sachiko and Yukiko were left alone on one bank. From the other, now brought in clear and now blotted out by the wind, came Etsuko's call, "Koi-san, Koi-san," and Taeko's answer. There was something child-like in the sport, and when it came to child-like things Taeko was the most enthusiastic of the sisters. Etsuko always joined forces with her.

Even now, here inside, Sachiko could hear the voices, blown across the river. "Mother—where are you, Mother?" "Over here." "And Yukiko?" "She is here too." "I have twenty-four already." "Well, be sure not to fall in the river."

Sugano pulled up some grass along the path and tied it into something like a broom. To keep fireflies in, he said. There are places famous for fireflies, like Moriyama in Omi, or the outskirts of Gifu, but the fireflies there are protected, saved for important people. No one cares how many you take here. Sugano himself took more than anyone. The two of them, father and son, went boldly to the edge of the water, and Sugano's bunch of grass became a jeweled broom. Sachiko and the rest began to wonder when he might be ready to think of going back. "The wind is a little cold— do you think perhaps". . . "But we are on the way back. We are going back by a different road." On they walked. It was farther than they had thought. And then they were at Suganos' back gate, everyone with a few captured fireflies, Sachiko and Yukiko with fireflies in their sleeves.

The events of the day passed through Sachiko's mind in no particular order. She opened her eyes. She could have been dreaming. Above her head, in the light of the tiny night bulb, she saw the framed motto she had noticed earlier in the day: the words "Pavilion of Timelessness," written in large characters and signed by one Keidō. Sachiko had no idea who Keidō might be. A flicker of light moved across the room. A firefly, repelled by the mosquito incense, was hunting a way out. They had turned their fireflies loose in the garden, and they had been careful to chase the last from the house before closing the shutters for the night. Where might this one have been hiding? In a final burst of energy, it soared five or six feet into the air, and glided across the room to light on Sachiko's kimono, spread on the clothes rack. Moving over the printed pattern and into the sleeve, it flickered on through the dark blue-gray cloth. The incense in the badger-shaped burner was beginning to hurt Sachiko's throat. She got up to put it out, and, while she was up, moved on to see to the firefly. Carefully she took it up in a piece of paper—the idea of touching it repelled her—and pushed it through a slot in the shutter. There were almost no fireflies left (had they gone back to the river?) of the scores that had flickered through the shrubbery and along the edge of the lake earlier in the evening. The garden was lacquer-black.

Still Sachiko tossed, listening to the breathing of the other three. They were apparently asleep. Taeko lay next to her, and Yukiko and Estuko on the other side of the room. Someone was snoring gently. Yukiko, she decided. A slight, delicate little snore.

"Are you awake?" It was Taeko.

"I have not slept a wink."

"Neither have I."

"You were awake all the time?"

"Because of the strange house. I never can sleep in a strange house."

"Yukiko at least is asleep. Listen to the snoring."

"Like a cat's purring."

"Exactly. Bell might snore that way."

"But how can she be so calm, with the *miai* tomorrow?"

When it came to sleeping, thought Sachiko, Yukiko was sounder than Taeko. Taeko was an extraordinarily light sleeper, awake at the slightest disturbance, whereas Yukiko could sleep sitting up on a train. Yukiko was surprisingly sound in many ways.

"He is coming here?"

"At eleven. We are to have lunch together."

"What shall I do?"

"You and Estuko are being taken to Sekigahara. The three of us will meet him."

"Have you told Yukiko?"

"I did mention it a little while ago."

Sachiko had not been rid of Etsuko long enough to talk to Yukiko, though the two of them were alone those few moments on the far bank of the river. "Tomorrow is the *miai*," Sachiko said. Yukiko gave her usual vague answer and Sachiko could think of no way to begin again. And as Taeko pointed out, Yukiko, with her quiet snoring, did not seem in the least upset. "I suppose when you have been through as many *miai* as Yukiko, you learn not to worry."

"I suppose so," answered Taeko. "But she could be just a little more helpful."

5

"YOUR MOTHER and Yukiko have been to Sekigahara any number of times, but Koi-san was very young and would like to see it again. Suppose you go off with Koi-san, then, and we will be waiting here for you."

Etsuko knew that something was afoot. Usually she would have whined and coaxed to have Yukiko go with her, but this time she set out quietly in a cab with Taeko, Sōsuke and his father, and the old man who had charge of the lunch. In the Pavilion of Timelessness, Sachiko helped Yukiko dress. Soon Tsuneko came to tell them that the gentleman had arrived.

They were led to the fartherest part of the house and into a large, old-fashioned room with low paper-paneled windows. From the wide boards of the veranda, polished to a dark luster, they looked out at the garden on which only the one room fronted, at the tiles of the memorial hall through the fresh green of the old maple tree, at the luxuriant growth of rushes between the pomegranate in bloom by the veranda and the shiny black stones along the pond. Sachiko asked herself whether there had always been this room and this garden, and memories began to come back. She wondered if it was not in this very room that they had slept when they first visited the house twenty years before. The cottage had not yet been built. She had forgotten everything else, but she remembered the rushes, the thin green stems all across the forepart of the garden like lines of rain in the air.

Sawazaki was introducing himself to Mrs. Sugano. When all the introductions were finished, he took his place at the head of the table. Sachiko and Yukiko faced the garden and Mrs. Sugano was at the foot of the table opposite Sawazaki. Before sitting down, he turned to examine a scroll hanging in the alcove above the flower arrangement, lilies in a metal vase. The sisters had a chance to study him from the rear: a small, thin gentleman whom they would have taken for the forty-four or forty-five he was said to be, and whose complexion suggested a glandular disorder. His way of speaking, his bow, his gestures were all quite ordinary, and there was no hint of ostentation in his dress. In comparison with Sachiko and Yukiko he was even a little too carelessly dressed: a brown suit not quite bulging, but worn a little thin here and there; a silk shirt yellowed from repeated launderings; silk socks the stripes of which were beginning to fade—all evidence that he was not taking the *miai* seriously, and at the same time that he lived a most frugal life.

"A fine Seigan [1] piece," he said, whether or not he had finished reading the poem on the scroll. "I understand you have a great many."

Mrs. Sugano giggled modestly, and her face softened. This was the flattery that worked best. "I am told that my husband's grandfather studied calligraphy under Seigan."

For a time the two discussed historical and artistic matters: the Sugano family had several pieces by Seigan's wife Kōran, screens and fans and the like, as well as several pieces by that Ema Saikō who was famous as a lady disciple of the poet and scholar Rai Sanyō. There had apparently been intercourse between the Suganos and the Emas, who were physicians to the head of the Ogaki clan, and Mrs. Sugano still owned a letter from Saikō's father. When the talk turned to Sanyō's love for Saikō, his days in this province of Mino, and Saikō's posthumous Chinese poems, Sawazaki had much to say. Mrs. Sugano, though her answers were short, gave evidence that she was not ill informed herself.

[1] Yanagawa Seigan (1789–1858) was a poet in the Chinese style.

"My husband was very fond of a bamboo ink wash by Saikō. He used to bring it out for guests, and he talked so much of Saikō that in the end I remembered everything myself."

"Mr. Sugano had very good taste. I used to play chess with him, and he asked me several times to come for a look at the new cottage. I've often thought I would trouble you to show me his collection."

"I would have liked you to see the cottage today, but these ladies are staying there."

"It is a beautiful room." Sachiko saw her opportunity to enter the conversation. "So quiet, off in the garden by itself, really much better then a special suite in the best hotel."

Again Mrs. Sugano laughed modestly. "It is hardly that good. But please stay and enjoy it as long as you can. My husband in his last years came to like quiet places more and more. He spent almost all his time out in the cottage."

"And how did you choose the name?" asked Sachiko.

"Suppose we ask Mr. Sawazaki. He will know more about it than I do." Mrs. Sugano seemed to be examining Sawazaki in the classics.[2]

"Well . . ." Sawazaki was obviously uncomfortable.

"Might it be something about a Chinese woodcutter?" Mrs. Sugano suggested.

"It might, I suppose." There was by now a distinct frown on his face.

Mrs. Sugano laughed and gave up the interrogation. A strangely perverse laugh, it rather chilled the conversation.

Tsuneko poured saké from a green porcelain decanter for Sawazaki and then for the others.

Mrs. Sugano had said that Tsuneko would cook lunch, but most of the lunch seemed to have come from a caterer. In such warm weather, Sachiko would have preferred fresh vegetables cooked at home to an uninteresting meal from a country caterer. She tried a bit of the sea bream and found it soft and pulpy. Extremely sensitive to the good and bad in sea bream, she hastily washed it

[2] The name of the garden cottage is literally "Pavilion of the Rotted Axe-handle," a reference to a Chinese woodcutter the handle of whose axe rotted as he stood watching a supernatural chess game.

down with saké, and laid her chopsticks aside for a time. Only the trout seemed really edible, and they were not from a caterer: she gathered that Sawazaki had brought them on ice.

"Suppose you try the trout, Yukiko."

Since it was her unfortunate question that had spoiled the conversation, Sachiko wanted to make amends. She found Sawazaki thoroughly unapproachable, however, and in desperation she turned to her sister. Yukiko had been looking at the floor since they came in. She only nodded.

"Yukiko is fond of trout?" asked Mrs. Sugano.

Yukiko nodded again, and Sachiko answered for her. "We are all fond of trout, and Yukiko more than anyone."

"How nice. We didn't know what to offer you, way out here in the country. And then Mr. Sawazaki brought the trout."

"We don't often see such beautiful trout," said Tsuneko.

"And packed in all that ice. You must have been loaded down. Where did you say they were taken?"

"In the Nagara River." Sawazaki was feeling better. "I telephoned Gifu last night and had them brought to the station."

"What a great deal of trouble."

"And so thanks to you we have our first trout of the year," said Sachiko.

Though the conversation moved a little more smoothly and there was desultory talk of famous spots in Gifu Prefecture—the Japan Rhine, Gero Spa, the Waterfall of Filial Piety—and of the firefly hunt, it required a great effort to string the pieces together. Sachiko, who could always drink, would as soon have had more saké. There was some excuse for Tsuneko's not having noticed, with the guests rather far apart in the large room and with but one man among them, and the weather was too warm for much saké. Still it seemed a little extreme that Mrs. Sugano and Yukiko should have their first cups cooling before them, and Sachiko should have had an empty cup since she washed down that piece of sea bream. Concentrating on Sawazaki, Tsuneko had decided that the women could take care of themselves. Perhaps Sawazaki was not in a drinking mood, perhaps he was being reticent, perhaps he was not much of a drinker. In any case, he allowed his cup to be filled only once in three times Tsuneko presented the decanter. He could not in the end have drunk more than two or three cups. All through the meal he sat with the stiffest formality, almost like a soldier at attention.

"Are you ever in Osaka or Kobe, Mr. Sawazaki?"

"Never in Kobe. I do go to Osaka once or twice a year."

Unable to keep from wondering why this millionaire had agreed to the *miai*, Sachiko was on the watch for defects. Nothing so far had struck her as especially peculiar, though it was a little comical to see how he hated to be asked something he did not know the answer to. He hardly needed to pout—but maybe such was the nature of rich men. The prominent veins along the bridge of his nose, just below the eyebrows, suggested a quick temper. And there was something a little furtive about the man (was it Sachiko's imagination?), something a little effeminate, brooding, even timid, about the cast of his features. She could see how little interest he had in the *miai*. She had noticed that he turned a searching eye on Yukiko several times during his conversation with Mrs. Sugano. Afterwards that dark, cold glance scarcely bothered with her at all. Mrs. Sugano and Tsuneko being at great pains to bring the two together, Sawazaki would occasionally say a word or two to Yukiko—and promptly turn to someone else. Yukiko's monosyllabic answers were partly to blame, but there could be little doubt that he was not pleased with her. Sachiko concluded that the principal reason was that left eye. In spite of Sachiko's hopes that the spot would have faded, it was only darker today. Yukiko had started to put on her usual thick powder, and Sachiko had had to restrain her—was it not just a little too thick? Sachiko had tried various tricks, adding a touch of rouge and thinning the powder, but there was no hiding the spot. Mrs. Sugano and Tsuneko gave no sign that they noticed. Yukiko was seated on Sawazaki's right, however, and the brilliant early-summer light set the mark off sharply. Her own indifference helped a little: she behaved as though the spot were the most natural thing in the world, nothing to be apologetic or embarrassed about; but Sachiko, sure that it was darker than the day before, did not see how she could leave her sister exposed much longer.

"I am awfully sorry, but I have to think about train time." Sawazaki stood up abruptly when lunch was over, and Sachiko thanked him from the bottom of her heart.

6

"Now THAT YOU are here, you must stay another night. Tomorrow is Sunday, and we can have someone show you the Waterfall of Filial Piety. You remember we talked about it at lunch."

But the sisters refused politely. As soon as Etsuko and Taeko were back, they began getting ready for the 3:09 train, which would have them in Gamagōri at five-thirty. Though it was a Saturday afternoon, the second-class car was almost empty. They found seats together, and the exhaustion from the day before overtook them. No one felt like talking. The car was oppressive and sticky in weather that announced the coming of the rainy season. Sachiko and Yukiko dozed off, and Taeko and Etsuko turned in a companionable way to the weekly magazines.

"Etsuko, your fireflies are running away." Taeko took up the firefly cage that hung by the window, and set it in Etsuko's lap. The old man at the Sugano house had made Etsuko a cage to take along, a tin can with gauze stretched over the open top and bottom. The gauze had come loose, and one or two fireflies were crawling out.

"Let me do it for you." Etsuko was having trouble with the cord around the gauze. By shading the cage, one could see the green light of the fireflies even in the daytime. Taeko peered inside.

"Look, look." She passed it back to Etsuko. "You have lots of things besides fireflies."

Etsuko took her turn. "Spiders, Koi-san, spiders!"

"You are right." Tiny, rather engaging spiders about the size of grains of rice were trailing after the fireflies. Suddenly, Taeko jumped up with a shriek and dropped the can in the seat. Sachiko and Yukiko opened their eyes.

"What is it, Koi-san?"

"Spiders, big spiders!" There were enormous spiders among the little ones. All four were aroused by now.

"Throw it away somewhere, Koi-san."

Taeko picked the can up gingerly and threw it to the floor.
A grasshopper jumped out.

"Poor fireflies." Etsuko looked mournfully at the can.

"Let me take care of your spiders." A man of perhaps fifty—
he had on a kimono and seemed to be from the country near by—
had been watching with amusement from diagonally across the
aisle. "Give me a hairpin or something." Sachiko gave him a hairpin, and he took out each spider and stamped on it. There was a
little grass mixed in with the crushed spiders, but not many fireflies escaped. "Several of them are dead, Miss," he said, tilting the
can from side to side when he had retied the gauze. "Take it to
the bathroom and sprinkle it."

"Wash your hands while you are there, Etsuko. Fireflies are
poisonous."

"And they smell." Etsuko sniffed at her hands. "Like grass."

"Don't throw the dead ones away, young lady. They make good
medicine."

"For what?" asked Taeko.

"Keep them and dry them, and then mix them with rice and
put them on cuts and burns."

"Really? And does that help?"

"I haven't tried myself, but they tell me it does."

Sachiko and the rest had never been through this part of the
country except on an express, and it bored them to have the train
stop politely at little stations they had not known existed. The
way from Gifu to Nagoya seemed interminable. Soon Sachiko and
Yukiko had dozed off again. "Nagoya, Mother. Look at the castle,
Yukiko." Etsuko set about waking them up. Opening their eyes
long enough to see the new passengers, they were asleep again
before the train was out of Nagoya. They did not notice that it had
begun to rain and that Yukiko had closed the window. The car
being even stuffier with all the windows closed, most of the other
passengers were soon dozing off with them. A young army officer
across the aisle some four seats ahead began singing Schubert's
"Serenade."

> "Softly flows my serenade
> Through the night to you. . . ."

There was nothing boisterous about the singing. Sachiko, opening her eyes, thought someone had brought a phonograph. Though
they could see only the back of the uniform and part of the face,
they knew that the officer was young, still in his twenties, and
shy. He had been aboard at Ogaki, and they had not yet seen his
face—even when, in their troubles with the fireflies, they had the
attention of the whole car. He evidently was proud of his voice.
Still it was a little strained, as if he were aware of the pretty
ladies behind him. When he had finished he looked at the floor
for a time, and began Goethe's "Wild Rose" to the Schubert
setting.

> "A boy once found a wild, red rose.
> Rose upon the heath. . . ."

Sachiko knew the songs from a German movie called "Unfinished Symphony." One of the sisters, they did not know which,
was soon humming with the young officer. As their voices grew
louder someone joined in with the harmony. The officer's neck
was scarlet. His voice was louder, and had a distinct tremor. Their
seats being a convenient distance away, the sisters sang on quite
as the spirit took them. When the concert was over, a startling
silence fell over the car. The officer looked bashfully at the floor,
and at Okazaki he fled from the car.

"And we never saw his face," said Taeko.

This was Sachiko's first trip to Gamagōri. She had heard a great
deal about the Tokiwa Inn from Teinosuke, who made a trip
or two a month to Nagoya, and who often said that he must take
them all to the Tokiwa some time. He was sure that Etsuko in
particular would enjoy it. They had made all their plans two or
three times before, but always something had come up. It was
Teinosuke's idea that they should now go to Gamagōri without
him. He was always too busy to keep them company even when
he was in Nagoya, he said, and this would be their chance. He
telephoned for reservations. Sachiko, who had learned to travel
without her husband on the trip to Tokyo the autumn before, was
childishly pleased with her new boldness and most eager to make
the trip. When she reached the inn, she felt even more grateful to
her husband. The *miai* had left a bad taste that would have stayed
with her had she said goodbye to Yukiko in Ogaki, and aside

from her own unhappiness, it would have been too cruel to send
Yukiko forlornly off to Tokyo after such an experience. Teinosuke's
idea had been a splendid one indeed. Sachiko was determined not
to let herself think about what had happened, and she was greatly
relieved to see that Yukiko—with Taeko and Etsuko—meant to
enjoy herself. The rain had stopped, and they had a beautiful
Sunday. As Teinosuke had expected, the games at the inn and
the scenery along the coast, everything about the place in fact,
delighted Etsuko. Still more pleasing to Sachiko, enough to make
the trip really worth-while, was the bright, placid Yukiko, no longer
in the least disturbed about what had happened the day before.
In Gamagōri Station at about two the next afternoon, they
boarded trains that passed within fifteen minutes of each other,
one for Tokyo, the other for Osaka.

Yukiko took a local train after seeing the others off. Never
having travelled such a distance on a local, she expected to be
bored, but it had seemed a nuisance to order an express ticket
and change at Toyohashi. She had a volume of short stories by
Anatole France to keep her company. Too listless to know what
she was reading, she put the book down and looked absent-
mindedly out the window. She was feeling the strain of the last
two days, and she was suffering a reaction from the gaiety of but
a short time before. And now she would have to spend several
months in Tokyo. She had been so long in Ashiya that she had begun to think she might escape having to go back, and here she was,
deposited by herself on a slow train in a strange country station.

"See me off as far as Ashiya," Etsuko had said, half jokingly.
Even as she dismissed the remark with a promise to come again
soon, Yukiko had for a moment thought seriously of going back
with them and putting off her return to Tokyo.

The second-class car being even emptier than the day before,
she had a whole section to herself, but her neck was so stiff that
she could hardly move, and she would doze off only to wake up
again. In a half hour or so she was wide awake. For some time
she had noticed a gentlemen across the aisle four or five seats
away. She had opened her eyes because she sensed that he was
staring at her. As she sat up in some confusion and slipped her
feet into her sandals, the man turned to look out the window, but
something seemed to be on his mind. Before long he was stealing

glances at her again. At first rather annoyed, Yukiko began to wonder if he might not have his reasons. She began to feel that she had seen him before. About forty, he was wearing an open-necked shirt and a gray suit with white stripes. He was small and thin and he had a swarthy complexion; his hair was neatly combed, and all in all his appearance suggested the rustic gentleman of means. At first he had been sitting with his chin on his hands, which were folded over the handle of the umbrella between his knees. Now he was leaning back. There was a new white Panama hat in the rack over his head. Who was he, why could she not remember? The man seemed to be asking the same questions. He would look away when she glanced in his direction and look back again when she was not watching. She could not remember knowing anyone in Toyohashi, where he had boarded the train—and then she thought of that Mr. Saigusa whom her brother-in-law had suggested as a possible husband more than ten years before. Saigusa had belonged to a well-to-do Toyohashi family, there was no doubt about it, nor could there be much doubt that this was he. Displeased with the man's rustic appearance and what she took to be evidence of scant intelligence and learning, Yukiko had brushed aside Tatsuo's suggestion and insisted on having her own way. The man was as rustic as ever. He was not especially unattractive, and, old beyond his years even then, he had not aged much, but his country air was even more pronounced. Because of it Yukiko was able to call up that particular face from all the dimly remembered faces in all the dimly remembered *miai*. The man apparently began to suspect the truth at about the time she recognized him. He turned abruptly to the window. But he still did not seem convinced. Taking care to choose moments when Yukiko was not looking, he would now and then steal a sidelong glance at her. She had met him several times at the main house in Osaka, and, determined as he had been to marry her, he should not have forgotten her even if she had forgotten him. What was puzzling him, perhaps, was that she had changed so little since the *miai*, and that she was as youthfully dressed as she had been that day. Even so it was not pleasant to be stared at. What if he knew how many *miai* there had been since, what if he knew that just yesterday there had been another, and that she was on her way home from it? She shuddered at the thought. And unhappily, she was wearing a less radiant kimono than that of two days before, and she had been rather careless with her make-up. Knowing that she showed the wear of travel more than most people, she wanted to retouch her face, but she thought it would be a sign of weakness to walk down the aisle past the man, or to steal a look at the mirror in her compact. He was probably not on his way to Tokyo, since it was a local train. At each station she hoped that he would get off. At Fujieda he stood up and took his Panama hat from the rack. After a last look at her, quite open this time, he turned to leave the train.

Thoughts of that *miai* and all that happened before and after chased through her tired mind. Had it been 1927? No, 1928 seemed more likely. She must have been about twenty. And was that her first *miai*? Why had she taken such a dislike to the man? Tatsuo tried every argument: the Saigusa family was one of the wealthiest in Toyohashi; the man was the oldest son; Yukiko would want for nothing; it was too good a match for what the Makioka family had become; and now that the discussions had come so far Tatsuo's position would be most difficult if she were to refuse. But Yukiko went on shaking her head, and her reason was more than the man's dull manner: though they had been told that he had been unable to go on to school because of illness, they knew that his poor record in the middle school was in fact responsible; and even as the wife of a wealthy man, Yukiko thought, it would be dreary to rust away in a little city like Toyohashi. Sachiko, who quite agreed with her, protested even more strongly. It would be unbearably sad to send poor Yukiko off to the back country. Then too, without saying so even to each other, they wanted to annoy Tatsuo. His foster father but recently dead, Tatsuo had begun to flex his muscles. All three sisters, Taeko with the others, had been most annoyed at the way he seemed to think he only needed to use force. They had formed a league of three to show him how mistaken he was. What angered Tatsuo most of all was Yukiko's refusal to give a definite answer until he had gone almost beyond retreating. Then, suddenly, she became stubborn. To his reproaches, she replied that young girls preferred not to express themselves openly on such matters, and that he should have known from her manner whether or not she wanted to marry the man. Even so, she could not deny that, in part, she had been thinking of the fact that an executive in Tatsuo's bank was acting as go-between. She purposely made her answers evasive to embarrass her brother-in-law. Through no fault of his own, the man Saigusa thus became ammunition for a family quarrel. Yukiko had neither thought nor heard of him since. No doubt he had several children by now. And what if she had married the rustic gentleman? More than sour grapes, she was sure, made her know that she would not have been happy. If he spent his life on slow trains between one out-of-the-way little station and another, she could not believe that she would have been happy with him. Her decision had been the right one.

Reaching the Shibuya house at about ten that night, she said nothing of the encounter to either Tatsuo or Tsuruko.

7

SACHIKO had much to think about on the train back to Osaka. More than of pleasant things—the firefly hunt two evenings before, the night and morning in Gamagōri—she found herself thinking of the forlorn figure they had just left in Gamagōri, of that thin face, the dark spot over the eye as prominent as ever. With the face and figure came back all the impressions of the unhappy *miai*. She did not know how many times in the last ten years she had seen Yukiko through a *miai*. Counting informal meetings, she thought five or six would probably be too modest an estimate. Never before had the Makiokas been so humbled. Always they had felt that the advantage was with them, that the other side was courting their favor—always it had been their role to judge the man and find him lacking. This time their position had been weak from the start. They should have refused when the first letter came, and they had begun to retreat then, and Sachiko had retreated again when there was still some possibility of refusing. She had, in the end, gone through with the *miai* out of deference to Tatsuo and Mrs. Sugano. Why then had she felt so intimidated? Always before she had displayed Yukiko proudly, a sister of whom she need never be ashamed, and yesterday she had trembled each time Sawazaki looked at Yukiko. There was no evading the fact that Sawazaki had been the examiner and they the examined. That fact alone was enough to make Sachiko feel that she and Yukiko had been insulted as never before. What weighed even more on her mind, however, and quite refused to leave her was the thought that Yukiko carried a blemish. A blemish hardly worth considering, perhaps, but there it was nonetheless. They might as well forget about this *miai*. What of future ones? Something must be done about that mark over the eye. Could it be removed, and did it not make Yukiko's prospects even worse? Or had the mark been especially dark yesterday, and conditions—the light, the angle—impossibly bad? One thing was certain: they would no longer enter a *miai* with the old feeling of superiority. From now on it would be as yesterday: Sachiko would tremble as she saw her sister exposed to the stare of the prospective husband.

Evidently guessing that this silence was more than a sign of fatigue, Taeko gave herself up to her own thoughts.

"What happened yesterday?" she asked in a low voice, taking advantage of a moment when Etsuko had gone to water the fireflies.

Sachiko did not want to talk. After a minute or two, as though she suddenly remembered that a question had been put to her, she answered: "It was over in a great hurry."

"And what will come of it?"

"Well, you remember how the train broke down."

Sachiko fell silent again, and Taeko asked no more questions.

Though she gave Teinosuke a general account of what had happened, Sachiko did not go into all the unpleasant details. The thought of living them again was too much for her. The man was certain to refuse, said Teinosuke, and they might take the initiative and refuse first, before they were made fools of. But that was only talk. They had to think of their relations with Mrs. Sugano and the main house; and in secret Sachiko still held out a hope that somehow, perhaps . . .

Before they had time to make their plans—almost as if to chase Sachiko home—a letter came from Mrs. Sugano.

June 13

DEAR SACHIKO:

It was good of you to come all the way out into the country. I fear we did nothing to entertain you, and I hope you' will forgive us and come again, possibly for the mushrooms this fall.

I am enclosing a letter I received today from Mr. Sawazaki. Nothing but trouble has come of my feeble efforts. I have no apology, and I can only repeat that I hope you will forgive me. Upon asking an acquaintance in Nagoya to investigate, my son was yesterday informed by letter that whatever desires there might be on the other side, there was some doubt as to what you yourselves would be thinking.

It is in any case not a particularly fine match, and I am only sorry to have brought you all this distance for nothing. Please pass this on to Miss Yukiko.

Sincerely yours,

SUGANO YASU

This letter was enclosed from Sawazaki:

June 12

MY DEAR MRS. SUGANO:

I was happy to find you well in this gloomy weather.

Thank you very much indeed for your troubles of day before yesterday.

About Miss Makioka: since, upon conference, we have concluded that the answer must be negative, I should be most grateful if you would so inform her. I am answering immediately lest I cause you further trouble.

Thank you again for your kindness.

Sincerely yours,

SAWAZAKI HIROSHI

These two oddly formal notes added to the unpleasantness in a number of ways. The Makiokas were, for the first time, being told they had failed an examination. For the first time they were branded the losers. Prepared though they had been in advance, the tone of the letters annoyed them, as did Mrs. Sugano's way of ending the negotiations. It did no good to complain, of course, but Sawazaki's letter was written in pen and ink on a sheet of very ordinary paper (the earlier letter to Mrs. Sugano had been in brush on more elegant paper). Although he said that the decision had been reached "upon conference," he could probably have given his answer the day of the *miai*. Be that as it may, he was not writing to the Makiokas, and could he not have thought of a less stiffly formal way to explain his reasons to Mrs. Sugano? Aside from the enormity of calling people a great distance only to reply that "the answer must be negative," was it not an insult to the Sugano family not to give an explanation? "Since . . . we have concluded." And what was that "since"? "Upon conference," he said, and he seemed to mean: "I have talked the matter over with my relatives and we have decided that it is no match." Such perhaps was the way with millionaires. That glib "since" clause made them yet unhappier. What could Mrs. Sugano have had in mind, enclosing the letter? If they had not known what Sawazaki said, it need not have worried them. Why then had she found it necessary to show them a letter that was not even addressed to them? There may have been nothing in it that disturbed her. But one could have expected of a woman her age that she quietly tuck it away and report the failure of the negotiations so as not to hurt the Makiokas. It was little comfort to have a forced explanation tacked on. "My son was yesterday informed by letter that whatever desires there might be on the other side, there was some doubt as to what you yourselves would be thinking. It is in any case not a particularly fine match." Though without doubt Mrs. Sugano belonged to an old and well-placed family, Sachiko and Teinosuke had to conclude that she was an insensitive rustic who simply did not understand the feelings of the city-dweller. It had been their mistake to be drawn into marriage negotiations managed by such a person. And the main responsibility rested with the main house in Tokyo. The Ashiya house had gone into the negotiations because they trusted Tatsuo. Should not Tatsuo, presumably familiar with his sister's disposition, have done a little preliminary investigating, and determined for himself just what the prospects were? The important thing was Mrs. Sugano's kindness; to ignore it would be to put Tatsuo in a difficult position—the details would come later. So Tsuruko had said in her letter. Had it not been irresponsible of Tatsuo to have Mrs. Sugano's message relayed to

them without considering Yukiko's position and without bothering
to see whether or not Mrs. Sugano had investigated her candidate?
Teinosuke and Sachiko and Yukiko had been made unhappy to
no purpose whatsoever. It was possible to feel that they had all
been used to save face for Tatsuo. Whatever might be the effect
on Sachiko and himself, Teinosuke was secretly troubled lest the
affair lead to more unpleasantness between Tatsuo and Yukiko.
He could only be grateful that the two letters had been sent to
Sachiko and not to the Tokyo house. Sachiko followed his suggestion and waited a couple of weeks before writing to Tsuruko.
At the end of her letter she spoke casually of word from Mrs.
Sugano that the negotiations with Sawazaki did not seem to be
going well. She hoped her sister would tell Yukiko in a tactful
way, she added, but the matter might as well be dropped.

8

EARLY IN JULY Teinosuke had to spend two or three days in
Tokyo. Worried about Yukiko, he found time to visit the Shibuya
house. He did not see Tatsuo, but Tsuruko and Yukiko both
seemed in good spirits. Though he talked alone to Tsuruko while
Yukiko was out making ice cream, the question of the *miai* did not
come up. He thought the main house might have had some hint
from Mrs. Sugano of the reasons why Yukiko had not pleased the
man, but Tsuruko did not seem to want to discuss the *miai*.
Possibly no word had come; possibly she preferred to keep it secret.
She talked a great deal of how, since it would soon be the
twenty-second anniversary of her mother's death, they would all
have to go to Osaka for memorial services;[1] and perhaps Yukiko's
unexpectedly good spirits were due to the fact that she could
count on returning to Ashiya soon.

They had decided, said Tsuruko, to move the day up from
September 25, the anniversary of her mother's death, to September

---

[1] On certain anniversaries, memorial services have a special significance.

24, a Sunday, and have services at the Zenkeiji Temple. She and
Tatsuo would therefore go to Osaka on Saturday, September 23.
The problem was which of the children to take. Six would be far
too many. Teruo, the oldest, would of course have to go, and
though they could leave behind the other three of school age,
Masao and Umeko would have to go too. And whom to put in
charge of the house? It would be ideal if Yukiko would agree to
stay in Tokyo, but one could hardly order her away from memorial services for her own mother. They had no one else to ask,
there was nothing to do but leave the maid O-hisa in charge. Did
he think it would be all right?—for only two or three days, after
all. There would be six of them in Osaka, then, and where should
they all stay? Probably at two houses. Six people would be more
than they could have descending on one house. Tsuruko would
ask to be put up in Ashiya. So she rambled on, worrying about an
event more than two months off.

Sachiko herself had been wondering what the main house
meant to do about the memorial services, and had thought of
writing to Tokyo before long. In December 1937, on the twelfth
anniversary of her father's death, Tatsuo had had simple services
in a Tokyo temple of the same sect as the Zenkeiji. The main
house had just that autumn moved to Tokyo and faced all the
problems of the new life, and it would not have been easy to
return to Osaka. Formal greetings and lacquer incense bowls
for memorial offerings were sent around to relatives: though
aware of the impropriety, Tatsuo meant to have memorial services
for the late Mr. Makioka in Tokyo; he would be delighted to see
anyone who happened to be in the city, but he could hardly ask
a special trip; and he hoped rather that everyone would visit the
Zenkeiji during the day. The reasons given were valid, and Sachiko
sensed too that Tatsuo, who knew how lavish services in Osaka
would have to be, feared the expense. Their father had been a
patron of the arts, and actors and geishas in considerable numbers
were present at services as late as the second anniversary. The
second-anniversary banquet at the Harihan Restaurant, complete
with professional entertainers, made one think of the Makioka
family at its most prosperous. His lesson learned, Tatsuo sent out
invitations for the sixth-anniversary services in 1931 to a small
and select circle, but many remembered and more heard by

chance, and the modest plans for refreshments at the temple had to be dropped in favor of another banquet at the Harihan. Although there were those who rejoiced in the display ("Father loved extravagance so, it is good to spend a little money on him—think of it as filial piety"), Tatsuo complained that the question was whether he should or should not spend beyond his means. The Makioka fortune no longer being what it once was, the services should have been more modest, as he was sure Mr. Makioka in his grave would agree. Everything considered, it seemed likely that he had special reasons for staying away from Osaka on the twelfth anniversary. The family elders all criticized him severely: what was this, not coming down from Tokyo for a parent's memorial services? The people at the main house had become wonderfully economical, it was true, but was not a memorial service rather special? With Tsuruko caught in the cross fire, Tatsuo's final excuse had been that he would make amends by having the sixteenth anniversary services in Osaka. Sachiko had therefore been wondering what he meant to do on this twenty-second anniversary of her mother's death. It was less that the other relatives would complain than that she herself would be most dissatisfied if services were again held in Tokyo.

Tatsuo had no strong personal feelings in the matter, not having known his mother-in-law. Sachiko's own feelings about her mother were rather different from her feelings about her father. Her father, who died of apoplexy in December, 1925, at the age of fifty-four, had not lived an especially long life. Her mother's life was short; she died in 1917 at the age of thirty-six. Sachiko herself was just at that age, it occurred to her, and Tsuruko was already two years older, and yet she remembered her mother as far more beautiful than either herself or Tsuruko today. The circumstances of her mother's illness and death had something to do with the fact that Sachiko, fourteen at the time, saw her mother as fresher and younger than she actually was. Though victims of lung diseases often become repulsively pallid and emaciated, Sachiko's mother preserved a strange charm to the end. Her face, a cleaner white, took on no shadow, and her hands and feet, thin though they were, still carried a warm glow. She had fallen ill shortly after Taeko's birth. Sent at first to the seashore, to Hamadera and Suma, she was finally moved to a little

rented house in the hills at Minoo when it became evident that
the sea air only made her worse. Sachiko was allowed to see her
mother in the last years only once or twice a month, and then
for a very short time. She would find after she went home that the
image of the sick woman lingered on and on in her mind, joined
to the lonely sound of the waves or the wind in the pines, and
it was thus that she came to idealize her mother, and her mother's
image became the focus of her affections. Because the family
knew after the move to Minoo that the mother would not live
long, Sachiko's visits were not restricted as they had once been.
There was a telephone call one morning, and she was dead
shortly after Sachiko and the rest arrived at her bedside. The
autumn rain, which had been falling for several days, beat against
the glass doors at the veranda. The little garden sloped gently
off to a mountain stream and all down the slope autumn *hagi*,[2]
beginning to shed its blossoms, was pounded at by the rain. With
the water rising and people talking excitedly of a flood, the sound
of the rushing water was far stronger in their ears than the sound
of the rain. Sachiko would tremble as a stone in the bed of the
stream, grinding against another, shook the foundations of the
house, and she would wonder what to do if there should indeed
be a flood. But at the sight of the quiet, utterly tranquil face of
her mother going away as the morning dew, she quite forgot her
fears, and felt as though something cool had swept over her, as
though she were being drawn in by a vision and washed clean.
It was sadness that she felt, but a sadness divorced from the personal, with a sort of musical pleasure in it, at the thought that
something beautiful was leaving the earth. Though they had
known that their mother would not live through the autumn, the
grief would have been scarcely endurable, the darkness far more
intense and persistent, had the dead face been less beautiful.

Sachiko's father, early addicted to pleasure, had been married
at the age of twenty-eight, rather late for the time, to a woman
nine years younger than himself. According to the family elders,
it was such a happy match that for a time he stopped going to
the teahouses. The two stood in complete contrast to each other,
the husband a lover of gaiety and lavishness, the wife, born of a
Kyoto merchant family, in every sense the fragile, self-effacing

[2] *Lespedeza japonica.*

Kyoto beauty. For all the contrast, people looked upon them as a couple to be envied. But Sachiko had no memories from so early a day. She remembered rather that her father was always away chasing after his pleasures, and that her mother, the docile, long-suffering townsman's wife, managed the house with no hint of dissatisfaction. The addiction to pleasure, verging on debauchery, only became more shameless with the mother's illness, and yet Sachiko knew that it was the Kyoto beauty her father liked best. He chose Kyoto more often than Osaka for his pleasures, and he sometimes took Sachiko with him to a Kyoto teahouse. And he loved Yukiko more than Taeko. No doubt he had all sorts of reasons, but one must have been that of the four sisters Yukiko most resembled her mother. Tsuruko too resembled her mother, while Sachiko and Taeko were like their father. Although Tsuruko's face reminded one of the Kyoto beauty, she was tall and generously built, and quite without her mother's fragile grace. Less than five feet tall—a woman of the last century —the mother had had tiny hands and feet. The graceful fingers reminded one of a delicately wrought miniature. Taeko, the shortest of the four daughters, was taller than her mother had been, and Yukiko, an inch taller than Taeko, was rather large by comparison, but she more than the others had inherited her mother's good points. She had about her a sort of perfume to remind one of her mother.

Sachiko heard of the memorial services only through her husband. Nothing came directly from either Tsuruko or Yukiko until the formal invitation arrived in mid-September. It struck her as a little odd, on reading the invitation, that the main house meant to move the sixteenth-anniversary services for her father up two years and hold them at the same time. Teinosuke too was surprised—nothing had been said in Tokyo of memorial services for the father. But whatever Tsuruko might have had in mind, there seemed little doubt that Tatsuo had meant from the start to combine the two services. It was not unusual to move up services for one parent or the other. Still Tatsuo, who had been criticized for the inadequacy of the earlier services, had promised to make amends when the sixteenth anniversary came. One could not deny, if confronted with the argument, that times had changed and that lavish display was improper in a national crisis, but if that was what worried Tatsuo, should he not have consulted the more troublesome relatives? To wait until the last minute and abruptly announce his decision—was it not a little tactless? The invitation said simply that the family would be much honored if such and such a person could be at the Zenkeiji Temple, Shimodera-machi, Osaka, at ten o'clock on the morning of September 24, for memorial services, the sixteenth and twenty-second respectively, for the late Mr. and Mrs. Makioka. It was not until some days later that Sachiko heard the details from Tsuruko over the telephone: although they had had no such plans when Teinosuke was in Tokyo, Tatsuo had suggested that it might be well to have the father's services this year too, reckless spending for memorial services being difficult to reconcile with National Spiritual Mobilization; even so they had made the change in plans only recently, after they had begun the invitations, and after Tatsuo had decided that with a war on in Europe and no one able to say how long Japan could stay out, and with the China Incident, now in its third year, showing signs of becoming part of a world war, they must economize and tighten their belts a bit more; since there were to be so few guests they had not thought engraved invitations necessary, and they had had to call in clerks from the bank to help with the rewriting; there had been no time for consultations, but Tsuruko did not think they would again be criticized—and she agreed completely with her husband. When she had finished this elaborate chain of apologies and explanations, she went on to tell of her own plans. She and Yukiko, with Masao and Umeko, would take the Swallow Express on the twenty-second. They hoped they might stay with Sachiko. Tatsuo and Teruo would take a night train on Saturday, return on Sunday night, and thus be no trouble to anyone. As for Tsuruko herself, it had been two years since she was last in Osaka. Inasmuch as she could leave the house in O-hisa's hands this time and did not know when she could leave home again, she would really like to stay four or five days, but unfortunately she had to return on the twenty-sixth at the very latest. What of refreshments, asked Sachiko. Yes, refreshments—they had taken a room at the temple, and they would have a caterer bring in lunch. She had telephoned all the instructions to Shōkichi, whose father was taking care of the Osaka house. There were not likely to be

366   THE MAKIOKA SISTERS

complications, but to make very sure, could Sachiko check again
with the temple and the caterer? Expecting some thirty-five guests,
she had ordered lunch and saké for forty. They might ask the wife
and daughter of the priest to warm the saké. They would have
to serve it themselves, however, and she hoped Sachiko would
be willing. Tsuruko, who rarely telephoned, talked on and on
when she did. She would think of something more and something more that had to be said. Both Yukiko and Taeko would
be at the services. How embarrassing to have people see the two
of them, still unmarried. And what sort of presents should she
bring to the family? It was Sachiko who finally said: "I will see
you day after tomorrow, then."

9

THE MATTER TOUCHED upon at the end of the conversation—that
it would be a trial to display the two sisters for whom husbands
had not been found—probably troubled both Tatsuo and Tsuruko.
One could see here another reason for their lack of enthusiasm.
Tatsuo had wanted to have at least Yukiko married before this
twenty-second anniversary—Yukiko, who was still "Miss" at thirty-
two, while all the younger cousins were married and some of them
mothers already. At the sixth-anniversary services in 1931, it had
not been easy for Tsuruko and Tatsuo to hear how Yukiko "had
not aged at all," and this time the discomfort would be still more
acute. True, Yukiko looked as young as ever, and she did not
seem in the least humiliated at having been overtaken and passed
by cousins. For that very reason people pitied her, and turned to
reproach the main house. What a shame that such a woman
should be so long unmarried; her dead mother and father must
be lamenting in their graves. A good half of the responsibility was
her own, thought Sachiko, who thoroughly sympathized with her
brother-in-law.
But she was upset at the thought of the approaching visit for

reasons that had nothing to do with Yukiko. There had been another change in Taeko's affairs.

For a short time after Itakura's death, Taeko had seemed dazed and apathetic. In a week or two, however, she had to all appearances recovered. She had been stunned by the death of a man for love of whom she had been prepared to brave all opposition, but she was not one to brood. Soon back at sewing school, she was as healthy and energetic as ever. Sachiko was filled with admiration: this time even Koi-san had been shaken, and it was fine of her to show it so little. With all these projects of hers, said Sachiko to Teinosuke, Koi-san could do things she herself could never hope to imitate.

One day toward the middle of July, Sachiko had lunch with Mrs. Kuwayama at her favorite Kobe *sushi* restaurant. Koi-san had just called to make reservations for two, said the old man. Sachiko had no idea where she might have called from, since she had left the house that morning, and had equally little idea who the other person might be. Several times recently, added one of the boys, Koi-san had been in with a gentleman. Startled, Sachiko would have liked to hear more, but with Mrs. Kuwayama beside her she could only smile and change the subject. And the truth was that she was a little afraid to know who the man was. Leaving Mrs. Kuwayama after lunch, she went to a French movie she had seen once before. When she left the theater at five-thirty, she could hardly keep herself from wandering back toward the restaurant—Taeko would just then be arriving with her gentleman friend. Instead, she went straight home.

A month later, toward the middle of August, Teinosuke, Sachiko, Etsuko, and O-haru went to see Kikugorō, playing that month in Kobe. (Taeko rarely accepted Sachiko's invitations to a play or a movie. She meant to go, she would say, but some other time.) As they climbed from the taxi and started to cross the street, Sachiko and O-haru were held back by a red light. A taxi passed, and they had a glimpse of Taeko and Okubata inside —in the bright summer sunlight there could be no mistaking them. Lost in conversation, they did not know they had been seen.

"O-haru, you are not to tell Mr. Makioka or Etsuko," said Sachiko in consternation. Noting the change in Sachiko's expres-

sion, O-haru nodded with great seriousness and looked at the
ground. Sachiko deliberately held back. She wanted her heart to
be pounding a little less violently when she overtook Teinosuke
and Etsuko, a block or so ahead. Always in a crisis she felt the
tips of her fingers go cold. She clutched at O-haru's hand.

"O-haru." She had to say something. "Have you heard rumors
about Koi-san? She hardly ever seems to be at home any more."

O-haru only nodded.

"If you know anything, please tell me. Are there telephone
calls from that man?"

"No calls—that I know of," said O-haru with some hesitation.
After a pause, she muttered hastily: "Two or three times in
Nishinomiya . . ."

"You have seen him?"

"Him . . . and Koi-san too."

Sachiko said no more. After the first act she had a chance to
question O-haru in the lobby. O-haru had taken two weeks'
vacation the month before to nurse her father, who had been in
a Nishinomiya hospital after an operation for piles; and once or
twice every day she had had to go home for food and other supplies. She always took the bus on the National Highway. Three
times she met Okubata, she said, once as she got off the bus, twice
while waiting for a bus. Each time Okubata took a bus in the
opposite direction, for Kobe. O-haru thus crossed the road from
the south and waited on the mountain side of the road, and Okubata came down through the *mambō*, crossed from the north,
and waited on the side toward the sea. (O-haru had used the word
mambō, an old dialect word that survives only in the Osaka
district. It describes a short tunnel, a sort of underpass, and it is
believed to have come originally from the Dutch. To the north
of O-haru's bus stop was a railway embankment through which,
just behind the bus stop, had been cut a tunnel barely large
enough for one person to pass.) The first time she saw him, she
was wondering whether or not to speak when he smiled and
raised his hat. The second time neither bus came for some
minutes, and he strolled over for a chat. He seemed to run into
her often, he said, and asked what she might be doing in the
neighborhood. When she explained her business, he smiled and
said that she should call on him some time. He lived just over

there, he said, pointing through the *mambō*. Did she know the Ipponmatsu, the Lone Pine? He lived just beside it—she would have no trouble finding the house, and she really must come to see him. Though he evidently had more to say, O-haru's bus came to cut him off. (O-haru, when she told a story, had a way of mimicking the conversation that brought it vividly to life.) She met him three times, always at about five in the evening, and always alone. Another time, again at five in the evening, she met Taeko at the same bus stop. Taeko came up and tapped her on the shoulder. "Where have *you* been," O-haru asked, immediately overcome with confusion at her own question. Since Taeko had managed to steal up unnoticed, it seemed fairly clear that she had come through the *mambō*. When would O-haru be back, Taeko asked in return. And how was her father? "Kei-boy said he saw you," added Taeko, smiling broadly. O-haru wondered what she could possibly say next. Taeko only told her to hurry back, however, and crossed over to take a Kobe bus, whether for home or on business in Kobe, O-haru did not know.

That was the whole of the story in the theater lobby. Suspecting that O-haru knew more, Sachiko called her into the parlor two mornings later, after Taeko had left the house and they had sent O-teru out with Etsuko. It was the morning for Etsuko's piano lesson. O-haru said she knew nothing more, although she had thought it strange that Okubata should have a house in Nishinomiya—she had thought he lived in Osaka—and she had gone through the *mambō* one day and up to the Lone Pine to find that he did indeed have a house, a little white-walled red-tiled house with a low hedge in front. The sign at the gate said only "Okubata." From the newness of the wood she guessed that he had but recently moved in. It was fairly dark, after six o'clock, and a bright light was shining through the white-lace curtains in the open second-floor windows. A phonograph was playing. As she listened she thought she could make out the voice of someone besides Okubata. It seemed to be a woman's voice, though she could not hear well because of the music. (Yes, she even remembered the record. That one, the one Danielle Darrieux sang in "Return at Dawn.") She had meant, if she had time, to go for another look, but two or three days later her father left the hospital and she returned to Ashiya. And she had fretted a great deal, she said, over whether or not to tell Mrs. Makioka. Neither the gentleman nor Koi-san had made any attempt to silence her, and she thought perhaps Mrs. Makioka already knew. Might it not seem odd, then, if she said nothing? Still one should be careful about talking too much. But did Mrs. Makioka not agree that Koi-san was very probably spending much of her time in that house? O-haru could, if necessary, go see what the gossip was in the neighborhood.

Sachiko had been caught off balance by that glimpse of Taeko and Okubata in the cab. Calmer reflection suggested that even though Taeko had turned away from him at the time of the Itakura affair, she had not broken with him completely. Now that Itakura was gone, it was not really surprising that the two should occasionally be seen together. Some ten days after Itakura's death, Sachiko had come upon a notice in the newspapers of the death of Okubata's mother. "I see that Kei-boy's mother is dead." She glanced at Taeko, who nodded vaguely. "Was she ill long?" asked Sachiko. Taeko wondered. And had Taeko seen Kei-boy? Taeko shook her head. Sensing that her sister did not want to talk about "Kei-boy," Sachiko was careful afterwards not to mention his name. Taeko had not said specifically that she was refusing to see him.

Fearing a second Itakura, Sachiko thought it a good thing—natural and proper and far less likely to arouse hostile criticism—for Taeko to have taken up with Okubata again. It was a little premature, on the basis of only O-haru's story, to conclude that she had in fact done so. But what could be more likely? And did it not seem possible (assuming that Sachiko's suspicions were well-founded) that Taeko, who could count on the approval of Sachiko and the people at the main house, thought she had nothing to conceal? Embarrassed at having to discuss Okubata after having once lost patience with him, had she not hoped that O-haru would tell Sachiko everything? Such in general were Sachiko's conclusions.

A few mornings later she and Taeko happened to be alone in the dining room.

"You passed us in a cab the other day," said Sachiko lightly. "The day we went to see Kikugorō."

Taeko nodded.

"And you went to the Yohei?"

"Yes."

"Why does Kei-boy have a house in Nishinomiya?"

"His brother threw him out of the Osaka house."

"Why?"

"For no very good reason."

"His mother died not long ago."

"That has something to do with it, I suppose." Bit by bit, Taeko told of the new house: the rent was forty-five yen, Okubata was living alone with his old nurse.

"When did you start seeing him again?"

Taeko had visited Itakura's grave every seventh day for some time after his death. The month before, early on the morning of the forty-ninth day, she had set out for Okayama. Okubata was waiting at the station when she came back from the temple. He had known she would be there, he said. She rode back with him to Sannomiya Station, and relations between the two, broken off at Itakura's death, were thus resumed. She added that she had in no way changed her opinion of Kei-boy. Much pleased with himself, he boasted that since his mother's death he had come to know what the world was like. His brother had thrown him out, and he had finally had his eyes opened. But Taeko paid little attention to what he said. With Okubata quite alone in the world, she for one would not be cruel to him. What she felt was not so much love as pity.

10

SINCE TAEKO had spoken with obvious reluctance, Sachiko did not try again to question her. She thought even so that she had the explanation for a great deal that had attracted her attention: more and more Taeko had taken to coming home late at night, and it was far from clear where she spent her time. She no longer seemed part of the family. Sometimes when she came home she did not bother to take a bath, and the color of her skin suggested that she had had a bath wherever it was she had been. Until then a lavish spender, she had become thrifty when the Itakura affair began—even when she had a permanent wave, she would hunt out the cheapest beauty parlor possible. But all that had changed: she was most extravagant again with her cosmetics and her clothes, down to the smallest accessory. Sachiko noticed that in the last two months the old wrist watch, the rings, the handbag, the cigarette case, and the lighter had all been changed for new. On the thirty-fifth day after Itakura's death Taeko had received that prized Leica—the one that had been thrown to the floor in Mitsukoshi Hall—and she had carried it about for a time. Now she had a new chrome Leica. Sachiko had at first assumed that with the death of her lover, Taeko's view of life had changed and she had abandoned her policy of saving money, but the matter, when one thought about it, seemed more complicated. Taeko had recently shown little interest in doll-making, and she had even turned her studio over to a pupil. It appeared too that she was absent from the sewing school more often than not. For a time Sachiko thought it best to view Taeko's affairs from a distance. But if Taeko and Okubata were quite openly seeing each other again and going out boldly in public, there was no telling when Teinosuke would run into them. Teinosuke, with his intense dislike for Okubata, would have opinions of his own, and very strong ones too. She therefore told him everything. He looked as unhappy as she had expected, and two or three mornings later, when she went into the study, he asked her to sit down. He had information for her about Kei-boy's relations with his family. That part of the story having aroused his suspicions, he had made inquiries and learned that in collusion with certain clerks Kei-boy had taken goods from the Okubata shop. This was not the first time, but always before his mother had persuaded the oldest brother to forgive him. The most recent incident had so infuriated the brother that he threatened to have Kei-boy arrested. The family somehow pacified him, and when the thirty-fifth-day services for the mother were over Kei-boy was thrown out of the house.

He did not know how much of this Koi-san had learned, said Teinosuke, but should not Sachiko and the people in Tokyo review their plans for having her marry the fellow? Certainly Tatsuo, strait-laced person that he was, would have second thoughts. Sachiko and the others had been tolerant—had perhaps even been glad that Taeko was carrying on with Kei-boy—because they saw marriage as a solution to all her problems. But if plans for marrying her off must now be abandoned, it did not seem proper that the two should be keeping company. Even if Sachiko herself and Tsuruko and Yukiko continued to think that Okubata would be better than some nondescript person of whose origins they knew nothing, Tatsuo was not likely to agree, at least until Kei-boy was forgiven and taken back into the Okubata family, and a marriage arranged with the family's consent. In any case, something had to be done. Okubata had once had his mother and his brother watching over him. Now, disinherited, he had a house of his own, small though it was, in which to do quite as he pleased. Probably he had received a certain amount of consolation money, and did it not seem likely that he was living on that, with no thought for the future? And that Koi-san was helping him spend it? If she did not love the man—Teinosuke did not like these suspicions—it was possible to imagine that her motive was not pity but something far less admirable. And what if they found some day that Koi-san and Okubata were living together? Or what of a possibility not quite so extreme: Koi-san was seen at the Nishinomiya house every day, and what if Okubata's brother were to hear of the affair? What would he think of the Makiokas? There was nothing to be done if Koi-san came to be thought loose, but what of Sachiko and himself, who were supposed to be watching her? Would not accusing eyes be turned on them too? He had always preferred to withdraw, said Teinosuke, when Taeko's behavior came up for discussion, and this time too he would rather not interfere too aggressively, but if Koi-san meant to go on seeing the man, they would have to tell Tatsuo and receive his permission—at the very least his tacit permission. Otherwise they would find themselves with no excuses to offer.

Teinosuke had taken up golf, and it embarrassed him to meet Kei-boy's brother on the links.

"You really think Tatsuo would pretend not to notice?"

"Hardly."

"And so?"

"We will have her stop seeing Kei-boy."

"It would be very fine if she would. But what if they go on meeting in secret?"

"If she were *my* daughter or sister, I think I would throw her out of the house."

There had been tears in Sachiko's eyes for some time. It was true that by turning Taeko out they would have satisfied the public and the Okubata family, but would they not be inviting the possibility Teinosuke found most distasteful? Taeko was twenty-eight and quite capable of taking care of herself, he said, and it would be a mistake to try to control her. They might best turn her out for a time and see what happened. If she went to live with Kei-boy—she went to live with Kei-boy. Once they began worrying about such eventualities there would be no end to their worries. But Sachiko could not bear to think of sending her sister away labeled an outcast. Could she, who had consistently protected Koi-san from the fury of the main house, really throw her out at so late a date for reasons so trivial? Teinosuke was being ungenerous. Whatever you said of her, Koi-san was the sheltered daughter of a well-to-do family, and at heart she was weak and a little too good-natured. And she had never had a mother. Sachiko had hoped in her inadequate way to serve as a substitute, and now, just as they were thinking of memorial rites for their mother, could Sachiko even consider turning her sister out?

"I am not saying she has to go," Teinosuke added a little hastily as he saw the tears. "I only said 'if she *were* my sister.'"

"I wish you would leave everything to me. I will talk to Tsuruko. I can reason with her."

But Sachiko did not really know whether or not she would tell Tsuruko. In any case she would wait until the services were over. On the evening of the twenty-second, when the guests from Tokyo arrived, she broke the news to Yukiko only, and asked her advice. If they were seeing each other again, said Yukiko, what could be better? There was no need to worry about Kei-boy's having been disinherited. What if he had taken something that did not belong to him? It was from his own shop, after all. One could expect as much from Kei-boy. The family only meant to teach him a lesson and would be welcoming him back in no time. It might not be entirely proper for Taeko and Kei-boy to be appearing in public together—but why not look the other way if they agreed to behave more circumspectly? Yukiko was opposed to telling Tsuruko. Tsuruko would only tell Tatsuo.

Though Sachiko did not like to criticize the main house, there was something unsatisfying about their plans for the services. Partly to supply what was missing, partly to entertain the sister so long away from Osaka, Sachiko hit upon the idea of a quiet little party with her sisters. At noon on the twenty-sixth, two days after the services, she would take a room at the Harihan—the restaurant called up such fond memories of her dead mother and father—and even Teinosuke would be asked to stay away. She would have only her sisters, Aunt Tominaga, and the latter's daughter Someko. The famous Kikuoka and his daughter Tokuko would play for them. Taeko would dance "Perfumed Sleeves" to Tokuko's accompaniment and "Moon at Dawn" to Sachiko's koto and Kikuoka's samisen. For two weeks Sachiko had been practicing the koto, and Taeko had been going to Osaka for dancing lessons.

Early on the twenty-third Tsuruko went out to shop and pay calls, taking only Umeko with her. She did not come back until late that night. She had been invited to dinner somewhere. On the twenty-fourth all nine of them set out from Ashiya at about eight-thirty in the morning: Tsuruko, Masao, Umeko, Teinosuke, Sachiko, Etsuko, Yukiko, Taeko, and O-haru. The women were in formal clothes, Tsuruko in black, the three younger sisters in varying shades of purple, and O-haru too in dark purple.

Kyrilenko, hairy legs protruding from under his shorts, got on the train a few stations later. He glanced at the colorful assembly, and came over to speak to them.

"Where are you all going?" He hung from a strap before Teinosuke. "You seem to have the whole family with you."

"This is the day my wife's mother died. We are all going to the temple."

"Oh? And when did she die?"

"Twenty-two years ago," said Taeko.

"Do you hear anything from Katharina?" asked Sachiko.

"I'm glad you reminded me. She asked in her last letter to be remembered to you. She's in England."

"She has already left Berlin?"

"She was there just a little while. Then off to England. And she has seen her little girl."

"How nice. What is she doing in England?"

"Working in an insurance company. She's the president's secretary."

"And the little girl is with her?" asked Teinosuke.

"Not yet. She's suing to get the girl back."

"Do give her our regards when you write."

"I imagine with the war on it takes a long time for letters to come through."

"And your mother must be worried," said Taeko. "There will be air raids, you know."

"There is nothing to worry about." Kyrilenko too fell into the Osaka dialect. "Katharina can take care of herself if anyone can."

For those who remembered the gaiety at the Harihan, the banquet after the services was a little lonely. Even so, the effect was not as chilling as one might have expected. Forty guests were seated in a long hall made by taking away the partitions separating three temple rooms. A number of people who had been close to the family were present: among them were Tsukada the master-carpenter, Shōkichi, representing his father, and two or three men who had worked in the old Semba shop. Although the sisters should have been pouring the saké, the cousins and Shōkichi's wife were so diligent that they hardly had to leave their seats. The tall white *hagi* shedding its blossoms in the garden made Sachiko think of that garden at Minoo and the day her mother had died. For the most part the men talked of the European war. The women, though not as if to be critical of Tatsuo, spoke again of how young "Miss Yukiko" and Koi-san looked.

One of the clerks from the shop, a man named Tomatsuri, had drunk a little too much.

"They tell me you are still single, Miss Yukiko," came a thick voice from the lower end of the room. "Why is that?"

There was silence for a moment.

"We are already behind schedule," said Taeko, always in control of herself, "and we think we might as well take our time and look around for someone really good."

"But you are taking a little too *much* time."

"Come now. Is it ever too late?"

Ladies giggled nervously here and there. Yukiko only smiled at the exchange. Tatsuo pretended not to notice.

"Tomatsuri, Tomatsuri." Tsukada the carpenter had taken off his civil-defense jacket and sat in shirtsleeves. Gold teeth flashed from the sunburned face. "I hear you made a killing in the stock market."

"Not yet. I am still thinking about it."

"You have some good ideas?"

"This month I go to China. My sister was working in a dance hall in Tientsin, and the army noticed her and made a spy of her."

"Oh?"

"And now she has married an old China hand, and I hear she does very well. She sends a thousand or two back every now and then."

"I ought to have a sister like that myself."

"She says this is no time to be loafing around in Japan. There is money waiting to be made in Tientsin."

"Take me with you. I could stop being a carpenter almost any time."

"Any sort of business that makes money is all right with me. A string of girls, maybe."

"You have to be ready for anything, I always say. O-haru, how about a drink."

In the Ashiya house, a little drunk on the saké O-haru poured for him, Tsukada would always set about courting her. Would she marry him? He would turn out the woman he already had, whenever she said—he was not joking. O-haru would laugh happily, and so the game would go on. Today he was a little too persistent in trying to make her drink.

"Let me see if they are heating more saké." She fled to the kitchen in spite of Tsukada's protests, and from there out to the weed-choked back garden. Hidden in the underbrush, she took a compact from her black satin obi and retouched her face, a little flushed from drink. Then, sure no one was watching her, she took out an enamel cigarette case, the gift of a favored shop clerk, lit a cigarette, had a few hasty puffs, and, slipping the butt back into the case, went inside again.

II

Tsuruko said it was absolutely necessary for her to leave on the twenty-sixth. After the party at the Harihan and a stroll through the entertainment district for an hour or so, Sachiko and the others took her to Osaka Station.

"Will we see you again soon?"

"Not unless you come to Tokyo." They talked through the window of the third-class car. With the children along she could not sleep even if she took a berth, she said, and if she had to sit up there was no difference between second-class and third. "Kikugorō will be playing next month."

"He was in Kobe last month, but somehow it was different from seeing him in Tokyo or Osaka."

"They say he means to use real cormorants next month for a fishing scene on the Nagara."

"It must be a new play. But the dancing is what I like best."

"Speaking of dancing, Aunt Tominaga was delighted with Koi-san. She said she had no idea Koi-san was so good."

"Isn't Yukiko getting on the train?" Masao had a crisp Tokyo accent.

Yukiko, standing on the platform behind the rest, smiled and started to say something. She was drowned out by the bell signalling train time. Since they all knew that she meant to stay in Ashiya, Tsuruko had not made a point of taking her along, and Yukiko had offered no apology. The matter had been settled automatically.

Sachiko took Yukiko's advice and said nothing of Taeko's affairs, and Taeko, apparently interpreting to her own advantage the fact that she had heard nothing from Sachiko, went more and more openly to Nishinomiya. Her daytime visits were bad enough, but Sachiko was much pained at the dark looks she got from Teinosuke when Taeko was away from the dinner table too many nights running. Teinosuke and Sachiko, and Yukiko too, did their best to avoid the word "Koi-san." The silence only made them more uncomfortable, however, because each knew what the others were thinking. And then there was the question of the effect on Etsuko. Though she had been told by her mother and Yukiko that Koi-san was busy making dolls, it was clear that she did not believe a word of the story. Without having been warned by anyone, she too became shy of mentioning Taeko's name. Sachiko several times asked her sister to keep her affairs hidden from Teinosuke and Etsuko. Taeko would nod, and, after coming home early for two or three nights, would fall back into her old habits.

"Did you tell Tsuruko about Koi-san?" No longer able to contain himself, Teinosuke brought the matter up one evening.

"I meant to, and then I had trouble finding the right time."

"Why?"

"As a matter of fact I told Yukiko, and she thought it would be better not to say anything."

"Why?"

"She seems to sympathize with Kei-boy. She is willing to look the other way."

"Whether or not you sympathize with him ought to depend on the facts. Does Yukiko see the effect this sort of thing has on her own chances?" Teinosuke frowned fiercely and said no more, and Sachiko had trouble guessing his thoughts.

Toward the middle of October, he was again in Tokyo for two or three days.

"Did you go to Shibuya?"

"Yes. And I told Tsuruko everything." Tsuruko had said only that she must give the problem some thought. Toward the end of the month an unexpected letter came.

October 25

Dear Sachiko,

I am afraid we were a great bother to you. Besides everything else, you gave that extremely pleasant party at the Harihan. I came away thinking what a good place Osaka was. I was too busy even to write afterwards, and now I find that I must write a letter I would prefer not to. I find that there are things I must say, distasteful though they are—about Koi-san of course. I was thoroughly shocked when I heard Teinosuke's story. He said he would leave nothing out, and told me everything, from the affair with the man Itakura on down to Kei-boy's being disinherited, and I was more shocked the more I heard. I have occasionally picked up rumors about Koi-san, but I had no idea that she was so thoroughly bad. I had thought that she would not go too far with you watching her. I see now that I was wrong. I have worried a great deal about making a good girl of Koi-san, and each time I have tried to intervene I have found you protecting her. She is a disgrace to the Makioka name. And I understand that even Yukiko said there was no need to tell me. Yukiko and Koi-san have insulted us by refusing to come home, and now what do they have in mind? I cannot help thinking that the three of you are deliberately trying to make trouble for Tatsuo— though we are probably at fault ourselves. We have not done as much for you as we might.

I have let myself run on. I have felt that I must tell you exactly what is on my mind, however, and if I have hurt you I am sorry.

The question now is what to do with her. We once agreed with you that the best solution would be for her to marry Kei-boy. We can no longer consider the possibility. It may be that there will be room for argument once he is taken back into his family, but as matters stand now we must insist that she stop seeing him. If she really has her heart set on marrying him, she ought to know that seeing him now can only alienate the Okubata family. Since she cannot be trusted even if she says she is no longer visiting his house, Tatsuo says, we must have her come to Tokyo for a while. It may not be easy for her. As you know, our house is small and we do not live as well as you do, but this is no time to worry about trifles. Explain everything to her, and send her to us. Tatsuo says that it was wrong of us to think we were too crowded. Yukiko is to come back too, and we will all bear the inconvenience together.

I must ask you to be stern with her at least this once. Even if she refuses to come to Tokyo, we do not mean to leave her with you. This is Tatsuo's view, and I quite agree with him. He adds that he hopes this time you will be on our side and help us be firm, and that we have made up our minds and want no stalling. We would like an answer before the end of the month on which of the two it is to be: does she come to Tokyo, or is she

thrown out of the Makioka family? Since we would of course
prefer to avoid the second possibility, we hope you and Yukiko·
will do your best to persuade her. I shall be waiting for an
answer.

As always,
Tsuruko

"I have had this letter from Tokyo, Yukiko. Read it." Sachiko's
eyes were red. "It is a very strong letter. And she seems to be
unhappy about you too."

"Tatsuo made her write it."

"But she was the one who did the writing."

"We insulted them by not going to Tokyo, she says. But that
all happened so long ago. He has never really wanted us since
he moved to Tokyo."

"And he as much as said that he did not mind having you,
but Koi-san would be a nuisance."

"Where would they find room?"

"They talk as though I were the one who made Koi-san a
delinquent. I knew she would never listen to them, and I
thought if I stood between and watched over her I could keep her
from going too far wrong. Tsuruko can say what she likes, if I
had not been here to step in, who knows what might have happened? I have only been thinking of Koi-san and of the people
in the main house, and I have tried to keep from hurting anyone.
I have only done what I could."

"And it is all so simple, they seem to think. If it is not convenient to have her around, just throw her out and everything
is settled."

"But what shall we do? She will never go to Tokyo."

"There is no need even to ask."

"What shall we do, then?"

"Wait a little while."

"Not this time, Yukiko. Teinosuke is on their side."

Sachiko would see what Koi-san had to say, then, and it would
be good if Yukiko could be with her. The three sisters shut themselves into Taeko's bedroom the next morning.

"Koi-san, would you think of going to Tokyo for just a little
while?"

Taeko shook her head like a spoiled child. "I would rather be
dead than have to live with them."

"But what shall I tell them?"

"Whatever you like."

"You can say so, Koi-san, but Teinosuke is on their side. They
are not going to forget."

"I will live by myself for a while."

"Not with Kei-boy?"

"I will see him, but I certainly will not go to live with him."

"Why do you put it so strongly?"

Though she did not answer, it seemed that she did not want
people to misunderstand, to think she was in love with the man
when she only pitied him. Sachiko and Yukiko suspected too that
she was reluctant to admit her mistake. In any case, since she must
leave the house, it would better satisfy appearances if she were at
least for the moment to live alone.

"You promise, Koi-san? You promise to take a room somewhere?" Sachiko's relief was apparent in her voice. "I hate to say
so, but that might really be best."

"And if you have a room somewhere I can look in on you now
and then," said Yukiko.

"Yes, Koi-san. There is no reason to make a real issue of it. We
can just say that you have reasons for wanting a room of your
own, and there will be no need to tell anyone you have left home.
If you come in the daytime when Teinosuke and Etsuko are
away, we will always be glad to see you. And we can send O-haru
around to look after you."

There were tears in Sachiko's eyes and Yukiko's. Taeko alone
was calm, her face quite expressionless. "What shall I do about
my things?"

"You ought to take along the things people will notice—the
chest and dresser. But you can leave your valuables here. Where
will you live?"

"I will have to think about that."

"The Matsuzumi Apartments?"

"I would rather not be in Shukugawa this time. I can find something if I look."

After her sisters had left, Taeko sat in the window and looked up at the clear late-autumn sky. Soon there were tears streaming over her cheeks.

12

TAEKO took a room north of the Motoyamamura bus stop. It was, according to O-haru, a newly finished house, bare and gaunt in the rice paddies, and still without complete utilities. In Kobe with Yukiko some three days later, Sachiko called Taeko for lunch, and found that she was out. Again from O-haru, they learned that she was generally out unless one called early in the morning. She would be around soon, thought Sachiko, but the days went by without a glimpse of her or a telephone call from her.

Perhaps Teinosuke thought that the sisters had quite severed relations with Taeko, or perhaps he knew that a certain amount of secret intercourse was inevitable. In any case, he seemed satisfied now that Taeko had at least outwardly been expelled from the family. Told that Taeko had taken a new studio and would live there, Etsuko accepted the explanation with reservations. Sachiko and Yukiko tried to convince themselves that they had seen little of Taeko anyway and that the change was therefore of no importance. Indeed if a blank space had opened in the house it had opened some time before and had not been specifically the result of the recent unpleasantness. Still they found it sad to think that one of them was living in a shadow.

To forget the sadness, they would go to Kobe every other day or so and search out old movies and new movies, and sometimes they even saw two movies a day. Among the movies they had seen in the last month alone were *Bagdad. Das Mädchen Irene, Hélène, Burgtheater, Boys' Town,* and *Suez.* They kept thinking they might run into Taeko. Disturbed at the long silence, Sachiko finally sent O-haru off to make inquiries. O-haru reported that she had found Taeko still in bed, evidently quite well. Mrs. Makioka and Miss Yukiko were worried, Koi-san must visit Ashiya,

said O-haru. Taeko laughed and said there was nothing to worry
about. She would be around before long. In December, Sachiko
and Yukiko went to see the French movie *Prison sans Barreaux,*
for which they had been waiting impatiently. Sachiko had to stay
at home nursing a cold for some time afterwards.

On the morning of the twenty-third, with Etsuko's vacation to
begin the next day, Taeko appeared for the first time in nearly
two months. After talking for about an hour, she went off with
a suitcase full of New Year clothes. She would be around in
January with holiday greetings, she said. On the morning of
January 15, she came for New-Year's porridge. Afraid of a chill
since that cold, Sachiko stayed close to the house. Yukiko, fond
though she was of the movies, was always reluctant to go out
alone. She was extremely shy for her rather mature years, and
she wanted someone to be with her on the most trivial errands.
To keep her at calligraphy and the tea ceremony, Sachiko had
been going with her for lessons. Even such quick sortees were
dangerous, however, and often Yukiko was sent off alone. And
they turned to something they had long been thinking needed
attention: Yukiko went every other day for injections to clear
the spot over her eye. Dr. Kushida gave her hormone and vitamin
injections recommended by a skin specialist at the Osaka University Hospital. This much Yukiko had to keep her busy, and in
addition a review, twice a week, of Etsuko's piano lessons.

Left to herself, Sachiko would sit down at the piano, or go
upstairs to practice her calligraphy, and she would sometimes
call O-haru in to practice the koto. O-haru had begun her koto
lessons two autumns before with the songs a girl of six or seven
learns in Osaka: "Flowers of the Four Seasons," or the one
about the princesses brought from their cloisters for the Doll
Festival. Sachiko gave her a lesson now and then as the spirit
moved her, and they had moved on to "Black Hair" and "Manzai"
and the like. O-haru, who had so disliked school that she asked
to be sent out as a maid instead, found this sort of school more
congenial. On mornings when Sachiko had promised a lesson, she
would rush through her house work. She had also picked up
dances from Taeko—"Snow" and "Black Hair"—so that she
could make her way through them with some competence. Now
she was learning "The Call of the Crane." One phrase—"Is it a

lie, is it the truth?"—gave her trouble, and she was set to practicing it over and over for two and three days running. Soon Etsuko was humming the accompaniment.

"I will get even with you this time, O-haru." She had been annoyed at the way O-haru would hum piano melodies she herself had difficulty with.

Late one morning toward the end of the month, Taeko appeared again. Sachiko was listening to the radio.

"Yukiko?" Taeko pulled a chair up to the fire.

"She has gone to Dr. Kushida's."

"An injection?"

"Yes." Sachiko had been taking down recipes said to be good for the season. Now someone was reciting a Nō play.

"Would you turn it off, please, Koi-san?"

"Wait. Look at Bell." Taeko pointed her jaw at the cat, asleep by Sachiko's feet.

Bell was drowsing happily in the warmth from the stove. Taeko had noticed that its ears twitched at each drum beat. Only the ears were affected, it seemed, by a reflex of no concern to the rest of the cat.

"What do you suppose does it?"

"Very strange."

They watched, fascinated, as the ears twitched an accompaniment to the Nō, and when the Nō was finished Taeko turned off the radio.

"An injection? Does it seem to be doing any good?"

"I wonder. Yukiko is not the sort to go on with injections."

"How many will she need?"

"The doctor only said we would have to be patient."

"Will it leave before she is married?"

"Dr. Kushida seems to think there is a possibility."

"But I wonder if injections will ever really take it away. That reminds me. Katharina is married."

"You had a letter?"

"I saw her brother yesterday in Kobe. He came running after me, and said they had word two or three days ago."

"And who is her husband?"

"You remember she was secretary to the president of an insurance company? Well, she married him."

"She caught someone, did she."

"She enclosed a picture of her house, and told her brother and
mother to hurry to England. Her husband would take care of
them. She would even send travel money. The brother said the
house looked like a palace."

"She did very well for herself. A tottering old man, I suppose?"

"As a matter of fact he is just thirty-five, and this is his first
marriage."

"Not really!"

"You remember how she told us she would catch a rich husband
when she got to Europe?"

"When did she leave Japan? Hardly a year ago."

"The end of March."

"Only ten months ago, then."

"And she has been in England no more than six months."

"She did very well for herself in six months. It pays to be
beautiful."

"Beautiful? There must be any number of women better looking than Katharina. Or do you suppose there are no good-looking
women in England?"

"Are Kyrilenko and the old one going to England, then?"

"I gather not. The old one says they would embarrass Katharina.
If they stay in Japan, the husband will never know how poor they
are."

"Westerners worry about that sort of thing too, do they?"

"Oh, yes, and she got the first husband to give her the child."

There was no particular reason for Taeko's visit; she only
wanted to tell of Katharina. Though Sachiko pressed her to stay
for lunch—Yukiko would soon be home—Taeko seemed to have
an appointment with Okubata and she left after about a half
hour. Sachiko sat for a time staring at the fire. The news of
Katharina's marriage did indeed seem important enough for a
special visit. It was only in the movies, Sachiko had thought, that
rich young executives fell in love with and presently married their
newly-hired secretaries. As Taeko had remarked, Katharina was
not outstandingly beautiful, nor did she seem to have extraordinary talent. If even she could be so fortunate, were similar cases
then common in the West? That the president of an insurance
company, thirty-five, unmarried, and the owner of a fine man-

sion, should marry a woman quite without roots, a vagabond about whose family and breeding he knew nothing, a woman he had hired but six months before—Japanese common sense would simply not permit it, however beautiful the woman might be. She had heard that the English were conservative. Were they nonetheless liberal on the subject of marriage? When Katharina said she would find herself a rich husband, they had laughed at her as a romantic girl who knew little of the world, but she had known more than they, and had left Japan in complete confidence that her looks would see her through.

It would be a mistake to compare a White-Russian refugee with a cloistered lady from an old Osaka family. But how ineffectual they all seemed in comparison with Katharina! Even Taeko, the scapegrace, the venturesome one, did in the final analysis fear criticism, and had not succeeded in marrying the man she wanted. And Katharina, probably younger than Taeko, had left her mother and brother and home behind and set off across the world, and promptly made herself a future. Not of course that Sachiko envied Katharina—Yukiko was far better than any Katharina—but how feeble and spineless they seemed, two older sisters and two brothers-in-law, unable to find Yukiko a husband! Sachiko would not want her quiet sister to set about imitating Katharina—the fact that she could not do so even under orders was what gave Yukiko her charm—but should not Yukiko's guardians, the people at the main house and Teinosuke and Sachiko herself, feel humble before the Russian girl? They were utterly useless, Katharina might laugh, and what could they answer? Sachiko remembered how Tsuruko, returning to Tokyo the year before, had heaved a deep sign and said to Sachiko when no one else was listening: "I only hope *someone* will marry her. It hardly matters who any more. Even if it ends in divorce, I hope someone will marry her."

Soon the doorbell rang and Yukiko came in. Her face already flushed from the heat, Sachiko bent nearer the stove and wiped the tears from her eyes.

13

IT WAS SOME two or three weeks later. Yukiko and Sachiko were still regular customers at Mrs. Itani's beauty shop, and "Itani" still worried about Yukiko. One day she asked whether Sachiko knew an Osaka lady named Mrs. Niu. And how did Itani happened to know Mrs. Niu, Sachiko asked in return. Itani had met her just the other day. The two had chanced to be at a farewell party for a soldier going overseas, and Itani, learning that Mrs. Niu knew Sachiko, had exchanged reports with her. Mrs. Niu said that she had once been very close to Mrs. Makioka, but that for some reason they had not seen each other recently. She and two or three friends had called at the Ashiya house and found Mrs. Makioka in bed with jaundice—but that was long ago, possibly three or four years ago.

Sachiko remembered the incident well. There were Mrs. Niu and Mrs. Shimozuma and someone else whose name she had forgotten—that fearfully stylish lady just back from America, the one with the strange accent. Really too ill to see them, Sachiko had not been especially polite, and she had sent them off without dinner. Perhaps Mrs. Niu was annoyed. She had not come again.

"I was very rude to her. Did she say anything?"

"No, she seemed more worried about Miss Yukiko. She wondered if Miss Yukiko was married yet, and said she had a good prospect. She thought of the man when Miss Yukiko's name came up. She said she was sure he would interest you."

Itani talked on. Meeting Mrs. Niu for the first time, she had no idea what the lady might consider "a good prospect." Still a friend of Mrs. Makioka's was to be trusted, and Itani therefore ventured to ask her good offices for Miss Yukiko. The man, Itani learned, was a doctor who had lost his first wife. Except for a daughter twelve or thirteen, he had no immediate family. He was not practicing medicine at the moment, but worked as director of a pharmaceutical company. That, said Itani, was all she had heard, and she had replied that it seemed to her not a bad prospect at all, and had urged Mrs. Niu to act immediately, since not a moment was to be lost. Itani herself would be glad to do anything she could, and she doubted that the Makiokas would make the demands they once had. She would see then how the man felt, said Mrs. Niu. That was very well, said Itani, but should they not now frame their plans in a general sort of way? Mrs. Niu replied that she would guarantee to produce the man—she did not think he would have objections, and if he did she would drag him out by force—and she wanted Itani to take responsibility for producing the Makiokas. A simple, quiet dinner party could be arranged, somewhere in Osaka. Mrs. Niu had the next two or three evenings open. In any case she would telephone. A splendid idea, Itani agreed, and Mrs. Makioka too would be pleased. As they left, Itani again urged Mrs. Niu to hurry. Itani was sure she would receive a telephone call very soon. She would visit Sachiko when she did.

Both Mrs. Niu and Itani were rather aggressive women, and Sachiko was sure she would soon hear more. At about ten o'clock three mornings later there was a call from Itani. Mrs. Niu had just telephoned to ask whether Itani could bring Miss Yukiko to a certain Japanese-style restaurant that evening at six. It would be no formal *miai*. Miss Yukiko need feel no more constraint than if she had been invited out to dinner. Mrs. Niu hoped Yukiko would agree to go alone, but if someone had to be with her it should be Teinosuke and not Sachiko. Beside her radiant sister, Yukiko would leave but a dim impression. Itani agreed, and hoped very much that Yukiko would go alone. Though it was rude of her to bring up such an important matter over the telephone, she added, they had covered the ground already, and haste was so important. She wanted her answer immediately. Sachiko asked her to wait an hour or two.

What did Yukiko think, she asked. It was true that so hastily arranged a party did not seem entirely felicitous. Still they must not be rude to Itani, who had been thinking of Yukiko all this time. And Mrs. Niu, hardly a friend of but a day, knew them well enough not to suggest too outrageously inappropriate a man.

But they really knew so little, answered Yukiko. Should Sachiko not talk to Mrs. Niu, even over the telephone? Sachiko

immediately called Mrs. Niu and learned that the man's qualifications seemed surprisingly good: his name was Hashidera, he was
from Shizuoka Prefecture, and he had two older brothers, both
doctors; he had studied in Germany; he rented a house in Tennōji Ward, where he lived with his daughter and an old housekeeper; the daughter, a student in the Sekiyō Hill Seminary, had
inherited all her mother's elegance and grace; the man lived well,
inasmuch as he had very probably received a share of the family
property (the two brothers were both successful men, and the
family was one of the more important in Shizuoka Prefecture),
and he probably had a sizable income besides as director of the
East Asia Pharmaceutical Company; the man himself was well
groomed and more than prepossessing—indeed one would not
be wrong in calling him truly handsome. And how old was he?
Probably forty-four or forty-five. And the daughter? She would be
in about her second year in the seminary. And did he have any
sisters? Any younger brothers? Mrs. Niu did not know. What of
his parents, then? Mrs. Niu wondered whether they were still
living. It gradually became clear that Mrs. Niu and the man's
wife had shared the same hobby, and had come to know each
other as members of a group that studied batik dying. Mrs.
Niu said that she had not visited the house often. She had met
the husband once while the wife was living, she believed, and
again at the funeral, and at memorial services on the first anniversary—four times in all, counting a visit the day before to
discuss the meeting with Yukiko. She had told him that there was
no point in mourning his wife forever—she had a fine girl she
wanted him to meet. He replied that he would leave everything
to her, and now if the Makiokas were to refuse . . .

Mrs. Niu was adept at both standard Tokyo speech and the
Osaka dialect, and could change back and forth to suit the occasion; but for some reason (was she using only standard speech
these days?—Sachiko remembered their last meeting) it was an
even swifter torrent of Tokyo speech than usual that assailed
Sachiko over the telephone.

Sachiko was coaxed into standard speech herself. Mrs. Niu was
really too unkind, she said. Had Mrs. Niu not insisted that
Sachiko stay away from the party? No, that had been Mrs. Itani's
idea. Mrs. Niu herself quite agreed, but because the idea had

been Mrs. Itani's, Sachiko should be angry with Mrs. Itani if she must be angry with someone.

"That reminds me," Mrs. Niu said, "I met Mrs. Jimba the other day, and when one of us happened to mention you she said she had tried to arrange something for you once herself."

Sachiko was startled. "What did Mrs. Jimba say?"

"Well—" Mrs. Niu hesitated. "She said she was turned down rather sharply."

"She must have been angry, then," said Sachiko.

"Possibly so," Mrs. Niu said. "But if it's no match, it's no match, and you can never arrange anything if you are going to be upset at each little failure. I'll never be so unreasonable myself, and if you don't like the man you can just come out and say so. Anyway, tell Yukiko that she has to meet him. I'll be very unhappy if she won't meet him."

Mrs. Niu added that she had already made reservations, and would be there with the man at the appointed hour. They needn't telephone again. She would be expecting them.

Sachiko thought it a little undignified to accept an invitation for that very night, an invitation as startling in its way as a covey of birds flying up at one's feet. If they chose not to worry about dignity, however, there was no reason why they should not send Yukiko off. Yukiko would not want to go alone, but Teinosuke had gone in Sachiko's place before and could go again if he was free that evening. The problem was only that they did not want to seem vulgarly eager. They wanted an excuse to postpone the *miai* two or three days, to give it a little dignity. But they had to worry about Mrs. Niu and what she would think if they looked coldly upon a project that filled her with enthusiasm. One of her remarks had upset Sachiko: that Mrs. Jimba was angry. Sachiko felt even more timid about refusing. They had refused Nomura two years before with the utmost circumspection: they had said that the main house was a little dissatisfied— but the refusal had apparently carried stronger overtones than they had meant to put into it. Sachiko had for some time wondered whether Mrs. Jimba might not be angry, and had even felt that she had reason to be angry. Mrs. Niu's remark therefore struck home. And why had Mrs. Niu brought the subject up? She liked to talk, of course, but it was more than the usual chatter when she suddenly introduced a complete outsider into the conversation and passed on a report she ought to have kept to herself. Perhaps Sachiko was being threatened.

"What shall we do, Yukiko?"

Yukiko did not answer.

"How would it be if you were to go?"

"And you?"

"I would like to go with you, but they say I am to stay home. Will you go with Itani?"

"With Itani?"

"We can have Teinosuke go with you, then." Sachiko studied Yukiko's expression. "I know he will go if he has nothing else to do. Shall I telephone him?"

Yukiko nodded very slightly, and Sachiko put in an emergency call to Osaka.

14

TOLD THAT Yukiko and Itani would arrive separately at his office no later than five-thirty, Teinosuke had nothing in particular to suggest, though he knew how prompt Itani would be and insisted that Yukiko too arrive on time—or better, some twenty minutes or a half hour early. He was much disturbed when, at five-fifteen, there was still no sign of Yukiko. He knew that his wife and Yukiko paid no attention to time, and he knew too that Itani's impatience would be trying. Yukiko must surely have left the house by now. Still, to make very sure, he put in a call to Ashiya. Before the call went through, Itani arrived with Yukiko behind her.

"Fine, fine. The two of you together. I was just going to phone."

"As a matter of fact I went by to call for Miss Yukiko. Shall we go? We have so little time, and I've kept the cab waiting."

Teinosuke had heard the details of the *miai*, but only by telephone. Though he knew Mrs. Niu's name, he was not at all sure he had met her. He felt as if he were plunging into a fog. On the way to the restaurant he asked about the man, and of Itani's relations with him. Itani would have to leave such matters to Mrs. Niu, she was afraid. What then of her relations with Mrs. Niu? Itani had met Mrs. Niu but once, and that once but recently. Teinosuke felt that he had ventured into a new sort of fairyland indeed.

Mrs. Niu and Hashidera were waiting at the restaurant.

"Well, well. Here you are already. Have we kept you waiting?" Itani's manner was wonderfully familiar considering that she had met the woman only once.

"We just this minute arrived," answered Mrs. Niu pleasantly. "But aren't you remarkable. It's exactly six."

"I'm always on time. I was worried about Miss Yukiko, though, and went around to fetch her."

"Did you have trouble finding the place?"

"None at all. Mr. Makioka here knew it immediately."

"How are you? I believe we've met." Teinosuke remembered having seen this face in his parlor.

"I'm afraid I'm not being very friendly these days. It's a long time since I've seen Sachiko—not since we found her in bed with jaundice."

"It was then, was it. That must have been three or four years ago."

"At least. Three of us rushed in and forced her out of bed. I'm sure we looked like female gangsters."

"Gangsters is the word for it." Hashidera, who had on a brown suit and was waiting to be introduced, glanced sideways at Mrs. Niu and smiled. He turned to Teinosuke. "My name is Hashidera. As a matter of fact, the lady is exactly what she says she is—a gangster. She told me I had to come, and she dragged me out before I knew what was happening to me."

"Please, Mr. Hashidera. Be a gentleman. You're here, and you don't talk of such things."

"Quite right," agreed Itani. "You don't go making excuses. After all, men are supposed to behave like men. And you are really being a little insulting."

"So it goes with lady gangsters. Ganging up on me again."

"Nothing of the sort. We're thinking of your own good. You'll only ruin your health, sitting around all day staring at your wife's picture. You need to go out now and then. You must know that there are plenty of women just as beautiful."

Teinosuke was afraid to look at Yukiko. But Yukiko was by now a veteran, and she only smiled.

"We'll stop arguing and sit down at the table. You are over there, Mr. Hashidera, and I'll sit here myself."

"With two gangsters after you, it won't pay not to do as you're told."

Teinosuke suspected that, like Yukiko, Hashidera had been dragged out against his will. Far from sure that he wanted to remarry so soon, he had been pounced upon by Mrs. Niu, a woman with whom he was not particularly friendly, and forced to act before he knew what he was doing. His conversation was full of words like "startled" and "confused." And yet the show of confusion was not at all displeasing. Teinosuke saw that the man knew how to handle himself in polite society. Offering a card on which he was announced as a physician and a director of the East Asia Pharmaceutical Company, Hashidera smiled: "I'm no doctor. I'm the chief clerk in a drug store." There was little of the physician about him. He rather suggested the able entrepreneur. Although he was said to be forty-four or forty-five, the skin on his face and hands down to the tips of his fingers had a youthful firmness. A regular-featured, round-cheeked, good-looking man, the solidness of whose figure gave him the full dignity of his years. In appearance at least he would rank first among the candidates they had reviewed for Yukiko's hand. He also seemed to be a good drinker, though not quite a match for Teinosuke, and he could always be persuaded to have another cup of saké. Usually there was a certain stiffness and restraint among people so recently introduced. Partly because of the two bold lady gangsters, however, and partly because the man himself was so completely at ease, the conversation flowed smoothly.

"I must come here oftener. Look at all the food." The saké was having its effect on Teinosuke, whose cheeks were a pleasant pink. "It's getting harder and harder to find anything decent to eat or drink. Is the food always so good?"

"I doubt it," said Hashidera. "Mrs. Niu probably threatened them with violence."

"That's not *quite* true. But my husband is a steady customer, and they generally let us have our way. And I thought the name of the place might bring us luck."

"Happy Omen," the restaurant was called. Mrs. Niu pronounced it "Kitchō."

"Isn't it 'Kikkyō,' Mrs. Niu?" asked Teinosuke. "It's not pronounced quite as it's written. Probably easterners like Mr. Hashidera here have never heard the word, but here in Osaka we have what we call a *kikkyō*. Do you know what it is, Mrs. Itani?"

"I'm afraid I don't."

"*Kikkyō?*" Hashidera too looked puzzled. "What is it?"

"I know," said Mrs. Niu. "*Kikkyō*—one of those things. You know, the things you buy at the Ebisu Fair in Nishinomiya or Imamiya. A little piece of bamboo with coins and good-luck pieces dangling from it."

"That's right."

"At the Ebisu Fair you can buy . . ." Mrs. Niu took up the jingle for the Ebisu Fair.

> *"Balloons and saucers and*
> > *pocketbooks too.*
> *Pennies and pocketbooks and high hats too . . .*

All of them dangling from a sprig of bamboo. And *kitchō* we ignorant Osakans call *kikkyō*. Right, Mr. Makioka?"

"Quite right. How do you happen to know?"

"I may not look it, but I'm an Osakan too."

"Really?"

"And I know at least that much. But do people still pronounce it the old way? Here in the restaurant they seem to say *kitchō*."

"Let me ask you another. In that jingle you just gave us, Mrs. Niu, what is a *hazebukuro*?"

But Mrs. Niu had pronounced it *kazebukuro*, and thought it meant "balloon."

"No, *hazebukuro* is right."

"Is there such a word?"

"A bag to roast *haze* in," ventured Hashidera. "*Haze* is a sort of puffed rice. In Tokyo children eat it on the day of the Doll Festival."

"Mr. Hashidera knows more than any of us."

For a time the conversation was of customs and dialects in the east and the west, and Mrs. Niu, who had been born in Osaka and reared in Tokyo and who later had moved back to Osaka, was the best informed of all. She called herself an amphibian, and she quite justified the claim as she switched from Tokyo speech for Itani to the Osaka dialect for Teinosuke. Itani, who had spent a year or so in America learning her trade, talked of how it was "over there," and Hashidera told of his visit to the Bayer plant in Germany: the place was enormous, he said, and had among other things a movie theater at least the size of the Osaka Shōchiku. Presently Itani set about bringing the conversation back to its original purpose. She asked Hashidera about his daughter and his family in Shizuoka, and contrived to make him exchange remarks with Yukiko. The subject of his remarrying came up again.

"And what does your daughter think?"

"I haven't asked her. The important thing is that I haven't made up my own mind yet."

"And so I keep telling you to make up your mind. You'll have to marry again some time."

"I suppose you're right. But then you know how it is. I don't feel in the mood to start having a new family in such a hurry."

"And why might that be?"

"No special reason. I just can't quite take the step, that's all. But with someone like you to prod me on, I suppose I'll find myself married again in no time."

"You leave everything to us, then?"

"I'm afraid it's not so simple."

"Aren't you slippery. I'm sure it would please your wife, if she knew, to see you married again."

"I'm not really brooding as much as you seem to think I am."

"Mrs. Niu," put in Itani. "This gentleman obviously has to have someone put the plate in front of him and take up the spoon for him. We won't argue with him. We'll go ahead and arrange everything our own way."

"And when the time comes we'll not take any excuses."

Teinosuke and Yukiko could only watch smilingly as the lady gangsters attacked Hashidera. The dinner was the informal one they had been promised, and there was little to suggest a *miai*. But to drag out a man who was not sure he wanted to marry, and to play out the little drama with which Teinosuke and Yukiko were being entertained—this was an art that only a lady gangster could have mastered. Teinosuke could not help thinking that they were in an extremely peculiar position themselves, and what astonished him most was that Yukiko had somewhere learned to smile and enjoy herself. The old Yukiko would scarcely have been able to endure it—she would have been a flaming red and on the verge of tears, and she might even have stood up and left the room. Women like Yukiko seemed to keep their freshness and innocence through the years. Had the accumulated *miai* brought a certain callousness, however, a certain brashness even? No, it was only natural that a lady of thirty-three should have become calmer and more poised. Aware only of her continued youthfulness and of the youthful clothes she wore, Teinosuke had failed to notice the change.

That aside, what did Hashidera have in mind? Even if he felt only that he had nothing to lose by taking a look at Mrs. Niu's young lady, one might with some justice assume that he was more "in the mood" to remarry than he admitted. He need not have come at all if he was so reluctant. There was something a little exaggerated about his confusion, and no doubt he felt that if Yukiko was a girl to suit him, he might consider marrying her. In any case, it hardly seemed likely that he had come just to tease them. But he was clever enough to justify Mrs. Niu's use of the adjective "slippery," and his manner gave not a hint of the impression Yukiko had made on him. While the other four talked quite easily, Yukiko, just a little abashed, stayed outside the conversation. As always, she made no attempt to exploit openings the others gave her. Hashidera for his part was far too busy with the gangsters to offer her more than two or three polite remarks through the meal. The Makiokas took their leave quite perfunctorily, without even knowing whether or not they would see him again, but Itani, who was with them on the train, was confident. She would bring her mouth to Teinosuke's ear and whisper over and over again that everything must be left to Mrs. Niu and herself, that they would see the affair through successfully, that they would take no excuses from a man who had come so far, that he was most pleased with Miss Yukiko. Itani had seen it all.

15

THAT NIGHT Teinosuke reported his impressions to Sachiko: to judge from appearances, the man must be given a perfect mark, and seemed quite ideal for Yukiko, but they could only wait, since he was still debating whether or not he wanted to remarry, and since the prospects were in no sense as bright as Mrs. Niu and Itani seemed to think. Teinosuke and his wife had become very timid about *miai* since the year before—if they put too much faith in the ladies they might be made fools of again. But the next morning Itani came calling. She had already had a telephone call from Mrs. Niu, and she wondered what Miss Yukiko thought of the man. Following Teinosuke's advice, Sachiko said only that the man had made a very good impression indeed, but that he did not yet seem to have made up his mind, and . . . No need to worry about that, said Itani. There was one difficulty, though: Mrs. Niu had that morning had a call from Hashidera, who said that Miss Yukiko struck him as a little moody. He preferred bright, lively, sparkling girls. But Itani had explained everything. Miss Yukiko impressed people as a little moody at first, but she was in fact not moody at all. Mrs. Niu must be sure to tell Hashidera so. Miss Yukiko might be a little reserved, but she was certainly not moody. She was so gentle and quiet that she sometimes made the wrong impression on strangers. When one got to know her, however, one found her surprisingly —perhaps, said Itani, that was not a tactful adverb to have chosen —anyway, surprisingly bright and modern and sophisticated. She was exactly the sort of girl Hashidera wanted. If he did not believe it he had only to see her more often. In music she liked the piano, in food she preferred the foreign, and she loved foreign movies. She knew English and French. What more could Itani say to demonstrate that Miss Yukiko was a bright and cheerful girl? It was true that she wore Japanese clothes, but did not the fact that gay clothes so became her show that there was something gay in her nature? If he would only take the trouble to know her, he could see for himself. Girls from good families simply did not talk when they met strange men, that was all. Itani had rambled on and on, she said, and put coin after coin in the telephone. But if the truth must be told, Miss Yukiko was too quiet, and she was likely to be misunderstood. She should muster up her courage and talk a little more. Itani would arrange to bring the man around soon. She wanted Miss Yukiko to leave a bright, happy impression this time.

Sachiko had been secretly apprehensive about that spot over the eye, though it had not been particularly noticeable the day before. But was there really much hope? She wrote off a good half of Itani's story as idle chatter. The next day at about three, she had a telephone call: Itani was in Osaka, and in an hour she and Mrs. Niu would bring Mr. Hashidera to call on Sachiko. Were they coming here? asked Sachiko in some confusion. They were indeed, said Itani. Mr. Hashidera had very little time and could stay no more than twenty minutes or a half hour, and there was no other convenient place to meet. And then Mr. Hashidera wanted to see the family and the house. That would be very pleasant, of course, but might they not . . . ? Itani cut her short. They could only stay twenty minutes or a half hour, and they would not expect to be entertained. With Mr. Hashidera beginning to show signs of interest, it would put him out of sorts if the plans had to be changed.

Sachiko had to consider Yukiko's feelings. What should they do? They could send Etsuko off to Kobe with O-haru, of course. But Yukiko proved surprisingly tractable. Etsuko and O-haru had already guessed everything, she was sure. Very well, then, they would be waiting, Sachiko said to Itani. She immediately telephoned Osaka to ask if Teinosuke could be home in time.

Back before the guests arrived, Teinosuke said that he too had had a call from Itani. Mr. Hashidera was starved for a taste of home, Itani had said, and would like to meet Sachiko and the rest of them at the Ashiya house that afternoon. But what surprised and pleased Teinosuke most was the change in Yukiko. Was it not remarkable that she had agreed to see the man?

Soon the three guests were in the parlor. Itani called Sachiko out into the hall. Was Koi-san at home? Startled, Sachiko answered that Koi-san was unfortunately away at the moment. Then they would like to see at least Etsuko, said Itani. Mr. Hashidera had wanted to bring his own little girl, but the plans had been too hurried. Next time he would surely do so. The girl and Etsuko were quite ideal for each other. They would soon be friends, and Mr. Hashidera would find that he was interested. Itani exuded confidence.

Since Yukiko had permitted it, Teinosuke agreed that they might call in Etsuko and have her impressions too, and presently the four of them, Teinosuke, Sachiko, Etsuko, and Yukiko, were facing the guests. Again Hashidera's manner suggested that he had been dragged out against his will. He had not approved of the visit—he had thought it most rude to sweep down thus uninvited, and his arguments had been quite overruled by the lady gangsters. And, he added (one hardly knew how to take the remark), a plain office worker like himself did not deserve such a bride.

Yukiko was no longer as difficult as she had once been, but she was not likely to lose her reserve overnight. It was as though she had paid no attention to Itani's orders. She made no effort to be friendly, and as always she barely answered questions that were put to her. Teinosuke thought to bring out an album of photographs from the Kyoto cherry-viewing the year before. Sachiko had to do most of the explaining, with Yukiko or Etsuko shyly adding a detail now and then. If only Taeko were here with her quips and burlesques, thought Sachiko. She could not help suspecting that the other three shared her wish. Twenty minutes went by, and a half hour, and after an hour Hashidera looked at his wrist watch and said he must go, and Mrs. Niu and Itani too stood up. Might the two ladies not be able to visit a little longer? asked Sachiko. Itani was always busy, but Mrs. Niu—it had been so long since she last called, and though they really could offer very little . . . Perhaps she would stay, then, said Mrs. Niu. Would they feed her? If she did not mind potluck, said Sachiko. Splendid, said Mrs. Niu, and stayed for dinner.

Yukiko and Etsuko left the three to talk by themselves. Sachiko too was pleased with Hashidera. She and her husband, quite without prearrangement, found themselves praising him and assuring Mrs. Niu that, though they had not yet heard Yukiko's views, they did not expect her to have reservations—somehow they felt sure that she would not object to such a man. As they learned the results of Mrs. Niu's investigations, they felt more and more that this was a proposal they would like to see through, but what still disturbed them was the fact that Hashidera himself seemed so unenthusiastic. It was Mrs. Niu's feeling, however, that he was striking a pose as a sort of defense against the noisy women around him, and that deep in his heart he was not a little interested. But to be honest, he had been deeply in love with his first wife, and he worried a great deal about the daughter she had left behind. Probably, then, he wanted to be pushed forward until there was no retreating. He wanted someone to prod him into a step he could not quite take by himself. If he really was so unenthusiastic, he hardly needed to let them bring him out twice. For all of his protests that it did not make sense to run off to the house of a young lady he had met but once, he had in the end allowed himself to be brought, and was that not evidence that he was interested in Yukiko? Sachiko and Teinosuke had to admit that there was much to the argument. Since he was so worried about the little girl, continued Mrs. Niu, no objection could prevail against a lady of whom the girl approved. She would arrange next time for the girl to meet Yukiko, and she would like if possible for young Etsuko to be present—the two children would become great friends. With that Mrs. Niu took her leave. Sachiko told Teinosuke afterwards that of the many prospective husbands they had inspected for Yukiko, this man seemed the best. All of their conditions were satisfied, and his family, his position, his way of living were neither ridiculously high nor ridiculously low by Makioka standards. Such a candidate was not likely to come again. And if, as Mrs. Niu suggested, he was deliberately holding back and hoping that they would go out after him, they might try being more aggressive. She seemed to be asking for brilliant suggestions from Teinosuke, but Teinosuke, though he agreed with her, could only wonder what was to be done. The real difficulty was that Yukiko was so passive by nature. They could expect no help from her. She could have put on an abler performance this afternoon, for instance. But they would think of something.

In Osaka the next day, Teinosuke looked for an excuse to stop by and become better acquainted with Hashidera, whose office was not far from his. In the course of the conversation the day before, he remembered, Sachiko had said that because of the war she was running short on German vitamins and sulfamine, of which she always liked to have a supply on hand, and Hashidera had urged her to use the sulfamine made by his company. Unlike most Japanese medicines, it produced absolutely no secondary reactions, he said, and he felt sure that it was quite as effective as the German product. Since his company made Vitamin B, she might give that a try too. He would send a package around immediately. Teinosuke protested that he was in Osaka every day himself and could just as well pick it up. Please, any time—if Teinosuke would but telephone, Hashidera could always arrange to be in. Though Teinosuke had not been serious, it now occurred to him that without seeming forward he could go around and say that his wife would be most grateful for a little of the medicine. Leaving his office early, he walked down Sakai Boulevard. He picked out the building as he turned west off the boulevard, the only reinforced-concrete building in a row of old earth-walled shops. Hashidera promptly ordered a boy to go off and wrap up so many packages of this medicine and so many packages of that. His office was not really suitable for receiving guests, he said, and if Teinosuke would wait a few minutes possibly they could go out together. He seemed to be leaving orders with two or three employees, and he came out coatless and hatless. Waiting in front for perhaps five minutes, Teinosuke saw from Hashidera's way with the employees that, in theory only one among several executives, he in fact ran the company. He suggested that they call on him if anything else were needed, and handed Teinosuke the package. Embarrassed at not being allowed to pay, Teinosuke withdrew apologetically, but at Hashidera's suggestion that they talk for a little while, he found himself following along, afraid he might miss an opportunity to hear something important. They would have a cup of coffee together, he assumed. Instead they turned into an alley and climbed to the second floor of a little restaurant one would have taken for a private house. Teinosuke thought he knew Osake well, but he had not known of this alley and this restaurant. The second floor, only one small room looking out over clusters of roofs and here and there a tall building, gave one the sense of being in the very heart of the old Semba district. Probably it was a favored spot

for merchants, and especially the owners and managers of the
pharmacies in which the district abounded, to talk business over
a light lunch. A poor place to be taking a guest, said Hashidera,
but unfortunately he had a little work to do before he went
home, and he could not stray far from the office. Having in effect
invited himself to dinner, Teinosuke was more and more embarrassed.

The food was cleverly prepared though not remarkably good—
some five dishes, and two or three flagons of saké. It was early
when they sat down, and Teinosuke, sensing that Hashidera was
extremely busy, meant to take his leave early. There were still
traces of light in the early-spring sky when they left the restaurant.
The meal could have taken no more than two hours. Although it
was clear that Hashidera was only returning a courtesy, and although the conversation, of the most desultory, touched on none
of the significant matters Teinosuke had hoped it might, he did
learn something of Hashidera: his specialty was internal medicine,
and in particular the gastroscope; he had chanced upon his return
from Germany to become acquainted with this pharmaceutical
company, and circumstances had compelled him to give up medicine and turn instead to business; the company had a president,
who was never seen; Hashidera did most of the work; when he
went out into the provinces to sell new medicines, the confusion
of the customer who had assumed he was not a doctor, and
learned in the course of the conversation that he was, could
sometimes be very amusing. Hashidera did not once ask about the
Makioka family, and Teinosuke found it difficult to speak of
Yukiko, but when fruit was brought he gathered his courage and,
working his remarks into the conversation so that they did not
sound like an apology, mentioned the fact that his sister-in-law
was far from the moody girl she at first impressed one as being.

16

THE NEXT DAY Sachiko had a call from Mrs. Niu. So Teinosuke had visited Mr. Hashidera. It was splendid that he had gone ahead by himself. She hoped that he would keep up the work and that they would become close friends. The Makiokas had been in the habit of leaving everything to others—hence their reputation for haughtiness. Mrs. Niu and Mrs. Itani had brought matters thus far, and it remained to see what their own efforts would do for them. The work of the two ladies, she thought, was at an end. They would withdraw for the time being. She was sure everything would be arranged beautifully. The Makiokas should do their best and see what came of the negotiations. And she would be waiting to hear the good news. She even offered congratulations. To Sachiko and Teinosuke, it hardly seemed that they were ready to be congratulated.

Immediately afterwards they had a visit from Dr. Kushida, who was passing the house on his way to see a patient. He had the information Sachiko had requested. Sachiko had some time before remembered that Dr. Kushida and Hashidera were both alumni of Osaka University, though not in the same graduating class, and had thought to ask about the latter. Always busy, Dr. Kushida did not even take off his coat. He handed Sachiko a piece of paper. She would find on it all he could tell her, he said, and left. Fortunate to have a classmate who was a very close friend of Hashidera's, Dr. Kushida had been able to make detailed inquiries about the man, his family in Shizuoka, and even the daughter, a quiet, docile girl whose reputation at school was far from bad. In general the information agreed with what Teinosuke had already been able to gather. As he left, Dr. Kushida added that he could give the man his highest recommendation.

At last Yukiko's luck had turned, said Teinosuke to his wife. They must do something to bring the negotiations to a happy conclusion. Though aware that he might seem wanting in common sense, therefore, he sat down and wrote Hashidera a letter some five or six feet long. He must apologize for his rudeness in discussing so delicate a problem by mail, and yet he must tell Hashidera about his sister-in-law. He had been on the verge of speaking the day before. Now, quite without regard for the proprieties, he would unburden himself. The question was this: why had his sister-in-law reached such an age without marrying? Possibly Hashidera suspected something dark in her past or something wrong with her health. There were no such complications. One reason, and one reason alone, explained her not having married, and perhaps he had already heard of it from Mrs. Niu or Mrs. Itani: the people around Yukiko, even though they belonged to a family of little importance, had chosen to be fussy about position and pedigree, and had succeeded in making themselves unpopular by turning down good proposal after good proposal. The result he would not attempt to disguise: people no longer brought word of likely candidates. It would be ideal if Hashidera would investigate for himself until his last suspicions were cleared away. The responsibility lay with the people around her. Yukiko herself was unblemished and had a perfectly clean conscience. He knew that he might seem to be boasting too much about a relative, but he could give Yukiko good marks in intelligence, learning, deportment, artistic ability. And what touched him particularly was that Yukiko was fond of children. Teinosuke's own daughter, ten this year, was actually closer to Yukiko than to her own mother. It seemed only natural that she should be. Yukiko watched over her school work and piano practice, and was a devoted nurse when she was ill. Here again he hoped that Hashidera would investigate and see for himself. And the matter of whether or not she was moody: as he had suggested the day before, she was not. Hashidera need feel no uneasiness on that score. If he might be permitted to speak quite openly, continued Teinosuke, he was prepared to offer it as his opinion that Yukiko would in no way disappoint Hashidera. There was no doubt that she could at the very least make the little girl happy. He was aware that in writing with such warmth of a relative he might embarrass Hashidera, but it was his desire to see Yukiko married that compelled him to write. He hoped again that Hashidera would forgive his unconventional behavior.

Such was the letter, which Teinosuke took great care to write in the gravest and most formal language. Confident since his student days of his ability to write, he had no particular trouble discussing the most delicate matters in the most circumspect fashion. This time, however, he was afraid of over-writing. He labored to avoid seeming importunate on the one hand and stiffly reserved on the other. The first draft was too strong and the second too weak, and immediately after he had mailed the third draft he began to wonder whether he had made a mistake. If Hashidera did not want to remarry, the letter was not likely to change his mind; and if he was interested, the letter might alienate him. It might have been better to wait.

Not really expecting a reply, Teinosuke found himself on edge even so when two or three days passed and he heard nothing. The following Sunday he left the house after telling Sachiko that he was going out for a walk. He found himself in a cab at Osaka Station and ordered it to Tennōji Ward. Though he had no real intention of calling on Hashidera, he remembered the address and thought he would just wander by for a look at the house. Leaving the cab in what he took to be the neighborhood, he walked along reading the names at the gates, and, possibly because the air felt like spring, his step became brisker, and the future seemed bright. Hashidera's house was relatively new, a cheerful house with a sunny southern exposure. It was one in a row of three or four trim two-storey houses, each with its board fence and its pine trees, far from badly built for houses to rent—a little suggestive in their way of the house one might choose for setting up a mistress. Perhaps even so small a house was too large for a middle-aged widower with only one daughter. Teinosuke stood for a time looking up through the pine needles, each separate needle aglitter in the morning sun, at a half-open upstairs window. It seemed a shame to have come so far for nothing. He pushed open the gate and rang the bell.

The housekeeper, fifty or so, led him upstairs.

"Good morning."

He turned and saw Hashidera at the foot of the stairs, a spruce kimono pulled over his nightgown. "Could you wait just a few minutes? I seem to have overslept."

"Please, please. It was rude of me not to warn you."

Hashidera bowed genially and started toward the back of the house. Teinosuke was much relieved. He had felt that he could not rest until he saw the man again. The letter had obviously not offended him.

Teinosuke waited in the front room on the second floor, apparently the parlor. There were no flowers in the shelved niche, but the wall-hanging, the porcelain below it, the framed motto over the door, the double screen, the sandalwood table, and the smoking set were carefully arranged and in good taste, and the fact that the paper-panelled doors and the mats on the floor were spotless and had none of the shabbiness one associates with widowers' apartments suggested what sort of man Hashidera was, and suggested too what his wife must have been. The house had seemed bright and cheerful as he looked up from the gate, and it was even brighter than he had expected. The door panels, white with a leaf pattern in mica, turned off the sunlight brilliantly. The air was crystal clear to the farthest corners of the room, the smoke from Teinosuke's cigarette hung motionless in a sharply defined spiral. Though he had felt a little forward as he handed his card to the housekeeper, he was glad now that he had come. It was something to be a guest in the house, and to see that the master was not out of sorts.

"I'm sorry to have kept you waiting."

Some ten minutes later, Hashidera came back in a carefully pressed blue-serge suit. It was warmer on the veranda, he thought —he led Teinosuke to wicker chairs from which they looked out over the street. Not wanting it to seem that he had come for an answer to his letter, Teinosuke meant to leave immediately, but the sun was warm through the glass doors, and Hashidera as always made it easy to stay on, and presently an hour had gone by. Teinosuke did finally mention the letter, for which he said he must apologize. Hashidera answered that on the contrary he had been most grateful. For the rest, the conversation flowed in an effortless detour around the really significant matter. Teinosuke roused himself and stood up to leave. Hashidera was going to the movies with his daughter, however, and if Teinosuke had no other business he might go at least that far with them. Anxious for a glimpse of the daughter, Teinosuke accepted the invitation.

Cabs were becoming scarce. Hashidera called a Packard from a garage he knew, and Teinosuke rode with him as far as the Asahi Building. Hashidera would of course be glad to see him to the station—if he had no other plans, though, suppose he join them. Teinosuke was uncomfortable at the thought that he would be one more meal in debt. But he did want to know the daughter, and it was such a good opportunity to become friendlier with Hashidera too.

For another hour or so they talked over dinner. This time, with the daughter along, the conversation was little more than innocent chatter about movies and the Kabuki, and American actors and Japanese actors, and school. The girl was thirteen, three years older than Etsuko, and much more poised. Though she still wore a student's uniform and there was no sign that she used make-up, her face was no longer that of a little girl. It was the delicately molded face of an adult, rather long and thin, with a proud, high nose. Inasmuch as she did not look like Hashidera, Teinosuke suspected that she took after her mother, who must have been a beauty. Probably Hashidera saw in the girl the image of his dead wife.

Teinosuke tried to pay the bill. No, the invitation had been Hashidera's, and Hashidera would pay. Very well, said Teinosuke, the next party would be his. He would like to show them Kobe. He left them at the elevator with a promise to meet again the following Sunday. The girl was to be along too. That promise was the gift he brought home from his expedition.

17

SACHIKO laughed at news of this remarkable success. He was becoming rather brazen these days, she said, but secretly she was very pleased. There was a time when she would have been furious at this lack of restraint, and Teinosuke himself, knowing that until recently he would not have been up to such forwardness, could only marvel at the change their search for a husband had brought. But he had gone far enough. He would wait to see what came of the Sunday meeting. In the meantime there was a telephone call from Mrs. Niu. She had heard that Teinosuke had met the girl too, and she could not tell them how delighted she was at the brightening prospects. And Hashidera and his daughter were to be their guests. Mrs. Niu hoped everything would be done to make them feel welcome. She hoped especially that Yukiko would do her best to cancel out that first impression of "moodiness," an impression that had troubled Mrs. Niu deeply. It seemed then that Hashidera reported each new development to her. He could not be entirely cold to the proposal.

On Sunday, the Hashideras stopped by the Ashiya house for an hour or two, and a party of six set out in a cab for Kobe. The Makiokas had debated at some length what to eat—Chinese food, Western food at the Oriental Grill, or Nagasaki food—and had decided that the Kikusui, a Sukiyaki restaurant, was most like Kobe. Lunch was over at four. After a stroll through the city and tea at Juchheims, the Hashideras left for Osaka. The Makiokas went on to see the American movie *Condor* at Hankyū Hall. It was not to be expected that one meeting would bring any real intimacy between the two families, and in fact they had scarcely gotten to know one another's faces.

The next afternoon Yukiko was upstairs practicing her calligraphy.

"Telephone, Miss Yukiko." O-haru came running up.

"For Mrs. Makioka?"

"He said he would like to speak to Miss Yukiko."

"Who is it?"

"Mr. Hashidera."

Yukiko put down her brush in great consternation. She hovered at the foot of the stairs, her face a flaming red, and went no nearer the telephone.

"Where is Mrs. Makioka?"

"She stepped out for a minute."

"Where?"

"To mail a letter, I believe. She left just this minute. Shall I call her?"

"Quick! Go call her. Quick!"

O-haru hurried out the door. Half for the exercise, Sachiko generally went out to mail her own letters, and while she was about it to take a stroll along the embankment. O-haru found her just around the first corner.

"Mrs. Makioka," she panted. "Miss Yukiko wants you."

"Why?"

"There is a telephone call from Mr. Hashidera."

"From Mr. Hashidera?" This was quite unexpected. "For me?"

"No, for Miss Yukiko. But Miss Yukiko sent me to call you."

"Did she go to the phone?"

"She was standing by the stairs when I left."

"Yukiko is so odd. She could just as well go to the phone herself."

Most unfortunate, thought Sachiko. Yukiko's dislike for the telephone was no secret, and when—rarely—there was a call for her she usually had someone else do the talking and went to the telephone herself only on very special occasions. No one had objected up to now, but this was one of those special occasions. Whatever Hashidera's reasons for calling, it seemed imperative, since he had asked for her, that Yukiko take the call. He would receive quite the wrong impression if Sachiko were to talk to him instead. Yukiko was after all not a sixteen-year-old. Though her sisters understood this shyness, they could hardly expect a stranger to understand. They would be lucky if Hashidera was not offended. Perhaps Yukiko had gone to the telephone, timid and protesting? But to go reluctantly after having made him wait, to say almost nothing—she was even worse over the telephone than she was face-to-face—and as a result to have him break off the negotiations—the better alternative might be to let him go on waiting. There was always that stubborn core. Possibly she had refused to go near the telephone, and was waiting for Sachiko to rescue her. Even if Sachiko were to rush home, however, she would probably find that he had given up, and if he had not, what could she say by way of excuse? This was one time when Yukiko herself should have taken the call, and promptly. Something told Sachiko that this trivial incident could mean the end of the negotiations on which they had worked so hard. But surely Hashidera, polished and amiable gentleman that he was, would not exaggerate the incident. If Sachiko had only been at home, she could somehow have dragged Yukiko to the telephone. Wretched luck that he had picked a time—no more than five or six minutes—when she was out of the house.

The receiver was back on the hook, and Yukiko was nowhere in sight.

"Where is Miss Yukiko?" she asked O-aki, who was making cakes for tea.

"She went upstairs, I believe. She is not in her room?"

"Did she answer the telephone?"

"Yes, ma'am."

"Right away?"

"She waited and waited, and then finally . . ."

"And did she talk long?"

"No more than a minute or so."

"When did she finish?"

"Just this minute."

Upstairs, Yukiko was studying a copybook.

"What did Mr. Hashidera want?"

"He said he would be waiting at Osaka Station at four-thirty, and he wanted me to meet him."

"I suppose he wanted to go for a walk with you."

"He said he was thinking of walking through Shinsaibashi and having dinner somewhere, and he wondered if I would go with him."

"And what did you say?"

Yukiko did not answer.

"Are you going?"

Yukiko muttered something that sounded very much like "No."

"Why?"

Silence again.

"You do not agree, Yukiko, that it might be a good idea to go?"

Sachiko knew her sister well enough not to need an answer: it would be unthinkable for Yukiko to go walking alone with a prospective husband, a man she had met but two or three times. And yet Sachiko was angry. No doubt Yukiko disliked the thought of having dinner with a man she did not know well, but did she feel no obligation to Sachiko—more important, to Teinosuke? If she would only consider the embarrassment and the humiliation Teinosuke and Sachiko had endured, she ought to think of doing something for herself. It had been bold of Hashidera to make the call in the first place, and it must have been a deep disappointment to be turned away so brusquely.

"You refused, then?"

"I said I was very sorry."

If she had to refuse, she could have refused gracefully, but the art of graceful refusal was foreign to Yukiko. Tears of resentment came to Sachiko's eyes at the thought of the strained, inept reply Yukiko must have made. Angrier and angrier the longer she looked at her sister, Sachiko turned abruptly and started downstairs. She went out to the terrace and on into the garden.

Yukiko might still try to recover the lost ground by calling Hashidera immediately, apologizing for her rudeness, and offering to meet him in Osaka that evening, but there was very little chance that Sachiko's arguments would move her. They would only quarrel if Sachiko tried to use force. Should Sachiko go to the telephone herself? Could she offer an explanation ingenious enough to convince him that Yukiko had good reasons for not meeting him today? Suppose they meet tomorrow, then, he might say, and what could she answer? Yukiko would continue to refuse until she felt that she really knew the man. Giving up the thought of immediate remedies, might Sachiko succeed in pacifying Hashidera if she went to Mrs. Niu the next day, explained Yukiko's feelings and general nature very carefully, and had Mrs. Niu pass the explanation on? Yukiko was in no sense keeping aloof from Hashidera, she would explain, and did not object to walking with him. She had simply led too sheltered a life, and she lost her self-possession when she met strange men. And was that fact not evidence of something pure and clean in her nature?

As Sachiko walked through the garden turning these various possibilities over in her mind, she thought she heard the telephone ring.

"Telephone, Mrs. Makioka," O-haru called down from the terrace. "From Mrs. Niu."

Startled, Sachiko turned to go into the house. She decided to take the call from Teinosuke's study instead.

"Sachiko. I just had a call from Mr. Hashidera. He was furious."

Mrs. Niu's tone was ominous. That crisp, assured Tokyo speech was even crisper when she was aroused. She did not know exactly why, but he was furious. He did not like spineless, quivering, old-fashioned women. Mrs. Niu had said that Yukiko was bright and lively, but where in the world was the liveliness she spoke of? He wanted no more talk of his marrying the woman, and he hoped Mrs. Niu would tell the Makiokas immediately. Mrs. Niu did not know exactly what had annoyed him, but he had evidently wanted to have a good conversation alone with Yukiko, and had invited her to go for a walk that evening. The maid who answered the telephone said that Yukiko was at home, and then there was no Yukiko. He waited and waited. When she finally came to the telephone he asked if she was free that evening. "Well," she said, and it was impossible to tell whether she meant yes or no. As he pressed her for a clearer answer, she finally said, in a voice he could barely hear, that there were reasons why she could not see him. She said not another word. He left the telephone in great anger.

Such was his story, said Mrs. Niu. And what did the lady have in mind, he had asked—was she intent on making a fool of him? He was really furious. Mrs. Niu hardly stopped for breath as she reported the conversation.

"And so I'm afraid there's nothing more we can do."

"I am terribly sorry. Terribly sorry—after all the trouble you have gone to. If I had only been at home. I stepped out for just a minute."

"Even if you weren't at home, Yukiko was."

"That is very true. I am really terribly sorry. And I suppose there is nothing to be done now."

"Nothing."

Sachiko would have liked to crawl away and hide. She could only listen, and now and then offer a hesitant, incoherent answer.

"I know I shouldn't say all this over the phone, Sachiko, but I don't think there will be any point in seeing you to talk about what has happened. I hope you won't mind." Mrs. Niu seemed ready to end the conversation.

"Really, really. I will be around to apologize. And you are quite right to be angry." Sachiko hardly knew what she was saying.

"You needn't apologize, Sachiko, and there's no reason for you to come and see me." Mrs. Niu wanted to hear no more. She cut Sachiko's apologies short and said goodbye.

Chin in hand, Sachiko sat for a time at her husband's desk. When Teinosuke came home, she must tell him the unpleasant news. Or should she wait until tomorrow, when she would be calmer? She knew how disappointed he would be, and what worried her most was the thought that the incident might turn him against Yukiko. He had always tended to dislike Taeko and to sympathize with Yukiko. Might he not come to dislike both of them? Taeko had someone else to watch over her, but what would Yukiko do if Teinosuke were to abandon her? Sachiko was in the habit of going to Yukiko when she had to talk about Taeko, and to Taeko to talk of Yukiko. She suddenly felt very lonely. How inconvenient it was not to have Taeko with her!

"Mother." From the doorway, Etsuko looked curiously at her mother. Coming home from school and finding the house quiet, she had sensed that something was wrong. "What are you doing?" She came into the room and peered over her mother's shoulder. "What are you doing, Mother? Tell me what you are doing."

"Where is Yukiko?"

"Upstairs reading. Is something wrong?"

"No. Suppose you go talk to Yukiko."

"You come too." Etsuko tugged at her mother's hand.

"All right." Sachiko stood up. Back in the main house, she sent Etsuko upstairs and sat down at the piano.

Teinosuke came home about an hour later. Sachiko was still at the piano when she heard the bell. She followed him out to the study.

"Something terrible has happened. And after you went to all that trouble."

Not sure whether she would tell him today or wait until tomorrow, Sachiko had found when she saw him that she could not keep the news to herself. His expression changed for a moment, and she thought she heard a sigh. For the rest he listened quietly, showing no sign of displeasure. In the face of this composure, Sachiko felt her resentment at Yukiko well up again. Who had caused them all this trouble? she thought bitterly. There was nothing to be gained by going over the whole story again, she knew, but it seemed clear that Hashidera had been in a mood to marry. Even though he refused to give a definite answer, there could be no doubt that he was interested in Yukiko. Why else would he have called today to invite her out? The telephone incident seemed too unfortunate—she wanted to stamp her feet and wail like an angry child. But wailing would do not good. The opportunity was gone, forever. Why had she not been at home? She might not have been able to make Yukiko accept the invitation, but she could at least have seen that her sister was polite to the man. And the negotiations would have progressed smoothly. Perhaps a formal engagement was in sight. She did not think she was dreaming when she said so. The chances were, or should have been, eight or nine in ten. And then came that call, when Sachiko was out of the house for no more than five or six minutes. That the merest trivialities should determine a person's future! Sachiko was inconsolable. She even seemed to blame herself for having left the house. And it had been Yukiko's unhappy fate that the call came at that time of all possible times.

"I am furious, of course. But poor Yukiko."

"It happened because Yukiko is what she is. I imagine it would have been the same even if you had been there to answer the telephone."

Teinosuke set about comforting his wife. Even if Sachiko had been with her, Yukiko would not have been able to talk to the man. And short of her accepting the invitation and going out with him, it did not seem likely that he would have been satisfied. The ultimate source of the trouble was to be found in Yukiko's nature, and not in the simple question of whether or not Sachiko was with her at the telephone. Even if they had made their way safely through this crisis, there would have been others ahead. The talks were doomed to failure from the start. Yukiko had not managed to change herself.

"Do you mean that she will never marry?"

"Not at all. A girl too shy to go to the telephone has good points of her own. There are men who would never think of calling her spineless and old-fashioned—men who would see something very charming in her shyness. And only a man who sees her good points is qualified to be her husband."

Sachiko's anger subsided. Noting that she was not so much comforting her husband as being comforted by him, she felt more apologetic than ever. She made a special effort to feel sorry for Yukiko, who had come downstairs and was sitting on the parlor sofa with Bell in her lap. But some of the anger returned— Yukiko was really *too* lackadaisical.

"Yukiko." Sachiko flushed from the strain of keeping back her anger. "I had a call from Mrs. Niu. She said Mr. Hashidera was furious and wanted nothing more to do with us."

"Oh?" Yukiko showed little concern. Possibly she was feigning an indifference she did not feel. She rubbed the throat of the purring cat.

"And not just Mr. Hashidera. Mrs. Niu too, and Teinosuke, and myself," Sachiko wanted to add. Somehow she held herself back. Did Yukiko agree that she had blundered? If so, she might at least offer a word of apology to Teinosuke. But Sachiko knew that Yukiko would never apologize even if she knew she should. The resentment rose anew.

18

THE NEXT DAY Itani came to Sachiko with all the details.

She knew that Hashidera had called Mrs. Niu, and as a matter of fact he had called her too. She felt almost as though he were springing at her throat (he was such a gentleman, too), and, guessing that the matter was no ordinary one, she immediately set out for Osaka to see both Hashidera and Mrs. Niu. And when she heard the story, she agreed that Hashidera had reason to be angry. His dissatisfaction was a result not only of what had happened the day before. It had had its beginnings the day before that, when Hashidera and his daughter had gone to Kobe with the Makiokas. As they were walking back toward the station, Hashidera and Yukiko were cut off for a few minutes by a parade

in honor of the expeditionary forces. Glancing at a haberdashery
window, Hashidera remarked that he thought he would buy some
socks. Would Yukiko mind helping him? Yukiko stammered and
stuttered, and looked back for help from Sachiko, fifty yards
away. Finally Hashidera, much annoyed, went into the shop and
bought the socks by himself. The incident took no more than
fifteen or twenty minutes, and no one else noticed, but for
Hashidera it was most disagreeable. He tried to take a liberal
view, to convince himself that such was Yukiko's nature and
that she did not especially dislike him. Still it weighed on his
mind, and since the weather was so good and he happened
to have time to spare, it occurred to him the next day that he
might telephone and see whether she did indeed dislike him.
And so, as they knew, insult was piled on insult. He had thought
the first time that she was only embarrassed and uncomfortable.
When he was treated with similar disdain a second time, he
could only conclude that she disliked him thoroughly. Her abrupt
refusal amounted to asking if he was too dull to see the point.
She could surely have found a more graceful way to phrase it.
The young lady was trying to wreck the talks on which the
people around her had worked so hard. He was most grateful for
Mrs. Niu's kindness and Itani's—and Sachiko's and Teinosuke's
too, he added—but however much he wanted to please them,
there was little he could do. He did not feel that he was breaking
off the negotiations—he felt rather that Yukiko had broken them
off. But it had been Mrs. Niu who was really angry, said Itani.
She could not approve of Yukiko's attitude toward men. Because
she had thought an impression of "moodiness" highly probable,
Mrs. Niu had especially advised Yukiko to leave a warm, lively
impression instead, and Yukiko had refused to take her advice.
Mrs. Niu found it even harder to understand Sachiko, who
allowed Yukiko to have her way. Such aloofness was no longer
permitted to a princess even, or to the daughter of a noble
family, and what precisely did Sachiko think her sister was?
So Mrs. Niu had said. Sachiko suspected that Itani was putting
her own resentment into Mrs. Niu's mouth. Severe though the
reproaches were, Sachiko had no answer. There was something
mannish about Itani, however, and once she had had her say she
felt better and moved on to more comfortable topics. It was not

such a tragedy, she said, noting Sachiko's dejection. She did not know about Mrs. Niu, but she herself meant to go on doing what she could for Miss Yukiko. In the course of the conversation, that spot over Yukiko's eye had come up for discussion. Although he had seen her three times in all, Hashidera had noticed nothing, said Itani, and the daughter had first called the spot to his attention. They need not worry, then. It made no difference whatsoever.

Sachiko told Teinosuke nothing of the incident in Kobe. Telling him could only have the effect of alienating him from Yukiko. Teinosuke for his part wrote a letter to Hashidera of which he said nothing to Sachiko. He had no apologies to offer, he wrote, and he knew his letter might sound querulous, but there was one thing at least that he must be allowed to explain. Perhaps Hashidera thought that they, his wife and Teinosuke himself, had pushed the marriage talks without attempting to learn Yukiko's views. That was far from the case. Yukiko did not dislike Hashidera, and they had cause to believe that her feelings were the opposite. If Hashidera wanted an explanation for her strange manner of a few days before, or for her manner over the telephone, then her general shyness before men was explanation enough. There was no evidence of any dislike for him. Though it would seem ridiculous to outsiders that a woman past thirty should be so shy, her family, those who knew her well, saw nothing whatsoever to be surprised at. She had always behaved thus, and her fear of strangers had if anything begun to leave her. They knew, however, that they could not expect people to understand, and he had no apologies to offer—especially for that telephone incident. He had denied that she was moody and had insisted that at heart she was gay and bright, and even now he felt that he had not been mistaken, but for a woman past thirty to be incapable of the simplest greeting was evidence of bad training in the extreme. Hashidera had every right to be angry. If he had been forced to conclude that she was not qualified to become his wife, then there was no quarreling with his decision. Teinosuke would have to admit that Yukiko had failed the test. He did not have the impudence to ask that Hashidera reconsider. Improper upbringing had left her behind the times: she had early lost her mother, and she had still been

young when her father had died—and of course a good part of
the responsibility lay with Teinosuke and his wife. Though it
was possible that he had come to overrate Yukiko, he did want
Hashidera to know that he had no recollection of having resorted
to distortion or falsehood in his efforts at matchmaking. He hoped
that Hashidera would soon find himself a good wife, and that
something would be arranged for Yukiko too, so that they
could both forget the unpleasantness, and he hoped that one
day they might all be friends. Since it had been such a pleasure
to know Hashidera, it was an irreparable loss that through so
trival an incident they might not see each other again.

That was the substance of the letter. Almost immediately a
polite answer came from Hashidera. He was most grateful for
Teinosuke's admirable letter. Teinosuke was being modest when he
said that his sister-in-law had been reared in an outmoded manner.
The fact was that Yukiko could never really be at home in the
modern world. She would therefore always retain something pure
and maidenly. What she needed was a husband who would place
a proper value on her virtues, someone who would see it as his
duty to cherish and protect them, and unfortunately the deep
understanding and the delicate sensibility required were quite
lacking in a countrified boor like himself. He had therefore
come to believe that a match would make neither of them happy.
He would be most distressed if he thought he had said anything
about the lady that might seem insulting, and he was most
grateful for all their courtesies. The tranquil happiness of the
Makioka family was something for the world to envy. Because
she was lucky enough to be a member of such a family,
Yukiko had become the gem she was. Like Teinosuke's, the
letter was carefully written in brush on Japanese paper. Though
it was not in the most formal of language, no one could have
taken exception to the careful, polished sentences.

In Kobe with the Hashideras, Sachiko had picked out a blouse
for the daughter and asked to have an initial embroidered on it.
Some days after the marriage talks were broken off, the blouse
was delivered. Thinking Hashidera might find it strange if she
let the matter drop, Sachiko sent the gift through Itani. When
she visited Itani's beauty shop two weeks later she was given
a manila-wrapped package that had been left by Hashidera, and

when she got home she found that it contained a crepe singlet from the Eriman in Kyoto. It was exactly right for her—perhaps Mrs. Niu had done the selecting. They concluded that it was in return for the blouse, and they thus had further evidence of Hashidera's scrupulous attention to the proprieties.

Though it was not easy to tell how Yukiko felt, outwardly she was neither disappointed nor apologetic. One would have said—she might have had a guiltier conscience than she chose to reveal—that she appreciated what Sachiko and the others had done for her, and yet, since she was incapable of doing more for herself, she was not one to grieve over a man who could reject her on such grounds. Sachiko found that the opportunity to speak of her resentment had passed, and soon the two sisters slipped back into their old relationship, though Sachiko still felt a vague rankling. She would have liked to tell everything to Taeko. Unfortunately it had been some twenty days since Taeko's last visit. She had come on a Tuesday early in March, the morning after the fateful telephone call; had stayed only long enough to hear that again it was "no match"; and had gone away looking bitterly disappointed. Afraid that Itani and Mrs. Niu knew a good deal bout Taeko and were hoping to learn more, Sachiko gave carefully evasive answers each time they asked what had happened to "Koi-san." She did not want it to be known that Taeko was living out, and yet she had to be prepared, if Taeko's relations with Okubata attracted notice, to say that Taeko was no longer one of the family. Now that her efforts in Yukiko's behalf had come to nothing, she found herself wanting intensely to see Taeko. What might have happened to Koi-san—ought they to telephone her? They discussed the matter over the breakfast table one morning, and that morning O-haru, who had taken Etsuko to school, was some three hours coming home.

Sachiko and Yukiko were alone in the parlor.

"Koi-san is ill," said O-haru in a low voice.

"Ill? What is the matter?"

"It seems to be either intestinal catarrh or dysentery."

"Was there a telephone call?"

"Yes, ma am."

"And you went to see?"

"Yes, I . . ."

"Is she in her room?" asked Yukiko.

"No, ma'am." O-haru stared at the floor.

This was the story: O-haru had gotten out of bed to answer the telephone that morning. The call was from Okubata, who said that two days earlier Koi-san had taken ill at his house. At about ten o'clock in the night she began to run a high fever, well over one hundred, and she was seized with violent chills. When she tried to leave he kept her back and made her go to bed. She got worse, and the next day he called a doctor who practiced in the neighborhood. The doctor had trouble with his diagnosis. It looked like influenza, he said, or possibly typhus, but in the middle of the night she was taken with violent abdominal pains and diarrhea, and the doctor decided she had intestinal catarrh or dysentery. If it did prove to be dysentery, they would have to move her to a hospital. For the time being she would be at Okubata's, however, since they could hardly send her back to her room alone. Okubata was telling only O-haru. Though Koi-san was in great pain, there was no immediate danger, and there was no reason why they could not take care of her in his house. He would let the Makiokas know of any change in her condition—not of course that he expected a change. O-haru decided to see for herself, and went to Nishinomiya after taking Etsuko to school. Taeko was much worse than Okubata had suggested over the telephone. She had had some twenty or thirty attacks of diarrhea in the night. Braced against a chair, she was in fact spending all her time over the bedpan. The doctor said that this would never do, that she should rest quietly in bed and use an insertable bedpan, and after O-haru arrived they forced her to lie down. There were several attacks of diarrhea during O-haru's visit, violent spasms that produced nothing and only added to the suffering. The fever was still high, about one hundred two at the latest measuring. The stool was being tested at Osaka University, and they would have the results in a day or two. When O-haru suggested that it might be a good idea to call Dr. Kushida, Taeko answered that she did not want Dr. Kushida to see her in such a place. And she did not want to worry her sisters. O-haru was not to tell Sachiko. O-haru replied only that she would come again some time during the day.

"Was there a nurse?"

"No. They said they would call a nurse if it seemed that she would be in bed long."

"Who is taking care of her, then?"

"The young master takes care of the ice bag." For some reason, O-haru had begun calling Okubata "the young master." "I took care of disinfecting the bedpan and tidying her up afterwards."

"Who does it when you are not there?"

"I wonder. The old woman, I imagine. She is very good—the young master's housekeeper."

"And she does the kitchen work too?"

"Yes, ma'am."

"But it might be dysentery. I should think it would be dangerous to have her handling the bedpan."

"Do you think I should go and help?" asked Yukiko.

"Suppose we wait a little longer."

If it was dysentery, something would have to be done, but there was no cause for confusion if it was only an attack of catarrh which would pass in two or three days. For the time being they would only send O-haru off to help, said Sachiko. Should they then tell Teinosuke and Etsuko that sudden business had called her home, and that she would be gone for two or three days?

"What sort of doctor do they have?"

"I have no idea. Somone from the neighborhood, they said. They had never called him before."

"It would really be better to have Dr. Kushida," said Yukiko.

"It would indeed," Sachiko agreed. "If only she were in her own room. But with her at Kei-boy's . . ."

Taeko had insisted that O-haru was not to tell the family, but Sachiko suspected that she hoped O-haru would ignore her orders. Surprisingly weak at times, Taeko knew how good it was to have a family. She would be lonely with neither Sachiko nor Yukiko beside her.

19

O-HARU hurried away after an early lunch, careful to thank Sachiko for the two or three days she was to have off. As she started for the door, she was called into the living room and given careful instructions: she was not to fall into her usual carelessness; she must wash her hands after she touched the patient, and she must sprinkle the bedpan with lysol each time it was used. And these instructions were added: though Sachiko wanted to be kept thoroughly informed, Okubata had no telephone; it would be awkward if a call were to come while Teinosuke and Etsuko were in the house, and O-haru was therefore to call at least once every morning; and even if it was possible to use a telephone in some near-by shop, she was to go to a public telephone.

Since it was already afternoon, they could not expect a call that day. The next morning seemed a great distance off, and the first call came at about ten. Sachiko took it in Teinosuke's study. The connection was very bad, and from time to time they were cut off. It was a very great effort to acquire very little information. There seemed to have been no particular change, except that the diarrhea had become worse during the night—some ten attacks every hour. The temperature showed no sign of falling. Was it dysentery? They did not know yet. What about the tests at Osaka University? They had no report. What about the stool —did there seem to be a mixture of blood? There did seem to be traces of blood, and besides the blood there was a thick, white mucus. Where was O-haru calling from? A public telephone. There was no public telephone near Okubata's house, and it was most inconvenient, and she had been late because two or three people were in line ahead of her. She would try to call again that day. She would call the following morning at the latest.

"If there is blood, it must be dysentery," said Yukiko, who was standing beside the telephone.

"I suppose so."

"Is there blood with intestinal catarrh?"

"I doubt it."

"It must be dysentery. Ten attacks an hour."

"I wonder if the doctor is good."

Convinced that it was dysentery, Sachiko debated what to do. The second call did not come that day, nor did it come the following morning. Toward noon, O-haru appeared at the kitchen door.

"What is it?" Noting a certain tenseness in O-haru's manner, the two sisters led her into the parlor.

"It does seem to be dysentery."

The report had not yet come from Osaka University, but the doctor, who had called the night before and again that morning, said it seemed to be dysentery. The Kimura Hospital on the National Highway had an isolation ward. Should the doctor have Taeko sent there? They were on the point of asking him to do so when the green grocer happened to tell O-haru that they might better choose another hospital, and upon inquiring around the neighborhood, O-haru found that the Kimura Hospital had a bad name. Dr. Kimura was almost deaf and incapable of a really thorough examination, and his diagnoses were often wrong. Though he was a graduate of Osaka University, his record had not been good, and it was even said that his graduation essay had been written by a classmate. The classmate, who was practicing not far away, sometimes boasted of having written two essays. Much disturbed when O-haru passed this information on to him, Okubata set about looking for another hospital. Unfortunately no other in the area had an isolation ward. How would it be, he suggested, if they said that she had intestinal catarrh and nursed her at home? They could hardly expect the doctor to agree, dysentery being an infectious disease. Surely not every dysentery patient was sent to the hospital, argued Okubata; a great many were treated at home. It made no difference what the doctor said: they would treat her at home, and he would have to agree. But they should consult Mrs. Makioka. Very well, said O-haru. Knowing that a telephone call would not do, she hurried back to Ashiya.

Sachiko wanted to know more about the doctor. He was a graduate of Osaka University, said O-haru, and seemed to be two or three years younger than Dr. Kushida. His father, who was still living, had long been practicing in the neighborhood, and father and son were both well thought of, but it seemed to O-haru that he lacked Dr. Kushida's brisk assurance. He was fearfully slow and deliberate in his examinations, and it was not easy to force a definite answer from him. His slowness had been one reason for the delay in the final diagnosis, and another had been the fact that for dysentery the fever was rather too high, and the diarrhea had begun a full day after the first symptoms appeared. There had thus been some possibility that it was typhus. The attack of dysentery was more serious than it would have been with a prompter diagnosis.

"But where did she pick it up? Did she eat something?"

"She said she thought it was the mackerel."

"Where did she have mackerel?"

"That evening she and the young master were walking in Kobe, and they had mackerel in a *sushi* restaurant called the Kisuke."

"I have never heard of it. Have you, Yukiko?"

"Never."

"Koi-san said it was in one of the geisha quarters. She had been told that it was very good and she had been meaning to go there for some time. They were on their way home from a movie."

"And nothing happened to Kei-boy?"

"The young master never eats mackerel. Koi-san had mackerel by herself, and they are sure that that was it. But she only had a little, and it was not the least bit old or spoiled."

"I am always afraid of mackerel. You never can tell about mackerel, no matter how fresh it is."

"The darker it is the more dangerous, they say, and she had two or three slices of dark meat."

"Yukiko and I never eat mackerel. Only Koi-san."

"And Koi-san eats in too many places."

"*That* is the truth. She hardly ever had dinner at home, and now see what happens to her."

And what was Okubata thinking? However calm he might seem, was he not upset at having on his hands a patient with an infectious disease? When he found that it was not, as he had supposed, a light attack of catarrh, had he concluded that he

had more than he could manage, and had he hoped to send her
back to Ashiya? Sachiko remembered his behavior at the time
of the flood, two years before. But O-haru replied that he did
not seem in the least upset. Rather the dandy, he had not
wanted to spoil his trousers in the flood, but he did not seem
to fear infectious diseases. Perhaps, remembering how the flood
had helped turn Taeko against him, he was determined to show
his devotion this time—in any case, O-haru could not believe
that it was empty talk when he urged Koi-san to stay with him.
And he noticed the smallest details. He would sometimes give
instructions to O-haru and the nurse, or help with the ice bag
and the bedpan himself.

"I am going with O-haru," said Yukiko. "No one can possibly
mind."

People did not die of dysentery. Besides, Okubata himself had
been the first to urge that Koi-san stay with him, and they
really had nowhere to move her. There seemed nothing wrong
with leaving her in Nishinomiya, then, but they could hardly
disclaim all responsibility. Whatever Teinosuke and the people
in the main house might think, Yukiko and Sachiko did not mean
to leave Koi-san unattended. There could be no objection if
Yukiko went on her own initiative. She would feel better if
Okubata had had Dr. Kushida in, said Yukiko, but with only a
strange doctor and nurse—she had to help. She would take O-haru's
place, and O-haru could be used as a messenger. Since it was so
difficult to learn the truth by telephone, they only worried the
more, and since there would be any number of things lacking
in a bachelor's house, O-haru would have much running back and
forth to do. Yukiko immediately went to get ready. After a light
lunch, she left the house without asking Sachiko's permission.
Probably she did not want to trouble her sister. Sachiko agreed
with her completely, and made no effort to stop her.

Etsuko was told in an offhand way that Yukiko had gone
to have an injection and afterwards to do some shopping in
Kobe. Such a story would not do for Teinosuke, however, and
Sachiko told him everything, down to Yukiko's decision, quite
without prompting from Sachiko, to go to Nishinomiya. Teinosuke
frowned and said nothing. He could only accept the decision in
silence. At dinner, Etsuko was told a little of the truth—that

Yukiko had gone to take care of Koi-san—and she immediately began digging for more: where was Koi-san, and what was the matter with her? Koi-san was ill in her apartment, and Yukiko had gone because Koi-san was all alone. And it was nothing serious, nothing for a child to worry about—Sachiko's manner became a little impatient. Etsuko said no more. Not at all sure that the child believed them, Teinosuke and Sachiko tried to interest her in other subjects. She answered their questions without enthusiasm, and now and then she would glance cautiously up at one or the other. Although she had been told that Koi-san, who had disappeared the end of the year before, was very busy, she had heard much of the truth from O-haru, and indeed it was convenient not to have her in complete ignorance. Two or three days later, worried that there was no sign of Yukiko in spite of all O-haru's trips back and forth, she began nagging at O-haru to tell her how Koi-san was. Finally she accosted her mother.

"Why is Koi-san away from home? Have them bring her home, right away."

Thus Sachiko found that she was the one being scolded. She tried to calm the child. "Yukiko and I are taking care of Koi-san, and there is nothing for you to worry about. Children are not supposed to talk about such things."

But Etsuko was aroused. "How can you leave her there?" she screamed. "She might die on you. She might. How can you leave her there?"

The fact was that Taeko's progress was not satisfactory. She was getting worse. With Yukiko at her bedside, she did not want for nurses, but O-haru reported that she was getting weaker day by day. The results of the tests had come from Osaka University. Among the germs were germs of the most virulent sort. And for some reason her temperature rose and fell any number of times every day. At its highest, it went up to one hundred four, and with the fever came violent chills. Partly this was because she had been given medicine to stop the diarrhea and the violent abdominal pains. When the diarrhea subsided, the ague began and the fever rose. And when on the other hand the diarrhea returned, the fever fell, the pain became intense, and she strained at the bedpan to produce only a thin, watery

substance. Told that the heart seemed to be affected, Yukiko
was quite beside herself. Would Taeko recover? It did not seem
to be simple dysentery—might there be complications? She suggested that the doctor try injections, Ringer's solution or vita-
camphor, but he only replied that matters were not yet so
serious. Sure that Dr. Kushida would by now be giving injection
after injection, Yukiko asked the nurse's opinion, and was told
that Dr. Saitō, influenced by his father, disapproved of injections.
He would give an injection only in a real crisis. Miss Yukiko,
said O-haru, now felt that it no longer mattered what people
thought, that they must call in Dr. Kushida, but she wanted Mrs.
Makioka to come for a look. O-haru added that in the last five
or six days Koi-san had gotten thinner and thinner. Mrs. Makioka
would be shocked.

Sachiko had been hesitating because she feared infection and
because she did not want to worry Teinosuke. Now, however, she
decided to go with O-haru that very morning, and to say nothing
to her husband of the visit. Just before she left, she thought to
call Dr. Kushida and ask his opinion. She explained briefly that
Taeko had taken ill in the house of an acquaintance, that there
were reasons for leaving her there, that they had called a doctor
named Saitō in the neighborhood, and that her progress had been
far from ideal. At such times, replied Dr. Kushida with his usual
briskness, one gave the patient shot after shot of Ringer's solution
and camphor. Otherwise the patient only became weaker. Sachiko
must tell the doctor to hurry with injections before it was too late.
She might have to ask Dr. Kushida to pay a call, said Sachiko.
It was not as if he did not know Saitō, replied Dr. Kushida,
and if Saitō had no objection he would call whenever they
needed him.

Some hundreds of yards east of Narihira Bridge, a cherry tree
over an earthen wall to the north of the National Highway was
in full bloom.

"How beautiful," murmured O-haru.

"This is always the first tree to bloom," said Sachiko. She
looked at the pavement, from which shimmering waves were
rising as in midsummer. They had hardly noticed in all the
excitement, but here it was April, and in another ten days the
cherries would be in full bloom. And would the whole family

go to Kyote as usual? If only they could; but did it seem likely, even at the most sanguine estimate, that Koi-san would be up in time? Perhaps she would be well for the late cherries at Omuro. Etsuko had come down with scarlet fever the year before, Sachiko remembered. Though the child had waited until after the cherry viewing, and her illness had not interferred with that particular pleasure, it had kept Sachiko from seeing Kikugorō. This month Kikugorō was coming to Osaka again. He would be dancing "Wistaria Maiden," and she had meant to go whatever happened. Would she have to miss him this year too?

The cab moved along the embankment. In the distance, Helmet Mountain rose through a spring mist.

20

TAEKO was in bed upstairs. Yukiko and Okubata had heard the cab and were waiting at the foot of the stairs.

Okubata signalled to Sachiko and led her to the rear of the house.

"Excuse me for being so abrupt, but there is something I have to tell you."

Dr. Saitō had just made his call, and as Okubata saw him to the door, the doctor had said that Taeko's heart was weaker. The symptoms were still far from clear, he added, and he might be imagining things, but it seemed to him that the liver was swollen. She might just possibly have anthrax. And what was anthrax? Okubata had asked. A disease in which pustules form in the liver. The extreme temperature fluctuations, the chills and ague, Dr. Saitō had said, could only be explained by anthrax. He did not feel confident alone, however, and wondered if he might call in a specialist from Osaka University. Okubata learned more of anthrax: germs from other lesions, occasionally from dysentery, attach themselves to internal organs; if there is but one pustule it is easily treated; unfortunately the pustules tend to multiply, and the disease can be very troublesome when numbers of pustules form in the liver. If the pustules break in the internal organs, all is well, but if they break against the diaphragm, the bronchial tubes, or the peritoneum, almost nothing can be done to save the patient. Though Dr. Saitō avoided a direct statement, there was little doubt that he considered his diagnosis certain.

"Well, let me see her." When she had heard the story from Yukiko and Okubata in turns, Sachiko headed for the stairs. The six-mat room, which faced south, had a little balcony and a foreign-style hinged door. Though the floor was matted in the Japanese fashion, the room was otherwise occidental but for a closet with sliding doors; there was no alcove, the walls and even the ceiling were white. As for furnishings: a triangular cupboard stood in a corner of the room, and on it a dirty candlestick, apparently a foreign antique, covered with drops of wax; two or three other knickknacks, probably from second-hand stalls; and a faded French doll that Taeko had made long before. As for hangings, there was only a painting on glass. It would have been a singularly ugly room but for the thick crepe-covered quilt of large scarlet-and-white checks, like a blaze of flowers in the sunlight that poured through sliding windows some two yards wide. The fever had fallen, it seemed. Taeko lay on her right side with her eyes fixed on the door, waiting for Sachiko. Sachiko had dreaded this first encounter, but, perhaps because O-haru had prepared her well, she found Taeko less wasted than she had expected. Yet there was no denying that Taeko had changed. The round face had become long and thin, and the swarthy skin was even darker. And the eyes seemed to have grown as the rest of the face shrank.

Something else caught Sachiko's attention. It was natural that Taeko, unable to bathe, should be a little dirty, but there seemed to be rather a special kind of uncleanness about her. Ordinarily she was able to hide the effects of her misbehavior under cosmetics. Now, as a result of the emaciation, a certain darkness, a shadow of what one might call dissoluteness, had come over the face and throat and wrists. It must not be supposed that Sachiko was immediately conscious of all this, but there her sister lay, like a charity patient picked up in a gutter, her arms lifeless on the bed, as though she were quite exhausted from something besides the dysentery, from her intemperance over the years. A woman Taeko's age, long in bed, often seems to revert to the pretty little girl she was at twelve or thirteen, to take on a cleanness, a spiritual quality almost. With Taeko it was the opposite: she had lost her youthfulness, and she even looked older than she was. And, strangely, that fashionable modern air had disappeared. She reminded one of a servant in some teahouse or restaurant, a not-too-proper establishment at that. Though she had always been the different one, the scapegrace, no one could have denied that there was something fresh and girlish about her, and now this muddy, sagging skin—a skin that seemed to hide some loathsome disease, and made one think of a fallen woman. The brightness of the quilt set the diseased look off more sharply. It occurred to Sachiko that Yukiko must have noticed, and that she had quietly been watching "the diseased look" develop. When Taeko had had a bath, Yukiko refused to use the tub afterwards. She would borrow the most intimate garments from Sachiko without thinking twice, but she never tried to borrow anything from Taeko. Sachiko had noted all this vaguely, whether or not Taeko had, and she had noted too that Yukiko's squeamishness had begun at about the time a rumor came to them that Okubata had chronic gonorrhea. Taeko was fond of saying that her relations with both Itakura and Okubata had been nothing but "clean," and Sachiko had made it a point not to challenge her. Yet Sachiko had trouble accepting these protestations, and it seemed that Yukiko, without saying a word, had for some time been critical and even contemptuous of her sister.

"How are you, Koi-san?" Sachiko asked lightly. "They said you had wasted away to nothing, but you really look much better than I expected. How often have you used the bedpan today?"

"Three times since this morning." Her face as expressionless as ever, Taeko answered in a low but distinct voice. "Only pains, and nothing comes out."

"That happens with dysentery. 'Tenesmus' is the word doctors have for it."

"Oh?" Taeko was silent for a moment. "I hope I never see another mackerel." She smiled for the first time, albeit faintly.

"I quite agree with you. Never have mackerel again." Sachiko's manner changed a little. "There is nothing to worry about, but

Dr. Saitō says we must be careful, and he wants to call in another doctor. I thought we might ask Dr. Kushida."

The three of them had decided downstairs that, since Taeko did not know how serious her condition was, a direct statement might upset her less than a long explanation, and that, though Dr. Saitō had suggested calling a specialist from Osaka University and there was much to be said for the suggestion, they might only succeed in frightening her. It would not be too late to call a specialist after they had heard what Dr. Kushida had to say. Taeko listened vacantly, her eyes on the floor.

"Do you mind, Koi-san?"

"Dr. Kushida is not to see me here." She spoke with sudden determination, and there were tears in her eyes. "I would be ashamed to have him see me here."

The nurse was tactful enough to leave. Okubata and Sachiko and Yukiko stared in surprise at the tears that were streaming down Taeko's face.

"Let me talk to her alone." In much confusion, Okubata cast a pleading glance at Sachiko. His eyes swollen from lack of sleep, he sat across from Sachiko in a flannel nightgown over which he had thrown a blue-gray silk bathrobe.

"Never mind, Koi-san," said Sachiko. "We can do without Dr. Kushida." The important thing was to avoid exciting her. Sachiko could not help feeling that she had gone too far already, and though Okubata probably knew what had caused this outburst, Sachiko had no idea.

It was almost noon, and she had come without Teinosuke's permission. An hour or so later, when Taeko was quiet again, she picked her moment to withdraw. Meaning to go home by bus or streetcar, she walked south through the *mambō* of which O-haru had spoken. Yukiko was beside her and O-haru a little to the rear—they would see her part of the way.

"Something strange happened last night."

So Yukiko began. It was at about two in the morning, she said. Yukiko and the nurse were sleeping across the hall. (They usually took turns with Taeko. The latter having gone comfortably to sleep at about twelve, however, Okubata suggested that the two have a good night's sleep. He would take care of the patient himself. They had left everything to him, and he must have been dozing beside the bed.) Suddenly they heard a loud groaning from the other room. Was she in pain, was she having a night-mare?—but Kei-boy would surely be watching over her. As Yukiko jumped out of bed and opened the door across the hall, she heard Okubata trying to rouse Taeko, and she heard Taeko call out for Itakura: "Yone-yan," she said, using the affectionate nick-name. She said no more. Evidently the dream had passed. But there could be no doubt about that cry: "Yone-yan." Yukiko closed the door and went back to bed, and for the time being everything was quiet. At that point the full force of her exhaustion struck her, and she slept until, at about four, the diarrhea began with intense pains, and Okubata, unable to manage alone, came to call her. She had been up ever since. She was surer and surer that "Yone-yan" was Itakura, and that Taeko had been frightened by a dream of the dead man. The first anniversary of his death was approaching—he had died in May. One knew, from the way Koi-san visited the grave in Okayama every month, that she still thought about him, possibly because he had died so horribly, and one could not help suspecting that it must trouble her, with the anniversary approaching, to be seriously ill in the house of his rival. Koi-san had depths beyond depths. It was not easy to know what she was thinking. Still it seemed fairly certain that this much at least was on her mind, and that she had had a nightmare somehow related to Itakura. Or possibly Yukiko was imagining things—she could not really be sure she was right. The physical anguish since that morning had left Koi-san no room for mental anguish; and when, finally, the pain subsided, she only lay apathetic. And Kei-boy was an even better actor than Koi-san, and from his manner one would never have guessed that anything untoward had happened. But if even Yukiko had noticed, did it seem likely that Kei-boy had not? And that outburst this morning: this was pure conjecture on her part, said Yukiko, but did it not seem likely that Koi-san, having been tormented by Itakura's ghost, was afraid to stay with Oku-bata? Might she be thinking that she would not recover while she was here—that she would grow weaker and die? If so, might she be telling them less that she did not want to see Dr. Kushida than that she wanted them to move her?

"You may be right."

"I might try to find out more. But Kei-boy is always around."

"I just happened to think. If we have to move her, how would Dr. Kambara's hospital be? I am sure he would take her if we explained."

"Of course he would. But can he treat dysentery?"

"If he will let us have a room, we can have Dr. Kushida come in."

Dr. Kambara had a surgical hospital between Osaka and Kobe. Long before, when the sisters had been girls and Dr. Kambara himself a student in Osaka University, he had frequented the Osaka house and the Semba shop. Old Mr. Makioka had learned that he was a very gifted student and that he was short of money, and, going through a suitable intermediary, had offered help. When Dr. Kambara returned from Germany to open his hospital, part of the capital came from the Makiokas. With all the qualities of a great surgeon and with complete confidence in himself, he soon prospered. Before many years he was able to repay the debt in full, and afterwards when someone from the Makioka family or the shop would go for treatment he would accept only a small part of the usual fee. He was in part still repaying the old debt, of course, but he had about him a fatherly expansiveness, and a natural warmth that told of his east-country origins. If Sachiko were to explain what had happened, and ask him to find a suitable pretext for taking Taeko in, he would not be likely to refuse. They would have to trouble Dr. Kushida to look in on the patient now and then, since Dr. Kambara had only surgeons on his staff. Fortunately Dr. Kushida and Dr. Kambara were classmates, and on good terms.

As Yukiko and O-haru saw her through the underpass, Sachiko worked out her plans: she would call Dr. Kushida and Dr. Kambara; because Taeko was growing weaker, and because Dr. Saitō had even suggested that they might expect the worst, they could no longer leave her at Okubata's even if she had wanted to stay; they could not be too careful, and Yukiko was to approach Dr. Saitō and insist on injections; and if Yukiko could not prevail by herself she was to talk to Okubata. At home, Sachiko called Dr. Kambara. Quite as she had expected, he said he would have a room ready, and they should bring the patient immediately. Dr. Kushida was a different matter: always busy, he was difficult to

catch. After following him around from patient to patient, Sachiko found him at about six in the evening. She was all for moving Taeko immediately. There were all sorts of details to be
arranged, however, and she had to explain everything to Teinosuke, who seemed worried in spite of his silence, and make him
agree to pay the expenses, and the move finally had to be put off
until the next morning. Sachiko called Nishinomiya at about
seven in the morning. O-haru, back at noon with messages from
Yukiko, reported new developments. First the illness: chills and
tremors had begun again shortly after Sachiko left, and the temperature for a time rose above one hundred four. In the evening
it was still over one hundred. Okubata went to the phone and insisted on injections, and Dr. Saitō said he would give them a try,
but it was his father who appeared and who, after an examination
and some deliberation, said that the time had not yet come for
injections, and shoved the hypodermic needle (the nurse had it
ready) into his case. Convinced that they must change doctors,
Yukiko waited until Taeko seemed relatively comfortable and suggested again that they call Dr. Kushida. Her suspicious were confirmed: Taeko did not want to be in Okubata's house—though
she did not give her reasons. She wanted to be moved to a hospital
or even back to her room. She would not mind seeing Dr. Kushida
afterwards, but she would not see him here. Because Okubata was
sitting tensely beside the bed, she talked with great reluctance.
Much annoyed, he tried several times to make her reconsider:
she was not to say such things, she was to stay in his house, there
was nothing to worry about. She ignored him and talked only to
Yukiko, and finally he lost his temper. Why did she dislike it here,
he asked, his voice rising. Suspecting that Taeko's nightmare had
brought emotional complications, Yukiko tried to calm him without touching on what had evidently upset him. She was most
grateful for his kindness, she said, but they could not leave Taeko
on his hands forever. And then Sachiko had said—and Yukiko
told of the arrangements with Dr. Kambara. In the end he was
somewhat calmer.

21

THERE WAS ANOTHER small incident when at eight the following morning Taeko was taken away in an ambulance. Okubata insisted that he would go with her. It was his duty to see her to the hospital. Sachiko and Yukiko took turns arguing, almost pleading, with him. They quite understood, but they wanted him to leave everything to them. Though they would not keep him from seeing Koi-san afterwards, the relationship between the two was not publicly recognized, and Koi-san herself worried about appearances, and the sisters hoped he would leave her with them for a time, and try to stay in the background. They would let him know of any changes, and they would always welcome telephone calls from him. After a great struggle, they made him promise to telephone only in the morning, to ask only for Sachiko or O-haru, and not to telephone the hospital directly. Sachiko explained everything to Dr. Saitō and thanked him for his trouble. He was most agreeable, and offered to see Taeko to the hospital, where Dr. Kushida would be waiting.

Yukiko rode in the ambulance with Dr. Saitō, while Sachiko stayed behind to clean house. An hour or so later, after paying the nurse and tipping the old woman, Sachiko followed by cab. That indescribable tension when someone near her was sent to the hospital, that terrible foreboding—Sachiko had experienced it before and feared it again now, and she could not fight off a growing heaviness of spirit even as she looked out at scenery that would ordinarily have left her buoyant and gay: the spring sunlight was more radiant than the day before, the Rokkō mountain chain carried a still heavier spring mist, and here and there magnolias and forsythias were in bloom. Taeko had changed dreadfully in one short day. Yesterday Sachiko had been able to tell herself that Dr. Saitō was trying to frighten them. Today she began to wonder whether it was not just possible—those fixed, staring eyes, quite unlike the eyes of yesterday. Taeko did not have a really expressive face at best, but that morning she looked numb and apathetic. Those strangely wide eyes seemed fixed on a point in the air, like the eyes of one who watched death. Sachiko could not look at them without feeling a new wave of terror. Yesterday Taeko had wept, and argued with some warmth, but during that discussion this morning—should Okubata go along, should he stay behind—she had only stared blankly ahead, as though the matter did not concern her.

Dr. Kambara had said over the telephone that he would have a special room for her, and her room was in fact an expensive one in the pure Japanese style, the main room of an outbuilding joined to the main hospital by a covered corridor. Built originally as Dr. Kambara's residence, it had become a sort of rest house when, the year before, he bought a mansion a half mile or so away, and now, since it could easily be turned into an isolation ward, Taeko was offered a luxury suite: an eight-mat room and an adjoining four-mat room surrounded by wide verandas, with access to kitchen and bath. Sachiko had called the agency to ask if they might have the "Mito" who had seen Etsuko through scarlet fever, and Mito was available. She came on duty that same morning. The popular Dr. Kushida was a different matter: although Sachiko had been most careful to specify the time, he did not come and he did not come, and again they had to chase him from patient to patient, and call two or three times to hurry him. Though Dr. Saitō did look at his watch occasionally, he waited politely and left after turning Taeko over to Dr. Kushida. The conversation between the two doctors, full of ponderous German words, was not entirely clear to the others. Dr. Kushida's diagnosis seemed to differ considerably from Dr. Saitō's. The liver was not swollen, he said, and he could not believe that Taeko had anthrax. The violent temperature fluctuations and the chills went perfectly well with amoebic dysentery, and were not so extremely unusual. She was making good progress, he added, but there was no denying that she was weak. He would give her injections of Ringer's solution and camphor, and afterwards "Mito" would give her prontosil. He would call again the next day. There was nothing to worry about. Sachiko, not wholly convinced, saw him to the gate and asked in a tearful voice if everything was *really* going as well as he suggested. Of course, of course, he said, overflowing with confidence. But might they not call in a specialist from Osaka University? No, Saitō was exaggerating. If it seemed necessary Dr. Kushida would call a specialist. Everything could be left to him. But, persisted Sachiko, Koi-san had changed even to the layman's eye. Only yesterday she had seemed so different. Did she not have the look of one who faced death? Dr. Kushida refused to consider the possibility. Exactly that expression came at some time to anyone who was seriously debilitated.

Sachiko paid her respects to Dr. Kambara and returned to Ashiya. Sitting in her hushed Western-style parlor, with Teinosuke, and Etsuko, and Yukiko, and O-haru all out of the house, she found her uneasiness coming back. Dr. Kushida had taken care of them for many years, and not yet made a mistake. She ought to believe him—and there were any number of reasons why she wanted to give more weight to his opinion than to Dr. Saitō's. But just this time—in Taeko's eyes there had been something that tormented Sachiko, and filled her with forebodings only a person who shared the same blood could understand. She had come home to write a difficult letter, thinking that it would be best to take her fears seriously and tell Tsuruko everything. But she would need two or three hours, and only after lunch was she able to drag herself upstairs: to explain, with suitable embellishments, what had happened since they turned Taeko out, and why, when they heard she was ill, they had felt that they had to take care of her. The most talented calligrapher among the four sisters, and the master of a polished style as well, Sachiko was never reluctant to write letters. Her brush would sweep over the paper, leaving behind bold, powerful strokes. Unlike Tsuruko, she never bothered with a first draft. But this time she made two or three false starts before she finally finished her letter:

April 4

DEAR TSURUKO,

It has been a very long time since I last wrote. And now it is spring again, the pleasantest time of the year of this part of the country. Every day there is a mist over Rokkō, and I find it hard to stay in the house. For the most part we have been well, as we hope you have been.

I must tell you unpleasant news. Koi-san has amoebic dysentery, and her condition is serious.

I have told you, I believe, that after your letter we turned

her out with orders not to come back. Perhaps I told you too that
she did not, as we had feared, go to live with Kei-boy, but took a
room of her own. Though we worried a great deal, we neither
asked about her nor had word from her. It would seem that O-haru
visited her in secret, and learned that she still had her own room
and that she was seeing Kei-boy, though she never spent the night
in his house. With that news we felt a little easier. Then, toward
the end of last month, Kei-boy called O-haru to tell her that
Koi-san was ill. She was ill at Kei-boy's, and it was not possible to
move her. At first we paid little attention, but gradually the symptoms of dysentery became clearer. Even then we could not decide
what to do—we had turned her out, after all, and we did not
know whether we should take her from Kei-boy's house or not.
O-haru was most upset, and reported among other things that it
was dysentery of the worst kind, that Kei-boy had called in a rather
unreliable doctor from the neighborhood, that the treatment was
far from satisfactory, that Koi-san had a high fever and was in
great pain from diarrhea, and that she was so thin one would almost take her for a different person. For a while I did nothing.
Without my permission, Yukiko went off to help take care of her,
and finally I went myself. I was thoroughly shocked when I saw
her. The doctor said that she seemed to have a disease called anthrax along with dysentery, and suggested that we call in a specialist. If it was anthrax, he said, she might even die. Koi-san, when
she saw me, began wailing and begging to be moved. I could not
help thinking she meant that she did not want to die in Kei-boy's
house. Yukiko too has a theory: with the first anniversary of the
other man's death coming, she suspects, Koi-san has the idea that
he—the photographer, Itakura—is somehow putting a curse on
her; she seems to have had nightmares about him. Possibly Yukiko is right, and possibly too Koi-san has thought how difficult it
would be for the rest of us if she were to die at Kei-boy's. In any
case, it takes more than a slight indisposition to leave someone
like Koi-san so helpless. Since yesterday she has lain staring into
space, not a muscle on her face moving—she has the look of
death, you might say. That expression terrified me when I saw her
this morning. I felt that I had to follow her wishes. Taking full
responsibility on myself, then, and asking Kei-boy to keep his distance, I had her moved to Dr. Kambara's hospital in an ambulance

today. All of the isolation wards were full, and Dr. Kambara
agreed to take her in, though secretly. Dr. Kushida, whom I be-
lieve you know, has charge of the case.

This, in general, is the situation. Whatever Tatsuo thinks,
I know you will admit that we could have done nothing else.
Teinosuke seems to agree with me, and to be greatly worried, al-
though he has not yet been to see her. I will telegraph you if the
end seems in sight (I trust I will not have to do so), and I want
you to know that the worst predictions are not entirely out of the
question. The expression on her face, and her general appearance,
are like signs that something terrible is coming. I hope I am
wrong. I am sure this is a confused letter, but I have felt I must
give you the whole story, right down to this moment. I am about
to leave again for the hospital. I have not been able to fix my mind
on anything, and Yukiko has accomplished far more than I. At
times like this she is a real tower of strength. She has been up
night after night, hardly closing her eyes.

I will write more later.

As always,
SACHIKO

Though she felt certain qualms at frightening her genial sister,
Sachiko exaggerated the illness a little to win sympathy for Taeko.
There could be no doubt, however, that for the most part she was
writing what she felt. When she had finished the letter, she started
for the hospital. She wanted to be out of the house before Etsuko came home.

22

ONE COULD SEE the improvement within a few days after Taeko
was moved. Strangely, that look of death lasted but one day. The
day after she entered the hospital, the frightening shadow had
disappeared. As though roused from a bad dream, Sachiko remembered Dr. Kushida's confidence, and could only be impressed

anew at his prowess as a diagnostician. Thinking too how she must
have frightened Tsuruko, she immediately sent off a second letter.
Tsuruko was delighted. This time there was none of the usual
slowness—a special delivery letter came two days later.

April 6

DEAR SACHIKO,

Your most unexpected letter was such a blow that I did
not know how to answer. Now your second letter has come, and
I cannot describe my relief. I could not be happier, for Koi-san,
of course, and for the rest of us too.

I may tell you now that I really did not think Koi-san
would live. I should not say so, perhaps, but I could not help
thinking that she was gone, that this was the punishment for the
trouble she has caused all these years. If she had died, who would
have arranged the funeral? And where would it have been? Tatsuo
would refuse, I am sure, to take charge, and it would have been
still more unreasonable to ask you, and we could hardly have had
the funeral at Dr. Kambara's. I was extremely worried, and I
thought how Koi-san would be a problem to the very end.

But now we are rescued from the dilemma, largely through
your labors and Yukiko's. Do you suppose Koi-san is grateful? If
she is, she might take this as the occasion for a clean break with
Kei-boy, and the opportunity to begin a new life. Has she any
mind to?

Dr. Kushida and Dr. Kambara have been a great help. It
is very sad not to be able to thank them openly.

As ever,
TSURUKO

Sachiko made a special trip to show Yukiko the letter.
"I have had this." She quietly took the letter from her handbag as Yukiko was seeing her to the door. "Read it here."
"How like her," said Yukiko.
Sachiko did not know exactly what that meant, but the truth
was that the letter had made an unfavorable impression on
Sachiko herself. Tsuruko had unwittingly revealed how very little
affection she had for Taeko. Her chief concern was to protect the
family, and while she did have a point, Sachiko had to feel sorry

for Taeko. Perhaps Taeko was being punished. Yet it seemed that she had already had punishment enough: as became a child of storm and violence, she had nearly died in a flood; she had lost the lover for whom she was prepared to throw away her good name, and she had suffered time and time again in a manner hardly imaginable to her more decorous sisters. Sachiko doubted whether Yukiko or herself could have endured as much. And she could see only too vividly Tsuruko's initial confusion, and the immense relief described in the letter. She found herself smiling at the picture.

Okubata telephoned the Ashiya house the day after Taeko was moved. Sachiko reported Dr. Kushida's diagnosis in detail, and added that they had reason to feel more hopeful. For the next two or three days there was silence. On the evening of the fourth day, after Sachiko had left for home, Yukiko and Mito were at the bedside and O-haru was heating gruel over a hot plate in the next room. Someone, probably from the family, had come to see them, said the old man who took care of the house. The caller would not give his name, but maybe it was Mr. Makioka. "Teinosuke?— that hardly seems likely," said Yukiko, looking at O-haru. Just then there were footsteps outside, and a figure appeared in the shrubbery: a showy double-breasted blue suit, dark glasses with gold rims (though there was nothing wrong with his eyes, Okubata had taken to wearing dandified dark glasses), and that cane, swinging as always. The outbuilding had its own entrance, but people who called for the first time usually came through the main hospital. Somehow Okubata had learned of the separate entrance and come directly to it, and while the old man was bringing his message had, uninvited, gone around to the garden. (They heard later that he had abruptly asked where Miss Makioka Taeko's room was, and had dismissed the old man's questions rather airily: "Just tell them I am here." How did he know that Taeko was in this separate building, and how had he found the way through the grounds to the second entrance? At first they suspected O-haru, but it later seemed less likely that he had had a secret informant; he had probably done his own detective work. Since the Itakura incident he had been strangely interested in spying on Taeko, and no doubt he had hovered about the place until he had the information he wanted.) The garden ran in an L-shape around the

east and south verandas. Brushing against the spiraea, then in full
bloom, he came up to the front veranda and pushed the glass
door open—it was already open a crack—through which he could
see Taeko's face. He took off his glasses, smiled, and announced,
not quite apologetically, that he happened to be in the neighborhood and thought he should stop by. Yukiko was reading a newspaper over a cup of tea. Noting Mito's fright at this strange in-
truder, she went out to speak to him as though there were nothing
to be surprised at. He was standing on the steps in some discomfort, and his manner suggested that he would like to come in.
She hastily pushed a cushion out to him. Ignoring his attempts at
conversation, she withdrew to the next room, and, putting on a
kettle in place of the gruel O-haru was heating, made him a cup
of tea. She thought of having O-haru serve it, but reconsidered
when it occurred to her that O-haru's good nature might cause
trouble. "You may go, if you like, O-haru," she said. "I can manage by myself, I think." She went back into the smaller room after
she had served the tea.

It was the sort of warm, overcast day one expects when the cherries are in bloom. The doors on the inside of the veranda were
open. Lying with her face toward the garden, Taeko had seen
Okubata. She watched him impassively. A little embarrassed at
being deserted by Yukiko, he lit a cigarette. As the ash grew longer,
he started to drop it at his foot, then hesitated, and, peering into
the room, asked no one in particular if there was an ash tray.
Mito brought him a saucer.

"I hear you are better." He brought a foot up to the veranda
and rested the heel on the frame of the open door. The stylish
shoe was in full view. "You were really in danger, I can tell you
now."

"I know, I know." Her voice was stronger than it had been.
"Just a step this side of hell."

"When will you be up? You are missing the cherry blossoms."

"I can do without them. I am more worried about Kikugorō."

"If you are healthy enough to worry about Kikugorō, we can
stop worrying about you." He turned to Mito. "Will she be up
by the end of the month?"

"I wonder." Mito too seemed disinclined to talk.

"I had dinner with Kikugorō last night."

"Oh? Someone had a party?"

"Shibamoto."

"Oh, Shibamoto. He has always been a Kikugorō man."

"He said a long time ago that he was going to have Kikugorō for dinner and wanted me to come too. Kikugorō is not easy to get, you know."

A restless, inattentive person unable to concentrate on any one thing, Okubata went to the movies but found the legitimate theater rather hard work. For all that, he loved to be with actors, and in the days when he had had money to spend he had frequently taken this actor or that actor to a teahouse. Very friendly with Mizutani Yaeko, Natsukawa Shizue, and Hanayagi Shōtarō, for instance, he would visit the dressing room when one of them came to Osaka, even if he had not bothered to see the play. He had been wanting to meet Kikugorō less because he admired that actor than because it was fun to know popular actors.

He proudly told of the dinner party, embellishing his narrative with imitations of Kikugorō. It seemed clear that he had come especially to boast of this new adventure. In the next room, O-haru was entranced. Yukiko would suggest that she hurry back to Ashiya, and O-haru would nod and go on listening. When Yukiko pointed out that it was five o'clock, O-haru saw that what must be must be, and stood up to leave. She generally came in the afternoon, did the cooking and washing, and returned to Ashiya in time for dinner. How long would young Mr. Okubata go on talking? she asked herself as she walked toward the National Highway. He was not supposed to come to the hospital. Mrs. Makioka would be very, very surprised. And what would Miss Yukiko do if he stayed on? Miss Yukiko would have trouble scolding him for the broken promise. While O-haru was waiting for a streetcar, a cab driver she knew happened to go by in the direction of Osaka. The cab was empty—if he was on his way back, would he mind taking her? He made a detour to deliver her at the corner below the Makioka house, and she came panting up to the kitchen door. Where was Mrs. Makioka? Had Mr. Makioka come home yet? She sped through the kitchen, where O-aki was making an omelette. "A terrible thing," she said dramatically. "Young Mr. Okubata has been to the hospital." She found Sachiko alone, resting in the parlor.

"Mrs. Makioka," she said in a hushed voice. "The young master has been to the hospital."

"What!" Sachiko jumped up in alarm. O-haru's tone, far more solemn than the occasion demanded, had caught her off guard. "When did he come?"

"It was just after you left for home."

"Is he still there?"

"He was still there when I left."

"What can he be thinking of!"

"He said he happened to be in the neighborhood. And he came in through the garden without waiting for the old man to show him the way. Miss Yukiko ran off and left him, and he stayed and talked to Koi-san."

"And was Koi-san put out?"

"She seemed to be enjoying herself."

Sachiko went out to telephone from the study. (Yukiko at first sent Mito to take the message, and went reluctantly to the telephone herself when Sachiko said that she must speak to Yukiko, much though it pained her to be so insistent.) Kei-boy was still there. When it began to grow chilly, he had moved in from the veranda without being invited and closed the door behind him, and now he was sitting by the bed. Koi-san did not seem in the least annoyed. Yukiko had finally moved back into the main room, where she sat listening to the conversation—she could not wait in the next room forever. Hoping to suggest that he ought to be going, she poured him another cup of tea, and made it a point not to turn on the lights even after the sun had gone down. Paying no attention whatsoever, he chattered on. The man was shameless, said Sachiko. Unless they protested he would come again and again. Should Sachiko herself go see what was to be done? No, said Yukiko. It was time for dinner, and besides, knowing that Sachiko had called, he would be leaving soon. There was no need for Sachiko to make a special trip. Teinosuke would be coming home, moreover, and Etsuko would be after her, wondering why she was going out at that time of the night. Very well, then, said Sachiko; she would leave everything to Yukiko, and she hoped Yukiko would get rid of the man. Sure that Yukiko would say nothing, she could only wonder what had happened afterwards. The evening went by, and she did not find another chance to telephone. As she started upstairs after Teinosuke, O-haru came up behind her.

"He seems to have left about an hour after you called."

"You called, did you?"

"I went out a little while ago to a public telephone."

23

AT THE HOSPITAL the next day, Sachiko learned that even after her call, Okubata had showed no sign of leaving, and Yukiko had again withdrawn into the next room. Since it was by that time really dark, she finally had to turn on the lights. Meanwhile Taeko's dinner hour passed, and Yukiko had Mito take her a bowl of gruel. Okubata seemed quite at home. Did she have an appetite? And when would she be able to eat heavier things? He was a little hungry himself—would they mind ordering him something to eat? What would be good? he wondered. Some time after Mito too had fled, he apparently became really hungry, and, calling his apologies for having bothered them, went out the way he had come. Yukiko opened the door a crack and pointedly refrained from seeing him to the gate. She would guess that he had been inside with Koi-san two hours, from four to six, and in all that time could Koi-san not have said one word to suggest that he was not welcome? Coming in on them from the garden with that supercilious way of his (Yukiko had said before that Okubata became a different person when Sachiko was not present; and he was particularly disagreeable that day)—Mito must have thought it very strange. Surely, knowing how he was embarrassing them all, Koi-san could have said something. Would it not have been natural for her to say something? Such were Yukiko's views. She did not confront Taeko, however, but complained rather to Sachiko.

Fearing that Okubata would come again before long, Sachiko thought it might be better to visit him and ask him to stay away, and she still had a duty call to make. Okubata had evidently paid

Dr. Saitō's bill, and miscellaneous expenses—medicine, and food
for the nurse, and so on—must have mounted up in the ten days
he had Taeko in his house. There were many small items besides:
taxi fares for the doctor, tips for the driver, supplies of ice. All in
all he must have paid rather heavily, and Sachiko had not even
been around to thank him. He probably would not take money.
She would of course make him take money for the doctor's bill,
but the rest would have to be paid in gifts. How much would it
all come to? She asked Taeko one day, and Taeko answered that
she would pay back everything herself, that Sachiko was not to
worry. It was only right that she should take care of all the expenses both at Okubata's and now in the hospital, she continued.
Because she could not conveniently draw money from the bank
while she was in bed, she was letting Okubata and Sachiko pay
in her place. She would clear all her debts when she recovered,
and Sachiko was not to worry.

But Yukiko pointed out that Taeko had been living by herself
for six months and would have used up the better part of her
savings. She could hardly carry out her grand promises. Although
they need not have worried about arrangements that concerned
only Taeko and Okubata, the older sisters were now involved.
Everything, money and goods, must be paid back, and as soon as
possible. Sachiko might think Kei-boy had money, added Yukiko,
but she herself, in the days she spent in his house, had seen many
signs that he was very hard pressed indeed. The food, for instance,
was astonishingly plain: in the evening only soup and one vegetable besides rice, for Kei-boy and Yukiko and the nurse as well.
Occasionally O-haru would bring back something a little more
elaborate from the Nishinomiya market, and Kei-boy would have
his share of that. When Yukiko made it a point to tip Dr. Saitō's
driver herself, Kei-boy pretended that he had not noticed. A man
could feign a certain insensitiveness to small details. It was the old
housekeeper, thought Yukiko, of whom they had to be careful.
She was a gentle, docile old person, devoted to Okubata and extremely considerate of Koi-san as well, and she wasted not a cent
in the kitchen. It was Yukiko's feeling, however, that agreeable
though the old woman was, she was secretly hostile to the Makioka
family, and especially to Koi-san. Not that she gave even a hint
of displeasure. Yukiko simply had her intuitions. If Sachiko wanted

further details, she could have them from O-haru. O-haru and the
old woman were always talking together. In any case, the old
woman *was* a problem, and they should not remain in Okubata's
debt.

Vaguely worried, Sachiko called O-haru into the parlor and
asked what the old woman seemed to think of them. Had O-haru
heard anything? If so, she should hold nothing back. Her face
most solemn, O-haru looked uncertainly up at Sachiko. Would it
really be all right to tell everything? Assured that it would be, she
timidly began her story.

The fact was that she had been wondering whether she ought
to tell Mrs. Makioka. The month before, when she had been in
and out of Okubata's house, she and the old woman had become
very friendly. With the patient to take care of, they had been too
busy for a really good talk. But after Taeko was moved, O-haru
went to pick up the last of the baggage; Okubata was out, and
the old woman, all alone, asked her to stay for a cup of tea. The
woman was warm in her praise of Sachiko and Yukiko, said O-haru.
How lucky Koi-san was to have such fine sisters! The conversation moved on to "the young master." No doubt he had his faults.
Still, turned out by his brothers after the death of the old mistress,
he was much to be pitied. He had only Koi-san in the whole
world, said the old woman, choking with tears. If Koi-san would
become his wife—O-haru should do what she could to see that a
marriage was arranged. Hesitantly, the old woman went on to
say that the young master had made many sacrifices for Koi-san
these last ten years. She even hinted, though with great circumspection, that Taeko was at the bottom of the incident that had
led to Okubata's being disinherited. What astonished O-haru most
was the allegation that for some years Koi-san had been receiving
financial help from Okubata. Almost every day since she left the
Ashiya house, she had been coming to Okubata's in the morning
before breakfast, staying for three meals, and going back late at
night to sleep in her own room. She said she was supporting herself and cooking for herself. As a matter of fact she was a free
boarder, and she even brought laundry for the old woman to do,
or cleaning for the old woman to send out with Okubata's. And
their pleasures outside the house—the old woman did not know
which of the two paid the bills, but she thought she had evidence

in the fact that, though Okubata generally kept one hundred or two hundred yen in his wallet, she would find it empty after he had been out with Koi-san. What Koi-san actually paid from her savings, then, was probably her room rent and little more. Noting that O-haru did not seem convinced, the old woman went into her room and brought out a sheaf of bills and receipts of the last year or so. "While we are talking about it," she said, and she proceeded to point out how the bills had gone up since Taeko became a "boarder." The gas bill, the electric bill, cab fares, the green grocer's bill, and the fish monger's bill had all jumped astonishingly since November, and did indeed suggest how carelessly Taeko was spending Okubata's money. Bills from department stores and clothes shops too were largely accounted for by Taeko's purchases. O-haru was astonished to find a bill for the camel's hair coat Taeko had had made at an expensive Kobe shop the December before, and the voile afternoon dress made for her at the same shop in March. Of a fine material, very light for its warmth, the coat was reversible, brown on one side and bright red on the other. When she had come to show it off in Ashiya, Taeko had said that it had cost three hundred fifty yen, and that, to pay for it, she had sold two or three kimonos that now seemed too bold. O-haru remembered wondering at the time whether Koi-san could really afford such luxuries on her own resources, and she thought she understood for the first time what had really happened.

The old woman insisted that she did not mean to condemn Koi-san, that she only wanted to show how desperate the young master had been to win Koi-san's favor. She was beginning to touch on matters that embarrassed her, continued the woman, but even the pampered Okubata was after all the third son of the family, and he did not have a great deal of money to spend on himself. He had managed well enough while the old mistress lived. Now his funds had been cut off. The master in Osaka (Okubata's oldest brother) had given him a modest solatium upon his being disinherited, and he had been eating into his capital ever since. The end was near; the young master, in his blind determination to please Koi-san, showed no concern for the future. He expected someone to come to his rescue. Unless he had a change of heart and set about making an honest living for himself, however, it did not seem likely that he would regain the sympathy of his family.

The old woman kept urging him to find work, even if it brought
him no more than a hundred yen a month. But his head was too
full of Koi-san. Only if he could marry Koi-san was there a possibility of his reforming. The old mistress and the master in Osaka
had been opposed to the marriage at the time of that newspaper
incident, and the woman had quite agreed with them, but now,
as she thought of the years since, she could not help feeling that
they had been wrong. If the marriage had been permitted, the
young master might not have gone astray. He might have had a
happy family by now, he would be working with the best of them.
Though for some reason the master in Osaka had never taken
kindly to Koi-san, and even now would not be pleased at the marriage, there was no point in worrying about him. The opposition
would not last forever. Marriage would open a new road for the
young master. There was still one great difficulty, however, and it
concerned the master in Osaka less than Koi-san herself: in the
old woman's view, Koi-san did not really mean to marry the young
master.

She might seem to be criticizing Koi-san, the old woman said
over and over again, but she did not mean to be. Finally she asked
what the Makiokas thought of the young master. He was pampered and he knew little of the world, and if they chose to look
for faults there was no doubt that they could find many, but the
old woman would swear to one thing: that his affection for Koi-
san was as steady as it had ever been. He had, it was true, first
known the joys of the teahouses when he was but sixteen or
seventeen, and his conduct had not always been exemplary. In
the days when he was separated from Koi-san his dissipation had
been extreme. The old woman hoped they would understand nonetheless that he had only been despondent over his inability to
marry the woman he had chosen. Perhaps Koi-san, whose intelligence was on a level far above his, who had sound judgment, and
who was almost too talented for a woman, had become impatient
with his general uselessness. That of course was understandable,
but after all a relationship that had lasted more than ten years
was not to be broken off so easily. Koi-san must see that the young
master, so unswerving in his affection, would really be too forlorn.
And if she did not mean to marry him, he might have resigned
himself to that fact had she broken cleanly at the time of the

Yonekichi affair (the old woman called Itakura "Yonekichi"). Instead she had managed to make it seem that she meant to marry
Yonekichi and that she did not mean to, and that she was still
fond of Okubata and that she was not. It was the same now that
Yonekichi was dead—what exactly did she mean, leaving the impression that she did not want to turn the young master away,
and at the same time that she did not want to marry him? Could
one help thinking that she was after his money? Not entirely
satisfied with this summation of the case, O-haru pointed out that
whatever the old woman had been told, the Makiokas had heard
that Koi-san wanted to marry Itakura, and that Kei-boy stood in
the way. Koi-san, she said, had told them among other things that
she meant to wait only until Miss Yukiko was married. Leaving
aside the problem of Miss Yukiko, answered the old woman, it
astonished her to hear that the young master had stood in the way.
Even while Koi-san was keeping her affair with Yonekichi secret
from the young master, she was meeting the latter without telling
Yonekichi. She was always—the old woman knew for a fact—
telephoning the young master. Koi-san had used the two of them
with consummate skill. In her heart, perhaps, she liked Yonekichi
better. Still she seemed to have reasons for holding on to the
young master as long as possible. The woman was in effect charg-
ing that Taeko had used Okubata for what she could wring out of
him. But as the old woman knew, protested O-haru, Koi-san
had her dolls, and she made enough to take care of herself and
even to put money in the bank. Where then was the need to use
the young master? So Koi-san said, retorted the old woman, and
O-haru believed her, as did Miss Yukiko and Mrs. Makioka, but did
it seem possible that a woman alone, with the income from work
that was child's play, could feed, clothe, and house herself in such
luxury, and have money left over to put in the bank? The Makioka
family naturally overestimated her ability to support herself, what
with the fine studio she was said to have, and the foreigners, even,
she had among her pupils, and her lavish advertising through pictures Yonekichi took for her, but it did not seem probable that
she really made much money. Though the old woman had not
seen Koi-san's bank book, she could guess that the balance was
not impressive. Or if it was, that could only be because she was
squeezing the young master to build up her own savings. The old

woman would not be at all surprised if it should prove that Yonekichi had been behind the scenes, urging her on. If Koi-san was
receiving help from the young master, then the burden on Yonekichi would be lighter. Perhaps he knew all along that she was
seeing the young master, and chose to look the other way.

More humiliated at each revelation, O-haru sought to defend
Taeko, but the old woman had unshakable evidence. How about
this, and how about this, she would say, lining up her exhibits.
O-haru did not have the courage to tell Sachiko the worst. It was
too awful, she would rather not talk about it. Even so she offered
an item or two. The old woman knew exactly how many jewels
Taeko had, and what sort of jewels they were. (With the China
Incident in progress, people no longer wore jewels, and Taeko
kept hers in a box as precious to her as her life. She had left it
with Sachiko rather than risk keeping it in her room.) Every
single one had come from the Okubata shop, said the old woman.
She herself had any number of times seen the old mistress come
to the young master's rescue when it became known that he had
stolen another ring. Sometimes he would give a ring to Koi-san,
sometimes he would sell a ring to give her money, and now and
then a ring Koi-san had sold in secret would be found back in the
shop. Not all the jewels went to Koi-san. Some he sold for his
own spending money, but one could assume that most of them
were for Koi-san. And it seemed moreover that she knew perfectly
well what he was doing and even urged him on, describing in
exact detail the ring she wanted. (Besides rings, there had been
wrist watches and compacts and broaches and necklaces.) The old
woman, who had been with the Okubata family she did not know
how many years and who had nursed Kei-boy himself when he
was a baby, knew everything. There was no end to the evidence
she could offer. It seemed, nevertheless, that she was not telling
the story out of bitterness. She wanted rather to show how devoted
the young master had been. The Makiokas thought ill of the
young master because they did not know the facts, she said; hence
they opposed the marriage. If they would only consider the real
reason for the young master's troubles, their opposition would very
probably stop. She was not saying that Koi-san was bad or good.
If Koi-san was important to the young master, then she was important to the old woman too. The latter only hoped that they

would all work to win Koi-san over. She had again found someone
she liked, it seemed, and she might again be preparing to brush
the young master aside. Perhaps she had noted that his pocket
book was a little thin.

O-haru was startled. The conversation had taken an unexpected
turn. How did the old woman know that Koi-san had found "another man she liked"? The old woman could not answer for sure,
but Koi-san and the young master quarreled a great deal these
days, and in the quarrels she often heard the young master mention the name "Miyoshi" with some warmth. Miyoshi seemed to
live in Kobe, though it was not clear what part of Kobe, or what
sort of work he did. The young master often spoke of "that bartender." And what, the old woman wanted to know, was a bartender? Evidently the man worked in a Kobe bar. She knew nothing more, and O-haru did not press her.

So much for O-haru's story. In the course of the conversation,
she added, she had learned that Koi-san was a heavy drinker. In
Sachiko's presence, Taeko drank a half pint of saké at most. It was
the old woman's story that with Okubata she could drink easily
a quart, and up to a third of a bottle of whisky. She rarely lost
control of herself, though it was true that sometimes, more frequently of late, Okubata had to carry her home. The old woman
had no idea where they might have been drinking.

24

IT TOOK a great deal of self control on Sachiko's part to hear the
story through. From time to time she would feel herself flushing,
and she would want to cover her ears and say: "That will do,
O-haru." There was probably a great deal more she could have
heard if she wished, but she found a convenient breaking point.

"That will be enough, O-haru. You may go." She leaned against
the table, waiting for the agitation to subside.

Was it true, then? Was what she feared true? One always takes
the part of those near one, and Kei-boy to the old woman was a

454 THE MAKIOKA SISTERS

pure, clean youth. It did not seem likely that he had really been so unswerving in his love for Koi-san. No doubt Koi-san and Teino-suke had reason to call him a profligate. Even so, Sachiko could not ignore the old woman's description of Taeko, the vampire. Just as the woman made too many allowances for Kei-boy, so the Makiokas made too many allowances for Koi-san. Sachiko had felt certain unpleasant suspicions each time there was a new ring on her sister's finger, but the suspicions had disappeared as she saw how pleased Koi-san was at having been able to buy a ring with her own money. And Koi-san had had her studio, and Sachiko had seen her dolls sell for surprisingly high prices, and, after helping with the accounts at the exhibitions, Sachiko had found herself believing what Koi-san said. Even when the latter turned to sewing and her income from dolls was cut off, she told her sisters that she had saved enough to go to Europe or to open a dress shop, and that she had no trouble meeting her expenses. Thinking how sad it would be for Koi-san to use up her savings, Sachiko ordered clothes for Etsuko, and took orders from people she knew in the neighborhood, and in general saw that Koi-san had money to live on. She had gone out of her way to believe Koi-san, who boasted that she was able to support herself quite without help from the family. Had Sachiko made too many allowances because it was her own sister, had she refused to believe the truth? But what had Koi-san said of Okubata? Had she not said that she could not expect to rely on so incompetent a person, that indeed she would have to support him once they were married? Had she not said that she received nothing from him, not a fraction of a cent, and that she even tried to keep him from touching his own money? Had those fine words been to deceive the world, and her sisters too?

But perhaps it was not Taeko they should blame. Perhaps it was the sisters, easily convinced, wholly unworldly, easy, trusting, foolish. Sachiko had to admit the truth in the old woman's arguments, now that it was here before her: one simply did not live in luxury on the income from a girl's hobby. Sachiko had had her suspicions, and her refusal to pursue them, one was forced to conclude, was less foolish than cunning. She had refused to believe that she could have such a sister, and her refusal had caused all the trouble. She felt her cheeks burn at the thought that the world, and still more the Okubata family, must have interpreted her motives differently. She had not been able to restrain her annoyance when she heard how strongly Okubata's mother and brother were opposing the marriage. Now she saw their reasons. Taeko was to them a vampire, and the family behind her was wholly disreputable. How to account for sisters and brothers-in-law who let the girl behave so? Sachiko had to agree that Tatsuo had been right to dismiss Taeko from the family. She remembered too that Teinosuke always tried to have as little as possible to do with Taeko's affairs. He would only say that Koi-san was too complicated, that he could not understand her, and probably he had guessed something of these darker matters. Possibly, in his roundabout way, he had been suggesting as much to Sachiko. If so, he could have spoken more plainly.

She decided not to visit Okubata that day. Complaining of a headache, she took a pyramidon tablet and retired to her bedroom. She avoided Teinosuke and Etsuko for the rest of the day. After seeing Teinosuke off to work the next morning, she went to bed again. She had visited the hospital at least once a day since Taeko was moved, and she thought she might go around for just a few minutes in the afternoon. Somehow the being known as "Taeko" had changed form, however, had become distant and vaguely evil. Sachiko was frightened at the thought of meeting her sister. At about two O-haru came upstairs. Was Mrs. Makioka going to the hospital? Miss Yukiko had just called, and asked if Mrs. Makioka could bring along the copy of *Rebecca*. Still in bed, Sachiko answered that she would not go herself. O-haru should take the book—it was on a shelf in the six-mat room. She called O-haru back: since Koi-san no longer needed much care, she said, O-haru might suggest that Yukiko come home for a rest.

Yukiko had been away for more than ten days. She had gone to Okubata's the end of the month before and from there directly to the hospital. Sachiko's message had its effect, and she was home in time for dinner. Trying to make it seem that nothing was amiss, Sachiko got up late in the afternoon. As a reward for Yukiko's labors, Teinosuke selected a very special bottle of white Burgundy, a rarity by then, from his impoverished wine cellar, wiped away the dust himself, and uncorked it with a pleasant pop.

"And how is Koi-san?" he asked.

"There is nothing to worry about. She is still weak, though, and it will be a while before she is really her old self again."

"Is she thin?"

"Very thin. She has a long, thin face—remember how round it was?—and the cheek bones stand out like this."

"I ought to go see her. May I go see her, Father?"

Teinosuke grunted and frowned. A moment later the frown was gone. "You can go, I suppose. But remember that dysentery is an infectious disease. You are not to go till the doctor says you can."

Because he was in especially good spirits, Teinosuke let them talk of Taeko before Etsuko, and even made it seem that the girl was not forbidden to see her aunt. But even allowing for the good spirits, Sachiko was startled. She suspected that Teinosuke's attitude toward Taeko was changing.

"I understand Dr. Kushida is taking care of her." He turned to Yukiko again.

"He was, but we never see him any more. He says there is nothing to worry about. When the patient begins to look a little better, you see no more of Dr. Kushida."

"Then there should be no need for you to go again yourself."

"None at all," Sachiko agreed. "Mito is there, and O-haru can go every day to help."

"When are we going to see Kikugorō, Father?"

"Any time. We were only waiting for Yukiko to come home."

"Next Saturday?"

"But first come the cherry blossoms. Kikugorō will be here all month."

"We see the cherries on Saturday, then. You promise, Father?"

"Yes, yes. If we wait any longer, the cherries will be gone."

"And Mother too, and Yukiko? Promise?"

"We promise."

It made Sachiko a little sad to think that this year Taeko would be missing. If there had seemed any possibility that Teinosuke would agree, she would have liked to suggest waiting until the end of the month, when Taeko would be out of bed, for a trip to see the late cherries at Omuro.

"What are you thinking about, Mother? You must want to see the cherries."

Teinosuke knew what she was thinking about. "Would Koi-san be able to go even if we waited? If she is up by then, we might take her to see the late cherries."

"But she will hardly be able to walk around the room by the end of the month," said Yukiko.

Yukiko had noticed that Sachiko was not sharing in the general good spirits.

"Did you go to Kei-boy's?" she asked when they were alone the next morning.

"No. As a matter of fact, I want to talk to you about that." Motioning Yukiko upstairs, she told the whole of O-haru's story. "And what do you think, Yukiko? Is the old woman telling the truth?"

"What do you think?"

"I think she is."

"So do I."

"It is all my fault. I trusted Koi-san so."

"But that was only natural." Yukiko's eyes clouded over, and Sachiko was already in tears. "It is not your fault at all."

"And what can I possibly say to Tatsuo and Tsuruko?"

"Have you talked to Teinosuke?"

"How can I talk to him? It is all too humiliating."

"I imagine he is beginning to think he should have been easier with her."

"It seemed so last night, certainly."

"And I imagine he knows well enough what she has been up to. He probably knows, and thinks it will only be worse if we have nothing more to do with her."

"If Koi-san would only reform, now that he has begun to change his mind."

"She has been the same Koi-san ever since I can remember."

"And is not going to change now, whatever we say?"

"Not Koi-san. Think of the number of times we have tried to change her."

"The old woman is right. It would be better for both of them if they were to marry."

"I doubt if there is any other answer."

"Do you think she really dislikes him so, then?"

Though both sisters were thinking about the bartender "Miyoshi," mention of the name would only have added to the discomfort.

"I have no idea. She refused to stay in his house, and then she talked on and on when he came to the hospital. Not even a hint that he ought to leave."

"Maybe she pretends to dislike him when she is really very fond of him."

"I almost hope so. But probably she feels in debt to him. She could never tell him to leave even if she wanted to.

Yukiko went back to the hospital to fetch *Rebecca*, and for two or three days afterwards she rested, read, and went to movies in Kobe. That week-end the four of them, Teinosuke, his wife, Etsuko, and Yukiko, made their annual pilgrimage to Kyoto for the cherry blossoms. Because of the national crisis, there were few drunken cherry viewers, and the cherries were left to those who really wanted to see them. The Makiokas had never before quite known the beauty of those weeping cherry trees in the Heian Shrine. It was a most elegant cherry viewing, quiet and wholly without ostentation.

Two or three days later Sachiko sent O-haru to pay Okubata for the cost of Taeko's illness.

25

OKUBATA called at the hospital again, and O-haru, alone with Mito, telephoned Ashiya for instructions. "Be less cold than last time," answered Sachiko. "Smile pleasantly and invite him in." Back home that evening, O-haru reported that he had stayed some three hours. Three days later he came again, and when, at six, he showed no sign of leaving, O-haru ordered food and a flagon of saké from a restaurant on the National Highway. He was thoroughly delighted, and talked on until after nine o'clock. But Taeko was annoyed. Such kindness was quite uncalled for, she said. If you were the least bit kind to the man, he took advantage of you. O-haru found it hard to understand why she was being scolded—after all, Koi-san and Okubata had been chatting most agreeably until but a moment before.

As Taeko had predicted, Okubata was encouraged by the un-expectedly kind treatment. He came again two or three days later, had dinner ordered from the same restaurant, and at about ten o'clock said he thought he would stay the night. After a hurried call to Ashiya, O-haru spread the bedding Yukiko had used—it would be a tight fit, she said, there beside the patient and the nurse in the larger of the two rooms—and, ordered to stay the night herself, found some cushions to sleep on in the next room. Remembering how she had been scolded before, she apologized the next morning for not even having a slice of bread in the house, and offered him tea and fruit. He had his breakfast at some leisure.

A few days later Taeko was released from the hospital and moved back to her room. She still had to rest, and every day O-haru would be with her from morning until late at night to take care of the cooking and cleaning. The last of the cherries, early and late, had fallen, and Kikugorō had left Osaka. It was the end of May before Taeko could really go out. Though he had not publicly "forgiven" her, Teinosuke made it clear that he would not object to her being seen in the Ashiya house. Anxious to put on weight, she came for lunch almost every day through June.

Meanwhile the world was shaken by new developments in Eu-rope. In May came the German invasion of the Low Countries and the tragedy of Dunkirk, and in June, upon the French sur-render, an armistice was signed at Compiègne. And what, through all this, had happened to the Stolz family? Mrs. Stolz had pre-dicted that Hitler would manage to avoid war, and what would she be thinking now? And Peter must be old enough for the Hit-lerjugend. Might Mr. Stolz have been drafted? But perhaps all of them, Mrs. Stolz and Rosemarie too, were so intoxicated with vic-tory that they refused to let family problems bother them. Such speculations were always on Sachiko's mind. And then one could never know when England, cut off from the continent, would be attacked from the air, and the possibility of air raids brought up the problem of Katharina, now living in a suburb of London. How unpredictable human destinies were! No sooner had the Russian refugee, until then living in a tiny doll's house, made

everyone envious by marrying the president of a large company
and moving into a house like a castle, than the English people
found themselves facing an unprecedented calamity. Since the
German attack would be concentrated on the London area, Katharina's castle might be reduced to ashes overnight. Even worse
disasters were in prospect: she might find herself without food or
a rag to wear. Might she not be thinking of the distant skies of
Japan? Might she not be thinking of that shabby little house, and
wondering whether she would have done better to stay there herself?

"Suppose you write to Katharina, Koi-san."

"I must ask her brother for the address next time I see him."

"I ought to write to the Stolzes too. I wonder who would
translate for me."

"Why not ask Mrs. Hening again?"

Sachiko wrote a long letter to Mrs. Stolz, the first in a year and
a half. She wrote of many things: they were overcome with pleasure at the military successes of a friendly nation; each time they
read of the European war, they thought and talked of the Stolz
family; the Makiokas were well, although with the China Incident
dragging on they were gloomy at the thought that they too might
soon find themselves in a real war; they could not but be astonished at how the world had changed since the days when the
Stolzes were next door, and they wondered wistfully if such happy
times would ever come again; that dreadful flood had perhaps left
the Stolzes with bad memories of Japan; such disasters were rare
in any country, however, and they should not be deterred from
returning to Japan once the war was over; the Makiokas wanted to
see Europe at least once, and they might all appear in Hamburg
one day; since they hoped to give Etsuko the best possible musical
training, they meant to have her study in Germany. Sachiko added
that she was sending Rosemarie some silk and a fan by separate
mail. The next day she visited Mrs. Hening and asked to have
the letter translated, and some days later, on an errand in Osaka,
she bought a dance fan at the Minoya and sent it off to Hamburg
with a piece of silk crape.

On a Saturday early in June, Teinosuke and Sachiko went to see
the spring greenery in Nara. Sachiko had been busy since the year
before with one or the other of her sisters, and Teinosuke wanted

to give her a rest. He thought too that for the first time in a very great while they could be alone, just the two of them, husband and wife. They spent Saturday night at the Nara Hotel and the next day went from the Kasuga Shrine to the Hall of the Third Moon and on to the Great Buddha and the temples west of the city. From about noon Sachiko was troubled by a swelling and itching behind her ear. The discomfort grew as her hair brushed against the irritated spot. It was rather like hives, but she suspected that, making her way through the green foliage at the Kasuga Shrine and posing five or six times for Teinosuke's Leica, she had been stung by a sand fly. She really should have worn something over her head—she regretted not having brought a shawl. Back at the hotel that night, she sent a bellboy out for carbolic liniment. There was no such medicine, the boy replied, and she tried Mosquiton instead. It was quite ineffective. She could not sleep for the itching, and the next morning she sent for zinc ointment. Teinosuke went directly to his office from Uehonmachi Station, while Sachiko returned to Ashiya. Toward evening the itching subsided. When he came back from work, Teinosuke called her out to the terrace to have her ear examined in a strong light. It was no sand fly, he snorted. It was a bedbug. What! Where could she have picked up a bedbug? In the Nara Hotel, answered Teinosuke. He had felt a little itchy himself that morning—see? He rolled up a sleeve. There could be no doubt that it was a bedbug, he said. If Sachiko would look at her ear she would find two bites close together. Sachiko held a mirror behind her ear, and saw that her husband was right.

"You are absolutely right. A fine sort of hotel—rude maids and waiters, terrible service, and bedbugs."

She was furious at the Nara Hotel. It had spoiled the whole week-end.

They must go on another trip to make up for it, said Teinosuke. June and July passed. Late in August he had business in Tokyo and suggested an outing somewhere along the main Tokyo-Osaka Line. Sachiko had for some time been wanting to make the round of the Fuji Lakes. They planned, then, that Teinosuke would go ahead and Sachiko would follow two days later to meet him at the Hamaya Inn, and that they would return to Osaka via the lakes. Teinosuke advised a third-class sleeper. Nothing was better

than a third-class sleeper in hot weather, he said. There were no
smothering curtains, the cool breezes passed freely. Third class was
far better than second. Perhaps she was too tired, however, for
there had been an air-raid drill that day and she had found herself
in a bucket brigade. In any case, she would doze off and dream
of the air-raid drill and wake up only to doze off and dream the
same dream again. It seemed to be the Ashiya kitchen, and yet it
was a far more up-to-date American-style kitchen, all white tiles
and paint, and sparkling glass and chinaware. The air-raid siren
would sound, and the glass and chinaware would begin snapping
and cracking and breaking to bits. "Yukiko, Etsuko, O-haru, this
is dangerous," she would say, and flee into the dining room, away
from the shiny particles in the air. Coffee cups and beer steins
and wine glasses and wine and whisky bottles would be snapping
and cracking in the dining room too. This is just as bad—she
would lead them upstairs, where they would find all the light bulbs
exploding. They would then run into a room with only wooden
fixtures—and Sachiko would be awake. She had the same dream
she did not know how many times. Finally it was morning. Someone had opened a window and she had a cinder in her eye. Tears
streamed down her face. She arrived at the Hamaya at nine, to
find that Teinosuke had already gone out. She thought of making
up for the lost sleep, but there was that object in her eye. Each
time she blinked the tears started again. Eyewash did no good.
She finally asked the landlady to call a good eye doctor and had
the cinder removed. The doctor ordered her to wear a bandage
for the rest of the day and to call again the following day. What
in the world had happened, asked Teinosuke, back for lunch.
Thanks to him, she had had a dreadful time. She would never
take a third-class sleeper again. Something always seemed to go
wrong with their second honeymoons, laughed Teinosuke. He
would finish his business so that they could leave early the following day. How long would she have to go bandaged? Only that
day, but there was danger, if she was not careful, of injury to the
eyeball, and she was to see the doctor again the following day.
What ought she to do if they were leaving early? A bit of dust
in one eye, scoffed Teinosuke. The doctor was out after their
money; the eye would be all right by evening.
Sachiko called the Shibuya house while Teinosuke was out.

They had arrived that morning and would stay only the day, she explained to her sister. Shy about her bandaged eye, she asked if she might trouble her sister to come to the inn. There were reasons why she could not leave the house, answered Tsuruko, much though she would like to see Sachiko. Tsuruko then asked for news of Koi-san. Koi-san had recovered, said Sachiko. Feeling that they should not be too harsh about "disinheriting" her, they were letting her come to the house, though not openly. Sachiko really could not discuss the matter over the telephone. She would be in Tokyo again soon. Very bored, she waited until the streets were a little cooler and went out for a walk on the Ginza. *History is Made at Night* was playing. She had seen it once before, and she suddenly wanted to see it again. Because she had only one eye, she found that Charles Boyer did not look like Charles Boyer. Those beautiful eyes were without their usual charm. She decided to take off the bandage. Her eye seemed to have healed—there was not a sign of a tear. He had been quite right, she said to Teinosuke that evening. And the doctor had made so much of it. Doctors were all alike. They wanted to hang on to you, if only one day longer.

They spent the following two nights at Lake Kawaguchi. This "second honeymoon" more than made up for the failure at Nara. After the heat of Tokyo, they had a clean autumn breeze at the foot of Mt. Fuji, and it was enough just to go for a stroll along the lake, or to lie looking from the second-floor window at the mountain. The native of Tokyo cannot imagine the fascination of Mt. Fuji for someone like Sachiko, who barely knew the east-country—an exotic fascination like that of "Fujiyama" for the foreigner. They had chosen this Fuji View Hotel because Sachiko was drawn to the name. And there was Fuji, right before the hotel, almost hanging over them. For the first time Sachiko could look up from the base of the mountain and watch all the changes, morning and evening, as she would. Both the Fuji View and the Nara Hotel were finished in unpainted wood, after the fashion of the classical Japanese mansion, but there the resemblance between the two hotels ended. The Nara Hotel was old and the wood had become dark and gloomy. Here the walls and pillars to the farthest corners of the room were fresh and clean, in part because the hotel was new, but also in part because the mountain air was so incomparably clean. After lunch the second day, Sachiko lay gazing up at the ceiling. On one side she could see the top of Fuji, and on the other the undulations of the range around Lake Kawaguchi. For some reason, she thought of a lake she had never seen, and of the prisoner of Chillon. It was less the mountains and the color of the sky than the touch of the air that made her feel as if she had been set down in a far-off country. And she felt too as if she were at the bottom of a cool lake, as if the mountain air were tingling carbonated water. Little clouds passed over the sun. The light would go and suddenly burst forth again, and at such moments the whiteness of the walls seemed to work its way past her eyes to make her mind itself as clear as the air. Lake Kawaguchi had until recently been noisy with refugees from the heat. Since the twentieth the number of guests had fallen off sharply, and now the large hotel was empty and quiet. There was not a sound, however one strained one's ears. In the silence, watching the light go and come and go and come again, Sachiko lost consciousness of time.

Teinosuke too had been staring at the ceiling and tasting the silence. He walked over to look out at Mt. Fuji.

"This is very interesting," said Sachiko.

"What is?"

Sachiko was looking at the nickel-plated thermos bottle on the table beside her pillow.

"Come look. See what a palace we are in."

The polished surface of the thermos bottle was a convex mirror reflecting the smallest details of the bright room. Everything was thrown out of perspective, however, so that the room had become a hall of state with an infinitely high ceiling. Sachiko, now sitting up in bed, was very far away.

"Look at me, will you." She shook her head and raised an arm, and in the convex mirror a far-away figure shook its head and raised its arm—the elf in the heart of a crystal, or the dragon queen in her palace below the sea, or a princess of the blood in her royal chambers.

How long had it been, he wondered, since his wife had seemed so youthful. They were back ten years and more, and on their honeymoon again. After a night at the Fujiya Hotel in these same mountains, they had driven around Lake Ashi, with Fuji in the background, and no doubt the surroundings called them back to that trip long years before.

"We must come here often," whispered Sachiko in bed that night. Teinosuke agreed. The bed-time talk also touched on soberer matters. With her husband in such a good mood, it would be a great shame to miss the opportunity. Sachiko quietly brought up the question of Taeko. Teinosuke ought to see her himself. He quite understood, said Teinosuke. He had been too harsh, and with someone like Koi-san harshness could only bring embarrassing complications. He would henceforth play no favorites.

<hr />

26

IN SEPTEMBER Teinosuke carried out the promise he had made on that "second honeymoon." He saw Taeko for the first time since she had been turned out of the house. Though he had allowed her to come and go, he had chosen not to see her himself. Now they had a pleasant dinner party, the five of them, husband and wife and sisters and daughter. Sachiko and Yukiko, still troubled by the story they had heard from O-haru, felt a certain constraint with Taeko. They were nonetheless determined to forget the unpleasantness, and, close to their sister for an evening at least, they drank more saké than they usually allowed themselves. The dining room was very lively indeed. Without having discussed the matter, Sachiko and Yukiko had come to much the same conclusion: they would say nothing to Teinosuke and they would not reprimand Taeko herself. Since a good part of the responsibility lay with them, they would be warm and affectionate in their efforts to win back this erring sister. Why not stay the night? suggested Etsuko, and Teinosuke and the others promptly took up the suggestion. It was decided that Taeko would stay the night. Etsuko was delighted—she and Yukiko and Koi-san would all sleep together. Easily aroused, she found such occasions particularly exciting.

Taeko's old charm had returned. When Sachiko had seen that

decaying face, and the muddy skin that seemed to cloak a vene-
real disease, she had wondered whether the freshness would ever
come back, but Taeko was once more a lively, full-cheeked modern beauty. Out of deference to the people in the main house,
said Teinosuke, Taeko should keep up the form of living out, and
she would spend part of her day in the Ashiya house, returning to
her room at night. Her old room upstairs having been given back
to her, she would sit by the sunny window immersed in her sewing, much of it on orders brought in by Sachiko. Sometimes she
rushed through dinner and went upstairs again in the evening.
Hoping to keep down Okubata's expenses, Sachiko went quietly
out in search of orders, and as she watched Taeko at work, affection for her youngest sister welled up again. Koi-san *did* like to
work. This very aggressiveness, it was true, had led her astray.
Still, if they watched her, they might turn her talents to something good and constructive. She was so clever with her hands;
she could master new skills so quickly. When she took up dancing
she was soon a good dancer, when she took up dolls she was soon
making really fine ones, and now see how it was with her sewing!
Not many girls barely thirty years old had mastered so many
skills.

"You are so patient with it, Koi-san." Often, when the machine
was still humming at eight or nine in the evening, Sachiko would
go upstairs to look in on her sister. "But you really should stop.
Etsuko will have trouble getting to sleep, and you will be stiff in
the morning."

"I thought I could finish it tonight."

"Oh, finish it tomorrow. Do you really have to make so much
money?"

Taeko laughed quietly. "As a matter of fact, I do need money."

"Whenever you do, just tell me, Koi-san. Please. I can always
give you spending money."

Because Teinosuke now had an important account with a muni-
tions company, Sachiko's purse was fat and she had considerable
latitude in managing the house, and Teinosuke had pointed out
that they were taking care of Yukiko with virtually no help from
the main house, and they might start looking after Taeko too.
Whenever she had a chance, then, Sachiko mentioned the possibility of an allowance, but Taeko always turned the suggestion

off lightly, as though she had too much pride to accept the offer, as though the last thing she wanted to do was depend on others.

Neither Sachiko nor Yukiko could guess from Taeko's manner what had happened to Okubata. Though Taeko came to Ashiya every day, she always spent part of the day elsewhere. She would come either late in the afternoon and spend the evening, or come in the morning and leave in the afternoon. Perhaps she was seeing Kei-boy, perhaps not. The two sisters worried a great deal, but neither sought to question Taeko. They agreed with the old woman: the only solution was to see Taeko and Okubata married. It would be rash to make the suggestion openly, however, and they only hoped that in the course of time Taeko would have a change of heart. Then one day—it was early in October— she brought home a report that Okubata was leaving for Manchuria.

"For Manchuria?" Sachiko and Yukiko asked in unison.

"It is very funny." Taeko laughed and told her story:

She did not know all the details, but it appeared that an official had come to recruit twenty or thirty Japanese for the Manchurian Imperial Household. "Officials," they were to be, but certainly not high officials. Dignified manservants, rather, to see to the Emperor's personal needs; neither intelligence nor learning was required. The men had only to be of good bourgeois origins, personable and well-mannered—pampered young men of family, in a word, who might even be a little stupid. Kei-boy fitted the order. His brothers were most enthusiastic. Since it would be in the service of the Manchurian Emperor, they need not worry about what people would think, and since the work would in no sense be difficult, it should be just right for Kei-boy. If Kei-boy agreed to go to Manchuria, they might welcome him back into the family. They would all want to wish him well.

"How nice. But it seems odd that he agreed to go."

"Oh, his mind is not made up yet. Everyone is urging him on, but he is holding back."

"That is not surprising, Koi-san. A boy from Semba going all the way to Manchuria—think of it."

"But he needs money. He will have to move, and no one in Osaka will hire him, and he has to do something. This is his chance."

"I suppose so. It is not work just anyone could do."

"Exactly. And that is why the pay is so good. And why I keep urging him on. I tell him he only has to stay a year or two. His brother will be over the grudge by that time, and people will start trusting him again. I tell him to pick himself up and go."

"But it will be so lonely. Is the old woman going along?"

"She says she wants to, but she has her sons and grandchildren to think of."

"Suppose you go, Koi-san," said Yukiko. "You ought to be willing to, if it means giving him a new start."

Taeko snorted and frowned.

"He would probably go if you promised to go with him, even for a little while—say six months, until he settled down. You must, Koi-san, if it means helping him."

"Yes, do, Koi-san," Sachiko joined in. "Even his brothers would thank you."

"This is my chance to break with him." Taeko's voice was low, but the words were clipped and distinct. "Otherwise we would go on and on. It would be far the best thing for him to go alone. And so I keep arguing with him."

"Koi-san," said Sachiko. "We are not trying to make you marry him. We are only suggesting that you stay with him for six months or a year. When you see that everything is going well, you can come back by yourself."

"If I went all the way to Manchuria, it would be harder than ever to leave him."

"Possibly. But surely you could make him see what had to be. And if he refused to understand, you could run off by yourself."

"And is there a doubt in the world that he would throw everything over and run off too?"

"I see what you mean, of course. But after all you do owe him something, and if you are going to leave him you should do your duty first."

"Do I owe him so much?"

Seeing that they were headed for a quarrel, Sachiko said no more. But Yukiko pressed on: "You really can say you are not in debt to him? Everyone knows what you have been to each other all these years."

"And I wanted to leave him long ago, and he kept tagging after me. In debt to him! He has been a nuisance."

"It is not true, then, that you have had a great deal of help from him? This will annoy you—but have you had money from him?"

"What a question. Absolutely not."

"Really?"

"I have never needed to. You know perfectly well that I supported myself, and even put money in the bank."

"So you say. But there are people who might not agree. I have never once seen your bank book myself, and I have no idea how much money you have."

"You are quite mistaken if you think Kei-boy is making money. I might even have to support him."

"Let me ask you this." Yukiko was toying with the chrysanthemum in the glass vase. Though she avoided her sister's eye, her voice was calm, her hand was steady, and she showed no sign of excitement. "The camel's-hair coat last fall—did Kei-boy have it made for you?"

"I told you that it cost three hundred fifty yen and that I sold two kimonos and a coat to pay for it. I can even tell you which kimonos."

"But the old woman says Kei-boy paid for it, and she has the receipt."

Taeko did not answer.

"And the voile afternoon dress. She has the receipt for that too."

"You believe everything people like that tell you?"

"I would rather not. But she has evidence for everything she says. If she is lying, possibly you can show us your accounts to prove it."

Taeko, as always, was impassive. She stared at Yukiko, and did not try to answer.

"And she says that it has been going on for years, and that he has given you more than just clothes. Rings, too, and compacts, and broaches. She remembers every single item, and she says that Kei-boy was turned out by his brother because he took jewelry from the shop for you."

Taeko still did not answer.

"And you have had any number of chances to break with him. When you were seeing Itakura, for instance."

"What would you have said if I had left him then?"

"It is true that we wanted you to marry him. But we might have reconsidered if we had known that you were taking money from him even while you were seeing Itakura."

Sachiko agreed with Yukiko. Koi-san needed a scolding. Unable to go so far herself, however, she watched with astonishment and admiration. This was the second time she had seen Yukiko perform thus. The other attack, some five years before, had been aimed at Tatsuo. What was it that brought about the transformation? Sachiko had seen the vacillating Yukiko suddenly become positive and forceful, and in the end Tatsuo was crying for mercy.

"He was not making money, of course, but can you say you are not in debt to someone you have had stealing jewels for you? Someone who had no other way to make money? In case you are coming to the wrong conclusions, I ought to point out that the old woman did not say a thing out of bitterness. She only said that after he had done so much for you we ought to see that you married him. And now that we know everything, we agree with her."

Taeko still said nothing.

"You use him as long as you can, and then you say you know a good place for worthless young men, and try to send him off to Manchuria. How can you do it, Koi-san?"

Whether she had no answer, or thought that to answer would be a waste of time, Taeko remained silent. Yukiko talked on and on, until she began to sound repetitious. Presently Taeko was weeping, though her face was as expressionless as ever. She seemed not to notice the tears trickling down over her cheeks. Then, suddenly, she got up and left the room, slamming the door so hard that the house shook. A moment later they heard the front door slam.

27

THIS REMARKABLE SCENE took place just before lunch. Teinosuke and Etsuko were away, and O-haru happened to be out on an errand. The argument, in the closed dining room, had sounded so much like an ordinary conversation that the maids suspected nothing. That slam was far from ordinary, however, and O-aki ran startled into the hall. It was already empty. Opening the dining-room door a crack, she was surprised to see that Taeko had disappeared. Sachiko and Yukiko were spreading the tablecloth for lunch.

"What is it?" asked Sachiko.

"Nothing." O-aki was confused.

"Koi-san has left. There will be only Mrs. Makioka and myself." said Yukiko. "It does her good to be talked to now and then," she added when O-aki had left. With that she seemed to forget the incident, of which the sisters said nothing to Teinosuke and Etsuko. Etsuko and O-haru were mildly surprised that Taeko did not appear the next day. Had Koi-san caught cold, they wondered. Very strange that she was not at work, answered Sachiko. She thought they might not see Koi-san for a time, but the next morning Koi-san was with them, as composed as ever. She greeted Yukiko as though nothing had happened, and Yukiko answered pleasantly. Okubata had decided not to go to Manchuria, said Taeko. Yukiko nodded, and neither had more to say of the incident.

Some days later, Sachiko and Yukiko chanced to meet Itani in Kobe. They heard unexpected news: Itani was going to sell her beauty shop and go to America again. Some of her friends pointed out that the international situation was most unstable, and that there might be trouble between the United States and Japan. Should she not wait a little longer? But Itani answered that the possibility of trouble with America was not likely to vanish overnight, and that she would hurry off and be back before the trouble began. It was not easy to get a passport, but Itani had her ways. She meant to be gone six months or a year. There was really no

need to sell her shop if she was to be back so soon, but she had
long wanted to go into business in Tokyo, and this was her opportunity. Sachiko and Yukiko were not entirely surprised, since
they vaguely remembered having heard of such plans when Itani's
husband, long abed with palsy, had died the year before. Now that
the first-anniversary memorial services were over, she had decided
to act. It was always her way, once the decision was made, to push
ahead briskly. She had found someone to take the shop, made all
the arrangements for the sale, and even reserved passage to America. People would want to give her farewell parties and the like,
but parties were inappropriate these days, and besides, she was
leaving in too much of a hurry. She even thought she might have
to be excused from farewell calls.

Whatever she said, Itani was well known in Kobe. It hardly
seemed possible that no one would organize a farewell party. If a
larger party was not in prospect, said Sachiko to Teinosuke that
evening, they themselves must at least invite Itani to dinner—she
had done so much for Yukiko. The next morning, however, they
received a printed announcement which, among other things,
firmly refused farewell parties and similar courtesies. Itani was
leaving the very next evening for Tokyo. She would be at the
Imperial Hotel until she sailed, and she would have no time for
parties. That was that—the three sisters would go around with a
farewell present some time that day or the next. Because they
had great trouble deciding on a present, they did nothing the
first day. Sachiko and Yukiko were deliberating the problem the
next morning when Itani suddenly appeared. How nice of her—
she must be so busy—the three of them had been thinking they
would call on her. But there was no need for them to call, she
answered, and even if they had called they would have found
the shop turned over to someone else, and the house in an up-
roar; her brother was moving in. She had decided to say good-bye
to a few choice friends. Since time was so short, she had made it a
policy only to look in at the door, but somehow with the Makiokas
—only the Makiokas—she wanted to stay longer. And there was
something she had to tell them about. "Do come in, please," said
Sachiko. Itani glanced at her watch and went into the parlor—
she could stay ten or twenty minutes at the most.

She would be back in Japan almost before they knew she was

gone. Still, it made her sad to think she was leaving Kobe for
good. And in particular—she hoped they would forgive her for
saying so—she had grown so fond of them, of Mrs. Makioka, and
Miss Yukiko, and Koi-san. (She talked as rapidly as ever, and allowed no interruptions.) Each of the Makioka sisters had her own
special qualities: three fine sisters, alike and yet different. The
truth was that she had few regrets at leaving Kobe, but one thing
did make her sad. She would no longer see the Makiokas, who
she had hoped would continue to put up with her presence. It
was a great delight to see two of the sisters today, and it was most
unfortunate that Koi-san was not in. Koi-san would be around
soon, said Sachiko. Should they try calling her? No, said Itani,
standing up as Sachiko started for the telephone. It was unfortunate, but would they just pass on her regards? She was not sailing
for ten days, she added. Might they be able, all three of them, to
come to Tokyo? Not that she was asking them to see her off, but
there was someone in Tokyo she wanted them to meet.

This is the story Itani told, after stopping to catch her breath:
She wondered about the propriety of saying so to the person
most concerned, but what weighed on her mind, now that she
was moving from Kobe, was that she would have to leave unmade
the match she had hoped to make for Miss Yukiko. Each time she
considered—no, she was not trying to flatter them—how few
girls were as fine as Miss Yukiko and how few had such remarkable
sisters, she felt that she was shirking her duty, and she wanted at
least to make a beginning toward absolving herself. She had a new
candidate. They must have heard the name: Mimaki, an old court
family. Old Viscount Mimaki had figured in the Meiji Restora-
tion. The present viscount, his son, was well along in years. Once
active in politics (he had served on investigating committees in
the House of Peers), he had retired to the old family seat in Kyoto.
Itani had chanced to meet one Minoru, a Mimaki son by a concubine. This Mimaki Minoru was a graduate of the Peers School
and had studied physics at the Imperial University, which he left
to go to France. In Paris he studied painting for a time, and
French cooking for a time, and numerous other things, none for
very long. Going on to America, he studied aeronautics in a not-
too-famous state university, and he did finally take a degree, it
seemed. After graduation, he continued to wander about the

United States, and on to Mexico and South America. With his allowance from home cut off in the course of these wanderings, he made a living as a cook and even as a bellboy. He also returned to painting, and tried his hand at architecture. Following his whims and relying on his undeniable cleverness, he tried everything. He abandoned aeronautics when he left school. Though he had had no regular work since his return to Japan some eight or nine years before, a house he designed half for the fun of it had attracted attention and he was known as an architect of some ability. He had even opened a small office in Tokyo. His houses cost money, however, being in the latest Western fashion, and orders fell off as the China Incident began to have its effect. Now he was a man of leisure again, forced to close his office after but two years in business. Such was the man's story; and he was looking for a wife—or rather, the people around him were insisting that he had to have a wife. He was forty-four, Itani had heard. He had spent long years abroad, and he was used to the easy informality of bachelorhood in Japan. It seemed, therefore—not that they knew much about his life abroad—that he had never had a wife or a substitute for a wife. Since his return he had frequented the teahouses. But only until the year before, Itani added hastily. He no longer had enough money. In his youth he had received a settlement from his father, and he had been enjoying himself since. A man who knew how to spend and not how to earn, he was today in no position to waste money. Though somewhat late in making a start, he had hoped to earn his living as an architect, and if the times had been more favorable he would no doubt have succeeded. Now he faced an impasse. But he was a sort not uncommon among children of the nobility, sociable, witty, wide in his interests, thoroughly easygoing and rather inclined to think of himself as an artist, and his difficulties worried him not at all. It was because he was too easygoing that people said he must marry. This life would not do.

Itani met Mimaki through her daughter Mitsuyo, who had graduated from Japan Women's University the year before and was now working on the magazine *Women's Japan*. It seemed that the president of the publishing company, a Mr. Kunishima, was extremely fond of Mimaki. The friendship had begun when Mimaki designed a house for Kunishima, and Mimaki was now a frequent visitor at the house, a friend valued as highly by Mrs. Kunishima as by her husband. The offices of the magazine being near Mimaki's office, he had been in the habit of calling almost every day, and he had come to know the whole staff, and especially Mitsuyo. Mitsuyo was a great favorite of Kunishima and his wife, almost a member of their family. When, on a trip to Tokyo, Itani went to pay her respects at the Kunishima house, she found Mimaki there. He was most amusing even on first acquaintance, and he and Itani were soon friends. Itani really had little business there, but, with her daughter doing so well, she made three trips to Tokyo before the end of the year, and she visited the Kunishima house each time. Two of the three times she saw Mimaki. It was Mitsuyo's story that the Kunishimas were extremely fond of gambling. They would stay up all night over bridge or mahjong, with Mitsuyo and Mimaki for their partners. Itani knew she should not boast of her own daughter, but Mitsuyo *was* a bright girl, precociously gifted at gambling, and she could stay up two nights running and still work twice as hard as anyone else in the office. Hence the Kunishimas liked her. Itani had been to Tokyo several times recently to arrange for her trip abroad, and she had had Kunishima's help with her passport. She had seen Mimaki several more times. Each time she visited the Kunishima house, the talk, with Mimaki at the very center, turned noisily to "the question of Mimaki's wife." The Kunishimas were among the more aggressive advocates of marraige, and Kunishima, who knew Mimaki's father, said that he himself would undertake to talk the Viscount into a new settlement if Mimaki agreed to marry. For the time being, then, the couple need not worry about money. Kunishima always asked Itani for word of likely candidates. She must let him know immediately when she thought of someone.

Itani, who had been talking steadily, glanced at her watch and said she must hurry through the rest of her story. She had immediately thought of the Makiokas—this was exactly what they wanted for Miss Yukiko. But the timing was so bad. If she had planned to be in Japan herself, she would have said that she knew exactly the girl, that she would arrange everything, but here she was going abroad. She finally decided to say nothing, though Miss Yukiko's name had been on the tip of her tongue. But the problem still troubled her—such an ideal match, if only it could be arranged.

She must tell them more about Mr. Mimaki. She had already told them that he was forty-four, probably a year or two younger than Mr. Makioka. As was so often the case with men long abroad, he was growing bald. He was also rather swarthy—one could not call him a handsome man, but one could say that his face told of his breeding. He was well built, a little stout—a strongly built man who had never been ill and who boasted that he could go on working whatever happened. And there was that most important matter, his finances: he had lived alone from his student days on a settlement of something over a hundred thousand yen, and one could say without exaggeration that not a yen was left. He had several times gone crying to the Viscount, who had given him money two or three times. That money too was gone. Not one to keep money when he had it, he would soon be as impoverished as ever. It was useless to give him money, the Viscount had said. And indeed no man past forty should be living in aimless bachelorhood, argued Kunishima. It was only natural that the Viscount and the world in general should look upon him with suspicion. The first step was to find steady work, however small an income it brought. The Viscount would then feel better, and possibly even help him. Since there had already been so many requests for money, the help would be of very small proportions, but Mimaki would not need much. In Kunishima's opinion, Mimaki was a man of really outstanding talent when it came to designing Western houses, and there was no doubt that he had a fine future as an architect. Though Kunishima did not claim that there was much he himself could do, he meant to back Mimaki to the very limits of his ability. Mimaki was having trouble because times were bad, but one need not be gloomy. The crisis would soon pass. Kunishima would see (and he thought the prospects were good) whether the Viscount would agree to pay the wedding expenses, to buy the couple a house, and to give them an allowance for two or three years. That, then, was the story. Itani thought— would they not agree?—that while they might have certain misgivings, Mimaki was the husband they were looking for. He had many merits: it was his first marriage; though he was the son of a concubine, his family was descended from the great Fujiwara clan and his relatives without exception were illustrious men; he had no one to support (she had forgotten to tell them that his mother died very soon after he was born, and he had no memories of her); and he was a man with refined and varied tastes, well versed in the speech and customs of both France and America. Though she herself had known him but a very short time and it would be well for the Makiokas to conduct their own investigation, she could say from what she had seen of him that he was an amiable, likable man with no apparent defects. He was a great drinker. She had seen him in his cups two or three times, and she had found that the more he drank the wittier and more entertaining he became. Thinking over and over again what a shame it would be to let this opportunity pass, she had cast about for someone to act as go-between in her place. Finally she had decided that, since the man moved so easily in polite society, the business of go-between need not be complicated. Once an introduction was arranged and matters began to look promising, Mr. and Mrs. Kunishima would see that the negotiations went smoothly. And Mitsuyo could help too. Mitsuyo was young, but she was a bold, forward girl, just the sort to help with marriage negotiations. They would find her of considerable use if they chose to make her their messenger.

"Dear, dear." She looked at her watch again, and stood up to go. "And I meant to stay only fifteen minutes."

And still she talked on. She had said what she had to say. She hoped they would think everything over. Kunishima was going to give a little party for her, and if they were at all interested in her story, would they consider representing Kobe at the party?— Mrs. Makioka and Miss Yukiko, and, because nothing could be better than having all three sisters, Koi-san too, if possible. With the farewell party for their excuse, might they not at least meet the gentleman? Their answer could wait. She would call from Tokyo, perhaps the next day, to let them know the exact time of the farewell party. She barely said good-bye as she flew from the house.

28

ITANI had been in too much of a hurry to tell them her train time. Sachiko called the house, only to find that she was out. The person at the telephone was most secretive. Itani had left strict instructions that no one was to see her off. In the evening, Sachiko managed to catch Itani herself. After all that Itani had told them, said Sachiko, they wanted to see her at least once more—and finally Itani let it be known that she was taking the nine-thirty express from Sannomiya Station. The whole family went to the station, and for the first time since the memorial services the autumn before, Teinosuke found himself escorting the three sisters, all in their most elaborate dress.

"Why does Koi-san have on a kimono?" Fascinated, Etsuko stared across the dinner table. Taeko was wearing a silk print, large white camellias on a green background. Surrounded by all this finery, Etsuko was as excited as at the annual cherry-viewing.

"And how do I look in my kimono, Etsuko?"

"You look better in foreign clothes."

"A kimono makes you look fat, Koi-san," said Sachiko.

Taeko was beginning to wear Japanese dress even around the house. She had good legs, and when she wore Western clothes there was something of the pretty little girl about her. In kimono, with her legs hidden, she looked dumpy. In her efforts to gain weight, she was perhaps eating too much. Though she had always had rather good circulation, Taeko explained, her feet and legs had been unbearably cold in foreign clothes ever since her illness.

"When women are young they like foreign clothes," said Teinosuke, "but when they get older they turn back to kimono. Koi-san is getting old."

"Look at Itani. She has been to America, and in her business she ought to wear foreign clothes. But do you ever see her in anything except kimono?"

"Never," said Sachiko. "But then she is *really* old. What answer shall we give her, by the way?"

"Suppose we do this: there is no need to talk much about hus-

bands, but you ought to see her in Tokyo. You would have had
to even if the other matter had not come up at all."

"I quite agree with you."

"I ought to go myself, but I am too busy. You and Yukiko go,
and if Koi-san can go too that will be even better."

"I would like to go," said Taeko. "When was I last in Tokyo?
I wonder. And this is such a good time of the year, and I have to
make up for the cherry blossoms."

Unlike her sisters, Taeko was not in debt to Itani. She was a
steady customer at the beauty shop, but she complained that Itani
was too expensive, and occasionally went elsewhere. Even so, she
liked Itani's free and open manner, that touch of bravodo so unusual in women. Turned out of the Makioka family the year before, Taeko had come to feel that the world was harsh, and that
people with whom she had once been friendly were looking coldly
on her. Only Itani was unchanged, as motherly and sympathetic
as ever. There could be no doubt that Itani, whose shop was a
rumor mart, knew all the details of Taeko's misbehavior, and yet
she chose to concentrate on what was good in the girl. Taeko was
thoroughly delighted, then, when she heard that Itani had especially asked for "Koi-san" and urged that she too go to Tokyo.
Each time a prospective husband appeared for Yukiko, Taeko felt
like the skeleton in the family closet, and she read into Itani's invitation the implication that the youngest sister was no discredit
to the Makioka name, that the family should see her virtues and
set her out on display. Taeko really must go to Tokyo.

"You go too, then, Koi-san. The more the better."

"But the most important person of all . . ." Sachiko looked at
Yukiko, who was smiling quietly. "The most important person of
all seems unenthusiastic."

"Oh?"

"She says that if all three of us go, Etsuko will be left alone."

"But Yukiko has to go if anyone does. Etsuko can stay and take
care of the house for two or three days," said Teinosuke.

"Oh, no need to worry about me." Etsuko was quite the adult.
"I can watch the house. And O-haru will be here."

"Yukiko has one reservation, though."

"What is that?"

Yukiko only laughed, and Sachiko went ahead for her. "She

says she has to go for Itani's sake, but she is not to be left behind afterwards."

"There is that problem, of course."

"Suppose we stay away from the Tokyo house," said Taeko.

"No, that will never do," objected Teinosuke. "There will be trouble when they find out."

"Yukiko says we are to tell them that she will be sent to Tokyo later, but that this time I am bringing her back with me."

"But if you hate Tokyo so," put in Taeko, "what chance is there that you will be interested in this man of Itani's?"

"Yes, what about that?" Etsuko agreed with Taeko. "Maybe you have to get married, but why to someone in Tokyo?"

"You understand such things, do you, Etsuko?"

"But will Yukiko like Tokyo? Will you, Yukiko?"

"Possibly you should be quiet, Etsuko," said Sachiko. "But I feel this way myself: Mr. Mimaki comes from a court family and Kyoto is in his blood. I imagine he might be willing to move west. After all, he only has a rented room in Tokyo."

"Especially if we find him work in Osaka. There *is* that Kyoto blood."

"But even coming from the same part of the country," continued Sachiko, "Kyoto people and Osaka people are so different. Kyoto women are all right, but I have never found much to say for Kyoto men."

"This is no time to go looking for faults," said Teinosuke.

"Maybe he was born in Tokyo. And he has spent so much time in France and America. Maybe he is different from most Kyoto men."

"I never have liked Tokyo," said Yukiko. "But I imagine Tokyo people have their good points."

They could wait until the Tokyo meeting to give Itani her farewell present. Upon Teinosuke's suggestion, the five of them set out after dinner to buy a bouquet in Kobe. Etsuko was to present it. Though one would have expected the station to be alive with well-wishers, it was in fact rather lonely, the departure time having been kept secret. Even so there were twenty or thirty people at the train, including Itani's brothers and their wives. The Makioka sisters, noting the rather sombre nature of the assembly, felt constrained to keep their cloaks on, and in the end they had no opportunity to display their carefully chosen kimonos. Sachiko managed to have a few words with Itani. They were most grateful for the visit that morning, she said. She had told Teinosuke of it, and they agreed that there was no way to thank Itani enough for worrying over the sisters to the very end, and now, more than ever, they felt that all three of them must be at her farewell party. Teinosuke added his thanks to Sachiko's. How splendid, said Itani. All three of them! She would be waiting, and they could be sure that she would telephone the details the next day. She leaned out the window to repeat her assurances as the train pulled out of the station.

There was a telephone call the next evening from the Imperial Hotel. The farewell party, said Itani, was to be three evenings later, at five o'clock, at the Imperial Hotel. There would be nine guests in all: Itani and her daughter Mitsuyo; Mr. and Mrs. Kunishima and their daughter; Mr. Mimaki, and, representing Kobe, the Makioka sisters. And where, asked Itani, would they stay? Possibly at the main house in Shibuya—but since it would be so much more convenient, suppose they too stay at the Imperial. With a festival in progress to celebrate the twenty-six-hundredth anniversary of the founding of the Empire, every hotel in Tokyo was crowded. Fortunately, relatives of Mr. Kunishima's had taken a room and had suggested that they might let the Makiokas have it and go themselves to stay with the Kunishimas. Taeko would be going and Yukiko did so particularly want to avoid the Tokyo house and to conceal the reason for the visit. Sachiko therefore felt that, selfish though it was of her, she must ask Itani to arrange for a hotel room. They would leave for Tokyo either the next evening or two mornings later. Although they would like to see Itani off from Yokohama, they could not be away from Ashiya for very long, and they must ask her to forgive them for going only to the farewell party. They would stay two nights, including the night of the farewell party. But they would want to see the Kabuki and it was just possible that they would stay a third night. Itani answered that she might want to see the Kabuki herself. Should she reserve seats?

They were able to get berths for the next evening, and all that day they were busy getting ready. Sachiko and Yukiko needed permanent waves. They did not know where to go, however, with

Itani no longer in business. If Koi-san were there she could recommend a place. Why was she so late? And so the morning passed,
and at two in the afternoon Taeko appeared, her hair neatly
waved. Always one to lay her plans carefully, she had gone off to a
beauty shop by herself. How nasty of her. They had wanted her to
take them along. But Taeko was not disturbed: there would be a
beauty shop in the Imperial Hotel. Quite true—consoled, they
turned to decide what clothes they would take, and packed a large
and a small suitcase and a bag. When they had finished dressing,
it was nearly train time.

29

"Mrs. Makioka?" In Tokyo Station the following morning, a
small young woman in Western clothes came briskly up and attached herself to Sachiko. "I'm Mitsuyo."

"Oh, Mrs. Itani's . . ."

"It's been a long time. Mother should have come to meet you,
but she had all sorts of things to do." Mitsuyo glanced at the baggage. "Shall I call a redcap?" She pounced on a redcap. "And
this will be Miss Yukiko, and this Koi-san. How long has it been,
I wonder. You've all been so good to Mother. Thank you for coming—just think, all three of you. Mother was so happy when she
spoke of you last night."

Two or three miscellaneous pieces—cosmetic cases and the like
—were left when the redcap had taken the larger baggage. "Let
me have them. Come on, let me have them." Mitsuyo seized the
pieces the sisters were carrying and darted off into the crowd.

Sachiko and the others had seen the girl once or twice when
she was in a Kobe high school. There was no sign now of the old
provincial manner, and they would never have recognized her if
she had not announced herself. Itani was tall, though rather
slender. Mitsuyo on the other hand had been small as a child, and
she had hardly grown at all. Sachiko remembered her as swarthy
and round-faced, and just a little plump. Now the face seemed

much fairer, and Sachiko would have said that the body had even
shrunk. The hands were no larger than those of a twelve- or thir-
teen-year-old. Mitsuyo was only an inch or so shorter than Taeko,
but by contrast with Taeko, heavy in kimono and cloak, she
seemed tiny and bird-like. And, as her mother had said, she was
just a little "forward." Her speech was almost laughably like her
mother's. The glib flow suggested a too-knowing child. Yukiko
squirmed each time this girl ten years her junior called her "Miss
Yukiko."

"How nice of you to come to the station. You must be so busy."

"It's nothing, nothing. But as a matter of fact we *are* rather
busy this month, with the celebrations and all. And then along
comes Mother."

"I understand there was a naval review the other day."

"And the day after that a meeting to organize the Rule Assist-
ance Association. And the festival at the Yasukuni Shrine is going
on, and on the twenty-first there is a parade. Oh, Tokyo is just
full of excitement. All the hotels are overflowing. That reminds
me—the Imperial Hotel has twice as many people as it can handle. We got you a room, but not much of a room."

"Anything will do."

"It's a tiny little closet of a room, but it's all they have. We did
complain when we saw that there were only two single beds, and
we got one changed for a double."

Mitsuyo told them all this as they drove through the city, and
much besides: that she had tried to find Kabuki tickets for that
day, but, with Tokyo in such a stir, tickets were not to be had by
ordinary means for a full ten days ahead; that, through her magazine, she *thought* she had tickets for two days later; that she and
her mother and Mr. Mimaki, whom she believed her mother had
described to them, would ask to go along; and that it would
probably be impossible to have six seats together.

"Well, here it is. Hardly any sunlight—but try not to mind too
much." Mitsuyo saw them to the room, put down the baggage,
and started for the door. "Mother should be back any time now.
She said to tell you she would call. If you'll excuse me, then, I do
have to go to the office. I'll stop by later. Is there shopping I can
do for you? Just let me know—here is my number." Mitsuyo
reached into her purse for a calling card. The fingernails on the

tiny hand were as bright a red as one could hope to find anywhere.

Sachiko wanted if possible to have her hair taken care of that
day, but they ought to rest. With Itani about to call, they could
not expect to catch up on their sleep. Even so, they might loosen
their obis and lie down for a while. Sachiko was less worried
about herself than about Yukiko. Possibly because of the injections, the spot over Yukiko's eye was much less conspicuous,
though it had not entirely disappeared. The dangerous time of the
month was coming, however, and the spot tended to be darker
when she was tired. Sachiko looked at the worn face and concluded that the most important thing was to let her sister rest.

"Shall we wait until tomorrow, Yukiko? You must be tired."

"Today will be all right."

"But the party is at five, and we can always find time tomorrow.
Suppose we rest a little and go out to the Ginza. We have our
shopping to do."

"I am going to lie down." Taeko was sprawled in the armchair
that was clearly the most comfortable in the room. She had occupied it as soon as they came in. While her sisters were talking, she
undid her obi, and, with only a narrow sash holding her kimono
together, threw herself down on the double bed. She would once
have been the last to show her exhaustion. She would have left her
less energetic sisters behind and set off on her business; but the old
liveliness had disappeared. On the slightest pretext she would fall
into a chair and fling her feet out before her, or lean heavily on
an elbow and yawn and sigh, and otherwise show that her manners, never good, had become worse of late. Not quite over her
illness, she had perhaps fattened herself too indulgently.

"You lie down too, Yukiko." Yukiko nodded and, putting aside
the cloak and obi Taeko had thrown across the armchair, sat down
without undoing her obi. She would have to sleep with Taeko,
but she did not feel in the mood to lie down beside her sister
now. The bed, though double, was smaller than most double beds,
and she meant to leave the single bed for Sachiko. It was nonetheless Yukiko and not Taeko who was presently asleep.

Whether or not she noticed this evidence of Yukiko's thoughtfulness, Sachiko lay down on the single bed. Yukiko slept happily
in her chair, and Sachiko and Taeko lay awake on the beds.

"Suppose we have our baths, Koi-san." Yukiko slept on while they had their turns at the bath. They woke her for lunch, and there was still no sign of Itani. At about three they decided to go shopping. They absolutely had to find that farewell present. Nothing Western seemed appropriate—they must find something uniquely Japanese that would please foreigners. After much perplexed searching they decided on a mother-of-pearl jewel box that could be Sachiko's present, and a tortoise-shell broach set with pearls, from Yukiko and Taeko. The search left them exhausted.

"No more, no more." Taeko headed for the hotel after tea at the Colombin, though they still had shopping to do. In the hotel room (it was by then four-thirty) they found an orchid, and beside it a note on Itani's calling card: "Telephone me when you come in. We can have tea together."

"No more tea!" Taeko was not to be pried from the armchair, which she had occupied again. The other two sat on the beds. Not ten minutes later the telephone rang.

"It must be Itani," said Sachiko as she picked up the receiver. Itani had been out since early that morning, and she hoped they would forgive her. She had come back a few minutes before. She would order tea, and they were to meet her in the lobby.

"Thank you, thank you. I was about to call you. Thank you. We will be right down."

"Leave me here," said Taeko. "The two of you can have tea with her."

But they must not be rude to Itani, said Sachiko. The others were just as tired as Koi-san. Soon all three went down to the lobby.

30

ITANI immediately began talking, and while they were having tea she managed to tell them everything. She had just been informed by telephone that she had Kabuki tickets for the day after tomorrow. Only the three Makiokas would be able to sit together.

She herself would sit with Mitsuyo, and Mimaki would have to sit by himself. In the course of what seemed the most idle chatter, they learned many important details: Itani had not only spoken of Yukiko to the Kunishimas and Mimaki, she had even shown them the *miai* photograph Sachiko had left with her; the photograph had been extremely well received; at Kunishimas' the evening before, everyone had agreed that Yukiko looked far younger than she was; already Mimaki was convinced that she was the wife for him; if the Makiokas had no objections, he was prepared to marry her whenever she said; since Itani wanted to hide nothing, she had told them all she knew of the Makioka family, of relations between the Shibuya house and the Ashiya house, and the unpleasantness between Yukiko and Taeko on the one hand and Tatsuo on the other; Mimaki seemed quite undisturbed, and there was no sign that this new information had weakened his decision; a man who enjoyed life, he was more reasonable than most, and perhaps he was above fussing over small family matters—in any case, she found him extremely easy to talk to. Yukiko and Taeko, sensing that the conversation was moving toward more delicate topics, left as soon as they had finished their tea.

"I told him about that spot." Itani lowered her voice and glanced at Yukiko's retreating figure. "I told him everything. It would not do to have him find out later."

"Quite right of you. We will all feel more comfortable. Of course Yukiko has been having injections, and, as you see, the spot hardly shows any more. And it will go away entirely once she is married. Could you explain that too?"

"Oh, I've already explained. He said he'd enjoy watching it go."

"Did he really!"

"And then—about Koi-san. I don't know how much you've heard, but there are all sorts of rumors. But even if they're true, we needn't worry. Someone in every family is a little different, and I think myself it's better that way. Mr. Mimaki says it makes no difference at all. He says he's not marrying the sister."

"That seems very reasonable of him."

"Oh, you know, people who've had their fun always understand. He said he had nothing to do with the sister, and that I could tell him everything. Not that he wanted to hear everything if I would rather not tell him." Noting the relief on Sachiko's face, Itani plunged on. "But what is Miss Yukiko thinking? That is the real problem."

"Yes. As a matter of fact. . . ."

As a matter of fact, Sachiko was for the first time really interested. Until then she had been most emphatic in making the farewell party the chief reason for the trip. Her rather tepid attitude toward the *miai* itself—though it had not been entirely out of her mind, she was determined to take it seriously only after they had met the man—was owing to a fear that they might once again go too far and be disappointed. She had not really talked to Yukiko. Assuming that conditions were otherwise good, one thing was sure to make Yukiko hesitate: the fact, touched upon earlier, that the man lived in Tokyo. Or rather, to be quite honest, they could no longer let Yukiko have her way, and Yukiko was not likely to be stubborn; and it was Sachiko who secretly hoped that they could find Yukiko a home somewhere in Osaka or Kobe. She hated the thought of sending her sister off to Tokyo. Just for her own information, said Sachiko, she wondered where Mr. Mimaki meant to live. She had heard that his father in Kyoto would buy him a house, and where was it likely to be? Though she was in no sense raising objections, she wondered if it must be in Tokyo. Might he not live farther west? That *was* a point, answered Itani. She had not thought to ask, but she certainly would now. She suspected that it would be Tokyo. Did they dislike Tokyo?

"No, not really." Sachiko hastily revised her answer: "No, not at all."

She would see them later, then, said Itani. It was possible that Mitsuyo would be around with Mr. Mimaki after dinner, and Itani hoped they would all come to her room. At about eight there was a telephone call: Itani knew they would be tired, but Mr. Mimaki had just arrived, and she hoped all three sisters would come to meet him. Sachiko helped Yukiko change. While she and Taeko were dressing, Itani called to hurry them.

"Come in." Mitsuyo opened the door. "The place is in a terrible clutter, I'm afraid. You'll have to forgive us."

The room was overflowing—five or six suitcases and trunks, cardboard dress boxes, farewell presents, supplies to be taken to America.

"Please, please. This will be fine for me." Mimaki sat down on a steamer trunk when the introductions were finished. There were but four chairs in the room, and they were assigned to Itani and the Makioka sisters. Mitsuyo sat on the bed.

"Now you have a real audience." Mimaki picked up the conversation the sisters had interrupted. "Suppose you give us a demonstration."

"No, sir."

"Oh, but I'm going to see you aboard ship, and you'll have to show me then."

"I will not. I'm wearing kimono the day I sail."

"Come, now. All the way across?"

"Maybe not *all* the way. But I don't mean to wear foreign clothes if I can help it."

"A very bad idea. Why did you have them made?" Mimaki turned to the sisters. "We've been talking about how Mrs. Itani dresses. Have you ever seen her in foreign clothes?"

"Never," said Sachiko. "She has never given us even a glimpse. We have often wondered why."

"We all have. Even Mitsuyo here says she's never seen her mother in foreign clothes. We have to see her at least once." He turned to Itani again. "Don't you think you should have a trial run, with all of us here to watch you?"

"I am to strip down right in front of you?"

"Yes, please do. Or maybe we could wait in the hall."

"You must stop teasing Mother, Mr. Mimaki. You don't really care what she wears."

Itani saw her opportunity to squirm loose. "I've noticed that Koi-san is wearing kimono these days."

"Don't change the subject."

"Yes, Koi-san has been wearing kimono a great deal. Oftener than foreign clothes, even."

"They tell me it is a sign of age." Like Sachiko, Taeko was quite unashamed of her Osaka accent.

"I hope you'll forgive me for saying so." Mitsuyo inspected the bright kimono from top to bottom. "But I think Koi-san would look better in foreign clothes. Not that she doesn't look good in kimono, of course."

"I thought the lady's name was Taeko. What is this 'Koi-san?' "

"Really! You're from Kyoto, and you don't know what 'Koi-san' means!"

"But 'Koi-san' is an Osaka word," explained Sachiko. "I doubt if it is used in Kyoto."

Itani brought out a box of chocolates, evidently a present from someone, but they had just had dinner and wanted only tea. "Mother, we must order something for Mr. Mimaki." Mitsuyo had her mother ring for whisky. Mimaki was not reluctant to drink. "Just leave the bottle here," he said to the bellboy. As he talked he poured happily from the bottle of Scotch at his elbow. Itani guided the conversation smoothly. She asked, among other things, whether his new house had to be in Tokyo, and he told them much about himself and his future. Mitsuyo had said that he was a Kyoto man, but as a matter of fact the family had lived in Tokyo since his grandfather's time, and he himself had been born in Tokyo. Though his father was of pure Kyoto blood, his mother was from the old downtown section of Tokyo, and he was therefore half the child of Kyoto and half the child of old Edo. He had in his youth been quite indifferent to Kyoto. He had been drawn to Europe and America, but he had recently begun to feel something like nostalgia for the city of his ancestors. Perhaps that was inevitable: his father too had come to love Kyoto, and had left the Tokyo house and retired to Saga, on the outskirts of Kyoto. Mimaki's own tastes were turning toward the Japanese. He was beginning to recognize the beauty of old Japanese architecture, and he meant, before he became an architect, to study what was uniquely Japanese, and later to give his designs a strongly Japanese flavor. He had begun to wonder whether, for his studies, he might not do better to seek work in the Kyoto region and to live there for a time. And it had also occurred to him that the Kobe-Osaka area would be more congenial to the sort of house he hoped to build. With but a little exaggeration, then, one might say that his future lay in Osaka and Kobe. What part of Kyoto would they recommend? Sachiko gave her opinion, and asked where his father was living, and it was concluded that the only parts of Kyoto to be recommended were the Saga plains to the west and the eastern hills around the Nanzenji Temple. Thus they talked on into the night. Even after a third of a bottle of whisky,

Mimaki was completely in control of himself. He only became wittier as he drank. Mitsuyo was a good adversary, and the two of them happily threw barbs back and forth. The entertainment was almost professional, so good that the Makiokas quite forgot their weariness. It was nearly eleven when Mimaki suddenly jumped up. Terrible—he was about to miss the last streetcar. Mitsuyo said that she too must go.

The sisters slept until nine-thirty the next morning. Unable to wait for the dining room to open, Sachiko had toast in her room, and afterwards set out with Yukiko for the Shiseidō beauty shop. Though there was a beauty shop in the basement of the Imperial Hotel, Mitsuyo had suggested the night before that they go to the Shiseidō, where they could have the Zotos cold wave and avoid scorching their hair. There were some twelve or thirteen customers ahead of them, and it was impossible to know how long they would have to wait. In Itani's shop they could have had their way—the waiting list could always be juggled—but here such stratagems were impossible. The waiting room was full of strangers, women of the Tokyo breed, none of whom seemed ready to strike up a conversation. Ashamed, even when they talked in hushed voices, to have their west-country accents overheard, the sisters felt as if they were in the heart of the enemy country. They could only sit and listen timidly to the brisk Tokyo speech around them. Wasn't it crowded, said one woman. Of course, answered another—it was a lucky day for weddings, and every beauty shop in town was full. The horoscope was good today, Sachiko remembered. Perhaps Itani had deliberately chosen the day to bring Yukiko luck. More and more customers poured in, and two or three managed to move ahead in the line. They were very sorry, but they simply had to be ready at a certain hour. It was two, and the sisters had come before noon, and they began to wonder whether they would be ready by five. She would never again come to the Shiseidō, thought Sachiko. Though she managed to hold back her anger, it was now clear that she had not had enough breakfast. She was ravenously hungry. And it was even worse for Yukiko. Yukiko liked to say that she had "a smaller stomach than most people," and it was true that she ate little at any one time, but it was also true that she was hungry again sooner than most. Sachiko looked nervously at her sister, silent and dispirited. Might

Yukiko faint with hunger? Would she be able to stand the ordeal of a permanent wave? Finally their turns came, and Yukiko went first, and it was nearly five when Sachiko was finished. As they were about to leave, there was a telephone call for "Mrs. Makioka." Not ready yet? But it was already five. Taeko was calling from the hotel. "Yes, yes, we are on our way," Sachiko slipped into the Osaka dialect in spite of herself. The two sisters ran for the door.

"Remember, Yukiko, never to go to a strange beauty shop on a lucky day."

As she hurried through the hotel to the farewell party, she passed at least five women, all in formal dress, whom she had seen at the Shiseidō that afternoon.

"Never go to a strange beauty shop on a lucky day," she said to Itani.

~~~~~~~~~~~~~~~~~~~~~

3 1

ON THE THIRD DAY, their last in Tokyo, they were busy all morning and into the afternoon.

Sachiko had at first planned to leave this day open for the theater, and, visiting the Shibuya house the next morning and finishing her shopping in the afternoon, to go home on the night train. She had had enough of night trains, however, and the lack of sleep was beginning to tell. She wanted only to be back in her own bed as soon as possible. It was Taeko who said so first, and Yukiko immediately agreed. And they wanted to make the visit to the Shibuya house as short as possible. It seemed, then, that they would take the Swallow Express back the next morning, and, between shopping in the morning and the Kabuki in the afternoon, they would dash out to Shibuya and keep the cab waiting no more than five or six minutes. Sachiko knew how her sisters felt. Taeko had always disliked the main house, and Yukiko had been back in Ashiya now for more than a year. The autumn before, when the order came from the main house that Taeko must decide whether to come to Tokyo or to leave the Makioka family, very much the same choice had been presented to Yukiko, but the order was not clear in Yukiko's case, and, remarking that she could not know how serious they were, she had chosen to ignore it. No word had come since to remind her. Possibly Tatsuo, who had had trouble with Yukiko before, had decided not to risk angering her, or possibly he considered her disinherited along with Taeko. In any case, Tsuruko was likely to mention the problem, and Sachiko was therefore as reluctant as Yukiko to go to the Shibuya house. On her trip to the Fuji Lakes, she had only telephoned her sister, partly because she was having trouble with her eye, but very largely because she feared being caught in a cross fire. Tsuruko might transmit an order from Tatsuo, and Yukiko might well ignore it again. And Sachiko had her own reasons for staying away from her sister. Though she may not have been entirely conscious of the fact herself, she had been chilled by the reply to her letter about Taeko's illness. For all these reasons, she would as soon have gone back to Ashiya without seeing the people in the main house at all, but Teinosuke had said that there would be trouble if they learned of the visit later. And it was just possible this time that Yukiko's marriage talks—the people at the main house should be given some slight preparation. The truth was that Sachiko herself had not been particularly hopeful. Now she had had an evening with Mimaki, and she had met the Kunishimas, who seemed happy to act as intermediaries, and had seen what sort of atmosphere they moved in. The old feeling that the Makiokas must not venture too far had left her. She had a distinct impression that, quite without their having planned it so, the meeting the night before had been a true *miai*, and the results had been pleasing to both sides. What delighted her most was the civility with which both Mimaki and Kunishima treated Taeko. They took the greatest pains, almost by turns, to talk to her in a most agreeable and unchallenging manner. They seemed prepared to overlook her faults, and they even seemed to be sympathizing with her, and, since nothing in their manner suggested condescension, Taeko too was completely open and relaxed, and quite ready to entertain them with the witty remarks and imitations that were her speciality. Sachiko felt her eyes growing moist at the thought of the affection for Yukiko that made Taeko thus play the comedian. It seemed that Yukiko too noticed. For

Yukiko, she was remarkably lively. Though Mimaki said several times that he would buy a house in Kyoto or Osaka, Sachiko now felt that with such a husband it would make no difference where Yukiko lived, in Tokyo or in Osaka.

Waiting until she was sure Tatsuo would have left for work, Sachiko called Tsuruko and gave her a summary of all that had happened: these were Itani's plans, and the three of them had come to Tokyo for her farewell party; they would leave on the express the following morning; they were going to the Kabuki with Itani, and, because they would have only that time open, they would like to stop by the Shibuya house for just a few minutes before the theater; and there had been mention at the farewell party of a possible husband for Yukiko, though Sachiko still had little concrete information to report.

The sisters wandered about the Ginza all morning. After they had passed the main Ginza intersection some three or four times and had lunch at the Hamasaku, they hailed a cab. Taeko had been complaining of fatigue all the while. In their private dining room at the Hamasaku, she lay down on the straw matting with a cushion for her pillow, and as her sisters got into the cab she said she thought she would not go after all. The family had thrown her out, and Tsuruko would only be embarrassed, and she herself had no desire to see Tsuruko. Possibly so, answered Sachiko, but it would be a little insulting if Koi-san alone were to stay behind. However Tatsuo might feel, Tsuruko at least would not be fussy about the matter of the "disinheritance." She would be delighted to see Koi-san, especially since the latter had been so ill. Koi-san must go with them. But Taeko answered that it was far too much trouble, that she would have a cup of coffee somewhere and go on ahead of them to the Kabuki Theater. Presently they left without her.

He would rather not wait, said the driver when they arrived at the house. They had to plead with him—it would be no more than fifteen or twenty minutes, and they would of course pay for his time. They went up to the second-floor parlor. The vermilion table, the Rai Shunsui motto over the door, the decorated-lacquer shelves—everything was as it had been. Since all of the children except Umeko, now five, were in school, the house was much quieter than Sachiko remembered it.

"But you could at least send the taxi back."

"Would we be able to find another?"

"There used to be all sorts of taxis. But you can take the subway. It is no walk at all from the subway to the Kabuki Theater."

"Next time we can stay longer. We will be coming again soon, I am sure."

"What is at the Kabuki Theater this month?" The question was a little unexpected.

" 'Briar' and 'Chrysanthemums' and—what else, I wonder."

Umeko had come upstairs. Yukiko took the child downstairs to play, leaving her two sisters alone.

"And Koi-san?"

"She was with us till just now, but she said she thought it would be best if she stayed away."

"Why? She should have come."

"I thought so too. But we have been so busy these last two or three days, and she seems terribly tired. She is not really well yet, you know."

From the moment Sachiko began talking to her sister, her vague resentment left. One could be displeased with Tsuruko from afar, but face to face one found her the same genial Tsuruko. Suddenly asked what was playing at the Kabuki Theater, Sachiko thought it somehow malicious to leave only one of her sisters out of the theater party. She would not have worried if she had thought Tsuruko was her usual impassive self, but Tsuruko, in some ways rather childlike even now, had very probably wanted to go along as soon as she heard the word "Kabuki." And did it not seem likely too that, since the carefully guarded property of the main house had almost vanished with the collapse of the stock market, Tsuruko could go to the theater only on very special occasions—occasions like today, for instance? To console her sister, Sachiko exaggerated Yukiko's prospects a little. Mimaki was most enthusiastic, she said, and only waited to know what the Makiokas thought. If they were willing, there could be no doubt that a marriage would be arranged. This time surely they would have good news for Tatsuo and Tsuruko. In any case, Sachiko would have more to say after Teinosuke had met the man.

"Mr. Mimaki and Itani and her daughter are going to the Ka-

buki with us." Sachiko stood up to leave. "We will see you again
soon, I am sure."

Tsuruko followed her downstairs. "Yukiko really *must* try to
be more entertaining."

"She was different this time, very lively. She talked and talked.
I know everything will be all right."

"I do hope so. Here she is thirty-three."

"Goodbye, then. We will see you soon." Yukiko, waiting downstairs, flew out ahead of her sister.

"Goodbye. Say hello to Koi-san." Tsuruko saw them to the
gate, and talked on after they were in the cab. "So Mrs. Itani is
going abroad. I wonder if I should see her."

"You hardly need to. After all, you have never met her."

"But should I at least introduce myself, now that I know she is
here? When does she sail?"

"The twenty-third. But she says no one is to see her off."

"Shall I go around to the hotel?"

"It hardly seems necessary."

As the driver stepped on the starter, Sachiko noticed that her
sister was in tears. Very odd—why should she weep for Itani?
The tears flowed steadily, and the cab moved off.

"She was crying," said Yukiko. "Why should she cry over Itani?"

"It must have been something else. Itani was an excuse."

"Do you suppose she wanted us to invite her to the Kabuki?"

"That must have been it. She wanted to see the Kabuki."

Though ashamed to have them catch her crying over the Kabuki, it would seem, Tsuruko had in the end been unable to control herself.

"Did she say I was to come back?"

"Neither of us said a word about it. She was too full of the Kabuki."

Yukiko was relieved.

Their seats at the Kabuki being separated, the sisters and Mimaki
had little chance to become better acquainted. He was with them
in the dining room, however, and during the five- and ten-minute
intermissions he would ask if they might not like to step out into
the lobby. Well-versed though he was in things foreign, he confessed that he knew absolutely nothing about the old Japanese

theater. They did not find it hard to believe him. Mitsuyo was most scornful when it became apparent that he could not even distinguish the two main styles of singing.

This would be goodbye, then, said Itani when she heard that they were taking the morning express. She was delighted at having been able to leave behind such a "present," and, though there were numerous details she would have liked to tend to herself, she was sure Mitsuyo would soon be writing to them. Mimaki suggested that they walk back toward the hotel together. Itani called Sachiko apart from the others, and as always said a great deal in a very short time: as Sachiko could see, Mimaki was most enthusiastic; the Kunishimas, after having met Yukiko the evening before, were if anything more in love with her than Mimaki himself was; Mimaki hoped to visit Ashiya some time during the following month, and to meet Teinosuke; and Mr. Kunishima, once he had the informal permission of the Makiokas, would arrange an interview with Viscount Mimaki. Promising to be at the train the next morning, Mimaki and Mitsuyo left the others after tea at the Colombin. The three sisters and Itani walked back to the hotel.

Itani, talking all the way, had seen them to their room, Sachiko had had her bath and Yukiko had gone in for hers. Still in her theater clothes, Taeko lay sprawled against an arm of the chair, a newspaper spread on the floor below her. The walk back had been a strain, but this exhaustion was a little too extreme.

"I know you are not really well yet, Koi-san, but might something else be wrong with you? Suppose you see Dr. Kushida when we get back."

Taeko nodded apathetically. "I know what is wrong without calling a doctor."

"Oh? What is it, then?"

Her face against the chair, Taeko looked sluggishly up at her sister. "It looks as though I am three or four months pregnant." She spoke with the usual calm.

Sachiko gasped, and stared as though to bore a hole through her sister's face. It was a moment or two before she could ask the question: "Is it Kei-boy's?"

"Miyoshi's. I think Yukiko heard about Miyoshi from the old woman."

"The bartender?"

Taeko nodded. "I am sure that is my trouble."

As always, after a shock, Sachiko felt the blood recede from her fingers. She was trembling violently. Thinking that the most urgent business was to quiet the pounding of her heart, she said no more to Taeko. She staggered over to turn out the ceiling light, switched on the bed lamp, and crawled into bed. She pretended to be asleep when Yukiko came out of the bathroom. Taeko at length picked herself up and went for her bath.

32

YUKIKO, who had heard nothing, soon went off to sleep, and Taeko apparently followed her. Sachiko lay awake all night with her new problem. Now and then she dabbed at her eyes with the edge of the blanket. She had sleeping medicine and brandy in her bag, but she knew they would do no good.

Something happened every time she came to Tokyo. Was it simply that she and Tokyo did not go together? Two autumns before, on that first trip to Tokyo since her honeymoon, she had been startled by the letter from Okubata telling of Itakura, and she had passed just such a night as this, and again, early in spring the year before—it was true that the incident had not directly concerned her—they had been paged at the Kabuki Theater and told of Itakura's illness. Something always went wrong in any case when Yukiko had a *miai*, and Sachiko had been uneasy at having a *miai* in Tokyo. Tokyo boded ill. Since it had been unlucky twice, it must be unlucky three times. She had tried to tell herself, when her third trip to Tokyo had been such a success—indeed her first really happy trip with her husband in years—that the bad luck was broken. And then she had tended to shrug Itani's proposal off as hopeless in any case, and it had seemed foolish to worry about omens and oracles. Now she knew again that, for her, Tokyo was the devil's corner. Nothing more was needed to ruin Yukiko's prospects. Such an interesting proposal too—what wretched luck that they had had to pick Tokyo for the *miai*!

Sadder and sadder for Yukiko, and angrier and angrier with
Taeko, Sachiko wept tears of sorrow and resentment.

Again—it had happened again—again she had been hurt by
this sister. But again, did the blame not rest rather with those who
should have been watching her? If she was "three or four months
pregnant," then it had happened perhaps in June, after she recovered from dysentery, and there must have been a period of
morning sickness. Had pure carelessness kept the others from
noticing? Was it obtuseness on Sachiko's part that with this sister
before her for three or four days now, hardly able to lift a fork,
tired at the slightest motion—that with all this she had not even
suspected the truth? She saw now why Koi-san had given up Western clothes. No doubt Sachiko seemed ridiculously simple to Koi-
san, and did Koi-san's conscience then not bother her at all? From
those remarks earlier in the evening, Sachiko was left to suspect
that the pregnancy was not accidental, that Taeko and this man
Miyoshi or whatever his name was had planned it carefully. Had
they not planned it so that they could present an accomplished
fact to both Okubata and the Makioka family—to make Okubata
accept the inevitable and to wring permission to marry from the
Makiokas? That had been very clever of Koi-san. For Koi-san, that
was the only course possible. But should they forgive her? After
all Sachiko herself, her husband, and Yukiko had done to protect her from the main house and its commands, did it please her
to shame them before the world? Sachiko could bear the damage
to her own name and to Teinosuke's, but was Yukiko's future
to be ruined? Why did Koi-san make them all suffer, time after
time? How completely devoted Yukiko had been during that illness! Did Koi-san not see that it was really Yukiko who had saved
her? It was to repay the debt in some measure, Sachiko had
thought, that Koi-san had performed so well at the *miai* the
evening before. She had judged her sister too generously; Koi-san
had been gay only because she was drunk. She thought of no one
but herself.

The cold determination of the girl, prepared to take whatever
extraordinary measures served her interests! Probably she had considered the fact that Sachiko would be angry, and the fact that
she would again alienate Teinosuke, and the fact that for Yukiko
the damage would be incalculable. Given Koi-san's view of life,

one had to accept the extraordinary measures as inevitable, but why did she have to choose a time when Yukiko's fate hung in the balance? True, it could not have been part of her plan to make her pregnancy known at the moment Yukiko was having a *miai*, but if she was sincere in saying that she would wait until Yukiko was married, that she would do nothing that might embroil Yukiko, then could she not have waited until Yukiko's future was secure? Why had she not been tactful enough to stay behind in Ashiya? In her delight at once again being accepted as a Makioka daughter and in her gratitude to Itani, who had given her the opportunity to step forth in the role, she had forgotten how easily she tired and, with her usual confidence, had told herself that she could stand the trip. Finally the exhaustion had gotten the better of her, and she had seen her chance to confess. Be that as it might, a woman three or four months pregnant was very likely to attract the attention of the outsider, even though people who saw her every day noticed nothing, and it had taken great confidence indeed for her to go out nonchalantly to a dinner party and even to the theater, where great crowds of people would see her. And this was the most dangerous time of all. What had she meant to do if, shaken by the train ride, she had had a miscarriage? Koi-san herself would not have minded, but what of the confusion and the shame for Sachiko and Yukiko? Sachiko's heart went cold at the very thought of such a possibility. Someone must have noticed Taeko, perhaps at Itani's party, and without their even knowing it, they had already been disgraced.

There was nothing to do now; Sachiko had been made a fool of. Having kept the secret so long, however, could Koi-san not have chosen a more appropriate time and place to make her confession? Here Sachiko was, off on a trip, in a cluttered hotel room, thoroughly exhausted and wanting only to rest. Was it not cruel to choose such a time for a disclosure that might be said to have turned her world upside down? Koi-san was lucky that Sachiko had not fainted. What a complete lack of consideration, what thorough heartlessness! Pregnancy could not be concealed forever, and Sachiko was grateful to be told so soon, but what a moment Koi-san had chosen! A moment when Sachiko was quite defenseless, when, with the three of them in one small room in the dead of night, she could neither weep nor rage nor even run away. Was this the way to treat a sister who had done her best, small though it was, over the months and years? The slightest consideration should have made Koi-san endure the discomfort and wait until they were back in Ashiya. There, after a good rest, Sachiko would have been calmer. Sachiko asked little of her sister, but was it unreasonable to ask this much?

She heard the early streetcars and saw daylight through the opening in the curtain, and she was as wide awake as ever. She kept turning the problem over in her mind. Soon Koi-san's condition would be clear to everyone, and something would have to be done. What, then? They might move in darkness from one secret to another and tell no one, but it seemed, from Taeko's earlier remarks, that she would never agree. It might not be wholly impossible for someone to make her see the evil of her selfish ways, to make her agree, for the Makioka name and for Yukiko's future, to sacrifice the child, and it might not be impossible to force her into an abortion even against her will. But someone as weak-willed as Sachiko could not hope to move her sister. And there was another difficulty: until two or three years before, any doctor would have operated without hesitation. There were now strong social pressures to be considered, and even with Taeko's consent it would not be easy to carry the plan out. They would have to send Taeko away, and let her have the child in secret. She would be forbidden to see the man, and she would be under the strict supervision of the Makiokas, who would pay all expenses, and in the meantime Yukiko would be married. At the thought that she must tell her husband—she would have to have his help—Sachiko was wearier than ever. Much though her husband loved her and trusted her, could she tell of this new misstep without the deepest shame? As she thought how Teinosuke—only a brother-in-law, after all, and at that a brother-in-law in an entirely different position from Tatsuo—had looked after Yukiko and Taeko as a real brother might have, and how this devotion was, in the final analysis,—she knew she could be accused of conceit when she said so— a product of his affection for Sachiko herself, she felt both grateful and apologetic. Teinosuke too had been made unhappy, and Taeko's affairs had brought discord to their otherwise peaceful home. And now, just when he was feeling friendlier toward Taeko, and had allowed her back in the house—and when Sachiko herself was looking forward to taking home the present that would make him happiest of all, news of the successful *miai*—to have unpleasant news again! Being the man he was, Teinosuke would contrive not to add to the humiliation. He would seek to console his wife, but Sachiko would only be unhappier, knowing that he was restraining his own feelings.

The inescapable conclusion was that Sachiko would have to tell her husband and trust his tact and understanding. What upset her most was the thought that Yukiko might once again miss her chance. Always it was the same: negotiations would progress smoothly, and at the very last minute difficulties would arise. Even if they sent Taeko off to some mountain resort, would they be able to avoid notice? Might not Mimaki learn the truth? If, as their negotiations with Mimaki became more active, Taeko vanished from the scene, could they keep him from having suspicions, however they sought to cloud the issue? And might they not expect opposition from Okubata? He could hardly be angry with Sachiko and Yukiko and yet, in his chagrin, might he not consider the whole Makioka family his enemy? Not above having his revenge, he might take steps to let Mimaki know everything. Would it be better to tell the truth, and hope Mimaki would understand? He had said that Taeko's affairs were no concern of his, and a confession might be better than a clumsy attempt at concealment that would later be exposed. He might be surprisingly liberal when he heard. No, no. Mimaki himself would perhaps be indifferent to the ugliest facts about Taeko, but what of his friends and relatives? What of the Viscount and the Kunishimas? Could they help frowning upon the proposal once they knew the truth? The Viscount in particular—could he possibly consider an alliance with a family that had produced such a woman?

Again, again, it would come to nothing. Sad for Yukiko, but . . .

Sachiko heaved a sigh and turned over in bed. When she opened her eyes the room was bright. In the next bed, Taeko and Yukiko lay back to back, as when they were children. Yukiko, still asleep, faced Sachiko. Sachiko gazed on and on at the white face, and wondered what her sister was dreaming.

33

TEINOSUKE heard the news when his wife returned from Tokyo. The moment she saw his face, she knew she could no longer keep it to herself. (She had told Yukiko that morning, when Taeko was out of the room for a short time.) Calling him upstairs before dinner, she told him everything, from Yukiko's *miai* to Taeko's pregnancy.

"I wanted to bring back good news this time. And now I have to upset you again."

Sachiko was in tears, and Teinosuke sought to comfort her. It was a pity, he said, that the troublesome matter should have come up just when they were ready to congratulate Yukiko. Even so, he could not believe that because of it Yukiko's hopes would be destroyed. Sachiko need not trouble herself; she should leave everything to him. He wanted two or three days to deliberate. He said no more, and some days later he called her into his study. How would it be, he asked, if they did this:

No doubt Taeko was, as she said, three or four months pregnant. Still, the first thing was to have her see a specialist and learn exactly when the child would be born. They would then have to move her, and on the whole Arima Springs seemed most convenient. Since she was living in a room of her own, they could, for the time being, forbid the man Miyoshi to see her; and they would send her off to Arima Springs some night in a cab. It was not easy to decide who should attend her, but he thought they might send O-haru, after giving her very strict instructions. At Arima Springs they would not use the Makioka name. They would say that Taeko was a housewife away for her health. She would stay until her time approached, and she could have the child at Arima or, if there seemed no danger of having the news leak out, she could be moved to a hospital in Kobe. It would be necessary to have the consent of both Taeko and Miyoshi. Teinosuke would see them and persuade them to agree. He felt that Taeko must in the course of time marry the man, and he had no objections to the match himself. They could not let it be known, however, that without the consent of her family she had become pregnant, and for the time being the two should not see each other. Taking full responsibility for Taeko's safety, Teinosuke and his wife would see that the delivery went smoothly. Afterwards they would send Taeko and the child off to Miyoshi and do their best to win the approval of the main house. The marriage need not be postponed long, only until Yukiko's fate was decided one way or the other. In general, that was the plan he would present to the two. Taeko would stay out of sight, and everything possible would be done to keep the affair secret. According to Taeko, only Miyoshi, Okubata, and Taeko herself knew or had guessed the truth, and there were also Teinosuke and his wife and Yukiko, and it would be impossible to keep the news from O-haru and the other maids. But they should make absolutely sure that it spread no farther.

Because Sachiko was still worried about Okubata, Teinosuke said he would talk to the man. If Okubata decided that he did not mind sacrificing his own good name, said Sachiko, there was nothing he could not do. He might even resort to violence—to swordplay, so to speak—and he might give damaging information to the newspapers. Teinosuke laughed at these fears. She was imagining things. It was true that Okubata had a criminal streak in his nature, but he was nonetheless the pampered son of a good family, and he would not be capable of "swordplay." Whatever extravagant ideas he might have, his courage would in the end fail him. And had the Okubata family or the Makioka family ever approved of his relations with Taeko? He was in no position to make demands. Since Taeko had lost her affection for him, Teinosuke would say in the friendliest way, and since she had become pregnant by another man, there was nothing for him to do but break with her cleanly. Sad though it was, he would have to resign himself to the inevitable. He would surely understand, thought Teinosuke.

The next day Teinosuke went into action. He visited Taeko in her room, and Miyoshi in a Kobe rooming house. What sort of person was he, asked Sachiko. A young man who made a surprisingly good impression, said Teinosuke. They had talked for less than an hour, and Teinosuke had not been able to study

him in any detail, but on the whole he seemed more honest and
sincere than Itakura. Quite of his own accord he admitted his responsibility, and he apologized most politely. Teinosuke suspected
that Miyoshi had not taken the initiative, but had been seduced
by Taeko. Though it would seem cowardly of him to be making
excuses, said Miyoshi, and he should certainly have had more
will power, he hoped Teinosuke would understand that he had not
gone out aggressively after Koi-san, but had found himself in a
position from which he could not retreat, and so the mistake had
been made. If Teinosuke were to ask Koi-san, he would find that
Miyoshi was not lying. Teinosuke added that he believed the story.
The man accepted Teinosuke's proposal, and even seemed grateful. He was not qualified to take Koi-san for his bride, he said, but
if the Makiokas would agree to the marriage he could swear to
make her happy. Aware of his responsibilities, he had been wondering what to do if they should indeed give their consent, and
he had saved a little money. He meant to open a bar of his own,
even a tiny bar—a not-too-vulgar bar catering to foreigners. Koi-
san would go on with her sewing, and they would not be a burden to the Makioka family. All of this Miyoshi said, and Teinosuke
passed on to his wife.

The next day Taeko went to an obstetrics clinic in Kobe, and
learned that she was not yet five months pregnant and that the
child would be born early in April. Because she would soon be
attracting attention, she was sent off to Arima Springs with O-haru
one evening late in October. Sachiko purposely called a cab
from a stand some distance away, and had her sister change to
another cab in Kobe for the trip across the mountains. She gave
O-haru detailed instructions: Taeko was to be in Arima for several
months, under the name Abe; O-haru was to call her Mrs. Abe
and not Koi-san; for liaison a messenger would be sent from
Ashiya, or O-haru herself would come back, and no one was to use
the telephone; O-haru was to understand that Miyoshi and Taeko
were not to see each other and that Miyoshi was not to be told
where Taeko was staying; and O-haru was moreover to watch for
strange letters, or telephone calls or visitors. When she had finished,
Sachiko received a shock: she supposed it was all right to say now,
remarked O-haru, that they had known about Koi-san since before
the trip to Tokyo. How had they found out? O-teru had been the

first to suspect; there was something strange about Koi-san, she said. Might it not be that? Only the maids knew. They had told no one else.

Some time after Taeko left for Arima, Teinosuke came home to report that he had seen Okubata. He had heard that Okubata was living near the "Lone Pine" in Nishinomiya, but had not found him there. Someone in the neighborhood remembered that he had moved to a place called the Pinecrest Hotel. At the Pinecrest Hotel, Teinosuke was told that Okubata had been there for only a week and had moved on to the Eiraku Apartments. There Teinosuke finally found him. Although the talk did not go as smoothly as Teinosuke had hoped, the results were in general satisfactory. It was a disgrace to the Makioka name, Teinosuke began, to have so wanton a sister, and he could only sympathize with Okubata, whose great misfortune it was to have become entangled with her. Okubata at first seemed most agreeable. Where was Koi-san, then? Was O-haru with her? With a show of indifference, he probed for news of Taeko. He was not to ask, said Teinosuke—they had not even told Miyoshi. Okubata fell silent. Would it be unreasonable to expect him, continued Teinosuke, to take the view that Koi-san's whereabouts was no concern of his? With that, Okubata was openly annoyed. He had given up in any case, he said, but did they really mean to let her marry such a man? He had heard that the man was a bartender on some foreign steamer before he found his present job, and beyond that no one knew a thing about him. In Itakura's case they had at least known where his home was. Okubata could not remember having heard anything about Miyoshi's family. Who could guess, seeing that the man had been a sailor, what sort of past he had? They were most grateful for this kind advice, said Teinosuke, and they would give it careful attention. He must make bold to ask a favor: Okubata had every right to be angry with Koi-san, but her sisters had committed no crime, and might Teinosuke not ask, for the sake of the sisters and of the Makioka name, that he keep the matter of Taeko's pregnancy secret? If it should become known abroad, the most seriously injured would be Yukiko, for whom as he knew they had not yet found a husband. Would he agree, then, to tell no one? There was no cause for concern— Okubata seemed a little hesitant, but his answer was clear and

positive. Since he had no grudge, even against Koi-san, he had no
intention whatsoever of troubling the sisters.

There the matter seemed to rest, and Teinosuke, much relieved,
set out for his office in Osaka. Soon there was a call from Okubata.
Okubata had a favor of his own to ask, and he would like to call
on Teinosuke. Almost immediately he was in the waiting room.
He fidgeted for a time; then, his face suddenly doleful, he began
to speak. He knew that there was nothing for him to do but accept the facts that Teinosuke had described that morning, and
yet he hoped that Teinosuke would try to imagine the inexpress-
ible sorrow of losing one's love of ten years. And that was not all:
as Teinosuke perhaps knew, it was because of Koi-san that he had
been turned out by his family, and, as Teinosuke had seen, he had
given up his pretty house in Nishinomiya and moved into a
shabby room, where he lived all by himself. If he was now to be
cast out by Koi-san, he had literally no one on earth he could call
a friend. All of this he said with tragic intensity. Then he broke
into a half-smile. He was rather troubled for money, embarrassing
though it was to make that admission, and—this really would be
very hard to say—he had in the past been of some service to Koi-
san, and he wondered if he might have the money returned to
him. Not that he had meant at the time for her to pay it back—at
this point even Okubata flushed a little—and if he had not been
so hard pressed he would never have thought of asking for it now.
He should of course be paid back all the money he had lent Koi-
san, said Teinosuke. How much had it been? He hardly knew,
answered Okubata, and if Teinosuke were to ask Koi-san—but
suppose they say two thousand yen. Teinosuke thought he might
indeed ask Koi-san. He concluded, however, that two thousand
yen was not a high price for silencing Okubata and warding off
future trouble. Suppose I pay you now, he said, and wrote out a
check. And you will remember your promise, of course—we will
be most grateful if you say nothing about Koi-san's condition.
Okubata replied that he understood, and that they need fear
nothing from him, and left. And so it seemed that Taeko's affairs
were at last under control.

In the midst of this excitement, a letter came from Itani's daughter Mitsuyo. After thanking the three sisters for coming so far to
the farewell party, Mitsuyo reported that her mother had sailed

in the best of spirits, that Mimaki planned to go to Osaka about the middle of November, that, since he meant to visit Ashiya, she hoped Teinosuke would find time to inspect him, and that Mr. and Mrs. Kunishima sent their warmest regards.

About a week later, a note came from Tsuruko. Tsuruko wrote only when there was something important on her mind, and Sachiko wondered what it would be now, but, strangely, the note was a random assortment of inconsequentialities:

November 5

DEAR SACHIKO,

I hoped to have a good talk with you for a change, and I am sorry you were in such a hurry. I know you enjoyed the Kabuki. Take me with you next time.

What has happened to Mr. Mimaki? It has seemed too early to say anything to Tatsuo, but I do hope everything goes well. Though there can hardly be any need to investigate a man from such a good family, we will do whatever you suggest. I always feel guilty about leaving the hard work to you and Teinosuke.

With the children growing up, I find I have time to write letters for a change, and now and then I practice my calligraphy. Are you and Yukiko still taking lessons? I am rather hard up for a practice book, though, and I am wondering if you have an old one you could send me. I would be especially grateful for one with the teacher's notes in it.

And while I am begging, I wonder if you would mind sending underclothes you no longer need. I can always find a way to use things you might not want yourself, and I would be grateful for clothes you are thinking of throwing away or giving to the maids. And Yukiko and Koi-san too—underclothes, bloomers, whatever you have. I have more spare time as the children grow up, but they take more and more money. I have to pile economy on economy. It is not easy to be poor, and I often wonder when life will be more comfortable.

Somehow I wanted to write today, but I see I am complaining. I had best stop. I will be waiting for good news about Yukiko. My regards to Teinosuke, Etsuko, and Yukiko.

As always,

TSURUKO

As she read the letter, Sachiko thought of the tears streaming down Tsuruko's face outside the cab window. Probably Tsuruko *had* felt like writing, and then she had things to ask for; but it seemed too that she had not forgotten the theater party. Perhaps she was subtly making known her resentment at having been left out. Tsuruko's letters in the past had been in the nature of magisterial pronouncements, and Sachiko was always impressed at how this sister, so gentle when one was talking to her, had to censure one or another of them whenever she took up her writing brush. It was odd that she should now be writing this sort of letter. Sachiko immediately sent off a package to Tokyo, but she did not answer the letter for a time.

Mrs. Hening's daughter Friedl was to go to Berlin with her father, it appeared, and in mid-November Mrs. Hening called on Sachiko. Though Mrs. Hening had great misgivings about sending her daughter off to a Europe at war, Friedl, intent on studying the dance, quite refused to listen, and Mrs. Hening had finally given up when her husband said that he would take the girl if she was so set on going. They had found traveling companions, and there seemed nothing to worry about on the road at least. The father and daughter would be visiting the Stolz family in Hamburg. They would be glad to pass on any messages. Sachiko had had Mrs. Hening write a letter in German and had sent it to Hamburg with a dancing fan and a piece of white silk, and she was uneasy that there had been no reply. This would be her chance to send something more. She would be around with a gift for the Stolzes before the daughter sailed, she replied. Some days later she selected a pearl ring for Rosemarie and delivered it to the Hening house with a letter for Mrs. Stolz.

As Mitsuyo had led them to expect, one evening toward the twentieth there was a call from Mimaki, who was at the Viscount's house in Saga. He had come from Tokyo the day before, he said, and he meant to stay two or three days. He would like if possible to visit them and meet Teinosuke. Any evening, at his convenience, answered Sachiko. He suggested the next evening, and appeared at about four. Teinosuke, who had come home early, talked with him for the better part of an hour, and afterwards the two went with Sachiko, Etsuko, and Yukiko to the Oriental Hotel for dinner. Mimaki was much as he had been in Tokyo,

open, expansive, and witty—in general an easy man to talk to.
He drank even more than before, refilling his whiskey glass time
after time. His drollery was inexhaustible. Etsuko was more delighted than anyone, and took his hand as they walked to the
station. He would make a good husband for Yukiko, she whispered
to her mother. And what had Teinosuke thought of him? He had
certainly not disliked the man, Teinosuke answered after a moment's thought. Indeed the first impression had been entirely
favorable. The man was most engaging. But genial, polished gentlemen could often be difficult, and it was their wives who suffered. The type of which he was thinking was particularly common among pampered sons of the aristocracy. It would not do to
fall recklessly in love with the man. In short, Teinosuke was
cautious. He did not think it necessary to investigate the family,
but it might be well to investigate the man himself—his character,
his behavior, the reasons why he had not married sooner.

34

AWARE THAT HE was being tested, Mimaki did not mention the
marriage proposal. He talked about many other things: architecture and painting, the old gardens and temples of Kyoto, the
grounds of the Viscount's mansion, foreign food, liquor,
stories his father had heard from his grandfather about the Emperor Meiji and the Dowager Empress Shōken. On a Sunday
morning some ten days later, Mitsuyo suddenly appeared. She had
business in Osaka, and she had been asked by Mr. Kunishima and
by Mimaki himself to see whether Mimaki had "passed the test."
Sachiko answered that upon Teinosuke's suggestion they were
investigating the man. Teinosuke planned a trip to Tokyo in
December, at which time he would talk to the people in the main
house, and call on the Kunishimas. And on what points were they
in doubt, asked Mitsuyo, as aggressive as her mother. There was
no one she saw oftener than Mimaki, and since she knew all his
merits and faults, Sachiko could ask whatever questions came to

her. Unable to manage the girl by herself, Sachiko summoned Teinosuke. Mitsuyo's manner invited questions, and Teinosuke was quite unreserved. These facts became clear: though Mimaki was on the surface a very polished gentleman, he was surprisingly touchy, and sometimes very irritable; his relations with his half-brother, the Viscount's heir, were particularly bad and they often quarreled; Mitsuyo could not claim to have witnessed such violence, but it was said that he had even struck the half-brother; he was too fond of his liquor, and drink sometimes made him pugnacious; now that he was older, however, he rarely drank too much; and because he had lived in America and was exceedingly polite to women, Mitsuyo could assure them that, however drunk, he never raised his hand against a woman. Without being asked, Mitsuyo volunteered another fault or two: though the man was extremely knowledgeable, he had not been able to pursue any one thing to the end; he was fond of entertaining people and otherwise doing favors, and good at spending money, but unfortunately he was not much of a hand at making money. Teinosuke replied that he could guess, from all he had heard, what sort of man Mimaki was. To be quite frank, he was worried about money: how would the couple live after they were married? He hoped she would forgive him for saying so, but the man seemed to have lived as he pleased on money he begged from his father. He had done nothing for himself. Teinosuke could not help being uneasy, then, as he asked himself whether even with Mr. Kunishima's backing Mimaki would be a success as an architect. There was no place these days for the sort of architect Mimaki hoped to become, and it seemed unlikely that conditions would improve in say the next three or four years. How would they live in the meantime? Through the good offices of Mr. Kunishima, he understood, the Viscount would help them for a time, but they could hardly expect him to go on helping them indefinitely. The crisis might last five or six or even ten years. Or perhaps they would in fact be dependent on the Viscount to the end, and that prospect was far from pleasant. He knew he was sounding a little petulant, but to be quite frank the Makiokas were interested in the proposal and had almost decided that they would ask Mimaki to marry Yukiko. In any case, Teinosuke meant to go to Tokyo the following month, and he could discuss the problem with Mr.

Kunishima then. She understood, said Mitsuyo, and she thought it quite right of Teinosuke to have these misgivings. Since she could not give him an answer herself, she would tell Mr. Kunishima everything and see if Mimaki's future could not be guaranteed to the satisfaction of the Makioka family. And she would be waiting for the visit in December. She had to take the evening train to Tokyo, she said, declining Sachiko's invitation to stay for dinner.

Early in December, Sachiko and Yukiko bought an amulet at the Kiyomizu Temple in Kyoto. As if by prearrangement, Miyoshi sent an amulet from the Nakayama Temple to Teinosuke's office, with instructions that it was to be delivered to Taeko. The two amulets were entrusted to O-haru, who came to Ashiya at just the right time and brought Sachiko and the others their first word of Taeko in a very long while: except for a morning walk she stayed quietly in her room; when she went out she avoided the main part of town and chose mountain paths where she was not likely to meet anyone; in her room she read novels, or worked again at the dolls she had once given up, or made clothes for the baby. There had been no suspicious calls, and not a single letter.

"I saw Mr. Kyrilenko today," said O-haru.

Kyrilenko was standing at the gate when she got off the train in Kobe. He remembered her and smiled, though she had met him no more than once or twice, and she nodded back. Was she alone, he asked. She was—she had just been up to Bluebell Hill. And how were all the Makiokas, and what had happened to Taeko? They were all very well—O-haru thanked him for asking. He must apologize for his remissness, he continued. He hoped O-haru would pass on his regards. Adding that he was on his way to Arima, he started for the tracks. Had he heard from Katharina, asked O-haru. London seemed to be suffering terribly from German air raids, and they were worried about Katharina. That was very kind of them, he answered, but there was nothing to fear. Only the other day he had received a letter posted in September. Though her house in the suburbs was on the bombing route and every day and every night fleets of bombers flew over, Katharina herself found the war rather enjoyable. She had a deep and luxurious air-raid shelter, and they turned on the bright lights and put records on the phonograph, and danced and drank cocktails. As O-haru could see, there was nothing to worry about. How like Katharina, thought Sachiko. She was both amused and distressed, however: the talkative O-haru might have let the secret slip out. Did Kyrilenko say anything else about Koi-san? No, nothing more. You are quite sure, O-haru? You are sure you said nothing you did not have to say? And did it seem that he knew about Koi-san? Not at all—O-haru was emphatic, and in the end Sachiko was satisfied. She sent O-haru back with careful instructions not to let anyone see her. It would be bad enough if she happened to be alone, but when she went out walking with Taeko she must heap precaution upon precaution to be sure that they were not seen. Who could know when they might run into someone?

December was nearly over. It was the twenty-second when Teinosuke set out on a business trip to Tokyo. Having made inquiries about Mimaki's character and behavior, and his relations with the Viscount and his half brothers, Teinosuke was by now sure that Mitsuyo had not lied to him, but on the problem of Mimaki's livelihood, not even the visit to Kunishima resulted in what he could call concrete guarantees. Kunishima had not yet seen the Viscount, and there was little he could say definitely, though he did think he could promise that the Viscount would buy the house and give Mimaki a certain amount of help for the time being, and that, to see that the money was not spent recklessly, he himself would take it in charge and give Mimaki a monthly allowance. And as for what was to happen later, might he not ask Teinosuke to have faith in him? He would see that Mimaki was never in serious financial trouble. He had great confidence in Mimaki's talents as an architect, and he would do everything possible when times were better to see that lost ground was recovered. Everyone had his own pet theories, of course, but Kunishima could not believe that the crisis would last much longer. Even if it did, Mimaki's friends should at least be able to piece together a livelihood for him. Kunishima said in effect that he stood behind Mimaki, whatever that fact might be worth. Teinosuke was shown through the Kunishima house, said to have been designed by Mimaki, but, knowing almost nothing about architecture, he could not really say how much talent it revealed. But if so well-placed a man as Kunishima was prepared to guarantee the man's future, there was nothing to do but trust him. It was clear, moreover, that Sachiko was even more enthusiastic about the proposal than Kunishima himself. There could be no doubt that she found Mimaki most engaging and that, though she had not actually said so, she was delighted at the prospect of an alliance with a noble family, and Teinosuke could imagine her disappointment if he were to step in and break off the negotiations. He too was beginning to think that this was the very best match they could hope for. He would leave everything to Kunishima, then, he said, but since in the natural order of things he must have the permission of the main house, and he ought to make very sure how Yukiko felt—he knew that she would have no objections—he hoped Kunishima would wait a little longer before telling Mimaki that they meant to accept his proposal. He would send his answer (the merest formality) early in the New Year. Kunishima might for practical purposes consider the negotiations concluded today. Kunishima answered that he would call upon Viscount Mimaki when he had Teinosuke's formal answer. Teinosuke went directly from 'Kunishima's to the Shibuya house, told Tsuruko in detail of the talks, and asked her to tell him about Tatsuo's views as soon as possible.

On January 3, Mitsuyo again appeared in Ashiya. She was spending the holidays with her uncle in Okamoto, and she had been asked by Mr. Kunishima to deliver a message. Kunishima, who had come to Osaka the day before on business, was now at the Miyako Hotel in Kyoto. He hoped that he might have the promised answer before his return to Tokyo. He would then call upon the Viscount and ask him to invite the Makioka family to Saga. Mitsuyo was to visit Ashiya and if possible to give Kunishima an answer the following day. The Makiokas might think Mr. Kunishima a little hasty, said Mitsuyo, but he seemed to feel that the permission of the main house and the assent of Yukiko herself were only formalities. Perhaps Mitsuyo could have her answer that very day. Though Teinosuke had, it was true, promised an answer early in the New Year, he had not thought of taking action before the holidays were over, and he had not yet had word from Tokyo. But Tsuruko had seemed thoroughly delighted at the news—so Yukiko was finally to be married, and to a member of such a fine family—the Makiokas were rising in the world—no one could look down on Tatsuo now—

and all because of Teinosuke. The years of waiting had not been
in vain. Sure that Tatsuo would have no objections at this late
date and that the answer had been delayed only by year-end
business, Teinosuke decided to act on his own initiative. But
he did have to talk to Yukiko. Yukiko's feelings were not hard
to read, and yet she might be hurt if it seemed that she was
being ignored. With many apologies, then, Teinosuke said that
he would call Tokyo for Tatsuo's views, and that he would have
to trouble Mitsuyo to come again the following day. They would
have an answer for her by then. The "telephone call to Tokyo" was
only an excuse. Still, because he did have time, it seemed a
good idea to call. Tsuruko came to the telephone and said that
Tatsuo was out making New Year calls. Had he sent off his
answer, asked Teinosuke. She thought not, what with the year-end
confusion and all, but she had told him Teinosuke's story in
the greatest detail. And what had he said? Well—Tsuruko hesitated—there was no possible fault to find with the man's family,
but Tatsuo was worried about the fact that he did not have
regular work. Tsuruko had replied that they could no longer
worry about such trivialities, and Tatsuo, having admitted that
she was right, seemed now to approve of the match. Mr. Kunishima's messenger was waiting, said Teinosuke, and he would
answer that there were no objections from Tokyo. But to make
quite sure that the negotiations went smoothly, Tsuruko should
have Tatsuo send off his formal permission with the greatest
possible haste.

Confident that Yukiko would be satisfied if they but made a
show of respecting her wishes, Teinosuke and Sachiko spoke to
her that evening. Her answer did not come as easily as they
had hoped. She wanted to know how much time she was being
given to consider the proposal. Mitsuyo would be coming again
the next morning, said Teinosuke. Yukiko frowned. He meant
that she was ordered to give her answer overnight? But it had
seemed clear, said Sachiko, that Yukiko was not displeased with
the man. Yukiko replied that she meant to marry whomever
Teinosuke and Sachiko told her to marry, but she thought a
person ought to be allowed two or three days' thought about
what was after all her whole future. They knew even so that
her mind was made up, and the next morning they at length

extracted her assent. She gave it only because Teinosuke had ordered her to make up her mind overnight, she announced peevishly. She took care not to show the slightest pleasure, and above all not to let slip a word of thanks to those who had worked so hard for her.

35

MITSUYO came for her answer on the morning of the fourth, and called again on the evening of the sixth. She had expected to leave for Tokyo after telephoning her reply to the Miyako Hotel on the fourth, she said, but Kunishima had ordered her to put off her return. She would have to act as go-between in her mother's place. She was now able to report that Kunishima's talk with Viscount Mimaki had gone splendidly, and that the Viscount would like to have Yukiko and her family come to Saga, if possible at three o'clock on the afternoon of the eighth. The Viscount himself would be present, and Mimaki, who would come from Tokyo, and Kunishima and Mitsuyo, and probably two or three Mimaki relatives from the Kyoto-Osaka region. Kunishima was most apologetic for rushing them so, said Mitsuyo, but, busy as he was, he hoped to arrange everything immediately. Viscount Mimaki would like to have Etsuko and Koi-san come too, if they were free. Unfortunately the main house would not approve of Koi-san's being present, answered Sachiko. It was decided that Etsuko would come home early from school, and that the four of them would go to Saga.

They changed trains at the Katsura Palace, and at Storm Hill they crossed the river by a footbridge. This was a district they knew well from their annual cherry-viewing expeditions, but now, in the dead of winter—and the Kyoto winter is harsh—even the color of the water made them shiver. Walking west along the river to the wharf from which excursion boats leave, they turned in toward the Temple of the Heavenly Dragon and soon came upon the sign they had been told to look for: "Hermitage of the Sounding Rains." The house, one-storeyed and thatched in the classical manner, did not seem especially large, but the garden, with Storm Hill in the background, was magnificent. When Kunishima had finished the introductions, Mimaki suggested that they go for a stroll about the grounds. His father would be pleased, and, cold though it was, there was no wind. His father, he said, was especially proud of the fact that the garden seemed to give directly on Storm Hill. One would never guess that a road and a river lay between. Even in spring, when cherry-viewers came in such crowds, the place was as secluded as a mountain hermitage. One wondered where the noise could possibly be coming from. The Viscount had purposely refrained from planting cherry trees. He preferred to enjoy the distant cloud of blossoms up the side of Storm Hill. They must see it themselves this year, said Mimaki. They could have lunch here and look out at the hill. His father would be thoroughly delighted. Presently they were called in for tea, served by a lady who appeared to be Mimaki's sister, and who had married into a wealthy Osaka family. It was growing dark when they moved on to the dining room. The food had been prepared with the utmost care—it would be from a well-known caterer, thought Sachiko, who knew all about Kyoto food. The old Viscount, with his long, thin face and an ivory skin that reminded one of a Nō actor, was exactly what a nobleman should be. His swarthy, full-faced son seemed not to resemble him at all, and yet, upon looking closely, one could see a trace of a resemblance about the eyes and the nose. Their dispositions were more completely opposed than their faces. The son was gay and lively, the father stern and withdrawn, the true "Kyoto gentleman." The Viscount was worried about catching cold. Apologizing for his rudeness, he wore a gray silk muffler through dinner and sat on an electric pad with an electric stove at his back. Well preserved for his more than seventy years, he spoke from time to time with quiet dignity, and it seemed that he was at some pains to be cordial to both Kunishima and the Makiokas. At first the party was rather stiff. As the saké began to have its effect, Mimaki, beside his father, brought their two faces up for discussion. It was said that they did not look in the least alike, and he wondered what the opinion of this audience might be. There was some laughter, and everyone felt a little

more at ease. Teinosuke exchanged cups with the Viscount, as
courtesy demanded, and moved on to exchange cups with Kunishima. Meanwhile Mitsuyo, in foreign dress, sat shivering, her
legs and feet next to naked. (Of the others, only Etsuko was
not in kimono.) Today, for a change, she was quiet and respectful.
Isn't Mitsuyo behaving like a lady—Mimaki pressed saké on her.
Protesting all the while that today at least he was not to tease
her, Mitsuyo was soon a little drunk and talking as fast as ever.
He could offer no white wine, but he knew how well they drank,
said Mimaki, pouring saké for Sachiko and Yukiko. Neither
refused. Yukiko managed to have her share and still be poised
and proper. Though she smiled and said nothing, Sachiko saw
in her eyes an excitement not usually to be detected there.
Mimaki occasionally spoke to Etsuko, who seemed lost among
all the adults. As a matter of fact, she was far from bored. She
was a high-strung child, but at such times she would be turning
an innocent gaze on the adults around her and studying in
detail their gestures, speech, and expressions, and their clothes
down to the smallest accessory.

Dinner was over at eight. The Makiokas were the first to
take their leave, and the Viscount called a cab to see them to
Kyoto Station. Perhaps she would go too, then, said Mitsuyo,
who was returning to her uncle's, and Mimaki climbed in beside
the driver and insisted on seeing them to the station. In great
good spirits, he talked on and on and puffed away at a cigar.
Etsuko had already accepted him as an uncle. His name was
Mimaki and hers was Makioka—funny that both names should
have the syllables "maki" in them. Very clever of her to notice—
Mimaki was delighted. What more proof did they need that
there was a bond between Etsuko's family and his? And, put
in Mitsuyo, Yukiko would not have to change the initials on her
baggage. Yukiko laughed with the rest.

The next day Kunishima telephoned from Kyoto. The party
had been a complete success, and he could not tell them how
pleased he was that both families were satisfied. He would be
returning to Tokyo that night with Mr. Mimaki, and they would
soon be making arrangements through Miss Itani for the formal
betrothal. The Viscount had said the evening before that the
Sonomura family, into which his daughter had married, was pre-

pared to sell him a house near Osaka for the bride and groom. Everything was as the Makiokas had hoped, then—Mimaki would be working in Osaka or Kobe, and Yukiko would be near Ashiya. Though the house was at the moment rented out, the Sonomuras would take steps to have it vacated.

Teinosuke was disturbed that he still had no answer from the main house. Possibly Tatsuo did not approve of the proposed marriage. Or might there be other reasons for the delay? After some days he sent off a letter. No doubt Tatsuo had heard all the details from Tsuruko, he began. The fact was that Teinosuke himself did not consider the match ideal, but, since they were in a weak position and could expect nothing better for the time being, it had seemed to him that he must leave everything to Mr. Kunishima. The Ashiya family had gone to Saga and met the Viscount (Teinosuke believed he had said over the telephone that they might soon be meeting him) and was now ready to consider plans for a formal betrothal. It worried Teinosuke to think that Tatsuo might be offended at having been left out of the negotiations. Though it was too late now, what he really must apologize for was a matter left over from the year before—no, from even longer: he had been unable to send Yukiko back to Tokyo in spite of repeated hints from the main house. He had not meant to cross Tatsuo—the problem had been a constant worry to him—but there were all sorts of reasons. In brief, Yukiko hated being in Tokyo and Sachiko seemed to sympathize with her, and, short of very strong measures, it would have been impossible to carry out Tatsuo's instructions. Even so, the final responsibility was Teinosuke's, and because he felt it so keenly he had been determined to do what he could to find Yukiko a husband. Was it not natural that Tatsuo himself could do little for a sister who went against his orders, and did it not follow that responsibility for looking after her lay with Teinosuke? If Tatsuo accused him of meddling, he would have no answer. These had long been his views, however, and if he could but have Tatsuo's consent to the match, he thought he should take care of the wedding expenses himself. But he must make it quite clear that he did not mean to have Yukiko marry from his house. She belonged to the main house. What he had said was entirely confidential, and all the forms would be observed: Yukiko would go forth as the daughter of the main Makioka family. He would be most grateful, then, if he might have Tatsuo's consent. He had not expressed himself well, but he hoped Tatsuo would understand his motives and give him an answer soon. Though he hated to seem importunate, there really was very little time left.

Tatsuo apparently understood. Four or five days later a most agreeable answer came. He thanked Teinosuke for his letter, and he was delighted with all the arrangements. He had through the years grown away from his sisters-in-law, and, though it had never been his intention to abandon them, he had done little for them. He could only apologize for having let them become a burden to Teinosuke—they were so fond of Teinosuke and Sachiko. There had been no particular reason for the delay in his answer. It worried him that Teinosuke should time after time be inconvenienced, however, and he had not known what to say. He had never thought of blaming Teinosuke for not sending Yukiko back, and he certainly did not think it Teinosuke's responsibility to pay the wedding expenses. If anyone was to blame for anything, it was Tatsuo himself, but what good would it do to go blaming people at this late date? Since Mimaki came from such an illustrious a family, since so eminent a person as Kunishima was willing to act as intermediary, and since Teinosuke himself was enthusiastic, Tatsuo did not think it his place to raise objections. He would leave everything to Teinosuke. He hoped Teinosuke would proceed with arrangements for the betrothal. As for the wedding expenses, he meant to do what he could, but, because Teinosuke's kind offer came at a time when he was rather hard pressed, he thought he might ask Teinosuke for help, provided of course that the latter did not think it his duty to help. They could discuss the details when they met.

Teinosuke was much relieved. Now he had only Taeko to worry about. Not trusting Okubata in spite of those promises, he wanted to hurry through at least the formal betrothal. Unfortunately there would have to be a delay: Mrs. Kunishima was seriously ill, Mitsuyo reported. A severe cold had turned into pneumonia. There was also a very polite letter of explanation from Kunishima. The Viscount had bought the house, and the deed had been turned over to Mimaki—this last fact they learned from Mimaki himself. Though the tenants had not yet moved, they would move very shortly. Mimaki hoped, when the house was vacant, to have a look at it, and he hoped too that Sachiko and Yukiko would join him. His father had offered to send a maid who would stay on after the wedding.

Mrs. Kunishima's condition was critical for a time, but by the end of February she was out of bed and off for a two-week change of air. She had worried over the betrothal and even talked of it in her delirium, said Mitsuyo, who in mid-March appeared in Ashiya to discuss plans for the ceremony. There was, first of all, the question of whether the betrothal and the wedding should be in Kyoto or in Tokyo. It was Kunishima's view that, since the Viscount's main house was in Tokyo and since the main Makioka family was living in Tokyo, both ceremonies should take place there, the betrothal if possible on March 25, the wedding in mid-April. Teinosuke, who had no objections, telephoned the news to Tsuruko. The main house was thrown into consternation: the children had made the place a pigpen, and doors had to be repaired and floors refinished and walls replastered.

Sachiko again had misgivings about Tokyo. She could think of no reason to object, however, and on March 23 she left with Yukiko. Teinosuke had to stay behind on business. The betrothal ceremony took place two days later, and Kunishima sent off a cable to Itani in Los Angeles. Leaving Yukiko to take her leave of the main house, Sachiko returned to Ashiya alone on the morning of the twenty-seventh. It was about noon, and both Etsuko and Teinosuke were out. In the bedroom she found two letters, already opened, that had come by Trans-Siberian Railroad. Beside them were several pages of Japanese and a pencilled note from Teinosuke: "We were surprised by letters from Mrs. Stolz and the Hening girl. Etsuko was in a great hurry and I opened them. Mrs. Stolz's is in German. I had a friend in Osaka translate it."

36

DEAR MRS. MAKIOKA,

I *have been telling myself for a great while that I should
write you a good, long letter. We often think of you and dear
Etsuko. She must be a big girl by now. Unfortunately I hardly
have time to lift a pen. As you know, there is a shortage of
manpower in Germany, and it is very difficult to find a maid.
Since last May we have had a girl who comes in three morning
a week to clean, and beyond that the lady of the house does
everything for herself: cooking, buying, sewing, mending, and so
on. Once I had time to write letters in the evening. Now I must
get out a basket of stockings, all with big holes and little holes in
them. In the old days I would have thrown away worn-out
stockings, but now we must economize. We must work together
to win through, and each of us must do his part, however small
it may be. I understand that life is harder in Japan too. A friend
from Japan was here on vacation not long ago, and he told us
about all the changes. But we must bear the burden. We are
both young nations fighting our way up, and it is not easy to
win a place in the sun. And yet I do believe that we will win
in the end.*

*I was delighted and deeply grateful that you wrote your
letter of last June in German. I suppose you can have some good
friend translate this for you, and I hope he can read my writing;
perhaps next time I can use a typewriter. It is too bad that the
silk and fan never arrived, but my Rosemarie was overjoyed when
she received the beautiful ring. We had a letter from Miss Hening
saying that she had the ring, but that she did not know when she
would be able to visit Hamburg. The other day a friend brought
it back from Berlin. It is lovely. In Rosemarie's place, I want to
tell you how very grateful we are. We are not letting her wear
it for the time being, however. We mean to keep it until she*

is a little older. A person we knew in Japan is going back in April, and we will send something with him for Etsuko. It will be the merest trifle, but each of the girls will have something to wear in memory of their friendship. When we win our victory and everything is normal again, you can visit Germany. I am sure that Etsuko will want to know the new Germany. It would be a very great pleasure to have you as honored guests in our house.

You will want to hear about the children. They are as healthy as ever. Peter has been in Upper Bavaria with his class since November, and seems to like it very much. Rosemarie has been taking piano lessons since October. She is very good. Fritz plays the violin, and he is now the largest of the children. He is a very entertaining lad. He too is in school, and doing very well. During his first year he thought of it half as a game, but now he has learned to take it seriously. The children all have to help in the house. Each has his own little job. Fritz must polish the shoes every night and Rosemarie must dry the dishes and polish the silver. They are all doing their very best. Just today I had a long letter from Peter, and it seems that there is polishing and mending in his camp too, and that each of the boys must take care of his own clothes and socks. Young people need that sort of training. But I am afraid that when he comes home he will leave everything to Mother again. My husband has taken over an import house and seems to be at home in the new work. He imports from Japan and China, though there are all sorts of war-time restrictions. This has been a long winter, but not as cold as last year. There are few sunny days here—the sun has hardly shown its face since November. But soon it will be spring. How warm it always was in Japan! We often long for that pleasant climate.

It will be a great delight to hear from you again. Tell me everything you are doing. How sad that we are not allowed to send photographs. Rosemarie will soon be writing to Etsuko. On week days she has a heavy load of homework, and letter writing must wait until Sunday. I believe Peter will write from Bavaria. They seem to be enjoying nature there, and they spend little time indoors. That is very fine. Here in the city we all live in caves.

Give Etsuko our love, and especially the children's. And

*please, Mrs. Makioka, accept assurances of my warmest regards
for you and your husband. Thank you for continuing to think
of us.*

Sincerely yours,
HILDA STOLZ

The letter from the Hening girl was in English, so simple
that even Sachiko could puzzle it out.

Berlin
February 2, 1941

DEAR MRS. MAKIOKA,

*Please forgive me for not having written sooner. I was
busy finding a place to live, and I had absolutely no time to
write. We have finally moved in with an old gentleman we know.
We were friendly with his son in Japan. He is sixty-three years
old, all by himself in a big apartment, and, being very lonely,
he said he thought we might want to live with him. And so we
moved in, and we are very happy.*

*We reached Germany on January 5, after a long but
pleasant trip. The quarantine in Russia was not pleasant, but
I am sure that the Russians were doing their best. The food was
very bad. Every day we had black bread, cheese, butter, and a
vegetable soup called borsch. We spent our time playing cards
and chess, and on Christmas Eve we lit candles and ate our
usual bread and butter. You cannot imagine how I longed for
Japan and my mother and brothers. Finally the six days were
over, and we were taken to our train. Father and I had a large
new seat all to ourselves. In the next seat were some boys from
the Hitlerjugend on their way back from Japan. We had many
interesting things to talk about and forgot what a long trip it was.*

*Here in Berlin, we hardly feel that there is a war on.
The restaurants and theaters are full, and there is plenty of good
food. When we go to a hotel or restaurant, there is usually more
food than we can eat. The change in climate has given me a
great appetite, and I am in danger of getting fat. We have been
surprised only at the great number of soldiers in the streets. How
handsome they all are in their uniforms!*

This month I started Russian ballet at a school only ten

*minutes from where we live. The teacher studied in Petersburg
and is very kind. She is always giving recitals. I practice from
eleven in the morning to twelve-thirty, and from three to four-
thirty in the afternoon. I hope I shall make much progress. Her
older and more talented pupils have just come back from a good-
will mission to Romania, and soon they will be going to Poland.
I hope that in two or three years I shall be a member of the
troupe myself.*

*I was able to have the ring delivered to Rosemarie. I
was afraid to mail it, and two or three days ago a friend of
Father's came from Hamburg, and I asked him to take it back
with him. Today I had a card from Mrs. Stolz saying that they
had received it, and that Rosemarie was most grateful. I enclose
the card.*

*It has been very cold, but from now on it will be warmer,
they say. In January it went down to zero. You can imagine how
we suffered. We have steam heat, however, and it is pleasant
and warm indoors. German houses have double windows and are
far better built than Japanese houses. We are not bothered by
wind through the cracks!*

It is time for my practice, and I must close. Please write.

Sincerely,

FRIEDL HENING

In the envelope was a card from Mrs. Stolz saying that the
ring had arrived.

37

YUKIKO was in Tokyo until the end of March. She could have
stayed on until her wedding day, but she wanted a leisurely
farewell to Sachiko and the Ashiya family. She slipped away
toward the end of the month, bringing word from Kunishima
that the wedding had been set for April 29, the Emperor's

birthday; that it would be in the Imperial Hotel; and that Viscount Mimaki, too old to make the trip, would probably be represented by his heir and the latter's wife. Though the Mimakis wanted to avoid ostentation, the reception at least was to be in keeping with their high position. Besides friends and relatives from Tokyo, there would be many guests from the Osaka-Kobe region. It was but natural, then, that all the Makiokas from Osaka, and Tatsuo's family from Nagoya, and even his sister, Mrs. Sugano, from Ogaki, should also be present. The reception would be a most elaborate one for the times. Mimaki, in Osaka for a visit, invited Sachiko and Yukiko to go with him for a look at his house. It was a fairly new one-storey house some blocks north of the electric line, just the right size for a married couple with one maid. What particularly pleased them was the large garden. After discussing the furniture and decorations, Mimaki described his plans for the honeymoon: they would spend the wedding night in the Imperial Hotel and leave the next morning for Kyoto; they would stay in Kyoto only long enough to pay their respects to his father; and, going on to Nara, they would spend two or three days enjoying spring in Yamato.[1] But if Yukiko thought she already knew Yamato well enough, they could choose a place near Tokyo. Sachiko knew Yukiko's answer without asking: Yukiko had had enough of the east-country; Mimaki should take her to Nara. Near though they were, they knew little of the Yamato ruins and monuments. Yukiko had never seen the wall paintings at the Hōryūji Temple, for instance. Sachiko remembered those bedbugs, and would have recommended a Japanese inn if Mimaki had not made the suggestion first. Mimaki also told them that Kunishima had found him a job in the East Asia Aircraft Corporation, which had a factory near Osaka; that his diploma in aeronautics had been his chief recommendation; that he was a little worried because he had done no work in aeronautics since his graduation; and that he was even more uneasy at having been offered a rather high salary, again thanks to Kunishima. To see his way through these difficult times, however, he meant to hang on. He would go to work as soon as he returned from the

[1] The present Nara Prefecture. Yamato was the center of Japanese culture until the late eighth century.

honeymoon, and he would study traditional architecture in his spare time and one day re-establish himself as an architect.

When he asked about Koi-san Sachiko started up in alarm. She managed to answer with a show of indifference that Koi-san was not in at the moment, but that she was well. Whether or not he knew the truth, he asked no more. He stayed but half a day. Taeko had come in from Arima with O-haru, and was in a Kobe maternity hospital. Afraid of attracting attention, Sachiko had not gone to the hospital, and had not once telephoned to ask how her sister was. Late one evening a day or so after Taeko entered the hospital, O-haru suddenly appeared. The child was in an abnormal head-up position, she reported. The chief obstetrician said that the position had definitely been normal when Taeko left for Arima. Possibly the automobile trip over the mountains had done the damage. Had he known sooner he might have corrected it, but now, with the birth so near, the child had settled into the pelvic basin and there was nothing to be done. He added, however, that they were not to worry. He would guarantee a safe delivery. There appeared to be little cause for alarm, said O-haru, who returned to the hospital after telling her news. Sachiko had no word through early April, when the child should have been born—first births are often late. Time passed; the cherry blossoms were beginning to fall. With Yukiko to be married in another fortnight or so, they regretted the passing of each busy spring day. They considered the possibility of a special celebration by which to remember these last days, but celebrations were harder and harder to arrange. Caught by the austerity edicts, they were unable to have new wedding kimonos dyed, and finally had to have the Kozuchiya hunt up old ones. That month rice rationing began. Kikugorō was not making his usual spring visit to Osaka, and they had to be satisfied with an even quieter cherry viewing than the year before. But it was an annual rite, and summoning up their determination and taking care to dress as unobtrusively as possibly, they made a one-day trip to Kyoto on Sunday the thirteenth. After a look at the weeping cherries in the Heian Shrine, they rushed out to the western suburbs and went through the form of seeing the cherries there. This year they did without their party at the Gourd Restaurant. Taeko again was missing. The four of them spread a sad little lunch by Ōzawa Pond and had a rather solemn drink of cold saké from the lacquer cups, and when the excursion was over they hardly knew what they had seen.

A day later Bell had kittens. Already eleven or twelve years old, Bell had had trouble the year before, and the veterinary had given her injections to induce labor pains. This year again she had been trying all night to have her kittens. Making a nest in a downstairs closet, Sachiko called the veterinary. When, with great difficulty, a head appeared, Yukiko and Sachiko took turns tugging at it. They said nothing, but they were doing their best for Bell to bring good luck to Taeko. From time to time Etsuko, pretending to be on her way to the bathroom, would peer in at them. Go away, they would say; it was no place for a child. By about four in the morning they had succeeded in delivering three kittens. They washed their bloody hands with alcohol and changed from their smelly kimonos, and just as they were ready for bed the telephone rang. Sachiko rushed for it in alarm. The call was from O-haru. What had happened? Was it all over? Not yet, said O-haru. It seemed to be an extremely difficult birth, and Taeko had been in labor for something like twenty hours already. The chief obstetrician had said that the pains were too light and was giving injections, but, perhaps because he was out of German medicine and had to use Japanese instead, the results were unsatisfactory. Koi-san only writhed and groaned. She had eaten nothing since the evening before, and she was vomiting a strange substance, dark and bilious. She knew they could not save her, she would say. This time she was going to die. Though the doctor was reassuring, the nurse was worried about Taeko's heart. Even to the layman it was obvious that a crisis was approaching, and O-haru had determined to telephone in spite of Sachiko's injunctions. The situation was not entirely clear to Sachiko. She concluded nonetheless that Koi-san needed German medicine, and she was sure there would be a way to find it. Every hospital had a supply hidden away for very special patients. If she were to plead with the chief obstetrician . . . Yukiko was beside her, urging her to go to the hospital. This was no time to worry about gossip. Teinosuke, who had gotten up, agreed with Yukiko. Since they had assured Miyoshi that they would be responsible for Taeko and the child, they had to do something. He bundled

Sachiko off to the hospital and set about notifying Miyoshi.
   The head obstetrician was said to be well trained and thoroughly conscientious. It was Sachiko who had recommended him
to her sister, but Sachiko did not know him personally. She took
along certain medicines, prontosil and betaxin and coramine
and the like, that were by then becoming rare. Miyoshi was
already at the hospital. It was good of her to come, said Taeko,
her eyes filling with tears. The two sisters had not seen each
other in six months, not since the autumn before. She hardly
thought she would pull through this time—Taeko was weeping
quite openly, and she seemed to be in great pain. From time to
time she vomitted an indescribable substance, horribly thick and
muddy. Miyoshi had been told by the nurse that poisons from
the child were coming out through the mother's mouth. To
Sachiko it did look very much like a child's first stool or like the
offal one finds in a crab shell.
   Sachiko immediately went to see the chief obstetrician. Pre-
senting Teinosuke's card and bringing out her medicine, she
assaulted him in a carefully shrill voice. She had finally gathered
this medicine, but she had been unable to find the particular
German medicine they needed. She wanted him to search through
the whole of Kobe for it, whatever the price. Somewhere, someone . . . The good-natured doctor soon surrendered. They had
one injection left, literally one injection, he said, bringing the
medicine out with great reluctance. Strong labor pangs set in not
five minutes after the injection, and Sachiko had a demonstration
of the relative merits of German and Japanese medicine. Taeko
was taken to the delivery room. Sachiko, Miyoshi, and O-haru,
on a bench outside, heard her moan once or twice. The doctor
ran to the surgery room with the child in his hands. From time
to time during the next half hour they heard a determined
slapping, but that first cry failed to come.
   Taeko was taken back to her room, and the three of them
sat tensely around the bed. They could still hear the slapping,
and they could imagine the doctor at work. After a time the
nurse came in. It was a great pity—the child had been alive,
and had died at the moment of birth. They had done everything
possible to revive it—they had even given an injection of the
German medicine Sachiko had brought—and all to no avail. The

doctor would tell them the details. He wanted to dress the child
in the clothes the mother had made, said the nurse, taking a
dress Taeko had brought from Arima. Almost immediately the
doctor came in with the dead child. He had no excuses to offer.
It had been entirely his fault. Since the position of the child
was abnormal, he had pulled at the feet and—how could it have
happened?—his hand had slipped, and the child was strangled.
He had promised them a safe delivery, and now to have blundered.
He had no excuses, he said again, wiping the sweat from his
forehead. Sachiko could not feel angry at a doctor who confessed
his responsibility and went on with apologies he could as well
have avoided. He talked on, and showed them the child. A
girl, he said. And what a pretty girl. He had delivered many
children, but he could say with no exaggeration that he had
never seen a sweeter, prettier little girl. It made him sad to think
what a beauty she would have become. The hair was brushed
to a gloss, and the child had on the dress the nurse had taken,
and almost anyone would have cried out in sorrow at the rich,
black hair, the fair skin, the cheeks with a rosy flush still on them.
The three took it up by turns, and suddenly Taeko was weeping
bitterly, and the others with her, Sachiko and Miyoshi and O-haru.
Just like a doll, said Sachiko. But as she looked at the clear,
waxen skin, almost weirdly beautiful, she wondered if the child
did not bear the curses of Okubata and Itakura.

Taeko left the hospital a week later. Teinosuke said that he
had no objections provided she stayed out of sight for a time,
and she immediately went to live with Miyoshi in second-floor
rooms they had rented in Kobe. She came quietly on the evening
of the twenty-fifth to take her leave of the Ashiya family and of
Yukiko, and to gather her things. The room that had once
been hers was gay with Yukiko's trousseau. The alcove was jammed
with presents from Osaka relatives and acquaintances. No one
would have dreamed that Taeko would be the first of the two
sisters to have her own home. After rummaging through the
belongings she had left with Sachiko, she packed what she would
need, talked to the family for a half hour or so, and was off to
Kobe.

O-haru returned to Ashiya when Taeko left the hospital. It
appeared that her family had found her a prospective husband.

She would like two or three days off, she said, after Miss Yukiko was married.

Thus the future was settled. At the thought of how still the house would be, Sachiko felt like a mother who had just seen her daughter married. She went about sunk in thought, and Yukiko, once it had been decided that she and Teinosuke and Sachiko would take the night train to Tokyo on the twenty-sixth, had even more regrets than her sister at the passing of each day. Her stomach had for some time been upset, and even after repeated doses of wakamatsu and arsilin, she was troubled with diarrhea on the twenty-sixth. The wig they had ordered in Osaka arrived on schedule that morning. Yukiko put it in the alcove after trying it on, and Etsuko, back from school, promptly tried it on too. "See what a small head Yukiko has," she said, going down to entertain the maids in the kitchen. The wedding kimonos arrived the same day. Yukiko looked at them and sighed—if only they were not for her wedding. Sachiko remembered how glum she had been when she was married herself. Her sisters had asked for an explanation, and she had retorted with a verse:

"On clothes I've wasted
Another good day.
Weddings, I find,
Are not always gay."

Yukiko's diarrhea persisted through the twenty-sixth, and was a problem on the train to Tokyo.

JUNICHIRŌ TANIZAKI

Junichirō Tanizaki was born in Tokyo in 1886, and studied Japanese literature at Tokyo Imperial University. His novels suggest that his student days were ostentatiously bohemian, in the fashion of the day. In his youth he was strongly influenced by Poe, Baudelaire, and Oscar Wilde.

He lived in the cosmopolitan Tokyo area until the earthquake of 1923, when he moved to the gentler and more cultured Kyoto-Osaka region, the scene of *The Makioka Sisters*. There he became absorbed in the Japanese past, and abandoned his superficial Westernization. Japanese critics agree that this intellectual and emotional crisis changed him from merely a very good writer to a great one. In *The Makioka Sisters* his personal crisis is reflected in the forced move of one sister from the beloved Osaka region to Tokyo.

Tanizaki's most important novels were written after 1923. By 1930 he had gained such fame that his "Complete Works" were published. He received the Imperial Prize in Literature in 1949.

Tanizaki began the long writing of *The Makioka Sisters* toward the end of the war, partly out of despair, and partly out of nostalgia for the last good times on earth. To console himself, he reached out across the great gulf of the war and re-created the beautiful world of *The Makioka Sisters*. "I tried to limit myself to what was attractive," he has said, "but I was not able to withdraw completely from the enveloping storm. This was the necessary fate of a novel born of war and peace."

Tanizaki died in 1965.

A NOTE ON THE TYPE AND PRODUCTION

The text of this book is set in ELECTRA, a Linotype face designed by W. A. DWIGGINS (1880–1956), who was responsible for so much that is good in contemporary book design. Though much of his early work was in advertising and he was the author of the standard volume Layout in Advertising, Mr. Dwiggins later devoted his prolific talents to book typography and type design, and worked with great distinction in both fields. In addition to his designs for Electra, he created the Metro, Caledonia, and Eldorado series of type faces, as well as a number of experimental cuttings that have never been issued commercially.

Electra cannot be classified as either modern or old-style. It is not based on any historical model, nor does it echo a particular period or style. It avoids the extreme contrast between thick and thin elements which marks most modern faces, and attempts to give a feeling of fluidity, power, and speed.

Printed and bound by American Book-Stratford Press, New York, N.Y. Typography and binding based on designs by CHARLES E. SKAGGS.